PRAISE FOR A.G SLATTER

"Slatter displays a rare gift for evocative and poetic prose."

PUBLISHERS WEEKLY, starred review

"Slatter's work is excellent, and eminently readable. The world that her creations live within is excellently depicted, and the characters easy to relate to. It's easy to see how she's managed to make such an impact on the genre and garnered a British Fantasy Award and numerous other nominations."

BRITISH FANTASY SOCIETY

"[Angela Slatter] has carved a niche as one of the best writers of short stories of dark fantasy... Slatter combines darkness, passion and beauty to leave the reader at turns amused, confronted and horrified."

THE AUSTRALIAN

"A collection of stories in which each individual work is a perfectly crafted gem... As of today's date, I rate The Bitterwood Bible and Other Recountings the best book I have read so far this year."

BLACK STATIC

"Wonderful prose and... enticing narrative style, where words are musical notes and the stories are symphonies."

BLACK GATE

"Like Aickman, her sense of the fantastic serves to show us the weird world we hold within our own psyches."

RICK KLEFFEL, American Public Radio Books

"Slatter's fairy tales have a ravishing quality which leaves the reader totally spellbound by their elegance and imaginative power."

BOOKGEEKS

ALSO BY A.G SLATTER
AND AVAILABLE FROM TITAN BOOKS

All the Murmuring Bones

The Path of Thorns

The Briar Book of the Dead

The Crimson Road

The Cold House

A Forest, Darkly

THE SOURDOUGH COMPENDIUM

A.G. SLATTER

TITAN BOOKS

The Sourdough Compendium
Print edition ISBN: 9781835415993
E-book edition ISBN: 9781835416006

Published by Titan Books
A division of Titan Publishing Group Ltd
144 Southwark Street, London SE1 0UP
www.titanbooks.com

First edition: June 2026
10 9 8 7 6 5 4 3 2 1

This is a work of fiction. All of the characters, organizations, and events portrayed in this novel are either products of the author's imagination or are used fictitiously. Any resemblance to actual persons, living or dead (except for satirical purposes), is entirely coincidental.

A CIP catalogue record for this title is available from the British Library.

EU RP (for authorities only)
eucomply OÜ, Pärnu mnt. 139b-14, 11317 Tallinn, Estonia
hello@eucompliancepartner.com, +3375690241

Designed and typeset in Times New Roman by Richard Mason.

Printed and bound in Great Britain by
CPI Group (UK) Ltd, Croydon, CR0 4YY.

TABLE OF CONTENTS

THE BITTERWOOD BIBLE AND OTHER RECOUNTINGS

SOURDOUGH AND OTHER STORIES

THE TALLOW-WIFE AND OTHER TALES

AUTHOR'S NOTE

This compendium originally began life as three separate mosaic collections, birthed as I began to work out the landscape of the Sourdough world for myself. *Sourdough and Other Stories* was written and published first, but when I began writing *The Bitterwood Bible and Other Recountings* I realised that it was a set of prequel stories. *The Tallow-Wife and Other Tales* was, thankfully, a sequel to both. So here for the first time are the stories presented in that order.

Thank you to Rosalie Parker and Raymond Russell of Tartarus Press, for publishing the original editions of these mosaic collections, and thank you to Titan Books for giving them their next life.

THE BITTERWOOD BIBLE
AND OTHER RECOUNTINGS

Once there was,
and twice there was not...

THE COFFIN-MAKER'S DAUGHTER

The door is a rich red wood, heavily carved with improving scenes from the trials of Job. An angel's head, cast in brass, serves as the knocker and when I let it go to rest back in its groove, the eyes fly open, indignant, and watch me with suspicion. Behind me is the tangle of garden – cataracts of flowering vines, lovers' nooks, secluded reading benches – that gives this house its affluent privacy.

The dead man's daughter opens the door.

She is pink and peach and creamy. I want to lick at her skin and see if she tastes the way she looks.

'Hepsibah Ballantyne! Slattern! Concentrate, this is business.' My father slaps at me, much as he did in life. Nowadays his fists pass through me, causing nothing more than a sense of cold ebbing through my veins. I do not miss the bruises.

The girl doesn't recognise me although I worked in this house for nigh on a year – but that is because it was only me watching her and not she me. When my mother finally left it became apparent she would not provide Hector with any more children, let alone a son who might take over from him. He decided I should learn his craft and the sign above the entrance to the workshop was changed – not to *Ballantyne & Daughter*, though. *Ballantyne & Other*.

'Speak, you idiot,' Father hisses, as though it's important he whisper. No one has heard Hector Ballantyne these last eight months, not since what appeared to be an unseasonal cold carried him off.

The blue eyes, red-rimmed from crying, should look ugly, unpalatable in the lovely oval face, but grief becomes Lucette D'Aguillar. Everything becomes her, from the black mourning gown to the severe, scraped-back coiffure that is the heritage of the bereaved, because she is that rare thing: born lucky.

'Yes?' she asks as if I have no right to interrupt the grieving house.

I slip the cap from my head, feel the mess it makes of my hair, and hold it in front of me like a shield. My nails are broken and my hands scarred and stained from the tints and varnish I use on the wood. I curl my fingers under the fabric of the cap to hide them as much as I can.

'I'm here about the coffin,' I say. 'It's Hepsibah. Hepsibah Ballantyne.'

Her stare remains blank, but she steps aside and lets me in. By rights, I should have gone to the back door, the servants' entrance. Hector would have – did so all his life – but I provide a valuable service. If they trust me to create a death-bed for their nearest and dearest, they can let me in the front. Everyone knows there's been a death – it's impossible to hide in the big houses – I will not creep in as though my calling is shameful. Hector grumbled the first few times I presented myself in this manner – or rather shrieked, subsided to a grumble afterwards – but as I said to him, what were they going to do?

I'm the only coffin-maker in Great Glimmerton.

They let me in.

I follow Lucette to a parlour washed with tasteful shades of grey and hung with white lace curtains so fine it seems they must be made by spinners with eight legs. She takes note of herself in the large mirror above the mantle. Her mother is seated on a chaise; she too regards her own reflection, making sure she still exists. There is no sign of the oldest child, a son, Lucien who is studying in one of the university towns, and never spoke two words to me when I was part of the household. Lucette joins her and they look askance at me. Father makes sounds of disgust and he is right to do so. He will stay quiet here; even though no one can hear him but me, he will not distract me. He will not interrupt *business.*

'Your mirror should be covered,' I say as I sit, uninvited, in a fine armchair that hugs me like a gentle, sleepy bear. I arrange the skirts of my brown mourning meetings dress and place my hands on the armrests, then remember how unsightly they are and clasp them in my lap. Black ribbons alone decorate the mirror's edges, a fashionable nod to custom, but not much protection. 'All of your mirrors. To be safe. Until the body is removed.'

They exchange a glance, affronted.

'The choice is yours, of course. I'm given to understand that some families are delighted to have a remnant of the deceased take up residence in their mirrors. They enjoy the sensation of being watched constantly. It makes them feel not so alone.' I smile as if I am kind. 'And the dead seem to like it, especially the unexpectedly dead. Without time to prepare themselves, they tend to cling to the ones they loved. Did you suspect your husband's heart was weak or was it a terrible surprise?'

Madame D'Aguillar hands her black shawl to Lucette, who covers the mirror with it then rejoins her mother.

'You have kept the body wrapped?' I ask, and they nod. I nod in return, to tell them they've done only just enough. That they are foolish, vain women who put their own reflections ahead of keeping a soul in a body. 'Good. Now, how may I be of assistance?'

This puts them on the back foot once again, makes them my supplicants. They must *ask* for what they want. Both look put out and it gives me the meanest little thrill, to see them thus. I smile again: *Let me help you.*

'A coffin is what we need. Why else would you be here?' snipes Madame. Lucette puts a hand on the woman's arm.

'We need your services, Hepsibah.' My heart skips to hear my name on her lips. 'We need your help.'

Yes, they do. They need a coffin-maker. They need a death-bed to keep the deceased *in*, to make sure he doesn't haunt the lives they want to live from this point on. They need my *art*.

'I would recommend an ebony-wood coffin, lined with the finest silk padding stuffed with lavender to help the soul to rest. Gold fittings will ensure strength of binding. And I would affix three golden locks on the casket, to make sure. Three is safest, strongest.' Then I name a price – down to the quarter-gold to make the sum seem considered – one that would cause honest women to baulk, to shout, to accuse me of the extortion I'm committing.

Madame D'Aguillar simply says, 'Lucette, take Miss Ballantyne to the study and give her the down payment.'

Oh, how they must want him kept under!

I rise and make a slight curtsey before I follow Lucette's gracefully swaying skirts to the back of the house.

I politely look away as she fumbles with the lockbox in the third drawer of the enormous oak desk her father recently occupied. When she hands me the small leather pouch of gold pieces, her fingers touch my palm and I think I see a spark in her eyes. I believe she feels it too, and I colour to be so naked before her. I slide my eyes to the portrait of her dearly departed, but she grasps my hand and holds it tight.

Oh!

'Please, Hepsibah, please make his coffin well. Keep him *beneath*. Keep us – keep me – safe.' She presses her lips to my palm; they are damp, slightly parted, and ever-so-soft! My breath escapes me, my lungs feel bereft. She trails her slim, pink cat's tongue along my lifeline, down to my wrist where the pulse beats blue and hard and gives me away. There is a noise outside in the hall, the scuttling of a servant. Lucette smiles and steps back, dropping my hand reluctantly.

I remember to breathe, dip my head, made subservient by my desire. Hector has been silent all this time. I see him standing behind her, gnarled fingers trying desperately to caress her swan's neck, but failing, passing through her. I feel a rage shake me, but control myself. I nod again, forcing confidence into my motions, meeting her eyes, bold as brass, reading a promise there.

'I need to see the body, take my measurements, make preparations. I must do this alone.'

* * *

'Stupid little harlot.' Hector has more than broken his silence, again and again, since we returned to the workshop. I have not answered him because I sense in his tone *envy*.

'How hard for you, Father, to have no more strength than a fart, all noise and wind.'

If he were able, he would throw anything he could find around the space, chisels and planes and whetstones, with no thought for the damage to implements expensive to replace. The tools of our trade inherited from forefathers too many to number. The pieces of wood purchased at great expense and treated with eldritch care to keep the dead *below*.

I ignore his huffing and puffing and continue with Master D'Aguillar's casket. It is now the required shape and dimensions, held together with sturdy iron nails and the stinking adhesive made of human marrow and boiled bones I'm carefully applying to the place where one plank meets another to ensure there are no gaps through which something ephemeral might escape. On the furthest bench, far enough away to keep it safe from the stains and paints and tints, lies the pale lilac silk sack that I've stuffed with goose down and lavender flowers. This evening, I will quilt it with tiny, precise stitches then fit it into the casket, this time using a sweet-smelling glue to hold it in place and cover the stench of the marrow sealant.

We may inflate the charge for our services, certainly, but the Ballantynes never offer anything but their finest work.

I make the holes for the handles and hinges, boring them with a hand-drill engraved with Hector's initials – not long before his death, the drill that had been passed down for nearly one hundred years broke, the turning handle shearing off in his hand and tearing open his palm. He had this one made at great cost. It is almost new; I can pretend the initials are mine, that the shiny thing is mine alone.

'Did you get it?' asks Hector, tired of his sulk.

I nod, screwing the first hinge into place; the dull golden glow looks almost dirty in the dim light of the workshop. Soon I will light the lamps so I can work through the night; that way I will be able to see Lucette again tomorrow without appearing too eager, without having to manufacture some excuse to cross her threshold once more.

'Show me.'

I straighten with ill grace and stretch. In the pocket of my skirt, next to a compact set of pliers, is a small tin, once used for Hector's cheap snuff. It rattles as I open it. Inside: a tooth, black and rotten at its centre and reeking more than it should. There is a sizeable chunk of flesh still attached to the root and underneath the scent of decay is a telltale hint of foxglove. Master D'Aguillar shall enter the earth before his time, and I have something to add to our collection of contagions that will not be recognised or questioned.

'Ah, lovely!' says Hector. 'Subtle. You could have learned something from them. Cold in a teacup – it wasn't very inventive, was it? I expected a better death, y'know.'

'It wasn't a cold in a teacup, Father.' I hold up the new hand drill. 'It was the old drill, the handle was impregnated with apple seed poison and I filed away the pinion to weaken everything. All it needed was a tiny open wound. Inventive enough for you, Hector?'

He looks put out, circles back to his new favourite torment. 'That girl, she doesn't want you.'

I breathe deeply. 'Events say otherwise.'

'Fool. Desperate sad little fool. How did I raise such an idiot child? Didn't I teach you to look through people? Anyone could see you're not good enough for the likes of Miss Lucette D'Aguillar.' He laughs. 'Will you dream of her, Hepsibah?'

I throw the hand drill at him; it passes through his lean outline and hits the wall with an almighty metallic sound.

'I kept you wrapped! I covered the mirrors! I made your casket myself and sealed it tight – how can you still be here?' I yell.

Hector smiles. 'Perhaps I'm not. Perhaps you're so lonely, daughter, that you thought me back.'

'If I were lonely I can think of better company to conjure.' But there may be something in what he says, though it makes me hurt.

'Ah, there's none like your own family, your dear old Da who loves your very skin.'

'When I have her,' I say quietly, 'I won't need *you*.'

Ghost or fervid imagining, it stops him – he sees his true end – and he has no reply but spite. 'Why would anyone want you?'

'You did, Father, or has death dimmed your memory?'

Shame will silence even the dead and he dissolves, leaving me alone for a while at least.

I breathe deeply to steady my hands and begin to measure for the placement of the locks.

* * *

'The casket is ready,' I say, keeping the disappointment from my voice as best I can. Lucette is nowhere in evidence. An upstairs maid answered my knock and brought me to the parlour once more where the widow receives me reluctantly. The door angel did not even open its eyes.

Madame nods. 'I shall send grooms with a dray this afternoon, if that will suffice.' But she does not frame it as a question.

'That is acceptable. My payment?'

'Will be made on the day of the funeral – which will be tomorrow. Will you call again?' She smiles with all the charm of the rictus of the dead. 'I would not wish to waste your time.'

I return her smile. 'My customers have no choice but to wait upon my convenience.' I rise. 'I will see myself out. Until tomorrow.'

Outside in the mid-morning sun I make my way down the stone front steps that are set a little too far apart. This morning I combed my hair, pinched colour into my cheeks, and stained my lips with a tinted wax that had once belonged to my mother; all for naught. I am about to set foot on the neatly swept path, when a hand snakes out from the bushes to the right and I'm pulled under hanging branches, behind a screen of sickly strong jasmine.

Lucette darts her tongue between my lips, giving me a taste of her, but pulling back when I try to explore the honeyed cave of her mouth in turn. She giggles breathlessly, chest rising and falling, as if this is nothing more than an adventure. She does not quake as I do, she is a silly little girl playing at lust. I know this; I know this but it does not make me hesitate. It does not make my hope die.

I reach out and grasp her forearms, drawing her roughly in. She falls against me and I show her what a kiss is. I show her what longing is. I let my yearning burn into her, hoping that she will be branded by the tip of my tongue, the tips of my fingers, the tips of my breasts. I will have her here, under the parlour window where her mother sits and waits. I will tumble her and bury my mouth where it will make her moan and shake, here on the grass where we might be found at any moment. And I will make her mine if through no other means than shame; her shame will bind us, and make her *mine*.

'Whore,' says Hector in my ear, making his first appearance since yesterday. Timed perfectly, it stops me cold and in that moment when I hesitate, Lucette remembers herself and struggles. She steps away again, breathing hard, laughing through a fractured, uncertain smile.

'When he is *beneath*,' she tells me. A promise, a vow, a hint, a tease.

'When he is *beneath*,' I repeat, mouthing it like a prayer, then make my unsteady way home.

* * *

I stood in the churchyard this morning, hidden away, and watched them bury Master D'Aguillar. Professional pride for the most part. Hector was beside me, nodding with more approval than he'd ever shown in life, a truce mutually agreed for the moment.

'Hepsibah, you've done us proud. It's beautiful work.'

And it was. The ebony-wood and the gold caught the sun and shone as if surrounded by a halo of light. No one could have complained about the effect the theatrics added to the interment. I noticed the admiring glances of the family's friends, neighbours and acquaintances, as the entrance to the D'Aguillar crypt was opened and four husky men of the household carried the casket down into the darkness.

And I watched Lucette. Watched her weep and support her mother; watched them both perform their grief like mummers. When the crowds thinned and there was just the two of them – the lord of the house buried too quickly for the only son to return from his studies in time – and their retainers to make their way to the black coach and four plumed horses, Lucette seemed to sense herself observed. Her eyes found me standing beside a white stone cross that tilted where the earth had sunk. She gave a strange little smile and inclined her head just-so.

'Beautiful girl,' said Hector, his tone rueful.

'Yes,' I answered, tensing for a new battle, but nothing came. We waited in the shade until the funeral party dispersed.

'When will you go to collect?' he asked.

'This afternoon, when the wake is done.'

He nodded and kept his thoughts to himself.

* * *

Lucette brings a black lacquered tray, balancing a teapot, two cups and saucers, a creamer, sugar boat and silver cutlery. There are delicate almond biscuits perched on a ridiculously small plate. The servants have been given the afternoon off. Her mother is upstairs resting.

'The house has been so full of people,' she says, placing the tray on the parquetry table between us. I want to grab at her, bury my fingers in her hair and kiss her breath away, but broken china might not be the ideal start. I hold my hands in my lap. I wonder if she notices that I filed back my nails, made them neat? That the stains on my skin are lighter than they were, after hours of scrubbing with lye soap?

She reaches into the pocket of her black dress and pulls forth a leather pouch, twin to the one she gave me barely two days ago. She holds it out and smiles. As soon as my hand touches it, she relinquishes the strings so our fingers do not meet.

'There! Our business is at an end.' She turns the teapot five times clockwise with one hand and arranges the spoons on the saucers to her satisfaction.

'At an end?' I ask.

Her look is pitying, then she laughs. 'I thought for a while there I might actually have to let you tumble me! Still and all, it would have scratched an itch I've had since… and Lord knows it would have been worth it, to have him safely away.' She sighs. 'You did such beautiful work, Hepsibah, I am grateful for that. Don't ever think I'm not.'

I am not stupid enough to protest, to weep, to beg, to ask if she is joking, playing with my heart. But when she passes me a cup, my hand shakes so badly that the tea shudders over the rim. Some pools in the saucer, more splashes onto my fingers and scalds me. I manage to put the mess down as she fusses, calling for a maid, then realises no one will come.

'I won't be a moment,' she says and leaves to make her way to the kitchen and cleaning cloths.

I rub my shaking hands down my skirts and feel a hard lump. Buried deep in the right pocket is the tin. It makes a sad, promising sound as I tap on the lid before I open it. I tip the contents into Lucette's empty cup, then pour tea over it, letting the poisoned tooth steep until I hear her bustling back along the corridor. I fish it out with a spoon, careful not to touch it with my bare hands and put it away. I add a little cream to her beverage.

She wipes my red hot hand with a cool wet cloth, then wraps the limb kindly. Lucette sits opposite me and I pass her the cup of tea and give a fond smile for her, and for Hector who has appeared at her shoulder.

'Thank you, Hepsibah.'

'You are most welcome, Miss D'Aguillar.'

I watch her lift the fine china to her pink, pink lips and drink deeply.

It will be enough, slow acting, but sufficient. This house will be bereft again.

When I am called upon to ply my trade a second time I will bring a mirror with me. In the quiet room when we two are alone, I will unwrap Lucette and run my fingers across her skin and find all the secret places she denied me and she will be mine and mine alone whether she wishes it or no.

I take my leave and wish her well.

'Repeat business,' says Father gleefully as he falls into step beside me. 'Not too much, not enough to draw attention to us, but enough to keep bread on the table.'

In a day or two, I shall knock once more on the Widow D'Aguillar's front door.

THE MAIDEN IN THE ICE

Rikke does not like crossing the ice.

Even during the harshest of winters, when the surface of the lake seems changed to bedrock, when it is frozen so thick you cannot see what lies below, even then, she does not like it. Ice is tricksy; it cannot be trusted. Rikke knows this – has known it ever since her little brother Geir went through four years ago. She still remembers, still re-imagines each year as the seasons change and grey frost-filled clouds gather, as the air cools and the stream and the lake become sluggish, until they stop moving altogether and households must break off chunks of freeze to dump in a pot above the fire for fresh water. She thinks how he looked, when they finally found him, days after an unseasonal thaw, at the spot to which the currents draw all debris, at the break in the earth where the flow spits out unwanted things. He was small, so terribly small, which meant he didn't get caught on some sunken obstacle and stay beneath until the flesh and muscle decayed and released his bones to the depths. He was small and whole and pale, not even beginning to bloat, and his eyes had turned snow-storm white.

No, Rikke does not trust the ice.

But this day she is on it because she is in trouble. She'd forgotten to collect more singing winter grass. When Aggi called from bed for tea made from the stalks, preserved lemon curls and fresh snow-melt, Rikke's heart sank and cooled. Her mother was unwell, her mother was bedridden, her mother was pregnant (again) and with such hopes for another boy to replace the son Rikke had let drown. So, fearful of hearing every fault of her eleven years recited once more (certain her mother would *know* she had been distracted by the same activity – reading – on both occasions), Rikke yelled back that the water was not quite ready, and slipped quietly out the door. Her usual route on the firm ground around the shore's edge would have taken far too long and Aggi would have known something was wrong. But if she went as the crow flies, it would be mere minutes before she made it to the patch of song-fine stalks, and a heart's breath for her to return. Screwing up her courage, Rikke stepped out.

Her boots are stout, the winter ones, with tiny ridges of metal embedded in the soles to clutch at the slippery surface, and she moves quickly with the light cautious step of a fox approaching a henhouse. Her ears almost hurt from the effort of listening for the slow, dark moan that will tell her the floe is about to betray her. For a while she tries to keep her eyes firmly fixed on her destination, on the silver-ash clump of sedge not so far – yet so very far – away. But the panic she's tamped down hard gets the better of her, and she looks to the sparkling, treacherous ground upon which she moves, seeking the cracks, the veins, the fissures that are surely forming there.

But what she sees is something entirely different.

An oval face; skin sallow – in the sun it will become olive; dark-flecked, large eyes; thick straight brows; an unbalanced mouth, the top lip thin, the bottom full; and hair as black as Rikke has ever seen. Black as nightmares, black as a cunning woman's cat, black as the water she is trying to escape. Older than Rikke, caught between girl and woman, and suspended in the solid lake as if she's a statue, standing; head titled back, one arm reaching up, the other pointing downward.

Rikke shrieks. She forgets the singing winter grass, her mother's tisane, her mother's disappointment; she forgets all her fears of a permafrost death, of cold and hoar. She spins about and runs, boots throwing shredded ribbons of rime behind, body moving faster, so much faster than her little legs it is a wonder she does not fall. She clatters into the house making such a noise that Aggi drags herself from bed and Rikke's father, Gamli, comes running in from outside where he has been seeing to the chickens and the goats. When they decipher their daughter's shouts, Gamli leaves the little cottage, yelling at the top of his lungs.

The cry goes up from house to house. 'Someone's in the lake!'

More men join him at the shore and they move carefully on and out, even though the substance beneath their feet is utterly silent. They find the place and stare down at the peerless face of the maiden. The ice is thick; experience tells them they can break through it – but to what end? She is surely dead. When the weather changes, she will come loose of her own accord.

And so, the villagers wait. And as they wait, they watch. Every day of winter, no matter the snows or the sleet, the winds or the frost, at least one person from Iserthal goes to visit her, to marvel at the colour of her skin, how her hair and the frozen black fathoms seem to be enmeshed, at the extraordinary planes of her face. At how her agate eyes, just sometimes, seem to flicker if they aren't *quite* looking at her. Some notice how strangely clear the ice around her is, but they keep their thoughts to themselves.

At some point, though, in the days and weeks and months, it becomes clear that she is *moving*, coming up a little at a time, a tiny bit every day – not so one marks it in the short term, but those who visit her only once a week notice and comment. The others, after consideration, agree. Perhaps it is the currents beneath, warming and wearing away at her gelid prison.

They wait. They wait until the spring thaw comes and the hard crystal surface begins to creak and crack and thin. They wait until the morning when a single slender arm and a clenched fist are seen by three feckless youths to break through the now-weakened layer of cold on top of the water. Having snuck away from their 'prentice duties to miller, butcher and smithy, but unable to find mischief to make, they are kicking a straw ball about by the shore. Upon noticing the arm raised like a flag, they run for their parents – the currents that have freed the body should surely have swept it away. Soon a small red dory is despatched to negotiate the rapidly melting, floating chunks of ice, to the centre of the pool.

* * *

Aggi refuses to have her in the house, as do all the women of the town, including Hebe the innkeeper's wife, so the nameless girl is sleeping in the barn loft behind the home of the largest landowner. Make no mistake, they laid down clean, fresh straw, and every household gave up at least two thick blankets so the warmth could be brought back into her limbs. All the goodwives sent broths and fresh bread – which she ate – and healing infusions, which she sniffed then refused, but none of them would have this strange damozel, this survivor of certain death, in their homes. Some whispered *fossegrim*, but others hushed them – she looked nothing like such a creature.

Aggi, upright, and conscious not so much of the miracle as of the fact that it was one denied to her Geir, had taken a sweeping look at the limp young woman in her husband's arms, at the long lashes on the cheeks, at the dark red of toe nails, the dirt clumped beneath her finger nails, and shook her head, a single sharp jerking motion that told Gamli in no uncertain terms that the girl would not cross their threshold.

Only Rikke, hiding behind her mother's skirts, felt the terrible weight that Aggi held up, knew that her mother's strength was the sole thing keeping the strange girl from their door. Gamli and every other man gathered around him had an unfocused gaze pinned on the pale form in his grasp, wrapped in Wurdin's dory blanket, the one with holes, that smells like fish and elderdamson rum. In case her meaning was lost, Aggi said quite clearly, 'No,' and Gamli reluctantly nodded. Thus began a meandering procession through the town, which was finally resolved at Adhemar's door – his wife was away so he took the refugee in. Even though he knew there would be heated words upon Mairen's return, he could not quite stand to turn the sallow lass entirely away.

* * *

Within four or five days, the girl is up and about, wearing cast-off dresses. Her long locks have been brushed and untangled by the resentful fingers of Adhemar's unwilling wife; Mairen will not have a member of her household, no matter how unwelcome, wander about unkempt. The maiden does not smell like a being of the water, which put paid to whispers that she's some breed of mari-morgan or merrow. Her perfume is earthy, rich and dark, like rotted roses; a sweetness at first, then a potency, then grown too strong, and finally the hint of decay as she moves past the folk in the streets, those in the markets. Storeowners open all their windows and doors after she has gone, to try and get rid of the scent, but it never *quite* goes.

They are calling her the damozel, or 'Damozel' to her face and she seems to accept it, to answer to it.

As she goes, male and female gazes follow her. Children in particular watch for they have never seen such a pretty creature – nor have they ever known, in their short lives, anyone who has escaped the ice. Their fascination, for the most part, overcomes their fear. She smiles, caresses them if she can get away with it, stroking hair and cheeks, holding small hands and faces, giving them gentle words, singing snippets of songs no one knows, in a language no one recognises. Her smile broadens as they break into answering grins, until their mothers pull them away. The three youths who saw her dragged from the icy lake watch her too, as she passes their places of work, but do not pursue her. Rikke thinks they are afraid.

Rikke follows her, but at a distance. She has not, since that first day, gotten close to the stranger. Rikke does not understand why she shadows the damozel so furtively, why she observes so closely – she comprehends only that the girl should not be alive, that she should not be hale and hearty. That she should not draw Gamli's eyes towards her, nor those of the other men, for it is a regard from which the will and intellect are absent. It is a look that Rikke, young as she is, knows to be dangerous – it's the stare of someone not paying proper attention. She suspects it was her own the day Geir was lost.

At night, Rikke hears her parents, after they think her asleep, arguing as they never have before. Aggi berates her husband for the thoughts she believes he harbours, and Gamli swears she is wrong. He wants no one but Aggi, but his wife… except, when he sees that girl, those flecked eyes, something happens; it's like he's being pulled forward, downward, then further downward. Only he doesn't want it, he doesn't want to go, but it's as if he has no choice. He will, he promises, stay away from that girl so he cannot see her, cannot feel that feeling, cannot think those thoughts, cannot *want* to surrender.

When he says that word, that last word, that's when Aggi shrieks and it is a sound such as Rikke has never heard. But she can recognise pain, a searing soul sickness; she can recognise jealousy.

So perhaps Rikke *does* know why she follows the one who smells like death and flowers. She simply ignores the reason, or perhaps, is still too young to know precisely why she feels the need to protect her mother. She tracks the damozel, hiding herself behind carts and stalls, behind the fountain with the statue of a bear and a wolf shaking paws; she darts between women's skirts and men's trousered legs, she glues herself to the corners of stone buildings, thinking herself thin and beneath notice. She watches as the nameless girl follows the same path she's taken since she rose from the clean straw and the mountain of second-best eiderdowns. She goes into every shop in exactly the same order each day, then visits each stall and barrow, again in the same order. She buys nothing – then again, she surely has no coin – and she speaks very little, but smiles a lot. When she finishes her rounds of the town square, she takes the cobbled street that leads to the lake shore – she stands here for a good few minutes, shading her eyes against the reflection of the sun on the water, and stares out at the place she was once entombed. Then she invariably turns around, and wanders home to Adhemar and Mairen's, sometimes into the kitchen where Mairen has her help, sometimes straight to the barn.

This day as the girl stands poised on the edge of the lake, its waters, still frigid, lapping at her toes, Rikke, behind a tree, watches the taut back, the head held just-so on the slender neck. The damozel is still so long that Rikke's caution slackens, just for a moment, and the object of her scrutiny turns, faster than Rikke would have thought possible, and the child is pierced by the other's gaze, frozen until the maiden from the ice grins and waves her slim fingers, mocking, beckoning. Rikke breaks cover and bolts.

* * *

Rikke is woken not by a scream but by an exhalation. Almost inaudible, it is the sound of surprise, of a soft agony, an agony which will build once its moment of bewilderment has passed. She rolls from her blankets and tiptoes to the door of her parents' bedroom.

Light streams through the single window and highlights Aggi, flat on her back, stomach protruding, knees bent and parted beneath the covers. Her breathing is fast, sharp; she puffs with intent, trying to breathe the pain away. Gamli is nowhere in sight and Rikke remembers that today he is hunting deer.

'Water,' gasps Aggi. 'Water.'

In the kitchen, Rikke stirs a mix of powder into a cup carved from a bull's horn: willow bark, vervain leaf, and yarrow flower, crushed fine as dust, to ease her mother's suffering. Aggi has coached Rikke, has taught her what to do, shown her where all the bandages and rags are, told her which herbs need to be prepared before the birth, which should be administered during and after, which should be used to make a poultice to stem the bleeding when the afterbirth has gone. How to wash the baby and make sure his nostrils are clear and his lungs are full – how to carefully hang him upside down, his feet in one hand, and slap his little bottom with the other. This is the part Rikke fears the most – what if he is slippery? What if he wriggles? What if she drops this new baby on the flags of the floor and splits his skull like a summer melon? Rikke does not think she could bear the weight of another lost soul on her conscience. She straightens her back and shoulders, sets her face with determination and takes her mother the water, then begins the process of productive bustling.

At first, things go well. She holds Aggi's hand when the

contractions are at their worst and does not cry when her fingers are crushed. She administers the medicaments as and when she should, she wipes the sweat from her mother's face and puts cold compresses on her burning brow. She checks at regular intervals to see if the child is crowning, but after four hours there is no sign.

'He will not turn!' shouts Aggi and Rikke can hear all her mother's hopes escaping in that one sentence. She is seized by the fear that the child will never come out, that he will rot inside Aggi, trapped there as Geir was trapped beneath the ice. Rikke thinks her heart will explode, it is beating so hard in her chest; she thinks she can hear its thud against the breast bone, against the cage of her body, trying to flee. She runs, followed by Aggi's scream, and flies out the front door, desperately looking around for someone, anyone.

The agate-eyed damozel is standing at the edge of the cottage's garden, bending over the heads of the new roses as if examining them, but her stare is on Rikke, as if she has been waiting. The little girl pauses only a heartbeat before she sobs, 'Help us.'

There is no hesitation. The young woman herds Rikke inside, then she pauses at the collection of herbs on the sideboard, some in large bottles, the rarer ones in small vials, others hanging bundles of dried flowerings and shrivelled bulbs. She hesitates as she looks in the mirror embedded in the sideboard, staring at her reflection, then reaching to touch the glass. Her fingers skim across its surface and she seems surprised, put-out. From the bedroom comes a moan and the damozel shakes herself.

'Angelica?' she asks, for it is nowhere to be seen. It is out of season and Rikke knows Aggi keeps her supply hidden at times such as this – it's too important a herb with which to be generous.

Rikke digs the alabaster urn from the bottom of a trunk where their best clothes and cloaks are folded. She hands it over with shaking hands. 'Please,' she begs, and is answered with a smile.

Aggi has passed out by the time they enter the bedroom. The girl stirs a mix of angelica, honey, lemon, vinegar and crushed nettle; Rikke observes the portions carefully, filing the knowledge away for later. The damozel holds Aggi's head up and makes her drink; Rikke thinks it a good thing her mother is delirious – had she known this woman was in her house, she would scream fit to bring the thatched roof down. When Aggi has taken in the tincture, her midwife sits back and waits. Rikke wants to ask questions, so many questions, but her throat is closed by fear, and not a little excitement. Her breath stops, just for a second, as she wonders if the girl will do Aggi harm – if this is the moment she has chosen for revenge on a woman who has set the tone for her reception in Iserthal. When Aggi begins to moan and move, Rikke is certain that she has been poisoned. But there was nothing, *nothing* she tells herself, in the potion to harm either her mother or the baby.

'The child is turning,' says the dark girl in a low voice. She glances at Rikke as though she can sense her thoughts. 'The child will come; they will be safe.'

And so he does and so they are.

A fine boy, sturdy and heavy. The damozel wipes his feet and ankles with a damp cloth then hands him to his sister; she watches as Rikke holds her new brother upside down and slaps his rump with not a little satisfaction. Then they prop him on his mother's chest while she sleeps, exhausted, and he finds the nipple straining against its load and latches on. They wait until he is full and drowsy, a trail of liquid white slowly making its way down his chin, then the damozel supervises as Rikke swaddles him.

'Not too tightly,' she says, fingers twitching at the bindings to loosen them, 'you want him to grow tall and straight and strong.'

They place him in the wooden cradle that once held Rikke, then Geir and now Orvar – this is the name Aggi chose months ago. Rikke covers him with a light comforter and looks up to thank the girl, but she is already gone. There is the light thud of the door settling back in its frame, and footsteps outside, scuffing on the stones of the garden path. Rikke, torn, checks on Orvar, then Aggi; both sleep deeply.

Rikke makes her choice.

Out in the golden light of the late afternoon, she casts about, and finally catches sight of the deep green of the damozel's hand-me-down gown disappearing between the trees, moving away from the lake and the town. Rikke follows, quickly at first, hastening to catch up with the girl and thank her for her help, but as her curiosity grows, her pace slows; she becomes more cunning, waiting until her quarry is well away, the flash of green just barely seen before Rikke continues her pursuit. She walks lightly, carefully as Gamli has taught her on those occasions when he thought to show her how to hunt and stalk; she makes sure she does not step on any friable twigs, is careful not to trip and fall. When her skirt is caught on a branch, she is patient and unhooks it rather than tugging at it so that it might rip and cause the slightest noise. Out here, she is cautious in a way she never was in town. Out here, she hopes hunting this prey will hold the prize of knowledge.

It is an hour before they reach a clearing surrounded by alder trees; one of them, the largest, shines like angel wings. In the centre of the glade stands… something. Shaped like a man, as tall as Rikke's father twice over, wearing a crown of stripped whistle-wood branches, each finial topped with rich black alder-buckthorn berries that catch the last of the light like gems. He wears a pitch-hued cloak that moves and circles like smoke in the wind; his hair is long and inky as the damozel's, and his face is a shifting landscape of features made from soot vapour and dust and ash. Rikke has heard, has read, enough tales to recognise him. His eyes are deep holes, their orbs sunken but polished, fastened on the girl who steps fearlessly towards him.

'My king,' says the damozel, her tone light, pleased. 'Father.'

The Erl-King does not answer, but the substance of him billows, whirls, like an animal trying to make itself bigger, more threatening.

'Oh, Father, don't be angry. You can't still be angry.' The girl laughs. Rikke realises she thinks herself safe; she does not think her father a threat. But Rikke saw what Adhemar did to *his* daughter with a briar switch when she spoke back to him; she saw what Wurdin did to *his* daughter when she was caught with the butcher's boy behind the mill; she remembers what Gamli did to her the day Geir's body floated free.

Still the great beast does not speak.

The girl sighs, harrumphs, pirouettes, arms held out as if she's flying. She does a little jig, the most graceful thing Rikke has ever seen. She twirls and twirls and twirls, one foot anchoring her, the other used to leverage herself round and round and round. She finishes suddenly, hands thrown back and down as if folding away her wings and she laughs once more, a high, ringing sound.

'Father, oh, Father. I just wanted to know what this upper-earth was like. I just want to be merry for a while, Father, to feel the sun on my face.' She moves closer and closer to the behemoth of haze. 'I just wanted to see *everything*.'

A voice finally rumbles up and out of the Erl-King. 'You had *everythin*g beneath, daughter. You had it all in my kingdom and you disdained it to come *here*.'

'Oh, not a punishment, not another – weren't those months in the ice enough for you?' She laughs again and Rikke can hardly bear it. 'Come, Father, let me return home. I have had my time here, I am content. I will return with you now.'

The head shakes, a slow movement back and forth that makes Rikke think of a neck being sawn through. 'No. What you threw away can only be re-earned, daughter. Your name is forfeit. Your place in under-earth is gone. Your power over men will be no more than that of an ordinary woman – you must learn to live as such.'

'Father, no!' Panic now as realisation dawns, but the dark voice continues unabated.

'You shall be called "Ella" – you want *all* and now it shall be your name. Let it be a reminder of your loss.' He raises a hand gnarled and knotted, fingers tipped with long sharp nails, coal-black, pointing at his daughter's face, his benediction a curse. 'You cannot return until your penance is done. All mirrors are closed to you. The shadow trees will not bear you.'

The girl reaches out, up, then, sensing no mercy, stops, draws in on herself.

'How shall I ever come home?'

'All things have a price. You know mine.'

The Erl-King gestures at the largest alder, the shining one. Its bole splits, widens, exposing such a black profundity that Rikke cannot see inside, not even in the light of the radiant tree. The breach stretches and stretches until the Erl-King can step through, then the wound closes over as softly and surely as petals curling around themselves as evening falls. The girl, Ella, throws herself at the now-whole trunk, weeping and wailing, hammering at the bark with clenched fists.

Rikke is torn: quietly slip away or show herself? The heartbreak in the girl's cries makes her decision.

With quiet steps she crosses the clearing and rests a hand on Ella's shaking shoulder. The girl pauses, startled, then continues with her distress. She howls until she is exhausted, with Rikke now crouched beside her, arms wrapped around the girl whose own arms encircle the unfeeling bulk of the alder tree. When her storm is passed, she pulls away from Rikke, sets her face as if nothing has happened.

'If you tell anyone about this,' she begins in a voice of iron, and Rikke shakes her head. Ella purses her lips, then nods. 'I do not forget kindnesses.'

She walks off through the copse and disappears in the rough direction of Iserthal. Rikke waits until she can be seen no more, then takes another, longer, path home.

* * *

Rikke does not tell her parents about Ella.

Oh, she tells them it was the damozel to whom they owe the lives of both Aggi and Orvar, and her mother does not speak for several hours. But she does not tell them about the Erl-King or the shining tree or the girl's unbearable loss. She does not tell them that the girl now has a name, a new one and that it has changed her.

All the townsfolk notice is that the young woman has become *different*. That, although Ella still keeps her routine, moving and shifting along her usual path, she is altered – perhaps diminished. The eyes of the men are no longer unfocused as they watch her – and they do not watch her for long, or no longer than any man graces a woman with his considering gaze. And the women notice this. They begin to dislike her less. They are, if not overly kind, then at least they are not unkind. Mairen gives the girl more chores to do, trusts her to make the household purchases in the markets. Mothers no longer pull their children away when the girl gives them a sad smile, and sings to them in the language they no longer care they do not recognise. Aggi says *thank you* to the damozel; she touches her hands and holds them for a long while.

The 'prentices overcome their fear of the girl; they begin to make their presence known, at first in the way of boys, with loud jokes and bragging. They follow her trying to engage in conversation, but she does no more than give them a smile and continue on her way. Unable to understand that she cannot possibly be interested in them, the miller's boy, the butcher's boy and the smithy's boy become bitter. Their japes turn to abuse, their hints become overtly sexual and crass, their teasing turns to torments. The townsfolk frown, reprimand the youths loudly. It merely serves to make them crafty.

Rikke wonders if, one day, she will speak to the girl again, and call her by her new name. Perhaps she will ask her about her father and the name to which Ella lost all right. Rikke might ask how she could return home, and if perhaps Rikke might help her to do so, to thank her. But she stops following the damozel; her interest wanes as the girl dwindles at the word of her father. But some weeks after Orvar's momentous birth and Aggi's great saving, and when the girl seems no more than a usual part of the town's life, things go horribly wrong.

* * *

Perhaps, Rikke would later reflect, if she had continued to follow Ella then nothing would have happened. Perhaps she'd have been safe. Perhaps the 'prentices would have lost interest in punishing the dark girl for her disregard. *Perhaps, perhaps, perhaps* – Rikke found herself, years afterwards, writing this over and over in a book in which she was supposed to be recording a history of legendary figures for the *Murcianii*. Perhaps if she *had* followed that particular afternoon instead of simply stumbling across them there would have been no history to write – or at least not her part of it.

The noises coming from Adhemar's barn were distressing in the extreme; though mingled with giggles and guffaws, the sounds of mirth were not kind, were not good-natured, but mean-spirited, feral. Rikke, walking swiftly towards the millhouse with her family's share of grain in a heavy sack hefted over her shoulder, heard the other sounds, the under-sounds, a woman in extremis. Moreover, she recognised the sobbing, having heard it once before.

She did not creep, she did not run away. She threw off her customary reticence, her shyness. Rikke became an adult on that day when she burst into the barn, swinging the sack of wheat like a weapon and knocking over both the smithy's lad and the butcher's boy before they knew what hit them. The sack slid from her sweaty palms and the miller's boy looked at her in shock; somehow she knew there were but seconds before they recovered and turned on her. The pitchfork hanging on a hook by the door proved her saviour and when she began to slash the air with it, the youths fled.

Ella had crawled to the darkest corner she could find, and covered herself with straw. Rikke, adrenaline gone, her moment of bravery exhausted, sat beside the shivering shaking mound of dirty yellow and waited. She was not prepared to leave Ella alone – she kept her eyes on the doors, the pitchfork resting on her lap should the boys think to come back and silence them both. When Adhemar and Mairen came in later, wondering why Ella had not prepared their supper, they found both girls still in the same positions.

Rikke told them what had happened. She told them though her stomach ached with the fear and the force of the telling. She told them as she knew she would have to tell others again and again, for such a truth would not bear simply the one recounting. She knew she would have to speak for Ella refused to do so.

Later that night when Ella, attended by Mairen, was ensconced in a makeshift bed set up in the corner of Rikke's room – when they'd tried to move her into Adhemar's house, she'd howled and fought; it was simply in too close proximity to the place of her undoing – Rikke addressed the gathered inhabitants of Iserthal in the meeting hall.

She spoke well and clearly, her voice steady and ringing against the oaken walls, not betraying her nerves at all. Her voice was a clarion, a bright peal of truth, and when she had finished, the silence that descended on the hall hung like a storm cloud that would not break. The 'prentices stood in a corner, shame-faced, examining their boots. There was no doubt what had been done to Ella and they offered no denial.

And the townspeople mirrored the boys and examined their own boots. In their faces Rikke could see, but did not at first understand, that there would be no remedy; that Ella was an outsider and the youths, no matter what they'd done, were Iserthal natives, the town's future, children of its fine citizens. The adults listened and they did nothing.

Aggi and Gamli, with curses of shame aimed at their fellows, hurried their daughter out when she began to yell.

* * *

Today is the first day Ella has risen from her bed, the first day Rikke has left her alone in the house, under the care of Aggi. The younger girl has been a constant nurse to her charge, driven as much by pity as by guilt for what the townsfolk have allowed to go unpunished. Rikke has, much to Aggi's pride and concern, almost worn herself out with caring. She urged her daughter to rest, and Ella, unsteady on her feet but supported by Aggi, and speaking for the first time in weeks says, 'Go.'

Rikke, sitting in the trunk of a great oak tree, reading, misses lunch, and does not emerge from the world of her book (in which a cat talks and wears boots and is far cleverer than her master and where danger is contained within pages) until she hears a high, thin sound.

It is a noise that continues and as it persists grows fat, fills out with grief, becomes saturated with pain. As she takes the path towards Iserthal at a run, the book clutched to her chest, the scream is multiplied like so many images in an arrangement of mirrors. It is torn from many throats, male and female, unalloyed by shame or self-consciousness.

Rikke bursts from the forest like a bird flushed from cover and enters the small maze of deserted streets that will lead her home. What is missing? What is missing, she wonders then rounds the corner and enters the semi-circle of the town green. All the inhabitants – all the adults – mill about, howling. To one side of that sad group, not part of it, are Aggi, holding tight to tiny Orvar, and behind her, Gamli, arms wrapped around his wife and son. They are, Rikke notes, the only parents with a child, but Aggi is still weeping and wailing with the rest of them and Gamli has tears running down his cheeks into the golden curls of his beard. Then Aggi espies her daughter, paused beneath the seamstress's sign, and her scream turns to a sound of joy, of triumph. Rikke's little family breaks away from the mourning masses and sweeps her up.

Other parents gather around, demanding to know where their children are – was she alone, might there be others? Rikke must shake her head and feel the weight of disappointment that her answer brings to so many. A further search of the town confirms the fact that Rikke and Orvar are the only ones under the age of eighteen to still inhabit Iserthal. Hours later, the blameworthy youths will be found, not spirited away, but their debts paid in full: each one hanging from the branches of a tree in the alder stand where Ella's father disowned her.

It is the day when a tiny piece of cold takes up residence in Rikke's heart – she knows this because she thinks but does not say *This is what you all deserve.* Just as Ella remembered kindnesses, she did not forget cruelties.

Aggi never again complains about Rikke's reading; she never again calls her daughter lazy or recites her list of faults. Orvar is precious to her but not more so than Rikke, for Aggi knows that the girl's actions saved them all from the terrible fate of Iserthal. She and Gamli keep her in books, stretching their income to ensure she has not only volumes to read, but also shelves on which to put them.

One day, the townsfolk will begin to breed anew after a suitable interval of mourning, but they will never forget that Rikke's family was untouched by what happened. The good citizens will resent them, but they will also never forget that they were complicit in their own downfall, and this will stay their hands.

One day, a man, blond and handsome, will come to Iserthal. He will ask questions about the dark damozel who defied death. He will try to winkle out the *why* and the *how* of her survival, but no one except Rikke knows the girl's secrets and she will not tell them to *this* man. Eventually, he leaves, certain that Rikke is an idiot child, that she holds no arcane mysteries he might learn.

One day, Rikke, however, will decide she wishes to record what happened, and Gamli will travel to Lodellan, to the street where the books are born, and brings her back handmade notebooks and fine knives for sharpening her quills, inks and pots and a fine leather satchel to carry them all in.

And one day, Rikke will begin to write, and she will inscribe the words *It is six years since the children left.* It is the start of a work that, in times to come, will bring the Blessed Wanderers to the door, seeking her for their ranks.

THE BADGER BRIDE

The tip of the quill scratches its way across the parchment, a sound that sets my teeth on edge.

One might think I'd be used to it by now. The black marks it leaves in its wake make no sense to me – indeed the entire book makes no sense – then again, I am a mere copyist and mine's not to question why. Although I do.

Frequently.

Much to my father's despair.

When he brought me this commission, I turned the tome over and over – a difficult enough task, for the thing is heavy, aged and fragile, the ebon cover tacky to the touch, the pages brittle – and a smell rose from the skin of the thing that was quite unpleasant. The name of the author and the title of the book were utterly obscured, a thick stygian gum had been smeared across them and it was hard to perceive whether this application was intentional or the result of mere carelessness. The inner leaves confirmed intent – no extant title page waited within, merely the remnants of a folio torn from the binding, tiny sad folds of paper with ragged edges.

So, an anonymous book.

'Who is the client?' I asked my father, Adelbert, once Abbot of the monastery of St-Simeon-in-the-Grove, who rolled his eyes and bid me *Just do the job.*

'But, Father, it is very old, very frail, and the ink is faded – fading as I watch if my eyes don't deceive me.' I manoeuvred the article in question so he could better see. 'Is it the last of its kind? Who is the owner? What does he expect?'

'He expects, like your father, that you do not ask questions, little prying thing. That you take this volume and copy it as quickly as you might!' He took a deep breath and roared, 'Else I'll put you out in the cold, Gytha!'

I harrumphed, and left his study. He will not put me out; he will do no such thing. I am the only child in Fox Hollow House who earns her keep, after all. Aelfrith spends her days draped across the couch, sighing for a husband, and Edda devotes her time to exercising and grooming the six horses in the stables. I alone understood and adopted the scholarly arts Father had tried to teach us; and I alone adopted the trade he learned at the monastery – and at which, he freely admits, was terrible. People come from all around, from as far away as Lodellan, to have me copy their books, their precious, unique, failing books; to have me adorn and enhance them, to add vines and flowers and strange animals in the margins; to change the existing illustrations they cannot bear (modestly clothe a naked Eve, paint out grandmother's warts on her nose, give uncle a chin that does not slope so straight from lower lip to clavicle). Copy, edit, amend, ameliorate, augment and occasionally, if the pay is right, forge.

I will make a book what they want it to be, either more or less itself.

So many since I was very small – so small that Father had to lift me onto the stool piled with two firm fat cushions that I might be able to sit at the tilted desk and reach the inks and shafts, the paints and tints, the papers and parchments that required my attention.

My fingers are stained from the mixing of hues of slate and blue, flashes of umber and gold, red and green; the same fingers are scarred, fletched with nicks from sharpening my very fine goose feather quills. When I copy, I wear white cotton gloves, each pair washed in the hottest of hot water after use. I have spectacles, thick half-moons of polished glass to magnify the things I must discern and craft; these perch on the end of my nose only when I am mid-copy. Aelfrith says I look like someone's granny, for all my smooth skin and dark hair.

'No one,' she taunts, 'would ever believe you young.'

Edda merely grunts at that and adds that I need to get out more – that both Aelfrith and I need to take in the healthful air, and undertake some exercise as she does. We three have different mothers, so we are more like to be dissimilar than if we shared a maternal imprint. Fathers have so much less influence.

The scratching of the nib, which has almost hypnotised me, now has a rival: the tap-tap-tapping of a bare frozen branch from the wild cherry tree by the side of the house.

With a tiny bed cupboard in one corner, my scriptorium is located on the second floor, in the room with the most windows so I might steal all the light I can. The cherry tree is naked and frosted; it looks dead, as if it will never bloom again. The cold coming from the glass panes might just convince me this is true – this place cannot be too warm, so I may have only the smallest of fires, banked low in the grate, which is why I prefer to not work in winter.

I have spent the day copying this wretched thing, stopping but once to read a couplet aloud, hoping that speech might add some meaning, but it remained nonsense. Looking up I blink hard until my eyes stop watering at the change in focus, and watch the thin branch as the wind pushes it this way and that; any moment now, any moment, it will snap. But no, the thing is hardier than I would have thought. It endures.

I stand, stretch, arching my back until I hear the four distinct cracks that say my spine is aligned once more. I take stiff steps over to the window, where a cushioned seat awaits, draped with shawls, and survey the garden. White as white can be, its purity is broken only by the shadowy things there's not *quite* enough fall to cover: the chopping block, the wood pile, the swing we use only in summer and only when we are feeling particularly frivolous. And at the edge of the lawn, a dark mobile thing the size of a small dog or a large cat, is inching its way forward, terribly slowly, shaking the snow off its gentleman's coat quite determinedly.

A badger; no creature should be left to suffer in this weather.

All stiffness is gone from my limbs and I fly from the room, down the staircase with its carved banister and hideous newel post (the head of a green man, but not as cheerful as it should be), making a great commotion that brings my family from various directions. I don't even worry about a cloak, but fling open the door and charge out into the white.

For precious moments I'm lost, blinded, then I catch sight once more of the determined lope – almost a waddle, with his limbs so chilled – of the black fur and the hoary streak down his back. I stumble through the cold powder and catch up the poor creature. He is heavy; he smells strongly, oh so strongly; he looks at me with bleary-eyed distrust.

'There, there,' I croon, stroking one hand over his head and face as I trudge towards the front door, where Father and my sisters wait. 'You're safe here, little brock, little badger.'

And the poxy little whoreson bites me.

Not viciously – it was merely a warning nip – and only on the one finger but still he breaks the skin and it wells red and stings. Then he snuggles against me, smugly content.

* * *

Edda washes and salves my wound. While she applies a bandage to the two sharp punctures, I glare at the animal, curled snug in a blanket-lined basket by the kitchen fire.

His eyes are closed, his breathing even and he is making a deep throaty noise somewhere between a grunt and a purr. One lid lifts, a brown orb stares at me, then is slowly sheathed again. In a bowl in front of a hastily-emptied basket are slices of preserved apple and cherries, tepid milk, porridge and honey. His left hind foot is bandaged; a deep cut slashed its fat pad. The cold had stopped the bleeding, but once inside, the flow started again. He let us bathe the limb with warm water and apply a rosemary ointment to it before Edda swaddled him like a baby. He didn't bite *her*.

'He must have gotten lost,' says Aelfrith, admiring his coal coat. He is a young male, not a cub, but not a fully grown boar. The streak of white from snout to tail is clean as clean can be. All things considered he is a very *hygienic* badger; well, except for the smell, which is not unpleasant, merely strong and musky.

Edda nods. 'Yes, he's wandered away from his sett.'

'Or perhaps he's been driven out – old boar and new boar can't live in peace,' I say, flexing my finger in hope of loosening Edda's tight wrapping. 'Especially as he seems to be a biter.'

'He only bit *you*, Gytha.'

'I'm sure it was just to say *hello*,' laughs Aelfrith.

I give my sisters the look they deserve and am about to serve up a retort when Father's bulk hoves into view. 'Still fussing with that confounded animal?'

'O God, how manifold are your works!' I quote.

'In wisdom thou hast made them all,' follows Edda.

Aelfrith chimes in with, *'The earth is full of your myriad blessed creatures.'*

'Yea, blessed!' we chorus, our mockery taking on the ring of a hymn.

Adelbert regrets (many times daily, I suspect) teaching his daughters scripture, for we have ended up with firm beliefs, but also varied means of arguing with him on his own terms.

'Gytha, don't you have work to do? You know the client expects that book by season's end.'

'And yes, I've been meaning to talk to you about this, Father. Winter work and no say to me in the deadline! It's not acceptable.' I frown.

He sees that bluster and bullying will not get him far this day, so he softens his tone. 'Gytha, I am sorry, but this is a special job. No more like this, I promise – but with the coin from this one commission, we need not work for two whole years!'

'*We* don't work, Father. *I* work,' I grumble, but turn on my heel and stride from the kitchen.

In the scriptorium, the fire has gone out and I have only a few more hours of usable light left. I poke at the embers and stir them up until flames lick at the twigs I throw on. When it is crackling, I defiantly add a larger log than I normally would and watch it catch with satisfaction.

I rub my hands together until they warm, carefully massage the fingers, then sit down to begin once more. Page ten: a drawing of a young woman, who seems to be sleeping, but for the fact there is a great tear over her heart; words in a language I do not understand, but which make me nervous nonetheless, are written around her corpse.

I manage the rough outline of the body before there is a scratching at the door.

I curse and pull it open. No one is there. Then: a furry weight as Master Brock crosses the threshold and treads over my feet, to sit himself on the rug in front of the fire.

We stare at each other for a moment, until he closes his eyes.

I shrug and return to my desk.

* * *

I come down to a scene of high circus the next morning, the badger limping at my heels. I stop in the kitchen doorway and he peeks out from behind my skirts.

'The cheese is gone!' Father shouts.

'The cheese?' I ask.

'All the cheese!' says Edda.

'All our lovely, lovely cheese,' wails Aelfrith.

'The cheese?' I repeat, thinking perhaps I am not awake, but still dreaming. I did not sleep well, and the welt on my finger throbbed throughout the night.

Father looks at me as though I am an imbecile. 'The cheese has been eaten. Our entire winter supply. Gone.'

Father is fond of his cheese.

'And no sign of a thief. No doors unlocked, no windows broken,' says Edda knowingly.

'Well, don't look at me.' I traipse down the narrow stairs to the cellar, which is a surprisingly small room, half the size of the kitchen, and lined with shelves laden with bottles of preserved fruit and vegetables from last summer, wrapped parcels of salted fish and pork, sacks of flour and sugar, small jars of salt and ground pepper, three kegs of Father's cider, one of his brandy, and a distinct lack of the five large wheels of cheese I set there at the beginning of winter.

I look closely at the walls, the floor, as if I might find a secret passageway heretofore unsuspected, then I shake my head. It's probably Aelfrith, wandering in her sleep again and now feeding her frustrations by eating. She'd best stop or we'll be well out of food before the snows end. Turning to go back up, I find myself pinned by a dark gaze in a curious face. I narrow my eyes and wonder at the badger sitting patiently at the top of the stairs. The cheese was on the highest shelf, my head height, and badgers are not known for their climbing ability, nor for their love of dairy. I shake my head once more and return to the kitchen, wondering how to phrase my suspicions of Aelfrith politely.

But this drama, it seems, has passed and another, quieter one has taken its place. Father is nowhere to be seen, and my sisters have moved themselves to the parlour, where they sit expectantly. Aelfrith, in particular, is preening.

'Where's Father?'

'In his study and not to be disturbed,' says Edda.

Aelfrith nods. 'He's with a client – *the* client.' She takes a deep breath, which she exhales with words riding upon it, 'He's ever so handsome, Gytha!'

Even Edda nods and I've not seen her enthused about the appearance of anything but a horse for many a year. Then again, we don't get too many men passing by, only the occasional monk, old friends of Father's, random clients, and tinkers. Certainly none from the burnt-out bones of Southarp village.

I make a move towards the door and Edda leaps up, terribly distressed and barring my way. 'Oh, no! You mustn't disturb them – Father said so.'

I narrow my eyes and stomp off to my workroom. Honestly, she doesn't know me at all. I sit at the window seat and watch, noting the absence of either horse or carriage. It doesn't take long before I hear the front door open and see a figure step out from beneath the storm porch, firmly settling a tricorn hat upon thick golden hair.

He gets a good head-start while I fight with the frozen casement latch and eventually clamber down the stout limbs of the cherry tree. I follow his tracks, deep footprints, and huddle against the shawls I threw hastily around my shoulders. Soon, I'm into the woods; icicles hang where leaves should be, and the patches of sky glimpsed through the bare tangle of branches are grey and unwelcoming. If I do not find him soon I will give up – I'm no fool. He will visit again and I will be waiting; next time I will charge into Father's study and take the golden-haired man's measure.

I'm cold and shivering. The moment I turn around, there he is, grinning like a wolf.

I see none of the handsomeness Aelfrith was mooning over, merely appetite and a will to do whatever he wishes. In his hands, a knife, long and thin, a stiletto blade; his knuckles are white around the ivory handle.

'The book,' I blurt and his expression alters. Ah! Here it is, that beautiful mask. But I've seen what it covers and I will not be deceived. 'I wanted to ask you about your book.'

Smoothly he hides the knife into the sheath at his belt, tucks it out of sight as if it might be easily forgotten. He is richly dressed, his cloak lined with ermine.

'My apologies – I could only hear someone following me and thought to defend myself from footpads. I did not mean to frighten you.' He points and I follow the direction of his kid-gloved finger. 'My coach is there.'

And so it is, on the road above where we stand in a hollow. Black and shiny as ebony, with four black steeds, a driver and a footman, both blank faced as they peer down at us. I find myself shaking and will it to stop. I clear my throat.

'The book – I was wondering if you knew its name and author? Only – I've been wondering. Professional curiosity,' I say, trying to look scholarly and serious.

He gives me a brilliant smile and shakes his head. 'Afraid not, Mistress Gytha – it is Gytha, yes? My copyist? I am – a collector. The book took my fancy; its value is purely ornamental and sentimental. It reminds me of someone very dear. But its ink is fading, the cover is derelict. I require a copy.'

'But I can re-ink the text, clean the cover, fix the bindings.'

'No, no. My memory hinges on the contents, not the container. New is best.' His expression tells me that he does not like old things; he is one of those who prefer possessions to be pristine and unused when they come to his hand. No true collector, he. An old book is not the artefact for him – the knowledge therein is what he wants, but he desires it in a splendid new repository. I notice his clothing – blue breeches, gold and cream waistcoat, white silk shirt, silver-grey frock coat and highly polished boots – not one item seems overly worn. Indeed, there is no sign of anything having been worn before at all; there is no fading of colour, nor weakening of nap, no hint of threadbare at the collar and wrists, and certainly no wrinkles or folds that might come with habitual attire. This man likes his things *shiny.*

'Where did you find it?'

He smiles again and does not answer, effortlessly striding up the slope to his conveyance. He tips his hat and climbs in. He leans out the window and says, 'I shall return in the spring, Mistress Gytha, to claim my book. I trust you'll not disappoint me.'

I stand shivering for some time after he is gone.

* * *

St-Simeon-in-the-Grove is a small monastery, all things considered. A mere twenty monks, aged from twelve (two boys left on the doorstep some years ago) to ninety-five (the librarian).

Edda has let me take our oldest horse, a tall beastie, with feathered feet and a mane like a blanket. Hengroen moves slowly and surely – it's a bit like being on a very sturdy boat, his gait is almost floating, which makes me feel both safe and seasick after an hour on his broad back. My rear protests as I dismount and groan loudly. The young monk who comes forward to take Hengroen looks astounded as I tip back the hood of my thick travelling cloak – obviously he has been brought up to believe women are crafty creatures, both fragrant and evil, but not given to terrible bodily noises. He should hear Edda after a meal of beans.

'Larcwide will see me,' I say, before he begins the speech about how my kind are not allowed in the monastery. A rule instituted since – in fact because of – my father's tenure. 'I'm bringing a book.'

Of course, I'm *assuming* he will see me as he has done before – that he will not remember that little fracas a few years back. This young man knows the librarian collects tomes, is consulted on them regularly, is an authority on things that hold words in one place. I'm banking on the very good chance that he has been terrified by at least one of the old man's tirades, and will be too afraid to refuse me.

'Don't worry,' I say, and pat his hand. He shivers the way a horse does when a fly lands on its hide. 'I'll take the side entrance so as not to cause a fuss.'

I'm rewarded with a flash of relief and he nods, leading my great mount to the stables for a rest. I dart across the rectangle of snow that in summer is a patch of green, keeping my head down, but I needn't bother – most of the brothers are at prayer this time of day. At the base of a tall tower – not the one with the bell in it, the one opposite – there is a small slender door, overgrown with winter ivy, which in this season looks deceased, as if the wall is shedding its skin, but a sharp eye will note the grey handle twisted about with dead vines, almost invisible. I get splinters, but the ingress opens with relative ease. Inside there is a set of black stone steps curving around and up. The air is dry and cold, but warmer as I rise. I can smell ink and paper, and old man.

The librarian is shuffling back and forth between cases, twitching folios from the shelves which line the walls, muttering, sliding them back into place or shifting them to another spot. In the centre of the tower is a series of platforms, weighted down with even more tomes, reached by a sort of elevator and pulley system, that creaks above. As I watch a thin monk steps onto the third platform, nimbly balancing an armful of volumes. Larcwide glares upward as dust particles drift down.

'I told you,' he yells, 'to clean your shoes! And did you? Did you?'

There is a muffled and indecipherable reply from aloft, and the old man swears softly.

'Father Larcwide?'

He swings around in surprise and squints at me. He won't rant about me being a woman, although he may well rant about my incursion. He shared in many of my father's adventures, but his continued presence at St Simeon is testament to both his inability to produce offspring and to his unassailed position as bibliognost. By virtue of his irreplaceable knowledge, his transgressions could be – and have been – overlooked. Unfortunately for Adelbert's career, he lacked the librarian's uniqueness – anyone can be an under-enthused abbot and mediocre copyist.

'Father Larcwide, I need to talk to you,' I say and hold up the satchel hanging at my side. His eyes sparkle and he gestures for me to come closer.

He peers at my face and recognition dawns. 'Adelbert's girl? The clever one.'

I grin and nod. 'Gytha. I need you to look at something.'

'Why me?' he grumps, contrary for the sake of it.

'Because there's none like you.' His ego, duly stroked, allows him to lead me along a maze of shelves to an alcove just big enough for a writing desk and two chairs. He sits and invites me to do the same. I draw the thing out of the bag, and unwrap it from the layers of shawl, then place it on the table between us. Larcwide leans forward to read the now-visible title. I have been working at it, testing out a variety of oils and soft cloths, trying to wear away at the black mess. It was slow toil: if I used too much of the lubricant, too much pressure as I rubbed, the stuff would have simply eaten its way through the cover. It is a capricious mix, with a peculiar personality all of its own, bought from the strange little man who travels in spring and summer and brings me supplies of the things that are hardest to find. I cleaned the surface, one letter at a time. So carefully. So very carefully, until:

Murcianus: Magica: A Book of Craft.

Larcwide's hands shake as he reaches out but does not touch the tome. His fingers are blue and brittle, stained with age spots. They hover over what I have so painstakingly cleaned.

'Do you know what this is? Of course you don't,' his voice quivers. Then, 'Where did you get this?'

No, I don't know, although, I have a suspicion, have had since I reached a page I recognised: a drawing of a hand with candles set in the tops of all the fingers and the thumb. A hand of glory. But I choose to act the innocent and answer only his second question. 'A client. A commission my father took on.'

He shakes his head. 'Oh, Adelbert. Will you never learn?' He closes his eyes, no more than a blink, but he looks exhausted when he opens them again.

'What is it?' I ask.

He nods. 'A *grimoire*. A book of craft. And this one…' He finally picks the thing up and rubs his fingers on the back cover, in the right-hand bottom corner, finding what I already know is there: the subtle relief of an embossment. *M.* He almost drops the book, so great is his surprise. 'Belonged to *him*!'

I want to poke and prod, extract the information swiftly, but I wait. He looks at me dubiously, then with judgement. I don't know who *he* is.

'Murcianus. This is the Bitterwood Bible.'

And I stare blankly at him and Larcwide's expression rolls into utter despair.

'Murcianus, one of the greatest encyclopaedists ever known. Or rather of the arcane and the eldritch specifically. He wandered the world, recording and compiling every strange ritual, every bizarre being, every spell, curse, myth, legend, enchantment, magical locations…' the monk seems to run out of words. 'Everything!'

I remain silent.

'Those books, nowadays, are so rare you barely find one outside a private collection – or with those bloody women at Cwen's Reach,' he mutters. 'They are wonderfully illustrated, most erudite and informative, filled with wisdom and wit and scholarship.' He turns my tome over in his hands. 'There are other volumes, Gytha, like this one, written in the language of witches, comprehensible to only a few, but this one is a rarity. Full of knowledge best left unknown, things too dangerous to be writ down. There are places, Gytha, where his works are forbidden; where those who carry them are burned, their ashes scattered.'

His face reddens and he looks away, remembering to whom he speaks; remembering at last our argument when I asked him for information my father refused. The one occasion I managed to extract the name of my mother from Adelbert, he was in his cups. He'd called her *Hafwen* and told me she had been so briefly beautiful, then burned. She was his final indiscretion, the one that sent him from the monastery, lucky to leave with his life. That is all I was able to establish before he passed out; he woke the next day with a sore head and foul temper, and would tell me nothing more. When I asked Larcwide about it, tried to get an answer, he banned me from coming to see him. I'd hoped the intervening years and his age had dimmed the memory.

'And the book. Where would *this* have come from?'

He shrugged. 'Lost? Left behind? Stolen? Who knows. All I know is this isn't some harmless thing you're working on, Gytha.' He pauses, suddenly distrustful. 'You haven't read from it?'

I would like to deny it, but my blush makes a liar of me. Larcwide goes pales and pushes the volume at me, insistent. 'What did you read?'

Flicking carefully through the pages I find the relevant one, with the drawings of wheat sheaves and other plants. The old man's dark eyes skim the words and they seem to make sense to him as he sits back and puffs out a sigh of relief. 'Transformation, but it's just a season spell. Not much harm in it.'

'What's that?'

'To work change for a few months only, to make an animal shift its shape.'

'Not a person?' I worry at the bandaged finger, which has not healed these past weeks, but itches still.

'Oh no,' he flicks through the pages and points to a couplet. 'Here: this one will work on a person, but only one who is willing. A resistant subject requires far more effort, instruments and ingredients.' He rubs his hands together. Larcwide seems to know rather more about magic than he should, I think, but do not say. 'But you have no ability, so I shouldn't worry about it. Just don't do it again – some spells are so powerful they need only be spoken, without intent, for them to effect a metamorphosis, unwanted or otherwise. You should know, though, that every bit of magic leaves a trace, Gytha, no matter how small. Even the tiniest skerrick may rub off, leaving the potential for alteration in its wake.'

'Thank you, Father.' I take the book from him and begin to wrap it up once more. He leans across the table, grasps my wrist and says, 'What will you do with this?'

'This is a commission, I cannot simply make it disappear.' I lower my voice. 'And I fear this client, Father, I fear him greatly. I will not risk my life nor that of my family by refusing to give him what he has demanded.'

'But, child, it's too dangerous. If you will not listen to sense, I shall have to tell the Abbot.'

'And if you do so, there's every good chance I will be burned – it won't matter that this book is not mine, it will simply matter that it is in my possession.' I hold his gaze for a long moment. I do not think he would like to see me as ashes.

'What will you do?' he asks quietly once more, defeated.

I shake my head. 'I'll think of something.'

* * *

I wipe my hands on a rag, then wash with hot water and Edda's whortleberry soap, massaging the cramps and the smell of ink and oil out of them. Passing my desk I survey the work: the replica is almost done. I am exhausted and my eyes ache; I have been copying by the light of the fire and as many lanterns and candles as I could find without leaving my family in darkness. Outside the black mirror of the window, the air smells of spring. The days have grown longer, warmer, but I have spent an eternity inside, slaving over this damnable book. The time is fast approaching and although I have not slept well since the client's last visit, it is not the sole reason for my sleeplessness.

The doors to the bed cupboard are open, just a little, and inside I can make out blankets and coverlets heaped up, mounded over the form of a slumbering young man with the thickest, blackest hair relieved only by a streak of white down the middle. He snuffles and snores, his hands curled like paws, batting at the pillows as he stirs, then stilling as he settles once again.

I struggle with the buttons of my dress, then drop it to the rug, half-undone. Crawling in beside him, I fit myself into the half-moon of his body and breathe deeply. He smells musky, slightly sweet. I close my eyes, nestling as his arms come around me.

'I want peaches,' he mumbles, breath warm in my ear.

'You ate them all, remember?' That was how I found him, in his night-time shape, late on the evening I returned from St-Simeon-in-the-Grove, crouched on the floor of the cellar, struggling with a bottle of preserved peaches. His hands seemed not to know quite what to do, and he dropped the bottle, which smashed impressively. He merely gave a grunt and neatly picked slices of the preserved fruit from the glass, carefully examining it for shards, then elegantly chewed it in tiny bites.

'It doesn't stop me wanting them,' he points out, in a reasonable tone.

'Ordinary badgers don't eat peaches.'

'Well, I'm no ordinary badger, obviously,' he says, and shrugs, a movement that takes his whole body, not just his shoulders.

Badgerish.

'You ate plenty this evening. I cannot believe how much food you put away – and Aelfrith insists upon feeding you twice a day. You won't fit in my bed soon.'

'Get a bigger bed.' As he cuddles comfortably into my back, I take hold of one of his hands, weave our fingers together.

'At least there's no cheese left.'

'Oh, that cheese! Terrible cheese. Awful constipation.'

'An ordinary badger doesn't eat *cheese*. Or indeed, spend his winter in a girl's bed.'

'An ordinary badger doesn't get hit by stray magic.' He nuzzles my neck, pauses. 'How long will this last, do you think?'

I shake my head, feeling dizzy as if I am dangling over a terrible pit where all the loss in the world resides. 'I don't know.' I squeeze his hands. 'What do you think about, in the day? When you're…'

'Four-legged and furred? Comfortable things: food and warmth, staying safe, about spring and blackberries and wild cherries.' He wiggles against me to suggest the time for talking is done and other activities should be considered.

Here is the problem with raising daughters so far from suitable mates: it makes them prey to roaming, transformed badgers. It makes their hearts easy pickings, like windfall apples.

* * *

I keep my eyes downcast, but watch through lowered lashes. Adelbert is trying to hide his surprise at my seeming modesty. He is also trying to hide his look of mistrust. We sit in his study, all three of us on separate over-stuffed armchairs.

The client has my work in his hands. He is appreciating the fine red leather cover I've added. It is different to the old one, but I see that I was right: this pleases him, this newness. There is neither title nor author on the front.

'Your workmanship is exquisite, Mistress Gytha. I commend you.' He pulls a heavy bag of coins from his belt, holding it in one hand to delay the moment of parting from it. Adelbert's expression turns soft, like a drunk seeing his first ale of the day. 'And the original?'

'I burned it,' I pipe up and two pairs of eyes turn on me. I hold a small box and shake it gently. 'The ashes. The book – the ink was almost unreadable by the time I finished and I did not think you would care, sir. It was old and not new.'

The man stares at me for long moments, then nods and brings out a tight smile. 'Yes, you're right, Mistress Gytha. Although, such a decision I would have liked to make myself.'

He does not care the original is gone, he merely cares about my high-handedness. I offer the box and manage to sound sincere, 'I apologise, sir. Would you like…'

He shakes his head dismissively and I nod. 'I *am* very sorry, sir.'

'But let no deed should go unpunished,' he says and dips into the bag of coins, pulling out a sizeable handful and letting them *chink* into his own pocket. Adelbert receives the remainder, unprotesting, watches as the man places the book into a leather case he has brought specifically for the purpose. 'I shall take my leave.'

Father sees him to the door, then returns to the study. Through the open windows comes the warm air of the first day of spring. I watch, just as I watched him that first occasion, as the client appears around the side of the house, then disappears into the green of the woods. I do not pursue him this time. I watch until the trees swallow him, until I am sure he is nearing his waiting carriage, waiting far from us so no one will know he has been here, has brought something here, so no one will question and perhaps hunt here, or to speculate on whatever he is doing.

'Well done, Gytha,' says my father. His good mood cannot be contained, despite the loss of part of our fee, and it makes me wonder if all this has been about more than mere money. He moves around the room, laughing and joking, pouring us both a glass from the last bottle of the summer-berry wine. He counts out my share of the coin into a smaller purse and gives it to me. I sit opposite and stare until he becomes uncomfortable. 'What is it?'

'Who is he, Father? How did he come to us?' I ask now because it has occurred to me at last that Adelbert did not tell me how this client found us. It is his usual habit to go into great detail about who they are and what drew them here, who referred them on. That I've only just thought of this is a sign of my distraction.

Adelbert gives a kind of half-hearted shrug. 'I knew him long ago, in my days at university. Before the seminary, before St Simeon's.'

'He looks too young,' I point out and he shrugs again.

'Some age better than others. Perhaps his life has been easier.' He scratches at his chin. 'As I said, I knew him *before*.'

'Before Hafwen?' I do not say 'my mother' for she has never been that, only ever an absence to whom I was able to put a name a few years ago. He makes a sharp sound and jerks his head to one side before bringing his gaze back to me.

'Yes,' he says.

'Well?'

'Well what?'

'Who was she?'

'A girl. Just a girl.'

'Was she a witch?'

I have never seen such grief in my father, such a terrible thing clawing its way up from inside and painting itself across his face. He lowers his head so I cannot see, then slowly raises it once more. Everything is gone but an awful blankness. I will get nothing from him.

'Enjoy the spring, Gytha, while there are no new commissions,' he tells me and looks away, staring resolutely out the window at the garden, but not, I feel, seeing it. His voice halts me at the door. 'Gytha, all you need to know is that your work has paid a debt that will plague me no more. Never think me ungrateful, daughter, but never ask me about *her* again.'

* * *

From the blanket box at the foot of my bed, I lift out several coverlets, folded winter dresses and shawls. At the bottom is the original Murcianus grimoire, its text and diagrams re-inked each day before I copied it. Every page has been dusted with a setting powder of my own devising. I run my fingers across the cover and wonder how long it will take me to learn the language of witches, to take the knowledge I need for my purpose. I wonder if Larcwide might be prepared to teach me. I wonder if I have any of my mother's blood in me to help.

I notice a four-legged absence. I look around for the badger. He is not in his usual spot, the rug by the hearth, but then as the days have grown longer he has been roaming about the house more, seemingly restless. Perhaps he is in the kitchen, begging food from Aelfrith. He will be so fat soon.

My sister is rolling out dough; a dozen apples sit on the bench, waiting to be peeled. Beside them, a bucket of blackberries, lush and dark. But there is no sign of the badger.

'Where is he? Where is Brock?'

Aelfrith looks at me in surprise. 'He wanted to go out.'

The kitchen door stands open. From the threshold I survey the green grass and the plants, growing thickly in the house-garden.

No track, no trail, no hint.

I run out, to the stables. Edda has a curry comb and is grooming Hengroen.

'Have you seen him? Have you seen the badger?' I ask, uncaring that my voice is breaking.

She shakes her head, and *tuts*. 'You knew he would go, Gytha. I know you're fond of him, but he's a wild creature. It's not as if he's a dog or a horse.'

I knew the spell would end. I knew he would change back, but I thought he would stay. I thought he would wait, that he would ignore whatever recalled him to the forest. I thought I could find something in the grimoire, some means to make him transform for good, to keep him with me.

A breeze starts up but the dancing air does nothing to lift my spirits. I did not think his badgerish instincts would lead him away from me so soon. The itching of my punctured finger is all I have left.

* * *

It is only three days later that I see the client again.

I thought I would have longer. I had planned to leave when he'd collected his finished product, when I had both book and badger. I had planned to run and find another life, but with my love departed, I had fallen into a funk. I had lost the will to move. I lost any care that the golden-haired man might try one of his new spells and find it did not work. That he would try another and it, too, would not work. And another and another until he realised that I had copied each and every enchantment, each and every curse, incorrectly. Just a tiny detail in each, a line missing, an ingredient changed, a direction left out, an instrument added.

Sitting on the window seat in my room, I see the man breaking out of the woods, his long knife catching the sun, and I finally rediscover the will to move. I bundle the grimoire into a satchel and drape the bag's strap across my chest. I clatter down the stairs, run into Edda, who protests, until I put a hand over her mouth, the bandage still on the finger that will not heal.

'Sister, if you never listen to me again, listen now. Lock the doors. Do not let anyone in, especially not that man, the handsome man. Don't let him in, Edda, no matter what. Keep all the doors locked. I am sorry for whatever I may have brought down upon you.'

I flee before she can answer. I tear out the door, creep around the corner of the house, then make sure the client catches sight of me. He gives a sound somewhere between a yell and a scream, but all rage, and pounds after me. It's the only thing I can do, to draw him away from my family. As I run, I feel myself pulled onward, my direction not as haphazard as I planned. My feet seem to have a plan of their own.

I know these woodlands far better than he. I know the paths both seen and hidden, I dart between trees, under hanging mosses, I hurdle over rocks and stiles and rills, but still he keeps on my trail. I think of the words I've practised these past weeks.

Then, all is silence. I stop, wait, turning, turning, turning, trying to see if he is anywhere in sight. From behind a huge oak, he lunges, the knife preceding him and slicing across my left side, not enough to kill, but to wound, to hurt. I swing the heavy satchel up at him and catch him in the face. He goes down like a sack of potatoes. I run.

I keep running, fleeing into the darkest, deepest part of the wood, bleeding, weakening, aching, my lungs burning, my legs shaking. Silently I mouth the spell, the spell on which I pinned my last hopes, try to feel it taking effect but there is nothing. In a green hollow, a spot dotted with mounds and slopes, I trip over a fallen branch and the breath *whumps* out of me. I hit my chin and bite my tongue and taste iron. Behind me I can hear the crashing, the swearing, the inexorable rampaging of the golden-haired man.

My injured finger tingles, twinges, burns. I hear a chittering, a squeak, a growl close by. Searching, I find the mouth of a hole and in that mouth a creature of black and white, a fine well-fed badger, who calls to me. At last I think *Make a noise, make a sound, if it cannot be heard it cannot be made*! and I finally I speak aloud the couplet Larcwide pointed out that day at the abbey. With a shaking voice I speak through blood that spatters the ground. I scramble up, try to stand, but my entire body convulses, arcs in on itself. The hand with the injured finger curls beyond my will, as does the other. They turn ebony with fur, the nails elongating, becoming hard horn. I drop on all fours and shudder as the transformation completes.

The boar's call changes, the noise more urgent. With the strap of the satchel still around my new shoulders, I scamper up the hillock, and follow my love down the tunnel and into the sett. The book is dragged along behind, getting caught now and then, but the corridors are wide enough for it to get through with a tug or two. We come to a large chamber filled with clean straw; the strap slips from me, the book's progress halting, pushing up a wave of the dry yellow covering that will eventually settle over it.

I can no longer hear the sounds aboveground of a man thwarted and driven beyond his patience. I cannot hear the raging and the cries of loss. I lie still and my mate snuffles at the wound in my side, licking it clean. He curves around me, our black and white fur a chessboard match. Even as I hope my family will be safe, I begin to forget Fox Hollow House. Ideas about books and inks and pages and covers all subside into a dim memory place. I begin to think of worms and beetles, of windfall apples, blackberries, and wild cherries. I begin to think badgerish thoughts.

THE BURNT MOON

Three days after Hafwen was turned to ash, the rats invaded Southarp.

They started at the Burnt Moon Mill, spilling up and out from a hole in the floor, climbing walls and clinging to the ceiling. They quickly spread through the town until the streets seemed an undulating carpet of dark fur. The good citizens could not move but that they put a foot down upon a squeaking, protesting rodent.

But that was three days after, three days after the fagots and sticks were lit beneath the giddy-headed girl, then fanned until the larger branches and logs caught. Until the flames flicked and licked at her toes, the soles of her feet; until they engulfed the ankles, calves, knees, thighs, the belly so recently flattened, up, up, the stomach, the breasts, the shoulders, neck and finally the head with all its lovely golden hair. And Hafwen, fair summer, was gone, cindered and sundered.

But that's by the by. The story doesn't start there, not with the rats, nor even with poor Hafwen's incineration. The story begins a whole week *before* the funeral pyre was sparked.

The story begins, as all good tales do, in a tavern with a kilderkin of mead, two monks speaking of foxes, and a wager.

* * *

'My dear Abbot, you cannot be serious,' Larcwide says to his tall, black-bearded, portly companion. Well, it was what he tried to say, but as he had been drinking – they both had, quite copiously – it came out rather differently, slurred, in no way enunciated. Fortunately, the language of the inebriated is one in which all drunks are fluent, and Adelbert had no trouble understanding his compatriot.

He nods sagely, as if Larcwide's statement is one with which he agrees wholeheartedly – Adelbert's favoured tactic for disarming opponents – then voices his passionate disagreement. 'The fox,' he begins, between hiccups. 'The fox is a finer vehicle for a witch than a hare.'

Adelbert proceeds to shore up his statement; he cites authorities from far and wide, across seas and mountains, time and cultures. He makes an argument so convincing, so powerful, so seemingly founded in the bedrock of fact, that even Larcwide – who knows his young friend is talking out of his fundamental orifice – is *almost* converted. Adelbert references vulpine cunning, sharp wit, keen sense of smell, speed, astonishing sight, ability to make itself almost invisible despite its flame-coloured fur, and talent at finding the tiniest of holes, slipping through it in order to get to what others don't want them to reach. Indeed, to save itself from what, to a lesser animal, would be certain death.

'It is well known and even you cannot deny,' concludes Adelbert, 'that foxes will gather where a witch lives.'

Larcwide shakes his head, as much to clear his mead-induced fug as to dislodge such rubbish from his ears. His abbot waggles a finger at him, as if the Librarian is a callow youth and not the older, wiser man.

'Indeed, I do believe Anselm the Adroit wrote of just such a transformation in his *bestiarum vocabulum*.'

Larcwide knows this is not true – he has read Anselm's bestiary from cover to cover many times, for he delights in the scholar's descriptions of strange beasts and their lands. He snorts and it spurs Adelbert on. Here is the abbot's downfall: in his cups, the determination to win overcomes all sense of caution. In trying to compel his audience, he goes too far, makes claims that can be easily disproved and the whole platform of his dissertation falls away.

'I'll wager you – just you see – I'll wager you it's true.'

'And what's the stake, Adelbert?' Larcwide sobers, just enough, at the thought of a bet.

'A copy…' Adelbert racks his brain, 'a copy of the *Incantations of Margaret the Barefooted*.'

'A rare tome, Adelbert,' warns Larcwide, becoming more alert by the second.

'I have one,' the abbot burps. Larcwide hides a smile as he bats away the smell of twice-fermented mead and the roasted goat Adelbert ate earlier. He knows Adelbert has the only *Incantations* within a three-week ride – a book, it should be noted, the possession of which is forbidden to individuals and the presence of which is even frowned upon in highly secure monasteries. While Adelbert's quality of trying to convince others to believe in things that can neither be seen nor proven is valuable in a man of religious habits, it is also a tendency that can cost him dearly. Combined with unwise gambles, it has, on more than one occasion, resulted in the growth of Larcwide's personal library.

The bibliosoph also knows there is a danger in speaking lies with such conviction. It may well amuse Adelbert to practise his powers of persuasion in the company of his oldest friend, a man of equal intellect who knows a joke when he hears one, but others are not so erudite. Not so attuned to the subtleties of a jest, to its depths and breadths, its meanings that lurk beneath the surface rather like warning rocks. Others, not so familiar with Adelbert and his tendency toward contrarianism, are assured, if not by the content and the actual words, then by the sheer seeming *belief*, and the fact that the man making the argument is the abbot of the not-too-near-but-not-so-far monastery of St-Simeon-in-the-Grove. Others may be persuaded entirely despite the fact that everyone *knows* witches transform into hares, not foxes, for foxes have such an emphatic will – they are too wild, too difficult a form from which to return. The witch who became a fox, wisdom has it, would either need to be tremendously strong-minded and in tune with the beast's nature, or so docile as to be subsumed beneath the creature's disposition. The hare was much stupider, easier to invade and therefore much more likely a vehicle.

Cern, the innkeeper, is not a witless man. He listens to all those who pass through his doors – as is the wont of his profession – he gathers nuggets of information, never truly discarding anything. He hoards this evening's conversation as he watches the two men. The monks come once a month, to Southarp, to oversee the grinding of the monastery's grain, the sale of its lambs and wool, its bottled fruits, its barrels of mead – as seasons change, so do the reasons for St Simeon's Abbot and Librarian to leave their posts and come to the village. They have a standing booking at the inn, the same relatively sumptuous rooms, and Cern welcomes them like old friends then leaves them to their own devices like a good host, reappearing only when they need more food or drink.

He watches them now as they sway to their feet, stand briefly straight, then begin the staggering walk required to get them upstairs. In their chambers, women wait: a red-haired waif for Larcwide, and in Adelbert's bed, Hafwen, sleek once more now their daughter is out.

* * *

Hafwen sings as she makes her way to the bakehouse for the first time since she gave birth. The market square with its bustling folk, bubbling fountain with a metal mari-morgan in the centre, and tall avenue of rose bushes, has fallen behind her; she passes rows of neat white and brown cottages, each with handkerchief gardens sweet with spring flowers. She follows the packed earth road to the edge of the village, past the inn, and soon enough she can hear the splash and slap of water hitting the mill wheel.

Beneath scarlet skirts, her hips swing in time with the tune, creating a hypnotising rhythm for any male who crosses her path. Cern watches her from the doorway of the inn; he polishes the silver goblet harder and harder as she passes. Hafwen gives him a half-smile, aware of the effect she has, but not considering its possible consequences.

A woven basket hangs loosely from the crook of her arm; beneath the green cloth is a side of bacon, a wheel of cheese, a block of butter, purchased from the market stalls. Now all she requires is to collect the bread she left as dough this morning with Cenred. In the pocket of her well-washed apron jingle the four copper bits he will demand for use of his oven – as if it's not enough that the village must pay him to grind their wheat to flour! But Hafwen knows, if she wishes, she could have all Cenred's services for free.

She does not wish, nor has she ever. Hafwen has not looked to the men of Southarp to receive her favours, not since she first felt stirrings between her legs. Luckily, she often thinks, Adelbert came riding into town, the thin librarian by his side, before Hafwen needed to consider one of the lumpen-brained villagers as a balm for her itches and aches. She cannot marry him she knows, but at this stage it does not trouble her. Mayhap in years to come she will experience discontent, certainly when the child is older and Hafwen's mother, Friðuswith, once again takes to the roads; when Adelbert's visits wane. Mayhap she will hear about his other two daughters and realise he has never ceased to visit *their* mothers.

But, for now, she is happy with her lot. And she forgets, conveniently, that before Adelbert's arrival, the miller had once seemed like a good match.

The abbot has returned to St Simeon for another month and her mother, curtailing her travels, is here to visit and help look after the child. In truth, Hafwen suspects Friðuswith does not trust her light-minded daughter to care for the baby. She has not revealed the length of her stay to Hafwen, who will not care if it is a very long one.

It is no hardship for the pretty, feckless girl to hand the babe over to someone else's care, and if it weren't for the heaviness in her breasts and the milk she can smell upon her skin no matter how often she bathes, she could almost believe herself childless once again.

She crosses the wooden bridge that spans the stream grown fat with spring run-off. The Burnt Moon Mill was built by Cenred and Cern's grandparents; it passed to the boys' father, and thence to Cenred. Cern got the tavern, which their mother had brought as her dowry.

Their sister, who is sweeping the stoop of the cottage, set between the bakehouse and the mill, received nothing. Wulfwyn remains a spinster, keeping board for her brothers; she has the worn look of woman ill-used. Her yellow-green stare at the abbot's mistress is blank, empty of either dislike or otherwise.

Hafwen passes her without acknowledgement.

She pushes the door to the bakehouse and breathes deeply the scent of fresh bread. The large square room is overly warm, even though the windows are open wide and the oven-fires have been banked for some hours. Her loaf, golden brown and sprinkled with seeds, waits on the sill where it is always left. She places it into the basket beneath the cloth. There is no sign of the miller; she plays with the copper bits. Hafwen is not one to leave hard-won coin lying about.

She crosses the yard then passes into the darkness of the mill. It takes a few moments for her eyes to adjust and the sudden sight of Cenred startles her. Residue from the grinding of the great millstone has rendered him ghostly pale. He is muscular and short, with shaggy brown hair that he ties with a ragged ribbon. His fringe hangs in his eyes, which are a blue so dark they're almost black. He is still, as if he has been waiting for her.

Hafwen giggles nervously. She retrieves the coppers from her pocket and rattles them against one another, then holds her palm out to him. But he doesn't take the coins. He wraps his large callused hand around her wrist and holds tight. Hafwen blinks, smiles.

'You look well,' Cenred says, voice gruff. He does not let her go. 'Beautiful. Beautiful again.'

Hafwen is miffed at the thought that pregnancy had rendered her somehow unlovely, and Cenred must see this in her face. He blushes beneath his coating of wheat-dust. 'I meant, I just meant—'

'Take your coins and let me be,' she says. If Hafwen has nothing else, it is the certainty that she is the prettiest girl in Southarp.

She doesn't care when other maidens snigger behind her back and cast side-long jade-tinged glances at her in the market square – they're just jealous and she knows this. But for a man – any man – to imply her looks were at any time less than powerful, less than compelling, less than arousing, is an insult she will not bear. And for it to be this man, this *little* man with his stench of sweat and flour. She tries to pull away, but he won't let go, his expression becoming desperate.

'Don't go! Please, Hafwen, listen to me!'

She stops struggling, gives him a suspicious glare. He has not loosened his grip.

'I only… Hafwen… you need… I want…'

'Spit it out, you halfwit!'

'I want to – look after you. And the child. I will take the child, too, for your sake,' he stammers and stumbles over his words, all his good intentions tripping him up. This was not how he planned to make his wishes – his generosity, his kindness to her – known. He babbles and as he does so, he begins to hate her, for the effect she has on him, for making him feel like a fool, for making him hard even now when he imagines he can smell that *priest* on her, for looking at him as if he is an idiot. 'I will take you to wife, make you decent.'

The girl's eyes widen, her green gaze disbelieving; her lips part and, still incensed, still seared by his perceived disrespect, she does the worst thing she possibly could.

Hafwen laughs.

* * *

Friðuswith dabs a cold damp cloth on her daughter's split lip. She used a moss poultice to stem the bleeding elsewhere. Hafwen will not speak; she has turned inward, shrinking from the horror of having something that should only ever have been given willingly taken so violently. In a cradle beside her bed, the baby is fussing, though not crying, the thick black hair inherited from her father already at shoulder length.

The village beadle left an hour or so ago. Summoned to see the state of Southarp's prettiest girl after Cenred had vented his frustration and wounded pride, the fat man's face darkened and he tapped his baton meaningfully against the top of his leather boots. He would, he promised Friðuswith, take the matter to the bailiff; then they would proceed to Burnt Moon Mill.

From the window of Hafwen's second floor bedroom her mother watches as the two officials step from the meeting hall, where the bailiff holds his court once a week, and head towards the edge of the village. They are accompanied by four able-bodied men: the blacksmith, the farrier, the church warden and the costermonger, all moving with purpose and carrying cudgels. Friðuswith feels a swelling in her chest: these are good men and they will get redress for what has been done to her daughter, her ruined child.

She runs through the list of herbs she will need to soothe Hafwen's hurts: comfrey for the bruises, lavender and aloe to help the cuts heal, hemlock to take away the swelling. Then belladonna for forgetting – no, celandine as it's less volatile – and valerian to calm her. Agrimony leaves under her pillow for the dreamless sleep she will so desperately need in the weeks to come, then St John's Wort to lift her spirits. Friðuswith twists her hands as she thinks, plots, schemes to make her daughter well; she has most of those things in her travelling pack, pressed between the leaves of her notebooks. Anything else she can find in the woods beyond the back of the house – this house where she once lived, long years until Eadmund finally died and set her free – in the hidden groves and gardens she herself dug and planted, nourished in secret. They will be overgrown now, but she does not doubt she will still find them growing wild. She is so distracted she does not notice, far, far down the street, that the group of good men, her avengers, are traipsing back from the mill. They do not have Cenred with them.

The baby wails and shakes her grandmother from reverie. Gathering up the little girl, Friðuswith rocks her until she quietens. There is a knock on the front door, almost unwilling, almost tentative, almost as if the knocker would prefer to slink away. With the child held tight against her chest, she goes downstairs and answers the reluctant summons.

'Friðuswith,' says the beadle. Behind him his supporters look intently at their feet, hands in pockets, scuffing their shoes in the dirt of the path leading to the little house with the dark green door. 'Friðuswith, there's a problem.'

When he tells her what that problem is, her scream is heard throughout Southarp, echoed by the child's howling wail.

* * *

Cern thought long and hard about denying that Cenred had even been in the mill, thought about claiming that his brother had been with him the whole time, but the Widow Albright had crossed the bridge just as Cenred stepped through the doorway, hitching up his britches and trying to wipe the blood from his white shirt, to stop the bleeding from the deep scratch on his face. At first the Widow thought he'd hurt himself, but then she noticed Hafwen dragging herself out after him, scarlet skirts in disarray, bruises beginning to darken her face, red seeping from her lip and other places. There was no denying that the girl had been violated. No one would believe it if he said his sibling was safely ensconced with him in the inn, counting barrels of mead in the cellar.

So Cern, knowing that his brother had harboured feelings for the girl for so very long, knowing that Cenred had cherished bright hopes long after they should have been dashed by the swelling of Hafwen's belly with another man's child, knowing that he could not bear to be left to run the mill, the tavern *and* the bakehouse on his own, did the only other thing he could think of.

'Witches turn into foxes,' he blurted much to the astonishment of both beadle and bailiff. 'The Abbot of St Simeon's said so, not two nights ago. And the Librarian agreed with him.'

'What does this have to do with what Cenred did to that poor girl?' demanded the beadle, clutching at his baton.

'Foxes gather where witches bide,' insisted Cern, his hands held tight in front of him to stop him from twisting the skin from the corners of his nails, a sure sign of untruth.

The bailiff shook his head in bewilderment and Cern saw his chance slipping away.

'Foxes gather outside Hafwen's house. She's a witch,' he fairly shouted. 'She bewitched Cenred, there's no other reason why he'd do that. He's been witched, I tell you.'

And while rape was indeed a crime and there was no doubt that the girl had been taken against her will, there was not a man in the group who didn't tremble at the thought of witchcraft; at the idea that his volition might be taken from him at any moment by a woman with wiles and will. And they all thought of the times when Hafwen had walked past them, with a sway in her step, a smile on her lips, and how their very thoughts betrayed them, how their very cocks, their very selves, responded like trained dogs without so much as a by-your-leave.

Yes, if there was witchcraft afoot in Southarp, then it was a serious matter indeed. If there was witchcraft afoot, then these good men all knew how to deal with such a problem. Fire was called for, for fire cleansed all.

'My brother would never touch a woman without her consent,'

Cern vowed – although their sister would tell a different story had anyone thought to ask her. Cern, unconsciously adopting Adelbert's speech patterns, the nodding of his head, the set of his gaze, had learned something about conviction. 'Watch by moonlight and you'll see.'

Which was how the beadle and the bailiff came to spend part of their evening crouched at the window of Hafwen's bedroom, the silent girl curled in the bed behind them, ignoring their whispered woes, their sotto voce plans. The two men watched the grassy expanse between cottage and woods, eyes darting hither and yon as they sought signs beneath the light of a witch's moon. First one, then two then three, and finally a dozen foxes grazed in the limpid brilliance. The creatures fed, sniffing and snuffling at the sedgy ground, scavenging whatever they could find. They gorged themselves on the mix that Cern had thrown there earlier that afternoon; they came attracted by the smell and the promise of over-ripe berries mixed with gamy meat; they came and unwittingly condemned Hafwen to the flames.

And no one thought to question why Hafwen would bewitch a man to do her harm.

* * *

The last thing Friðuswith is able to do before good men (each wearing a pouch filled with rowan and hawthorn twigs to keep them safe from magics) surround her house, is bribe the butcher's boy to take a message to Adelbert. He is only one in the village she can convince to do this – years ago her herb-lore saved him from being a cripple, but it still requires a push from his own mother to make him saddle the great draught horse and urge it along the road to St-Simeon-in-the-Grove. She sends the message praying that the abbot will be there, that he will return in time. It is the only hope she can have. Burnings do not delay in Southarp, lest a witch manage to influence townsfolk and judges before justice can be done. It is almost thirty years since the last conflagration and the village had thought itself free of the menace of sorcery. Serves them right, they admonished themselves, for becoming complacent, for not being more vigilant. For not paying attention.

So. The note is sent to Adelbert, who, due to a detour to visit one of his other mistresses, is not at the abbey. It is received the day after the young mother has become ash. The second day after Hafwen's burning, Wulfwyn knocks on Friðuswith's door. The hollow-eyed women stare at each other for long moments before Friðuswith steps aside and lets the other in. In the kitchen, the baby sleeps in a basket – her grandmother cannot bear to let the child from her sight and carries her from room to room – and Wulfwyn sits at the table, watching the infant sleep.

Wulfwyn does not pay attention as the older woman grinds leaves for tea. She does not see the calamus root and bergamot leaves, the liquorice root and elder flower, the blood root and the five finger grass all carefully measured and crushed to a fine powder. And even if she had paid attention, Wulfwyn would not have recognised them, would not have known that they are commanding herbs, plants which give dominion over the spirit and mind.

When she speaks, her tone uncertain, her voice is low, as if she is unused to its sound, as if she barely recognises it herself. Friðuswith listens, but she does not pause in her endeavours.

'He lied. They both lied, and I am sorry for it.'

'Why didn't you come forward before? Before my child was nothing more than a dying ember?' Friðuswith keeps most of the agony from her voice. Wulfwyn's thin shoulders travel up and down, but there are no tears to accompany the gesture, no sobs – she has none left, although her pain is real.

'They are my brothers. I would lose my home. Worse, they would kill me.' She picks at a thread on her apron, looking very young; she is, after all, no older than Hafwen was. 'Although, perhaps that would not have been so bad.'

Friðuswith pours hot water from the pot above the fire over the dried ingredients and a fragrance fills the air that makes Wulfwyn's heart lift. It is the sensation of surrender, of letting one's own will go, of allowing another to make all one's choices. It is a false sense of responsibility no longer being yours. She blows on the surface of the beverage, anxious to drink, and it is still a little too hot when she gulps it down, but she doesn't care; the burning in her mouth, the searing of her throat, the flaring warmth in her belly matter not a jot. Wulfwyn has abdicated and Friðuswith willingly takes the reins.

That night, Wulfwyn waits until her brothers are drunk and passed out at the dining table. They have done this each night since Hafwen's dishonouring. She tiptoes into the balmy air and steps through the velvety darkness as if she is dancing, light-footed and far more graceful than she ever is. Inside the mill, she finds the place, the spot where the wood has been rotting, decaying. It doesn't take much for her to knock a hole the size of a man's fist in boards the consistency of mouldy bread. From under her skirts, she takes the parcel Friðuswith tied there so no one would know. Inside the scarlet bundle – the cloth was cut from Hafwen's skirts and the girl's blood stands out as a darker hue against the field of red – she can feel long thin *things*, between four and six inches in length, organic and soft through the fabric. The scent of angelica is strong as is the smell of grave dust and spoor and decay. Wulfwyn knows not to unwrap Friðuswith's gift.

She pushes the parcel into the hole, makes sure it is secure then pulls a woven basket across to hide the breach. Wulfwyn goes to bed and sleeps the best she has in long, long years.

* * *

The rats are phenomenally destructive. No home is left untouched, except that of Hafwen – and by the time anyone notices, Friðuswith and the baby are gone.

It is night when Adelbert arrives at last. He sits in the back of a hay wain, which is outfitted by torches to light the way, drinking from a fine silver cup engraved with a hunting scene. At the edge of the village, the cart stops, the horses refusing to wade into the shifting sea of rats. A covered bucket is held firm between the abbot's feet so its contents may not slosh and spill. Some of the villagers have fled, others are stubbornly staying in their homes, stuffing cloth into previously unsuspected gaps in walls and floors, hammering planks over those same gaps as a double-measure, laying out poison in the hope that, in the morning, the number of rodents will be markedly less. The village cats have gorged themselves stupid and, fat and torpid, shun further mouthfuls of rat. Cenred and Cern were both found the morning after the first wave of the plague hit, in the cottage, chewed and chewed and dead. Of Wulfwyn, there was no sign.

The beadle and the bailiff attend upon the Abbot, who does not move from his padded seat in the wagon. He stares and waits for them to speak. A very young monk refreshes his goblet from an elaborate ewer.

'Your Grace,' begins the beadle.

'Your Eminence,' follows the bailiff.

Adelbert merely raises an eyebrow.

'Help us,' begs the beadle.

'Tell us what to do,' requests the bailiff.

At last the Abbot speaks. 'Fire is your fondest solution. Burn it. Burn it all.'

He hands his goblet to the boy beside him, then picks up the bucket, knocking away its lid. Adelbert stands and throws the contents – a liquid with a strange green luminescence, the recipe for which will one day cost him more than he can imagine – across the shivering, shuddering, juddering field of fur, then just as quickly detaches one of the flickering torches from the wain and hurls it at the creatures. The carpet of rodents lights up as if a great wyvern has breathed over them. The ignited bodies tumble and move, the flames dancing upon them, leaping one to the other. From the rats to the gardens, to the fences, thence the cottages, the shops, the market stalls.

Soon, all of Southarp is ablaze, and many of its citizens with it. Adelbert watches with an unconcerned stare.

And in the darkness at the forest's fringe, beyond where the Burnt Moon sparks and smoulders, Hafwen's mother sits, embraced by shadows, shifted to her travelling shape, wearing her dark red fur, four paws neatly placed. Friðuswith watches Adelbert. She could take this moment, she knows, to teach him a lesson, to avenge her daughter, but she knows in her heart he is not responsible for what happened to Hafwen; she knew he would not be able to respond to her missive in that brief sliver of time betwixt accusation and burning. She thinks he carries enough soul-sorrow with him now; the weight of Hafwen's death, and all those of the townsfolk not fast enough to escape the fire he set.

Her arms feel empty, the place where the baby has been held against her chest these past weeks is cold. She has left the little one, Gytha, at St Simeon, with the thin librarian, along with instructions she be handed to her father and a note that says *Gather your daughters to you, try to protect them better than you did mine.*

As for Friðuswith, the road calls once more, the silver benediction of the alder well racing through her veins. She has so many things to record, so many words and ideas, magic and wonders, needing to be committed to paper. She will not stop until she has written her fill, her due, her debt. Until she has done all she promised to do.

BY MY VOICE I SHALL BE KNOWN

If I still had a voice, I would cry out.

The fabric is thick and my needle blunt – I should have sharpened it before now – so I put too much weight behind my thrust and forced the point. Not only the quilt, but also my finger is impaled. I do not wail, though I long to, determined not to make the hideous grunt that is the only noise left to me. In my memory, I still hold the sound of my voice, but each time I *bellow* it lessens, chips away at the timbre so lovingly preserved in recollection. Slowly, carefully, I draw the thread fully through, then pull my injured digit off the silver shaft. A scrap of spare cloth is wrapped around the glistening blue-ruby drop, then the needle itself is assiduously cleaned. I set the bulky bundle of material aside and limp, my legs stiff from hours of sitting, to the basin in the far corner of the tiny room Mother Magnus has given me. Washing the injury, applying a salve, then bandaging the deep wound; I look out the window, not really seeing so much as remembering what is there before me.

Bellsholm sprawls along the banks of the wide Bell River, loose-limbed as a sleeping giant; a rough crescent with its northern tip truncated by the bulk of the Singing Rock. In the foothills that hug the edge of the town some few ramshackle houses have crept, not too high, and certainly nothing up on the majestic outcropping of the promontory. At the furthest boundaries there are farms to supply the markets and businesses best located away from the centre of town, such as the carriage maker, the foundry, the marble worker's studio, three carpentry and joinery firms, and Ballantyne's Coffin Emporium where the strange woman employs four apprentices and, rumour has it, keeps a locked room filled entirely with mirrors. There is also the hostelry, where travellers with no interest in the hamlet can rest, eat, exchange their tired horses for fresh ones, then continue their journeys. Down by the river are the docks, brimming and bobbing with great ships from afar filled with all the finest things a prosperous place requires, and small local boats that bring in fish and travel up and down the reaches too narrow for the caravels and barques.

I can hear, dimly, the melodies of the *rusalky*, wafting up from the base of the Rock, where they laze daily (except Sundays when the sound of church bells sends them into hiding) and serenade anyone who will listen. Murdered maidens, those unfortunate in love, gather their spirits to sit on the rocks, dangling luminescent toes in the water. The weak of will may traipse too close and fall in. Some drown. The natives are, by now, mostly inured to the strains and are all brought up to swim like eels – indeed, Léolin will tell you that as a young man only his strong stroke saved him on the day when he was distracted by a particularly lovely ballad. The greatest danger is to travellers, on ships and on the roads, unfamiliar with our ladies.

My finger aches and throbs and drags me back to the four-walled space with its thin-mattressed brass bed, ancient velvet-covered chaise, stand of drawers, and the single lantern to brighten my nights. I must ignore the pain and get back to my work. To the quilt, the wedding quilt; the wedding quilt that should have been mine.

* * *

Adlai made his money on the ships.

I cannot say when we first met, for it seemed he was always there beside me as we two orphans made our way in the world – but our whole time together, reason tells me, could not have been more than three years. So, perhaps we met soon after I first came here, hoping to find a home. I had a voice then. A voice with which to sing and shout, speak and chant, to laugh and sometimes lie. I had a voice to say 'Yes' when he asked me to lie with him, to say 'Aye' when he begged 'Marry me', to say 'Please' when asked if he should read to me that which I could not for myself, and to bid him 'Farewell, fair winds' when he sailed off on his very first journey. He – *we* – had scrimped and saved, set aside the fare for his passage and the funds needed for the silks and velvets, the barathea and the bayadere, the cashmeres and organzas he would bring back to Bellsholm.

We had not married – all our meagre capital went towards this endeavour, towards *establishing* Adlai – but it was, he assured me, only a matter of time. The first trip was a happy success; the exquisite bolts of cloth were demanded by *modistes*, interior stylists, furniture makers, and craftsfolk whose living lay in creating elaborate curtains and cushions and bed linen for those with more funds than sense. We made a profit, some of which was set aside and the rest reinvested in his next buying expedition.

Adlai's apprenticeship to a gentlemen's costumier did not satisfy him. He did not see any way that he might *rise* – even were he to inherit the business from his master some way down the track, he would not reach the heights he desired for himself. There would be no grand house in the Vines district (itself a tiny created island, surrounded by a diverted channel of the river, and accessed by six tidy bridges), no closed fiacre in red and black, no servants, no piles of gold gradually accruing interest in the Bellsholm Bank, and – did I but know it – no well-bred wife to admire it. All that life guaranteed for him was continued servitude to those above, measuring coats and breeches, cutting waistcoats from splendid cloth he himself would never wear.

As funds accumulated, so our accommodations grew finer – or rather, so *his* grew finer. From the garret atop the gentlemen's outfitter, to a small room in Mrs Xavier's Rooming House, thence to a larger chamber, then to a suite with two rooms, then three, then four, until finally he purchased a tall house in Lady's Mantel Court. It was three storeys high and, by all accounts, equipped with five bedrooms, an attic with space to store seven servants, a subterranean kitchen, and a large tidy garden out back. The façade was smoothed plaster, painted apricot and white, with shimmering filigree touches on the window and door fittings. A high wrought iron fence, black, with gold and silver finials on each spike, kept the common riff-raff on the street where they belonged. A riot of well-tended flowers bloomed in the front garden.

Adlai then handsomely paid those very same furniture makers and interior designers, curtain and linen and cushion makers, who had sought his wares so avidly, to decorate his home. The perfectly serviceable fittings and furnishings left by the former owners (an importer of wines and his wife and sons, fallen on hard times due to the predations of pirates) were thrown out on the streets, and quickly snatched up by those with less cash and more cunning. The old drapes were piled beside padded chairs, sets of drawers, myriad duchesses and chaises; these textiles, hardly faded, disappeared rapidly, only to reappear not many days later as dresses for girls and exuberant sailor suits for boys. Wallpaper, which had clung vertical for barely twelve months, was scraped off and burned in the basement furnace. Everything, it seemed, must be *new*.

In the end, the abode at Number 6 Lady's Mantel Court outshone its neighbours. Adlai Alveson's social status climbed as well – prosperity turned his humble origins into a mere bagatelle, easily overlooked. He became a member of the chamber of commerce, of the town council, and gained in short order a reputation as something of a philanthropist with donations to the orphanage and the home for sailors' widows. His betters (some still in full possession of their affluence, others rather impoverished but with breeding in spades), soon turned speculative eyes toward him. Few things open doors like a rapidly expanding fortune.

Why did I not move in with him as his lodgings changed? I asked – oh, I did ask! – and was assured it would happen, but not yet, not at *that* precise moment. He promised most faithfully that it should come to pass, but for the sake of propriety, it would only be after the wedding, the date of which seemed to shift like the horizon each time I enquired. And I did not push, for after all, wasn't Adlai the one doing all the work? Wasn't he the one who travelled and travailed to ensure our future? So I remained, faithfully, steadfastly, in the attic room above my place of employ, Sally Sanders Quality Quilts, sewing counterpanes for people's weddings, stitching in tiny spells and good luck charms to help happiness, fertility and longevity attach themselves to a couple's life together. Putting aside the money I made – for I wanted a wedding dress worthy of the name – and making my own quilt out of the lovely scraps my mistress let me harvest from the leftovers of the bedspreads I created for other women.

Adlai would visit, bringing gifts: kid gloves of deepest red, embroidered handkerchiefs, hats so thin they seemed spun of gossamer and wishes, a thimble, sharp scissors so beautifully crafted they appeared art rather than implement, and an enamelled brooch in the shape of a lovers' knot, which disappeared almost as soon as it arrived – Adlai said its clasp was loose, he would have it fixed, but it never again came into my possession. These presents, when they ceased, were soon replaced by small piles of coin before he left of a morning – or an evening – but I did not recognise them for what they were: payment for services rendered. He told me fewer and fewer of his dreams, rarely reading to me, never mentioning the time when we would marry and I would join him in his grand home.

Still and all, I welcomed him with open arms each and every time, greeted him with patience and trust – although truth be told I ignored the things that gave me pause. The fear of being alone was too great in those days, of being set aside – if I did not look directly at it, I felt certain I would not see it and if I did not see it then surely it could not exist. So I blinded myself quite willingly, showed him the designs I'd drawn for our wedding quilt, told him of the enchantments and charms I'd created just for us. How this would be my finest work, and we would be bonded more strongly than any lovers had ever been. I did not notice, then, how he changed the subject, nor how he failed to answer questions that pertained to our future. I filled the silences, the gaps between us with mindless chatter, busy useless noise. Had I but known my voice had only a short time to remain, I'd have chosen my words more scrupulously, used my breath more wisely, said things of importance.

* * *

I creep to the edge of the water, hang out over the bank like a weeping branch. The current is fast, the surface touched by a light cold mist that floats up towards me – it will burn off when dawn breaks properly. In the weak light, I can see my quarry, dozing on a horse-shaped rock but a long leap away.

In sleep, the *rusalka* has lost some of her form. In the sunlight, when they know they're watched, they are careful to keep the shape they had in life; slumbering, they grow forgetful and let the changes wrought by experience and death come to the fore. The skin has a greenish tint, the hair a will of its own – not a gentle undulation as if shifted by eddies, but an angry serpentine motion. I can see, if I look closely, the holes in her body where the rot has eaten through.

I select a pebble from the ground and take careful aim. The thing on the rock jerks awake when hit, all grace lost to surprise; she hisses, her teeth sharp, and eyes backlit by an unholy fire. I shudder, just a little, but I do not show fear when her glare lands on me. I straighten and begin my dumb show. She calms as she realises there is a deal to be made, and relaxes back into her daylight aspect: long-limbed, golden-haired, smiling, teeth as neat and white as pearls, gaze as blue as a summer sky.

I tap at my eyes, so she knows where things start, then my fingertips patter on my cheeks, miming rain. She cocks her head to the side, lifts an eyebrow; she knows what *I* want, but wonders what I will give in return. From the pocket of my apron, I draw an embroidered swathe of white cambric and slowly unfold its layers so she may view what lies therein. Her eyes go wide, and I hide a smile, knowing I will get my way in this thing. I look down at the long, thick plait of auburn-rose hair curled around and around, all three yards of it, thick as a baby's arm. The length that once hung down my back. I brushed it one hundred times to make sure it shone like richest cinnabar, then carefully plaited it before Magnus, protesting at the loss, cut it carefully off with the large, sharp scissors I reserve for shearing through dense fabrics. Magnus swore the murdered maids would find it irresistible, and I would need something irresistible if I was to gain the first ingredient.

The *rusalka* nods, this bargain too good to refuse, although I cannot imagine what she will use the tresses for; I do not care.

I pull a golden vial from my apron and carefully toss it towards her; she snatches it from the air, quick as a snake. She appears to concentrate and then, as if on cue, she weeps. No actress treading the stages of the great cities could do better. Sluggish silver tears creep down her cheeks and she holds the ampule up to catch them, first one side, then the next. She cries freely, generously. When she is done, she pushes the stopper home, making sure nothing can escape, then slips down the rock and swims to me in a flash of white skin-now scales, flashing feet-now tail. She reaches up and offers me the vial; I reach down and give her the coil of hair; we swap our treasures at the same moment.

We both smile, each certain that she has gained the better part of the bargain.

* * *

On the day the *Revenant* docked, I was placing the last stitches in *my* quilt, the silver thimble he'd brought me all the way from Lodellan shining on my pointer finger. Pure damask, a double wedding ring pattern embroidered in argent threads. Between the two internal layers of padding I had sewn a series of tokens: tiny sterling horseshoes, miniature bags containing sprigs of apple blossom, yet others of althea and balm of gilead, cardamom and clove, rose and lavender; love knots and bows, four coins (one for each corner), and seersucker clovers.

And it was white, so white, white as snow, white as bone.

I finished my task, dexterously folded the coverlet, wrapped it in a laurel green cloth, tied it all together with a silk ribbon, then gently placed it in the box of reinforced hunter-coloured brocade decorated with gold lace trim. The box with the tiny stain in one corner that was ruined for customers, but which Mistress Saunders was more than happy to let me have. I wonder now, as I did not then, why I was so willing to accept second best things.

Outside, the air was fresh and intoxicating after a morning of being cooped up in my attic room. I wandered down to the docks, thinking to buy some of the sweet small fish Léolin kept aside, perhaps a fresh loaf of bread, which would be delicious today and passable tomorrow. As I neared, I could hear the sounds of ships creaking against moorings, of men shouting to one another, of cargo and baggage being hefted to and fro, and, beneath it all, the carillon peal of *rusalky* voices on the breeze. Salt aromas clung to hulls that had known the seas but days before, and I daydreamed of voyages I would take alongside Adlai.

'Careful, hen, or you'll fall in the drink. C'mon, pay attention now.' Léolin's rough voice was belied by the kindness in his tone. He was tall and broad, blonde and bearded, with skin red and rugged. He made a good living, but smelled like fish. 'You're looking pleased with yourself, and your feet are barely touching the ground.'

'I've finished my quilt, laid the last stitch,' I fairly sang, and his face darkened.

'You'll be looking for your man, then,' he observed, and shook his head, began adjusting the shiny grey bodies all lined up on the bench of his stall. 'Wait; I'm sure he'll have business hereabouts.'

He lifted his chin and I followed the direction of his gaze.

The *Revenant* was a clipper from Breakwater; it plied the seas then crept up rivers like ours, to despatch passengers and some cargo – mostly high end, expensive and small, cargo and passengers both – and it was a vessel on which Adlai had taken passage more than once. A party of five was tripping down the gangplank. A pretty pink miss with large eyes led them, with a parasol to protect her, an ecru and lapis dress with bustle and gold lace cuffs, her caramel-coloured hair all caught up in a net with the sheen of spider silk covered with morning dew, and a teeny-tiny hat perched on the crown of her head, tilted ever so slightly to the left. She was accompanied by an older woman, grey-haired, grey-gowned, with a black mourning veil wrapped tight about her face as if her private grief might never be allowed to escape; two girls – the miss's sisters? cousins? – not yet in their twenties, who looked like twin roses in coral dresses and white gloves; and there was a man, old, serious in appearance, with the air of a majordomo about him – a man used to organising affairs.

I watched and listened as arrangements were made for their effects to be decanted from the ship as soon as possible and delivered, post-haste, to the house at Number Six Lady's Mantel Court. As I pondered this there was the sound of a carriage clattering to a halt; a fiacre, shining with red and black lacquer and gold fittings, drawn by four night-coloured horses, each with ebony leather trappings studded with brass bits and fastened with brass buckles. The conveyance pulled up and Adlai, lithe and resplendent in pale fawn breeches, hand-crafted square-toed shoes, brocade tailcoat with emerald buttons, white silk shirt, golden cravat and a magnificent waistcoat of cream and cerise and wheat, stepped forth. He bowed so deeply to the lady at the centre of the party that I thought his fine tricorn hat (in shades of chocolate) might fall from his cinnamon curls. But no; it was judged perfectly, his obeisance, like all things Adlai had done – had *learned* to do – all the things that drew him further from me.

When he straightened, he was bold – but just the right amount – stepping in close to the pretty girl, one hand on her elbow, the other around her waist, his lips to her ear, almost touching, and I could see the wet glimmer of his tongue as he spoke words no one else could hear, but which I suspected I knew, for he had told them to me enough times. But to her – to her he would mean them. On her left hand glistened a fat sapphire set in gold, a piece I recognised. He had shown it to me and promised it would be mine, one day. And I noticed at that very moment, the flash of enamel at the join of her prim collar, twisted in the shape of a lovers' knot.

The *rusalky* chorus, which had been as steady a rhythm as an untroubled heartbeat, seemed to swell at that moment, impossibly high. Penetrating the air between their rocky domain and the docks, shocking all who heard it, making eardrums ring. Or perhaps that was simply my perception.

Then Adlai broke contact, and time moved again. He greeted the governess, the twins, the majordomo, and bustled them all towards the fiacre, which would be snugly packed, but he would sit so close, so close to the pretty girl, perhaps she would be almost in his lap – propriety suspended a little, after all, they were affianced and such a man could surely be trusted with a lady's honour. Certainly with a *lady's* honour. Not that, though, of a stupid illiterate quilter.

I watched. He was the last to climb into the carriage and he must have felt the weight of my gaze, for he turned and found me, standing in my faded lavender dress, with its made-over sleeves, patches and many-times-repaired hem, the white lace applied to make it seem not so poor. For I spent no money on clothes, setting it all aside at first for his voyages then later when he stopped needing it, for our wedding, *our* life. For all the things that would never happen.

He smiled at me, sadly, nervously.

I wondered how long he'd thought he could get away with it. Not even I could tell myself she was a guest, the daughter of a business partner simply passing through, being offered hospitality. Perhaps I would have tried, had it not been for that *look*, that last look as he turned his head and hauled himself into the carriage and I saw him seated beside the pretty girl, one hand lightly laid over her pale two.

Léolin's paw was heavy with sympathy on my shoulder and, did I but realise it, hope. I heard him say my name and it occurred to me, finally, that Adlai had not used it for some time.

* * *

After the sun had set and good folk were sitting down to their evening meal, I took one of the bridges to the Vines district. I was unsure what I would do. Whether I would knock on that pastel door, ask to speak to the master of the house. Whether I would simply stand on the corner cloaked in twilight and watch the windows as people moved past them, carrying tapers to light lamps and candles. Whether I would take one of the stones I had placed in my pockets and hurl it at those very same windows, purely for the joy of hearing the shattering of their expensive glass and the high-pitched shrieks of well-bred women.

As it transpired I had no chance to do anything.

From behind, hands grabbed me and pulled me into deeper shadows. A cloth came over my mouth and nose, stinking of belladonna. Sleep was swift.

* * *

I run a finger across the stump of my tongue. It no longer aches, the scars are smooth now with the stitches removed and the blood-crusts gone. Despite the absence I still sometimes think it yet remains – a phantom tongue to match my phantom voice.

Setting aside the quilt, I stand – this *new* quilt is all but ready, the two halves finely made, some strips and scraps of my old wedding quilt (salvaged by Magnus from the poor pile of my possessions left on the street after my "disappearance") worked in, so that skerricks of lost hopes and broken dreams will cling to it. It needs only to be pinned and sewn together, then the pattern I have chosen stitched, but the second ingredient is required.

From beneath my bed, I draw a cup of water. Last night it was clean and clear when I placed it there. Now it is black and churns of its own accord, filled with the nightmares that would otherwise plague me if I did not employ this simple piece of magic to draw them away and trap them. Carefully, I add it to the contents of the stout earthenware jar Magnus gave me. I slide the flat copper disk into place then heat the stick of red wax, and seal the container, blowing gently to cool and set it quickly. I move into the sitting room, which is filled with light from the large windows and thence to the lean-to which runs off the kitchen. This is where Magnus grinds her herbs, mixes her potions, and casts her spells; a small area, cramped, its shelves over-laden, and hanging from the ceiling are bunches of dried plants waiting their turn to be made into something *else*. I place the jar on the workbench where it will be ready for her when she returns, and hidden from Léolin when he arrives.

Mother Magnus is a hedge witch. She is not shunned, nor is she embraced. She is, however, accepted as an essential part of Bellsholm's daily to-and-fro. Her magic can shade from white to black, should she choose and should her clients pay enough. Her cottage, neat and tidy, is just at the edge of the town, just before the earth begins to climb, to roll up to the Singing Rock. There are no other dwellings nearby. This, perhaps, was why Léolin brought me here.

In the grey dawn, Léolin out in his dory, noticed what seemed a lavender sack floating downriver; then he recognised the rags of white lace, then the red hair stretching out like waterweed. When he pulled me aboard, I coughed and he had a brief hope, for it was a sign of life – but with that cough came a great gout of blood and a sound – oh, a sound he swears he never wishes to hear again. Something told him not to take me back to the town, not to try the doctors there, the doctors who socialised with Adlai. He made his way to the shore, then carried me to Magnus and begged her to save me.

And save me she did, although for a long while I would not have thanked her for it. She healed the cuts, helped the bruises fade faster, set the breaks in my arm and ribs, and stopped me choking on my own blood where they'd cut out my tongue. Léolin has told me since, somewhat unwillingly, that that particular part of me was taken as proof of my death, presented to my erstwhile beloved. I was fortunate; I suppose that they were too lazy to try for the heart as well. These are the rumours he collects, the whispers from the docks where worlds mix and mingle and good folk might hear terrible things about what has been done and covered up.

Magnus has tried, too, since that day, to mend the breaks in my spirit but I did not respond until she began to stoke the strange and terrible cold fire of revenge. She knew, I think, that it was the only way to keep me alive, the only way to keep me from sliding into the apathetic darkness of death – for I was determined to walk that path for the longest time.

'Do something,' begged Léolin as he sat beside my bed in those first days and weeks. 'Do anything.'

I wonder if he would have said the same thing if he knew what Magnus dangled before my dimly flickering soul in order to pull me back.

There is a knock, politely tentative. I wait and then the door opens, as always, and Léolin ducks his height under the lintel. He can stand straight inside, but must watch his head. He carries a posy of lilac roses and windflowers; the townsfolk surely must think he is courting Magnus. He blushes to see me and smiles. No matter that he plucked me from the river, that he saw me at my lowest, that he has seen me more in the past few months than he ever did in the time I lived in the town, that he has lain with me, he still flushes like a lad whenever he arrives.

'Hello, my dove, I like your hair.' He fingers its sheared edges in wonder. We do not kiss but we do all the other things a courting couple might. Léolin makes plans for us.

'When you're quite better, hen, we'll leave. I have enough for us both. There's anywhere in the wide world we can go; put your finger on a map, choose a compass point and that's where we shall be.'

I smile as he speaks and I listen. I wonder sometimes if this was how I sounded to Adlai. Léolin does not know how ruined I truly am.

After he leaves, Magnus discreetly returns, her basket filled with medicinal blooms and newly dug roots, a rabbit or two to feed us for the next few days. She has been trying to teach me my letters. I try, I do, but I cannot help but feel it is merely a distraction – that, having shown me a path, she now wishes to divert me from it.

Magnus is tall, her hair ash-white, but her face belies that colour, the skin smooth and creamy, a wide plum of a mouth – she has not yet crossed over that boundary into the shadow-land where women become invisible. Her figure is fleshy but shapely, her eyes the colour of honey and her smile is ready.

'I saw Léolin,' she says, 'on the road.'

I simply watch her. We have had this one-sided conversation before and I do not imagine its direction will change.

'He would take you, you know. Take you elsewhere, uproot his whole life all for your sake. You don't have to do what you've planned.'

We have made ourselves understood with signals and signs these past weeks and months. When I first came to her, it was she who offered me solutions, with me accepting and refusing alternatively with nods and head shakes. It was she who suggested the option I ultimately chose and now she asks if I am *sure*? I don't even nod, merely lift an eyebrow and look towards the bench in the lean-to, where she can see the earthenware jar awaiting her attention. Awaiting her ministrations so I might have my second ingredient.

I need her and her wide-reaching, her all-encompassing magics – the tiny spells I have always known are white as white can be. They are *good*. But what I need now must be black as the cat curled by the cold kitchen hearth. I pay Mother Magnus in nightmares, in *aqua nocturna*. All I ask in return is a little dust.

'He doesn't know, does he? You will not tell him?'

I shake my head and look away, find the cat regarding me with large green eyes.

'Are you sure?' she asks. 'Certain this is the path you wish to take?'

I nod, and stare at her so she cannot mistake the answer. She blows out a heavy breath and I think she deflates a little, seems to age, to bow and bend; then the moment is past and she inclines her head.

* * *

The bottom half of the quilt lies across my bed. I have covered my mouth with a cloth, as per Magnus's instructions, so I don't breathe in any of the dust made from the water of my nightmares. 'Do not waste a speck,' she said. Attentively, I upend the black pouch and sprinkle its contents over the fine white felt I have used as a warm lining. I make sure it is evenly distributed and as I watch each particle worms its way into the fabric, disappearing, embedding itself into the fibre and the future. When I can no longer see the argent-grey gilings, I lay the top half over and pin it in place. Then I pin the pattern that I will quilt, much as I did when I made my own, but this time I create a forest of trees, which a careful eye might note is actually a nest of serpents, but I ensure their long bodies look like trunks, their heads and tongues seem like flowers, all so intertwined that only the most alert, the most perspicacious might notice the malice sewn there. I place stitches with a silver thread, spun by Magnus from the *rusalka's* tears.

When I am finished, my eyes and hands ache. I show the coverlet to Magnus. 'Just in time,' she says, fingering the border thoughtfully.

* * *

While the inhabitants of Bellsholm are either at the wedding of Adlai and the girl I now know to be Edine, daughter of a rich Breakwater merchant, or celebrating it in one of the taverns, I will set foot in the house at Number Six Lady's Mantel Court for the one and only time. Covered and cloaked, I have wandered and stalked, meandered and crept through the town's streets and byways so many evenings these past months, moving like a spectre unseen and unsuspected. Magnus gave me a pair of soft slippers, their soles enchanted to muffle any noise I might make.

Now I move towards the Vines district in the dimness of dusk, my gift carefully wrapped and bundled on my back like a pack; I sidestep revellers and avoid any who might be sober enough to peer under my hood, perchance to recognise my face. And I slide through the tiny lane behind Lady's Mantel Court, where there is a back gate for deliverymen to use. I sidle up the gravel path, making not a sound, and thence inside through the servants' entrance, left unlocked so those preparing for the happy couple's return might enter and exit with ease. Up the stairs to the second floor, along the corridor towards the front of the house, where there is only one door – the master bedroom runs the width of the building.

The room is a symphony of grey-blues and creams, and all the furniture is of white oak: a roll-top desk, dresser drawers, a vanity complete with cushioned stool, two matching armchairs and a chaise longue placed around a delicate low table inlaid with mother-of-pearl. A walk-in dressing room and bathroom are at one end, and at the opposite, a canopied bed.

Upon it already lies a quilt. I look it over, wasting precious moments with professional contempt. The stitching is shoddy, the design mundane – flowers and rabbits – it may well be the work of my former mistress; she had not sewn since I began to work for her and it seems her skill has deserted her. I yank the spread away, rolling it tightly and pushing it under the bed, where the layers of ruffled valance will hide it from prying eyes. I replace it with the coverlet of my making. It is perfect; even if anyone should notice the change, no one will remove it – not so close to the wedding night when another might not be found, and certainly not when it is as exquisite as this.

When I leave, the eiderdown is lying inert, snowy and lovely, waiting for the third ingredient.

* * *

Back at the cottage I help Magnus prepare. We both know Bellsholm will not be safe after this night; we fill carpetbags with all the possessions she refuses to be without. I do not know why she aided me at such cost to herself. Perhaps she simply felt it is time to move on; perhaps her outrage at what was done to me is what made her act; perhaps, as she tended me when I first woke and voiced a sound to make the Devil weep… perhaps she cannot live here without hearing it over and again. We load the small sturdy buggy and harness the tall horse, then she says once again, hopelessly, 'Go to him. Now. He is a good man. He will take care of you.'

I hug her hard and let her go; she climbs into the buggy with a sigh. The black cat is perched on the seat beside her, eyeing me wearily. Mother Magnus slaps the reins and the horse, somewhat startled, moves forward with a snappy gait. I watch until they disappear into the darkness of the bend that accommodates the insistent bulk of the Singing Rock, then I go inside. Enough of her things are left in the cottage that any folk who seek her out, who believe her behind what will happen, will not think her fled. They will wait here for her to come home, and by the time they realise she is gone, pursuit will be futile, and I – I will be beyond them too.

As the dark hours creep by, I sit sewing pointless, shapeless samplers, using up threads and scraps, listening in vain for the great swelling arias and canticles floating from the *rusalky* damozels, the sopranos and contraltos, with the altos winging between. But they will not sing again until daybreak. Sometimes I make flowers, other times animals, yet other times geometric shapes layered on top of one another. I work thus until I doze upright in the armchair. With no glass of water beneath the bed my dreams run riot, but this night they are different; they transport me, it seems, to the bridal chamber, to unwillingly watch as Adlai takes Edine as gently as a husband might a new bride, he with soft caresses, she with noises all reluctant that are given lie by her heavy-lashed gaze and the hearty wet kisses she bestows on him. Then there is the moment, when she cries out, surprised that he has hurt her, surprised that the pleasure has ended in pain, in tearing, in the blood her governess warned her about but to which she had not truly given credence.

I wake when the maids by the Rock begin their vocal exercises, an acrobatic warming of throat and voice, and I have but half an hour at best. I wrap the cloak about me once more and run.

I am breathless by the time I reach Lady's Mantel Court, and the morning light grows brighter. I stand on the pavement across from that house and watch the windows, listen intently until there is a scream, muffled by glass and thick curtains. Moments pass like breath as folk throw off their slumber, then a male voice, a grunt and a howl. Adlai sees his bride, but not as he expected, not as he had seen her last night. I wonder at the horror I have created, for all my dreams since Adlai's men took my tongue and left me for dead have been of a spliced woman, her torso female, her lower half a serpent's tail. All it required was the third ingredient, which only the bride could provide: blood – so much better if it was virginal – to seal the spell, to make the nightmare dust and tear-threads come to life.

More bellows and cries now – they sound so like me! Servants waking, rushing, seeing Edine's shame – I am sorry for her, she did me no intentional harm, but she was the means to my end. Now she's a fine bride for a seafaring man.

I turn on my heel and pace steadily, smartly across the bridge opposite the one on which I came. I walk with my head held high, a smile on my face. If I could, I would sing – part of me wants to do it anyway, but I know all I would produce would be a caw even a crow would disdain. In my imagination, my voice, my true voice sounds, a rich contralto, exultant. In my mind, others hear me and turn to listen for as long as they can. I pass people as I go; they take second glances as they recognise me, recoil as if they've seen a ghost. I keep moving until I achieve the edge of the town, then begin to climb the steep winding path to the Singing Rock. The songs grow louder as I approach. I wonder if I will join them, the *rusalky* maids, when I am done. I recognise now that I've held this wish in my heart, refusing to look at it for fear it might be taken away. Now I admit it, acknowledge it, hope to find a place I belong.

I reach the peak and the breeze is strong – I can smell the brine, even though all I can see is the wide river snaking along, a green-brown band cutting its way through sometimes mountains, sometimes flat pasture, sometimes marshlands, sometimes land riven by many, many streams. I cannot see the ocean, though; it is too far away.

What I can see, when I turn my head, is the bright golden halo of Léolin's hair, far below as he knocks upon the cottage door. I hope he will be well, that my betrayal will not break him as I was broken by Adlai. I do not wait to watch him find the place empty.

I step to the edge. The drop is sheer, broken only at the bottom where the *rusalky* have their day nest and recline on stone couches. I can see shining hair in all hues, white blouses and long, long skirts in silver and gold. Perhaps there are bare feet flashing pale and pink or perhaps those are fish. I will be close enough to see soon enough. The wind picks up, buffets me. I wonder idly if Adlai was at all touched by the horror my nightmares bred or does he stride freely as a man with a crippled wife must? A smile lifts the corners of my mouth. How will he like his Edine now?

How long before she, too, chooses the water?

I take a few steps back, then run, throw myself out into the sky.

I plummet for such a short time, but I do not hit. That is not what stops me. I open my eyes. The songs from beneath rise, knit themselves together, catch at me as a golden net. They pull me down slowly, slowly, gently towards the surface of the river. I hover above it, unable to move either up or down, thwarted utterly, as the murdered maids watch me sadly.

'You have no voice. You cannot join us,' says the one, then the other, then another, then all the voices threading and weaving one into the next to make a chorus of the same words. The same ribbons of sound, wrapping around and around me, telling me that there will be no welcome here. One of them watches me with a spiteful gleam in her bluer-than-blue eyes, as if she knew my hopes and bided her time until they might be crushed; around her shoulders is a cloak woven of auburn-rose locks, lined with the tiniest chips of stars. Then the net is gone, that wonderful thing of light and sound disappears like a puff of smoke, and I am dropped into the Bell River. The current picks at me, the waters fill my skirts, making me heavier and heavier, pulling me *beneath*, and out towards the sea.

My nose and mouth fill. I give myself up to the flow – for a moment – then there is drowning and darkness and the actuality of a slow death and I begin to fight. I rip at the catch of my skirts, fingers numb, finally tearing at the band; the buttons wetly give way and all that complexity of petticoats, old lace and weary gingham fall away, down, a'down, into the depths of the Bell. Then my jacket is gone too, and the broderie blouse, and the clever, quiet slippers carelessly discarded after such good service. And here I am naked but for a shivering thin shift, a skin of muslin plastered to me by the press of the tide, which lifts me up and carries me downstream. Towards Breakwater, towards any of more than a dozen tiny places identical to Bellsholm, towards the open sea.

THE UNDONE AND THE DIVINE

The ghosts spend their days profitably, doing precisely what they did in life.

Trading, gossiping, building, baking, shoeing ephemeral horses with u-shaped things made of smoke and promises, sleeping when the sun sets and rising when it shows its face once more, fornicating as is only natural. Such coupling, however, is unsatisfying, for it produces nothing, neither pleasure nor offspring; ethereal fingers pass through gossamer flesh. Touches are felt no longer than the tiniest fragment of a second, with no lingering to allay the longing. At its heart, the village is broken and without purpose.

So when Delling, shaven-headed, in a faded blue travelling dress, crosses the burnt boundaries, steps over the earthy threshold still marked with deepest ash and visible under the grass and wild foliage after all the lonely years, the spectres go about their business, pretending that *she* is the insubstantial one. They ignore her when she says, quite loudly, 'Southarp' into the warm air. They ignore her although they yearn to know what she carries in the satchel hung at her hip and the sandalwood box slung across her back. They wonder why she looks familiar. They are even more curious to note that she does not run screaming when she sees them, for see them she does.

For a while, she stops and watches the phantoms as they do their dance of imagined life, taking in their faces and storing them in her memory. Then she moves along. Beneath the thick soles of her boots, Delling can feel things crunch and crumble; the last of the rats' skeletons, friable, but defiant against the elements and time. She strides past the shell of the Burnt Moon Mill where the wheel still hangs, precarious on the last few struts and wall fragments. It no longer turns, although slapped and batted by the water, but does not yield; the liquid gives up, splits and flows around the fluid-eaten paddles that have been submerged for so long they are covered with a green algae that seems fluorescent. Delling eyes the mill and the skeleton of the cottage that once housed Cenred and Cern and Wulfwyn. She continues on by the hunched shape of the inn, all collapsed in on itself with vines climbing thickly over it, like some great beast gone to sleep for too long and trapped. Along the streets she goes, accompanied by the crunch-crunch-crunching of her shoes as they grind down the past.

So many leftovers, so many burnt-out wrecks, so much loss, but the silhouette of the old is still there, the figure of the village remains. Just like the moving shadows and shades that hustle and bustle in the last of the afternoon sun, the goodwives nodding to each other, the menfolk closing their stalls for the day, penning up ghostly animals, picking spectral vegetables from gardens long since grown over. As she passes she can see them all disappearing into their cremated homes; through non-existent walls she watches them prepare for the evening, cooking illusory meals that can be neither tasted nor truly eaten, setting children tasks that no one will care to check. Soon, they will be abed. Delling wonders if ghosts dream.

At the end of the main thoroughfare, just beyond the burned border, stands the only untouched dwelling, two storeys high, small and neat, with cobwebs lacing the windows inside and out. But there are no signs of incineration, nor scorching. The timbers appear sound. The picket fence is no longer white, but the grey of silvered time. The front door, a peeling green, is firmly closed.

Delling hesitates here as she did not when she stepped into the haunted territory of Southarp. She knows what she must do. She knows this place – or rather she knows of it – this once-home was not where it started, not really. She knows her blood is telling her she has no right to cross this threshold. She knows she will do so, though.

The girl squares her shoulders and lifts her chin. She fixes her yellow-green gaze ahead and steps along the garden path. The handle turns upon the insistence of her fingers and the door, somewhat unwillingly, opens. Inside there is the smell of only gilings and years, dried herbs – perhaps cloves – no spoor, no mould nor decay. No scent of death. The dust lies deep across the sparse furnishings and she leaves boot-shaped prints as she drifts through the lower floor, taking in the kitchen, parlour, dining room, the tiny tacked-on laundry out the back. Upstairs, she finds two bedrooms. In the largest one, the mattress still wears the bloodstained sheets Hafwen was dragged from when they took her to the pyre. A baby's cradle beside the bed is full of ancient toys and frayed woollen blankets. The other room contains a single bed, neatly made with a hand-stitched quilt tidily pulled over it. There are tomes on a rough set of shelves: a few children's picture books, a herbal, two novels with no note of authorship. At the back of the second floor is a washroom, poky; Delling tries the taps but is greeted by silence. Nothing has flowed through its pipes for years. Tomorrow she will draw water from the fountain and bathe.

In the smaller room, Delling rolls the quilt back, careful not to disturb the dust any more than she must. She unhitches her own bedroll from beneath the sandalwood box and places it on top of the ancient sheets, then puts the box itself on the floor, relieved to be free of its weight. From the satchel she takes dried meat and a hunk of stale bread, a flask of water warmed by the day's journey. She eats a simple meal, occasionally letting her gaze fall on the chest, but not opening it. Outside the sun is almost gone.

She moves quietly from her chosen space to the other bedchamber, and looks down at the wildly overgrown back garden, barely distinguishable from the myrkwood behind the house. On the lawn, foxes gather, foraging for what they can find, conducting a wary, dainty dance around each other. Delling watches them until there is no more light to make out their russet shapes.

* * *

She wakes only when she is cold and shivering beneath her featherweight covering. The found candle beside her bed is long-since extinguished. Standing in a shaft of moonlight, there is a figure, short and broad, but the light passes through it almost as easily as it does through the window glass.

Slowly it turns and moves towards her. In spite of the darkness and the translucence of him, she can make out his features. Shaggy brown hair, skin as pale grey as a winter sky, thick lips, a scar – no, a deep scratch, unhealed before he died. Yes, there is the raised crust of a wound ill-cleaned.

It's the face she saw at her mother's sickbed, the face that made the woman weep and howl in her last weeks. There are other marks she thinks might be where the rats got to him. She keeps her eyes high, does not look down at his crotch, does not look to see if what her mother said happened, happened.

'I know what you did,' she says, voice steady. 'I know what you did to my mother and the other.'

The eidolon stops beside her bed, leans down. Delling does not flinch, she holds his gaze for what seems forever, then he grunts and slowly fades. For long moments she does not move, then Delling reaches down to find the discarded quilt. She pulls it up, heedless of its dust and dirt, of the way it feels as if it might crumble in her fingers at any moment. She curls into a tight ball, quivering. It is an hour or more before she closes her eyes again.

* * *

As soon as dawn has split the darkness, Delling sets up shop in the market square, beside the fountain which has never ceased to run, fed as it is by the mill stream. The sculpted mari-morgan at its centre is green with verdigris, and the top of the low wall around the pool is thick with moss, but the water in the fountain is clear and clean. All that remains of the rose avenue is a single stunted bush, heavy with lilac-coloured flowers, seemingly too weighty to grow to its intended height. Delling thinks it a miracle that anything survived at all.

From the laundry in Hafwen's old house, Delling has dragged a wooden box once used, if she but knew it, by Friðuswith to strike her seedlings – it is about a foot deep, two wide and three long. From her satchel, she takes a length of netting, not too fine, and stretches it across the mouth of the planter then holds it in place with the tiny tin tacks she has carried with her for so many weeks. As well as the box, she has commandeered a rake, a shovel, a large hammer, and a copper boiler, rectangular shaped with its corners rounded, handles at the thinnest ends and an ill-fitting lid. She rinses the boiler out with water from the fountain pool, then sets it aside to dry.

Sometimes she talks to the ghosts brushing past, mainly for the sound of a voice: 'Good day to you.' 'My, what a lovely dress/necklace/little child.' 'My, isn't this weather perfect?'

But they do not answer, although she sees how some of them must contain their gazes, make an effort not to look at her, not to ask *what are you doing, girl?*

Delling rolls the sleeves of her shirt up past the elbows, then hitches her skirts and tucks them firmly into her belt so they look like trousers. She wraps a scarf around her prickly skull to keep off the worst of the summer sun. Picking up the rake, she strides purposefully to the west boundary of the village, looking for the tell-tale signs of ancient embedded cinders. When she finds them, she lifts the head of the rake high then lets it fall hard to the earth so its teeth dig deep, and begins her work, raking everything that the tool collects towards the market square.

She is diligent, not merely attending to the streets and flat areas, but also stepping into the ruined houses, carefully tiptoeing around fallen beams and collapsed walls, unhinged doors, all blackened and half-eaten by flame. She works systematically, east, south, north, clearing the village in careful sections, fastidiously making sure nothing is left behind. In some places she finds white crystalline deposits, buried deep, under rocks or branches where they've been protected from rain and snow – she sniffs at them, wets a finger and tastes the grit. Salt. Someone has salted the borders of Southarp to keep the ghosts in. Delling looks up and stares into the trees, looks down the hard-packed road as if she might find the culprit, but she sees only the slight forms of busy apparitions as they go about their business, and so she returns to her endeavour.

It takes her all day. By the time she stops for a quick meal from her dwindling supplies, the sun has passed the horizon and there is only the last lambent glow to see by. There are four small mountains of dirt, ash, and general detritus piled in a semi-circle around her station by the fountain. As she eats, chewing slowly, feeling the sweat creep its way through the bristles of her hair, sliding slowly down her neck and back, she stares at the mounds, can see all manner of things there, all tumbled about.

Her task for the day is done. *Almost done*, she reminds herself, and looks towards the place where the mill, inn and cottage hulk in the darkness. The bakehouse is no longer in evidence.

Tomorrow, she thinks, *in the light*.

Quickly, she strips, piling up her filthy clothes, and stepping into the fountain. The water is blood-warm after the day's sunshine, but she welcomes it, enjoys the sensation of the dirt and sweat being washed from her. She stays, immersed, until the sense of being watched overwhelms her, and she hastily re-dresses. Delling goes back to Hafwen's house, leaving the results of her labours *in situ* – for who would take detritus?

She falls into the thin bed and sleeps so deeply that she does not wake when Cenred appears, nor does she stir when he reaches out to run his intangible hand across her scalp. When she wakes in the morning she finds her skin covered with a thin layer of ice, where her perspiration has frozen over.

* * *

She stretches, then hefts the shovel, digging its head into the closest mound of dirt and then tipping it gently onto the net-mouthed planter box. Soil and the fine particles fall through the gap-toothed netting, the larger items are left behind; these Delling sets aside in tidy drifts. The small ones – fingers, toes, vertebrae, teeth – are to the left. Adornments – rings, bracelets, necklaces, tie pins, brooches, earrings, belt buckles, buttons, warped pocket watches – are to the right. The big bones – femurs, ribs, pelvises like broken bowls – go into the fountain to soak clean, then are lined up along the low stone wall to dry.

By the time the sun passes the midpoint in the sky, she has finished sifting and sorting, so she turns toward the one area of Southarp she has not picked over. The Burnt Moon Mill, the cottage and the inn. She shoulders the rake and advances on this final destination. The inn first – she walks confidently past the shade of Cern at the broken doorway, polishing a ghostly goblet with an equally spectral cloth. Once inside, she creeps through its dark collapse, under beams, her bravado shrinking as she moves cautiously so as not to fall through the floor and into the cellar, down the unreliable stairs although she does not wish to, carefully, oh so carefully choosing her steps, placing her feet, freezing whenever the creak of the wood sounds too loudly, too urgently for her liking, then at last into the darkness where only the occasional shafts of sunlight come. She wishes fervently that she'd gone back to the cottage and taken one of the few candles in the kitchen cupboard. Still, she is fastidious in her efforts even though she would happily sprout wings and flee, even though she is certain there is very little here that she needs for what she must do. She makes an apron of her petticoats so she may carry her prizes with ease as she carts them back to the fountain area.

Delling does not pause but returns quickly to the dreaded precinct. She fords the stream, thigh-high in water, lifting her skirts to chest level so they do not become waterlogged and cause her to be swept away – there is no longer a bridge – and finds the cottage much easier to deal with, so small. There are two skulls, an assortment of large bones, two belt buckles, some buttons and that is all that endures of her uncles. Their remains join the piles she raked from the inn. At last, there is only the mill.

Across the door is a fallen beam and she must go on hands and knees to pass. The wooden floor was burned completely and she walks on the stone and dirt foundations. The skeletons of the rats are many here – as if they fled back to the site of their birth to try and escape the flames. Each step makes a sound like gravel and it shreds her nerves. She can see the stream has broken in through a weakened wall, and a small lake laps at the far side of the room. The grinding wheel lies, half-submerged, and on it sits Cenred, precisely as he was in her room the night before if she did but know it.

He stares at her and she begins to feel what she has avoided until now: terror. Perhaps his touch in the night, although unknown, left its mark after all. She was unafraid when she saw him by Wulfwyn's bedside, even as her mother screamed. She was merely enraged when she saw him beside her youngest sister's bed after they had laid their mother to rest, when she saw him reach his translucent hand out to try and touch Mercia's shaved head, the teardrop birthmark beneath her eye. Delling was utterly determined as she did her research, questioned the Little Sisters of St Florian at Cwen's Reach, and gathered the items she would need into the sandalwood chest Wulfwyn had kept all her life and filled with the tiny treasures she was too afraid to let anyone have.

Now, as the phantasm rises with an audible, unthinkable cracking of knees, Delling is filled with fear, even though she knows – *knows* – he cannot do anything tangible to her. Her nerve breaks and she flees, stumbling, tripping, but staying on her feet until she reaches the door and crawls out under the obstruction. Something grasps the back of her dress and she shrieks, certain that the apparition has her; she pulls hard and hears the tearing of the fabric as it is wrenched away from the ragged splinters of the beam.

Then she is out into the afternoon light, half-running, trying to peer over her shoulder yet not lose speed, seeing nothing, no pursuit and then she is stopped by a wall of flesh. She bounces back, falling to her arse and then tumbling like an ill-trained acrobat, and yelling, yelling, yelling no actual words, but sounds of panic and surprise.

When she stops rolling and pitching, when her stream of noise dries to a trickle, she looks up and sees a man staring at her with bewilderment. He is tall but stooped with age, his once well-fed features have drooped as he has become lean. His head is bare and the hair that encircles the naked patch of his tonsure has streaks of black among its sombre silver. He wears the long grey robe of a mendicant and clasped in both his hands are the ends of his belt, made of a series of wooden beads, which he tells as he watches her, as if she interrupted him and he will not be interrupted. At his side hangs the ash-tree baton his kind carry for protection from footpads and forest-wights alike.

She has nothing to fear from this man, she senses. When he speaks, there is no kindness, but equally no anger, merely a sort of exhausted exasperation.

'What are you doing, you fool?'

* * *

The old man watches morosely as she returns to her task, sieving the last of the dirt and detritus she took from the inn and the cottage. She immerses the big bones in the fountain as she did with all the others, and sets them to dry. Of the small things, there are the belt buckles, four brass buttons, two ivory ones, and random links of a chain on which Cenred wore his pocket watch. Delling could not find the watch itself, but she is certain she has enough for her purpose.

When all the skeletal parts are dry, she places them, large and small, in the copper cauldron. Then she takes the hammer she found in Hafwen's house and smashes it down on them – they fragment and atomise with relative ease. Soon there is but a thick mass of white dust settling in the base of the boiler, waiting while Delling pours in three careful measures of water from the fountain, stirs the paste, then hunts up wood and builds a fire, which she does not light.

'They burnt her here,' says the mendicant. 'This was where they always burnt them.'

'Hafwen?' she asks and he winces, his pain seemingly as fresh as it was that night long ago.

He nods. 'How do you know of her?'

'My mother told me,' Delling says, taking the scarf from her head and laying it out flat on the edge of the fountain. Into its centre she piles most of the found gems and settings, chains and pretty things, and begins to wrap them up, tying all four corners together like a tramp's swag. A small pile is set aside. After so many days of silence, here and on the road, she finds the talking a welcome relief.

'What are you doing?' asks the man sharply.

Delling looks askance at him. 'For the Sisters – the Little Sisters of St Florian. They nursed my mother in her last months. We could not pay them anything, but they helped us anyway. This,' she holds up the small swag, 'will go some way to recompense for all they did.'

He nods slowly. 'Who was your mother?'

She is slow to answer, uncertain of the consequences of her

revelation. 'Wulfwyn, sister to those who injured Hafwen, whom Friðuswith used for her revenge.'

And because one secret requires another, he says, 'I set the fire, you know – burning the village, not Hafwen.'

She nods, wonders whether to give him her own name, decides against it. 'I wondered if it was you – I mean, if you were the Abbot Adelbert.'

'No one has called me that for a very long time.' He shakes his head, giving a ghost of a smile. He stares down at his large hands with their ragged nails.

'Did you salt the border?' she asks, and watches him nod once more.

'After the flames died – and all the villagers as well as the rats – I couldn't bear the thought of them escaping. I couldn't bear the idea they might stop suffering. Now…'

'Now?' She prompts, as she fishes about in her satchel for the silver tinderbox.

'Now I think I managed to sour my whole life. I left my post at St Simeon and gathered my three daughters to me, good girls, but the best of them – the best of them disappeared. To avenge Hafwen, I made a promise in return. I got what I wanted and then for so many years nothing was demanded of me. It got so I thought I was free – then the man came to collect, and I lost Gytha too.' He rests his head in his hands, then continues, as if confession is good for the soul. 'The other two, when they married – oh, each wanted me to live with her and be looked after – I bethought to clear my conscience. I took to the roads, doing good deeds, giving comfort where I might, but I cannot keep the dreams at bay. I see her burn – not them, not the villagers, but her, my Hafwen, my summer breeze – even though I did not witness it. And I came to believe I would not be free – nor she – until I made recompense for the lives I took here, for all of them. I've come to pray, for whatever good it might do.'

She does not answer, merely strikes the flint and firesteel until orange sparks eat at the charcloth and finally catch the kindling, then the larger pieces of wood.

'Why are you here?' he asks belatedly.

'My mother… she spent her last weeks haunted by her brother – the worst of them, Cenred. She told me, in that time, what he had done – to her and to Hafwen. What Cern had said to protect him and how she had remained silent and let your love burn. She told me how she went to Friðuswith, who gave her tea to drink, to take away her cares and her will and how she did not fight – she did not care. She told me of the gift given her by Hafwen's mother, and how she, Wulfwyn, released the plague on Southarp, watched her brothers die although the rats did not come near her, and then she left.'

In the boiler, the white-grey mix begins to bubble and pop. She takes a metal rod scavenged from the smithy, perhaps once meant to become a sword, and stirs the admixture, her face turning rosy from the combination of heat and exertion. From her satchel she draws a jar of smoked glass, the length of her hand and the circumference of three fingers. Its gold lid is sealed with yellow wax, which she carefully cracks and peels away with a knife. She pours its contents – dark red, sluggish, smelling of iron – into the mix, watches it turn everything pink. Then she takes three handfuls of the sieved dirt from the planter – it is, for all intents and purposes, grave dust. The fire begins to die down. Gingerly, Delling, hands wrapped in her skirts as proof against the heat, removes the boiler from the flames; with Adelbert's unrequested aid, she heaves it up onto the fountain's low wall, then into the shallow pool, which is not full enough to spill over into the mix. Steam rises and the waters hiss their discontent for a while, then slowly sink to silence. When she judges the mixture sufficiently cooled, Delling and her new acquaintance lift the boiler out again, and place it on the ground.

She stirs it with the rod once more – it has become languid, lethargic, thick as bread dough. Delling dips her hands in and brings the whole lump onto her lap, where she begins to mould it, urgently, intently into a recognisable form. While she sculpts, and she and the once-abbot of St-Simeon-in-the-Grove talk, the ghosts of Southarp gather around them. Sitting close, leaning over shoulders, pushing and shoving each other for the best view, they watch attentively as the strange clay takes shape. It is not a child, nor a babe, but a creature to which she gives both breasts and a cock, a slit and two firm round balls. It will have – needs – no clothes. It is the sum of all the villagers, in some small part, bones, skin, dirt, death-dust.

When she is finished, she sits back and surveys her handiwork.

'What now?' asks Adelbert.

'Now this,' she answers, and sets the homunculus on the ground, then kneels before the sandalwood chest, which has quietly waited its turn.

She undoes the complex latch which must be turned this way, then that in a most particular order, then tenderly flicks back the lid. Inside, on a bed of watery blue silk, is the thing she and her sisters, Halle and Mercia, made, two days after they shaved their hair so their mother might not be naked at her burial, and three days before Wulfwyn died. They spent their time by her bed alternatively plaiting and weaving their tresses into the shroud Wulfwyn would wear to the grave, in accordance with the Little Sisters' exhortation that daughters should cover their mothers for the final passage, and constructing the other *thing*.

It is a boat, a ship, really, made of… tiny, tiny slivers of bone – no, horn, thinks Adelbert. Quickly, he realises his mistake: this girl has brought a *naglfar*, a boat of human nails from toes and fingers. A ship to take the dead home.

'People become superstitious – when they've brushed up against magic, but have no trace of it in their own make-up. Wulfwyn collected these each time she trimmed them, so no one might find them and have power over her. It is a strange and random belief, for she didn't collect her bloods – which I would if I were of such a bent.' She smiles and continues, 'Just the nails, without knowing what power lay within them.'

'Why bring it here?'

'Because by her bedside, Cenred appeared, saying nothing but by his mere presence tormenting her.' She carefully reaches into the sandalwood box and lifts out the *naglfar*, turning it around and around so he might see its every detail, from the tall single mast to the minutely crafted figurehead on the prow. He admires its craft, its impossibility, its madness and notes that the effigy she has made will fit neatly inside. 'Then when Mother still had breath, I found him one night perched beside Mercia's bed – she looks most like Wulfwyn – and I will not have *him* blight her life.'

On the word 'him', she nods and Adelbert turns to see one of the shades pressing through the un-substance of the other ghosts. Its eyes are fixed firmly on the ex-abbot, and they seem to gleam with the last embers of the fire that devoured Southarp. Adelbert stands and Cenred comes for him – neither the mendicant nor Delling are concerned, for what can this creature do? – until the ghost plunges his hand into the old man's chest and Adelbert begins to gasp.

Delling leaps up, tries to pull her uncle away, but her hands pass through him and she sees his lips lift in fiendish delight.

'No!' she cries, then realises there is only one thing she can do. She places the pinkish-grey doll into the stern of the *naglfar*, and the leftover pile of gems and buttons, buckles and bits into the bow, then runs towards the stream that circles the town, that feeds the fountain, that once powered the millwheel. Adelbert is dying, she can hear it in his cries. She trips, almost falls, recovers – her cargo, her duty, too important, too precious.

Delling reaches the wide, deep stream and kneels. She whispers a prayer and a farewell, then gently, gently places the *naglfar* into the clear, swiftly moving waters. The current catches the ship, makes it bob slightly, but the thing stays upright, stays watertight. As it floats swiftly towards where the millwheel still hangs, where the whole plan might well come apart, Delling sees a fog flow after it, into it. Looking back towards the fountain, she sees all the ghosts, all the shades, pulled out of shape, dragged towards the *naglfar*, sucked into it as if into a whirlwind. She sees Cenred, too, resisting, resisting, but finally wrenched away, through the air, then down, whirling, into the nail boat, into the tiny ship of the dead.

As she watches, she sees a wall of mist rise, just before the ship reaches the millwheel, just before it must surely run into the useless blades and shatter. The ship moves into the thick swirling whiteness, becomes itself as translucent as its ghostly cargo and disappears.

Delling returns to the fallen ex-abbot, and kneels beside him. He is gasping, clutching at his chest, at whatever Cenred was able to do to disrupt his existence, but his expression is beatific, his eyes pinned on one point before him.

'Can you see her?' he asks and his tone is that reserved for a hymn of joy. 'Can you see her? Just as she was, so lovely, my Hafwen, my summer breeze.'

Delling doesn't answer, doesn't know if the burned girl is truly there or if Adelbert's death shadows are kinder than those that have dogged his living years. She lifts his head into her lap and holds one rapidly cooling hand as he slowly breathes down to his last.

Southarp is silent once more.

THE NIGHT STAIR

The Steward is a tall man, entirely bald, gaunt in the face, yet rotund in the belly. His legs, in their loose fawn linen trews, look like a scarecrow's, sticking out under the awning of his gut – perpetually in shade perhaps they don't get enough light to grow. His tunic of padded green silk, his sable wool coat with its thick fur collar, are too warm even for the end of summer, but as marks of his office, must be *seen*, just like the yellow crystal hanging about his neck. Called the 'Steward's Gaze', it's the size of the top joint of a man's thumb, and has passed from incumbent to incumbent for as long as anyone has the will to recall. He puts it in his mouth and sucks hard when he thinks no one is watching. It's worth a king's ransom, and I'll warrant the gold chatelaine belt around his waist could buy the city's food for half a year.

His finery makes me aware of the state of my black dress – not that it's poor or made shiny by age, but it belonged to others before me. Both my sisters – my only full-blood siblings – wore it to their own choosing. I am certain I can smell them, their scents imprinted into the warp and weft of the fabric despite washing. The colour makes my skin paler, my eyes bluer, provides the perfect background for the tresses, which pour down my back like gold fresh from the smelter. I was careful, so careful with my toilette: brushing my hair, one hundred strokes; rubbing the cream that was my mother's (comfrey and rose to soften and plump, a little lemon balm for lightening) into my skin; drops of eyebright to ensure my gaze is clear. I refrained from pinching my cheeks – pale is best – but I did nip gently at my lips, to carmine them a little, so it seems as if all life is concentrated there. I will not be found wanting.

I stand in line with seven other girls who have been presented this day. We are of an age, none more than sixteen springs, and there is only one of them, perhaps two, who *might* outdo me. To my right is Essa, with her milky skin and eyes like the sky reflected in ice, hair bright platinum; even her nails seem to have a silvery sheen. She watches me from the corner of her eye, just as I watch her.

To my left is Dimity, whose eyes are bright green, her cheeks with the tiniest hint of pink. She keeps her regard firmly fixed upon her own feet. Our Lady best likes girls who resemble herself; that is not Dimity for all her snow-washed whiteness – the eyes are all wrong and the eyes count.

So, Essa. Essa is the one to beat – the Steward will surely select between the two of us.

Filling this large room in the city hall are parents, including my father, who's left the running of the mine's smelter to his deputies so he can see what deals might be struck. Behind him are three of my younger half-siblings, those not yet old enough to be exhibited, but deemed mature enough to watch proceedings in order to learn how to behave when – if – their time comes. Another ten still wait at home; not all will be offered, only those whose appearance is *right*, those whose behaviour does not mark them out as more trouble than they're worth. My father has twice made a small fortune from this process and I imagine he hopes to again – his tendency for taking new wives, sometimes before the old one is done, and his proclivity for procreation, his personal fecundity, constantly require more funds than his well-paid position provides.

Steward Oswain walks slowly up and down our line, as if inspecting troops. His brown eyes are considering, patient, although a little uncertain, as if offered several courses at a banquet and told he might only have one. He stops in front of the Toop girl and shakes his head (anyone can see she's too fat), then the Ansible twins (hair too dark), and then Mistress Garran's girl (whose neck is smudged by a red birthmark); a dismissal for each. At the back of the crowd I hear a woman crying; she is shushed and hustled out – I cannot tell if her weeping was of relief or despair. The desperate whirring of my own thoughts is far too loud.

I straighten my shoulders, lift my head a little higher, blink quickly so that tears of fear do not start and cause the coal-mascara on my lashes to run. The Steward takes one more pass; another. He stops in front of Dimity – Dimity! – puts a finger under her chin and makes her look at him. Her lips tremble; he smiles kindly and nods. Essa makes a noise, and this one I know for relief. The Steward steps back, turns away. All scrutiny has left us. Parents mill around the tall stork of a man to strike bargains; Dimity's mother to get the highest price, the others to find out when there might be another choosing – as if the Steward can predict our Lady's moods to a day and date! Only my siblings still watch, their eyes fastened onto me as if by hooks.

Dimity takes her first step forward as a chosen girl and I trip her. Essa's intake of breath is sharp. The green-eyed maiden falls so fast, is so surprised, that she does not put her hands out to save herself. Her face meets the floor with a satisfying *crunch* of bone and cartilage. There is that tiny broken moment when nothing happens, no one moves, when time is divided into *before* and *after*, then, as if a clock's hands click over, everything starts again, and the girl on the floor wails. I do not move.

Dimity sits up, blood pouring from her ruined nose. She stares at me all uncomprehending, hands twitching as if to point me out, but she catches my glance and I can see her crumple inside. She sobs a little more quietly and when an adult asks what happened, she answers with 'I fell'.

She will thank me; or rather, she would if she thought about it.

The Steward is displeased – she is no longer *acceptable*. He turns to Essa, and I glare for a few moments until her nerve breaks and she steps backwards, in effect removing herself from the field. I am thankful for I have no more tricks.

'You then,' says the Steward, giving me a calculating glance. He looks at my father, who nods approvingly (what kind of fool thinks I do this for him?). 'Perhaps you will do best. Your father's blood runs strong.'

It is not the sort of compliment I wished for, but I duck my head in assent, then notice that my half-siblings still watch, mouths agape.

Never let it be said I've taught them nothing.

* * *

'Never speak first.'

The Steward had continued his litany of rules as we made our way from Caulder's city hall to the hostelry where he'd left his tall grey horse. He mounted, then pulled me up to sit in front of him, perched uncomfortably on the saddle. 'Do not ask questions that are not invited.'

Wear only the clothing you are assigned.

Eat and drink only that which is offered to you.

Always answer when our Lady calls you 'daughter'.

Do not enter the undercroft.

Do not enter our Lord and Lady's chambers without invitation.

Do not correct our Lord and Lady.
Do not run along the corridors.
Do not take anything that has not been given to you.
Do not investigate locked doors.
Do not wish for more than is given.
Do not ask them to make you as they are.
Do not.
Do not.
Do not.

My head buzzed by the time we'd left behind the cobbled streets and begun to traverse fields yellow with wheat, pastures thick with cattle and sheep, enormous garden beds sown with all the things that can be stored in root cellars to tide the city over during winter. By the time we'd ridden to the far end of the horseshoe-shaped valley, to the sweet spot where the manor house with its great hall and single lofty tower rested in the curve of the 'u'… by the time we'd left the horse to the lad at the stables and entered the house… by the time I'd been led up to this very room… well, by then my head ached.

This bedchamber has windows that do not open, the shutters are nailed in place to keep the light out. If I feel the need for sun, I have been told, I may walk in the gardens, but for my own sake I should wear one of the muslin visages and a pair of gloves to protect my complexion, for even a light bronzing will ruin everything.

'That was your sister's sin,' says the Steward.

'Which one?'

'The first one.'

Sophie always did like to play outside. She'd have darkened so fast.

The bed is enormous, with a mattress thick and high, a satin canopy of deepest crimson, a matching coverlet, and so many pillows I may well suffocate if I don't remove them before I sleep. I think back to the bed I shared with my sisters when our mother would read to us in the evenings – before everything changed. It was barely big enough for all of us, sleeping like pups pressed against each other, breaths mingling, hearts beating in time; here we would lose each other. We shared a wardrobe, a washstand, a mirror, our clothes; we fought over hairbrushes and ribbons. Hardly a year apart, we were more like triplets, close enough to finish each other's sentences, to know the others' thoughts before they were spoken.

Here, there is a desk with a roll-top, a tall wardrobe, a long sofa with scarlet velvet bolsters, a tiny round table with mother-of-pearl inlay in a bird-and-girl pattern, and two wingback chairs set either side of it; all the furniture is a burnished mahogany. Through a door concealed by a *trompe l'oeil* design of a sunny sandstone courtyard packed with fruit trees and climbing vines, is a marble-floored bathroom, almost as big as the bedroom. There is a sunken pool, golden wash basins, and a corner where water flows in a continuous shower then runs out a cleverly decorated drain that looks like a posy of roses. I was delighted when I saw it. All this space just for me, but there are no bookshelves and no books. It is said that all manner of tomes are kept in the tower. I wonder if I will be allowed there – I do not ask, for then I cannot be refused.

'And April?' I ask and he gives me a look so blank my heart aches. By the time her body was returned to us she'd had a good run compared to others, such as Sophie, who'd lasted but a month. 'My other sister; she stayed here eighteen months.'

He shakes his head, quite sadly. 'I cannot remember them all. Some infraction, some upset to our Lady. Let it serve as a lesson to you, Adlisa, let all your steps be careful ones.' He plays with the crystal, almost popping it into his mouth – but he catches himself first and the slip makes him brusque. 'Now, I suggest you bathe – I will send one of the women to do your hair. There is a selection of dresses so you will surely find one to fit; fold your old one up and leave it at the foot of the bed. It will be returned to your family. And have a nap if you can manage – from this day onwards you live half in light and half in shadow. And I'm sure your mind is moving apace after the other candidate's misfortune.'

I meet his eye steadily, do not flinch. The Steward grips my arm and whispers, 'I have been here thirty years, girl. I have seen your kind come and go, the ambitious and the unassuming. None of them has survived.'

My expression does not change for I am neither one nor the other, although I am sure he must hear my heart clattering in my ribcage like one of the machines in the smelter that crushes chunks of rock and ore into smaller pieces. I raise my chin, just a fraction and he lets me go, straightening his coat before he leaves this room, which is mine however ephemerally.

* * *

'Call me "Mother", child,' says the alabaster woman.

Her voice is soft but the tone brooks no refusal. We are in the circular chamber that serves as her solar, its skylight open only at night. On her lap is a piece of embroidery, a fine stitching of black silk roses on snowy cambric.

That word has not crossed my lips in some years, not since my own mother disappeared in a night of shouting and rage after which my father ceased to speak of her. It was a title I'd refused to accord to any of Father's subsequent wives or concubines, despite all the slaps and bruises that defiance brought. The term conjures a shadowy, slippery, precious memory – an ache – but that isn't why I do not give it lightly. I keep it close, pristine and unused, for it has power; power for both she who gives and she who receives, and I must be careful about bestowing such potential. It is tricksy and dangerous, it can make one party think they are stronger than they are, when really it is a key to their heart. Our Lady would like to think it gains her the upper hand but in this conferral *I* alone acquire the advantage.

'Mother,' I say. It slides across my lips with barely a hiccup. And I smile, meeting her glacial blue gaze for the first time; I have kept my eyes downcast as a polite and chaste child should, addressing my Lady respectfully and shyly.

'Come closer, Adlisa,' she says and I step forward to where she reclines on a chaise longue; her watered silk gown in shades of oyster pink and dove grey drapes beautifully about her slender form, but she must lie on a slight angle to accommodate the beribboned bustle. Her hair is the same shade as mine, a good sign, gilded as the statues that stare down from the portico of the city hall. Her skin is so pale it's almost transparent – I wonder if I stare hard enough might I see the skull beneath this bleached canvas? – and her forehead high and domed, eyebrows fine as golden pin feathers, cheekbones sharp, lips a petulant pout even in repose. Her chin is a little weak and it appears she is aware of this for the tilt of her head seems a conscious combat against it. A thin hand with long digits reaches out and turns my head this way and that, not cruelly or painfully, but in a determined grip I could not break. If she wanted, she could shatter my jaw with the snap of her fingers.

'My, you are lovely. You do remind me of someone else, but I cannot think who.' Her lips lift at their corners. Her fingers toy with the soft curls the old woman Rikke left dangling by my cheeks when she swept the rest up in a great loose bun on top of my head.

I think of my sisters, wonder if she genuinely remembers them, but I do not say *My Lady, you ate them*. April and Sophie would have been afraid of her. They would have been scared and it would have finally got the better of them. At some point, she'd have called them to her and they would have shown reluctance; she with her predator's instinct would have smelled their terror, and that would have meant death. Our mad Lady, who has sought across so many years, in the faces of so many others, a replacement for her lost daughter, and found them all wanting. Sophie's tanning would not have offended nearly so much as the sight of her nerve fracturing. The shaking and shattering of our Lady's happy illusions would have broken her mother's heart anew. Like most folk, she loathes and destroys the things that make her see the truth, has done for three centuries or more. There is barely a family in Caulder that has been untouched; barely a family that hasn't had an inert, empty body delivered back to them.

'Mother, will you show me how?' I point shyly at the embroidery in her bloodless hands and she beams, patting the seat next to her. Her delight in my interest is childlike, unalloyed. I know that my survival depends on the illusion I create for her being flawless. I am careful not to prick myself with the sharp golden needle – it would not do to either ruin this piece of work nor tempt her with blood. We are there long enough that I am able to finish one black petal under her instruction.

'Shall I begin another, Mother?' I ask.

She looks at the elaborate timepiece on the mantle – a thing of porcelain and bronze, which disgorges three dancing maids on the hour – and shakes her head. 'No, no, I have let our time fly. Where is my sense? Come, we must to dinner.'

I walk a step behind her, but slip my fingers into the cold cocoon of her palm. She smiles down at me and leads me along corridors until we reach a narrow formal dining room with an extravagant fireplace, two magnificent chandeliers in crystal and gilt, and a terribly long table in polished ebony, with padded seats for fifty people – although how they would ever manage to find so many willing guests is anyone's guess. At the far end are three place settings and one man sitting at the head. He looks up and smiles at us, but his stare is cool – we are late. Behind him stand two plump girls with ruddy complexions and gowns of a better quality than the housemaids': winepresses, these, being fed on one night, then rested for six while they themselves drink strong red wines and eat rare meats to build up their blood once again. They look at me with wary boredom. How many day-daughters have they seen come and go? How many girls whose privileges hardly seem worth the price they all ultimately pay? How much better to be one of these, these valued *cattle* – kept and preserved, not drained and thrown away on a whim, like an empty Jeroboam. I can see they think themselves better than me, more permanent; there's an arrogance yet a wariness, for the day-daughters are still favoured if only for a short time. The day-daughters are *family* and no insolence will be tolerated from anyone, not even these precious casks.

So as we approach, the two girls bob curtsies, eyes hooded.

'Edward, my love. This is Adlisa.' Our Lady hands me forward as the Lord pushes back his chair, but does not rise. He surveys me and I drop into a deep curtsey, mirroring that of the drinking vessels. I do not look up until he says, after proper pause, 'Good evening, Adlisa.'

In his green gaze I see the same weariness as that of the winepresses; how many day-daughters has *he* seen? How many times has he indulged his wife's madness? He must love her a great deal to repeat this scene over and over. He is very handsome, with chiselled features, thin lips, and dark red hair. Any freckles that might have marred his complexion in life have been long-since faded by his death years.

He nods toward the only place that is set with food – roasted meats, piles of steaming vegetables, a platter of white bread with delicate curls of butter in a small dish by its side. 'Sit, it is well past time to eat.'

Our Lady ignores the gibe and seats herself, gaily chattering about how she taught me to embroider and what an apt pupil I am, learning so terribly quickly – it does not seem to occur to her that perhaps I learned well before I was chosen. But then, that is part of her fantasy – refusing to believe that there was any life for me before becoming hers. I play my part. 'Thank you for teaching me, Mother.'

She positively glows. Our Lord gives me a sideways glance, which I answer with a guileless smile and an innocent gaze. After a pause he nods towards my meal, and I carefully serve myself ladylike portions although I ache to scoff down as much sustenance as I can. I'm starving, but eating like a peasant will not make a good impression. There is no servant to attend me – as few witnesses as possible to see them feed, I suppose. A strange delicacy.

The girls move into position, one beside the Lord, the other beside the Lady, both of whom carefully flutter embroidered serviettes into their laps before taking the chubby wrists offered and fastidiously biting through the skin as one might a peach. I glimpse trickles of blood that are swiftly licked away and I concentrate on my own dinner, forcing myself to eat despite a sudden loss of appetite. There is no more conversation until the repast is finished and the winepresses are swooning dreamily, then our Lord says, 'Adlisa, as this is your first night, you will be tired. You may retire.'

His inflection tells me this is not suggestion and, despite the Lady's disappointed moue, I nod and stand, curtsey, and leave the room. The Steward is waiting outside the door and nods approvingly, but says nothing. It makes me wonder how badly other first nights have gone, that he thinks this meal a triumph.

* * *

Out in the garden, the small one behind the manor, between the kitchen door, the stables and the upward slope of the mountainside, I am sketching meadowsweet into the small leather-bound herbal that was my mother's – the only thing I brought with me, tucked deep into the pocket of my black dress. I run my fingers along the spine, feeling the outline of what has lain hidden there for decades. I carefully reproduce the plant's appearance and label all its parts; I jot down what I know of its properties, whether it may heal or hurt (it will assuage vomiting, fluxes and the pain of women's courses). I leave enough space to make new notes that reflect what I might learn of it in my lifetime (however long or short that might be), just as my mother did and hers before her. I wonder who will have it when I am gone, who will fill the empty pages at the back? I adjust the muslin visage, surreptitiously using it to mop the sweat from my face.

This is my time to myself, before the Lord and Lady rise at nightfall and after I have spent some hours helping the Steward with the tasks needed to keep the manor and the city – the whole demesne – running smoothly. I awaken late, past midday, in order to straddle day and night, eat, then present myself at Oswain's office, which is a chamber of middling size. I have been put to copying, neatly and tidily, invoices and payment advices into the huge account book that is chained to the broad desk, the record of all the Lord and Lady's incomings and outgoings during Oswain's tenure. Against the opposite wall are shelves lined with other books like it – those to the left are filled with the scribblings of Stewards past; those to the right are blank, awaiting the day when this one is full and the stroke of a pen will begin the process of recording anew.

There are two doors to this room, the one I use daily to enter and exit, and the other of black oak, which I spent most of my time studiously ignoring. It is, I was told severely, the entrance to the undercroft – beyond it lies the night stair leading to our Lord and Lady's crypt where they sleep during the day. I shall never see it, I am told.

Sometimes, when I finish my duties early, I go to the far end of the manor house, to where the stone tower of the library sits. I read the history books, the tales of how the estate grew into a village that grew into a town and finally a city. I read the stories of how the Lord and Lady *became*, of the dark man who passed through Caulder and left his mark in their blood, taking their only child and leaving them to wander forever. I read the diaries of the long-dead Stewards, the lists of the very first orders given to ensure the safety of the newly reborn Lord and Lady – such as the scouring of the hawthorn trees and the garlic plants, the burning of the tiny wooden church and how the priest was thrown on the pyre as extra kindling. How the system of pricing was established so that people were properly compensated for the service they paid to their overlords. Our Lord and Lady have long understood that a gentle hand and a slow corruption will keep them in position much longer than repression and tyranny; that ensuring the population is contented, compliant – bovine – is the way to retain power.

Make lives, for the most part, enjoyable; all it costs is a little blood. And if any should question, if any should complain too loudly, or say 'I do not wish to make this bargain for my child's life', then their voice is silenced. But cunningly – an outspoken individual can be made to seem a thief, a law-breaker, a disturber of the peace, so that when they are taken away, it is in broad daylight and all might see that this is not some secretive retribution, but an open and honest operation of the law of the land. The punishment is delivered not by the Lord and Lady, no, but by the council of our fair city, so we might think ourselves self-determining, living and thriving under a system fair and equitable.

Other times, all this reading hurts my head, all the knowledge I gain of consequences and injustices, of loss and mourning disguised as justice, of my sisters fed to an unnatural hunger, settles in my chest and swells there, making it hard to breathe. Those are the times when I take to the herb garden and let myself think on nothing but the plants, on keeping my hand steady and my drawings accurate. As I add a few more veins to a leaf my fingers, too long clenched, spasm and I drop the pencil. It rolls under the meadowsweet and I kneel to locate it below the lush foliage. At the base of the bush, quite well hidden, I find a tiny white flower, which I recognise but have never seen, at least not in its true form. I flick to a page in the back of the herbal, one that's folded in on itself and tucked behind the endpaper so only a sharp eye will see it. My grandmother's etchings of the garlic plant. Her notes tell me there will be bulbs beneath the earth. The flower is shrouded by the meadowsweet; no one will expect it, no one will know. It makes me lightheaded with possibilities. All the time spent planning to gain a place in this manor house, all the recent weeks looking for weaknesses, for some idea of how I might take my revenge and here is this unlooked-for boon, something for which I'd never thought to hope.

'Will you help?' A soft voice almost scares me to death and I look up, stricken. Rikke's gentle smile fades. She kneels beside me before I can rise, distract her, turn her attention elsewhere. 'What is it, Adlisa?'

And she catches sight of the tiny white flowers and the pupils of her grey eyes dilate as if she's taken a dose of belladonna. And I see that *she* knows what it is as no one from this city should. My heart hammers, then she climbs slowly to her feet, knees cracking and creaking, her white hair lifted by the breeze that seems to have started just for us. She makes sure the stalks of the meadowsweet cover the nascent blossoms, then offers her hand to me, and repeats, 'Will you help?'

I nod, scramble up.

'Another set of hands on our Lady's new dress will make the work go faster. And then you may help with dinner if you wish,' she says. As we move towards the kitchen door, she lowers her voice and adds, 'Be careful, Adlisa.'

And I wonder at her. She can't have been born here, recognising a plant that has not been seen in this area for generations. Do I perhaps remember she arrived here some years since and the Steward claimed her as his cousin? Our visitors are few and far between, and none come without invitation. Will she tell Oswain what she has seen?

* * *

In the library, on the third floor, there are many books of strategy and philosophy, well read, their pages thumbed, markings made in the margins, all by the Lord's hand. After the first few weeks as a day-daughter, I settled myself at the desk opposite the arched window, the one that looks out across the valley, and piled tomes in front of me – where the Lord might find me. He'd raised his brows and asked if I understood what I was reading; it was the first time he showed any interest in me beyond a polite 'Good evening, Adlisa' and 'Good night, Adlisa', beyond humouring his Lady.

'Some of it – the strategies mostly. I enjoyed *Deor's Art of War* best so far. The philosophy, though – it's beyond me.' I shrugged, fingers resting on the cover of the Angelic Bergevilde's *Philosophies and Mores*.

He questioned me about the *Deor*, trying to trip me up – but I have studied the book, more than once. My father had a copy – old, tattered, inherited from a grandparent I never knew – and I've read it cover to cover and back again. I particularly liked how it speaks of infiltrating the enemy's camp, sowing trust in order to reap revenge; how to make your adversary expect a warm hand in the dark, but find only cold steel. Oh, I know my *Deor*.

Tonight we discuss *Leofgod's Military Tactics* and the Lord shows his age – the book is over five centuries old if it's a day and it was ancient before the Lord himself became what he is. He is of a generation that believes battles are won on fields watered with blood and filled with men soon to become corpses, with weapons that catch the sun, while monumental music provided by drummers and buglers thickens the air. That land must be gained and lost several times before a victor is named. That all war should be out in the open, frank and honest. Deor's advices have passed him by – he has read them but finds them… ungentlemanly, and as such he has let them slip away like lightly held thoughts.

We debate the relative merits of the tacticians and I do not let him win. We argue to a stalemate and he sits back in his armchair with a satisfied air. He sees me, at last, as something other than an ephemeral day-daughter, a creature whose lifespan is determined entirely by how long our Lady remains fixated on me. I smile brightly, thinking only that he is one of those men who have never had to ride to war and cannot know that strategy survives only so long as one has no contact with the enemy.

He offers me his arm to go to dinner and I think, foolishly, how pleased my Lady will be to see that at last we are friends, for she has spent so much time trying to encourage him to pay attention to me.

'You're late,' snaps she when we enter the dining room. The winepresses – the same ones who witnessed my first triumphant meal here – cover their smirking smiles with raised hands. I can see the tiny scars around their wrists, cicatrices like bracelets.

'My apologies, my love,' says the Lord smoothly. 'Our daughter and I lost ourselves in the heat of intellectual intercourse.'

The hairs on the back of my neck stand to attention as he leads me to my seat before taking his own at the head of the table. My Lady looks daggers at me from across the silver filigree candle tree; she seems thinner, whiter, not quite well. Her eyes catch the tips of the flames and flash red. My Lord reaches out and strokes my hand – I pull away without thought. I fear it's too late to appease my Lady, for something has begun here that I had not foreseen. So smug I have been, that I too have forgotten that *a strategy survives only so long as one has no contact with the enemy.* I see now that I was merely her mouse to be dangled in front of the cat to torment it – not to make friends with it.

'Your hair,' she begins, 'is ghastly, Adlisa, all dressed and pomaded like a harlot.'

No matter that the coiffure is one she herself has asked me to wear.

'And your skin is looking… golden,' she says with distaste. 'You have been outdoors without your visage.'

I have not – I am as anaemic-pale as I ever was.

'And that dress is ugly. The colour does not suit you, it makes you look jaundiced.' That the dress was an especial present from her, seems to make no mind as she warms to her topic. I am lazy and tardy, selfish and slatternly in my person, ignorant and ungrateful, and I do not truly love her.

My Lord says nothing, merely smiling slyly and affixing himself to the wrist of this evening's fat girl – they have favourites, he and the Lady. I've noticed that they do not share, do not swap; always the same seven girls each, in the same order each week. He watches us over the barrier of porky pink flesh, and I rethink my opinion of him. Perhaps he has not dismissed all of Deor's lessons out of hand.

Answering back, trying to defend myself, will do no good. My only choice is to burst into tears, which I summon by thinking of my lost sisters. My Lord, overthrown by a woman's weeping – our surest weapon against which no man has a defence – tidily finishes his meal and leaves the room. Out of his presence and shocked by my sobbing, our Lady is contrite, tender, motherly.

'Oh, Adlisa, come here,' she cries, pushing back her chair so I may sit at her feet, my head in her lap. She caresses my hair. 'I'm so sorry, my darling – I'm a terrible mother. A terrible person. How can I say such things, such cruel things?'

'No, no Mother, you are the kindest, sweetest woman. I give thanks every day that you chose me,' I aver, words sticking in my throat. 'I did not mean to displease you, only I thought you would be happy, to see Father and I as friends.'

She slips to the floor, her silken apricot skirts pooling around her, and holds my face close to hers. As she speaks I catch the rankness of old blood seeping up from her stomach. She has not fed yet – she is paler than usual, and she would smell differently if she had – meatier, wetter. 'You must not trust him, Adlisa. You must not. That was the mistake the others made, thinking him harmless, a kind father. But if you trust him, he will… then I will…' She does not finish the thought, but rocks me back and forth as if I am a child and not almost a woman grown. She emits little moaning sounds that make the skin on my spine shiver and pucker. In the end, I gently pull away and call to the untapped winepress.

'Our Lady is thirsty. Our Lady hungers. My Mother must be fed,' I say and there is a grudging admiration in the girl's eyes, to see that I have salvaged myself at least for this night. She comes close and the scent coming off her skin is faint but I can detect it because I am looking for it. She offers her wrist and our Lady bites into it as if she is starving.

I stay until she is sated and the drinking vessel has all but passed out. Our Lady, despite her repletion, does not seem any stronger. I help her up and take her to lie on the chaise in her solar, where she drifts into an uneasy sleep until such time as Rikke or one of the lesser maids will wake her and escort her to the night stair before the day dawns.

* * *

'A visitor arrived for you this afternoon, my Lord. He has conducted previous correspondence with your good self, I believe.' The Steward's tone tells precisely what he thinks of this visitor, a blonde man perhaps in his mid-forties – vain, I can tell, for he wears make-up as women do to try and fill the furrows time has made in his face. I watched him, surreptitiously, from the kitchen while I was helping Rikke prepare for the evening meal. Some of the day-daughters, she has told me, have determinedly refused to undertake such tasks, acting as if they're born porcelain ladies and not temporarily elevated earthenware, but I have ever been willing to assist with meals for the entire household, taking it on myself to season the rich, meaty stews and roasts for the winepresses.

The sound of smashing drew my attention away from him – Rikke, stood behind me, eyes wide, expression disbelieving. When I asked her what was wrong, stooped to pick up the shards of the terracotta jar, she shook her head.

'I thought…' she began and shook her head again, summoned a smile. 'I thought I knew him, from a long time ago. But that's not possible, is it, with him unchanged?'

We gave each other a shaky grin – do we not live in the shadow of the unchanging?

The man was very handsome, his eyes terribly blue as they watched the slow spin of the Steward's Gaze at Oswain's chest, but lacking in warmth, cold as the depths of a sapphire are cold, and his lips were very full, overripe, and I did not trust his mouth. Everything he is resides there, in its petulance, its greed, its formation of want. I do not think him a friend to the Lord, but rather someone who wants something – and who resents having to ask for it. He does not wear the cloak of a supplicant well. Oswain gave him a guest room, for it is winter now and the Lord has been rising late – the Lady later still – and left him there to wait until someone came to lead him to the library for an audience.

I had not heard my Lord enter the Steward's office, but then one seldom hears either of them if they do not wish it so – although the Lady has become slow, more heavy-footed of late, liable to send vases and suits of armour crashing to the floor without any effort at all. Lord Edward stands in front of the great desk where Oswain sits hunched over one of his ledgers, while I sort a stack of invoices into their proper order at a smaller desk in one corner. I have been avoiding him, this strange father-figure, since that night when all my intricate planning seemed to go astray, when my steps appeared to leave the sure path I'd been so careful to stay on, and I could not divine the *why* of it. The library at night has been off-limits by my own design, and each evening I wait in the Lady's solar until she rises, then help her to the dining room. She is weakest and most disoriented after waking, so when I've seen her safely to her seat, I take a small sharp knife and tap the veins of her winepress, letting the thick rich red trickle into a crystal glass. It is still warm with an echo of life vibrating through, enough to give her some strength, but one must be quick for the heartbeat rapidly fades. Her mystery ailment has made her too feeble to feed straight from the source until she has had a little taste to energise her, to remind her that the *claret* is what she craves. And as I render this service, our Lord eyes me with displeasure but says nothing; his mood has deteriorated with our Lady's health. He no longer addresses me directly, but follows me with a gaze that broods and promises punishment.

For the moment, though, I am of no interest to him and our Lord fixes the Steward with a glare, ignoring mention of the guest, and jerks a thumb behind him as if to signify the rows of covered baskets in the hall.

'And what is all *this*, Oswain?'

'My Lord, there was a cave-in at the mine; three families lost sons and fathers. I have taken the liberty of having these supplies prepared to help tide the broods over until arrangements can be made for new husbands.' More than one woman has found herself widowed by the black rock of the mountain, then newly married a few days later to ensure no impoverished relicts mar our streets.

'You coddle them, Oswain! Surely they should be able to care for themselves without your constant attention?' The undertone is mean, petty, and I can see the Steward stiffen. His lips tighten, blanch.

'My Lord, I and my kind have kept your *cattle* alive, healthy and contented in the interests of keeping you and your Lady contented and healthy and… alive,' he stumbles, just a little, over that word. 'Few things will disturb your pleasant existence more than an untended populace, but if you truly wish me to change how I discharge my duty then the choice is yours.'

The Steward's tone is steely, and I hold my breath, fearful – I have become fond of him in these past months. He is stern but kind, and I have never seen him commit an act of cruelty. The moments stretch, scraping my nerves like a knife's edge on ligaments. Then the Lord grins ruefully.

'Oswain, you have the right of it, old friend. But be careful you do not overstep.'

'I am ever mindful of your wellbeing, my Lord.' Oswain bows his head, relief palpable. I sense that the Lord, too, did not wish a confrontation – did not wish to push against a limit, a barrier that might crack and break too easily.

'Add some bottles of tokay from the cellar to the baskets, as many as we can spare. And to send the visitor to the library – there will be no formal meal tonight, so make sure he is fed in his room.'

Oswain raises an eyebrow. 'My Lord?'

'Tonight, my Lady and I shall hunt,' he says, smiling and raising his hand to forestall the Steward's protests. 'Do not fear, Oswain, we will take the carriage and go beyond the boundaries of our demesne. None of your charges will be harmed.'

Oswain nods slowly. 'Make sure you choose an isolated farm so no one might raise an alarm. Leave no trace of yourself or your… meal.'

'I recall how to hunt, Oswain, though it has been an age.' He drops his voice. 'I fear for my Lady Marcella. I hope this – excursion – will help to heal her. Perhaps we have been too long sedentary, too long content to be fed; we have forgotten how to take something of the prey into us.' His eyes glitter and he looks like a feral thing, dangerous, struggling against the bonds he's put on himself. Then his face relaxes and the moment is passed.

But I cannot forget that expression, even when he smiles at me, seemingly once again the doting father who had indulged in mock argument with me, testing me and finding himself pleased. He turns his back and leaves.

After interminable seconds, Oswain stands and closes the door. I can see a fine beading of sweat on his bald pate.

'Why do you serve them?' I say, the words out before I can think better of it. For a moment I doubt he will answer.

'Because without them, there will be a vacuum and a vacuum must be filled. And we can never know that what might come along isn't worse than this pair.' He hides his face in his hands. 'I do what I can as did my father and his before him and his before him. This is a *business* upon which an entire city depends, and as long as we remain clever and careful, we will survive.'

'Why Dimity?' I ask. It's been bothering me for so long now and he seems inclined to talk. 'She doesn't look like our Lady.'

He shakes his head. 'No. She looks a little like our Lord, though. But it was… I thought it might preserve a life. She would not interest our Lady much, and consequently nor our Lord. She might have simply faded into the domestic staff or become a winepress… anything's better than me having to deliver another hollow body to parents who had higher hopes for their child.'

I had not thought about it that way – I had not thought the choice of Dimity might be calculated. Steward Oswain is a good man doing his best under a mighty burden. I respect him and I pity him. Once I'd thought to take revenge on him, for it was he who chose my sisters. But now, having seen how he aches… I cannot raise my hand against him.

'What is wrong with our Lady?' I ask.

He shrugs. 'They are *old*, Adlisa. Nothing is meant to live that long. Perhaps it is simply death catching up with them.'

'Are there others of their kind?'

Again, a shrug. 'Somewhere, I suppose, but I've not heard of any for the length of my life. My grandfather said the man who made them was not like them, not the same thing he turned them into. He – it – cursed them and stole their child. They've been changeless for so many centuries, but perhaps the curse is coming to its end and so are their lives?' Again he rubs his hands over his face, the sound of skin against stubble is loud. 'They were never bad rulers, Adlisa – if you've spent your time wisely in the library you will know that. And as they are now, they are nowhere near as bad as they could be. Time has made them strange.'

Silence falls and reigns, broken only by the ticking of the timepiece on the desk, a thing with a bird that coos the hours. I think we will stay there forever if I do not speak. 'Shall I have the baskets delivered?'

'No, I'll organise that. You go and collect the guest and take him to the library. After that, I think you might be best keeping to your room tonight.'

I pass through the kitchen and, from the small wooden box I've concealed behind the sacks of potatoes, I take three bulbs. I crush them quickly against the bricks of the fireplace while no one's looking and drop the garlic fragments into the thick, meaty pottage bubbling over the fire. The taste will be disguised by that of the leeks, chives and onions already in the mix. I scrub my hands carefully at the stone sink with lye soap, then splash some of the lemon juice wash Rikke keeps there for when she has been handling fish and needs to get rid of the smell.

The guest has been given a room three doors along from mine, an elaborate decor in greens and golds and bronze. When I knock, he is slow in answering, then makes me wait after I tell him why I am there – although he surely must know – but he takes his time putting on his seemingly brand-new velvet frock coat with its intricate enamel buttons, teasing the lace cuffs of his shirt sleeves out so they might be seen and admired. He pushes at his hair, this way and that, in front of the large gaudy cloisonné mirror over the fireplace, vain as a woman, as if such fussing might help his cause.

He does not engage me in conversation, but I can feel his eyes boring into the back of me as I lead him along corridors, down staircases, through smaller rooms until at last we reach the library.

'Thank you, Adlisa,' says my Lord when I introduce his guest. He grabs my upper arm without seeming to offer me violence, and strokes my face and curls. It is not the act of a father, and it makes me afraid, as if I'm being pulled towards something I cannot escape, a whirlpool, a drowning wave. As his wife fades, he grows more predatory. As she gives in, he fights against whatever is happening. He lets me go as if dropping me from a height. 'Off you go.'

'Pretty girl,' I hear the blond man say as I close the door. 'Rather reminds me of my sister…'

* * *

I waited until I heard the carriage rattle away; the Lord and Lady would be gone for hours. I waited until the house had quietened as the staff took the rare opportunity to rest earlier in the evening than was their wont. When all is quiet, I slip from my room and tiptoe along the corridor, carefully past the guest's room, then down one set of stairs and up another. Along a long landing; the door I'm seeking is at its end and I try the handle, find it unlocked, press my ear against the thick wood and listen intently, then push it open, quiet as can be.

There is a snuffle and a snort, a contented sleeper's noise, from the large bed beneath the window. In the winter moonlight, the thin form of the Steward is curled about Rikke's naked roundness. Not cousins, then. On the chest of drawers beside the door, right next to me, is the gleaming eye of the Steward's Gaze, and beside it the great golden pile of the chatelaine and keys, carelessly discarded for the night when he keeps it so carefully during the daylight hours. The cold radiates off it as I clasp it tightly.

Oswain gives a tremendous snore, fit to wake the household. I freeze, will myself invisible, wait to see if he rouses himself. He subsides into shallow breaths and sighs, and I slip out. Bouncing with nerves on my bare tiptoes, holding the chatelaine with both hands so it does not jingle and give me away, I scurry along the thin hallway rugs laid end to end; they muffle the sounds of my passage. I am so keyed up, listening so hard to the silent house that I almost overshoot my destination.

I unlock the office, and step inside. The room is dark except for the weak embers of the banked fire, but these weeks as a daughter in a house which comes alive at night have made my eyes sensitive to the darkness, as if I've become a cat. There it is: the black door, the locked door, the door that leads *down*.

I have no reason to go there, merely curiosity as hot and intense as flame. A desire to see a place where my sisters might have met their fate, where I might yet meet mine. I take a taper from the top drawer of the great desk, hold it to the glowing coals and let the wick catch. It glimmers weakly.

Five paces and the key is sliding into the lock easily, then the stygian wood is pushed back to reveal the night stair. There is no illumination here. The cold stone steps beneath my naked feet answer back a quiet *shhh* as I descend into the earth. The walls are pocked with burial niches, some with mouldering bones huddling sadly in corners, others with intact skeletons lying fully prone and relaxed in death. When I reach the bottom, I blink and stare into the deeper shadows. There are two empty biers made of marble. I step forward, tiptoeing although I know no one is here; I catch my foot on something frail and friable. There is the faintest *crack*. I look down and see I have stepped on a doll, swaddled in sepia cloth and wearing a lace bonnet of ancient style. I bend and sweep it up, hold it close to my frail taper, look into its face to find it is in fact a mummified baby, empty-eyed, hollow-cheeked, hungry-mouthed. Beneath the swaddling I can feel where I snapped one of its ribs. I look about for a place to hide it and notice at last the pile – mound – of more of the same, all dressed so sweetly in styles of different ages, all as dead as dust, all with that same expression.

I carefully bury the one I broke beneath its fellows and hope that my Lady does not go looking for it. A quick survey of the space yields nothing, and I am about to return to the Steward's office when there is the sound of scuffing, of shoes hastily making contact with stone. I am frozen, unable to blow out the taper, to hide. What good would it do me?

'Adlisa?' It is Rikke's voice, taut with fear. Rikke, who has been so kind. Rikke, who has kept my secret. Rikke, who asked if she might create a facsimile of my herbal so there might be more than one copy in the world. Gentle Rikke, who has followed me down into this Hell. 'Adlisa, what are you doing? Come, you must leave now. They have returned – I heard the carriage.'

We fly up the stairs. My hands shake too much and she must take the chatelaine from me and lock the black door, then the office too. She slips the heavy golden thing into the pocket of her brown woollen dressing robe. We are waiting in the entrance hall when the main doors are thrown open and the Lord, our Lady in his arms, charges in, both of them pale as the winter moon, but streaked with blood. The Lord's gaze is wild, the Lady's eyes are firmly closed.

* * *

'Drink this. Our Lady needs you,' I say to the plump winepress. She is still befuddled by slumber and does not question me, merely lifts the goblet I put in her hand, chugging down the red wine, not commenting on the taste. Ah, bless these gluttonous girls.

I don't not let her dress, lest the Lord think I did not fetch her swiftly enough, and lead her to our Lady's chamber. As I walk, in my pocket I can feel the weight of the item I've kept hidden inside the fat mattress of my bed ever since I lent Rikke my herbal. It hits against my thigh with each step, not heavy but still solid. Tap-tap-tap. Tap-tap-tap.

In the solar, our Lady is draped across the chaise seemingly in a faint, but her eyelids flutter when she hears my voice. 'My Lord, here is the girl.'

He, in all his blood-streaked glory, grabs the winepress's forearm and drags her over to his wife. He forces her to her knees and presses her wrist to our Lady's mouth. The winegirl yelps in surprise; this is the roughest handling she's ever had. The first time she's seen the Lord's true nature, which he has subsumed for so many, many years. Our Lady grimaces and turns her face away, batting the air weakly with hands grown skeletal. The Lord, seeing this, raises the girl's wrist to his own mouth and his teeth – those canines they've gone to such care to carefully cover, speaking with lips close together so only the barest tips can be seen – those teeth seem to lengthen, sharpen, and he tears at the girl's flesh with them. He offers the limb once again to his wife and this time she opens her mouth, roused by the rich scent, latching on like a leech.

Her lids flutter up, eyes widen as she watches me. Her throat convulses with each gulp, each swallow, the marble flesh undulating painfully. I wonder if she knows what is happening.

The Lord, now certain she is drinking, strides around the room.

'The hunt did not go well?' I ask quietly and he hisses at me.

'No! Fool child, it did not. We found a farm, but there were too many – we did not know. Once I could have counted the heartbeats in this entire city, but now… they came from nowhere and we… we have grown sluggish and lazy, feeding on these thin-veined, fat-arsed bitches.' His movements are jerky, graceless; his control is slipping. He paces past the drowsing winepress and offers her ample backside a kick, then changes direction. He has been less affected than his wife; perhaps his vessels have drunk less deeply or eaten less heartily of what I've prepared for them, or perhaps he is simply stronger. But now his face is thinner and his eyes stare, protrude just a little, the skin around his throat looser, perhaps. 'We will feed on you all – it will make her well. You see? You see how she is after feeding on one of them? Before they woke and turned on us, before one of them fetched her a blow to her poor head. You see?'

At this we both turn and look at our Lady.

The winepress lies on the floor, insensible; her wrist, beribboned in red, drops slowly to the carpet as its captor looses it. Marcella, her mouth a ravening hole, has tried hard, so terribly hard to get all the sustenance she needs, but the blood of the winegirls has been tainted for weeks now with garlic and belladonna, just small amounts in their own food and wine. It makes them terrible sleepy – although it does protect them against colds – and it's been building up slowly in them and then in my Lord and Lady – whose bodily functions no longer function, have neither excreted nor sweated nor vomited the poison out. The extra dose I put in the girl's wine before bringing her here finally had the desired effect.

I've watched as my Lady's grown weaker, more tired. I've stroked her lovely hair as she's clung to me like a child to a doll. I've whispered promises that she would grow well again soon and be strong. I've told her she would find peace. A thin shiver of guilt ripples through me until I think of all those tiny babies down in the undercroft, all those dried-up little creatures deprived of life and all their chances.

And now… and now, my Lady Mother lies there, replete, finished. Before our very eyes, her skin wrinkles like lace left too close to a fire. Her locks turn white faster than I can think, then drop away from the skull that is shrinking as its true age catches up with it. The body beneath her glorious burgundy evening gown diminishes, leave the dress too large, a hulking shell for a withering creature. The pale eyes glaze over, then shrink to tiny marbles, then disappear completely, and then… and then, she is nothing but brittle bones, then dust on a velvet couch, an empty dress, and discarded tresses shining like forgotten gold in the lambent light of the candles.

The Lord rushes towards the remains of his wife, stops, spreads his hands wide, but does not touch her – there is nothing, really, to touch. His howl is like that of a wolf, only worse, darker, deeper, blacker.

I step back, although I know I should use this moment when his attention is turned away from me. But I am so afraid, so afraid that my heart is a leaden thing in my chest; so afraid that it seems to have ceased to beat; so afraid that I fumble when I draw the wooden dagger from my pocket and drop it on the carpet between us.

It is so slim and simple, nothing to excite the interest, not especially beautifully or elegantly made, but it is compact enough to lie hidden in the spine of my herbal, its blade is honed to a fine sharp edge, and it is carved of hawthorn, one of the last of its kind, and, now, it seems so small and inadequate. But I cannot falter, I cannot fail. If I do not remove this creature then our whole city will suffer; all lives will change and not for the better.

I fall over myself to get to it, scrambling on hands and knees, my fingers touching, clutching the haft, just as the Lord wheels around and sees me. In the shortest of moments, he knows, he understands that somehow this has all been me, the viper in the nest of vipers. His expression is a swirling vortex of shock, bitter amusement, rage and hatred. He moves, fast, so fast, his right hand closing in on itself, all the nails becoming talons and gathered together like a spearhead. He draws his arm back and then drives the point through my chest and into my heart. All I have time to do is to bring my dagger, my tiny dagger up and across to slice through the skin and flesh of his throat. The cut itself cannot be mortal, but the substance of the knife – ah, now therein lies *cessation*.

I cannot look at him for there is blood pouring over me, in my eyes, my mouth, down my wounded chest, then there is a shower of grave dust. The rug beneath me is thick and soft as I draw my dying breaths. There is the sound of running footsteps and doors opening and closing, but all is muted to me. I'm not cold, but warm as death reaches for me.

But I don't mind. I don't mind dying with all my deeds done.

In front of me I think I see beacons, my sisters burning before me, April and Sophie, smiling. I think I see all the other girls, the day-daughters who have come and gone, the great rolling tally of years. I see them all though I do not know their names.

Then there is darkness and they fade from sight, and I see no more.

* * *

I did not expect to wake, and when I realise *why* I have, I want to weep.

The dark lies on me like a blanket, but I can see through it as if it's pure daylight down here. My throat hurts and my mouth is dry.

My chest aches where it was pierced, but when I put my hand to the torn place, feel through the ragged rips in the fabric of my dress, I find no holes, no rents in my torso, just smooth cold skin.

A tiny glimmer catches my attention, bobbing as it slowly descends the night stair. I am in the undercroft. I lie on a bed of marble.

Oswain's kind face looms over me; beside him is Rikke, her eyes sad and silver in the strange light. They seem reluctant to speak. Oswain offers a hand and helps me sit up. I can smell them both; they are *warm* and full of life. I push the thought aside, as hunger buzzes nastily in my head.

'The blood,' I say. 'His blood?'

Oswain nods. 'Entered your wounds. Healed you inside out. Changed you.'

I look around the undercroft so I do not need to see the pity in their eyes. My gaze comes to rest on the mound of mummified children.

'The babies?' I ask. The Steward glances away, blinking. Rikke peers at him, perhaps thinking it is his tale to tell, but when he opens and closes his mouth, once, twice, and no words come out, she explains.

'The Lord and Lady played games with each other – being as they were, all that time, anyone would begin to hate the other. The Lord tolerated his wife's obsession only so long. The fonder our Lady became of her day-daughters, the more perverse grew the Lord. He would begin to woo girls until finally he bedded them. Those that became pregnant thought themselves safe – he told them he loved them, that he wanted only them, that his Lady was old and desiccated.' She takes a breath, glances at Oswain, who is now sobbing quietly, his shoulders quaking.

'But as they grew great, as the evidence of what had been done came clear, the Lady knew herself betrayed and found her love diminishing; her daughters had failed her. When they gave birth, she took their children away and the Lord… the Lord dealt with the day-daughters. The Lady thought the babies adorable for a time, but they cry as babies do, then she found them too much trouble. Eventually, she would stop their crying the only way she knew how, but she still didn't like to part with them so she kept them here.'

We are silent for a while. I wonder which of the tiny dead dolls belonged to April. Sophie was not here long enough. I have a tiny niece or a nephew, lying there amongst the dead.

'You should kill me, Oswain,' I say gently. 'I do not wish to live like this. Even now I can smell you – your blood. Kill me and I will not fight you. There are garlic bulbs aplenty beneath the meadowsweet. And my knife – where is my knife?'

'Adlisa, we are a city of many souls. Do you remember when I spoke to you of vacuums? Who do you think might fill the one you've created? Hmmm?' I notice he does not answer me about the hawthorn dagger.

'You could. You are kind and wise,' I say, stretching my arms above my head, expecting to be stiff and sore but finding my cold limbs strangely limber, pliable, although my flesh is marble.

He shakes his head. 'My power derives only from being the representative of the manor house. Without a Lord and Lady, there is no figurehead, no sense of order from above. You have created this situation, Adlisa, you must fix it.'

I blink hard, thinking if I close my eyes for long enough everything will go away. Then a thought. 'The visitor? Our Lord's supplicant?'

Oswain's hand goes to where the Steward's Gaze usually hangs and I notice at last the jewel's absence. His fingers jerk, spider-like, seeking a phantom limb. He does not need to tell me that in the chaos of my making the guest snuck into the Steward's room much as I did earlier, that the gem is by now far away from Caulder.

Rikke looks at her feet, then into my eyes. 'You must feed, Adlisa. One of the winepresses?'

'You will need to find a new one. I fed them all on garlic and belladonna.'

Oswain nods. 'I'd wondered what you'd done. You terrible, clever girl.'

'I don't want to live like this,' I repeat, and there is a break in my voice and I wonder if I can cry now that I am *like this*. Or is it merely the echoes of the pity a dead thing feels for itself? Could I walk out into the sun or is the sleep that comes with the daylight too profound? Or is it simply that I am starting to feel what the Lord and Lady felt for so long: a desperation to hold onto life. A refusal, a denial of true death, a determined clinging to some sort of existence.

'Adlisa, we will find a cure,' says Rikke, and Oswain gives her a warning look. I know what he is thinking: *The girl is dead, make her no false promises*. She ignores him. 'There is a great library far from here, at Cwen's Reach, a repository such as few can imagine.

The women of St Florian's gather rare and arcane books, copy them to make sure the knowledge never passes from the world. I am sure, Adlisa, that in one of those books is the secret to curing you. I will write to my sisters, some will remember me there. You are not without hope.'

Her voice is so sincere, so filled with faith that I want to believe her. I want to believe her the way children believe the fairy tales they're told at their mother's knee. And I see how it will be for me for some years, listening to the stories she tells me of this place, of her time there, of how she came there and why she left, of how the answer to my *unfortunate condition* lies there, and how, one day, we will find it.

Until then, my life will be darkness and blood.

NOW, ALL PIRATES ARE GONE

The sea is strangely silent tonight and this makes Maude and her crew nervous.

Beneath their collective worn canvas shoes, bare feet, and thick-soled boots, the brig's deck is steady as *Astra's Light* moves through the waters with nary a noise, and only the slightest *shhhh*'ing as the bow splits the flat mirror of liquid salt. Ahead of them, the island lies low, relaxed, a dark hunched thing against the blue-black sky, seemingly boneless as those chickens Maude's aunt sometimes bred, the ones that weren't quite right. But from the centre of Isla Caleuche rises a tower, straight and tall as a luring finger, saying *Come hither*.

The breeze that pushes them toward their goal is strong, warm – indeed, hot – and the night air is humid. Maude wipes at her face with an embroidered kerchief. The thing was not meant for such rough use and is frayed, discoloured after five hard years. Soon it will be little more than a rag, but she won't discard it for it was a gift from the mute woman with auburn-rose hair they'd plucked from the sea, back when the oceans were kind and full of bounty. When the business of piracy was at its peak and all but the worst captains could afford to, and did, display some compassion and a reasonable degree of generosity. The folk of the *Astra's Light* didn't know how long the woman had floated, and they couldn't figure how she hadn't drowned, but her skin had turned as furrowed as a crone's frown and it took days of pouring fresh water into her mouth and applying rich unguents (from Maude's own stock, thank you very much) to make her even begin to look human once more.

Grateful, the woman had made herself useful – darning ragged pants, shirts and skirts, socks and stockings. Making serviceable bunk-blankets for the whole crew out of the worsted wool, calico and felt from an argosy they'd 'lightened' but days before; and a fine coverlet of green and gold brocatelle for Maude and Sancha's bed. Men and women all began to regard her as something of a mascot, a pet to replace the cat that had disappeared in a storm a week earlier.

The woman couldn't write or speak, so Sancha had begun teaching her letters. By the time they'd set her ashore at Cwen's Reach, she'd made a silken shawl for Sancha and the fine cambric kerchief for the captain, Maude's initials embroidered in one corner and cleverly stitched now-mermaids-now-maidens gambolling around the edges, tail to feet and back again. Maude, who had the full complement of sailors' superstitions to give her ballast, came to regard the piece of fabric as something of a lucky charm. In her career, she'd had her share of accidents – a shoulder dislocated from hanging out a window, stab wounds from any number of ill-wishers and naval men, powder burns from unexpected and inconvenient explosions – but from the day the kerchief came into her possession she'd been unusually incident- and injury-free.

When they'd made harbour at Cwen's, Sancha had accompanied the woman, and left her with one of the Little Sisters of St Florian at the Citadel – which was the closest thing to a charitable institution the port town had. It seemed like the best place, Sancha later said, as she showed Maude the new ship's cat she'd acquired, a black and gold kitten five months or so old, standoffish and wise as it sat on the bed beside them, observing their state of undress with a kind of disdain. Or perhaps the distaste was for her name: Hieronymus.

It was only some time after she'd gone, the woman, and the seas seemed to change their tenor, that they wondered if she was the beginning of their ruin.

* * *

At first, no one really noticed – oh, comment was made that some of the sisterhood and the brethren were having awful luck. Aggie Firehead's *Dawn Maiden* mysteriously went down in deep beastie-free waters, with no other ships about; only Ignacio the cabin boy survived, and managed to tell the story to those on the ship that found him floating days later, barely alive. Bede Blackhand and his crew were caught by five Royal Navy ships and the *Angel's Breath* was fired upon without warning – almost all hands were lost, but this time the cook's girl held on.

From each disaster, one survivor, one lone bard to tell the story and sing the ballad of the lost. Storms such as had never been seen by neither woman nor man with salt in their veins rose out of nowhere, waves a hundred feet high, seabeds naked for long moments as the swells pulled back and up, higher and higher, skies black with clouds that blocked out the sun, and the only illumination to be seen.

was the lightning in its sundry forms: sheets, bolts, ball and sprite. St Elmo's Fire appeared and led mariners astray. Rocky shoals sprang up where none had ever been, and Navy boats suddenly seemed to know where wanted men and women would sail before they knew themselves.

One by one, pirates and their ships began to disappear either through accident, incident or unnatural selection. Some, sensing how things would go, settled into a comfortable retirement while they still had a modicum of their liberated bounty, finding houses by the sea so they could still smell the briny perfume of their mistress, but no longer setting foot on a boat. The oceans had turned against them – although the merchants positively prospered – and it was a foolhardy or brave individual who did not heed the warning.

The captain of *Astra's Light* was uncertain on which side of that divide she fell. Maude only knew that she'd been able to stay afloat longer than any other, whether through luck, good or dumb, timing or cunning, she could not say. But she knew she had a crew to care for, people to feed, Sancha to look after and love. The sea was all she knew and, until the sea spat her out, there she would stay.

Eventually, though, her reserves decreased, all the treasure she'd accumulated and deposited in respectable bank accounts started to run low; the spice warehouses filled with creatively acquired saffron, cinnamon and tamarind dust began to empty. Even though the competition had thinned to nothing, when it became obvious that hers was the last pirate ship abroad, even Maude had to admit her odds of avoiding disaster were getting smaller and smaller. But then there came a whisper, both heavy and light, of a treasure like no other. A treasure for which it was worth risking life and limb. A treasure that could keep a woman and her crew for several lifetimes.

If only it could be found.

* * *

There are five of them in the lifeboat. Back on the *Astra's Light*, the rest of the crew lean against the strakes, not speaking, not even in a whisper, simply watching the upstroke and dip of the oars plied by black-bearded Ambrose. In the little boat's stern are the twins Fralle and Seðryð, both tall and muscular – the former's pectorals and the latter's breast identical in size and firmness. Brother and sister are distinguishable only by their hairstyles, the one's head covered by long and flowing golden locks, the other's closely shaved. Their breeks and vests, once a bright elaborate brocade in red and green, are now frayed and worn; Fralle is barefoot and Seðryð wears black leather buckled boots that reach almost to her knees – expensively and especially made in more prosperous times by a cobbler in Breakwater, who carves his mark into the soles of every pair he produces so his work may be known. The others laughed at Seðryð for buying what she might steal, but she wore the boots proudly, and kicked anyone who sniggered in her hearing.

Maude, in the bow, twists around so she can glimpse Sancha on deck, the moonlight dripping down her midnight curls, revealing her pale face with its sharp chin. The still silhouette of Hieronymus sits beside her on the rails. Maude raises a hand, sees an answering gesture, and looks once more towards the island. Next to the captain crouches Helissente, the smallest member of the crew – an essential soldier when on raids such as this. Maude never knows when she might run into a situation that requires a thin, flexible, acrobatic girl, so she keeps one in perpetual readiness. The captain is nothing if not prepared.

But there is nothing that could have prepared her for what is about to happen.

As the lifeboat beaches with Ambrose's last powerful stroke, the silken *crunch* of ocean-blessed wood meeting compacted fine sand is not enough to cover the noise that splits the night. At first there is a rumbling, a bubbling, then a snap and a creak and finally a whistling sort of scream. All turn towards the *Astra's Light*, just in time to see – to see…

One tentacle, then another, spears up from the deck, having first pierced the curve of the hull, then anything between it and the sky, heedless of bunks, cargo, barrels, weapon racks, cannons. Those on the island watch in horror as a third, a fourth, a fifth appendage perform precisely the same destructive dance, then, not content with having turned Maude's ship into a large sieve, the fat oil-glistening limbs strain and *pull* sideways. *Astra's Light* tears as easily as paper, as a lady's handkerchief. Bodies, planks, casks, sails, masts, the other lifeboats, *everything* flies across the night firmament as effortlessly as the cow jumping over the moon.

Maude feels her heart rise and fall with those figures; feels it rend with the timbers of her ship.

When all is quiet again and there is only the whisper of the waves, Ambrose begins to push the little boat out but Maude lays a hand on his shoulder and shakes her head, though it is agony to do so. The sea is strewn with wreckage, with things that do not move of their own accord; on the wine-dark surface there is no sign of anyone trying to swim, to survive. Nor is there any sign of the great tentacles that tore the *Astra's Light* to shreds – the thing may well be lurking *beneath*, waiting for Maude to be lunatic enough to mount a rescue.

'But, Cap'n,' protests Ambrose. He is the newest member of her crew, not yet as unquestioning as the others. Fralle and Seðryð turn glacial gazes on him; the lack of action hurts them no less than Maude, but they are practical creatures – they believe one cannot aid the dead. Maude wonders how to explain that her mother, captain of the *Astra's Light* before her, taught that the care of others was based on priority, and the first priority was those who had the best chance of survival. She watches the waters for as long as she dares, hoping to see at least one form moving, splashing, swimming hard towards her – and she knows in her heart that she wants it to be Sancha, that she would trade every other life in her hands for it to be Sancha, and that shames her. But there is nothing. No one.

In the end, though it makes her ache, she simply says, 'There can be no survivors, Ambrose. Look to the living.'

As she turns away, Maude thinks about how she came to hear of the Treasure of Isla Caleuche, of how she'd been ready to retire, to leave *Astra's Light*, her sails changed to the innocuous colours of a merchantman, her crew dressed in seldom-used uniforms, to distract the authorities from thinking of them as pirates moored in Breakwater's harbour, to let her gather barnacles. The ship had rested there for weeks and months while her sailors marked time gambling, fishing, patronising the local brothels, doing odd jobs for legitimate merchants who didn't want their own men sullying their hands with illegal acts, and all the while Maude's fortune dwindled. And somehow – she couldn't quite remember how – word had come, as if drifting on the breeze, of the island and its treasure, supposedly unguarded, supposedly there for the taking, and Maude had thought perhaps one last voyage, one last sortie, and she could pay off her crew and see them safely set; buy a house, perhaps even sell *Astra's Light* to one of the great trading houses and give her a new life as an honourable vessel. To settle down with Sancha and Hieronymus and be a respectable woman, perhaps taking a stall in the marketplace, perhaps a little black marketeering on the side just to keep her edge.

And Maude ponders, now, if the promise of this one last journey wasn't simply the baiting of a trap.

* * *

They fight their way along an overgrown path, through a twisted mess of vines, branches and knee-deep leaf matter. As they approach the entrance to the tower, Maude thinks she hears something following them. She pauses, cutlass drawn, and waits as the others move past her and up the rough-hewn stairs. Head cocked, she listens hard, looks about and sees, too late, what Fralle and Seðryð have failed to notice. There is a slight dip on the broad stoop in front of the tower's red wooden door, a tell-tale depression in what is otherwise solid stone.

The twins' large feet hit the step, trigger the mechanism and the ground under them opens. They are gone so fast Maude hasn't time to take in a breath; they did not have time to cry out. Their captain sprints up the steps, stares into the hole in the moments before granite scrapes on granite, and closes over what is nothing more than a pit of black.

Ambrose, ashen-faced, rounds on Maude. 'We must turn back.'

'And go where? We have no supplies. We are five days from the nearest port and that's if we had *Astra's Light*. In the lifeboat? Under the sun with no water? No food?'

'It's too dangerous! Whatever is here – we can't eat treasure, Cap'n.' Ambrose, perhaps the least superstitious of her crew, is bug-eyed with fear. Maude can see traces of white foam at the corners of his lips. She pitches her voice low, trying to calm him.

'Ambrose, the only way is forward. We might find food inside.'

'Hard-hearted grasping bitch! You don't care what we lose!'

Maude grabs the front of his shirt, ripping it as she lifts him upward. 'I lost Sancha and I care greatly about that,' she hisses between gritted teeth, then lets him go. She can see he's too far gone. Maude wonders, now, which man or woman he'd loved on her ship, whose bunk he'd shared to make him grieve for them so – or perhaps it was simply fear that made him break so eaily.

The stocky man shakes his head, eyes growing ever-wider. 'No. No, no, no, no, no, no, no, no, no…'

He retreats, keeping his gaze fixed firmly on her face as if she might attack him the moment his back is turned. It's only when he reaches the edge of the clearing that he spins and plunges into the foliage. Maude wonders at this terror that leeches the trust from men. There is the sound of bushes being thrust aside, of twigs breaking as boots tread hastily on them, and then there is a wet noise, as of something large falling with intent from a height and crushing something not quite as large. There is nothing further from Ambrose, but Maude thinks she hears a fleshy tearing, a snapping of bones as an appetite is sated.

She looks at Helissente, who is shaking.

'Do you trust me?'

The girl nods with barely a hesitation and Maude takes heart from this, although she suspects she shouldn't. The child only joined them six months ago, anxious to flee the boredom of a life among the Little Sisters of St Florian; citing a hunger for adventure when she'd begged to be one of Maude's crew. *Plenty of that now*, thinks Maude grimly. Careful not to trigger the trapdoor, she tiptoes around the spot where the twins disappeared and cautiously pushes the door handle downward.

It opens easily as she remains cautiously to one side, pressed against the outer wall. Nothing falls, swings out or explodes at them. Maude examines the dim interior until she is satisfied, then moves into a space that reaches upward, a spiral staircase the only thing obscuring the view of the open sky for there are no upper floors. As above, so below, the staircase curls down into a darkness that is not complete, lit as it is by spilled moonlight and a strange luminescence from the algae on the walls. Maude leads, Helissente follows.

The stairs are solid if a little slippery and at the bottom the women splash into a foot of water that shimmers like mercury. There is an archway reached by four steps ascending into a dry passage of flagstones. Torches line the walls but they are long extinguished. Maude takes one and uses her flint to give them a frail and flickering light. The corridor ends in a large square kitchen, and off that run other smaller rooms: two bedchambers fitted with thin pallet beds, a chest at the foot of each, iron hooks for hanging thick coats that smell musty and old; a cold-room, terribly still and chill, where they find large wheels of still-good cheese, and milk in metal churns and earthenware jugs, some containing sour sludge, others dried lactic crusts; another area houses smoked fish and eels, hung on drying racks, with barrels of salt waiting in the corner; a cell filled with kegs of beer, casks of wine and water; storerooms lined with shelves of wizened fruit and vegetables, with jars of preserves, mouldy loaves of bread, brittle biscuits that turn to flour particles the moment Helissente breathes near them. It is not more than two hours since they last ate, but the threat of hunger, of going without, and the relief of finding at least some salvageable provisions make them ravenous. Maude stops the girl's hand and says, 'No'.

Reluctantly, Helissente nods. They must go on, Maude says, to the dark heart of this mystery. All other things must wait.

At the far end of the kitchen is another door, iron-bound and immoveable, its locks resistant. But above, cut into the lintel is a slight gap, a slit, through which a thin, flexible, acrobatic girl might well fit. Maude and Helissente's eyes meet; the captain's questioning, the girl's resigned. Maude makes a stirrup of her hands and the girl's weight barely causes them to bow as she is hoisted aloft.

Helissente grabs hold with her fingers, swings one leg up to the sill, then begins the tortuous process of wiggling herself through. Maude watches as the last of the girl's slender figure disappears, and she hears the light scuff of Helissente's bare feet on the other side, the *thunk* and *snap* of the lock as the bolt is shot, then a slap and a sigh as of all the air leaving a small body.

Maude pushes at the door; it resists, a little, but Helissente is light and it doesn't take much for the captain to dislodge her. She kneels and examines the child. There is no sign of violence, the eyes are blue and staring, the mouth ajar. Maude can barely swallow for guilt. The girl claimed herself an orphan, but the Little Sisters will expect word of their erstwhile charge.

Around her there is the sound of flames igniting. A legion of flambeaux burst to life, lighting the entirety of the high-ceilinged round chamber, which smells of fish and flesh. Maude is crouched on a pavement perhaps three feet broad that runs around the edge of the room; beyond its rim is a wide dark pool, and in its centre a raised island of flat stone. There is a four-poster bed, huge, hung with thick red velvet curtains; a coverlet stitched with silver serpents disguised as trees is thrown back and rumpled, and there are sheets, once bright white, now stained with the olive and ochre of mould. Maude can see, in the space under the bed, leather-bound chests, and piles of unrestrained gold and gems spill forth. The occupant of the mattress sits up from where she's been reclining on a wealth of pillows; the movement causes an avalanche of treasure, piles of coin tipping, falling, making a trail to the edge of the islet and plopping into the pool, where they sink slowly like dead golden fish.

'Are you the last?' the girl – woman, really – asks, barely above a whisper, but the acoustics of the chamber magnify her words. The voice is light and sweet; the face is small, the eyes large and blinking, the hair an untidy caramel-coloured chignon.

Maude, still staring at the fat green scaled tail that protrudes from the ragged hem of the woman's blemished pink silk evening gown, must pull her gaze away. 'What?'

'Is it you? Are you the last?' The tone becomes impatient, petulant. 'The last pirate? I've worked so hard, seeking out your kind, scouring the oceans.'

When Maude does not reply, the thick tail rises up, then smashes down, sending a spray of water over Maude, and the woman on the bed yells, 'Are you the last?

'Yes,' says Maude. 'I do believe I am.'

The woman sighs and it seems to shake the very air.

'Finally.' She smiles and her teeth are small and precise and sharp; she folds her hands on her lap and even from a distance Maude can see that their nails are black and encrusted with filth. Maude takes careful paces – not along the stepping stones that lead out to the bed-isle, but around the room, circumnavigating her interrogator.

'Why? Why do all this?' asks the Captain before she asks for a name, even as she wonders how long she has left. Maude is wary that any conversational misstep might be her last. 'Why the pirates?'

'Because,' says the woman-with-tail quite reasonably, 'he said when it was done, he would come back for me.'

'He?'

'Stop! Stay where I can see you – it's only polite,' the girl-serpent says sharply and Maude stops in her tracks, does not move beyond the creature's gaze, does not take the extra steps forward that would allow her to see fully what is forbidden. 'My husband, my lovely man. He said once the last of you was gone, he would return. He would find a way to change me back – but shouldn't we first take advantage of what I could do? See the bright side? That's what he said, and I'm happy to have been a helpmeet for him.'

From her position, Maude can just see the edge of a pile of long yellow-white bones strewn behind the bed, as if out of sight, out of mind. And there, she can just make out a glimpse of flesh, an arm, a leg, the heel and sole of a boot, engraved with a familiar cobbler's mark. She raises her eyes, seeking in the shadows of the ceiling the chute down which the twins took their fatal journey.

'He left you here alone?' Maude strides in the other direction, stopping before she incites anger. When she reaches the limit, she turns and goes back the opposite way; the woman's gaze follows her to and fro.

'Oh, no, there were servants,' the girl says, looking away. 'They took care of me.'

'I saw no servants on my way in. Have they abandoned you?'

'It all started with the first one, you see,' the woman begins and Maude senses that for all her monstrosity, this girl has no guile, that when asked a question she will answer quite honestly no matter how hideous or condemning the truth may be. 'He washed up, you see, and I wanted to talk to him, see how I was going – see how many of you were left. And he wasn't polite, but I didn't mean to, but he – he broke so easily. And I found myself so hungry, you see…'

Maude nods, although she doesn't quite know where this is going, and the speaker continues.

'Any road, they kept washing up and the servants kept bringing them and for a while there was such a feast! Then…'

'Then you found you had done your work too well.'

The woman-serpent nods. 'There were fewer and fewer and then there were none and I got so hungry and I couldn't stand the fish anymore, or the vegetables and fruit. And then the servants were gone – Adelmo was so insolent and deserved it, but I regretted Helen – and I was alone and I had no choice but to eat fish.' She gestures with dainty filthy hands to the pool and Maude can see that there are indeed shoals swimming cautiously by. 'I'm much more careful now. I can make them come, you see, the fish, even when they don't want to – anything that swims seems to do my bidding. But I can't talk to them and I've been so lonely, but now there's you – you'll do for a while. And Adlai. Adlai will come soon – he will realise that his ships are safe now that all the pirates are gone.'

Maude thinks of Helissente's body lying just inside the door, of Sancha on the seabed, and takes a deep shuddering breath that she cannot hide and the woman misunderstands.

'Oh, don't fear! You're quite safe. What I really want is company until Adlai comes.' She smiles again, quite winningly. 'But it's been so long. So long since I've seen him. I wonder when he will come.'

Maude thinks hard. There had been talk of an Adlai Alveson out of Bellsholm, a merchant, certainly. Maude remembered no whispers of a wife of this sort, but she recalled something else, and weighed up whether or not to impart the information.

'I'm Maude,' she says. 'What's your name?'

'Edine! Edine Alveson – Edine Braud, that was. Oh, it's so lovely to chat!'

'And when you married…?'

'I was not like this,' Edine says and begins to weep. Maude wonders how many tears she has shed over the years, whether it has made the seas rise, their salt content increase. 'Oh, I was not like this.'

And for a while there is only sobbing until, 'Have you ever loved, Maude?'

'Yes,' Maude answers. 'My beloved was on the ship you sank out in the lagoon.'

'Oh.' A little girl hiccupping sigh. 'Do you hate me?'

'No more than I pity you.'

'When Adlai comes he will make it better.'

'Adlai cannot raise the dead.'

The girl-woman ignores her and witters on, 'He will take us both home and all will be well.'

'Edine, I tell you this not because I wish to hurt you –' which Maude knows is a lie '– but to help you. Adlai Alveson is dead.'

'Dead? No, he can't be.'

'Dead and buried in Bellsholm.'

'What happened?' Edine wails, rocking back and forth, her tail raising waves.

'He was killed – murdered by a man who'd had a fish stall at the docks. Adlai had – pushed him out of business, so the story went.'

The sound that came from the girl was ear-splitting. 'Who was he? Tell me his name!'

Maude, knowing how this thing has reached out by magic means and destroyed her entire kind, is not about to give the man's name, so she lies as best she can. 'It doesn't matter, Edine, he was killed – killed by Adlai's bodyguards. You can't touch him, Edine, vengeance is already done.' But she remembers Sancha saying that the man, Léolin, had escaped, that the other folk of the Bellsholm docks had hidden him, and smuggled him away. They'd always collected gossip, careful to keep track of the lives of merchants whose ships they plundered.

The woman howls and howls until at last she subsides, whimpering, 'Well that explains why he never came back for me.'

Maude secretly thinks it an unlikely reason – that Adlai would never have returned to the wife he'd put aside and set to cleanse the ocean of the pirate scourge. Two birds with one stone. He'd taken another wife, she seemed to recall, not long before his murder – a tall blonde with a sizeable fortune – he would have gained nothing in reclaiming his serpent-spouse, with her tail, her strange appetites, and her childish mind quite turned by loneliness. Maude does not mention this second wife.

'What will I do?' sobs the woman. 'Whatever will I do?'

'You said you weren't always thus – seek a cure? You've fortune enough to pay.'

There is another roar. 'And be seen like *this*? By all those little people who would snigger behind my back? Take my money with one hand, and plan to stab me with the other?'

'Find the one who did this to you?'

'No one knew. No one ever knew. And with Adlai gone, there is no hope.'

There is silence.

'What will you do?'

'What can I do? I will die.' And Maude realises that this stripe of woman would rather expire than be seen as different. Would rather die than go to the effort of seeking a solution – all so she might not be seen *thus*. Maude knows that Edine's request is one she should have no trouble fulfilling, but pity will make it terribly, terribly hard.

'Will you do it?' asks Edine. 'Will you be so kind? I can hardly kill myself. I cannot drown. I cannot eat myself.'

They are both struck by the unlikely, grotesque image of Edine nibbling on her own tail, devouring herself bite by bite, and ridiculously, they burst into giggles. For the tiniest moment, they are friends, comrades, sisters. 'Will you?'

Maude nods; for a second she wonders if Edine is simply trying to get her near enough to catch, but the woman has no need to be close – Maude suspects the tail's coils are myriad beneath the soiled skirts and petticoats, and had she wished, Edine could have reached out and killed her at any time, the way she did Helissente. Maude takes the stepping stones to the island bed. Edine lays back on her pillows once more, her tiny hands primping at the damp disarrayed curls around her face, straightening the enamel lovers' knot at her breast. She smiles at Maude, and closes her eyes.

The cutlass is swift and sharp as it slides between Edine's ribs; she gives but a little cry. When she withdraws the blade, Maude wipes it with the worn kerchief then, she knows not why, places the now-thin fabric over Edine's poor face. The cloth flutters and for a terrible moment Maude thinks she struck awry, but then the material disintegrates, becomes nothing but a breath of dust motes that dance gold and silver up, up, up to the shadows of the ceiling. And when Maude looks down at Edine once again, she finds no tail, but two pretty feet peeking out from under the argent-pink lace trim of the dress.

* * *

Maude fills voluminous two sacks, one with food – salt fish, preserves, wheels of cheese – the other with coins and gems from Edine's hoard. She is not greedy; she takes nothing large or heavy, and only the finest of the small things, with the highest value. Things that will last her lifetime, should she manage to make it back to the lifeboat, then across the sea. She finds a roll of canvas, an old sail, that can be a shade against the sun, and uses it to swaddle up as many of the small water casks as she can.

She makes her way safely to the beach, cutlass drawn, a sack on each shoulder and the full sling dragging behind. There is no sign of whatever took Ambrose, but she sees dark brown stains on the path and she steps quickly over them.

Maude breaks from the undergrowth and stumbles into the soft dry sand at the edge of the beach. It seems days since she left, but it has been mere hours; hours since she said goodbye to Sancha, hours since she lost her love and her closest friends, hours since she'd walked more of those friends into a trap and watched them die. She will carry them with her until the day she herself shuffles off. She knows this and willingly accepts the burden, but for now she will not examine it. She cannot be distracted, for the only thing that counts at this moment is *living*, for Maude is a survivor. Sancha is a hole in her heart, yes, but she will not lie down and expire. She will not give up. Maude is not that kind of woman. She is the last of her breed, the last – although admittedly forcibly retired – of the buccaneers.

She takes a deep breath and turns towards where the lifeboat was left. To her relief it is there still, dark against the silvery sand. And beside it, a shape, sitting with knees drawn up under a sharp chin, dark eyes fixed on the black line of the horizon, the last of the moonlight cascading down midnight curls. And beside her, perched on the bow, a black feline silhouette, delicately licking a paw and washing it over a pointed ear.

Maude's throat fills so she cannot speak, cannot call out. She puts her head down and feels the heat of grateful tears against her cheeks as she trudges along the beach, across the obstructive sand, towards Sancha the sole survivor of *Astra's Light* who shall sing the tale, and Hieronymus the cat, who has more lives than one.

ST DYMPHNA'S SCHOOL FOR POISON GIRLS

'They say Lady Isabella Carew, née Abingdon, was married for twenty-two years before she took her revenge,' breathes Serafine. Ever since we were collected, she, Adia and Veronica have been trading stories of those who went before us – the closer we get to our destination, the faster they come.

Veronica takes up the thread. 'It's true! She murdered her own son – her only child! – on the eve of his twenty-first birthday, to wipe out the line and avenge a two-hundred-year-old slight by the Carews to the Abingdons.'

Adia continues, 'She went to the gallows, head held high, spirit unbowed, for she had done her duty by her family, and her name.'

On this long carriage journey I have heard many such recountings, of matrimony and murder, and filed them away for recording later on when I am alone, for they will greatly enrich the *Books of Lives* at the Citadel. The Countess of Malden who poisoned all forty-seven of her in-laws at a single banquet. The Dowager of Rosebery, who burned the ancestral home of her enemies to the ground, before jumping from the sea cliffs rather than submit to trial by her *lessers*. The Marquise of Angel Down, who lured her father-in-law to one of the castle dungeons and locked him in, leaving him to starve to death – when he was finally found, he'd chewed on his own arm, the teeth marks dreadful to behold. Such have been the bedtime tales of my companions' lives; their heroines affix heads to the ground with spikes, serve tainted broth to children, move quietly among their marriage-kin, waiting for the right moment to strike. I have no such anecdotes to tell.

The carriage slows as we pass through Alder's Well, which is small and neat, perhaps thirty houses of varied size, pomp, and prosperity. None is a hovel. It seems life for even the lowest on the social rung here is not *mean* – that St Dymphna's, a fine finishing school for young ladies as far as the world-at-large is concerned, has brought prosperity. There is a pretty wooden church with gravestones dotting its yard, two or three respectable mausoleums, and all surrounded by a moss-encrusted stone wall. Smoke from the smithy's forge floats against the late afternoon sky. There is a market square and I can divine shingles outside shops: a butcher, a baker, a seamstress, an apothecary. Next we rumble past an ostlery, which seems to bustle, then a tiny school house bereft of children at this hour. So much to take in but I know I miss most of the details for I am tired. The coachman whips up the horses now we are through the hamlet.

I'm about to lean back against the uncomfortable leather seat when I catch sight of *it* – the well for which the place is named. I should think more on it, for it's the thing, the thing connected to my true purpose, but I am distracted by the tree beside it: I think I see a man. He stands, cruciform, against the alder trunk, arms stretched along branches, held in place with vines, which may be mistletoe. Green barbs and braces and ropes, not just holding him upright, but breaching his flesh, moving through his skin, making merry with his limbs, melding with muscles and veins. His head is cocked to one side, eyes closed, then open, then closed again. I blink and all is gone, there is just the tree alone, strangled by devil's fuge.

My comrades have taken no notice of our surrounds, but continue to chatter amongst themselves. Adia and Serafine worry at the pintucks of their grey blouses, rearrange the folds of their long charcoal skirts, check that their buttoned black boots are polished to a high shine. Sweet-faced Veronica turns to me and reties the thin forest green ribbon encircling my collar, trying to make it sit flat, trying to make it neat and perfect. But, with our acquaintance so short, she cannot yet know that I defy tidiness: a freshly pressed shirt, skirt or dress coming near me will develop wrinkles in the blink of an eye; a clean apron will attract smudges and stains as soon as it is tied about my waist; a shoe, having barely touched my foot, will scuff itself and a beribboned sandal will snap its straps as soon as look at me. My hair is a mass of – well, not even curls, but waves, awkward, thick, choppy, rebellious waves of deepest fox-red that will consent to brushing once a week and no more, lest it turn into a halo of frizz. I suspect it never really recovered from being shaved off for the weaving of Mother's shroud; I seem to recall before then it was quite tame, quite straight. And, despite my best efforts, beneath my nails can still be seen the half-moons of indigo ink I mixed for the marginalia Mater Friðuswith needed done before I left. It will fade, but slowly.

The carriage gives a bump and a thump as it pulls off the packed earth of the main road and takes to a trail barely discernible through over-long grass. It *almost* interrupts Adia in her telling of the new bride who, so anxious to be done with her duty, plunged one of her pearl-tipped, steel-reinforced veil-pins into her new husband's heart before 'Volo' had barely left his lips. The wheels might protest at water-filled ruts, large stones and the like in their path, but the driver knows this thoroughfare well despite its camouflage; he directs the nimble horses to swerve so they avoid any obstacles. On both sides, the trees rushing past are many and dense. It seems a painfully long time before the house shows itself as we take the curved drive at increased speed, as if the coachman is determined to tip us all out as soon as possible and get himself back home to Alder's Well.

St Dymphna's School (for Poison Girls) is a rather small-looking mansion of grey-yellow granite, largely covered with thick green ivy. The windows with their leadlight panes are free of foliage. The front door is solid, a scarred dark oak – by its design I'd judge it older than the abode, scavenged from somewhere else – banded with weathered copper that reaches across the wood in curlicues.

Our conveyance slews to halt and the aforementioned front door of the house is opened in short order. Three women step forth. One wears a long black dress, a starched and snowy apron pinned to the front; her hair is ash-coloured and pulled back into a thick bun. The other two move in a stately fashion, ladies these, sedate, precise in their dress, fastidious in their person.

Serafine, too impatient to wait for the coachman, throws back the carriage door; she, Adia and Veronica exit eagerly. I pause a moment to collect my battered satchel, hang it across my chest; it puckers my shirt, adds more creases as if they were needed. I pause on the metal footplate to take everything in. There is a manicured lawn, with a contradictory wild garden ranging across it, then a larger park beyond and the forest beyond that. A little thatched cottage, almost completely obscured by shrubs and vines, hides in one corner, a stable not far from it, and the beds are filled with flowers and herbs. A body of water shimmers to the left – more than a pond, but barely a lake – with ducks and geese and elegant swans seemingly painted on its surface.

'Welcome, welcome, Serafine, Adia, Veronica and Mercia,' says one of the Misses, either Fidelma or Orla. I climb down and take my place in line with St Dymphna's newest crop, examining my teachers while I wait for their warm gazes to reach me. Both are dressed in finery not usually associated with school mistresses – the one in a dress of cloth of gold, the other in a frock of silver and emerald brocade – both wearing heavy gold-set baroque pearl earrings, and with great long loops of rough-cut gems twisted several times about their necks. Then again, were they ordinary school mistresses and this nothing but a finishing school, our families would not have gone to such lengths to enrol us here for a year's special instruction.

'Welcome, one and all,' says the other sister, her heavy lids sweep great thick lashes down to caress her cheek and then lift like a wing, as a smile blossoms, exposing pearly teeth. In her late forties, I'd say, but well preserved as is her twin: of the same birthing, but not identical, not the *same*. As they move closer, strolling along the line we've formed… ah, yes. She who spoke first is Orla, her left eye blue, the right citrine-bright. Neither short nor tall, both have trim figures, and peach-perfect complexions, but I can see up close that their maquillage is thick, finely porous, a porcelain shell. The cheeks are lightly dusted with pink, the lashes supplemented with kohl and crushed malachite, mouths embellished with a wet-looking red wax. I think if either face were given a swift sharp tap, the masque might fracture and I would see what lies beneath.

How lined is the skin, I wonder, how spotted with age, how thin the drawn-in brows, how furrowed the lips? And the hair, so thick and raven-dark, caught-up in fine braided chignons, shows not a trace of ash, no sign of coarsening or dryness. Their dresses have long sleeves, high necks, so I can examine neither forearms, nor décolletage, nor throats – the first places where Dame Time makes herself at home. The hands, similarly, are covered in fine white cambric gloves, flowers and leaves embroidered on their backs, with tiny seed-pearl buttons to keep them closed.

Orla has stopped before me and is peering intensely, her smile still in evidence, but somehow dimmed. She reaches out and touches a finger to the spot beneath my right eye where the birthmark is shaped like a tiny delicate port-wine teardrop. She traces the outline, then her smile blooms again. She steps away and allows Fidelma – left eye yellow, right eye blue – to take her place, to examine me while the other students look on, perplexed and put out. Serafine's lovely face twists with something she cannot control, a jealousy that anyone other than she might be noticed. Orla's next words offer a backhanded compliment.

'*This*,' she says severely, indicating the tear, 'this makes your chosen profession a difficult one – it causes you to stand out even more than beauty does. Any beautiful woman might be mistaken for another, and be easily forgotten, but this marking renders you unique. Memorable. Not all of our alumni are intent upon meeting a glorious and swift demise; some wish to live on after their duty is done – so the ability to slip beneath notice is a valuable one.'

I feel as if I have already failed. Adia laughs heartily until quelled by a glance from Fidelma, who says to me, 'Never fear, we are mistresses of powders and paints; we can show you how to cover this and no one will even suspect it's there!'

'Indeed. You were all chosen for virtues other than your lovely faces,' says Orla, as if our presence here isn't simply the result of the payment of a hefty fee.

At last, Fidelma too steps back and bestows her smile on the gathering. 'We will be your family for the time being. Mistress Alys, who keeps a good house for us, will show you to your rooms, then we'll sit to an early supper. And Gwern,' she gestures behind her without looking, 'will bring your luggage along presently.'

A man leaves the thatched cottage and shambles towards us. Tall but crooked, his right shoulder is higher than his left and his gait is that of someone in constant pain. He is attired in the garb of gardeners and dogsbodies: tan waistcoat, breeches and leggings, a yellow shirt that may have been white, an exhausted-looking flat tweed cap, and thick-soled brown leather boots. A sheathed hunting knife hangs at his waist. His hair is black and shaggy, his eyes blacker still.

In the time it has taken us to arrive and be welcomed, the sun has slid behind the trees, and its only trace is a dying fire against the greying sky. We follow the direction of Orla's graceful hands and tramp inside, careful to wipe our shoes on the rough stone step. The last in line, I glance back to the garden and find the gaze of the crooked man firmly on me; he is neither young nor old, nor is his a dullard's stare, but rather calculating, considering, weighing me and judging my worth. I shiver and hope he cannot see inside me.

We troop after the housekeeper along a corridor and she points out where our classrooms are, our training areas. The doors that are locked, she says, are locked for a reason. Then up a wide staircase, to a broad landing which splits into two thin staircases. We take the one to the right – to the left, we are told, leads to the Misses' part of the house, and the rooms where visiting tutors will rest their heads. We traipse along more hallways than seem possible in what is such a compact abode, past statues and paintings, vases on pedestals, flowers in said vases, shiny swords, battleaxes and shields all mounted on the wood-panelled walls as if they might be ready to be pulled down and used at a moment's notice. Yet another staircase, even narrower than the first, rickety and not a little drunk, leading to a room that should be the dusty attic, but is not. It is a large chamber, not unlike the dormitory I am used to, but much smaller, with only four beds, each with a nightstand to the left, a washstand to the right, and a clothes chest at the foot. One wall of the room is entirely made up of leadlight glass, swirling in a complex pattern of trees and limbs, wolves and wights, faeries and frights. The last of the sun-fire lights it up and we are bathed in molten colour.

'You young ladies must be exhausted,' fairly sings Mistress Alys in her rich contralto. 'Choose your beds, and do not fight. Wash up and tidy yourselves, then come down for supper.' She quietly closes the door behind her.

While my cohorts bicker over which bed covered with which patchwork quilt they shall have, I stand at the transparent wall, looking, taking in the curved backs of men hefting luggage from the top of the carriage, over the gardens, the lake and into the woods – to the place where my inner compass tells me the alder well lies.

* * *

The igneous colours of the afternoon have cooled and frozen in the moonlight and seem as blown glass across our coverlets. I wait until the others are breathing slowly, evenly; then I wait a little longer so that their sleep is deeper still. Exhausted though I am I will have no peace until I make my pilgrimage. Sitting up, my feet touch the rug, the thick pile soft as a kitten's fur, and I gather my boots but do not put them on.

One last look at the sleepers around me to make sure there are no tell-tale flickers of lashes, breaths too shallow or even stopped altogether because of being held in anticipation. Nothing, although I think I detect the traces of tears still on Serafine's face, silvery little salt crystals from where she cried prettily after being reprimanded by the Misses. At supper, I'd exclaimed with delight at one of the dishes laid before us: 'Hen-of-the-Woods!' and Serafine had snorted contemptuously.

'Really, Mercia, if you plan to pass among your betters you

must learn not to speak like a peasant. It's known as Mushrooms of Autumn,' she said, as if the meal had a pedigree and status. I looked down at my plate, hoping for the moment to simply pass quietly, but both the Meyrick sisters leapt in and explained precisely why Serafine was wrong to make fun of anyone. It was kind but almost made things worse, for it ensured the humiliation endured, stretched agonisingly, was magnified and shared. And it guaranteed that Serafine, at first merely a bully, would become an adversary for me and that might make my true task more difficult.

I tiptoe down the stairs, and slip out the kitchen door which I managed to leave unlocked after doing the evening's dishes. Fidelma said we must all take turns assisting Mistress Alys with cleaning and cooking – this is no hardship for me, not the unaccustomed activity it is to my companions, whose privileged lives have insulated them from the rigours of housework. Orla instructed it will help us learn to fit in at every level of a household, and doing a servant's tasks is an excellent way to slip beneath notice – which is a skill we may well be grateful for one day.

Out in the spring air I perch on the steps to pull on my boots, and sniff at the heady aroma of the herbs in the walled kitchen garden; I stand, get my bearings and set off. Do I look like a ghost in my white nightgown, flitting across the landscape? With luck no one else will be abroad at this hour. The moon is crescent, spilling just enough illumination for me to see my way clear along the drive, then to follow the line of the road and, stopping short of the town, to find the well – and the tree, its catkins hanging limp and sad.

There is a small peaked roof of age-silvered timber above a low wall of pale stone and crumbling dark mortar and, on the rim of the well, sits a silver mug attached to the spindle with a sturdy, equally silver chain. Just as they – the Postulants, Novices, Sisters and Blessed Wanderers – said it would be. I drop the cup over the edge, hear it splash, then pull its tether hand over hand until I have a part-filled goblet of liquid argent between my trembling palms.

The vessel feels terribly cold, colder than it should, and my digits tingle as I raise it. I swallow quickly, greedily, then gasp at the taste, the sear in my gullet, the numbness of my mouth as if I'd chewed monkshood leaves. The ice travels down, down, leaching into my limbs, taking my extremities for its own, locking my joints, creeping into my brain like icicles. My fingers are the claws of a raven frozen on a branch; my throat closes over like an icebound stream; my eyes are fogged as glass on a winter's morn.

For a time I am frost-bitten, a creature of rime and hoar. Still and unbreathing.

They did not say it would be like this.

They did not say it would hurt. That it would make me panic. That I would burn with cold. That I would stay here, dead forever.

They did not say it would be like *this*.

Then time melts, that which felt like an aeon was but seconds. My body begins to thaw, to warm and I feel new again, freshly born, released from all my ills.

This is what they said it would be like; that, in drinking from the alder well, I would feel renewed and refreshed, that I would view the world with clear vision and an open, receptive mind. And, having drunk of the wellspring, I would be ready, ready to join them – that those who had already partaken here, the Blessed Wanderers, would recognise the *flow* in me.

My exhaustion is gone, washed away. I stretch upwards, bathe in the moonlight, invincible, invulnerable, eternal – until I hear the crack of a fallen twig and I fold swiftly into a crouch. Trying to make myself small I peer into the gloom, my heart beats painfully, the silver in my blood now all a'bubble, seeming to fizz and pop. Through the trees I see a shape moving calmly, unconcernedly, tall but with one shoulder risen higher than its brother, the hair a shaggy halo around a shadowed face.

Gwern.

I hold my breath. I do not think he has seen me; I do not think myself discovered. He shifts away slowly, continuing on whatever night-time errand is his and his alone. When he is out of sight, I run, as swiftly, as silently as I can, back towards St Dymphna's. My feet seem to fly.

* * *

'While the folding fan may seem the least offensive thing in the world, it has been used in at least thirteen high-profile political and forty-five marital assassinations in the past three hundred years.' To underline her point, Orla produces a black ebony-wood fan and opens it with a sharp flick of the wrist. The item makes quite a sound as it concertinas out and she beckons us to look closer. The leaves are made of an intricately tatted lace of black and gold, the sticks are wooden, but the ribs, oh, the ribs look slightly different – they are metal, perhaps iron, and with subtly sharpened points. Orla draws our attention to the guardsticks: with a long fingernail she flicks the ends and from each pops a concealed blade. One delicate wave and a throat might be cut, one thrust and a heart pierced. I cannot help but admire the craftsmanship as we sit on the velvet-covered chaises lined against one wall of the practice room, which is located in the basement of the manor, a well-thought-out and thoroughly equipped space.

In front of us is a chalkboard covered with diagrams of innocuous-looking fans of varying designs and substances (iron, wood, reinforced linen, nacre), with the names of all their component parts for us to memorise. To our right stretches the far wall, with four practise dummies made of wood and hessian and straw, red circles painted over the heart of each one. To the left are weapons racks filled with everything one might need, including a cunningly constructed sword that breaks down to its separate elements, an orb that with the touch of a button sprouts sharp spikes, and two kinds of parasols – one that has a knife in its handle, the other which converts to a tidy crossbow.

Then there are the display cases which contain all the bespoke appurtenances a lady could desire: silver-backed brushes with opiate-infused needles concealed among the bristles; hairpins and gloves and tortoiseshell hair combs equally imbued with toxins; chokers and pendants, paternosters and sashes and tippets, garters and stockings, all beautifully but solidly made and carefully fortified so they might make admirable garrottes; boots with short stiletto blades built into both heel and toe; even porous monocles that might be steeped in sleeping solutions or acid or other corrosive liquid; hollowed-out rings and brooches for the surreptitious transport of illicit substances; decorative cuffs with under-structures of steel and whalebone to strengthen wrists required to give killing blows; fur muffs that conceal lethally weighted saps… an almost endless array of pretty deaths.

Fidelma hands us each our own practice fan – simple lightly scented, lace-carved, sandalwood implements, lovely but not deadly, nothing sharp that might cause an accident, a torn face or a wounded classroom rival – although at the end of our stay here, we will be given the tools of our trade, for St Dymphna's tuition fees are very grand. Orla instructs us in our paces, a series of movements to develop, firstly, our ability to use the flimsy useless things as devices for flirting: hiding mouths, highlighting eyes, misdirecting glances, keeping our complexions comfortably cool in trying circumstances.

When we have mastered that, Fidelma takes over, drilling us in the lightning-fast wrist movements that will open a throat or put out an eye, even take off a finger if done with enough force, speed and the correctly weighted fan. We learn to throw them, after first having engaged the clever little contrivances that keep the leaves open and taut. When we can send the fans spinning like dangerous discuses, then we begin working with the guardstick blades, pegging them at the dummies, some with more success than others.

There is a knock on the door, and Mistress Alys calls the Misses away. Before she goes, Orla makes us form pairs and gives each couple a bowl of sticky, soft, brightly coloured balls the size of small marbles. We are to take turns, one hurling the projectiles and the other deflecting them with her fan. As soon as the door is closed behind our instructresses, Serafine begins to chatter, launching into a discussion of wedding matters, dresses, bonbonniere, bunting, decoration, the requisite number of accompanying flower girls, honour-maids, and layers of cake. She efficiently and easily distracts Adia, who will need to learn to concentrate harder if she wishes to graduate from St Dymphna's in time for her own wedding.

'It seems a shame to go to all the trouble of marrying someone just to kill him,' muses Adia. 'All the expense and the pretty dresses and the gifts! What do you think happens to the gifts?'

'Family honour is family honour!' says Serafine stoutly, then ruins the effect by continuing with, 'If you don't do anything until a year or two after the wedding day, surely you can keep the gifts?'

The pair of them look to Veronica for confirmation, but she merely shrugs then pegs a ball of red at me. I manage to sweep it away with my fine sandalwood construct.

'What has your fiancé done?' asks Adia, her violet eyes wide; a blue blob adheres to her black skirt. 'And how many flower maids will you have?'

'Oh, his great-great-grandfather cheated mine out of a very valuable piece of land,' says Serafine casually. 'Five. What will you avenge?'

'His grandfather refused my grandmother's hand in marriage,' Adia answers. 'Shall you wear white? My dress is oyster and dotted with seed pearls.'

'For shame, to dishonour a family so!' whispers Veronica in scandalised tones. 'My dress is eggshell, with tiers of *gros point* lace. My betrothed's mother married my uncle under false pretences – pretending she was well bred and from a prosperous family, then proceeded to bleed him dry! When she was done, he took his own life and she moved on to a new husband.'

'Why are you marrying in now?'

'Because *now* they are a prosperous family. I am to siphon as much wealth as I can back to my family before the *coup de grace*.' Veronica misses the green dot I throw and it clings to her shirt. 'What shoes will you wear?'

I cannot tell if they are more interested in marriage or murder.

'But surely none of you wish to get caught?' I ask, simply because I cannot help myself. 'To die on your wedding nights? Surely you will plot and plan and strategise your actions rather than throw your lives away like…' I do not say 'Lady Carew', recalling their unstinting admiration for her actions.

'Well, it's not ideal, no,' says Veronica. 'I'd rather bide my time and be cunning – frame a servant or ensure a safe escape for myself – but I will do as I'm bid by my family.'

The other two nod, giving me a look that says I cannot possibly understand *family honour* – from our first meeting it was established that I was *not* from a suitable family. They believe I am an orphan, my presence at the school sponsored by a charitable donation contributed to by all the guilds of my city, that I might become a useful *tool* for business interests in distant Lodellan. I'm not like them, not an assassin-bride as disposable as yesterday's summer frock, but a serious investment. It in no way elevates me in their estimation.

They do not know I've never set foot in Lodellan, that I have two sisters living still, that I was raised in Cwen's Reach in the shadow of the Citadel, yearning to be allowed to be part of its community. That I have lived these past five years as postulant then as novice, that I now stand on the brink of achieving my dearest wish – and that dearest wish has nothing to do with learning the art of murder. That Mater Friðuswith said it was worth the money to send me to St Dymphna's to achieve her aim, but she swore I would never have to use the skills I learned at the steely hands of the Misses Meyrick. Even then, though, anxious as I was to join the secret ranks, the inner circle of the Little Sisters of St Florian, I swore to her that I would do whatever was asked of me.

As I look at these girls who are so certain they are better than me, I feel that my purpose is stronger than theirs. These girls who think death is an honour because they do not understand it – they trip gaily towards it as if it is a party they might lightly attend. I feel that death in my pursuit would surely weigh more, be more valuable than theirs – than the way their families are blithely serving their young lives up for cold revenge over ridiculous snubs that should have been long-forgotten. I shouldn't wonder that the great families of more than one county, more than one nation, will soon die out if this tradition continues.

'You wouldn't understand,' says Veronica, not unkindly, but lamely. I hide a smile and shrug.

'My, how big your hands are, Mercia, and rough! Like a workman's – they make your fan look quite, quite tiny!' Serafine trills just as the door opens again and Fidelma returns. She eyes the number of coloured dots stuck to each of us; Adia loses.

'You do realise you will repeat this activity until you get it right, Adia?' Our teacher asks. Adia's eyes well and she looks at the plain unvarnished planks at her feet. Serafine smirks until Fidelma adds, 'Serafine, you will help your partner to perfect her technique. One day you may find you must rely on one of your sisters, whether born of blood or fire, to save you. You must learn the twin virtues of reliance and reliability.'

Something tells me Fidelma was not far from the classroom door while we practised. 'Mercia and Veronica, you may proceed to the library for an hour's reading. The door is unlocked and the books are laid out. Orla will question you about them over dinner.'

She leaves Veronica and I to pack our satchels. As I push in the exercise book filled with notes about the art of murder by fan, my quills and the tightly closed ink pot, I glance at the window.

There is Gwern, leaning on a shovel beside a half dug-over garden bed. He is not digging at this moment, though, as he stares through the pane directly at me, a grin lifting the corner of his full mouth. I feel heat coursing up my neck and sweeping across my face, rendering my skin as red as my hair. I grab up my carry-all and scurry from the room behind Veronica, while Serafine and Adia remain, fuming and sulking.

* * *

'Nothing fancy,' says Mistress Alys. 'They like it plain and simple. They've often said "Bread's not meant to be frivolous, and no good comes of making things appear better than they are", which is interesting considering their business.' She sighs fondly, shakes her head. 'The Misses got their funny ways, like everyone else.'

I am taking up one end of the scarred oak kitchen table,

elbow-deep in dough, hands (the blue tint almost gone) kneading and bullying a great ball of it, enough to make three loaves as well as dainty dinner rolls for the day's meals. But I prick up my ears. It's just before dawn and, although this is Adia's month of kitchen duties, she is nursing a badly cut hand where Serafine mishandled one of the stiletto-bladed parasols during class.

The housekeeper, stand-offish and most particular at first, is one to talk of funny ways. She has gotten used to me in these past weeks and months, happy and relieved to find I am able and willing to do the dirtiest of chores and unlikely to whinge and whimper – unlike my fellow pupils. I do not complain or carp about the state of my perfectly manicured nails when doing dishes, nor protest that I will develop housewives' knee from kneeling to scrub the floors, nor do I cough overly much when rugs need beating out in the yard. As a result, she rather likes me and has become more and more talkative, sharing the history of the house, the nearby town, and her own life. I know she lost her children, a girl and a boy, years ago when her husband, determined to cut the number of mouths to feed, led them into the deepest part of the forest and left them there as food for wolves and worms. How she, in horror, ran from him, and searched and searched and searched to no avail for her Hansie and Greta. How, heartbroken and unhinged, she finally gave up and wandered aimlessly until she found herself stumbling into Alder's Well, and was taken in by the Misses, who by then had started their school and needed a housekeeper.

I've written down all she has told me in my notebook – *not* the one I use for class, but the one constructed of paper scraps and leaves sewn into quires then bound together, the first one I made for myself as a novice – and all the fragments recorded therein will go into a *Book of Lives* in the Citadel's Archives. Not only her stories, but those of Adia, Serafine and Veronica, and the tiny hints Alys drops about Orla and Fidelma, all the little remnants that might be of use to someone some day; all the tiny recordings that would otherwise be lost. I blank my mind the way Mater Friðuswith taught me, creating a tabula rasa, to catch the tales there in the spider webs of my memory.

'Mind you, I suppose they've got more reason than most.'

'How so?' I ask, making my tone soothing, trustworthy, careful not to startle her into thinking better of saying anything more. She smiles gently down at the chickens she is plucking and dressing, not really looking at me.

'Poor pets,' she croons, 'Dragged from battlefield to battlefield by their father – a general he was, a great murderer of men, their mother dead years before, and these little mites learning nothing but sadness and slaughter. When *he* finally died, they were released, and set up here to help young women such as you, Mercia.'

I cover my disappointment – I know, perhaps, more than she. This history is a little too pat, a tad too kind – rather different to the one I read in the Archives in preparation for coming here. Alys may well know that account, too, and chose to tell me the gentler version – Mater Friðuswith has often said that we make our tales as we must, constructing stories to hold us together.

I know that their mother was the daughter of a rich and powerful lord – not *quite* a king, but almost – a woman happy enough to welcome her father's all-conquering general between her thighs only until the consequences became apparent. She strapped and swaddled herself so the growing bump would not be recognised, sequestered herself away pleading a dose of some plague or other – unpleasant but not lethal – until she had spat forth her offspring and they could be smuggled out and handed to their father in the depths of night, all so their grandfather might not get wind that his beloved daughter had been so stained. This subterfuge might well have worked, too, had it not been for an unfortunate incident at a dinner party to welcome the young woman's paternally approved betrothed, when a low-necked gown was unable to contain her milk-filled breasts, and the lovely and pure Ophelia was discovered to be lactating like a common wet nurse.

Before her forced retirement to a convent where she was to pass her remaining days alternatively praying to whomever might be listening, and cursing the unfortunate turn her life had taken, she revealed the name of the man who'd beaten her betrothed to the tupping post. Her father, his many months of delicate planning, negotiating, strategising and jostling for advantage in the sale of his one and only child, was not best pleased. Unable to unseat the general due to his great popularity with both the army and the people, the lord did his best to have him discreetly killed, on and off the battlefield, sending wave after wave of unsuccessful assassins.

In the end, though, fate took a hand and the lord's wishes were at last fulfilled by an opportune dose of dysentery, which finished off the General and left the by-then teenage twins, Fidelma and Orla, without a protector. They fled, taking what loot they could from the war chests, crossing oceans and continents and washing up where they might. Alas, their refuges were invariably winkled out by their grandfather's spies and myriad attempts made on their lives in the hope of wiping away all trace of the shame left by their mother's misdeeds.

The records are uncertain as to what happened, precisely – and it is to be hoped that the blanks might be filled in one day – but in the end, their grandfather met a gruesome death at the hands of an unknown assassin or assassins. The young women, freed of the spectre of an avenging forebear, settled in Alder's Well, and set up their school, teaching the thing they knew so well, the only lesson life had ever taught them truly: delivering death.

'Every successful army has its assassins, its snipers, its wetdeedsmen – its Quiet Men,' Orla had said in our first class – on the art of garrotting, 'And when an entire army is simply too big and too unwieldy for a particular task one requires the Quiet Men – or in our case, Quiet Women – to ensure those duties are executed.'

'One doesn't seek an axe to remove a splinter from a finger, after all,' said Fidelma as she began demonstrating how one could use whatever might be at hand to choke the life from some poor unfortunate: scarf, silk stockings, stays, shoe or hair ribbons, curtain ties, sashes both military and decorative, rosaries, strings of pearls or very sturdy chains. We were discouraged from using wire of any sort, for it made a great mess, and one might find one's chances of escape hindered if found with scads of ichor down the front of a ball or wedding gown. Adia, Seraphine and Veronica had nodded most seriously at that piece of advice.

Mistress Alys *knew* what her Misses did, as well as did white-haired Mater Friðuswith when she'd sent me here. But perhaps it was easier for the dear housekeeper to think otherwise. She'd adopted them and they her. There was a kind of love between them, the childless woman and the motherless girls.

I did not judge her for we all tell ourselves lies in order to live.

'There he is!' She flies to the kitchen window and taps at the glass so loudly I fear the pane will fall out of its leadlight bedding. Gwern, who is passing by, turns his head and gazes sourly at her. She gestures for him to *come in* and says loudly, 'It's time.'

His shoulders slump but he nods.

'Every month,' she mutters as if displeased with a recalcitrant dog. 'He knows every month it's time but still I have to chase him.'

She pulls a large, tea-brown case with brass fittings from the top of a cupboard and places it at the opposite end of the table to me.

Once she's opened it, I can see sharp, thick-looking needles with wide circular bases; several lengths of flexible tubing made perhaps of animal skin or bladder, with what seem to be weighted washers at each end; strange glass, brass and silver objects with a bell-shaped container at one end and a handle with twin circles at the other, rather like the eye rings of sewing scissors. Alys pulls and pushes, sliding them back and forth – air *whooshes* in and out. She takes the end of one length of tubing and screws it over a hole in the side of the glass chamber, and to the other end she affixes one of the large-gauge needles. She hesitates, looks at me long and hard, pursing her lips, then I see the spark in her eyes as she makes a decision. 'Mercia, you may stay, but don't tell the Misses.'

I nod, but ask, 'Are you sure?'

'I need more help around here than I've got and you're quiet and accommodating. I'll have your aid while I can.'

By the time she returns to the cupboard and brings out two dozen tiny crystal bottles, Gwern has stepped into the kitchen. He sits and rolls up his sleeves, high so that the soft white flesh in the crooks of his elbows is exposed. He watches Alys with the same expression as a resentful hound, wanting to bite but refraining in the knowledge of past experience.

Mistress Alys pulls on a pair of brown kid gloves, loops a leather thong around his upper arm, then pokes at the pale skin until a blue-green relief map stands out. She takes the needle and pushes it gently, motherly, into the erect vein. When it's embedded, she makes sure the bottom of the bell is safely set on the tabletop, and pulls on the pump, up and up and up, slowly as if fighting a battle – sweat beads her forehead. I watch as something dark and slow creeps along the translucent tubing, then spits out into the bottom of the container: green thick blood. Liquid that moves sluggishly of its own accord as the quantity increases. When the vessel is full, Alys begins the process again with the other arm and a new jar which she deftly screws onto the base of the handle.

She pushes the full one at me, nodding towards a second pair of kid gloves in the case. 'Into each of those – use the funnel,' she nods her head at the vials with their little silver screw tops, 'Don't overfill and be careful not to get any on yourself – it's the deadliest thing in the world.' She says this last with something approaching glee and I risk a glance at Gwern. He is barely conscious now, almost reclining, limbs loose, head lolling over the back of the chair, eyes closed.

‘Is he alright?’ I ask, alarmed. I know that when I lay down to sleep this eve, all I shall see is this man, his vulnerability as something precious is stolen from him. Somehow, witnessing this has lodged the thought of him inside me.

She smiles, pats his cheek gently and nods. ‘He’ll be no good to anyone for the rest of the day; we’ll let him sleep it off – there’s a pallet bed folded in the pantry. You can set that up by the stove when you’ve done with those bottles. Shut them tightly, shine them up nice, the Misses have buyers already. Not that there’s ever a month when we have leftovers.’

‘Who – what – is he?’ I ask.

She runs a tender hand through his hair. ‘Something the Misses found and kept. Something from *beneath* or *above* or *in-between*. Something strange and dangerous and he’s ours. His blood’s kept our heads above water more than once – folk don’t always want their daughters trained to kill, but there’s always call for *this*.’

I wonder how they trapped him, how they keep him here. I wonder who he was – is. I wonder what he would do if given his freedom. I wonder what he would visit upon those who’ve taken so much from him.

‘Hurry up, Mercia. Still plenty to do and he’ll be a handful to get on that cot. Move yourself along, girl.’

* * *

When I hear a board creak, I glance at the two hands of glory, and notice that of the seven fingers I lit, only six still burn and my heart ices up.

I have been careful, so careful these past months to quietly pick the lock on the library door, then close it after me, pull the curtains over so no light might be seen in the windows, before I kindle one finger-candle for each inhabitant of the house, then lay out my quills and books, the pounce pot, and open the special volume Mater Friðuswith gave me for this specific duty. Generations of St Florian’s abbesses have asked many, many times for permission to copy *The Compendium of Contaminants* – rumoured to be the work of the first of us – yet time and again the Misses have refused access.

They guard their secrets jealously and this book is alone of all its kind. Their ownership of the only extant copy is an advantage they will not surrender, even though the *Murcianii*, the Blessed Wanderers, seek only to record and keep the information. There are to be found *fragments* of this greatest of poisoners’ bibles, yes;

copies with pages missing, edges burned, ink run or faded – but none *virgo intacto* like this one. None so perfect, so filled with recipes and instructions, magical and medicinal properties and warnings, maps of every manner of plant and where it might be found, how it might best be harvested and then propagated elsewhere, how it might best be used for good or ill, how it might be preserved or destroyed. Without it our Archives are embarrassingly bereft, and with only one single copy in existence, the possibility of its destruction is too great for us to bear.

And this is why I am here; this is my initiation task to earn my place among St Florian's secret sisters, the *Murcianii*, the collectors, the recorders, the travelling scribes who gather all manner of esoteric and eldritch knowledge so it might not pass out of the world. Folktales and legends, magic and spells, bestiaries of creatures once here and now long-gone, histories and snippets of lives that have intersected with our efforts, our recordings… and books like *these,* the dark books, the dangerous books, the books that some would burn but which we save because knowledge, *all* knowledge, is too important to be lost.

If I bring a copy of this book back to Mater Friðuswith then my position will be assured. I will *belong.*

But all that will be moot if I am discovered; if my betrayal of two of the most dangerous women of the day – indeed other days, long ago – is found out.

The door opens and Gwern stands there, clothes crumpled from his long sleep, hair askew, the marks of a folded blanket obvious along his jaw line. He sways, still weak from the bloodletting, but his eyes are bright.

'What are you doing?' The low voice runs through me. Part of me notes that he seems careful to whisper. He takes in the *Compendium*, propped on the bookstand, all the tools of my trade neatly lined up on the desk (as untidy as my person may be, I am a conscientious craftswoman), and the hands of glory by whose merrily flickering light I have been working.

And I cannot answer; fear stops my throat and all I can think of is Fidelma and Orla and their lethal ornaments, the choking length of a rosary about my neck, a meal infused with tincture of Gwern's lifeblood, a down-stuffed pillow over my face as I sleep. He steps into the room, closes the door behind him then paces over to lift me up by the scruff of the neck as if I am a kitten who's peed in his shoes. Not so weak as he seems, then. He shakes me 'til I think my head will roll off, until he realises I cannot explain myself if I cannot breathe. He lets me go, pushing me back until I sit on top of the desk and draw in great gasps of air, and he asks me again in that threatening tone, 'What are you doing?'

And I, in fear of what might happen if two Quiet Women should find out what I've been doing, how I've been taking from them what they've refused – and hoping, perhaps, after what I'd witnessed this morning that he might not have much love for the Misses – I tell him almost everything.

And when I am finished, he does not call out and rouse the Meyrick sisters. He does not bend forward and blow out the gory candles, but rather smiles. He leans so close that I can smell his breath, earthy as freshly mown grass, as he speaks, 'I knew it. I knew when I saw you that night.'

'Knew what?' I demand, momentarily brave.

'That you were different to them; different to the others who have come here year upon tiresome year. When I saw you in the moonlight, I *knew* – none of the others ever venture out past the walls at night, certainly don't wander to the well and drink its contents down so sure and so fast. They don't make brave girls here – they make cowardly little bits who like blades in the dark, poison in the soup, pillows over faces.' He straightens, rolls his uneven shoulders. 'I knew you could help me.'

'Help you do what?' I ask, mesmerised by his black gaze.

Instead of answering, he goes to one of the shelves and rummages, finds a slim yellow volume and hands it to me. *A Brief History of the Alder Well*. He says nothing more, but runs a hand down the side of my face, then leaves, the door closing with a gentle *click* behind him. I feel his fingers on me long after he's gone.

* * *

The alchemy laboratory is situated on the ground floor; it has large windows to let in light and equally large shutters to keep out the selfsame when we work with compounds that prefer the darkness. We each have a workbench, honeycombed with drawers filled with plants, powders, poisons, mortars, pestles, vials, and the like. On mine this morning, I found a rose, red as blood, its stem neatly sheared on an angle, the thorns thoughtfully removed; my heart beats faster to see it, that kindness. Indeed there's been a floral offering every day for the past three weeks, roses, peonies, lily of the valley, snowdrops, bluebells, daffodils, all waiting for me in various spots: windowsills, shelves, under my pillow, on the kitchen bench, in the top drawer of my bedside table, hidden among the clothes in my chest. As if I needed anything to keep their giver in my thoughts; as if my dreams have not been haunted. Nothing huge, nothing spectacular, no grand bouquets, but something sweet and singular and strange; something to catch my eye alone – no one else seems to notice them. Not even Serafine with her cruel hawk's gaze.

We have a new teacher for this sennight, who arrived with many boxes and trunks, cases and carpet bags, and a rectangular item neatly wrapped around with black velvet. When her driver seemed careless with it, she became sharp with him. It must be delicate, perhaps made of glass – mirror? A painting? A portrait?

The poisoner is fascinated by Serafine. In fact, we others may as well not be here. She hovers over the sleek blonde girl's work-table, helping her to measure powders, cut toxic plants, heat solutions, giving her hints that we may or may not hear and take advantage of. My copying of the *Compendium* means my cognizance of poisons and their uses is greater than my companions but I cannot show off; cannot appear to have knowledge I should not possess.

We are not working with killing venin today, merely things to cause discomfort – a powder sprinkled over clothing or a few drops of liquid added to someone's jar of night cream will bring up a rash, afflict the victim with itches and aches that appear to have no logical source. One must be careful, Hepsibah Ballantyne tells us in a rare address to the whole class, not to do things that disrupt a person's ordinary routine – that is what they will remember, the disruptions: the tinker come to a door selling perfumes, the offer of a special new blend of tea from a recent acquaintance. When you wish to injure someone, do something that rubs along with their habits, their everyday lives – merge into the ordinary flow and simply *corrupt* one of their accustomed patterns. No fanfare, no drawing of attention to yourself or your acts. Do nothing that someone might later recall as out of the ordinary – it will bring the authorities to you faster than you please.

Mistress Ballantyne arrives once a year to stay with the Misses and impart her venomous wisdom, although Alys tells me this is not her profession proper. She is a coffin-maker and most successful – she travelled here in her own carriage and four (the driver currently making himself at home in Alys's bed). Years and experience have made her a talented poisoner, although few know it and that's as it should be. I think she is older than she seems, rather like the Misses;

in certain lights her face is as lined as a piece of badly prepared parchment, in others it seems smooth. She has short blonde curls, and brown eyes that watched peachy-pink Serafine too closely from the moment she was introduced.

I take the apple seeds and crush them under the blade of my knife.

'How did you know to do that?' Hepsibah's voice is at my shoulder and I suppress the urge to jump guiltily. The recipe in front of us says to grind the seeds in the mortar and pestle, but the *Compendium* warns against that as weakening the poison – crush the seeds just once with a sharp hit to crack the carapace and release the toxin. I look into her dark eyes and the lie comes quickly to my lips.

'My mother. She learned herbcraft to support us after my father died.' Which is true to some extent: Wulfwyn did learn herblore at St Florian's after Mater Friðuswith offered her refuge, but our father had been well and truly gone for many years before that – or rather, my sisters' father. Mine hung around on moonlit nights, watching from the shadows as I grew. 'She wasn't a poison-woman, but she knew some things, just enough to help get by.'

Her gaze softens. I've touched a nerve; she's another motherless girl, I suspect. We are legion. She nods and moves away, telling me my labours are good and I show promise. Hepsibah gives Adia and Veronica's work a quick once-over and shifts her attention back to Serafine, resting a callused and stained hand in the small of the other's back. I notice Serafine leans into the touch rather than away, and feel an unaccustomed wave of sympathy for her, to know she longs for something she will not be allowed to have.

* * *

Standing outside the library door, one hand balancing a platter of sweetmeats, the other preparing to knock and offer the Misses and their guest an evening treat to go with the decanter of winterplum brandy I delivered earlier along with three fine crystal snifters. A terse voice from inside the room stops me. I slow my breathing to almost nothing, stand utterly still; if I've learned nothing else here it's to be undetectable when required.

'Sweet Jesu, Hepsibah, control yourself!' Orla's voice, strangely harsh and raised in an anger none of us have yet witnessed in the classroom no matter how egregious our trespasses.

'I don't know what you mean,' Mistress Ballantyne answers, her tone airy.

'I *saw* you in the garden this afternoon, busy fingers, busy lips, busy teeth,' hisses Orla.

'Jealous?' laughs Hepsibah.

Fidelma breaks in, 'We have told you that you cannot touch any student in our care.'

'That one was thoroughly touched and not complaining, besides,' retorts Hepsibah and I imagine a wolfish grin crossing her lips.

'Scandals! They follow you! It's your own fault – one then another, ruined girls, angry families and you must leave a city yet again.' Orla pauses, and I hear the sound of a decanter hitting the rim of a glass a little too hard. 'Lord, just find someone who *wants* your attention, who isn't already spoken for, and be content.'

Mistress Ballantyne snorts and I imagine she shrugs, raising her thin shoulders, tossing her neat, compact head with its pixie features and upturned nose. She might fidget, too, with those stained fingers and her small square hands; she asks belligerently, 'Where's the fun in a willing victim?'

Fidelma fairly shouts, '*He* has been seen. Not two counties away.'

And silence falls as if a sudden winter has breathed over the library and frozen its inhabitants. It lasts until Mistress Ballantyne breaks it, all swagger, all arrogance gone, her voice rises to a shriek, 'Has he been *here*? Have you *betrayed* me?'

Fidelma shushes her. 'Of course not, you silly bint, but people talk, rumours have wings. Those who live long and do not change as much as others become the target of gossip. Those who do not hide, who do not take care not to draw attention – they are the ones who stand out, Hepsibah.'

Orla sighs. 'And you know he's been searching for something, something other than *you* – in addition to you. *We* do not live in a large city, Hepsibah, we do not live in a grand house and parade along boulevards in an open-topped landau, begging folk to stare and take note. Few people know who we truly are, fewer still that the wars our father fought ended a hundred years ago.'

Fidelma: 'It's a wonder you survived in the days before you knew he was hunting you. You've never learned the art of hiding yourself – of putting your safety ahead of your baser desires.'

'You've had good service of me. I've shared my secrets with you, helped keep you young, taught your murderous little slatterns who think they're better than me.' There's a pause, perhaps she worries at a thumbnail. 'But if he's been seen, then I'm off.'

'But you've still got classes to teach!' protests Orla.

Hepsibah shrugged. 'Well, consider that I'm thinking of my own safety before my *baser desires*,' she sneers. 'Get Magnus, she's a good poisons woman if you can find her. Last I heard she'd berthed in Breakwater.'

There are quick footsteps and the door is wrenched open. I'm almost bowled over by Mistress Ballantyne, who shouts, 'Out of my way, halfwit,' and charges off towards her room. The Misses stare at me and I hold up the tray of sweetmeats, miraculously not thrown to the floor as Hepsibah passed. Orla gestures for me to come in, then turns to her sister. '*You* see if you can talk sense to her. I'm not teaching poisons.'

'You're the one who mentioned him. If it comes down to it, sister, you will.'

Fidelma sweeps out, taking a handful of sweetmeats with her. Orla slumps in a chair and, when I ask if there's anything else she needs, she waves me away, not bothering to answer. On the small table beside her are three discarded vials, red-brown stains in the bottom.

I will not make my nest in the library tonight. Mistress Ballantyne will take a while to pack her trunks and rouse her coachman from the warmth of Alys's blankets. The household will be in uproar this night and I shall take the chance to have a sleep uninterrupted by late-night forgery at least; there will be no guarantee that I will not dream of Gwern. One night without copying the *Compendium* will not make much difference.

* * *

Orla's grace has deserted her.

All the patience and fine humour she's displayed in the past is gone, replaced by an uncertain and somewhat foul temper, as if she's been tainted by the subject she's forced to teach. The Misses, wedded to their schedule, decided not to try for the woman Magnus, and it is as Fidelma threatened: Orla, having caused the difficulty, must now deal with the consequences.

Open on the desk in front of her is the *Compendium* as if it might solve all of her problems. I wonder if Mistress Alys with her fondness for herbs wouldn't have been a better choice. I keep looking at the book, suppressing shudders each time Orla's hands – filled with a toxic powder, wilted stalk or simple spring water – pass anywhere near it. It is unique, alone in the world and I feel it must be protected. Coiled, I wait to leap forward and save it from whatever careless fate Orla might bestow upon it.

The ingenuity and patience, which is so fully in evidence when teaching us how to kill using unthought-of weapons, has left no trace as Orla makes us mix concoctions, elixirs and philtres to cause subtle death. She forgets ingredients, tells us to stir when we should shake, to grind when we should slice, to chop when we should grate. We are not halfway through the first lesson when our tutor swears loudly and knocks over a potion, which pours into an alabaster mortar and mates with the crushed roots there. The reaction is spectacular, a fizz and a crack and smoke of green then purple fills the alchemy room like a sudden, vitriolic fog.

I throw open the windows, shielding my mouth and nose with the bottom of my skirt, then I find the door and thrust it to – the smoke begins to clear but all I can hear are the rasping coughs of my fellow students and teacher. Squinting against the tears, I find them one by one and herd them out into the corridor, where Mistress Alys and Fidelma, drawn by the noise, are in a flurry. When Orla is the last one out, I dive back into the room and rescue the book – it tore at me not to save it before any mortal, but common sense prevailed and no suspicions are aroused. I hold it tightly to my chest as we are all hustled outside into the fresh air.

'Well done, Mercia,' says Fidelma, bending down to pat her sister's heaving back. Orla vomits on the grass, just a little.

'There's no fire, Miss, just the vapour. It should clear soon – there's a good enough breeze,' I say.

'Indeed.' She stands and surveys the lilac-tinged vapour gently wafting through the door behind us. 'We are nothing if not adaptable. I think we shall leave the rest of our poisons classes until such time as Mother Magnus or a suitable substitute might be found – lest my sister kill us all.'

Orla makes an unladylike gesture and continues coughing. Mistress Alys, having braved the smog, reappears with a syrupy cordial of black horehound, to soothe our throats and lungs. We swig from the bottle.

Some time later, order has been restored: the house has been cleared of the foul-smelling fumes; pleural barks have been reduced to occasional rattles; Orla's dignity has been stitched together for the most part; and I have (with concealed reluctance) handed back the *Compendium* and been given by Fidelma a letter for Mother Magnus and instructed to deliver it to the coachman who resides in Alder's Well, begging him to deliver it to the poisons woman and wait for her reply – and hopefully her agreement to return with him.

I walk slowly there and even more slowly back, enjoying the air, the quiet that is not interrupted by the prattle of girls too silly to know they will be going to their deaths sooner than they should – too silly to know that now is the time they should begin mourning their lost futures. Or planning to run away, to fade from their lives. Gods know we are taught enough means to hide, to provide for ourselves, to change our appearances, to earn a living in different ways, to *disappear*. Sometimes I am tempted to tell Veronica about Cwen's Reach and the Citadel, about the Little Sisters of St Florian and how they offered my family refuge, and how, for a long time, no one found us, not even Cenred's ghost. How she could just as easily come with me and become one of the sisters or live in the city at the Citadel's foot as Delling and Halle do, working as jewel-smiths. But I know better. I know she would not want to lose her soft life even for the advantage of longevity; she will play princess while she may, then give it all up not for a lesser lifestyle, but for death. Because she thinks with death, everything stops.

I could tell her otherwise. I could tell her how my mother was pursued by her brother's shade for long years. How he managed somehow to still touch her, to get inside her, to father me well after he was nothing more than a weaving of spite and moonlight. How I would wake from a dream of him whispering that my mother would never escape him. How, even at her death bed, he hovered. How, until Delling did her great and pious labour, he troubled my sleep and threatened to own me as he had Wulfwyn. I could tell her that dying is not the end – but she will discover it herself soon enough.

I had not thought to go back by the clearing, but find myself there anyway, standing before both well and alder. They look different to that first night, less potent without their cloak of midnight light. Less powerful, more ordinary. But I do not forget the burning of the well's water; nor my first sight of the alder and the man who seemed crucified against it, wormed through with vines and mistletoe.

'Have you read it? The little book?'

I did not hear him until he spoke, standing beside me. For a large, limping man he moves more silently than any mortal should. Then again, he is not mortal, but I am unsure if he is what he would have me believe. Yet I have seen his blood. I give credence to things others would not countenance: that my father was a ghost and haunted my dreams; that the very first of the scribes, Murciana, could make what she'd heard appear on her very skin; that the Misses are older than Mater Friðuswith although they look young enough to be her daughters – granddaughters in some lights. So, why not believe him?

I nod, and ask what I've been too shy to ask before, 'How did you come here?'

He taps the trunk of the alder, not casually, not gently, but as if in hope that it will become something more. It disappoints him, I can see. His hand relaxes the way one's shoulders might in despair.

'Once upon a time I travelled through these. They lead down, you see, into under-earth. Down to the place I belong. I was looking for my daughter – a whisper said she was here, learning the lessons these ones might teach.'

And I think of the little yellow book, written by some long-dead parson who doubled as the town's historian. *The Erl-King who rules beneath has been sighted in Alder's Well for many a year. Inhabitants of the town claim to have seen him roaming the woods on moonlit nights, as if seeking someone. Parents are careful to hide their children, and the Erl-King is often used to frighten naughty offspring into doing what they're bid. My own grand-dam used to threaten us with the words 'Eat your greens or the Erl-King will find you. And if not him then his daughter who wanders the earth looking for children to pay her fare back home.' Legend has it he travels by shadow tree.*

'Did you find her? Where is she?'

He nods. 'She was here then, when I came through. Now, I no longer know. She had – caused me offence long ago, and I'd punished her. But I was tired of my anger and I missed her – and she'd sent me much… tribute. But I did not think that perhaps her anger burned brightly still.'

No one is what they seem at St Dymphna's. 'Can't you leave by this same means?'

He shakes his great head, squeezes his eyes closed. It costs his pride much to tell me this. 'They tricked me, trapped me. Your Misses pinned me to one of my own shadow trees with mistletoe, pierced me through so my blood ran, then they bound me up with golden bough – my own trees don't recognise me anymore because I'm corrupted, won't let me through. My kingdom is closed to me, has been for nigh on fifty years.'

I say nothing. A memory pricks at me; something I've read in the Archives… a tale recorded by a Sister Rikke, of the Plague Maiden, Ella, who appeared from an icy lake, then disappeared with all the village children in tow. I wonder… I wonder…

'They keep me here, bleed me dry for their poison parlour, sell my blood as if it's some commodity. As if they have a *right*.' Rage wells up. 'Murderous whores they are and would keep a king bound!!'

I know what – who – he thinks he is and yet he has provided no proof, merely given me this book he may well have read himself and taken the myths and legends of the Erl-King and his shadow trees to heart. Perhaps he is a madman and that is all.

As if he divines my thoughts, he looks at me sharply.

'I may not be all that I was, but there are still creatures that obey my will,' he says and crouches down, digs his fingers firmly into the earth and begins to hum. Should I take this moment to run? He will know where to find me. He need only bide his time – if I complain to the Misses, he will tell what he knows of me.

So I wait, and in waiting, I am rewarded.

From the forest around us, from behind trees and padding from the undergrowth they come; some russet and sleek, some plump and auburn, some young, some with the silver of age dimming their fur. Their snouts pointed, teeth sharp, ears twitching alert and tails so thick and bushy that my fellow students would kill for a stole made from them. They come, the foxes, creeping towards us like a waiting tribe. The come to him, to Gwern, and rub themselves against his legs, beg for pats from his large callused hands.

'Come,' he says to me, 'they'll not hurt you. Feel how soft their fur is.'

Their scent is strong, but they let me pet them, yipping contentedly as if they are dogs – and they are, his dogs. I think of the vision of the crucified man I saw on my first day here, of the halo of ebony hair, of the eyes briefly open and so black in the face so pale. Gwern draws me close, undoes the thick plait of my hair and runs his hands through it. I do not protest.

I am so close to giving up everything I am when I hear voices. Gwern lets me go and I look towards the noise, see Serafine, Adia and Veronica appear, each one trailing a basket part-filled with blackberries, then turn back to find Gwern is gone. The foxes melt quickly away, but I see from the shifting of Serafine's expression that she saw *something*.

'You should brush your hair, Mercia,' she calls slyly. 'Oh, I see you already have.'

I walk past them, head down, my heart trying to kick its way out of my chest.

'I suppose you should have a husband,' says Serafine in a low voice, 'but don't you think the gardener is beneath even you?'

'I'd thought, Serafine, you'd lost your interest in husbands after Mistress Ballantyne's instructive though brief visit,' I retort and can feel the heat of her glare on the back of my neck until I am well away from them.

* * *

Alys is rolling out pastry for shells and I am adding sugar to the boiling mass of blackberries the others picked, when Fidelma calls from the doorway, 'Mercia. Follow me.'

She leads me to the library, where Orla waits. They take up the chairs they occupied on the night when their nuncheon with Mistress Ballantyne went so very wrong. Orla gestures for me to take the third armchair – all three have been pushed close together to form an intimate triangle. I do so and watch their hands for a moment: Orla's curl in her lap, tighter than a new rose; Fidelma's rest on the armrests, she's trying hard not to press her fingertips hard into the fabric, but I can see the little dents they make on the padding.

'It has come to our attention, Mercia,' begins Fidelma, who stops, purses her lips, begins again. 'It has come to our attention that you have, perhaps, become embroiled in something… unsavoury.'

And that, that word, makes me laugh with surprise – not simply because it's ridiculous but because it's ridiculous from the mouths of these two! The laugh – that's what saves me. The guilty do not laugh in such a way; the guilty defend themselves roundly, piously, spiritedly.

'Would you listen to Serafine?' I ask mildly. 'You know how she dislikes me.'

The sisters exchange a look then Fidelma lets out a breath and seems to deflate. Orla leans forward and her face is so close to mine that I can smell the odour of her thick make-up, and see the tiny cracks where crows' feet try to make their imprint at the corners of her particoloured eyes.

'We know you speak with him, Mercia, we have seen you, but if you swear there is nothing untoward going on we will believe you,' she says and I doubt it. 'But be wary.'

'He has become a friend, it is true,' I admit, knowing that lies kept closest to the truth have the greatest power. 'I have found it useful to discuss plants and herbs with him as extra study for poisons class – I speak to Mistress Alys in this wise too, so I will not be lacking if – when – Mother Magnus arrives.' I drop my voice, as if giving them a secret. 'And it is often easier to speak with Gwern than with the other students. He does not treat me as though I am less than he is.'

'Oh, child. Gwern is… in our custody. He mistreated his daughter and as punishment he is indentured to us,' lies Orla. To tell me this… they cannot know that I know about Gwern's blood. They cannot know what Mistress Alys has let slip.

'He's dangerous, Mercia. His Ella fled and came to us seeking justice,' says Fidelma urgently. Her fingers drum on the taut armchair material. Whatever untruths they tell me, I think that this Ella appealed to them because they looked at her and saw themselves so many years before. A girl lost and wandering, misused by her family and the world. Not that they will admit it to me, but the fact she offered them a lifeline – her father's unique blood – merely sweetened the deal. And, I suspect, this Ella found in the Misses the opportunity for a revenge that had been simmering for many a long year.

'Promise us you will not have any more to do with him than you must?' begs Orla and I smile.

'I understand,' I say and nod, leaning forward and taking a hand from each and pressing it warmly with my own. I look them straight in the eyes and repeat, 'I understand. I will be careful with the brute.'

'Love is a distraction, Mercia; it will divert you from the path of what you truly want. You have a great future – your guilds will be most pleased when you return to them for they will find you a most able assassin. And when your indenture to them is done, as one day it shall be, you will find yourself a sought-after freelancer, lovely girl. We will pass work your way if you wish – and we would be honoured if you would join us on occasion, like Mistress Ballantyne does – did.'

The Misses seem overwhelmed with relief and overly generous as a result; the atmosphere has been leached of its tension and mistrust. They believe me to be ever the compliant, quiet girl.

They cannot know how different I am – not merely from their idea of me, but how different I am to *myself*. The girl who arrived here, who stole through the night to drink from the alder well, who regularly picked the lock on the library and copied the contents of their most precious possession, the girl who wished most dearly for nothing else in the world but to join the secret sisters. To become one of the wandering scribes who collected strange knowledge, who kept it safe, preserved it, made sure it remained in the world, was not lost nor hidden away. That girl… that girl has not roused herself from bed these past evenings to copy the *Compendium*. She has not felt the pull and burn of duty, the sharp desire to do what she was sent here to do. That girl has surrendered herself to dreams of a man she at first thought… strange… a man who now occupies her waking and slumbering thoughts.

I wonder that the fire that once burned within me has cooled and I wonder if I am such a fickle creature that I will throw aside a lifetime of devotion for the touch of a man. I know only that the *Compendium*, that Mater Friðuswith's approval, that a place among the dusty-heeled wandering scribes are no longer pushing me along the path I was certain I wished to take.

* * *

'Here, you do it!' says Mistress Alys, all exasperation; she's not annoyed with me, though. Gwern has been dodging her for the past few days. Small wonder: it's bleeding time again. She pushes the brown case at me and I can hear the glass and metal things inside rattling in protest. 'Don't worry about the little bottles, just bring me back one full bell. I'm going in to Alder's Well and I'll take the Misses Three with me.'

'But…' I say, perplexed as to how I might refuse this task of *harvesting*. She mistakes my hesitation for fright.

'He's taken a liking to you, Mercia, don't you worry. He'll behave well enough once he sees you. He's just like a bloody hound, hiding when he's in trouble.' Alys pushes me towards the door, making encouraging noises and pouring forth helpful homilies.

Gwern's cottage is dark and dim inside. Neither foul nor dirty, but mostly unlit to remind him of home, a comfort and an ache at the same time, I think. It is a large open space, with a double bed in one corner covered by a thick eiderdown, a tiny kitchen in another, a wash stand in another and an old, deep armchair and small table in the last. There is neither carpet nor rug, but moss with a thick, springy pile. Plants grow along the skirting boards, and vines climb the walls. Night-flowering blooms, with no daylight to send their senses back to sleep, stay open all the time, bringing colour and a dimly glimmering illumination to the abode.

Gwern sits, unmoving, in the armchair. His eyes rove over me and the case I carry. He shakes his head.

'I cannot do it anymore.' He runs shaking hands through his hair, then leans his face into them, speaking to the ground. 'Every time, I am weaker. Every time it takes me longer to recover. You must help me, Mercia.'

'What can I do?'

He stands suddenly and pulls his shirt over his head. He turns his back to me and points at the base of his neck, where there is a lump bigger than a vertebrae. I put down the case and step over to him. I run my fingers over the knots, then down his spine, finding more bumps than should be there; my hand trembles to touch him so. I squint in the dim light and examine the line of bone more carefully, fingertips delicately moulding and shaping what lies there, unrelenting and stubbornly… fibrous.

'It's mistletoe,' Gwern says, his voice vibrating. 'It binds me here. I can't remove it myself, can't leave the grounds of the school to seek out a physick, have never trusted any of the little chits who come here to learn the art of slaughter. And dearly though I would love to have killed the Misses, I would still not be free for this thing in me binds me to Alder's Well.' He laughs. 'Until you, little sneak-thief. Take my knife and cut *this* out of me.'

'How can I do that? What if I cripple you?' I know enough to know that cutting into the body, the spine, with no idea of what to do is not a good thing – that there will be no miraculous regeneration, for mortal magic has its limits.

'Do not fear. Once it's gone, what I am will reassert itself. I will heal quickly, little one, in my true shape.' He turns and smiles; kisses me and when he draws away I find he has pressed his hunting knife into my hand.

'I will need more light,' I say, my voice quivering.

He lies, face down, on the bed, not troubling to put a cloth over the coverlet. I pull on the brown kid gloves from the kit and take up the weapon. The blade is hideously sharp and when I slit him, the skin opens willingly. I cut from the base of the skull down almost to the arse, then tenderly tease his hide back as if flensing him. He lies still, breathing heavily, making tiny hiccups of pain. I take up one of the recently lit candles and lean over him again and peer closely at what I've done.

There it is, green and healthy, throbbing, wrapped around the porcelain column of his spine, as if a snake has entwined itself, embroidered itself, in and out and around, tightly weaving through the white bones. Gwern's blood seeps sluggishly; I slide the skean through the most exposed piece of mistletoe I can see, careful not to slice through *him* as well. Dropping the knife, I grasp the free end of the vine, which thrashes about, distressed at being sundered; green sticky fluid coats my gloves as I *pull*. I cannot say if it comes loose easily or otherwise – I have, truly, nothing with which to compare it – but Gwern howls like a wolf torn asunder, although in between his shouts he exhorts me not to stop, to finish what I've started.

And finally it is done. The mistletoe lying in pieces, withering and dying beside us on the bloodstained bed, while I wash Gwern down, then look around for a needle and strand of silk with which to stitch him up. *Never mind*, he says, and I peer closely at this ruined back once more. Already the skin is beginning to knit itself together; in places there is only a fine raised line, tinged with pink to show where he was cut. He will take nothing for the pain, says he will be well soon enough. He says I should prepare to leave, to pack whatever I cannot live without and meet him at the alder well. He says I must hurry for the doorway will stay open only so long.

I will take my notebook, the quills and inkpots Mater Friðuswith gave me, and the pounce pot Delling and Halle gifted when I entered the Citadel. I lean down, kiss him on his cool cheek, which seems somehow less substantial but is still firm beneath my lips and fingers.

The manor is empty of Alys and the girls and the Misses have locked themselves away in the library to mull over Mother Magnus's refusal, to work through a list of suitable names that might be invited – begged – to come and teach us poisons. I shall sneak through the kitchen, tiptoe past the library door, snatch up my few possessions and be well on my way before anyone knows I am gone.

All the things I thought I wanted have fallen away. The *Compendium*, the Citadel, the *Murcianii*, none of that matters anymore. There is only Gwern, and the ache he causes, and whatever mysteries he might offer me. There is only *that*.

All well and good, but as I step out from the kitchen passage into the entry hall, I find Orla and Fidelma standing on the landing of the main staircase. They turn and stare at me as if I am at once a ghost, a demon, an enemy. Time slows as they take in the green ichor on my white apron – more than enough to tell a tale – then speeds up again as they begin to scream. They spin and whirl, pulling weapons from the walls and coming towards to me, faces cracked and feral.

'What have you done?' screeches one – Fidelma, who carries a battleaxe. Orla wields a mace – how interesting to see what is chosen in fear and anger, for slashing and smashing. None of the subtlety we've been taught these past months. Not such Quiet Women now. Angry warriors with their blood up.

I turn tail and hare away, back along the passageway, through the kitchen and breaking out into the kitchen garden. I could turn and face them. I still have Gwern's knife in my pocket, its blade so sharp and shiny, wiped all clean. I could put into practice the fighting skills they've taught me these past months. But how many have they put beneath the ground and fed to the worms? I am but a scribe and a thief. And besides: in all they've done – to this moment – they've been kind, teaching me their art, and I've repaid them with deception, no matter what I think of the way they've treated Gwern. I would rather flee than hurt them for they have been my friends.

I cross the lawn and launch myself into the woods, ducking around trees, hurdling low bushes and fallen branches, twigs slashing my face. At last, I stumble into the clearing and see the well – and the alder, which is now different in its entirety. The ropes and ribs of mistletoe have withered and shrunk, fallen to the ground, and the tree shines bright as angel wings, its trunk split wide like a dark doorway. And before it stands… before it stands…

Gwern, transformed.

Man-shaped as before, but almost twice as tall as he was. A crown of stripped whistle-wood branches, each finial topped with rich black alder-buckthorn berries, encircles his head. His pitch-hued cloak circles like smoke and his ebony-dark hair moves with a life of its own. His features shift as if made from soot vapour and dust and ash – one moment I recognise him, the next he is a stranger. Then he sees me and smiles, reaching forth a hand tipped with sharp, coal-black nails.

I forget my pursuers. I forget everything. And in the moment when I hesitate to take what Gwern is offering me – what the *Erl-King* is offering me – in that moment I lose.

I am knocked down by a blow to the back – not weapon-strike, thankfully, but one of the Misses, tackling me, ensuring I don't have a fast, clean death. That I will be alive while they inflict whatever revenge they choose. I roll over and Fidelma is on me, straddling my waist, hoisting the battleaxe above her head, holding it so the base of the handle will come down on me. I fumble in my pocket, desperate and as she brings her arms down, I jam Gwern's knife upwards, into her stomach. I am horrified by how easily the flesh parts, sickened by the doing of something that until now has been an *academic* concern. There is the terror of blood and guts and fear and mortality.

Fidelma's shock is apparent – has no one ever managed to wound her? She falls off me and rolls into a ball. Orla, slower on her feet, shoots out of the trees and makes her way to her sister. The mace and chain swings from one hand as she helps Fidelma to her feet.

I look upwards at the pair of them, past them to the cloudless blue sky.

Fidelma spits her words through blood, 'Bitch.'

Orla raises the mace with determination.

I am conscious, so conscious of the feel of the grass beneath me, the twigs poking through the torn fabric of my grey blouse and into the bruised flesh of my back. I turn my head towards the alder tree, to the where the split in the trunk has closed; to the empty spot where Gwern no longer stands. I watch as the bole seems to turn in on itself, then pulse out, one two three, then in again and out – and out and out and out until finally it explodes in a hail of bright black light, wood, branches and deadly splinters sure as arrows.

When my ears stop ringing and my vision clears I sit up slowly. The glade is littered with alder and mistletoe shards, all shattered and torn. The well's roof has been destroyed, the stones have been fractured, some turned into gravel, some blocks fallen into the water. The next *Murcianii* pilgrim will have difficulty drinking from this source. I look around, searching for Fidelma and Orla.

Oh, Fidelma and Orla.

My heart stops. They have been my teachers, friends, mentors. I came to them with lies and stole from them; they would have killed me, no question, and perhaps I deserved it. They stole from Gwern long before I came, yes, kept him against his will; yet I would not have had them end like this.

Fidelma and Orla are pinned against the trees opposite the ruined alder, impaled like butterflies or bugs in a collection. Look! Their limbs so tidily arranged, arms and legs stretched out, displayed and splayed; heads lolling, lips slack, tongues peeking between carmined lips, eyes rolling slowly, slowly until they come to a complete stop and begin to whiten as true age creeps upon them.

I look back at the broken alder; there is only a smoking stump left to say that once there was a tree, a shadow tree, a doorway for the Erl-King himself.

He is gone, but he saved me. And in saving me, he has lost me.

I cannot travel through this gate; it is closed to all who might recognise it.

I will go back to the house.

I will go back to St Dymphna's and swiftly pack my satchel before Alys finds her poor dead girls. I will take the *Compendium* from its place in the library – it can be returned to the Citadel now the Meyricks will not pursue it. In the stables I will saddle one of the fine long-necked Arabian mares the Misses keep and be on the road before Alys's wails reach my ears.

Shadow trees. Surely there are more – there must be more, for how else might the Erl-King travel the land? In the Citadel's Archives there will be mention of them, surely. There will be tales and hints, if not maps; there will be a trail I can follow. I shall seek and search and I shall find another.

I will find one and let the shadow tree open itself to me. I will venture down to the kingdom of under-earth. I will find him and I will sleep in his arms at last.

THE BITTERWOOD BIBLE

All stories have a beginning, but beginnings themselves have many sparks, some slow to catch, others forest-fire fast.

Does this tale begin three hundred years ago, give or take, with the small child stolen from her parents? Does it begin the moment she ceases to cry for them, starts to forget them, loses her determination to find them again – for the best, really, so she will never know what they become? Does it begin when she is first ordered to pick up a quill, punished until she forms her letters correctly, beautifully? Does it begin when she starts to regard as *hers* the book in which she records everything for her master?

Or does it begin here, at the base of the cliff? At the breach through which only she can fit? Or in the tunnels that climb upward, honeycombing the substance of the promontory of Cwen's Reach, upon which the Citadel sits?

Murciana's palm is sweaty as she grips the torch, despite the glacial cold creeping through the tunnels. She makes dragon's breath with every exhalation, and her lungs ache from the icy air she takes in. Beneath the soles of her shoes, the ground is a mix of rubble and rime, depending on how much seawater has flowed through. The passages are thin, in some places she must turn her scrawny self sideways to pass by – even if there'd been no other reason for her to undertake this mission, her master would never have fit through half these ways. She has to be careful with the satchel, adjusting it thus and thus so its contents are not bumped and damaged.

Her other hand is equally sweaty, wrapped as it is around the ivory hilt of the misericorde, which she holds ahead of herself. Her master offered the knife, casually at the very last minute – he has never let her near weapons before, certainly not handed her one – along with the advice that she might encounter some kinds of creatures in the tunnels, perchance large rats, smaller wild cats, mayhap even a troll or ogre – they liked dark places, although she shouldn't worry too much as neither of the last three was overly fond of either sea or water. Oh, and she should look out for crevasses, subterranean lakes, uncertain earth and rock falls. With that he heaved her upwards and through the slim aperture, waiting only to pass the torch and dagger to her when her thin-wristed, ink-stained hand reappeared, questing for the light.

So far no crevasses, subterranean lakes, uncertain earth, nor rock falls. No large rats or even little ones, no smaller wild cats, nor troll nor ogre, although there had been times when she'd been certain of a stealthy footstep behind her, and she'd swung about, torch held high, blade jabbing at the dancing shadows. But there was nothing either mundane nor arcane trying to make itself known. She was alone, in the darkness, in the heart of a cliff, climbing upwards to ask questions of a thing of which she cannot quite conceive, although gods knew she'd seen enough miracles great and terrible in her short life.

'It will only speak to you,' her master had said as they'd trekked across marshlands and plains, through forests, up hill and over dale, until they came to that port city of Breakwater and negotiated passage to a small inlet two days' journey from Cwen's Reach. Far enough away, he'd sworn, that they wouldn't be noticed in the city of the Citadel. Another long walk along the ridges and clifftops, then down a rugged path and onto the sand and pebbles, struggling and stumbling until at last they came to the wide mouth of a cave. Inside the Magister cast a spell, throwing magelight across the damp dark space and searching until he found the ramp of scree that led up the hole in the rock wall. 'It will only speak to another woman.'

'That doesn't mean it will speak to me,' she said quite reasonably and was rewarded with a glare. 'I only mean to say, Magister, that just because I'm female doesn't guarantee its cooperation. What if it wants to know why I'm asking these questions? Why I'm copying down these spells? What do I plan to do with them? Surely saying "I shall give them into the hands of my master" will not be viewed well?'

She knew she was courting a beating, but couldn't quite help herself, not even after all this time. She wondered that part of her that refused to submit, to be obedient.

'Just ask it the questions, and write down the answers. It won't hurt you, but gods help you if you return empty-handed.'

It seems she'd been climbing for hours, and in her mind she goes over the questions she must ask. They form a kind of rhythm for her footsteps, even as she worries at them, concerned that the word order will escape her – they must be spoken firmly, confidently, insisted the Magister, not read out. Aloud, she almost sings:

How to transform things for a season?

How to kill without trace?

How to live beyond one's time?

She wonders if she might ask questions of her own? Would the Magister even know if she tried? After she's asked his questions, obviously, those to which she must bring back answers.

Some while ago the sloping path had given way to steps, at first rough-hewn, but as she rose higher their craftsmanship grew, the precision of cut and placement increased, the materials changing from rock, to polished stone, to something that looked like marble and sparkled in the light from her torch. The walls grew smoother, the passages broadened, showing obvious signs of tool marks, of someone caring how this area looked. And soon enough she began to hear a low rumble, the timbre of a voice echoing in an enclosed space.

When she comes at last to a dead end, she reaches out and feels about, taking so long to find the catch that she thinks perhaps the Magister's information had been incorrect. That she will have to go back through the winding underworld of the tunnels and bring him nothing after all his months and years of research and planning. That she will dash all his great hopes of finding what the tinker had told him was rumoured to be held in the deepest, most secret room of the Citadel. As she despairs, her fingers catch at it, the cold carven hook, which she pulls and feels it *click*.

There is a grinding, the painful sound of a mechanism unused for many years, and then the floor beneath her tips so she slips and is thrown forward into the space where the wall had been. She loses both knife and torch in the fall, and the bag lands heavily on her, knocking the wind from her. And she makes a noise, such a noise, with the dropping and the falling and the *whumping*.

Still and all, it doesn't seem to bother the women watching her too much. Well, the woman and her companion, who is also female – looks female – but lacks everything except a head. The woman, the actual one, has half-risen from a squat stone bench that encircles the basin where the other's head floats on a sea of flame. Or is it cloud, all saffron-hued and red-streaked? On closer inspection, it is a kind of pond, not too deep, but filled with roiling, aggressive fire-clouds, yet the head does not bob, is not buffeted, simply levitates, hovering in the same spot, looking at Murciana with curiosity but not disdain, not fear. That gives the girl heart, which surprises her.

'Good evening,' says the woman in a low, rich voice.

'Good evening,' echoes the head, in an equally mellifluous tone.

Scrambling to her feet, readjusting the heavy satchel, Murciana manages to nod several times before she stutters out an appropriate greeting. All eyes turn to the torch which is guttering on the ground and the misericorde, whose thin blade seems blood-covered in the ruby light. Suddenly, Murciana feels unutterably rude – it isn't a sensation with which she is too familiar, having not been trained in etiquette and having devoted large amounts of her time to perfecting a sly disrespect where the Magister is concerned. But before these women who've not batted an eyelid at her sudden arrival she feels callow and impolite.

'Are you all right?' asks the woman, gracefully standing, her long blue robe shifting as if it is a second skin. She has black hair, only the streak of white down the middle and at the temples says she is older than her face suggests; her eyes are very dark and, in certain angles, reflect the ruddy glow of the pond. She gestures with her hands, palms out, unthreatening, agreeable. 'Have you hurt yourself?'

Murciana shakes her head, unknots her tongue sufficiently to manage a strangled, 'No. I'm sorry.'

'You're sorry you're not hurt?' asks the head, perplexed.

Murciana feels that now, having been directly addressed, she can take a good look at the thing, can stare without appearing to do so. The head is large, about a foot high, as if it belonged on a statue of some sort. The skin is smooth and tinged a pale bronze, the eyes are the brightest of blue, the hair a deeper bronze, and her lack of eyebrows makes her look perpetually surprised. The face is lovely, but below her jawline is a long neck that simply ends in a kind of smudge where it meets the fire-cloud. She appears to be in her twenties, although Murciana doesn't doubt that the head had been subjected to some older, darker magic long ago – that once she had been an ordinary mortal.

The woman gives a chuckle. 'You must forgive our Beatrice, she's been a long time away from the ebb and flow of humanity. She has become very… literal.'

The head makes a sound rather like a *harrumph* and Murciana has the feeling that, had she been able, Beatrice would have happily turned her back in a huff.

'Hush, my dear, I'm only teasing,' continues the woman. 'Now, how may we help you, young pilgrim? What is so important that you interrupt our nightly meditations?'

Murciana thinks that terribly kind considering she is there to take by stealth. Memory of her mission makes her blush more than the embarrassment of her fall had. The woman smiles, and the head says, 'Ah, a thief, Mater Adela. Didn't I say we were overdue for one?'

'You did, Beatrice, you did. Although you said it would be a man,' agrees Adela. Murciana's expression must slip, twitch, let the truth show, for the older woman smiles again and nods. 'Ah, a puppet master then. Beatrice, you have the right of it once again.'

The brazen head looks smug.

'And you came by the dark path – has that breach opened once more?' Adela frowns. 'We must have that seen to.'

Mater Adela sits back down and pats the bench beside her. Murciana's eyes slide to the fallen dagger, and the older woman's eyebrows rise. 'Do you feel you need that? I'm quite happy for you to retrieve it if it will make you feel safer, although I'd like a promise that you won't use it.'

'I'm sorry,' says Murciana. 'I'm sorry.'

She resolutely drags her eyes away from the misericorde, and sits on the bench, carefully positioning herself so she can see both Mater Adela and Beatrice, not that she senses a threat from either. Lamely, she says again, 'I'm sorry.'

'We've established that,' says the head.

'Why have you come here, little thief, and do you have a name?' asks Adela.

The girl nods, finds her voice, unconsciously strokes the satchel. 'Murciana. I am Murciana and I have been sent to ask questions of Beatrice.'

'Sent by whom? Your parents?'

'I have no parents, or at least none I choose to remember.' The girl's tone becomes steely, her air of contrite helplessness lessens.

Mater Adela sees she has touched a nerve. 'Were you stolen?'

Murciana nods reluctantly. 'A long time ago. They did not look for me – or rather, they did not find me.'

That is the worst thing, the girl thinks, *that they did not find her*. A woman's face drifts into her mind: pale skin, smelter-gold hair, a high domed forehead, eyebrows fine as golden pin feathers, cheekbones sharp, chin a little weak, but lips full and pouting. A man, handsome with green eyes and red hair, features he's passed on to his daughter. And the girl shakes her head, dislodges the memories and they burst like glass bulbs. She will not think on them for they failed her, left her to the Magister.

Mater Adela asks no more. Enough girls have come to the Citadel seeking refuge from things over which they had no control, things they will not discuss for many years if ever, and Adela learned long ago not to push, but to let time and tide draw things out or leave them hidden in the depths.

'And this man to whom you are in servitude?' Adela is clever in her wording – to say *serve* would imply the child is willing, and Adela senses this is not so. She will direct the girl, gently, with the correct choice of words, as she has navigated the women under her command for the past twenty years as Mater of the Little Sisters of St Florian.

'The Magister, a magician, a mage, a collector of things, people, spells, souls,' mutters Murciana. 'We wander from town to town, wherever he learns there is something he wants.'

'You have no home?'

'There is a hut, a refuge near a town called Bitterwood. It belonged to witches, once, but he drove them out and they have not returned.'

Adela points at, but is careful not to touch, the satchel. 'And this is his?'

Murciana frowns. 'He has made me write in it since I first learned to scribe for him. Had me record every spell he has learned or made or stolen. But the writing is mine, the care of this book is mine.'

'Can you cast those spells?' pipes Beatrice, interest piqued. Murciana shakes her head.

'I'm untouched by magic, I have no ability there. But I am a scribe of great prowess,' she says proudly and opens the flap of the bag. She slides out a large book with a sturdy black cover. Part of her hears a warning voice saying she should not boast, she should not show this greatest of secrets to anyone; but the louder voice says someone should see what she does, should *witness* what she has made. Someone other than the Magister, who considers this merely a convenience, that he does not have to scribble and scribe for himself, that this book – her book – is merely a container.

Mater Adela is gentle and careful when she takes the tome, and she only does so with the girl's permission, with a nod of her head. Adela opens the volume in her lap; the inner pages are a pale ivory that will darken with years, the inks are mostly black, but here and there are blues and greens and reds and yellows to illustrate spells and instructions, to ensure someone reading a recipe will get blue willow-bark and not red. In some places marginalia cavort around the borders, strange animals and faces, making the thing far more than a mere ledger. It is written in the language of witches, some of which Adela understands, and there are others among the Sisters who will understand more still. The penmanship is lovely – even though the earlier pages show a less steady hand, that of a younger girl, fearful and tentative, it is in no way *diminished*. 'This is beautiful, Murciana.'

'He used to beat me until I got it right, until I made my letters perfectly and understood how to space things out, how to draw to scale.' She swallows, thinking of lessons learned hard. 'It took me a long time.'

Beatrice makes a *coo* of sympathy and Adela reaches out a gentle hand to touch the girl's shoulder. She would prefer to hug her, but fears such close contact might send the child fleeing back down the dark passages in the rock, and Adela does not want her to go. The girl belongs *here*. She has come to them wounded, like so many others; she has come to them at the right time, just as the path diverges before her. Adela recognises these moments, these pivotal points; it is one of her great talents. She takes a deep breath.

'Would you stay with us, Murciana? If you could?'

The girl's eyes widen, but there's disbelief, suspicion there – she has never been offered anything for free, has never been offered anything that didn't cost her more than she wished.

Adela recognises this and continues, 'Many women, young and old, come to us, come to join the Little Sisters of St Florian, or come for refuge, for respite, to learn new skills before they go elsewhere. Some come to be nursed, to be healed, or if they are too far gone then at least to die with ease. Some come to learn the art of being a scribe – we keep books here, we keep them safe, we copy them so the chances of their knowledge being lost is small. We send copies to other houses, to private collections, we send them out into the world so they are myriad and hard to track down by anyone who would destroy them.'

Murciana snatches the book off Adela's lap and she stuffs it back in its satchel clumsily.

'We do not want your book, Murciana – for it is yours and not his. He has not sweated over it, wept onto its pages, poured a little of himself into it through his very labours.' Adela watches as the girl's hands still. 'We would like to copy it, yes, but only with your permission. If you do not give that, then we shall not make a copy. The choice is yours.' She leans forward and puts a tender hand on the girl's closest wrist. 'But you have such skills! You could teach in the scriptorium, you could copy any book you liked for your own personal library, you could learn more from Sister Ubertina, our librarian and greatest copyist. We offer you a place, friends and sisters. You would never again be subject to the whims of the Magister and you would be free.'

Murciana wants to shout *Yes!* She wants to hug the woman, to never see the Magister again, to forget whatever life she's lived until now, but her existence has made her cautious whenever something is offered. Nothing has ever been easy, nothing has ever been without a price. She reminds herself that her only companion, her only constant for most of her years has been the old man, the shifting, nasty, selfish, smelly, violent old man. But still, she hesitates.

'You may ask three questions you like if it will help you decide,' says Adela kindly.

Murciana looks at the brazen head and says, 'Even of her?'

'Of course,' Beatrice says and looks attentive, inclining her head without seeming to have the means to do so.

'But we will ask you three questions in return – this will be your test. Beatrice will judge your honesty, Murciana, that is *her* gift.'

The girl nods slowly and directs her questions to Beatrice rather than Adela. 'Are you here of your own free will?'

There is a silence, then, 'Where else would I go in this state? But the answer is yes.'

'Did my parents look for me?' Murciana adds, keeping her voice light.

'Yes, they did.' Beatrice sees but does not tell her how long they looked, or how quickly their hunger overtook them. She does not tell the girl what they became.

'How did you become this way?'

'Mages are fast to anger and their vengeance is terrible.'

'St Florian's first Mater found Beatrice,' adds Adela. 'She has been here two hundred years and has been friend and guide to every leader since.'

'And you know everything?' asks Murciana.

Beatrice laughs. 'Oh, that's a fourth question! But no, I make half of it up.' Then she sobers. 'I see shadows and mists, Murciana. The past is most often clear, but the future… I see hints and fragments and sometimes I can piece things together. Mostly I cannot.'

Adela clears her throat. 'Now we will ask our questions. Are you ready?'

'Yes.'

'What did your Magister want you to ask, Murciana?'

'How to transform things for a season. How to kill without trace. How to live beyond one's time. '

Adela glances at Beatrice, who nods solemnly.

'What would you do amongst us?'

'What I am bid – and if I am allowed, I will travel and find new books to copy, new volumes to bring back to the Citadel, books in need of *us*.'

Both Adela and Beatrice smile at this. Again, the head nods, indicating the girl is truthful.

'And, finally, what would you bring to our order?'

'The book – this book.' Murciana holds up the satchel. 'Let it be copied, although I will have more to add to it.'

And when she smiles it is like a sunburst.

'And so, will you join us?'

Murciana nods and hands the tome back to Adela.

Adela hugs the girl tight. 'Now, if you go to the door over there, you will find Sister Vinica waiting outside. Tell her I have sent you and you are to be given a place in the dormitory. Tell her I shall speak with her soon, but first I shall finish my discussions with Beatrice, which you so fortuitously interrupted – and I shall see you in the morning, Murciana. You are most welcome.'

The girl appears uncertain.

Adela reassures her. 'Trust us, Murciana. Your place is here. You shall be taken care of – and your Magister cannot get inside our gates, nor wander up the narrow byways you took. You are safe.'

The girl smiles and nods. She goes to the door and pushes it open and a very surprised Sister Vinica looks at her, then askance at Adela, who simply inclines her head. Vinica offers a hand and Murciana takes it, seems suddenly very small, very young, very trusting.

Adela and Beatrice sit in silence for long moments, until the head speaks. 'What will you do? About him, I mean?'

'The Sykes girl, the new arrival, she's got enough magic in her skin to deal with him.'

'And then?'

'The new wing needs a certain something in its foundations. I'm happier not to take one of the townsfolk for they are our friends, Beatrice, even though they would gladly offer one of their number. I cannot bear the thought of burying one of them in the earth. But this

Magister, when Sister Constance strips him of his powers, his bones will lie well in our ground.'

'Will you tell the girl?'

'Of course,' says Adela, surprised. 'Otherwise she will spend her life looking over her shoulder, wondering when he might return for his revenge. I'll tell her, certainly, but after the deed is done. Let her get used to us, to learn to love us and her new position. Let her be safe and comfortable, then tell her that vengeance has been had.'

'Perhaps that's something she'd like to take herself,' warns Beatrice.

Adela nods. 'I know. That's why I'll have someone else do it. Blood on young hands never washes off, Beatrice, or have you forgotten?'

'I forget nothing despite my years. It's the future I have issues with.'

'Mark my words, Bea, that girl has potential, I can feel it.'

'She will need to prove herself; there are others here with potential.'

Adela nods. 'Very true, my dear, very true. But there is something about her, and her notion of wandering scribes – oh, Bea, she's been here five minutes and already a brilliant idea. Imagine what she'll be like once she's drunk from the alder well.'

'It is so simple, one of your clever women should have thought of it before,' says Beatrice tartly.

'Oh, hush, you old curmudgeon. I know you like her, I can tell, I've sat with you too many years not to know the insides of your mind – or at least some of the thoughts lying there. You like her and will be here to mentor and guide her as you did me and countless others before me.'

'Harumph,' grumps the strange woman. 'It's not like I have much choice – where else would I go?'

TERRIBLE AS AN ARMY WITH BANNERS

Dearest Elswide,

This is written in haste for the last boat is departing soon and I will not be on it, although I hope this will be. I beg you keep safe these pages, for they record an end – such an end, sister! Such an end – and I would have this chronicle preserved. If you can, have it copied and sent forth so it may be found and read, and the truth of our demise – the last days of the Citadel at Cwen's Reach – known.

You did not agree with my decision, sister, when I left home and joined the order. I know our silences have been long and fraught, but you are my blood and that counts for much. Your children are my family, too, and they should be told what I have done. They should know who the Little Sisters of St Florian were and they should be proud, though soon some will try to erase us from the world's memory. Elswide, I did not desert you, I did not betray our shared heritage by leaving. I followed the path that was, to me at least, obviously laid out, but you have ever been in my thoughts. I've not forgotten you.

Please know that I have never regretted my decision, not even now when the end is upon me, not even when I can hear the sound of the siege engines at the gates. Know that I did the right thing and that my place was always meant to be as part of this community. I was always meant to have a quill in my hand and my nose pressed close to a blank page that begged to be covered with words. I was always meant to be here at the end. I write this knowing that I am a thing, a final thing, an omega.

Do not despair, sister, for in all endings there are new

beginnings; from fire there comes new life, and from chaos, creation.

Your sister,

Goda

Amanuensis to Mater Dylis, last Mother Abbess of the Little Sisters of St Florian,

The Citadel at Cwen's Reach

* * *

Know all you who read this that it is the recounting of the last days of the Citadel at Cwen's Reach, the home for centuries past of the Little Sisters of St Florian, and their innermost circle the Blessed Wanderers, the *Murcianii*, whose diligence and bravery have brought so many books to us and therefore prevented their loss to the world. I write this now as events draw to a close – I would that you could hear the things I do as my pen scratches across the page: the roar of cannons, the crackle of flames, the sounds of men dying in the streets outside our walls. All you need know of me is that I am Goda, Amanuensis to Mater Dylis, who shall be our last mistress. I have lived here for almost fifteen years, at first as a postulant, then as a novice, finally as a full Sister and scribe – not as one of the wanderers, though, for I was never so blest – but I have faithfully served as I may.

Know also that the Citadel has been a refuge for women of all ages, from all walks of life, those who fled and looked for something better. Some found a place with us, others rested and recovered and learned the skills to set them on a newer, safer path. Some came to seek the counsel of the most sacred Beatrice – although at the time they did not know it for her existence has always been a closely guarded secret – who has given guidance to our Maters for so many, many years. Some came to learn, some to teach. Some came for the wrong reasons but, in the end, learned the right ones. Others still came to us for the balm of eternal sleep and it was given with tenderness and compassion.

We have been a repository, a shrine, a home, a fortress. We have been a beacon of learning, custodians of knowledge that might otherwise have passed away. Until now we have been unbiased in what we have preserved. Until now we have never knowingly destroyed any book, but circumstances have removed the luxury of such openness and inclusion.

For centuries, wars and battles have been waged around us

by lords and kings, petty and powerful, forgotten and renowned, yet we remained inviolate, neutral, untouched by these ructions. Requests have been made of us by these rulers, and our decisions to either grant or refuse access to volumes or scrolls or other such records, have been accepted and respected, if not happily received. Our walls have never been breached, we have never been attacked, and no man has ever set foot in the shrine of the *caput mundi*.

But now this man, this strange man, this darkness made flesh of whom Beatrice warned us almost too late, is coming. This terrible man who, it is whispered, has lived well beyond his time. This man who has refused to take *no* for an answer.

It began with a letter some months ago, polite, solicitous, begging an audience with Beatrice.

As is our rule, Mater Dylis denied knowledge of any Sister of that name among us, advised the supplicant he was mistaken. She replied that while he was most welcome to send his queries to us via correspondence – our scribes and librarians would be happy to research an answer for him – he would not be allowed to set foot in the Citadel. We thought, quite reasonably, that that would be an end to it, although there was much concern that anyone knew the name of our Beatrice – her pronouncements have always been voiced by our Maters and her presence never revealed to outsiders. She has been our most painstakingly kept secret, as much for her sake as for ours.

A second letter duly arrived, delivered by a potato-face man-at-arms in the company of a small detachment of finely dressed soldiers. They were from the army of a lord with whose name we were not familiar; but the request was not his, but rather from his general. We did wonder if his lord knew how the commander of his forces was using these resources. The tone of this missive began as wheedling, coaxing, trying to get Mater Dylis to change her mind. Then it shifted slightly, implying she was foolish to blindly follow traditions whose origins were lost in time. The writer advised he knew that Beatrice existed and that Mater should reconsider her position, lest she court consequences unforeseen.

The soldiers were sent from Cwen's Reach with a final reply, much in kind with the first and, after they had retreated, the outer gates to the Citadel were closed for the first time in over half a century. Mater Dylis hurried to consult with Beatrice, who had grown quiet in recent years. I do not know precisely what passed between them, for I have never been privy to their meetings and meditations – nor has any Amanuensis since Sister Vinica onwards. I only know that Dylis was changed ever after, for I do not doubt that she learned that the fall of the Citadel was in sight.

That day she began to issue orders such as had never been given in the confines of the Citadel. Any wanderers within range of a day's ride were to be recalled. The most experienced scribes and scriveners were directed to finish only their most urgent projects. Others were set to copying specific tomes, over and over, as many facsimiles as could be managed. Yet others were tasked with penning letters to any convents or abbeys, monasteries or priories of other orders known to be in sympathy with the Citadel's goals, and still more to private collectors, great houses, universities, and powerful families who owed something to the Little Sisters – letters that were to accompany certain books. The newest members were set to sewing stout satchels and sacks, and covers of oilcloth. The Prioress, Sister Agnes, was charged with the logistics of our endeavour: locating boats and horses, wagons and coaches, reliable men to direct their course, organising and scheduling the waves of the planned disapora.

The elaborate codices that listed our entire holdings were brought down from their shelves, the silver chains that kept them in place wrenched from the wood, and pored over by Mater, our chief librarian Sister Octavia and the other Sisters who held high office – Sister Vala the Almoner, Sister Hilde the Cellarer, Sister Ivalo the Physick, Sister Penelope the Sacrist – and the impossible selection begun. Books were sorted into categories: those that must (and could) be quickly copied, their simulacra spread far and wide; those that must be removed from the Citadel but remain extant in new homes; those that might be abandoned here as if unloved; and finally, those that must, for the sake of all, be burned rather than fall into the hands of the coming man.

All those volumes, those glorious tomes, now reduced to ash in the hearths of the Citadel!

So many histories, so many arcane secrets, solutions, spells, curses, so many dreams and promises and prophecies, destroyed by our hands. How can I recount them all so you may understand? How can I tell you all you need to know of the Maters who led us, of the Sisters who worked towards a single vision? How can I tell you enough of Mater Friðuswith who, after her terrible loss, wandered as a scribe for thirty years before she became our head? Of Sister Mercia, her protégé who returned to us the *Compendium of Contaminants*, that seminal and most extraordinary poisoner's doctrine, yet lost her way to pursue ghosts and gods and shadow trees? Of Mater Adela who brought into our fold Murciana, the first of the Blessed Wanderers, who brought us what became known as the *Bitterwood Bible*, a *grimoire* without equal – Murciana, whom men now call 'Murcianus' as if the myriad accomplishments of her hand cannot possibly be those of a woman! Of Sister Rikke whose writings drew us to her, who came to us so young and finally went into the lands of darkness? Of Mater Fiammetta who found Beatrice in the heart of the honeycombed cliffs – indeed, of Beatrice herself, who had refused the hand of a mage in marriage and was so awfully punished, abandoned by her family and left to wait and wait and wait. Of Sister Benedicte of cursed name, who, when tasked with copying the *Bitterwood Bible,* stole it instead. All of these lives, these annals of women whose works, no matter their magnitude, were a part of the complex tapestry of our existence, who were so important in what we did, who we were… and who we shall soon cease to be.

And those lives, those other little lives of which we've managed to capture tiny, shiny moments… the fish merchant Léolin who loved and lost and found again his silent bride with her auburn-rose hair… of Maude the last pirate and her wife Sancha, who brought tall tales of sea monsters and word of the woman Edine and her terrible mission… of the fearful, fearless Meyrick sisters and all those many, many murderous brides…

It makes me want to weep, to put my head down on the desk, overwhelmed by such a sea of loss. But I must not sob and howl. I am not here to wail, to mourn; I am here to witness, to record how we came to this pass; how we came to this eve when below the Citadel, all of Cwen's Reach lies in flame and ruin.

We were able to give early warning to the population of the city below, so they could elect to stay or go. Those who went, and were judged fit, were given the care of fastidiously wrapped parcels of books – and the youngest among our number. Such suitable families were allocated funds to help either deliver the girls to appropriate fosterage or to raise and educate them as kin. The young ones will pass without notice; they will seem to the untrained eye to be mere children, if a little more solemn than most are wont to be. Our adolescents were paired with older Sisters and sent forth, by boat or hay wain, by water or road, dispersed to the compass points to settle where they might as mothers and daughters. Instructed not to not draw attention to themselves, to build new lives, to be cunning women, storekeepers, physicks, fortune-tellers, forgers, witches or wives; to live quietly but never forget who they once were. To be seemingly ordinary women, to guard our secrets, but to copy the books in their charge in the darkest parts of the night, to make sure the replicas went out into the world so they may still be read.

But to be cautious, to always keep an ear rumour-wise, to tremble if word should come on the wind of the man who sought those who once trod the sacred earth of the Citadel. If the man who, upon Mater's third refusal, sent an army, or at least a good portion of one. The man who does not ride at its head, Beatrice tells us in one of her rare whispers, but waits. He bides his time at the back of the pack – when others have torn a hole in our throat, then he will come to drink his fill…

Mater Dylis calls me, I must go.

* * *

The last of the Sisters are gone, having trodden the narrow paths that wind down through the cliff, to the last of the boats at the small inlet. They take with them the last of the books for rescuing – so many last things! – but not this letter for I have not finished and I am determined that our end shall be *written*. I will leave it in the hidden niche by the gate, where any Sister who returns will know to look; I must trust to providence that someone will come back, even though all that remains here are the cinders of those volumes too dangerous to abide, the tomes too trivial to be destroyed, Mater Dylis and myself. And Beatrice, for she cannot be moved and Mater Dylis will not leave her, and I will not leave Mater Dylis.

The sounds of the fighting in the streets have stopped for the first time in hours. Those citizens who stayed behind mounted a stout defence, but I fear their time is done. I fear that the enemy are now rolling their canons up the long winding ways until they are at our gates. The walls of the Citadel are thick and stray artillery has not made much of a dent in them as far as I can tell, although some missiles have cleared our battlements and smashed into buildings that border the central courtyard, which is now strewn with broken glass and stone, marble and splintered wood. The main tower has been struck and damaged; I do not know how long it will stay erect. The kitchens, refectory and both the dawn and dusk chapels are in ruins, although the dormitories, the room in which I have passed much of my life, are still intact. The stables were hit and for a long time the horses too old to be sent forth screamed, and I could not get to them to help. The sound stays with me as a ringing in my ears.

Over the past months, since our state of frenzied preparation and siege began, I have taken some time from my duties to see what I may discover about our determined visitor.

Searching our records, our myriad *Books of Lives*, the tiny local histories we keep safe, I have found mentions, notations, small references, hints, whispers, anecdotes of encounters. He ghosts through our folios like a virulent breeze… but I can find nothing concrete. Nothing that constitutes proof that *these* men who have been written of in various places are *this* man who comes for us now.

Sister Rikke wrote of such a man who came to question her about the Plague Maiden, Ella, who stole the children of Iserthal; that he demanded to know of the girl's powers of survival. The jewel-smith, Delling, left a record of events in Southarp, of the deal struck by the once-Abbot Adelbert of St-Simeon-in-the-Grove with such a man. Tales of the defection of Sister Benedicte say she was seen in discussion with such a man not long before she disappeared.

Yet I feel certain it is him. By his deeds I know him, for men do not change the things they do by habit. He appears like lightning, seemingly respectable, trustworthy, a leader, then when his purpose is fulfilled or he is thwarted, he disappears just as quickly, leaving devastation in his wake. By his description, which is unchanging across time. He is blond and handsome, charming while there is something he desires, less so when his goal is attained. By the things he seeks, which are always of the same ilk. It is books, magical items, spells, powers, secrets. By all these things I *know* him though there is no hard evidence.

I find these traces only because I have searched, because I knew for whom I was looking, and I am certain that, given more time, I would find more. It has been there in our Archives, all this information, waiting to be discovered, to be pieced together, to be made relevant. To warn us. We have been undone by the sheer vastness of our knowledge, too few hints across too many tomes.

But now I can leave something important behind: a name.

General Lucien D'Aguillar.

* * *

[This page is dotted with bloody fingerprints and smears.]

I do not have much time.

Mater Dylis, who had been observing from the battlements for some short while, bid me open the gates, which I duly did.

Let him in, she said, *let him think he's won.*

We had finished all our duties, put everything beyond reach of the coming man, until at last there remained only to *see* him, to put a face to he who had brought the Citadel low. No – that gives him too much power – we made our own decisions, chose our own fate at Cwen's Reach, made our stand, and therein lies our strength. That we did not give him that for which he came.

We did not give in.

He entered the ruin of our home in triumph, his beautiful face shining, a company of bloodied soldiers at his back – what sort of man brings reinforcements against two women, one old and the other of middling age? It was a pleasure to see his expression shift as we led him through the remains of the library and he saw the cinders and ash, the last remnants of the books he'd thought to plunder. And though we led him to the shrine, though we led him to our Beatrice, he did not get his way, for she was not his to command.

The stone basin in which she'd passed so many centuries, in which she might have remained forever, was the secret. On Beatrice's instruction, Mater Dylis and I took to it with the largest of the blacksmith's hammers left behind by Sister Blanchefleur. We set to with a will and after much effort, finally one of its walls gave way. The fire-cloud flowed through the rupture as if anxious to be away, and Beatrice gave a great and heartfelt sigh, her final breath travelling out in one long, happy sound.

When the general found her thus, merely the shrunken skull of a dead old woman, not the terrible brazen oracle he had come to question… oh, rage! I believe Mater Dylis shared my satisfaction, my great good spite. But we did not have long to enjoy our exultation.

Mater Dylis died quickly, which is for the best.

He took his time with me – drawing the life from me, I don't know how, but I could feel it go! – not bothering to finish me off after I passed out. He knew I would not recover. When at last I woke in the darkness of the empty shrine, I managed to drag myself back here, to my cell, to where this account waited. These words I have added are important: they are my last.

I am tired, so tired. It is hard for me to grip the pen, to make coherent marks on the pages. I shall finish and fold them, put them into an oilskin pouch and secrete them in the niche in hope of discovery – I believe I can make it that far. I *will* make it. Perhaps then I shall sleep.

* * *

Note appended to the parcel delivered to Elswide Förstemann by a tinker eight months after the fall of Cwen's Reach:

Dear Elswide,

I was friend and Sister to your sister, Goda. I returned from a long journey to find the Citadel devastated and only dead leaves and burnt air among the ruins. I found your sister's body, too; she and Mater Dylis have been given honourable burial. I send this letter and chronicle to you in accordance with her wishes, and in the hope that you will respect those very same wishes with regard to the dissemination of this tale.

I took the liberty of making a copy for myself. I have waited some while before despatching it in the hope that, with the passage of time, the interest and attention of the man who took the city has waned and his search for my kind is losing momentum as he turns his eyes elsewhere for other, easier answers to his questions. I am told he has not been seen again in the land from whence he came, nor has he been heard of, so I can only imagine he has moved on once more to continue his search further afield.

Yours.

Sister Immacolata

BY THE WEEPING GATE

See here?

This house here in Breakwater, this one, by the Weeping Gate where men and women come to wait and weep for those lost to the sea. This house is very fine, given the notoriety of the canton in which it resides; indeed, given the notoriety of its inhabitants.

The front stairs are swept daily by the girl who tends to such things (more of Nel later); the façade is cleverly created, a parquetry of stones coloured from cream through to ochre, some look as red as rubies, all creating a mosaic of florals and vines (the latter use malachite tiles). There is nothing like it anywhere else in the port city and there are uncharitable souls who whisper its existence is owed solely to the artisans' truck with magic. The windows are always clean and shine like crystals, but none may see inside due to the heavy brocade drapes hung within.

Come to the door, look at its intricacies, all carved from ebony, bas-relief mermaids and sirens, perched upon jagged rocks with the sea throwing itself against those ragged angles. The knocker is surprisingly plain, as if some tiny attempt at good taste was made; it's merely brass (highly polished, of course), with a slight ripple pattern so it looks something like a piece of rope. The house was not built by its current occupants – they have shifted into it, grown like a kind of hermit crab into a new shell – but by a sea captain who quickly made then lost his fortune to the ocean and its serpents and pirates, its storms and violent eddies, its whirlpools and deceptive coasts with rocks sewn just beneath the surface. After that, another man purchased it, an ill-famed prelate with no flock, who spent his days delving into dark mysteries, talking to spirits and trying to create soul clocks so that, if he might not live forever, he could at least access another lifetime. His departure from the city was encouraged by a nervous populace. The abode lay dormant and lonely for several years until *this* woman came along.

Dalita.

Tall and striking with jet-black hair, skin the colour of wheat, and eyes like brown stones. She dragged behind her three small daughters, their features enough like hers and distinct enough from each others' to say they had different fathers. No one knew whether she bought the property or simply set up shop there – a lawyer did descend a few weeks after her presence was noticed, but by then her business was well established (it took only a week).

The solicitor rapped the knocker, peremptorily, a look of displeasure on his face and entered when the door was whisked open. He came out some time later, features quite changed and set in what seemed an unfamiliar arrangement of happiness. He walked somewhat stiffly, now, but this did not seem to bother him at all. He became a regular visitor and was content to leave Dalita to her affairs (and her offspring, who continued to increase in number), and if his wallet was a little heavier and his balls a little lighter each time he left, then so much the better.

For all its decorative glory, the house does not have a delightful marine aspect. Perhaps that is unfair. By peeking out one window, inching one's body sharply to the left and pressing one's face hard against the glass, one might see, through the tight arch of the Weeping Gate, a sliver of water. It is, it must be said, a strip of the peculiarly unclean, slightly greasy liquid that lines the port, infected by humanity and its waste. But then, no one who ventures this far comes for the sea view.

The house has no wrought iron fence, nor tiny enclosed garden; it simply sits cheek by jowl with its street, which is muddy in times of rain, dusty in times without. The cries of the gulls are not faint here, nor is the smell of fresh, drying or dying fish.

Once inside, however, incense and perfume, a heady opiate mix, negates any piscine odours (and others more personal, leisure-related), and anyone setting foot in the spectacular red entrance hall will immediately lose hold of their fears or concerns. The richness of the decor and the beauty of the girls, their charm, their smiles, their voices (coached to pitch low and light), combine to wash away all imperatives but one. After a single visit, even the most nervous of trader, wheelwright, tailor, sailor, princeling or clergyman – in short, anyone who can scrape up Dalita's hefty fee – will be content to wander the requisite dark alleyways to the house by the Weeping Gate.

And in truth, with time the locale became strangely safer – mariners keen to earn extra coin were easily recruited to run interference in the streets. Thieves and ruffians learned quickly not to trouble those walking in a certain direction with a particular gait, lest they find themselves faced with consequences they did not wish to bear. The longshoremen were known on occasion to shift some of the more inconvenient street-side debris further away from the house. No need to scare the punters.

Gradually, Dalita's clientele increased, and soon enough she took fewer *habitués* herself, becoming fussier, more miserly, with her favours. But as each daughter came of reasonable age, so too did the number of employees of the house; firstly Silva, then the twins Yara and Nane, then Carin, next Iskha, then Tallinn, and finally Kizzy.

Asha was kept aside, held back for finer things.

And Nel, too, was kept aside, banished to the kitchens.

Iskha, taking her fate in her own hands, ran away and should not have been seen again.

* * *

Nel has never feared the streets. They always felt more welcoming than the woman's house – she does not think of Dalita as her mother, possibly because she has never been encouraged to do so.

Nel is plain, astonishingly so – perhaps Dalita might have forgiven her if she had been ugly, for that would have been one thing or the other, but as plain as she is, Nel seems almost… nothing. A blank upon which looks did not imprint. Perhaps this causes the most offence – the other daughters all have some version of their mother's allure, enhanced cunningly with pastes and powders, dresses and corsets, all to make the best impression in the eye of the beholder.

But Nel… on the occasions her sisters tried to make her up, make her over, it seemed as if the colours they layered upon her face had no effect at all, merely sat on her skin effecting no more of an impression than the merest hint of a breeze. The lacy pink tea gown dangled listlessly on her as if it, too, could find nothing on which to *take*. Her hair, similarly, would neither kink nor wave even after a full night wrapped tight in rag curlers. When let loose, it simply hung to her shoulders in thick straight lengths, neither brown nor black nor blonde, but an unremarkable mix of all three. Of middling height, with middling grey eyes, she was a middling sort of girl and blended into her surroundings as well as a chameleon might.

She'd found in the avenues, the alleys, the seldom-used thoroughfares, the hidden ways *through*, a kind of home and a kinship with those who inhabited those places. Similarly invisible they recognised a fellow shadow. Some took the trouble to help. Not attracting the eye meant not attracting attention and there was safety in this. Mother Magnus, the cunning woman, showed her smidges of magic to help dampen the sound of her footsteps, to make darker shades cling to her as camouflage. Lil'bit, the cleverest thief, taught her how difficult locks might be encouraged to open, even though she did not indulge this new-found talent for nefarious purposes. Every little bit of knowledge was stored away, if not used immediately.

But the streets had become less welcoming in the past few months, the gloom seemed darker and deeper, the night silences heavier, and she was never sure now what she might find when she went abroad, either on ways of packed earth or cobbles.

Nel had found the first girl.

She'd gone to buy the week's coal, dragging the newly cleaned little red tin wagon behind (Dalita always insisted it be pristine no matter that the coal filthed it up within moments). Nel was always there earlier than Bilson's Coal Yard opened, but she knew how to subvert the lock on the rickety wooden gates, and Mr Bilson was happy for her to leave the small bag of brass bits and quarter-golds in a tiny niche beside the back door of the building.

Nel let herself in, every bump of the wagon on the ground making a loud protest against the quiet of the dawn, but it kept her company. She made her way over to the huge scuttle (the height of one man, the length of two and the width of three) with its metal lid and rolled the thing open to find a face staring back at her. As she looked harder into the dim space she could see a body carelessly laid across a bed of black, bare but for its dusting of coal, an expression of eternal bewilderment on the dead girl's face.

The Constable, fat and red-faced, was terribly cross with Nel because she couldn't tell him who had done this thing – which was going to make his job difficult. He normally dealt with nothing more than theft, and drunk and disorderlies. He studiously ignored runaways, vowing that they would return whenever hungry enough. He quietly took his bribes from those who ran the underbelly of the city – they were terribly good at self-regulation, which he appreciated. Any bodies that were the result of the criminal machinations tended to disappear. *He* did not have to deal with them. This… this was something new.

'I didn't see anyone,' she said for the third time. 'I just found her.'

‘And what are you doing out so early?’ he demanded.

She rolled her eyes. ‘Buying the coal for the house; and Madame Dalita will be looking for me by now.’

At the mention of her mother’s name, the Constable had realised that he didn’t need to detain her any longer.

Everyone hoped this murder was simply an aberration, but no. There had been five others since – or, at least, five who had been *found*. Nel had seen two of them, but only from a distance as they were hastily taken away to avoid public panic. One from the fountain in the city square (which was round), one from the garden at the bottom of the old Fenton House (deserted for many years), another in the orchard belonging to the widow Hendry on the outskirts of the city, yet another on the steps of the city hall and the final one tied to the prow of the largest ship in port, a caravel belonging to the Antiphon Trading Company. The young woman was wrapped around the figurehead as if holding on for dear life.

The girls were all poor, mostly without family, but very, very lovely, once upon a time. It didn’t matter, however, when they were lifeless and lying on the marble slabs of the Breakwater Mortuary, wrapped in black cloth so their souls couldn’t see to get out. All waiting for the coffins paid for by the city council – penniless girls, yes, but nothing puts more of a fright into folk than the idea of the restless dead. Those who in life had been destitute and dispossessed, when improperly buried, seemed to be more disagreeable, disgruntled and disturbing as revenants. So the council of ten, made up of four members of the finest families, three of the richest traders, two of the most vociferous clergymen, and the Viceroy, reached into their deep pockets and stumped up for properly-made coffins and decent burials.

The Viceroy began to make noises, after girl number two, found in the fountain – *people drank that water!* – and so the Constable was given two helpers to aid in his investigations. Unfortunately, the need to spend time in taverns asking questions also meant the under-constables found themselves unable to resist the temptation of drinking whilst working and managed, by sheer effort, to not help very much at all. The Constable traipsed daily to the Viceroy’s office, a hang-dog expression on his face, head sinking lower and lower into the setting of his shoulders, so much so that people wondered if it might simply disappear and he would cut peepholes in his chest so he could see out. He stood quietly while the Viceroy yelled.

Nel had watched with interest some of the Viceroy's performances.

He was in his seeming mid-forties, a handsome blond man with a poet's soft blue eyes. Tall and well made, he dressed with care and splendour, which set him apart from the previous Viceroy. He raged at the Constable. He ranted at the council members. He looked splendid doing it. He spoke gently to those who had lost daughters and paid out a blood-price to those who asked, even though, as people commented approvingly, it was not his place to do so. And he attended at the funerals of the murdered girls, eulogising each and every one, warmly praising the power of their youth and beauty, and lamenting their loss.

When Nel had first appeared at the door to the council chamber bearing her mother's initial missive, he had paused in his tirade at the Constable and given a vague smile. Now he did not bother, as if her plainness made his eyes slide away and he could no longer notice her. She wondered if he thought the notes floated to him all by themselves. Indeed, her approach excited so little attention that she often watched him unheeded, caught his unguarded expressions and was surprised by those times when it seemed his face was not his own, but a mask set loosely atop another. Nel would shake her head, knowing her eyes deceived her.

She would clear her throat and he would stop what he was doing – whether it be reading, writing, making decrees or fiddling with the large yellow crystal he sometimes wore as a pin in his cravat – stretch forth his very fine hand with its manicured nails for her to place the letter onto his pale, lineless palm. That fascinated her, the blank slate of flesh, as if he had neither past nor future. As if he had simply appeared in the world as he had appeared in Breakwater, six months prior, bearing all the right letters with all the right seals. Accompanied only by two potato-faced men, who spoke seldom and then in monosyllabic grunts, he tidily ousted the incumbent Viceroy – a man known for his indolence, drinking, fondness for young flesh and payments made under the table – in a coup that had delighted and surprised the citizens.

He was terribly good at organising things and wonderfully talented at shouting down opposition, so the city began to run smoothly for the first time in many a year. Grumbles about his dictatorial style gave way to admiring nods as the mail began to arrive in a timely manner, providores were obliged to clean up their kitchens, and slack or shoddy workmanship incurred painfully large fines.

When Dalita initially sent her on this errand (having waited in vain for the new Viceroy to attend her establishment), Nel wondered at the woman touting for business. She thought perhaps Dalita feared the man's next target would be to root out moral corruption and the like – he seemed the type. How else could one explain his absence from the house by the Weeping Gate? Dalita's product spoke for itself, attracted buyers and created its own momentum, and would have done so even without the little bewitching touches such as enchanted whispers blown across a crowded marketplace, and tiny ensorcelled chains of love-daisies slipped into pockets and baskets.

Eventually, though, Nel realised that this was something more than a simple marketing ploy; this was higher stakes. Dalita was offering something for a more permanent purchase, not merely a short-term *rental.*

Dalita was planning to move *up* in society.

At the outset, Nel simply waited for the Viceroy to sniff and snort, and send her out of the chamber with laughter echoing in her ears; but he did no such thing. He read the note, opened the locket which had weighted down the billet-doux and stared at the miniature portrait of Asha for a while, then gave a nod, and the words 'I will consider this proposition.'

She duly reported to her mother, who sat back on a padded recamier, with a well-satisfied look and a gleam in her eye. The speed with which this business-like courtship has proceeded surprises no one.

Now Nel visits the Viceroy every second morning or so with some wedding-related query. He does not give her a direct answer, but sends one of his men with a written reply in the afternoon.

What he *does* give Nel are his traditional sennight gifts for the bride-to-be (whom he has never met), one for each day of the week before the wedding.

These are strange, gaudy things that seem to have begun life as something else. A rusty iron coin, set in a fine filigree and hung on a thick gold chain. A rag doll dressed in a robe of impossible finery and carefully crafted miniature shoes, but the doll itself smells… wrong, musty, a little dead. A bracelet of old, discoloured beads, restrung on a length of rope of wrought silver. A brass ring with a piece of pink coral atop it. A shard of green, green glass set in a gilt frame as if it is a painting. A mourning brooch dented and tarnished, the hair inside ancient, dry and dusty, but a new stout pin has been affixed to the thing so it won't fall away. And finally, today, the earrings.

They are large, uncut dirty-looking diamonds, stones only an expert would recognise (and Dalita is such a one).

They hang from simple silver hooks.

They are ugly and the Viceroy insists his bride wear them for their upcoming wedding.

* * *

The attic stretches the length of the house. It is populated by six beds, narrow wooden things, but with fat soft mattresses and thick eiderdown duvets, satin coverlets and as many pillows as might be accommodated. To one side of each bed is a free-standing wardrobe, plain yellow pine lightly lacquered, barely able to be closed for the wealth of attire stuffed within: day frocks, evening gowns, costumes for clients with more particular needs, wisps of peignoirs for those who prefer fewer hindrances to their endeavours. To the other, bedside tables overflowing with jewellery, hair decorations, stockings, knickers, protective amulets, random votives, powders, paints and perfumes. Nel's thin pallet is in the kitchen, piled high with her sisters' cast-off quilts.

There is a space, too, where bed, 'robe and table no longer reside, but the marks of their feet are still visible. A gentle reminder of Iskha who always talked of running away and one day did. A space haunted by the glances the other girls give it, and by the presence of one of whom they now speak rarely and then only in whispers for fear their mother might hear. A space filled with yearning.

The wooden floors are covered with rugs of thickly woven silk – only naked feet may tread on these, so all the footwear for the ladies of Dalita's establishment is kept in the room, which takes up half the tiny entry hall to the attic (the other half is a curtained-off bathroom), and is lined with shelves stashed with rows and rows of all manner of shoes: slippers, boots, heeled creations, sandals of gold and silver leather, complex constructions of ribbons and bows that must applied to the foot using an equally complex equation of order and folds to ensure the wearer can walk.

Against the back wall of the long room is the shrine: one large bed with four posts, big enough to accommodate three fully grown adults, and hung with thickly embroidered tapestries to cut out the light when beauty sleep is a must. On either side of the bed rests a wardrobe, mahogany these, also tightly packed. To the left of this suite is a dressing table, complete with a stool, cushioned lest the buttocks of the chosen one be bruised. On the tabletop, rows and reams and streams of necklaces, bracelets, droplets of earrings and finger rings, all a'sparkle like a tiny universe of stars carelessly strewn. And amongst this are pots and bottles (carved of crystal in various shades), palettes and brushes to apply all the colours required to highlight eyes, emphasise cheekbones, give lips more pout than Nature intended, and an oil (expensive, rare) to make black hair shine like wet obsidian.

This is the space laid out for Dalita's special darling, her most beautiful child, the loveliest of them all; the one, Dalita believes, who most resembles *her*.

Asha's mane falls below her waist, its ends tickling the tops of her thighs when she stands; Nel, when she is not in the kitchen, spends many hours washing it, rubbing oil into it, washing it once more, then brushing it, brushing it again until it glistens.

Asha's eyes are just a little too large (like a doll's), and hazel, and in the company of men, frequently cast down as Dalita has taught her. Her skin is the colour of butter with a marked sheen – again, Nel spends many hours rubbing this skin with creams that contain tiny flecks of gold and silver. Asha's face is the shape of a heart, her nose pert and straight and her mouth an inviting purple blossom, lips always moist. She is secure in her position, in the knowledge that she's destined for something *more*. It does not make her unkind.

She is Dalita's gem, her pearl, her sole unspoiled child, for Dalita has greater plans for this daughter. Asha remains untouched and unbroken, a prize to go to the highest of highs. And at the moment, she is not in the room, which is awash with the noise of young women waking and dressing, bickering and bonding.

'Don't pull so!'

'Oh, hush.'

'You're never so rough with Asha,' whines Nane.

Yara, sitting opposite her, nods. 'No, never so rough.'

'I'm not rough,' protests Nel, 'but you will let clients mess up your hair like this. Honestly, it's a bird's nest – what do they do?'

'Naught you'll ever know about.' Nane laughs and pokes her tongue out. Nel catches sight of it in the mirror and tugs harder on the black tresses, smiling when her sister howls. Yara sniggers and earns a kick from her twin.

From one of the beds comes a growl. Silva sits up and glares. 'Shut up, you lot. Some of us are trying to get our beauty sleep.'

'Some need it more than others,' replies Tallinn silkily and a barrage of giggles and pillows explodes from Silva's bed. Her aim is excellent and her ability to throw in more than one direction at once is impressive. Only Nel is safe. As if the sisters know Dalita's treatment of the plain one is more than enough torment for anyone, they are always tender to their kitchen sister.

'There.' Nel draws the silver-backed brush through the now-smooth locks one last time, smiling at their lustre with contentment. 'Hurry, Yara, you're next, before Asha comes.'

'Oh, yes, Asha's big entrance. Gods forbid she ever slip *quietly* into a room.' Kizzy rolls out of bed and slides to the floor, a look of discontent painted on her porcelain face. She is rounder than her sisters, scrumptious and cuddly, and the youngest; as such she instinctively knows she should be the one who is spoilt, but Asha's pre-eminence has deprived her of this and she resents it daily.

Yara slips into the spot vacated by her twin, and lets her eyes close, feline, as the brush begins its work. Yara is as neat as Nane is untidy; with their faces so alike it's hard to believe that their natures are so different. Nane is robust, hoydenish; Yara is sleek, almost virginal (something truly precluded by her occupation, but the impression is more than enough to satisfy a particular kind of client).

'Someone help me with these stays,' howls Carin. 'Gods, Nel, can't you be more careful when you wash these things? You've shrunk my corset!' She struggles with the garment, tugging it this way and that, straining the tying ribbons until they threaten to snap. Nel puts down the brush and makes her way over the wildly struggling sister.

Calmly, she bats Carin's hands away and adjusts the corset, shifting a fold of fabric here, straightening a caught-up hem there, and finally pulling the ties into alignment and deftly doing them up. She pats her sister's face and kisses her cheek.

'I think you'll find the corset is the same size and you're one who's changed. How long since—'

'Oh, no!' Carin wails. 'Not again.'

'You're so careless,' says Tallinn, rippling a frilly green day dress over her head. 'Mother will make you keep this one – she said so last time.'

Carin slumps to her bed, head hung low, face covered with her hands. But she doesn't cry – none of Dalita's girls are given to tears for they redden eyes, puff up faces, coarsen complexions and fill sinuses with unpleasant fluids; no one looks charming thus.

'Maybe,' she mumbles through her fingers. 'Maybe it wouldn't be so bad?'

'And what life for it?' snarls Kizzy. 'What life?'

Nel looks at the youngest and frowns, putting a finger to her lips. 'Hush now, hush, Carin. We'll take care of it, don't worry. Dalita doesn't need to know.'

'Maybe,' says Carin, 'Maybe I could find Iskha?'

Carin's expression of hope hurts Nel's heart. She wonders if her other sisters suspect.

'I could go to stay with her? Do you think, Nel? Could we find her?'

'I *think* I'll make the appointment for next week. Mother Magnus will take care of it. Just keep your food down for a few more days, and give me one of those brooches the fat little Constable gave you last week.'

'What for?' demands Carin, affronted that any of her trinkets might be taken. Nel rolls her eyes.

'You have to pay for her services somehow and what money do you think I have?' she asks tartly. Carin subsides and reaches into the top drawer of her bedside table to pull out a square mother-of-pearl container filled with things that shine. She hands Nel a cameo, engraved with the head of a Medusa, lovely and serpentine, then insists, 'Could *you* find her, Nel?'

'I think she wanted to get away and if she doesn't want to be found, she won't be.'

Nel pats her shoulder and returns to Yara's hair, which she gives a final cursory brush and twists into a tightly elegant chignon. 'Now, all of you, neat and tidy! Lest *she* come looking and find you wanting.'

As if summoned, Dalita appears, with all the imposing poise of an empress. Her eyes sweep the room, finding nothing to complain about, all daughters dressed and coiffed, paints applied to faces, potions and perfumes to skin. In her hands (strangely square, mannish, very capable, ruthless – what might those hands not do?) is a box, ancient, highly polished, yet with its wood cracking under the weight of years, a gold clasp holding it shut. It is almost four of the afternoon and the clients will soon come a'knocking, but first there is this to be done, this important thing before tomorrow.

Behind her stands Asha, quietly dignified, her wedding dress, a great white confection, glowing in a ray of last sun pouring through the skylight above. Taught by her mother, she knows how to always present herself in the best possible way; she knows everything there is to know about lighting, position, composure, posture, how to dominate a room from the moment you entered to the moment you left.

One senses, however, that she is not at full power, that she has dimmed herself for this practice run; she conserves her energy until she needs to *glow.*

The dress – the result of seven seamstresses sewing sleeplessly for seven nights – is rather like a wedding cake, with its lace and frills, its layers and embellishments. Shiny white, reflecting with so many hand-sewn crystals it almost hurts the eyes. It is the first time she's seen it and Nel thinks it looks like a suit of armour.

No one but Dalita is to have the honour of preparing Asha for her wedding day, for Dalita trusts no one but herself. She certainly knows her craft: Asha is breathtaking; her sisters, even Kizzy (slightly green) stare in admiration and longing, and not a little envy.

Upon Asha's hair – which has been carefully coiffed, bouffed, backcombed, woven, plaited, twisted, tied and knotted and sculpted like spun black sugar – is a fringe tiara, a framework of gold-wrought wire. From it flows a veil of silk gossamer, spider-spun, almost to the floor, but somehow incomplete. The headdress fans across the crown of her head like a peacock's tail, with seven fine, hollow spikes as part of the structure, yet there is no adornment, none of the gems one might expect.

Dalita looks over her shoulder, gives Asha leave to move into the centre of the attic so she is encircled by her sisters (not Nel, though; Nel falls back, knowing her place is not *there*, and stands against a wall, quiet as a shadow-mouse). Dalita's fingers clutch at the casket, fumble with excitement as she flicks the clasp.

'This box,' she says, pauses, struggles. '*This* has not been opened for forty years, not since your grandmother wed. What is inside is a gift to the bride that only a family can give: protection and a dowry against the future.'

She lifts the lid and offers the contents to Silva, then Tallinn, then Yara, then Nane, then Kizzy, and finally Carin; she herself retrieves the last item. Apiece, they hold what looks like a very long hatpin (the length of a hand), topped with a gemstone, each a different colour. Dalita takes her diamond-tipped pin and approaches Asha; carefully she inserts it into the middle spindle of the headpiece. 'Long life to you, my daughter. Bring your family prosperity and pride.'

All the sisters do the same, and soon a rainbow arcs across Asha's tiara: blue, red, green, purple, orange, pink and the diamond, clear as light.

The earrings from Asha's betrothed hang like clumps of dirty water at her ears. Dalita adjusts her daughter's hair, just a little, to try to cover the offending ornaments. She frowns, making mental note to ensure the 'do is tweaked *just-so* on the morrow.

Dalita surveys her other daughters, does not speak, but merely waves a hand.

To a woman, they traipse out of the attic and down the stairs, past the two floors of the house holding Dalita's luxurious chambers as well as bedrooms equipped with a sturdy bed, themed decorations, and a discrete bathing corner, down to the three parlours on the ground floor, where they will drape themselves over chairs and long sofas. Yara and Nane will pull back the curtains in the front windows and settle themselves on the padded seats to watch for oncoming visitors, and smile and wave, welcoming the regulars and drawing new customers in. Kizzy and Tallinn will ensure the drinks trolley in each room is fully stocked and all the heavy crystal glasses of varying shape and sort and size are ready. Silva will hover to open the front door upon the third knock (always the third, any less is too hasty, any more too tardy – three is just enough to sharpen a client's anticipation, but not enough to stretch his or her patience). Carin will wait with her, ready to take coats and hats and canes and carefully put them away in the walk-in cupboard by the door. Tomorrow, they will have the day off, but not tonight.

'You,' says Dalita, pointing a finger at Nel, but not looking at her. Nel wonders if the woman suspects. 'Take this to the Viceroy.'

Nel nods, pocketing the letter.

'But first help your sister out of that dress.' Dalita's need to control extends only to the construction, not the deconstruction, of an illusion.

Nel nods again, although she knows this is neither required nor expected.

Dalita turns, her burgundy gown whispering, and lightly touches Asha's creamy cheek. She catches sight of herself in one of the mirrors hung on either side of the doorway and pauses, struck. Nel wonders how many nights the woman spends before her own reflection, watching the years converge upon her skin and begin to decay her beauty. Dalita shakes her head, closes her eyes for a moment, then leaves. Both girls let their breath go as soon as they hear her heels on the stairs.

'Is it heavy?' Nel asks. Asha nods gingerly so as not to dislodge the work of art on her head. Nel begins with the headdress, unclasping the veil first of all and tenderly draping it across the nearest bed. Then the tiara, laid beside it.

'Is he handsome? Up close?' Asha asks unexpectedly.

Nel pauses in the task of unbuttoning the two hundred tiny pearl buttons running down the back of the gown. Nel wonders if she should tell her about the times when she fancied the Viceroy seemed *other*, but decides against it. 'Yes. You've seen him from the window.'

'But that's not close up. Is he nice? You've spoken with him.'

'No, I've delivered things to him and that's different.' She considers. 'He seems… determined. He knows what he wants. He is polite.'

Asha sighs. 'I supposed it's the best I can hope for.'

Nel hugs her sister, pressing her plain pale cheek against Asha's butter-rose one. They are silent then, knowing that Asha has already had the best that can be hoped for in the house by the Weeping Gate.

* * *

Mother Magnus works and lives in a long narrow room, a forgotten roofed area, a lacuna between two larger buildings. Her bed and washroom are at the back, her workshop and store at the front; a ramshackle kitchen divides the spaces. To look at, Magnus is anyone's idea of a witch, hunchbacked and bent, a shuffling gait, one side of her face a mess of scars, the other still quite smooth. Her hair, though, defies expectation; it is silver-white, long, soft, luxuriant, and hints at a different past. She smells like lavender.

Nel picks up bottles and jars, then puts them down. She flicks through the yellowed hand-written recipe and spell pages Magnus sells, stacked in boxes on a bench. She shifts back and forth impatiently while waiting, batting at the dried plants hanging from the low ceiling.

'Stand still before I hex you, child.' The woman's voice is sweet, mellifluous and deep.

'I'll be late. Yet another letter to the bridegroom.'

'Can't hurry magic, girl. Hurried magic is messy magic. Messy magic is dangerous magic.' Mother Magnus points to the corrugated side of her face, then turns back to the mortar and pestle, attending to the task of grinding herbs with a particular intensity. Nel will ask her, one day, what happened, but she knows that now is not the time. The cunning woman's back is eloquent in its deflection of enquiries. There is a dry rustling as the crushed ingredients are shepherded into the neck of a small bottle, then a *glug* as a purple liquid is poured in after. Magnus stoppers the flask and seals it with black wax. She hands it to Nel, who, in return, counts five quarter-golds into her wrinkled palm.

'My thanks, Mother,' says Nel. A tisane for Asha, to help with conception. Dalita is determined that her daughter will be *embedded* in the Viceroy's life as soon as possible.

Nel finds herself staring at the ruined side of Magnus' face and, without thought, she blurts, 'Does my mother ever come to you?'

Magnus shakes her head. If the question surprises her she does not show it. 'Never. Although if ever there was a woman I thought would seek me out, it's her.'

'Why?' Nel thinks she knows the answer.

Magnus grins. 'Why, for a cure against woman's mortal enemy.'

'Time.' Nel nods, smiles a little; is thankful she doesn't have to worry about having beauty to lose.

'If ever I thought there was a woman who would want potions – if ever there was a woman I thought would seek a soul clock or some such…'

'A soul clock?'

'Steals the life – the youth more particularly, and all that goes with it. Done right, it will give you another lifetime, perhaps.'

'Perhaps?'

'I've never seen it done right.' Magnus rubs at her own face and turns away. She will not say more. 'Night, Nel.'

Nel is out of the street and heading up towards the finer part of Breakwater, where the houses rest at the feet of the mountains, when she remembers she neglected to mention Carin and her needs. No matter. There will be plenty of time after tomorrow.

* * *

The Viceroy, in preparation for his wedding, is not at the council chambers this day. Running of the city has been suspended as the townsfolk anticipate the celebration to come and no one has any complaint. The taverns have opened their doors and libations are free – courtesy of the Viceroy's fat wallet – and the brothels similarly are offering their services gratis (not Dalita's girls, though – there is no promise of a change of life for them). There is much laughter in the streets and good-natured camaraderie; petty arguments have been suspended, debts and obligations forgiven and forgotten, at least for a few days. A carousing city relaxes, lowers its guard.

As the afternoon shades to an evening-lilac, Nel finds the iron gate of the Viceroy's mansion secured. From her pocket she draws out a lockpick (a gift from Lil'bit), and has the lock clicking merrily in a trice. She slips in and wanders along the path, which rises slightly as it makes its way towards the white plaster and granite edifice. A mansion of twenty bedrooms for a single man and his two men servants. And soon, Asha; and soon Asha will have children. Nel dreams that she might leave the house by the Weeping Gate and look after Asha's babies.

The trail winds its way through the overgrown grounds of the house, which are somewhat tropical; the air here is hot and damp. There is the smell of rotting vegetation and something else. Nel thinks the garden needs work and wonders that a man who so generously spreads his fortune across his citizens, who is so concerned with an organised and tidy city, takes no such care in his own home. In the foliage, behind the trees and bushes, things move and her spine twitches with the weight of gazes she cannot see. Nel picks up her pace.

The stone stairs of the mansion are off-white (no one washes and sweeps *this* stoop) and in places cracks make deep veins where dirt has infiltrated, looking like black blood. Nel tiptoes over them, and towards the front entrance. She raises her hand and knocks – which causes the door to swing open.

'Hello?' she calls.

There is only silence. She steps into the wide entry hall. The floor is covered with a black and white chess pattern of tiles; dual staircases climb the walls, to the left and right of a strangely placed fireplace, where only cold ashes shift in the slight breeze that has snuck in behind her. To her left and right are double doors, ornately carved, painted dove-grey with gold filigree decorations around the handles. Nel chooses the left. The parlour is empty, silent and filled with stale air. She wanders through and finds another door, a single one this time. She pushes it open: a room lined with books and at the far end, two chairs (with curved armrests, slender legs and threadbare cushioning) wait, each with a large silver pan in front. In the pans is dust: two heaped piles of grey particles. On closer inspection, there is dirt, too, and what look like flakes of snake skin. On a delicate table between, two pewter ewers, filled with water and beside the chairs, a mound of clothes: the livery worn by the Viceroy's two attendants.

Nel slips a hand into her pocket and rubs at the thick paper of

Dalita's note. Her heart does not hammer, but its rhythm has become more certain, like a punctuation of every second she remains here. She backs away, turns, and sees something she missed before: a curtained alcove. There is the sound of a latch rattling, a handle turning and now her heart kicks like a startled horse. Without a thought, she slips behind the hanging and holds her breath.

The space is small, containing only her, a slim crowded shelf and a chest, a sea chest, not closed, with fabric spilling out. Nel reaches down and pulls at one of the rags; it's a dress, aged, dirty, with smears of coal dust across the skirt. Another dress, and another. All old, well-worn, as if by someone who could not afford to replace it; eleven in all. On the shelf, bottles. Phials half the length of her hand; she counts twelve and only one is empty. The others swirl with a roiling red-grey mist that seems to push against the very glass as if to get out.

Her attention is drawn away by footsteps. Footsteps and muttering; nothing intelligible, but determined. She puts an eye to the split between the curtains and watches the Viceroy pace, his back to her, to the chairs and their pannikins and pitchers. He kneels, grunting and groaning like a grandfather and pours the contents of a jug into a pan, whispering all the while.

A mist rises, swirling into a tall tower that takes on the shape of a man. The Viceroy moves to the other pan and, while the first thing is coalescing and firming, begins the process anew. He lifts his head and Nel sees his face in profile: the Viceroy, yes, with all the peaks and valleys of the features she knows, but old, so much older than he has presented himself. Furrows in a skin, blotched with age and malign intent. Nel, understanding her time is short, slips out of the alcove and through the open door.

Her mouth is dry as paper, her throat closed over as she sneaks from the house. A sudden breeze pulls the door from her numb grip and slams it. Nel is used to little magics, the tiny enchantments to help things along, the harmless brushes of conjuring; what the Viceroy has done – is doing – is beyond her understanding. She runs down the cracked steps, behind her she hears the front door pushed back against the façade of the house, and two sets of stumbling feet, as if their owners have just woken. Nel darts into the undergrowth, fear of what she knows is chasing her greater than that which she imagines might be lurking in the garden. She tiptoes through dank detritus, glances over her shoulder and in the process trips over an ill-covered lump, wrapped in a mouldering blanket.

The smell of *something else* is worst here, right by this thing, this cylinder-shaped thing that feels soft and giving beneath her shaking hands. Before she summons the courage to unwrap it, however, the sound of footsteps grows louder, more confident, rushing through the leaf-litter, following her tracks. The moment before they appear, the Viceroy's golems, there is a whisper and a sigh – no, *whispers and sighs* – and Nel is surrounded by grey, wispy women, made wan by death. Through them she can just make out the potato-faced minions, their heads moving back and forth, back and forth like confused bloodhounds. They cannot see her; the women have shielded her. The men servants shuffle off, back towards the path and the house.

Nel soughs her thanks, but the girls do not reply, merely watch her with sad, sad eyes. She glances at them, at the swirling number of them, trying to fix their features in her memory, until her eye lights on a face she knows too well. One for whom she packed a knapsack with warm clothing and food and drink; for whom, not six months since, she'd silently unlocked the door and watched as the other disappeared into the fog of the early morning. One she'd thought *free* of Breakwater and the house by the Weeping Gate.

She runs to her mother, not to the Constable, not any of the other council members. She runs to her mother, with the spectre of Iskha at her heels. To Dalita because she is the most powerful being Nel has ever known. No matter that there is no love there, Dalita loves Asha and Dalita will not allow her chosen daughter to be harmed.

* * *

Nel, propelled forward by the force of Dalita's large hands, keeps her balance until the final few steps. Then she trips and sprawls.

Her fall is broken by damp fabric; felt, soaked with water. There is the sharp, briny smell of salt.

'You will not ruin this for me!' Dalita howls like a cat impaled upon a hot poker. Her rage, her disbelief, when Nel told her what she had seen, what she feared, was something to behold.

At first Nel thought it directed towards the Viceroy, then a ringing blow to her head and a second to her face made her reconsider. While she was disoriented, her mother grabbed her by the hair and dragged her, half-crawling, half-walking through the house, then into the kitchen and down to the cellar. Nel was unsure what enraged the woman most: the idea that Nel might endanger the wedding or that she had helped Iskha flee.

'Liar! Ingrate! Knave! Bitch!'

Dalita threw open another door, in the floor – a sub-cellar.

And the terrible truth of this place is becoming clear, after Nel's drear hours in the dank dark room: this place is *tidal*.

There is a gap at the base of one wall, she can see, where the sea comes in, but there's no hope of escape: there is a crosshatch of bars across the opening. The water is rising, rising, rising.

Wailing and shouting have not helped – no one can hear her through the cold thick rock of the walls and ceiling. Anyway, her sisters are all a'flap with celebrations – there was no pause for them in the evening, business as usual, but today they wear wedding finery and act the dutiful daughters even though the streets will be filled with people who sneer and laugh at them behind their backs.

The hours have done nothing but make Nel colder, to bring her closer to despair; her teeth chatter, she shakes so badly she can no longer stand and beat at the wood of the trapdoor, which is sodden, but not soft, not rotten. Her hands are bruised and fingers bloody from that hopeless endeavour. There is no lock which she might finagle into compliance.

And the water has continued to rise mercilessly; inevitably; inexorably.

A wash of waves pushes Nel, and her bluish lips and nose scrape against the rock-carved ceiling. She tastes salt and metal; she smells mildew and death. In moments, the sea will replace the last tiny pocket of air and she will drown. It doesn't matter.

It doesn't matter anymore.

With this realisation she feels her body suddenly very heavy, her spirit suddenly very light. She ceases to fight, ceases trying to stay afloat, gives herself up to the water, and she bobs about, heedless as seaweed. The tide pushes against her again, once, twice, thrice and she feels this is the end.

Hands.

Hands, strong and insistent, many of them; and voices, crying, angry, relieved. Many voices, all at once and Nel is hauled upwards. Behind her the trapdoor is slammed back into place, the bolt shot as loud as a lightning strike.

And her sisters, all her sisters but one – but two – gather around her, clamouring, demanding, groaning with fear and relief, wanting to know what happened, where has she been, was this why she missed the wedding.

And she tells them, choking on seawater and bile and vomit;

shivering and shaking and desperately trying to pull her soul – which she so recently was preparing to let go – back into her body.

And they believe her; they believe her because she has never lied and because they *know* their mother and the length, breadth and height of her ambitions.

Nel hopes Asha is safe, that there is *time*.

'The Viceroy insisted they pay their respects to the morgue dead after the ceremony, while the city feasts.'

The mortuary, thinks Nel, so full of lost souls and spent lives, of untapped *power*.

And as they sit there, the seven of them, they hear in the distance the sonorous clang of the death-bell. Not a rhythmic beating, but a desperate clamour, a cacophony. A cry for help. It stills them, voices, faces, hands trying to dry Nel off. It stills their hearts and their minds for precious seconds. And then they run, all of them, even Nel in a halting, stuttering fashion.

They run up the stairs, through empty rooms. They tumble down the front steps like kittens released from a box; they process through the cobbled streets, fast and fleet and trailing diaphanous fabrics and long tresses behind them like banners. They run through the night streets like glorious, terrified ghosts, flashing past windows and open doors, glowing in the lamplight as they pass from shadow to light and back again.

Not far from their destination, the air is split by a rumbling and the lash of a whip; they are almost run over by a black carriage and four, ebony plumes waving in the air. In a blinking moment, Nel glimpses the Viceroy slumped inside, his white wedding attire bloodied and torn, his true age writ large upon his face. Then the conveyance is gone, on towards the city gates, and the sight gives wings to Nel's feet.

The sisters run until they merge with the gathering throng outside Breakwater's black marble and cardinal brick mortuary, threading their way through folk who, minutes ago, were celebrating all unawares.

Upwards the girls rush, pushing past the fat Constable and his slack-jawed deputies, along corridors embedded with the smell of death: mortification and preservation. Finally they crowd into a room, the room where all will one day go, lined with alabaster tables, each bordered with gutters and silver tubes leading to channels in the floor, stained rusty with all the years of bodily fluids. A room laid out not unlike their own attic sanctum. A room with windows set very high in the walls so no gawkers might peek at the frailty of the dead.

A room with a roughly drawn scarlet circle laid out before them, a star etched inside it with a bottle at eleven of its twelve points. Bottles filled with a churning red-grey mist, some fallen on their side as if collateral victims of a struggle, but none of them broken; none but the empty one lying beside Asha, who is draped across one of the tables.

Her wedding gown is worse for wear, and her tiara is askew and missing some of its pins. As the sisters approach, they notice her make-up has smudged and run, the lip wax is smeared, the kohl and mascara lie in lines across her face, her eyes seemingly bruised by the mess of dark smudges. One earlobe is torn and bloody, its earring gone.

The others stop; these are steps they cannot take. But Nel continues, her feet bare and muddy (her shoes lost in the depths of the sub-cellar), her dress saturated and still dripping on the cold marmoreal floor. Her soles jerk with the shock of being cut – glancing down, she sees shards of yellow, the crystal the Viceroy once wore, now destroyed. She notices that her sister still breathes laboriously, crimson vapour travelling on the exhalation. Nel gathers her up, heedless of the heart's blood spilling from the tear in her chest. Nel leans close and catches Asha's last words, 'I can see Iskha.'

As her sister relaxes into death, Nel lets her lie back down. She arranges Asha's limbs and clothing, gently closes her lids over staring eyes, tries to tidy the wildly dishevelled tresses. Clenched in Asha's right hand is one of the missing pins, the diamond-tipped one. Its long thin shaft is covered with rapidly congealing blood. Nel does not believe this is her sister's and she wraps the spindle in a piece of fabric torn from the wedding dress and buries it deep in her own pocket.

She then notices, around Asha's body, an aura, a silver shimmer that pours off the dead skin; a voice in her head says *no*, but she ignores it and touches once more the morbid flesh.

There is nothing. No bolt of lightning, no arching pain, neither scream nor shout nor moan. Nothing, but a kind of itch, across her scalp and her own skin, her own face. Nothing that hurts, nor is even uncomfortable, but simply the sensation of a change creeping on, slowly.

* * *

‘A soul clock,’ says Mother Magnus, her voice tunnelling through the dim front parlour of the house by the Weeping Gate. All the rooms have been dark for some weeks, all business dealings postponed, all noises hushed. Nel stands, staring out through the gap in the thick curtains. The view of the street has not changed, although there is a carriage waiting, not too fine, not too ordinary, simply one that will draw no attention. She lets the old woman reel out her explanation. Nel occasionally asks questions and wonders if the cunning woman should have – or did – notice the signs.

‘Why girls? Why not boys?’

‘Vanity? Convenience? Soft skin? Who looks for lost girls of suspect morals?’

‘And Asha? Why Asha?’ Nel’s voice trembles but does not break.

‘Who was more beautiful than Asha?’

Nel realises she is wringing her hands; she shakes them, stills them.

‘He was aging – I saw him. I think he was getting desperate. He was getting sloppy, stopped bothering to hide them.’ Nel rubs her face, still getting used to it. ‘I wonder what he’ll do now, where he’ll go.’

‘Like I said, hen, you can track him with *this*, if it’s his blood.’

Nel nods, because she is sure. She *wants* to be sure. She takes the item from Magnus.

‘*He* won’t recognise you, but it will be harder for you to hide.’

‘I know,’ says Nel, skin all goose bumps at the thought of being seen.

‘What about the other ones?’ the old woman asks.

Nel turns. Mother Magnus is pointing to the eleven bottles, now empty. Nel hopes the wisps of souls will forgive her. It will not be long, she tells them in her heart, and prays Iskha will intercede for her.

‘Home,’ she says. ‘They went home.’

Upstairs, Nel can hear her mother’s ruckus and she takes her leave of the cunning woman. Dalita, having disappeared after being given news of her darling’s demise, was found hours later screaming at the Viceroy’s mansion, yelling obscenities at the top of her lungs, banging at the doors and breaking the windows with anything she could find to hand. She has been abed ever since.

The first time she opened her eyes and saw Nel she recoiled, gibbering. Now she will take food only from this daughter’s hands.

For it is Nel, but not Nel alone.

The plain daughter is transformed. She is not the great and

terrible beauty Asha was, but something of the dead sister has passed over to her.

Her hair is now a decided black, her eyes are larger, but still grey. Her mouth has blossomed into something that demands attention and her figure has filled out, hips and breasts growing wider, just a little, and waist pinching in without the aid of a corset. She is dressed in Asha's clothes for her own no longer fit.

She is a different girl, touched somehow by the magic left on Asha's skin. She is no longer a girl who can live in the shadows, and she feels this loss. Nel no longer feels safe for there is nowhere she can hide from the gaze of those who would drink her in.

This morning, dressed in a grey velvet travelling dress (once Asha's favourite), a beaded purse hanging from one wrist, and a black lacquer fan which, when open, shows mermaids and sailors, on the other, she gives instructions to Carin, who insists upon interrupting.

'And what do we do,' asks Carin (now rounder than she was and determined to become rounder still), 'when she asks for you? When she refuses to eat?'

'Mix a little of the valerian in her food, it keeps her calm. Tell her I am doing what I must and she needs to be patient.' Nel pulls on kid gloves fastened with jet buttons.

'When will you come home?'

'When it is done.'

Her single carpetbag waits by the doorway. When she is in the shadowy confines of the carriage, when she can feel the rock and sway of the vehicle and knows they are beyond the city's boundaries, Nel will take the diamond-topped spindle from her reticule. She will place it on her palm and wait to see which way it spins, until it finds the direction she must follow.

Nel takes a deep breath, steeling herself to step outside, to move through the world and be *seen*.

See here?

See this girl?

She is a very fine girl indeed.

SPELLS FOR COMING FORTH BY DAYLIGHT

Four years, I think, refusing to believe it and so speak out loud: 'Four years.'

The folk milling around me in Half-moon Lane's broad expanse barely notice and those who do are adept at looking elsewhere. *Steady, Nel*, I think. This is the area of Lodellan where people know how to mind their own business – if they know what's good for them – which is in part why I sought it out. Also, it's cheaper to find a bed here, to eat once a day – should I so desire I can feel my ribs, count them with ease – and to go unremarked unless I fail to pay my bills.

Alas, that's becoming an all-too-likely event. Four years and the money, the valuables, have just about run out. I sold the last of the tiara gems almost twelve months ago and have been living frugally on the proceeds since. I bartered away the clothing, too, all those lovely travelling dresses, even Asha's favourite dove grey; now the only thing between me and public indecency is a well-worn pair of trews, an equally lived-in shirt, boots with emaciated soles (enchanted to keep my footsteps quiet), and a cloak grown thin with age – I'll be in trouble by the time winter comes. All in varied shades of brown, for brown turns aside the eye, excites no attention, and since my face changed, became more *pleasing*, I have been so anxious not to be noticed. The camouflage does seem to work, although crowds part when I walk through them even if no one seems to see me. Sometimes I wonder about this, but mostly I simply accept it as bonus of whatever magic rubbed itself on my skin. After the second year of fruitless searching, I sent the driver and coach back to Breakwater, and began walking the length and breadth of whichever land, county, country, the bloodstained pin directed. I've crossed mountains and oceans, marshlands and forests, borders and boundaries, followed faithfully to where it led, and look what it's gotten me: permanently callused feet, a tan that will never fade, wrinkles like canyons at the corners of my eyes, and hip joints that grind with every step. Perversely, I never thought I'd bewail the loss of what Asha passed on, never thought I'd be concerned for my looks, but it's strange: when suddenly you get something you never thought to have, never thought you'd care about, it becomes so stupidly precious. I never thought I would be that way. I never thought I would miss the smell of the sea, the stink of the port, the heady sweet miasma of home. I never thought I would miss the house by the Weeping Gate.

This city is landlocked, although there is a river running through and around it – it does not seem to have a name, just "the river" – and in the weeks since I've been here I have sat by its banks with my eyes closed, trying to persuade myself that the sounds of its rushing waters are like the gentle splash of waves breaking against the pylons of the wharves in Breakwater's harbour. Some days I am almost convinced; mostly I'm not.

This city is both old and new, its foundations deeply embedded in the past, its encompassing walls thick and ancient, built to house a smaller community in more generous surroundings, but the population has grown as populations are wont to do, and begun to fill the space. Not fully, no, but everything fits more snugly within the series of squares that make up the burg, will become more snug still as time passes. The palace of the local prince and his most recent bride is being extended, extra wings added to house who-knows-what, gardens improved upon and expanded, planted with ever-more exotic foliage that require ever-more gardeners to ensure they do not die in alien soil. And there is a magnificent cathedral being built to replace the tiny church that once was sufficient for the needs of the worshipful, but now no longer meets the requirements of either size or prestige. The Archbishop is apparently anxious for his holy accommodations to reflect his status. I passed by the building site last week, looked down into the great abyss they'd hollowed out, saw all the tunnels that will form catacombs and secret places, and shuddered.

This city, I fear, is the last place I have any hope of finding the Viceroy.

I seemed always to arrive too late. Sometimes it would be obvious he had been there before me – talk in the hostelries and marketplaces would be of a sudden abundance of murders in locales barely touched by such events, or of items of esoteric value disappeared or stolen. Yet when I described the man I sought no one would, or indeed could, tell me they had seen him. It made me wonder what new magic he had learned, to wipe people's minds so clear. Then again, perhaps he simply has not shown himself for whatever reason, perhaps his peculiar golems have been carrying his will into the world?

At any rate, I have not found him, have not caught up with him – at least until now. The bloodstained pin from Asha's wedding tiara – just the pin itself, mind you, the diamond at its apex was the last thing to go – did something it had not done before when I wandered into Lodellan: it stood straight up, balancing vertically in the palm of my hand. It has spun madly, spun slowly, lain dormant, but it has never done *this* – indeed it stands to attention still, on the rickety desk in my room in the boarding house – and I choose to see in this novelty a sign. That the end is here, that my road will be done, that Asha and Iskha and all the others will be avenged, that the danger of the Viceroy will be gone from the world, and that I will be free. I am unsure what I will do then – the threat of liberty has always seemed so far away.

I make my way along Myrtledove Walk, a tiny byway that leads, as if by magic, to the better part of town. It seems that I step across an enchanted threshold into Busynothings Alley. While the street is a little narrower than its downmarket, more criminally inclined counterpart, the stores here are fancier, tidier, their signs freshly and artistically painted, emblazed not merely with a drawing of the service offered, but also with the written description beneath. I would feel out of place if I thought myself more conspicuous; as it is I am a brown smudge of a woman, with a hood pulled low over my face, and a heavy satchel concealed under my cloak.

I think what it would be like to be here with the weight of excess coins in my purse, wearing a pretty dress – not a hand-me-down, but something made just for me – and wandering about with little else to do. No burden of obligation on my shoulders, no thoughts of home and my sisters and Dalita, no thoughts of last chances and all the tiny failures that have dotted my past forty-eight months. I think about all that and shake my head for such thoughts gain me nothing. I see the sign for Gisborne Street and hurry down it until it intersects with Whortleberry Lane, my destination.

Ermingard, the proprietress of thc Loathly Lady, the boarding house of which I am currently a well-tolerated patron, is a source of valuable information if one can but get her to open her mouth.

She knows more useful secrets and is in charge of more nefarious things than she will ever admit, but after I rendered her a small service – Lil'bit would be pleased to know I have not lost my touch with a lockpick – she has seen fit to answer my queries about the best place to try and sell a book of rare sort (ancient, black-covered, and smelling of badger). The purveyors of fine tomes to which I've been directed are, Ermingard assures me, both trustworthy and discreet.

Carabhilles' Fine Books is located halfway down the lane, a gem even among so many other finely appointed bookstores. The shingle depicts a book with legs, which makes me laugh aloud for the first time in an age. The windows of the shop are clean and sparkle brightly in the afternoon sun. Through them I can see shelves and shelves, rows of tables and desks, piles of volumes neatly stacked awaiting inventory and placement. Well-dressed men, women and children moved about inside with the polite greed of bibliophiles.

I take a deep breath and push the door, which makes the bell on the lintel give a genteel cry of alarm. Heads turn and take me in ever so briefly, then, having summed up my worth and found it wanting, they all return their attention to the things most deserving: the books. Or rather all but one: a youngish woman, not quite twenty, with light brown hair and angry amber eyes, is still staring at me as if that will send me back to whence I came. I shake off my hood and give her a bright smile in answer and nod to say I've seen her and *yes*, I will speak with her. I peel away the edge of my cloak so she can see the satchel beneath, see its size and estimate its heft. So she can imagine what might lie therein and her curiosity is caught, outweighing her annoyance. I was once not this manipulative, this set on getting my own way; I wonder what I would have been like had Asha's death never happened. A mouse, I suspect, a shadow all my life.

The woman moves towards me, her saffron gown flouncing with each step, and I towards her so we meet in the centre of the front room. Behind the counter from which she's just come stands another girl, younger still and wide-eyed, this one with white-blonde hair, a green gaze and a dress of amethyst hue that speaks to the prosperity of this establishment. I'd have thought they would look alike, for they are supposed to be sisters, but there is nothing to show a shared blood – I wonder which one takes after their mother?

'How may I assist?' Amber-eyes asks tightly.

'I wish to discuss the sale of a book.'

'You wish to buy a book?' Her expression says quite clearly I cannot afford even a bowl of soup.

'No, I wish to sell one to you.'

'What makes you think we're interested?'

'We'll neither of us know until you look at it, but Ermingard at the Loathly Lady said you might be. She said the Carabhilles could be trusted – I do hope her faith has not been misplaced.'

She doesn't bother to answer but waves a hand in a gesture that might mean *follow me* or something less polite. I am an optimist after all, so I choose the former and trail her further into the room, to a narrow polished table with a purple velvet runner down its middle. I open the satchel and extract the big black book, careful not to disturb the other item in there, and place it on the velvet, where it looks like a magnificent rock of a thing. The woman's eyes widen as she reads the front cover – *Murcianus: Magica: A Book of Craft* – then tries to hide her shock by turning away and rifling through a drawer to find a pair of white cotton gloves. When she faces me again she is mostly composed. If I had not watched her so closely, I'd think the gloves were to stop the musky badger scent from getting on her dainty hands.

'This is old,' she says, voice husky. She carefully opens it, gingerly leafing through each page, then pauses – she thinks I don't notice how her right hand slides beneath the back cover looking for the indentation, the *M* I already know is there. Her fingers rest on it, caressing the relief lovingly. How can she think I don't notice? What is this thing that all her caution, all her sangfroid evaporates like morning dew in the sun? I can only hope it means I will get a good price for it – I have no interest in keeping it, I cannot read the language in which it's written. It is a means to an end for me, to finance the final leg of this journey. Or at least to get enough to pay Ermingard for a bed for the next few weeks and to ensure a meal or two a day for that long. Perhaps enough for a new pair of stout boots and a new cloak that will see me survive winter. The more I think about it the more my list of needs grows, so I put the expectant anticipation from my mind.

'I will need to value this before we can discuss any sale,' she says. 'My mother and sister will need to be consulted, too, so we might reach an agreement. Will you be so kind as to leave the book with me and return this afternoon?'

I snort. 'I'm sorry, have I given the impression that I'm some sort of lackwit? I will not leave this volume here, no. I will wait for you and yours to do a valuation under my watchful eye, or I shall take the tome with me and see what other merchants in this street of books will offer for it.'

She looks as if I've slapped her. I take the heavy item from her seemingly nerveless hands and put it back into the satchel, then draw my cloak around it and myself and make to leave. Her fingers grab at me, hard into the flesh of my upper arm.

'No!' she almost shouts, then realises that her well-heeled clientele are staring. She lowers her voice and loosens her grip. 'No, please. Come in and wait.'

I pause for a long moment before nodding. I follow her through the stacks of polished oak, the beautifully bounded books all lined up like pretty maids, until we come to the back wall, which seems to be simply more book-lined shelves, or so I think. She touches a bright red spine with *Beata Beatrix* in gold lettering and there is a stealthy *click*. The wall swings back a little. She pushes it open and stands aside, showing I should go first.

And I do for, after all this time, I am apparently an idiot.

As soon as I step into what appears to be a dining room of moderate extravagance, arms snake around me and sharp steel is cold against my throat.

'Is this how you do business?' I say, trying to keep my voice steady. I can feel her hand shaking and the knife with it. She may well cut me through sheer nerves rather than intent, and that would be contrary to my desires. I have a dagger, too, slim and slender, and concealed at my hip, but I'm in no doubt that brandishing it will be counterproductive.

'You wanted to wait,' she hisses. 'So you will wait until Mother returns.'

There is a medium-sized table and she pushes me into a chair at one end, then takes up position at the head. Not exactly the best means of controlling me – and if the shoe had been on the other foot, I'd have tied me up – but then I've just shown myself stupid enough to give her the advantage, so what do I know? We sit in silence for a good few minutes, I rubbing my neck where it feels as if the cold of her blade has seared me.

'Where's your mother and when might she grace us with her presence?' I ask and she remains silent. 'Only, I've got somewhere else to be this afternoon…'

Still she does not answer, but glares at me as if she might be able to ignite my hair or eyebrows. The door in the wall opens and the other girl enters.

'Where are you, Cassia, leaving me with all those customers…' she trails off and stares at us. 'What are you doing?'

'She has the book, Flavia – Murciana's great book!' Her amber eyes are bright as fire. The younger girl turns a sceptical regard on me, and Cassia raises her voice, 'In the bag! Under her cloak. Get it, examine it!'

The other girl appears doubtful and I feel it's time to establish some boundaries, crossing my arms over my chest. 'If you come near me, I promise you broken fingers at the very least.'

That seems to decide matters – no hardened criminals or stand-over merchants these, just angry frightened children at heart. What are they hiding that makes them so fearful? A professional would have cut me a little, taken off a slice of flesh to encourage me to talk – and I would have! – but neither of them are certain of themselves. They have no ruthless disregard for life.

'Tell me where you got it?' Cassia almost begs.

I give her a long look, compressing my lips and narrowing my eyes. 'Since you were not polite enough to answer my questions, I will not answer yours. We shall wait for your mother to return – oh, and I'd suggest at least one of you goes back out to the shop floor. I didn't like the look of some of your customers for all their fancy attire, and books – well, we've ample evidence that they make people crazy.'

And so we wait.

* * *

'Again, I cannot begin to express how sorry I am for my daughters' behaviour.' Blanchefleur Carabhille, seated at the head of the table, looks nothing like her "daughters". But we have already established that there is no blood relation between them, a fact I would have worked out even if Cassia had not called her "Sister Blanchefleur" when she came through the door not long after sunset. She is not particularly tall, a stocky woman built like a bull, all muscle from neck to shoulders, chest, middle, hips and legs. She has changed from the suede trousers and cotton shirt she wore earlier into a green brocade dress, but there's no hiding she's a smith. Her hands are scarred and callused, with burns on them and her forearms, gifts of the forge she works each day. Not for her the books her young charges love; she has a smithy in the lower city, shoeing horses, crafting tools and, when it's called for, swords, maces and other weaponry. She is a round column of flesh with fading auburn hair and an open honest face scattered with tiny red freckles, older than she at first appeared, perhaps in her late fifties.

'They were afraid,' I say graciously, and admit, 'I may not have been terribly helpful.'

Upon coming home and finding her daughters had a hostage, she was very calm if not somewhat exasperated. She'd sent the girls to make dinner and while dishes were clattered and meats were carved, cheeses plated up and wines poured, Sister Blanchefleur, late of the Little Sisters of St Florian, pored over the book I had brought, and confirmed it was indeed of great interest to her.

She was, I felt, a person whom I could trust and I've not met too many of them in a long while. We'd exchanged our stories, each giving up secrets as a gesture of faith, quite a leap considering how our acquaintance had begun. I told her of the house by the Weeping Gate, of Dalita and my sisters, of Iskha and Asha, and the Viceroy and all he had done. In turn, she told me of the Fall of the Citadel at Cwen's Reach, of the disbanding of the order and the flight of the Sisters, of the new lives they were forced to live. She showed me the copy of the chronicle of the Blessed Amanuensis Goda, and we discussed the possibility that her General Lucien D'Aguillar was my Viceroy.

The book lies on the table between us; the hot sweet coffee, brandy and biscuits the girls brought for afters have been set well away. Sister Blanchefleur has said she will give me whatever I ask if only I will hand over this tome. I have assured her that I've no desire to bankrupt her, and we have come to an understanding satisfactory to both of us. Cassia and Flavia are sitting opposite me, quietly watching everything that occurs; they're like children aware that something is afoot and cautiously remaining silent so as not to remind anyone of their presence lest they be sent to bed. Now, with their superior in charge, they are happy to leave everything in her capable hands. All traces of resentment, of insecurity, anger and fear are gone.

'Do you think he had it?' I ask.

She touches the cover lovingly, fingers tracing the title. '*This* was added later, but we – that is, the *we* that was the Little Sisters of St Florian – searched for this for so many years. But we never found hide nor hair of it, nor Sister Benedicte afterwards, who was tasked with copying it.'

'Can you read it? Does it contain the sort of spells Goda says he looks for?'

'I can't read it, but there are those who can. It was written by the first of the wandering scribes, and it is said she called its contents spells for coming forth by daylight… spells to change the nature of things, to bring the dead back, to extend life, to do all the things one should not.'

'Why hold onto it then? It sounds dangerous,' I say.

'Oh, it is. But we were devoted to keeping all knowledge in the world, in case it should be needed.' She smiles sadly. 'We will make copies and then ensure they find other homes.'

I half-nod, half-shrug. The volume is no longer my concern.

'And you found it?' asks Blanchefleur, brow wrinkling.

'Purely by accident and I was lucky not to break my neck.' I take a sip of the bittersweet beverage. 'I followed the path of the pin, passing deserted towns, burnt villages and crumbled abbeys. I came to an empty, overgrown house with tiny lettering above the door that said *Fox Hollow House.* And I walked and I walked and I walked some more, into the woods until at last the ground gave out beneath me and I fell through a hole. It was an old sett and when I woke up I found myself lying next a satchel containing the book, and two small skeletons – badgers by the look of them. I wonder how they got the thing. I know they can be notorious thieves, but still…'

Silence all around as we file it under *we'll never know.*

'I wonder now if the pin doesn't just take me to where he is, but it's also sometimes taken me where he has been long ago. I'd always assumed it would be accurate, current. But perhaps not.' I sigh. 'And this man, this general, you didn't see him at Cwen's?'

Blanchefleur shakes her head. 'Mater Dylis insisted we be gone swiftly. The only reason we know what happened at the end is because of Sister Immacolata, who made it her mission to bring Goda's chronicle to us, and to any other Sisters she could find – you must remember that we left no record of where we all went when we dispersed, for our own safety. Any Blessed Wanderers who were on the roads knew nothing of what befell us.'

'Did Immacolata ever see *him* in her travels?'

'Not that I know of – but it's ten years since she stumbled upon us then went on her way, and twelve years since the Fall, Nel. I do not know what became of her. Few of the Sisters who've come to Lodellan have seen her and the chronicle, and even those who have haven't met her since, to my knowledge at least.'

'But you still find your Sisters?'

She smiles, a warm nostalgic ghostly thing. 'Yes. Mostly by chance at first, but over the years we have managed to trace each other. They come to stay for a day or two, we relive old times, talk about rebuilding, about making a pilgrimage to Cwen's Reach, and then they go on their way. We are ever mindful that this general might still be active, although in recent times we've grown hopeful that he has gone at last, found something else to occupy himself, something far away, or better yet, died – but if what you've told me is correct, perhaps we have been wrong to hope.'

'Yet there's been no one newly arrived here that might be him? No one handsome and bright as a lightning flash, with lineless palms, making waves, drawing admiration from all those around him? No mysterious murders, no sudden drop in the population of the homeless, the lost children, those at the bottom of society?'

'I must say no, with both relief and regret that I cannot help you.' She takes a long drink from the pewter goblet – it is engraved with books and sayings such as *verba volant, scripta manent*, which she told me earlier means *spoken words fly away, written words remain*, and others still about books and readers and their shared fates. 'There are new people here every day, some rich and important, others poor and beneath notice. We have seen no one who might be your Viceroy or our General D'Aguillar.'

I rub at my face, tired, frustrated. It's a long time since I've eaten so richly, drunk so deeply and it makes me feel slow, my mind lumbering as an ox. I wonder if perhaps he has learned to change his face? 'Is there anyone else who might know in this city? Any other refugee or traveller, gypsy or vagabond? Anyone different who might notice some… aberrance?'

She is quiet for a moment as she considers, 'There is Hepsibah Ballantyne, the coffin-maker. She is a strange woman, not given to company, but she has been a friend to us. Pay attention, Nel: she is *peculiar*. But perhaps she will have some clue. She has been in Lodellan several years now. On one occasion she asked that if I should learn of anyone looking for her to tell her immediately. She never gave a name for such a person, although now I wonder if she knew it but was simply keeping her secrets close. She might be able to help you, but remember, Nel, there are many women in this world fleeing many things.'

'Where can I find her?' I make to rise and she laughs at me.

'It's well past midnight, Nel! She'll certainly not open the door to you now. Sleep here tonight – we have beds aplenty.'

I can think of nothing worse than having to trudge back to Ermingard's establishment at this hour. She will not panic if I do not return tonight; she'll mind her business for I am paid up to the end of the week. If I do not return at all she'll wait a day or so then gather up whatever she can find and sell it off, or would do if I'd had enough things to leave any in that tiny room. I don't begrudge her this, it's the only sensible thing to do. I accept Madame Carabhille's offer graciously.

* * *

Newly outfitted in a sapphire blue dress, my hair brushed for the first time in months and twisted atop my head by a very patient Flavia – Blanchefleur says I will get nowhere with Mistress Ballantyne by looking like a beggar – new boots (carefully enchanted like the old ones) and a short cloak with silver embroidery around its hem, I am ready to face the day. Being tidied up has taken years off me and Cassia insisted on cleansing my skin and painting my cheeks and eyes. For former nuns they have certainly embraced the art of cosmetic deceit – when I step outside I know I will be *seen*. This morning I was reminded of being with my sisters, preparing them for their evenings, only for a change I was on the receiving end of being made presentable. It made me think about Carin and her baby who will be a toddler by now; it made me wonder if Dalita is still abed with mourning or if she has recovered and reasserted herself, reopening the doors of the House by the Weeping Gate. I wonder if my sisters have rebelled or knuckled under.

I walk with Blanchefleur for a while, until we reach the cross street where we must part, she for her smithy, and I for the upper reaches of the city. She is quiet as if trying to find a way to tell me something. Finally she comes out with, 'Hepsibah is a terrible snob, although I don't believe she was born to any kind of privilege. If you're insufficiently imperious she'll think you're not worth her time.'

I nod, adjusting the pretty leather gloves that hide my broken nails and reddened hands.

'And, Nel, she's… haunted by ghosts of her own making. I don't know how else to put it.'

'I'm not afraid of ghosts,' I say and then see that she knows I've failed to understand.

She shrugs and waves me off. 'Good luck.'

Mistress Ballantyne's business premises are located outside

the city walls – Lodellan prefers not to have its coffins prepared within the civic area for some reason or other – but she also has a very, very fine house not far from where the palace sits and the Cathedral will one day perch. It is a tall, thin abode built around a courtyard where a fountain plays, and I at first think to wander in under the archway, to knock on the tradesmen's entrance, but no. I must approach Mistress Ballantyne as a social equal. I think of Dalita and feel my spine stiffen, my chin raise so I might look down upon people. I roll my shoulders and think of Asha. I can feel the eyes of the folk bustling by become intent as they follow me. I can feel my sister's talents running through me, taking over, ensuring I am *visible*.

I raise my hand and rap the brass ring as if I've every right to be there. The knocker is in the shape of an angel's head and its eyes fly open to regard me with disdain. The door is unlocked by a short, pinched-face girl with dark hair and an ice green gaze, a black dress and a white maid's apron over the top. She stares at me and says, 'What?'

Obviously she's not been chosen for her manners.

'I am here to see Mistress Ballantyne,' I say, drawing myself up so I tower over her, then add, 'Mistress Carabhille referred me.'

She makes a noise that has no real translation but shows she's unimpressed, and slams the door in my face. I swear the angel smiles as it closes it eyes. At a loss, I wait a few moments then raise my hand to knock once again, but the door is pulled open before I manage to connect with the wood.

A small woman with a pixie's face, hard brown eyes and short blonde curls stares at me. Her dress is rich, rich, so rich! A golden brocade such as Dalita might have dreamed of for a grand ball, but never everyday wear. Her square, battered hands are covered in rings, her wrists in bracelets. She is perhaps in her fifties, well-preserved, but the years have settled in her neck; the skin of the throat is thoroughly furrowed and painted with age-spots. She's layered necklaces and chokers as if they might distract from the wreckage. I can see through her, though, I can see everything she does is a kind of armour, trying to make up for all the things she fears she lacks. Trying to fill a void she's borne her whole life. I'm careful to blink away my knowledge so she does not see what I know, so she doesn't realise how transparent she is to me. But I needn't worry: she merely looks me up and down, putting a value on me.

‘Well?’ she says and I can see where the maid learned her etiquette.

‘Mistress Carabhille sent me,’ I begin.

‘I know that – this little fool just told me. What do you want?’

So much for the benefits of a friendly referral.

‘I wish to speak to you about…’

‘Blah, blah, blah,’ she says, rolls her eyes and makes to shut me out.

I take a chance and blurt, ‘Lucien D’Aguillar.’

She freezes – it’s a small moment, a fragment of a second, but she’s terrified. Her face spasms, turns into a sneer to hide her fear. ‘Lucien D’Aguillar is dead, dust over a hundred years ago. Don’t waste my time.’

And the door is closed in my face for a second time.

I know when to cut my losses. I turn around and look into the street. A closed landau drawn by two dappled greys rolls past. Inside is an old man in ecclesiastical garb, the Archbishop presumably, who looks at me for what seems an age, then finally smiles. Beside him is another man, whose face I cannot properly see but there’s a flash of bright blond hair that makes my heart leap upwards. They are rolling away from the building site of the Cathedral, and continue along the short length of the street – which they could have easily walked – that terminates at the guarded entrance to the palace grounds. I could follow them, but have no better chance of getting into the royal residence than I do of getting into Mistress Ballantyne’s home. I watch the gates close and give up trying to get a glimpse of the two men.

My heart has slowed its beating and slid back down my throat, back down where it belongs in my chest. I need time to regroup. I must think.

I wonder what I might find were I to visit Mistress Ballantyne’s premises outside the city?

* * *

The building is low and long and deserted.

Sister Blanchefleur said Hepsibah works alone, takes no apprentices, and only toils when she has a commission. Located a good ten minutes’ walk outside the city, the structure is a functional thing of wood and brick. There are no neighbouring businesses and I make short work of the lock on the back door.

Inside it is a workshop much like any other, benches and tools, rows of brackets up one wall hold wooden planks of the finest oak and ebony, maple and mahogany. A tall set of itty-bitty drawers is filled with fittings in gold and silver, all exquisitely crafted. There are several coffins, each in a different state of completion. A heavy curtain covers a doorway, which leads through to another area, fastidiously neat and tidy and clean, where there is a chaise and a wide table covered with a large sewing box, various fabrics in myriad colours, silks and velvets, felts and blanket cloth. A series of shelves contains dried ingredients, a lot of lavender, asphodel, basil, elder, holly and other things I cannot recognise, but it reminds me a little of Mother Magnus' tiny shop. Another curtained entrance, and a third chamber where finished coffins wait to be viewed by grieving relatives come to select a death-bed. Varnished and polished to a high shine, the precious trimmings, hinges and locks look like gems against the lustrous wood, and inside each is a finely quilted silken lining, puffed with stuffing and smelling faintly of all the herbs needed to keep the dead beneath. But I find nothing to tell me any secrets.

As I'm leaving, I take one last look and notice something I missed before: hidden in one corner of the workshop is a large open-mouthed pot, and inside it, a collection of jagged mirror shards. On a slim shelf above it, an assortment of small bottles with cork stoppers, and in their bottoms a reddish-brown residue. What is a coffin-maker doing with mirrors on her premises? The recently dead should not be anywhere near such things… no bodies are here, of course, she does not run a mortuary, but still I find it strange. I look closely at the pieces, but don't reach in, don't touch them. This is not the place to spill blood.

I am careful to lock the door on my way out.

Back inside the city I stop by the Loathly Lady, to tell Ermingard of my change of address, but I also decided to pay her for another week's board just in case I should need a bolthole – with the heavy coin purse courtesy of the Carabhilles, this presents no problem. I approach the counter behind which she sits each day, knitting scarves and vigilantly scrutinising the comings and goings of her lodgers. She pulls me into the back room before I can open my mouth.

'I don't know what you've done, hen, but someone's looking for you.'

I feel my eyebrows rising. 'Who?'

'Two men in palace livery came to ask after you, but at least it wasn't a great legion of them. They've been asking around here, in all the inns and rooming houses.'

'What did they want?'

'To know if you were staying here and, if you were, for me to send someone to find them when you returned.' She points to the side of her face where I can now see the hint of a bruise coming through. 'Bastards. Told them I'd never seen you, wouldn't have you in my establishment even if I had.'

'Bless you.'

'No one tells the Loathly Lady what to do,' she said, eyes fierce. 'And don't think I don't know assassins when I see them. So, get out of here, girl, don't tell me where you're going, just in case.'

I try to give her a handful of gold bits but she waves me away, so I hug instead her, thinking, stupidly, of how I missed being hugged by my sisters. She tolerates it for a short time, then tells me to leave via the attic, which she's left unlocked. The room is close and dark, except for where one of the windows has been opened. It's an easy climb out and a scamper across the roofs. Things look different from up here, and I imagine I'm a great blot against the blue sky, that my shadow stretches to the ground and will give me away, so I need to be careful. I pass the north gate and notice that the number of guards seems to have doubled since I walked back through it so recently.

I've looked for such a long time for this man, and here I am running away. I'm not even sure it's him – although who else would send men-at-arms after me? I can't afford to be caught, to have my throat cut and be tossed into the river. I'll hide. I'll get outside the city walls somehow and I'll wait, I'll wait until he shits in his nest again and he has to leave. I'll be poised. But I can't go quite yet anyway – although the book is no longer my concern, the satchel and the rest of my funds are still at Carabhilles' Fine Books. At last I slide down the pitched roof, the tiles clawing at my backside and ruining the new dress. I slither earthward on the drainpipe and drop into the high-walled back garden, then slip in the kitchen door.

Inside, Flavia is surprised by my sudden entrance and drops the plate she is carrying with a little scream. I hush her, tell her what has happened, with little hope of a practical solution, but she surprises me.

'Is it him?' she asks quite sensibly and, though I cannot say for certain, I nod.

‘Right.’ She hands me a loaf of bread, a hunk of cheese and a flask of water, and leads me to the basement. A few moments pass as she fiddles and fidgets with a piece of carving then a door in the wall pops open. There is a sliver of a room furnished with bed and chair, candles and tinderbox on a table and a few books. It is considerably more comfortable than the last cellar I was in, but I still feel a sweat break out in the small of my back. She gives me a smile. ‘We’re prepared in case a Sister should come in need of a hiding place.’

‘My satchel,’ I say, ‘My things – should anyone search…’

‘I’ll bring them. We must appear to carry on as normal – Sister Blanchefleur has always said that a change in habit is the first hint that something is wrong, so we shall act as if nothing is amiss. This evening, we will make plans to get you out.’

When she closes the door on me, the room feels very, very tiny.

* * *

I sleep, though perhaps I should not, but if these past years of troubled travel have taught me nothing else it’s to grab a kip where and when I may. It’s night by the time the light of Sister Blanchefleur’s lantern creeps in. She smiles, though her face is strained and pale.

‘Comfy?’ she says.

‘Not really, but thank you for asking.’

We grin like idiots and she opens the door wide, gesturing for me to come out. From the chair I gather up the satchel, which Flavia must have delivered while I slept. It feels heavier.

‘No one has asked after you,’ she says as we climb the stairs to the kitchen. ‘I think perhaps no one has yet connected the grubby traveller who visited us yesterday with the stylish woman who left here this morning. They’re probably still searching the lower city. Though how long that will last is anyone’s guess.’

‘Small mercies,’ I say. On the kitchen table I spy my old clothes, washed and neatly folded. Blanchefleur helps me with the many buttons on the ruined dress.

‘We’ve packed you as much food as we could fit,’ she says, eyeing the satchel. ‘Fascinating urn in there.’

My hand goes to the flap of the bag. ‘You didn’t open it, did you?’

‘No. I’m smart enough not to go around opening sealed jars etched with prayers.’

I breathe a sigh of relief. She gives me a look, but does not ask why I have the item in question, and says instead, 'How are you at climbing?'

'Rather good.'

'Handy. There's one spot where the forest grows close enough to the ramparts to almost touch.'

'Almost? How much is almost? Because that's not climbing, that's jumping.'

'You can climb from the roof of the mill onto the walls without too much trouble – you'll just need to wait until the guards have done their rounds. Then I'd suggest you very briskly hop, skip and jump to the nearest tree. They're big and old; they should hold your weight.'

'You are not comforting me,' I point out, giving thanks, for once, for my skin-and-bones frame.

'They've been searching wagons and carriages at the gates, so we can't smuggle you out that way, I'm afraid,' she tells me apologetically. 'But you must go. Is it him, do you think?'

I can see her concern for me is genuine, but not for me alone. If Lucien D'Aguillar is somewhere in Lodellan, might he know that there are Little Sisters of St Florian hiding here? Will he care or are they no longer of interest to him? I fasten the cloak at my throat and pull the hood up. I can tell from the way her eyes narrow that I'm harder to see already.

'I don't know, but who else would look for me? You said yourself no one has come to this house and that's a sure sign, after all these hours, of them not having a clue about you. Just keep acting normally. Where are the girls?'

'Acting normally – they teach a calligraphy class tonight at the house of a prosperous matron with appalling handwriting. It wouldn't have done to cancel.' She opens her mouth, then hesitates.

'What is it?'

'I take it Hepsibah wasn't helpful?'

'That's putting it mildly.'

'Well, when I said no one had come looking for you I may not have been entirely truthful. Her maid turned up at the door earlier, begging your attendance on her mistress – her exact phrase and I've never heard a polite word come out of that little chit's mouth in a full twelve months.' She crosses her arms squarely over her chest. 'So, what's it to be? Over the wall as quick as you like, or a visit to Hepsibah first?'

'Do you trust her?'

She shrugs. 'Not entirely. The women I'm used to dealing with – the Sisters, I mean – they're helpful and supportive of other females. Hepsibah's out for herself; if she's aided us in the past it's been because there's been something in it for her. And because she's got her eye on Flavia. Personally, if it were me, I'd run like my arse was on fire.'

'Wise words. But I think your Mistress Ballantyne knows something that I need to know. I can't go until I've seen her. Wish me luck.'

'Luck and blessings,' she adds and hugs me hard.

'I'll go out the back.'

I shinny up the garden wall and take to the roofs again. It's a much faster way to get around and in the darkness; as long as I'm careful on the slopes, I don't fear exciting any comment or notice. The air is cool and clean, heady – I can almost imagine I'm free of obligations, a sense that lasts only until I have to drop to the street not far from Mistress Ballantyne's fine townhouse, and wait for a good long while, scanning the shadows for movement by any twitchy watcher. But there's nothing so either they are better than I or not there at all. I'll know soon enough. I slip through the night and sidle to the door, which I briefly consider picking the lock of, then decide that breaking and entering may not be the best way to further my cause.

The sour-faced maid lets me in without a word, and I step into a foyer free of all furniture but a large round table crafted from porcelain and mother-of-pearl. She starts up the polished staircase that crawls along one wall to become a long landing, and leads me past three doors then stops at another at the furthest end.

There are seven locks but the girl merely pushes and it swings to. Obediently, I follow and as soon as I set foot in the ill-lit bedroom I know it for a mistake. In the weak light of a single lamp I can see Mistress Ballantyne seated at a desk, half-turned away from me. To my left is a large bed, above it what looks to be a painting draped by black velvet, to my right a dressing table, and a door to a walk-in robe that sits ajar.

'Mistress Ballantyne?'

She doesn't answer.

I step closer, throwing a look at the maid, who is studying her feet. 'Mistress Ballantyne?'

The door slams and I swing about. More light floods the space as the wall sconces are lit by two potato-faced men in livery. Hepsibah whimpers and I look back at her as she jerks in the chair, to which I can now see she is tied by silken scarves. Her pixie face is bruised and one eye has turned to red jelly. Her fine golden dress is worse for wear and a rag torn from its hem is stuffed in her mouth.

'Is it you?' rasps a voice.

An old man in a white cassock trimmed with purple and gold, and stained with blood, moves slowly from inside the closet. His cloak is cobalt, and his head is bare of all but a few clumps of yellow hair. As he comes closer, I can see how very blue his eyes are, and he repeats, 'Is it you, my beauty?'

I drop back my hood so he can see I am not who he thinks I am… and then, staring into that burning gaze I realise that I *am*, in part at least. He stops in the centre of the room as he takes in the legacy Asha left me. It's the eyes: when I look at them and ignore the Archbishop's ancient frame in which they're set. It's the Viceroy, himself transformed, perhaps by the failure of the soul clock – I think of Mother Magnus touching her face as she spoke of what might happen if the magic goes awry.

I back away, find myself bumping against Hepsibah, who grunts with pain – I wonder how much of her he's broken. I wonder how much of this he did and how much his creatures – although the amount of red on him tells me he's probably got enough strength to injure me. I pull the gag from her mouth. She spits out crimson, teeth and curses.

'Are you all right?' I ask, and the words sound stupid in my ears.

She doesn't even look at me, but at the Archbishop-Viceroy-General-whatever-else he's been. 'There! She's here, I've given her to you, now let me go. Honour the bargain.'

Oh, you maggot.

'Ah, Hepsibah, when will you learn, little slattern?' He rubs his hands together. 'Princes of the Church don't make bargains with ones such as you.'

'You shit!' she screams, and he holds up a finger.

'Much more of that behaviour and I'll have that gag put back where it belongs,' he says. 'Now, hush, for the moment.'

He gives me his attention again. 'Is it you? Don't make me ask a fourth time.'

'I'm Nel,' I say and he looks puzzled, shaking his head. 'Asha was my sister, as was Iskha. You took them both – I am Nel.'

He peers at me, staring hard. 'No. Not the plain little thing who used to deliver that woman's letters?'

I nod. 'The very same.'

'But no, it can't be,' he says in a musing tone. 'I saw you today outside this house and I thought it was her…'

'Whatever you tried to do, something was left on Asha. It passed to me.'

'Asha! Little slut fought. Fought like none of them had; she wouldn't die, I couldn't get her soul into the bottle, and she ruined everything.' He shakes his head. 'She destroyed the crystal and the magic turned sour and I… I forgot who I was.' He shakes his head. 'Sometimes I would remember, snippets, bits and pieces of what I had done, of what I was trying to do, whom I was trying to find… but for long periods I was simply… blank.'

Was that why the pin had been wrong so many times – perhaps it would only work when he knew himself?

'I came here in one of those lucid moments. On one of the deserted old roads leading to the city I found the new Archbishop, almost safely at his destination. It was easy enough to take his place – after all, one old man is much the same as the next – but then I became lost again. In my defence, I have been an *excellent* Archbishop.' He waggles a finger at Hepsibah. 'I didn't remember who you were, Hepsibah Ballantyne, even though I've searched for you all these long years – not even knowing your name! But when I saw this one… she brought me back to myself.'

'You haven't tried again? With the soul clock?' I ask him what I've suspected, that he tries something only once and if it does not work he casts it aside, looks for something new. But Hepsibah has given a great shout of a laugh.

'A soul clock! Only an idiot would try that!'

'What have you done, draggletail? I've pursued you decade upon decade to find out. I needed something new, something stronger – all the other magics had lost their efficacy. All the things I'd attempted, they would work for a while, a decade or so, but then age would begin to reassert itself.' He looks at his hands as if they are strangers to him, looks at the palms that are lineless still, giving no hint of who he might be. His focus returns to the battered woman. 'But you, how have you lived for so long?'

'That's what you've wanted to know? That's why you've tracked me hither and yon all this time?' she asks in utter disbelief, then cackles, a little insanely. It's the sound of relief; of someone realising that only a *lesser* sin has been discovered. She calms and her answer is almost an aria: 'Don't know! Working with the dead, I expect. Don't know what I did, but something's kept me young.' It rings untrue to me, but I wonder if he hears the hollowness. 'And look at you, Lucien.'

'Don't address me with that familiarity!'

'Oh, we're all equal now. Look at what you've become – was it worth it, you dried-up old bastard?'

'Have you done any different?! Are you any better? I'll have the truth out of you, I swear.'

'What would your sweet sister think of you?' sneers the bloodied woman.

'Lucette is dead and gone,' he says, sorrowful, resigned.

'Rotting in the crypt back in Great Glimmerton, beside the father she and your mother killed?'

He looks as if he's been slapped. Such secrets between these two! Such awful hidden things that have spilled over so many years, washed across so many innocent lives. Such selfish, insane creatures.

'All that time you spent watching her when you were our scullery maid – did you think we did not notice? Did you think we did not laugh about you in the dark hours as we lay curled against each other?' His words hit home and Hepsibah goes pale, her lips quiver. I am grateful to be forgotten. Then she gives a crooked grin.

'Lucien, would you like to see her again? If you could?'

'Don't try to tempt me with foolish fantasies, crone.' His contempt is towering, yet she smiles and it is an awful thing.

'I thought she was the reason you'd followed me, you know. All this time I've known myself pursued and I believed it was because of her. But you didn't even notice, did you? After she was gone, you gave her no more thought than a sweet dream.' Her voice drops low, is surprisingly tender. 'Do you think I'd have let her go? When everything I've done has been to hold her, to have her?'

She looks at her maid, who has been crouched at the foot of a wall. 'Uncover it.'

The Viceroy's gaze follows the girl as she shakily stands and makes her way around to the thing and gently pulls away the velvet cloth.

It is a large mirror, gold-framed, and studded with gems. Against the shimmer of mercury stands a young woman of surpassing loveliness, delicate features, blonde hair and blue eyes making her the female twin of the Viceroy at his beautiful best. She turns to us with a haughty gaze.

'Lucette,' calls Hepsibah sweetly. The maiden in the mirror lifts an eyebrow in acknowledgement. 'Lucette, look who is here: your brother.'

The girl frowns, searching the room for the one who matches the memory of her Lucien. Her eyes light on the wrinkled mess that is the Viceroy and swiftly flit off. The Viceroy moves towards the mirror as if to a long-held hope, his hands held out. His henchmen watch, slack-jawed, dull-eyed. While all attention wavers I carefully slit the bonds around Hepsibah's wrists. I'll not leave her to this man, no matter what.

'That's himself, Lucette. Much changed isn't he?' Hepsibah's tone drips spite and she laughs as the girl in the glass peers at her brother, realises it *is* her Lucien. The exquisite face convulses with disgust and she presents her back.

The Viceroy stops. His shoulders slump with the weight of a disappointment a century or more in the making. I open the satchel quickly and bring forth the earthenware jar I'd taken from Magnus' shop before I left Breakwater. In the red wax seal words are engraved, both a prayer and a vow, to keep things in: *Until I am done*. I wrote them after I'd placed a mix of mint and blood in the bottom to attract the eleven spirits from their bottles as I'd opened them, swearing revenge and rest for them, if only they gave me more time. The murdered maids have been so patient.

The old man turns, his face twisted by hatred. He will kill us both, I am sure, then spill more blood attempting to fix his decrepit body. Perhaps he will take the mirror and pour more lives, more deaths into bringing his sister back into corporeal form so she might witness his triumph. I raise the urn high above my head then smash it down on the floor.

A red-grey mist rises, buzzing like angry insects, then splits into eleven separate entities. The wisps of souls fly, each in a different direction, reforming as ghostly women, who float between the Archbishop and I, waiting politely. I point at the old man. 'It's him. Just as I promised. Now have your vengeance and then take your ease.'

The droning becomes a collective howl and they dive at the General-Archbishop-Viceroy, passing through him like arrows of air, but taking great gouts of scarlet with them every time they surface from his skin. He doesn't have time to shout, so fast and powerful is their attack. Soon he is a bloodless husk on the floor of Hepsibah's elegant room. His golems disintegrate into dust without even taking a step to defend their master; his magic is broken, but who knows, perhaps they are tired of serving. The ghost girls hover over him briefly then begin to fade. They sketch a bow of thanks in my direction. I hope they find their peace now, their rest. I hope Iskha forgives me for carting her about for so long.

'Impressive,' coughs Hepsibah. 'I thought we were dead for certain.'

'If you had your way I would have been,' I point out. 'You tried to trade my life for yours.'

'No hard feelings,' she says and manages to get to her feet. She hobbles over to the bed, and looks up at the girl in the mercury, who is staring in horror at the desiccated corpse of her brother. Hepsibah, expression softening, speaks to her. 'Never mind, my darling, we're safe now. We can stay here, he won't be hunting us anymore.'

'You've been taking their souls,' I say slowly, thinking of the broken bits of glass and the vials at her workshop. She looks at me in surprise. 'You've been using small mirrors to catch the souls of those whom you measure for a coffin. You put a lure in the vials then break the reflective surfaces.'

She shrugs, shakes her head. 'They decant quite easily. I didn't know what would happen for a long while, then I started to experiment and it seemed to keep me young. No one was harmed, no one knew.' She gives me a carmined smile. 'They're dead anyway, I just drank them like gin, tasted the same.'

And I look at this woman who has caused so much pain through her selfishness; a trail of ruination and blood has passed in her wake, as bad as that of the Viceroy. And this girl, Lucette, trapped for so very long – it must be like going mad anew every single day.

There is an ink pot on the desk and I pick it up. It has a lovely weight, a lovely heft, and I fling it with all my might.

The glass shatters, a spider web of cracks spreads across its surface and the silent girl looks gleeful as a child. I watch as she squeezes herself out through the fissures of her prison, becomes a silver fog that throws itself down Hepsibah's mouth as it opens to scream, 'No!'

And the woman chokes. She chokes horribly. Blood trickles out the side of her mouth and when she finally stops moving there is only a line of argent steam that rises from her gaping lips.

The sour-faced little maid is sobbing in fear, though I have no doubt that when I'm gone she'll be stripping the rings from her erstwhile mistress's fingers. I will send her for Sister Blanchefleur, who will want to arrange for Hepsibah's funeral. The Archbishop will lie in the foundations of his cathedral – I'll bundle what's left of him up into a blanket and sling him into the deepest darkest pit I can find, behind one of those areas they've already finished.

I doubt the king's guards will have much interest in me now, but still. I'll be over the walls before dawn, and on my way to the next town. I'll hire a carriage and four and point them toward Breakwater.

I should be home by year's end.

SOURDOUGH
AND OTHER STORIES

What the ear does not hear,
will not move the heart...

THE SHADOW TREE

'Why are you so dark, Ella?' squeals Brunhilde, the king's daughter. She is thirteen years old. It is the fourth time she has asked me the question since she and her brother invaded my rooms this afternoon. They are both verminous brats, exactly the kind I seek. The other one, the youngest, is not out of swaddling cloth so I cannot yet judge him. Sometimes it is simply enough to leave them to do harm where they may.

'Yes, Ella. Why so dark? Do you roll in the dirt at night or sleep in the cinders?' Baldur is fourteen and equals his sister in unpleasantness, occasionally surpassing her. Platinum blonde hair and violet-blue eyes, they are shining, flawed metal, the worst that a royal house can offer: cruel, spiteful, selfish, beautiful, utterly confident of their position in life.

'Nigra sum sed formosa,' I answer, pleased at the blank stares they give. 'Does your tutor not teach you Latin, then?' I click my tongue, a gesture both despairing and scornful. I do not translate that I am dark but comely. 'Ignorant children, what a blot upon the world.'

Brunhilde throws herself at me, and hangs off my skirt, trying to tear the fabric. If she had eyes and mind to see beyond the ordinary, she would notice that the material was fine once, a heavy brocade embroidered with gold and silver thread. The filaments are so aged and dull now their shine is lost to all but the most observant. She begins a chant and will not stop. 'Why, why, why, why, why, why?'

'Shut up, Brunhilde.' Baldur sometimes sees further than his sister, sometimes he tries to dig. She drops away, sits on the cold floor and sulks. 'You do not know your place, Ella.'

'My place is here for the moment, for as long as I choose,' I say. I do not mention that warming their father's bed now and then gives me licence to say what I please – within measure. My position as herbalist gives me power, too. I supply the physician with the medicines upon which his reputation rests. Ladies of the court come to me for unguents to keep their skin soft, or for draughts to get rid of inconvenient pregnancies. The Queen occasionally asks for something to make her husband sleep and so relieve her of his demands for a night or two. Men want love philtres to help them do their best by their womenfolk, or to make them eloquent before the King. The Archbishop, Serenus, comes more often than most.

I have been here six months, threading my way through the life of the palace and this little city of Lodellan, which thinks itself large. Soon it will be time to go.

'You do not speak like a servant. You do not behave like a servant.'

'Yet I am a servant,' I finish curtly. 'Now, get out of my room, and take your squalling sibling with you.'

'You cannot order us about!' squeaks Brunhilde.

'I can and have. Now out, or there will be no stories tonight, nor for a sennight to come.' Here is my real power over them: the tales I tell. They have become small addicts, to our sessions and the drops of mandrake I put in their milk. The nights when I am not telling their father fables of a different sort, I spend beside their beds, recounting myths and legends to take into their dreams. Even though the children are vile, this weaving of words is a pleasure for me, and it furthers my ends. I suffer no illusions: they do not love me. As long as I provide an amusement, it will stave off the moment when they turn on me.

'Not like the one you told last night, Ella,' Baldur says warily. I shake my head, hide my smile. I gave them the history of the Erl-King and in the morning they both woke with tears on their cheeks.

'No, I'll tell you something exciting, something secret,' I promise.

When they have gone, I unlock the door to my workroom and step inside. A thin cat detaches herself from the shadows under one of the benches. She glides around my skirts, mews to be gathered up. She's black, with the greenest of eyes, tiny and frail still. I rescued her from the children a month ago; they were tormenting her in the stables, had already executed her kittens and dangled their limp bodies in front of her. For a long while, the cat wouldn't eat, but eventually I coaxed milk into her mouth and loved her into living. She is gentle and sad.

For their efforts, Brunhilde and Baldur spent two weeks vomiting and shitting, fed with one of my potions, and their sheets sprinkled with a compound that made them break out in red, itching spots.

The cat's face against mine is warm and she is soft in my hands.

I hold her like a child, and survey the room. It is dim because some of the plants and powders I work with do not like the light. It smells musty, but layered with sweetness and something bitter and dark at the very base, like rotted roses. In the end, it reminds me of home, a comfort and an ache at the same time, to remember a place and an exile from it.

Hesitantly, I uncover the mirror that waits in one corner. It's big enough to show my face and torso, faded dress, cat in arms. My skin is deep olive, burnt by the sun as I tramp the hills beyond the forest for herbs, my face an oval set with dark eyes and an unbalanced mouth – upper lip thin, the lower full. My brows are straight, and my hair as black as the cat's fur. I have the look of a gypsy, a wanderer.

I wonder if perhaps my time has passed and I can return. In hope, I touch the glass, feel it cool under my fingertips, wish that I could travel through it, through the doors between worlds, back to my own place. My exile isn't yet done. The surface remains hard, unbroken, impenetrable. The cat makes a soft noise, like sympathy. I bury my face in her fur.

* * *

The Queen seeks a sleeping draught, not for her husband this night, but for herself. She wears lines of trouble on her brow, drawn sharp around the corners of her mouth. Her eyes, the same colour she passed on to her children, seem darkened by her thoughts.

'Thank you, Ella.' She is polite and gentle and I am puzzled that she bred those two vipers. Sensing the direction of my mind, perhaps, she tells me: 'I worry about my children.'

'Madam?' I feign ignorance.

'I don't like them, Ella. I don't like my own children. What sort of mother does that make me?' Her voice holds pain and a kind of battered love.

'Quite a normal one, madam,' I tell her honestly. 'Parents see children as an extension of themselves, so when they go wrong, we often don't like them. Love them, yes, but like them, no.'

'Do I even love them? *Did* I love them?' she asks herself. 'How did they get so? They are cruel and thoughtless and selfish. I know what they did to that cat you've adopted.' She puts her face into her pale hands. 'How? Didn't I love them enough?'

'Sometimes that's where you do wrong, madam, too much love, insufficient discipline. They are spoiled, have been their whole lives.

They have been taught to think only of themselves, of no one else's desires or wants or needs. They think not to return love, but only to expect it.'

She looks at me like a coiled snake; I have gone too far.

'You asked me, madam. I answered you with truth,' I say quietly, lowering my head. She deflates and begins to weep. I try to temper her grief. 'There is the baby, madam. The smallest one may yet bring you happiness.'

I tuck the rich linens around her, whispering that the drink will help her dreams, but the posset remains untouched. She will take it, though, in her own time; she will wish for a brief oblivion. I leave. The King's page waits outside the door; I shake my head.

'Then you will do for tonight,' he tells me.

I lean close. 'It would be better for you to learn some respect. Else watch what goes into your food, my lad.' I take pleasure in the way he blanches, dip my head mockingly and make my way to the King's chambers.

He is a thin man, voracious in his appetites; amazing amounts of food disappear down his gullet but have no effect on his lean frame. He looks like an ascetic, but eats like a glutton. His hair is white-blonde, long and fine. He likes the way my dark skin looks against his pale flesh, he likes the things I do to him, fulfilling desires he dares voice to no one else. He knows that I am a well for the things he wishes to keep hidden. Funny that no one in this palace ever questions my ability to catch and keep secrets.

I think the children's shortcomings must spring from his blood. This twice-born man is not a good king.

* * *

'You're late,' accuses Brunhilde, sitting high against her puffed-up pillows, an enormous doll propped next to her like a silent sister. The doll's eyes move, the creature just barely animated by a tiny piece of soul. Baldur has crept across from his own bed and curls at the foot of his sister's like a lazy dog. The baby sleeps in a nursery elsewhere under the watchful eyes of three nurses. Governesses do not last with these older two, which is how and why I have gained such leverage.

'I was seeing to your parents. Now, hush, or there will be no tale.' I settle myself on a corner of the bed, my back resting against the carved post, my legs crossed under my skirts, my hands lying loose in my lap, waiting until the story needs them.

'I have told you before of the Robber Bridegroom and how he was defeated by a clever girl,' I begin. They nod, eyes growing wide as my voice takes hold. 'Before his demise, he was the finest thief in the land, and this is because he knew the location of a shadow tree.'

'What's a shadow tree?' they ask in unison. I put a finger against my lips to still their interruptions.

'Where is your milk? Have you had your milk?' They shake their heads and I take the jug of lukewarm liquid from the bedside stand and pour each a cup, dripping in mandrake juice from the vial in my pocket. Not enough to kill, but enough to make them sleepy and suggestible. They drink it down as I settle back in my spot.

'Shadow trees belong to the Erl-King – I have told you of him, also, and of his daughter who ran away and was punished with exile. The Erl-King's trees are his doors to the upper-earth, this is how he travels the land. But, if you know how, a shadow tree can also render you invisible.'

'How?' breathes Baldur. I knew this would pique his interest – imagine the mischief he could do if he could not be seen!

'What follows you everywhere and gives you away?' I ask.

'Your shadow,' pipes Brunhilde.

'Exactly. The Robber Bridegroom knew how to pin his shadow to the trunk – without it to give him away, he could come and go into people's homes as he pleased. He wandered in and out, doing as he would, causing great harm.'

Baldur's eyes shine. 'Is there a shadow tree near here? Do you know, Ella? Surely you must!'

I purse my lips as if to restrain the secret, which makes him all the more urgent. 'You must tell me, Ella! You must or I shall have Father *make* you tell me.'

I suppress a laugh – as if this pup could influence his father one way or another in regard to me! I feign fear and lean close. I whisper to them that *Yes, there is a shadow tree in the forest, not far from the city walls, in the clearing where they sometimes go to play, where the six standing stones wait.* I tell him it is best found in moonlight, when it will gleam like an angel's wings and, lo and behold, tonight is a full moon. I will not take them there, I tell them, and in this I am adamant. They will, I know, go without me. I tuck them into their beds, make them swear they will not go into the woods tonight and look for the tree. They promise me with lying lips. They will stray, like so many before them, and find the shadow tree, which will sense the mandrake in their veins. It will open the door in its trunk and the children, drugged and malleable, will wander in and down into the darkness. They will make the journey I cannot.

After leaving the room, I watch, pressing myself into an angle where corridor meets corridor. The door opens and they slip out, luminous in the dark, their hair washed by the lambent moonlight pouring in through the high windows. They walk down the hallway, now in shadow, now in light, disappearing and reappearing like ghosts. Turning right they escape my view, taking the passageway that leads into a tiny palace garden. In the garden is a folly, made like a miniature castle, and in its floor is a trapdoor, which leads to a tunnel that comes up in the forest outside the city walls. I wait until I hear the faint click of the latch behind them, then step from the shadows.

Another does the same, leaving her hiding place. In the Queen's hand is the posset I gave her. We stare at each other for a long time, so long that the cold begins to seep up from the flagstones into my feet. Perhaps we'll both freeze here forever. At last, she raises the cup to her lips and drinks, her eyes never leaving mine. She nods, backs away, and turns to continue the journey to her bedchamber.

I return to their father's bed and wake him with strange kisses; when his children go missing, what better alibi for me than the King?

Soon I will make my way to another palace, another castle, to observe and judge the royal children who dwell therein. Soon I may start again to tell the story of the shadow tree. I will travel for as long as I must, telling my tales, collecting children to pay my fare back across the dark path; staying in one place only until the rumours grow too loud and too frequent. Soon, I hope, my father will forgive me. Soon, I hope, the Erl-King will declare my exile at an end, my escape from his realm pardoned. Soon, I hope, I will be allowed to go home.

GALLOWBERRIES

There were too many apples.

Far too many for the age of the trees, the time of year and the brevity of my stay. The orchard was small, but every branch fair drooped with fat fruits, boughs hung low and heavy. I, perched atop a rickety ladder, my apron filled with fragrant balls of red, sang loudly. What I harvested would not, could not have been there but for my magic. I was entirely pleased with myself.

'Good day, mistress.'

His voice startled me.

Tall, olive-skinned and handsome, his expression was too dour and weary for his youth. His clothes, I noticed in the moment before I tried to climb down too fast, were sombre and travel-stained. I got tangled in my skirts and twisted a foot on one of the rungs and fell. Apples flew like hard rain.

Instead of crashing to the ground I was caught mid-flight. I felt muscles and the rub of rough fabric; the smell of man and horse was strong. He held me a moment longer than he needed to then put me carefully on my feet. I tried to stand but my ankle gave way and I found myself scooped up again.

'May I?' he asked belatedly and I nodded assent, fluttering my eyelashes. I wrapped my arms around him. The stiff white collar of his shirt was bright against the black of his jacket. Gently I touched the dark curls at the nape of his neck. He pretended not to notice, but from beneath lowered lids I could spy him stealing glances at me.

We rounded the corner to see Dowsabel feeding carrots to a long-legged ebony horse. She gave a cry and hurried forward.

'Bring her inside. What have you done, Gideon Cotton? Patience, are you all right?'

I nodded, surprised that she knew him and addressed him so familiarly. I had not seen many visitors in the time I'd been with her, mainly tinkers and travelling salesmen. Then again, a lack of callers did not mean a lack of acquaintances. Dowsabel may well have lived on the fringe of Bitterwood, but it stood to reason that the townspeople knew of her and she of them.

She led him into the parlour and he put me gently on a long couch. He lifted both of my legs onto the worn padding, then pushed my skirts up to my knees. The right ankle seemed to swell even as we watched, the flesh hot and ruddy. His hands touched the heated skin and I shivered, as much from excitement as from the coolness of his palms. Dowsabel made a disapproving sound and bustled him aside.

He blushed and stood awkwardly. His chin was raised as if to distance himself from the proceedings. I swallowed a smile.

'What happened, Patience? Did he hurt you?' Her words were harsh but her gaze told me it was more a joke than anything else; that she wanted to see how much leverage she might get out of his discomfort.

'No, Dowsabel. He startled me, but I fell through my own clumsiness.' I gave him the full force of my green eyes and he blushed ever darker. She had her back to him and shot me a grin he could not see. She put her slim hands around my ankle and I gasped for dramatic effect, all out of proportion to the pain I actually felt. The young man started guiltily.

Dowsabel rose and gazed at him. 'Are you satisfied? I told you before you charged off into the orchard there is only myself and my young cousin, come to help while my husband is away.'

The lies sweetly rolled off her tongue. I noticed his eyebrows raised at the word "husband", but otherwise he had the conscience to look ashamed.

'My apologies, goodwife. I have become – obsessive in my pursuit and now I have caused injury.' His shoulders sagged.

'What do you seek?' I asked, although I thought I knew the answer.

'Someone who fled Bitterwood three months ago.'

'Man, woman, girl, boy? Many pass through the town, Gideon, so you need to be more specific.' She laughed and annoyance at the thought that this woman did not take him seriously flew over his handsome face.

'How can you be ignorant of what happened, goodwife?'

'You know very well, Gideon Cotton. Who comes to exchange news, good or bad, with the likes of me?' she asked sternly, and he flinched. 'So, I ask again: who do you seek?'

'I don't know. I don't even know if the person exists. My father and the town council hanged – or tried to hang – a witch. Ever since that day our families have been afflicted – wells were poisoned. My parents and younger brother died. Cows were made barren and the fields are rotten with dead crops. I suspect she had an accomplice or a familiar, someone left behind to take revenge on us.'

'What happened to the woman?' I asked quietly.

'She disappeared. One moment she was there, the next gone. Some devilry.'

'So, why do you not think it was *she* who cursed you and yours? Why some invisible familiar?' Dowsabel's face had lost its customary gentleness but I couldn't tell if she disapproved of him or the possible escapee.

'I… we…' It seemed this had not occurred to him. She touched his arm and his face cleared. Apparently Dowsabel was not without her own magic. I had not suspected.

'Let me set your mind at ease, Gideon.' She touched his forehead, speaking low. 'We have seen none such as you have described, neither man nor woman, maid nor lad.'

He stood for a moment, enchanted. I was as transfixed by her as he was. Dowsabel smiled once more and said, 'There is only we two.'

He stared at me and even though I knew he could not identify me, could not possibly know *anything*, I held my breath and felt sweat prickle my palms. At last he shook his head and tried a limp smile, which Dowsabel returned, hers brilliant and designed to dazzle. 'Would you like refreshment before you continue on your way?'

'No. No, I thank you, goodwife. I have been hunting rumour for so long I no longer know how to behave civilly. You are wise – it must have been the witch and there will be no finding a woman who can disappear at will.'

* * *

The fruits grow lush and glossy, uniformly round and enticing, but they have no smell, which may make you suspect something is wrong. When you bite into them, you *know*. Perhaps they are so foul because they contain the essence of transformation, of ultimate change. The gallowberries taste, without exception, of rotting flesh and spent seed – their garden lies at a crossroads, under the gallows where criminals are hanged. The lives of such men shudder to a halt, their last breath and last pleasure simultaneous. With time the bodies rot, wind, rain, sun, air taking their toll on ephemeral flesh.

They break down, these gallowscrows, to all component parts – some of them are more useful this way. That is why my mother spent one of her evenings sixteen years ago lying beneath a gibbet, skirts about her waist, muttering words that made sense to few, but would have earned her a noose all of her own. The dead ones, she told me when I was old enough to understand, cause you far less trouble and seldom want anything in return. She was not beautiful, Wynne Sykes, and I think perhaps she found robbing the deceased easier than risking rejection. My looks, I was assured, came from a dead man; not his only gift.

'Crossroads, Patience,' my mother said one day as she gathered bright berries, 'are funny things. Gateways to all sorts of places and not just north, south, east, or west.' She held up one of the gallowberries with a grin. 'And these can help unlock all manner of gates.'

So, when she was finally caught, some months later, cutting the hand from a hanged man, she was able to escape the rope and the salivating burghers who wanted to see her last choking moments. I watched from my roost in a tree. She stepped carefully out of the cart they'd brought her in, keeping her eyes on the road, looking for a shift in the air, for an almost imperceptible line that would tell her a crossing space was there.

I knew by her face when she'd found it, the half-smile twitching her lips, and the toss of her thin, pale hair. She popped one of the gallowberries she habitually carried into her mouth. As she moved forward, she spoke a word or two, bit down hard and blinked out of existence. Gone just like that, leaving seven confused and terrified men milling about, and me lying along a branch, with a sense of satisfaction and loss.

Take that, you bastards, I thought viciously. I was angry, but not so angry that I came down before they had all gone back to their cosy homes and their warm, ample wives and their smug, self-righteous town. I stood on the spot where she'd disappeared then sat in the dirt, searching for the path she had taken. It was beyond my pitiful abilities, though. She never taught me how to find those doorways, never taught me the words that acted as keys to other places.

Eventually I knew it was time to move on, that the ache of being left behind would work against me were I to give in to it. To be found where the witch had last been seen – who knew what the fearful, tiny-minded clowns of Bitterwood might make of that?

In the velvet darkness I visited the houses of those seven *foremost* men, the members of the town council, who'd judged my mother and brought her to the crossroads. The night before her hanging, I sneaked to the back window of the place where they'd held her. Her jailer, she'd whispered to me out of the bars of the cell, had been kind, as had his wife. I was instructed not to touch them. The seven, though, those fine upstanding citizens, were to be taken care of – whether I punished them or their families was irrelevant. Those left untouched would live in guilt and fear of what might visit them in times to come; any future misfortune would be viewed as something resulting from this day's work. My mother had a fine mind for revenge.

I moved through the blackness like a fish through water, my eyes accustomed, pupils widening to swallow all the white. Perhaps this is the result of my strange conception, perhaps this is my father's dead gift to me: the ability to see like a cat or a creature of under-earth, and other things besides. I poisoned wells at three of the houses. At the next two homes, I spoke lovingly to the cows as I rubbed their udders with an oil to curdle the milk therein and I fed them a mix of grasses and herbs to render them barren. At the last two residences, I stood at one end of the fields, held a powder of salt and sulphur, breathed malignant words across my palm and blew. Caught by eldritch winds, the particles drifted across the earth to settle into the soil, to kill the crops and prevent any fresh ones.

I was exhausted. Unlike white magic, which rewards its maker as well as its object, malign magic sucks the strength out of you. I knew I had to find somewhere to hide, to lie low before the sun rose and my deeds were discovered. If I tried to run, drained as I was, they would hunt me down as surely as day follows night; but if I stayed close, hid in plain sight, I would have a good chance of surviving. No one had seen me, no one knew about me but if I were discovered walking determinedly away from the town with its ill-water and ruined livestock then questions would be asked. I did not want to return to the hut in which my mother and I had spent our last two nights together. I did not want to meet the memories that would surely wait for me there.

Once anger, grief and vigilance were dulled by time and fear, then I might again take to the roads.

I found a barn on the outskirts of town. It was rundown and inhabited by a few scrawny cows and ancient chickens, but the straw in the hayloft was fresh and soft. It would give me a relatively safe haven for the days I needed. I slept the sleep of the just – or the vengeful, depending on your viewpoint – and woke feeling refreshed and hungry.

In the darkness I hadn't really taken in the state of the house to which the barn belonged, but I wasn't entirely surprised to see it was equally depleted. A two-storey manor with grubby windows and shingles missing from the roof. The overgrown garden was beautiful though, filled with roses and jasmine, magnolias and the like. It was not close to its neighbours and was mostly shielded from view by tall hedges and large trees. I watched the yard between the cracks in the walls. The only activity was that of a single woman, perhaps in her thirties, with the bump of a child beginning to show. No sign of a husband or children, no sign of servants. I observed until the growling of my stomach got too loud to ignore. If nothing else I could beg stale bread; better though if I stole it, if no one saw me.

I waited until the woman headed to the small orchard set behind the house.

The cool of the stone-flagged kitchen welcomed me. I could smell fresh bread, just out of the oven. My nose led me to it, cooling on the bench. As my eyes adjusted to the dimness I saw the room was clean and tidy. A vase with bright yellow flowers sat in the middle of a rough table. Pots and pans, dented with age but scrubbed bright, hung from nails on beams above my head, and a tidy sideboard housed a collection of unmatched crockery. Pieces of coloured glass sat along the window sill eating the sunlight and throwing brilliantly tinted shafts around the room. A fireplace was cut deep into the wall and an iron cauldron hung over the cold remains of a fire.

I was reaching for the warm loaf when there was a small scream and the sound of something shattering.

Turning, I saw the woman silhouetted in the doorway. I stepped into the patch of light coming through the window so she would see me fully and know me to be no threat. I looked like a starveling cat, huge eyes, hollow cheeks and dark hair; no danger at all.

She gave a sigh, not angry but surprised. 'Oh, you did give me a start!'

I took heart and spoke. 'I'm sorry.' I bent down to help scoop up the pieces of broken plate. 'I'm so hungry,' I said as I carefully put the smaller shards onto the biggest one, trying not to cut myself.

'You had only to ask.' Her tone was reproving but she smiled and I could see she was older than I first thought. Her hair shone, a mix of gold and silver and grey. She must have been over forty. She put a hand to the small of her back and rubbed ruefully. 'You'll be wanting something to drink with that, I'd imagine.'

I told her I was alone in the world, travelling to the cathedral-city of Lodellan to look for work. She said her name was Dowsabel and she did not question me too closely. Just a few days, I begged of her, and she readily agreed. I think she was glad of company.

* * *

'He will return, you know.'

Dowsabel looked tired and old. She sat back in the armchair and pulled a knitted rug over her lap. I gave her a mug of tea; scents of cinnamon and ginger rose from it. Night had fallen and my ankle was strapped tight. I curled into a seat across the fire from her, hands wrapped around my own beverage – this one steeping herbs to numb pain.

I shook my head. 'He has no reason to – unless you put him under a spell,' I said archly. 'All big eyes and wide smiles, glamouring him so.'

'Is that the thanks I get?' She laughed. 'For saving your worthless hide, little witch?'

'A familiar! As if I'm a cat or a toad an old woman carries around in her pocket!' I took umbrage at that slight. 'Did you know? When first I came?' I asked, curious. *I* had not known *her* for what she was. Now here we were, our secret selves exposed.

She shook her head. 'Not at first, Patience. No, not at first, but when the animals began to prosper I suspected. When the apples kept coming, I knew.'

'Why did you not cast those spells yourself?' I asked.

'Those are not my magics,' she explained, astonished by my ignorance. 'What did your mother teach you?'

I stared at my hands; they looked so harmless just holding that cup. 'Revenge,' I said and told her my life, letting it spill out, from my unconventional birth to the recent blood on those self-same hands.

She was quiet for a while. 'My strength lies in glamours, in making people see what I want them to see.' She caught my look and laughed. 'Oh, not on you! You'd peer straight through that. Our kind knows very quickly when she's being glamoured – we do not react well to a rosy view of the world! It makes us suspicious.'

I snorted.

'And you punished the town?'

I nodded. 'The innocent and the guilty, it seems.'

'And your mother escaped?' she said cautiously.

'She knew the roads – the *other* roads. Never taught me though,' I muttered as memories of Wynne forced themselves to the surface. 'Left me behind to wander this world.'

'Perhaps her time here was done. And not everyone, Patience, can walk those roads. There's only a select few of our kind who know the ways through and the paths in between, and are strong enough for those journeys.' She reached across the gap between our chairs and patted my hand. 'Your mother couldn't take you with her.'

'Will she come back?'

Dowsabel shook her head. 'Step through the door and there is no returning. You pass by only once.'

I nodded, unsure whether to grieve or not. The few days I'd begged of Dowsabel had stretched, as if by magic into weeks, then months. I'd grown comfortable with a life in one place. The hole Wynne left had been quickly filled by my new friend. I had, I must admit, almost forgotten that I once had another mother. A life of hardship was softened and faded by the time I spent at the manor, and happy remembrances of myself as Wynne Sykes' daughter were few and far between. In my mind a new dam superimposed herself over the old: Dowsabel, kindly and caring, who never let me go hungry, who did not teach me to turn my skills into strange arts, who did not need me to hate and mistrust the world around me.

I'd known my life had been hard, but it was *all* I'd known. I realised that it had been an existence of deprivation, but I'd had nothing else to judge it by and thus find it wanting. *Soft cats*, my mother used to sneer at other people and I'd agree with her. Now I slept in a feather bed. I had more than one dress (Dowsabel's cast-offs, but better than my one gown with fabric so old that in places black had faded to green). I was warm and I was fed. I wore pliable leather boots Dowsabel said were too small for her. I no longer needed my feet filthy and bare to warn me that vibrations in the road meant a cart or carriage or horses so I should hide in the undergrowth; that damp soil might mean good crops, but I would leave a trail if I stole from an orchard.

I had found comfort and care and I had no desire to leave it. I thought perhaps I might fit into a normal sort of life, become a normal sort of girl. I *wanted*, heaven help me, to be a normal sort of girl. I did not want to practise the dark things I was so used to; I did not think to use magic for harm anymore. Dowsabel taught me lessons that almost took.

She had stopped speaking but, involved in my own thoughts, I did not realise it until she heaved herself to her feet. 'Come. Let's go for a walk.'

'It's late and you're tired and my ankle hurts,' I complained.

'And yet this must be done by moonlight. Come along, little liar, little witch.'

I pouted but complied. She linked her arm with mine as we walked through the overgrown garden and across the fields beneath an autumn moon. I exaggerated my limp and she laughed. The smell of apples was strong on the breeze.

'That man,' she said once again, 'will come back. I saw the look on his face and I saw the look on *your* face. He will come a-courting.'

'Who is Gideon Cotton when he's at home?' I asked, curiosity getting the better of me.

'His *father*,' she said pointedly, 'was a judge and on the town council – as you well know. Gideon has been studying law, although I think now he will take his father's position if he has not already done so. Bitterwood does love its lawgivers.'

'I killed his parents,' I repeated so we might both hear it aloud and remember.

'And his younger brother,' she reminded.

'I'm a murderess,' I said.

'*He* doesn't know that.'

'One day, he will see it in my face.'

'You'd be surprised how much you can hide from a man, Patience, and for how long.' We stopped at a tightly clustered copse, just before the hedgerows began. 'What do you see?'

I glanced around and up. 'Sky, moon, trees.'

'Look down. What there?'

I stared at the ground. Beneath the thick grass I could see the earth had been churned and dug over, not recently, but its disarray was evident to my night-eyes. I peered deep and found the rotting corpse, a man by the look of the clothes, worms still playing in his flesh.

Dowsabel breathed: 'Do you see him?'

I nodded.

'I thought as much,' she said with satisfaction.

'Is he your husband? Did you do it?'

'No and yes. It was many years before my parents would let me marry, would let me leave them – you can see I am not in the first flush of youth! On my way to my wedding I was… stolen by the man who lived here. Something in him made him proof against my power. Somehow he saw *through* and I could not change him.' She shook her head. 'By the time my family found me I was thoroughly ruined. I could have gone home but to what purpose? What place? I was his whore whether I willed it or no. I stayed here because I thought I deserved nothing better.'

'What happened? Is he the baby's father?'

She nodded. 'I stayed. I stayed for five years and never fell pregnant. He drank. One night not so long ago he hit me once too often. I grabbed a candlestick – one of those silver ones you polish so assiduously – and hit him back. I almost panicked, almost ran, but I remembered what I could do, how most people do not look beyond the glamours I put in front of them. I thought on how few visitors came, how badly they regarded this house. Only Gideon's father asked me where my *husband* was and no one questioned me after I'd said he'd gone away. I thought then perhaps I could go home but…'

'The baby?'

'The baby.'

'Would your family not take you back?

'*Before* I was simply ruined, but to bring them a child – proof of my whoring? No, I would not do that, to either them or myself. Or the child.'

We turned away and walked back to the warmth of the manor. I wondered that she could continue living there after what had happened to her. Perhaps sensing the direction of my thoughts, she said, 'I earned this house. No matter what happened to me here – or perhaps because of it. It's the one place I have that is *mine*.'

* * *

The days turned in upon themselves, the nights lengthened and winter threatened to oust autumn without making good. Dowsabel said I must stay (as if I ever looked like leaving!) for it was not safe to take to the roads with such weather coming on. There would be snow and I would be lost. I did not tell her I had lived through worse, that Wynne and I had tramped through snow drifts that sometimes rose above our heads. We had come so close to freezing that I knew death did not have a chill breath, but a hot one that made you feel consumed.

I thanked her and agreed to stay, telling her she was right.

She was right, too, with much smugness, about Gideon.

He returned many times, always with gifts: flowers, jewellery, ribbons. He paid me attention and listened when I spoke. I had known men before, when starvation threatened and survival left no other courses. They had meant nothing, but a heart unused to kindness is an easy victim for love.

'The witch,' I said to him tentatively. Our bodies were still slick with each other's sweat and I could taste him on my lips. I ran my fingers across the broad bas-relief of his chest, then down the tight stomach muscles until his hand stopped mine and I grinned.

'I swear, Patience, you are insatiable.'

'I did not hear you complaining before,' I said pertly.

'Not a complaint, my darling, merely an observation and a plea for respite so I may gather my strength.' The fingers of his other hand caressed my shoulder and his lips moved against my hair. I could feel him breathing deeply, taking in the scent of me. Even though I was without the magic of glamour, the art of seduction served me equally well.

I kissed his chest and angled my head to look at him, slanting my eyes.

'The witch,' I repeated unable to let the subject go. 'What was her crime? Had she harmed anyone?'

'She found was cutting a hand from a gallowscrow.'

'And?' I asked, all innocence as if I had not been trained to do the very same thing. 'She'd not actually *done* anything?'

'She hardly needed to, her intent was very clear.' His tone became impatient. 'They take the limbs and make foul things – hands of glory. A candle is placed on each finger and once lit, it will put all those who slumber into the deepest of sleep. Not a one of them can wake while the witch enters the house and does what she will, murdering people in their beds. She'd have used it herself or sold it to some blackguard.'

My mother would have used the hand to steal, certainly, never to kill though, not without provocation at any rate.

'Oh,' I said, lamely.

'Her kind are a blight on this earth.' He was warming to his theme; I felt anger coursing through him. He could not realise how all woman are, in one way or another, 'her kind', even his dear departed mother. 'Three members of my family are dead by her hand and they had done *nothing*.'

Mother and brother blameless, perhaps, but Father had reaped his just reward.

I kept my own ire in check, felt it balanced by sadness that this would always be between us. 'I know, my heart, I know. You are right.'

I tasted my own lies and found them rich and rotten. I rose up over him and put my mouth to his, distracting him the best way I knew how, thinking it was love.

* * *

I wondered where he told his remaining family (two sisters, one other brother, I was advised by Dowsabel) he went when he came to me. He would not have been honest. I knew enough of men to divine there was never marriage in his plans; I was not fool enough to think that.

Dowsabel informed me of the milk-pale girl his father had chosen for him, the priest's niece (some whispered his daughter, but not too loudly), and a very suitable match. When Dowsabel went into the town for the things we could not make or grow ourselves, people talked around her if not to her. She gleaned her knowledge thus, picking through the chatter and taking what interested her as if selecting the best grains from the chaff. She told me, too, when their wedding date had been set.

I would tease Gideon about it. Ask him how he would give me up when he'd wed his betrothed. He did not like to speak of it and did not like to be tormented, but I did not stop. Deep inside I wanted to be a chosen girl. Deep inside it made me angry that he assumed I would always be waiting for him. That the manor was a house of patient whores and I would be another woman as compliant as Dowsabel seemed. So my teasing had an edge and a heat and the longer he and I were together, the sharper I became in my pricking of him. More and more often he left in anger.

One morning I made one of my infrequent trips into the town. Dowsabel was unwell, coming so close to her time, and it appeared the effort of carrying the child had eaten all of her reserves. My friend looked like a ghost, a shadow, all of her vital force turned inward and sucked up by the parasite inside. She was craving honey cakes from the market. She was very pale when she sent me off.

'Will you be all right?' I worried. She laughed, but the sound was weak.

‘Of course, little witch. I’ve not lived this long to shuffle off now. Go! I’ve a mind for those cakes.’

A quick foray, I thought, straight to the stall and Mrs Hensley the baker’s wife, who didn’t look unkindly upon us. She often wore marks on her face, where Mr Hensley had written his displeasure. I handed her the bundle of herbs sewn into a small pillow no bigger than my hand (to take down swelling and suck the darkness out of bruises). She stuffed it quickly into the pocket of her apron and gave me a box of pastries in exchange.

I turned to go and saw them across the square.

Gideon, all swarthy-handsome, beside him a girl with the whitest hair I’d ever seen and a face untouched by any kind of hardship – it rendered her blank as a doll. She smiled at him and my heart twisted when he smiled back. Behind trailed his family.

The oldest girl, Anna, in her early thirties, eyed everything and everyone unpleasantly, picking things up from trestle tables and putting them down again, finding them wanting as a matter of course. She was pretty but dissatisfaction had made thin roads on her face and piety had rendered her features hard as if to ruin their attraction. The younger one, Elise, not quite flowering, followed her sister’s lead and showed every sign of becoming another such a one. And the boy, Balthazar, not yet a man, still sullen; his eyes followed not just other women, but also his sisters and his brother’s betrothed.

But I took that in quickly and all my attention returned to Gideon. The hardest thing you will ever see is your lover with the ones who possess him. The worst thing you will ever feel is the knowledge that *you* do not own him, that he will never be yours and that you have only ever been loaned a tiny part of him. That he is too much a coward to love you fully and openly; that you will always be hidden like a dark secret; and that as long as you let him, he will continue this way because he has everything and he cares not a jot that you have nothing but that which he deigns to give. And if you are lucky, oh so lucky, you will realise this and, though it breaks your heart, you will choose to walk away. You will leave him to a pallid existence and he will live forever with your contempt painted on his soul. That is the only power you ever have.

He felt my eyes upon him and I watched as he looked about for me; found me; blinked; looked away. There is always a point where lovers fail each other, one or the other or both. Funny how it feels like a broken heart will kill you, and it will if you let it; the milk-bride would have curled up and died, but *I* was not that sort of girl.

* * *

The manor was deathly quiet when I stepped inside.

I found Dowsabel upstairs in her room. She was sitting in a pool of blood, leaning against the bed she had failed to reach when the pains began.

I lifted her with difficulty and helped her lie upon the coverlet. Terror settled in my chest as I followed her gasped instructions. She was too old to be carrying this child. There was not enough life for both of them and in that moment as she lay gazing up at me, we both knew it.

'Look after her,' she begged, even though the babe had not yet shown itself to be girl or boy. She grasped my arm and held on with surprising strength. I nodded.

'Promise me,' she insisted and her desperation was awful. Her nails broke through my skin. 'Say it. Say you will look after her and she will come to no harm. *Promise* it.'

I nodded again. 'I promise. I swear. But you will get well, Dowsabel, you will. Some moments of pain and then you will sleep and all will be well.' Lies from my lips once more. She gave me a sad smile.

She bled a lot during the birth. I knew only small things my mother had taught me, how to stem the blood, which herbs and mosses would stop the flow and reduce fever. But I didn't know enough to save her, only enough to slow her death.

The child came, a pale wight of a daughter, who mewled for her mother's milk even as Dowsabel bled out. She held the baby weakly to her breast and the tiny girl latched on, sucking determinedly as if she knew time was short.

Weeping, I stretched out on the bed beside my friend and stroked her hair. She gave me a frail, beautiful smile and named her daughter, 'Olwen.'

I slid one arm under Dowsabel's head and curled the other over her to help hold the infant. We fell asleep that way.

In the morning Dowsabel was as cold as the tears on my cheeks. Olwen wailed. I picked her up and held her close; she was hungry but I knew enough not to put her to her mother's breast to see what she might drain from there. No child should drink from its mother's death. I milked one of the cows and dripped the warm liquid into the baby's eager mouth. She screwed up her face at the taste but drank nonetheless. Sated, Olwen slept.

I washed my foster-mother's body and laid her out, dressing her in her finest gown and then taking a long linen sheet and wrapping her around, but I did not cover her face. I did not want her to feel alone in that final darkness. I had not been able to perform this service for my own mother, but I was able to do it for Dowsabel and I felt in some way that I honoured them both. The simple rhythm of the offices of death gave me something to do, a way to distract myself.

I whispered to her that I remembered my promise and I would see that Olwen was taken care of, that she had a home and someone who loved her.

* * *

The grave was not deep for the ground had begun to harden with the oncoming cold. A mound reared up over Dowsabel's body. I did not think she would have appreciated lying with Olwen's father, once more all unwilling. It was late afternoon by the time I'd dug over a piece of earth in the garden where she would lie with the blossoms she'd so adored, all the things she'd taken such time and effort to nurture. When the weather changed and the flowers bloomed, she would be content. I had no words to give, no faith to suggest comfort.

I held Olwen and felt the weight of her gaze on my face. My tears dripped into her mouth. I could see her tiny lips moving, her tongue exploring the salty bitterness. She was too young to know why I cried; she was too young to know that the soul had been stripped out of her home.

I had made my promise to Dowsabel to look after her daughter. My kind have our own rituals, more effective than pouring water over a baby's head.

Upstairs in Dowsabel's empty room, I placed Olwen on the bed and took a knife of bone and iron from my pocket and sliced my thumb, just a small cut. Blood welled and I pushed the digit into the baby's mouth. She suckled as if it were a teat filled with milk. This was the best protection I could give her.

'Blood of magic, blood of my heart, bless this child.'

A gasp interrupted. Gideon stood at the door, staring.

The look on his face, the fear in his eyes. I knew all he saw now was a crone, a witch, something he hated. He saw his parents and brother dying in front of him and he divined my hand in the whole sordid tale. The woman who'd murdered his family, then warmed his bed, who'd deceived him – it didn't matter that I did truly love him. It didn't matter. He looked as though a hole had been punched through him.

The window was open behind me to let in fresh air. I could not take Olwen, could not flee and hold her at the same time – and all I could think of was to run. He would not hurt her. She would be safe. I *hoped* she would be safe.

I flung myself from the casement, and swung onto the trellis that clung to the front of the manor; roses covered its struts. Thorns pierced my palms, sliced my torso and thighs. I let go when the pain got too much and fell. My ankle protested at the impact, but in seconds I was running, engraved with scratches and embossed with bruises, aching but whole, and haring across the fields as fast as I could. The sun dropped swiftly and once I was among the trees only my peculiar eyesight kept me from falling over roots and debris.

Gideon would go to the town council. He would summon the priest and the constable and they would plot how to murder me. In the morning they would come with dogs. They would not hunt me at night, for fear that if confronted in my element they would all be lost. The battered copy of Murcianus' *Magica* my mother once carried cautioned 'Hunt not a witch in darkness.'

They would be huddled inside, planning and praying. Would they expect me to run? I had not last time. Surely no one would think me fool enough to stay again. There was one place I might be able to hide, if only for the few hours I needed. I had managed to stuff my knife in the pocket of my dress, even more miraculously I had managed to not stab myself as I fell. I would need it.

I stumbled as the woods broke abruptly to display a crossroads, a gibbet and three gallowscrows swinging in the gentle breeze.

* * *

The hut looked the same.

It looked safe.

I circled it twice, making sure no one else had taken up residence. There are places where my kind may find rest, where supplies are kept, where we might prepare for a task. Word of them is passed one woman to another.

Signs and sigils were scratched into the door and its frame; they helped render it less obvious to those who did not know it was there – they made the eye slide away. If you knew what you were looking for, though, if you knew where and *how* to look you might find refuge. If they came with dogs I was not sure the wards would keep the beasts at bay; might confuse them, yes, but for how long? Every hour I stayed risked more and more; I had to be well gone before morning.

All the things I needed would be inside. All the ingredients I thought I'd never use again. All the ingredients but the one I had to bring myself.

Hacking off a man's limb, even when he was dead, was not easily done.

I chose the freshest of the gallowscrows and set about taking his left hand. The sinister, the best one for my purpose. He was still hanging and it was difficult to hold him still enough to do what was needed, but ultimately I managed it, weeping all the while.

Now I waited outside the hut, putting off the moment. Night held me close, draped itself around me like a second skin, but nonetheless I was scared, listening hard for any sound. I held my breath and pushed open the door.

Empty and cold, the dust was undisturbed and covered any trace that I'd ever been here before. But there was Wynne's book, her copy of *Magica*, abandoned all those months ago and open at the very page she had required then and I required now. I pulled jars from the shelves, placed the hand on the uneven table, found a pair of leather gloves, thin with age, and fat-yellow candles in a wooden box that smelled like long-gone spices.

I worked quickly but carefully, uncertain that I could make it effective. My haste scared me, but I had no choice. While I waited for the thing to set, even though I was spent, I turned my attention to one last potion. My final defence; I pulled the gallowberries from my pocket.

* * *

I knew Gideon's house; the judge's house where I'd dripped poison into the well. I knew there was an orphanage, too, and I would have gone straight there but for an instinct that made me climb a tall tree in the garden of Gideon's home and watch the windows. I was quickly rewarded. Olwen was there, wrapped in sombre grey blankets as if they were trying to leech the joy out of her. Gideon's older sister carried the baby around, fed her, all the while her face set with nothing more than duty. No sign of affection, not even a flicker. This was cold charity.

I waited. I waited until the candles and lanterns had been snuffed, until I could detect no movement inside their fine abode, until I thought them asleep. I stood at the back door and lit all the fingers on the hanged man's hand.

The lock was easy, giving up under a simple spell and a breath of holly-ash that I blew into the aperture. I was careful as I moved through the corridors, the place where my sins had taken root. I traversed its rooms like a ghost, looking for the child I'd left behind, trying to honour the promise I'd made and already broken once.

She was in a bedroom at the top of the stairs. I entered quickly and closed the door behind me. She whimpered in her sleep, but the witchery of my candle kept her from waking. I set the hand on a chest of drawers and picked her up, warming her with the heat of my body and folding the blankets around her more tightly. What kindness would she find here? Would they keep her? Raise her as a servant? She deserved better. She deserved freedom. She deserved to know joy.

'Hush,' I whispered and she subsided into a deeper rest.

I reached out to pick up the hand and watched as the flames on top of the finger-candles fluttered. The door to the room had opened.

Once again, Gideon stood in a doorway, cutting off my escape. The light made his face look hollow, his eyes black and empty. Either he had not slept and so escaped the effects of my spell, or he was one of those who were proof against such things. Or perhaps the sense of me reached into his sleep and woke him. But there was no love there, no tenderness.

'You,' he spat and it felt like a slap in the face from one who'd said my name so sweetly. But this was what I had feared; this was what I had expected. Why was I surprised? 'Witch.'

I nodded. I put Olwen back in her crib and faced him once more. 'Yes.'

'You killed my parents, my brother.'

'And your father took my mother from me.'

'Another witch.' How he hated us! Me. How he hated *me*.

'And no harm to anyone.'

'Witch!' And I knew there would be no reasoning with him. His hatred and fear were burning inside him, feeding on one another. I glided toward him, slowly as a snake charms a bird. He did not move away, although I know he wanted to; he wanted to fall back beneath my advance but that would have been *openly* cowardly and weak. It made me smile, just barely. I stood close, so close. He neither flinched, nor softened.

'You won't escape this time.'

'Yes,' I said, 'I will.'

'I'll follow you.'

'I know,' I replied softly.

'I'll see you hanged,' he swore.

'No, you won't,' I soothed. 'I'm sorry, my love, truly sorry.'

I had slipped my gloved hand into the pocket of my skirt and unstoppered the small vial there. It tipped and the greasy fluid poured onto the glove. I reached up and touched his face. Determined not to falter, he felt too late the oily damp of the unguent. A small silver-grey smear was left behind, not much, but enough. His eyes widened and I spoke one word.

'*Canis.*'

There was nothing more from him, no last words of affection or loathing. He dropped to all fours and there were horrible moments while his bones cracked and reshaped, his skeleton reformed and a thick golden fur broke out all over his body. The grunts of pain he made became whimpers. He sat on his hind legs and looked up at me with amber eyes, no longer himself. Gideon as he was had gone, memory replaced by that of an animal, no recollections of love or hate, merely a loyalty he could neither understand nor question. I peeled off my gloves and ran my hands through his thick pelt. Soft and warm and comforting. He whimpered again and licked at my palms.

'Fenric,' I said. I could never call him *Gideon* again. He was remade and renamed. I rose and scooped up Olwen once more and bound her to my chest. I collected the glory hand and then clicked my fingers at the beast. 'Come.'

We walked from the slumbering house into the darkened streets. We walked into the maw of winter.

LITTLE RADISH

All I ever wanted was the tower.

I dreamt of it when night coloured the sky. When the sun threw gilded light over everything, I would lose myself in daydreams of the serenity of stone resting upon stone. Since I was small, the thought of it had been with me.

There was no such structure near my home. Not even a castle. We lived so deep in the woods there were only cottages scattered here and there. Neighbours were few and far between: woodsmen; old women deserted by their families, despised and feared; brigands; folk who simply liked the peaceful lull.

My mother loved radishes beyond reason, so it's only proper that I should have a mania all of my own.

I lived in quietude, but I longed for utter silence. I imagined an incomparable stillness, held in by granite, a barrier that nothing could penetrate. I desired air untroubled by the vibrations of sound, an impregnable vacuum.

My parents did not understand. Distance grew between us. We could sit in the same room yet not speak, not touch, not even breathe in time. They gave up trying to communicate with me and I happily wrapped myself in the fabric of utter quiet. My siblings delighted in making noise, rough and tumble like puppies. I would flee to the forest to sit and eat the *hush* of it all.

When I was sixteen I wandered from home. I would, I thought, find the tower – it *must* be there, I could not simply have imagined it. Whatever it cost me, I would find it, for that was where I belonged.

* * *

I spent four days lost before I stumbled into a clearing. A cottage sat, like a creature waiting for something to come; perhaps it wanted prey, perhaps company. Hunger and thirst propelled me and I fell against the door with a cry, crumpling to the stoop.

An old woman peered down at me. A walking stick held her

upright. She wore a dress that had once been the colour of dark leaves but had been washed back to a faded green, a cap, and an apron stained with yellows and reds. Her glasses were smudged and she wrinkled her nose to move them back into position on her face.

'Who are you?' she croaked. She cleared her throat and tried again, the melodious timbre restored. 'Sorry. Who are you?'

'Rapunzel,' I replied. She smiled.

'Is your mother the one who's nuts about radishes?'

I nodded wearily.

'Come in. I'm Sybille.'

She fed me thick, buttery cheese with stodgy bread and gave me tea to drink. When I had finished wolfing it all down, we spoke.

'So, what are you looking for, little radish girl?'

'A tower. *The tower.* The one I've dreamt of my whole life.'

'None of them around here,' she answered.

'Then I'll keep walking until I find one.'

'Stubborn.'

She sighed and got to her feet. A bookcase leaned haphazardly against one of the walls; she shuffled over, grabbed a thin tome from the warped shelves.

'There *used* to be one. Don't know if it's still there. Some years ago it became invisible after a nasty business with a king not paying his due to a wise woman.'

'You?'

'Maybe it was and maybe it wasn't,' she hedged, pointing her finger at me. 'Any road, there is a tower for the taking. As you seem determined, you may as well have it.'

'How do I find it if I can't see it?'

'Hold your horses, missy. Always in a hurry, young women.' She clucked her tongue, opened the book, and flicked through it, running a finger down each page and muttering 'nope' as she reached the bottom. After a time she gave an 'ah ha'.

'You'll need the key, of course,' she said and plucked one, ungainly and slightly rusty, from the back of the ragged book. 'Now, walk north for three hours and when you bump into something you can't see, then you're there.'

'And?'

'Say this: tower fair you seem not there, take pity on this girl and your glory now unfurl. That should do the trick.'

'And if I should want it invisible again?' I asked and she rolled her eyes.

‘Then – and make sure you’re inside first or you’ll have to mess about making it visible again so you can find it – say “tower clear and tower bright, fold yourself back into night”.’ She rolled a lump of bread and cheese in a cloth and handed it to me. ‘I’ll come see you sometime.’

She pulled two small, carved stones from her pocket and held them out.

‘If you need anything, send the cat or the raven. Blow on them and say ‘bid your mistress come to me’. Sometimes you might just want the cat for companionship, so blow and say ‘malkin black or malkin white, bring thy company to my sight’. He’ll sit around for as long as you want. To send him back try ‘malkin black or malkin white, get thy company from my sight.’

‘I’m not a witch,’ I said.

‘You’re a woman, aren’t you?’

I had to agree. I gave thanks and was on my way. She watched until I disappeared into the trees and, I suspect, for a long while after that.

* * *

I found the tower. Literally I walked into it.

The spell took a few moments to work, as if the words were thinking about whether or not they would do as bid; or maybe it was the edifice, so used to being unseen, that was unwilling to obey immediately. Soon enough the air shimmered as if a heat haze had strolled past; a grey shadow-shape formed, wavered, and finally solidified.

It was exactly as it had been in my dreams: beautiful dark grey stone, flecked with quartz that caught the sun and threw it back at the watcher. The door at its base was huge and banded with iron. A keyhole stared at me like a curious eye. I fitted the key Sybille had given me into the lock and it turned with only a small protest.

The bottom floor was a storeroom-cum-kitchen: bags of grain still lay there, holes nibbled in their corners by happy mice; jars of wine sat on shelves; and, amazingly enough, a family of chickens perched comfortably on a pile of fabric grown green with age. The floor was liberally sprinkled with years’ worth of chicken droppings. Gingerly, I picked my way across the midden and started up the stairs.

These were cold, hard, barely worn – the tower must have been relatively young when Sybille hid it from the king. The next floor held the library. Books ran around the walls like sentinels on guard; I had never seen so many. The cobwebs would have to go, of course. The spiders would not be happy, nor would the mice, but so be it.

The top floor held a four-poster bed, a vanity, a polished mirror the price of which would have fed my family for a year, a garderobe, and, at each of the four compass points, a window through which light and air flowed in a continuous stream. Sunlight shone through the wheeling motes of dust and danced happily on my new home.

I surveyed my kingdom and was overwhelmed by a housewifely urge. Cleaning began and, before the sun went down, I had a serviceable bedroom.

Over the next few days I cleared the chickens out and set them up in the lean-to coop they had abandoned some time ago. Buckets of water from the well eventually washed away the layer of fertilizer. I planted some of the seeds from the storeroom. Carrots, corn and all manner of green things made an appearance with relative speed.

I brought the cat out after the first day. He was a strapping black and white mongrel and I called him Malkin, well, because it was easier than giving him another name. I didn't put him back because I liked his noiseless comradeship and he discouraged the mice from making a return. He never made a sound, not a miaow, not a hiss. Just swirled in and out between my ankles and curled in my lap when I sat to read one of the old books from the library. The raven I kept on the shelf, just in case.

Life was silent and wonderful. The stillness was not oppressive: I welcomed it, swallowed it in great gulps as a thirsty man would water. I passed my days in reading, sewing bits of the surviving fabric together into dresses and hangings, petting Malkin, sitting at my windows and bathing in the silence I had always sought. It was perfect. For a short time, it was perfect.

* * *

He came one evening as spring danced in on the breeze and I sat at the north window, taking in the velvet of the sky. I saw him ride out of the woods and stop, stunned at the sight of the tower. When he had dismounted and tethered his horse near the briar patch, he approached and found the door unlocked.

I waited for him to reach the top of the stairs, unsure what to do. Malkin was glued to my ankles like a guardian.

The torchlight caught in his red-gold hair, and flickered on the gold tassels of his princely attire. He was a good deal taller than I and he smiled as he took in my pale oval face, and the black river of hair that hung straight and glossy down my back.

'This place was once my father's,' he said.

'He cheated a wise woman,' I replied. He scowled.

'A witch.'

'Not a witch. No more than your father was an honest man.'

He glared but said no more. His eyes roamed the room and I thought how it must seem to him, raised in wealth, and how it seemed to me, born in poverty. That which shone here must be to him tarnished, old, to be thrown aside as worthless; to me it was a treasure, a piece of sunlight caught and held in a solid object, to be kept safe. How must I appear to him? Dress made of twenty different fabrics, hand-stitched carefully, slowly; face and feet bare of any decoration, hands those of a girl who had scrubbed the very stones to claim them, not the hands of a princess. To him I must look like a gypsy playing at lady.

How did he seem to me? He was golden, royalty and richness incarnate. He was at ease, as if he belonged in *my* home. The thought made me angry.

'Who are you?' he asked. 'Who are you, maiden in the tower, so fair and fierce, who smells so sweet?'

'Rapunzel,' I answered reluctantly.

'Little radish.' He laughed, not meanly. Still, it enraged me, and I threw myself at him, a hissing, spitting mess of hair, teeth and nails.

It started with rage. At some point it was no longer a battle: it was clothing peeled away, skin sliding on skin, flesh against flesh and then flesh *in* flesh. Finally it was sighs and screams and sobs and a pleasant ache that demanded it all be done again.

In the end it was love, or so I thought.

* * *

He stayed with me a month. I still remember the taste of him then, like the freshest of sap from a stalk of spring grass. I remember the feel of him, and all the things I learnt straddling his lap or writhing beneath him.

I remember how the silence was no longer desired; as long as there was the sound of his voice, the touch of his skin, the salt of his sweat, the world was perfect. I could not believe that I had sought solitude when there was this sweetness, this honey, to be had in the company of another.

He told me tales of his family and his travels. I did not hear the utterances of a young man obsessed with himself and his own doings, I did not hear the hint of selfishness in his every word; all I heard were the tones of my love. I thought, stupid girl that I was – stupid, silent girl – that I was important to him. That I was of the same abiding importance to him as he was to me.

Then, one day, he announced it was time for him to leave. He had tarried long enough in my presence and must go back to his princely duties. He would visit me, of course, when he had both time and inclination. I was to lock the door after him and never let another man near, for I was the property of royalty now.

He finished dressing, finished speaking, and stood, silhouetted against the sky in my north window. I was naked, angry, sinuous as a snake. I launched myself at him and pushed hard.

I don't know if I meant for him to fall, to tip over the windowsill, to tumble down and land in the briar patch. My mind still strays away from looking too closely at that. He broke no bones but his eyes were put out by the thorns. He cried for help but I would not answer.

I watched him from the window; a fury perched on the sill. His horse came to his aid. He mounted the beast and set off between the trees.

It took a long time for my tears to fall but when they came, they came with a vehemence that threatened to unhinge me.

* * *

Men searched for me.

I had hidden the tower, and would watch them, my eyes hungry. I thought perhaps he might come himself but that was a wish made of cobwebs.

My days were spent in a silence that was no longer a comfort. I would sit at a window, my hand smoothing my growing belly, listening for the second heartbeat that thumped in time with my own, listening to the spaces between my breaths for something I did not understand. Listening for a new noise, a noise that would remind me of him, a noise I sought no matter how much it hurt.

Malkin was constant even though I was not pleasant-tempered. Now I wished he could talk, would talk, but he remained silent, still as stone. I'd wake in the night, heavy and sweating, my belly aching along with my heart, feeling myself utterly alone, but Malkin was always there, flush against me, not even a breath between his fur and my skin. I remember reaching out and burying my fingers in the softness of his coat, comforted for a brief while.

It seemed the child would never come and, when he finally began to move, he took three days. The pain was immense and I hoped I would die. Finally, I crawled to the shelf and sent the raven to fetch its mistress.

She arrived, black and feathered, shaking her head over my swollen, infected form. Sybille fed me brews and possets, applied compresses to my brow and stroked my belly gently to coax the child out. By then there was, I thought, no pain that I had not suffered. I was numb to everything as my body rebelled against me and the child. Sybille tried her best, brought all her skill, invoked all the powers she knew.

The baby died, caught too long between its mother's body and the air it needed.

The old woman took him away without letting me see. She cleaned off the blood and got rid of the cord, wrapped him in soft white wool and placed him in a small crystal chest she'd rummaged from somewhere. Sybille made him ageless; he would not decay and diminish before his mother's eyes. I would need to see him, she said, when the time came.

For the first month I could not bear to look. I threw a shawl over the chest and pushed it to the far side of the room. Over the weeks, though, I began to glance to the dark curve of the wall where my child lay. When spring again scented the air, the day came when I wanted to know his face.

He looked like a doll, my son, a sleeping doll. I thought if I poked him gently he would wake and cry and seek my breast and all would be right. But he did not wake, nor cry, nor feed and nothing was right.

* * *

Sybille went back to her cottage to check on things, staying away for longer and longer as I grew physically stronger. We would talk sometimes, to alleviate the now-hated silence, to draw the poison out of me. She did not condemn him, my prince, but suggested he was a product of his upbringing. Yes, he had been wrong to think me a toy to be played with and laid aside at whim. Yes, he had been selfish and foolish. But perhaps the loss of his sight had been punishment enough. Perhaps it had taught him things he would not otherwise have known. Perhaps he deserved knowledge of his son.

People, said Sybille, were not meant to be alone. Men and women, women and women, men and men, all should find each other. Solitude was for those broken beyond repair.

I looked hard at her.

'I wasn't always alone, little radish,' she gentled me. 'I had a husband for forty years, until three winters ago. Now he's gone. My sons live nearby and they come to see me often. Did you think me an outcast, an old witch with no love nor need for it?'

Yes, I had.

'You sought the silence because it was easier than being with someone else. You're a damaged creature in your own way. So is your prince.' She reached out. 'You're not meant for silence, Rapunzel. Your babe isn't meant for silence. You should go into the world. Be among life, not sitting here in a living death, with only your frozen child and a stone cat for company. This isn't living, little radish.'

This time, when the tears came, they seemed to wash the poison away. I thought perhaps I might breathe again.

* * *

With the child's coffin strapped to my back, I walked until I found the edge of the forest and stepped into a wide field. Far behind me was the tower, left open and plain for all to see.

I had never been anywhere that was not surrounded by trees. I had never seen such wide open space. I shook and felt sweat break out on my brow. But it was not entirely empty, I told myself. There was corn, green and lush, growing high. There was the path I must take, running alongside it. There were people on the road, walking, riding horses, plodding along in their drays and conveyances, heading toward the open gate in the city walls.

A woman in a cart smiled down at me and offered a lift. I climbed gratefully up beside her and settled myself, the weight of the child heavy on my back. Her eyes kept flickering to my tapestried patchwork dress, and my face, with its bones washed clean by pain, my eyes dark and endless. She sensed, I think, something awry in me, an emptiness occasioned by hurt, a heart with a layer peeled back, a vacuum searching for something to curl inside it.

To distract her, I asked about the prince. She smiled, happy to speak of him, although he was a prince no longer, his father having died over a year ago.

The prince, blind for two years, king for one, had spent his time wisely.

The wastrel had become a careful, considered young man. Where he had once laughed at the maimed, tormented the poor, spat on the beggars, he now bestowed kind words, placed alms in the bowls of those who asked, and built shelters for those who did not. His own terrible accident had turned his heart and mind toward better things.

He could not see but employed an army of learned men to read for him and he took in their words, acquiring them by rote. Another cohort he employed to take down his thoughts: his scholarship had become known far and wide.

'How,' I asked, 'can I find him?'

He held an audience every Tuesday morning, tomorrow. My companion invited me to spend the night with her family. It was a great charity, in this city, to offer hospitality to travellers.

In the late afternoon we rumbled through the main gate. After many turnings on the cobbled streets we stopped outside a tall, crooked building. I helped her unpack the wagon, and she showed me to a small room at the top of her house. When she left I unstrapped my burden and placed it gently on the bed. I pulled away a layer of cloth and stared at my son's face. The door opened and my Samaritan burst in, a small girl at her skirts, words dying on her lips.

Her eyes moved from the thing on the coverlet to my face and back again. She saw the cause of my emptiness and anguish, she saw how the hole had been made in me. She muttered an apology and backed out of the room.

I did not stay there that night. It was easier to huddle in a stable, nestled in the straw, with only the horses to watch as I curled around the chest, crystal panes separating me from the flesh of my child.

* * *

The audience was held in a great hall in the palace. I stood back, watching the supplicants come before him. Finally, when the hall was empty of all but the king and his short, round chamberlain, I stepped forward.

The official raised his palms to tell me 'no', I was too late.

The king's head moved swiftly, his nostrils twitching. His hand reached out and pulled the man away. 'Who are you, who smells so sweet, little radish?' Useless eyes moved as if they could see me.

He ordered the chamberlain to leave us, and the man did so, reluctantly. I had thought I would stay out of range, but the prince stretched forward to find me and caught at my arm. Though I expected pain, his touch was soft.

'I sent men to find you,' he said. 'At first, it was to have you punished, later I just wanted you beside me.'

'I'm sorry I hurt you. Forgive me,' I whispered. His fingers flitted across my face, reached my eyes and gently caressed them, cleverly cupping the unbroken tears in his hands.

'I cannot forgive you,' he said, 'when there is nothing to forgive. I did not truly see until my sight was gone, nor had I listened to my heart nor the hearts of others until my own had been wounded.'

I put the casket in his hands.

'If you can bear more pain,' I said, 'then know that this contains our child. He did not live long enough to breathe.'

He wept and begged me to open it and let him hold our son, just once. I slipped the catch and our tears fell onto the soft still face. The king's hands scooped the child up, to be held against his chest.

The air around us moved, swarmed, something shifted, tore, then mended. Between our sobs, I heard something: a catch of breath in once-stilled lungs, a surprised gasp from a baby new to the world. Then a cry and my son began to wiggle and to wail.

So live the blind king, his wounded wife, and their twice-born son.

DIBBLESPIN

Ingrid knows the woods better than anyone except me. She recognises every tree, rock, leaf and can easily tell one from another. The thick underbrush parts quite willingly when she walks through, because it recognises her in return.

'Dibblespin,' she says, 'things are moving in the forest.'

'Things always move there,' I reply.

She shakes her head, silvery hair rippling like water. 'Dark things. Something is awake. I hear wolves outside my garden at night.'

'Not your mother?'

Ingrid fears nothing in this place. She has lived there all her life. So did her parents and both sets of grandparents, who Ingrid says she sees sometimes, in new forms: Grandma Finkel is a squirrel; Grandpa Ezza is a bright-eyed bird with blue feathers; Grandma Pandy is the large toad who lives under the water barrel out back of the cottage; Grandpa Sidle is the tabby cat, spending his time by the hearth fire. Father is the dormouse who lives in the walls and her mother, Olwen (free of familial constraints) has become a grey-eyed wolf.

'Never my mother at night.' She hesitates. 'They seem to sing, but not with wolf-voices. They sound like children.'

For the first time, she *is* afraid. I can smell it on her skin; it seeps through the pores like sickness. She plays with the silver knife that hangs at her belt, its hilt shaped like a wolf's head.

I do not know what makes me ask again, but I say 'Your mother, Ingrid. Have you seen her?'

She lowers her green eyes and lies when she answers, 'No.'

My sole inheritance from our father are *my* green eyes and bright red hair. From my mother came my large nose, heavy brow, harsh chin, flappy ears, long fingers, monstrously big feet and hunched shoulders. Needless to say my mother was *not* Ingrid's mother. More than reason enough to hide from someone as beautiful as Ingrid, if she was not so kind – and more than reason enough to hide from Olwen.

* * *

That night I sleep sweetly in the arms of an ancient oak, thick of trunk and sturdy of limb. The trees are so densely branched and close together that I can travel through the treetops, stepping lightly from bough to bough, and make a bed of them when I need to.

I do not spend much time indoors. I do not like it. When my mother turned to stone (branches above broke and fell, letting sunlight pierce down like a lance to catch her on its point), I burned down her hut. I hated its dark corners and sour smells; nothing good ever happened to me there.

Ingrid's cottage was once in a clearing but the years have encouraged the forest to grow back and Ingrid's father and grandfathers had no inclination to argue. There is a small yard, a tiny garden, hedged in by young trees, not as much girth to them as the old ones, but trying hard to reach higher, grow wider. In the garden are all manner of flowers that bloom year-round to spite winter. Thc yellow ones keep the space around the cottage bright so the lack of sun doesn't matter much. At night, they close their lovely faces and go to sleep.

Ingrid knows eyes watch her from behind bushes and rocks, but it bothers her not at all. I like, sometimes, to simply observe my sister. She is so beautiful; I do not look at my reflection in the stream or pond. I pretend we share the same face. She doesn't call me "stinky" or "dirty" or "ugly" or "troll". When she smiles her teeth show straight and white; mine are snarled and yellowy.

I wonder still what her father saw in my mother. Part witch, part troll-wife, she lived in the deepest part of the woods, where no sun shone at all and no blossoms grew to give light. He did not spend all his time in Ingrid's cottage. For weeks at a time he would go into the city not far from here, with its great walls and imposing cathedral and neat palace, and live there. Perhaps he wandered on his journey, got lost, found the ramshackle hut the foul thing called home. Perhaps she threw an enchantment over him so he thought her palatable (if I am ugly, my mother was worse still). She let him go only when she knew he'd finally planted a seed. Nine months later I appeared, and Ingrid had a half-sister.

Her grandparents died, one by one; then our father. I saw him only a few times in my life, never close enough to touch. When chopping wood, he missed the block and took off his foot. No one was around to help stem the flow of blood. Olwen wandered away the very next day, making her way among the trees until she was just a speck of dancing red, and then nothing at all. She came back six months later to drink from the rainwater barrel, but on four legs instead of two, and politely ate pieces of meat from Ingrid's hand.

* * *

I am woken by the scuffling and snuffling at the base of my tree. There is a low growl and I can hear claws determinedly trying to reach my perch.

But I am up too high, and the shadowy thing with flashing eyes cannot climb. It has my scent though. I try to peer into the darkness, to discern what waits so impatiently. There is only the glow of eyes; more than one pair, a forest of red glares up at me.

One by one, the owners of those glittering orbs begin to sing. It starts as a howling, but soon enough the chorus melds and twines into a tapestry of voices, the unalloyed joy of children. They embroider a folk song, a fairytale set to music, so the ideas dance in my mind, sugar-pink girls and bold boys, hand in hand moving through the woods. There is nothing else to be done, so I let them sing me to sleep.

* * *

Unlike my mother I can bear the touch of the sun and like the sky above me, a clean breeze in my face. During the day, I happily sit as high up as I can and enjoy the light and warmth. The night, though, gives me the comfort of shadows, places I can hide.

At the edge of the forest it's a small leap to the walls of Lodellan. I jump, teeter, find my balance and melt into the black spaces of the ramparts. From here I can slip around the edges, shimmy down if I wish and move from rooftop to rooftop. I know the tall houses and some of their inhabitants: there is the woman who makes bread and her pretty daughter with hair so like mine; there is the inn where people purchase affection; the miller's dwelling filled with his entire extended family and the mill set in the back, straddling the stream that runs through the city; the spinster sisters' whose spinning wheels thrum long into the night; the schoolmaster's residence; the Archbishop's manor; the Smithy; the Treasurer's home; the Prime Minister's abode that takes up an entire block but contains only him and his servants; and so on.

I choose a smaller house close to the outer walls near the postern gate, not one of the big structures that dominate the inner cantons;

a domicile with a straw roof, not the hard tiles used on the others. Only one family lives here: the Woodsman's. Mother, father, son. I climb down to cling to the thatch, hook my toes into the woven fibres and listen.

People have no idea how many secrets slip up their chimney with the hearth-smoke. I like roofs; I like being up high and seeing the stars, and smelling the scent of eagerly roasting meat. I make these visits, sampling the sounds that rise. They vary: sometimes it's children playing, whispering and giggling before bedtime; other times it's lovers sharing confidences in the dark; yet others are slaps of discipline or love; hurtful words thrown across a room, sometimes regretted, sometimes not; and, if I'm lucky, it's bedtime stories, fairytales and the like. These are my favourites. I settle in and listen, pretend I have a mother, a father, a grand-dam to lull me to sleep with fables and rhymes.

Tonight, though, I seek no tales, only the truth or a hint of it.

I am mindful of Ingrid's fear, she who fears nothing. If she goes into the city the adults will ask her questions: where are her parents? Why does her mother no longer come to the markets? They will pat her golden head and tell her she is too young to live on her own. They will try to make her stay in the orphanage, where rich people send their cast-off clothes so they feel better about not loving anyone but themselves.

I cannot ask, cannot show my face; they will throw things at me, curse me. The only way I can learn what they want to keep hidden is to steal the knowledge. They think whispers released within four walls will remain inside like obedient pups.

I choose the Woodsman's roof, for who else will know better if the forest is changed, restless? But before I can pick up a thread of conversation there's a noise from the garden. A wolf stands below in a bed of white lilies, its pelt bristling, nostrils flared; a young male, almost grown out of his adolescent awkwardness but still likely to trip over his own large paws. He is beautiful beneath the moon, a phantom limned silver and grey; my heart thuds. I lean out further than I should.

One of my feet slips and pulls loose a hank of straw, which drops and falls in front the beast. The handsome head is swiftly raised and I'm pinned by scarlet eyes. He throws his head back and howls, incautious. From inside the house come the sounds of chairs being pushed violently back, of panic and, finally, of a door being thrown open.

The Woodsman is a blur as he charges out. The animal barely has time to react before a huge axe is swung, moonlight catching its edge. There is the dull wet sound of metal cleaving fur and flesh.

In place of the wolf lies a sad figure curled on the bed of now-red lilies. I recognise him. In death, the Woodsman's son has lost his wolf's coat; he's naked and pale, except for the blood seeping from his neck and his near-severed head.

I'm still clinging to the roof. From the corner of my eye I catch a movement. At the edges of other buildings shadows move, seeping from one puddle of darkness to the next until they are gone. The Woodsman's wife screams, throws herself on the body and weeps. The Woodsman himself raises his head to the sky to let loose his cry. He's sees me and I am frozen in the beam of his stare, held by his terrible grief.

His eyes catch the light, but there's no flicker of red there, merely the opalescent wash of the moon. His wife lies at his feet, her son's blood soaking into her clothes, covering her hands as if she herself killed him. The Woodsman is caught between her and I, between letting out his anger and comforting the wailing woman. We are trapped, he and I, immobile for long, long seconds until he hurls his axe upward in vain hope of hitting me, of finding an outlet for his rage.

But I'm moving before the first bellow charges from his throat. I bound upwards, scrambling across rooftops until the weeping grows faint and I can fling myself from the walls and into the welcoming arms of the trees.

* * *

I have been inside Ingrid's cottage before, at times when she has not been, at times when her whole family still lived but none of them were home. I suppressed my dislike of four walls. I touched their things, respectfully, longingly. I drew the scent of their lives into my nostrils and wept for all that was denied to me.

My half-sister has always been gentle with me and because of this, I make sure I wash in a stream before I go to see her. I sit and scrub myself with the fine grains I find on the streambed and let the water rush through my carroty mop of hair. I cannot change how I look but I am clean at least.

This morning I sit, still fresh and damp, on the doorstep and drink the tea she offers. She cooks the silver fish I brought her, fresh from the stream; I eat mine raw, neat as a cat. I tell her the fate of the boy. I tell her to lock her doors at night. I tell her to be careful.

Leaving, I walk along the paths into the deeper darkness of the forest. The flat packed earth of the trails makes me think of padded feet smoothing the dirt as they pass. Deep in thought, for a while I do not realise that the idea of padded feet has become a reality. I turn to look about when I should simply climb. Shaggy grey forms appear and take me down.

Stupid, stupid girl. I had not thought that daylight might be as dangerous as night.

They pile on top of me and I try to fight my way clear of the roiling, writhing mass of wolves, some cubs, some adolescents, all vicious. There are white teeth, scratching claws, muscular limbs that trample. I feel my ribs crack and a sharp pain in my left hand. I shriek. It seems to startle them, a reaction more human than wolfish, and they pause. Then there is a voice, lovely and low, that chills my blood.

The pack, reluctantly obedient, backs away.

Ingrid's mother is tall and beautiful; she is the sign of what Ingrid will become. Her hair, more silver-grey than blonde, is loose and wild. There is a moment when she is *between*, when four feet become two, when fur gives way to blindingly white skin, until at last she *shifts* a red dress, woven from her very flesh, across her nakedness.

She smiles. 'Little troll. Little filth. My husband's little bastard.'

I push hair out of my eyes, feel blood trickle onto my face. The thumb of my left hand dangles by a thin string of sinew. It hurts like fire.

'Bitch,' I say and red spittle comes out. I rub my tongue against a tooth and feel it try to wiggle free of my mouth. This, too, hurts.

Olwen laughs as if the compliment delights her. She nods and gestures to the pack. 'Yes, and look at what I can do: one nip and all these puppies.'

'Where do they come from? Don't their families look for them?' But I think I know the answer.

'These ones? No one looks for them; they are the refuse the city throws out and leaves on the streets. But I, *I* love them. I give them a home and gentle motherly kisses.'

'The Woodsman's son?'

'Ah, yes. He was sniffing around in the forest and saw us. At first I thought to kill him, let my children feed, but why should I waste such a fine young man?' She smiles, drawing her lips back over her teeth. 'What would *you* become, I wonder, if I bit you?'

She pretends to consider it, but I know she has only death for me, not change, not transformation. Desperate, I look about for an escape but with my injuries I cannot scale any of the trees, not with sufficient speed. With my other hand I worry at the dangling thumb. It comes away with a *snap* and I throw the meaty chunk over the lupine heads. They yip and howl, follow its arc with their narrow eyes, and leap as one when it hits the ground. Even Olwen is distracted by the treat.

I heave myself to my feet and I run, blood spattering from my wounds. Behind me, Ingrid's mother laughs and her voice dances after me, 'Not too quickly, my babies, don't let it end so soon!'

Fear makes me fleet in spite of the pain and I run off the path and into the undergrowth. Ingrid's cottage is not so far, but it seems like the other side of the world. I must trust my sister, but in truth I do not know how she will choose.

The chase is a wild hunt of green and brown, shafts of errant sunlight, flashes of grey and excited howls swirling around as if to trip me.

At last the bright spot of the sunflower garden is before me and I trip and fall, rolling and rolling until I slam against the stones of the cottage wall and feel a shoulder crack.

The wolves' frenzy dissipates and they stop just outside the invisible boundary of the yard. They stalk back and forth, watching, waiting, growling, teeth and curling lips dripping with saliva. I do not question the respite, am merely thankful for it.

I hear the latch on the front door lifted and Ingrid steps out. She kneels beside me and touches my hair, tries to wipe the blood and dirt from my face but merely succeeds in aggravating the grazes.

Olwen glides through the ragged horde of cubs. She smiles at her daughter's disapproving expression. She alone can step into the garden; she lived here once, this is her territory. The pack, however, has no such right.

I push myself into a sitting position, back against the support of the wall.

'Hello, my darling.' Olwen laughs and it's like a chime.

'Mother, you promised. You promised to leave her alone.'

Olwen pouts as if denied a longed-for delight. 'I lied.'

'She's my half-sister.'

'She's nothing to me!' Olwen's voicc riscs to a shriek of rage. With visible effort she calms, reinstates her smile. 'Come now, Ingrid. Come, my daughter. I ask such a tiny thing.'

‘Mother…’

‘Won’t you let me be rid of this one single thing? This remnant of your father’s betrayal? This constant reminder of my hurt?’

Ingrid hesitates and my stricken heart hammers. She glances between mother and sister. In this struggle I now know I will lose.

‘Darling girl,’ says Olwen.

Ingrid no longer looks at me, purposefully averts her gaze.

Olwen comes closer and closer still; she bends down in front of us. She leans in and I can feel her hot breath on my cheek.

‘I do not think you will be tasty, you ugly scrap. I wonder will you be rancid? Bitter?’ She opens her mouth wide and the teeth inside shift and elongate, her tongue becomes redder than a berry and her breath smells like something rotten.

‘You will never know,’ I tell her and jam the knife I’ve torn from her daughter’s belt between Olwen’s ribs. Its slender blade finds her heart and punctures it. With not even a growl of disbelief, Olwen slumps on top of me. I gasp as the weight crushes down on my cracked ribs.

From beyond the border of the garden comes a howling, then the noise of crying, naked children. Among them, though, I can see some who still retain their wolfish shape. Whether they are children in the skin of wolves, or wolves in the skin of children, I cannot tell. I fear some of them, though, mourn their lost fur and the freedom it gave.

Ingrid, too, begins to weep, if for her mother or for me, I neither know nor care. She says through her sobs, ‘There, there, Dibblespin. There, there, sister-mine. I’ll take care of you.’

But there was a test and she failed it. She had a chance and she betrayed me, would have given me up to her mother like a trophy; like a lump of flesh and bone to be played with and then devoured.

I struggle and stand. My hand has stopped bleeding and the pain is receding to numbness. I leave my half-sister there with her mother’s body. The wolfish-children and childish-wolves let me pass. I will find the stream and wash myself clean. Then I will climb the tallest tree and turn my face to the sun and the wind and I will not come down.

THE NAVIGATOR

Windeyer perches atop the mast, face to the wind, eyes (all pupils) unblinking. His shoulders twitch as if the stumps of his wings itch and ache. Some days, when he's aloft like this, I think I can see the sun shine through him, his bones a dark frame beneath his skin. Perhaps I imagine it. He should have been able to fly; they should have left him that.

Not many ships have Navigators such as he anymore; his kind began dying out twenty years ago. Pining, avian-human diseases, masters who got sick of having to retrieve runaways and, in frustration, transected them with a crossbow bolt. It was, I think, a kind of mass suicide, a tribal loss of the will to live. With their wings taken, with no freedom, what was the point?

He moves and I tense. In a fluid motion he dives from the mast, from the very top, into the waves. I watch, fearful that he won't come up, will founder like his father. That he will drink in the sea instead of the air and *choose* to sleep on the sandy bottom. At last, he surfaces.

I do not chide him. His cruelties are few and this is the worst of them: to endanger himself in front of me. Some days he won't talk. I feel, more and more, this distance between us, his lack of wings and mine.

'How much longer?' I ask as he hauls himself over the ship's rails. I'm relieved he doesn't consult the map. It's drawn on human skin and I do not wish to think on how he came by it. He reaches out and runs his fingers down my face, leaving salt and water there, writing my tears for me.

'Another day, another night. Afraid?'

I shake my head.

'It's not too late,' he says. 'We can still turn back. You can marry your way out of poverty.'

'Or I can sell you. That would clear all debts.'

It hangs between us, bitter fruit. I turn away and fix my eyes on the endless horizon. The feeling of the wheel under my hand is sweet.

* * *

Windeyer was sired on a human whore by Father's Navigator, Desidero. The woman had waited for a year until the *North Star* returned to the port at Breakwater. She presented the surprised sire with a babe in arms, whose metre-wide wing-span took the breath away. She demanded money in exchange for her son. Desidero begged my father to buy the boy.

Desidero was wild, his wings clipped late, but he found some bond with Balthazar Cotton and stayed. Behaved abominably but stayed. It must have been something more than a shared interest in whoring that kept them together, must have been a kind of friendship, for in spite of his wildness, Desidero never tried to run. He loved the ship and he loved my father. Perhaps it would have been better if he had fled for he died in a storm when his son was five.

I was born six years after Windeyer. Mother was a fine lady of good family who'd married a merchant and expired with the shock of giving birth to me. Balthazar Cotton didn't entrust me to a governess as a proper parent should: I was carried around in a small woven cocoon, hung on the nearest mast when he needed both hands free, always carefully shielded from the sun. My father, son of a landlocked city, discovered late in life that he loved the ocean; I was born to it. So much time did I spend at sea that solid land always felt foreign to me. The inland air I breathed when Father took me on occasional visits to his birthplace of Bitterwood was free of salt and soak; it tasted wrong.

Windeyer was given guardianship of me – to teach him responsibility – and he looked after me as well as a brother might. In those early years his wings had not been taken and he would sweep me up and we would fly above the water as the ship floated beneath us. This was his gift to me: to know what it was like to soar on the thermal currents, to see things the way the gods might, to feel unbounded by earth and dirt and gravity.

And I took that from him.

* * *

The night air is clean. I breathe it deep and hold it in my lungs as long as I can; as if every breath counts. We are anchored outside the reef surrounding the island of the Sirens. I would not risk the passage in darkness, so Windeyer has been forced to wait. He sulks in the bow, his back to me. I think I see the shadow his wings once cast.

‘I have a way out,’ he said not so many weeks ago. This is the only ship left in the fleet I inherited: a small sloop, just barely manageable by the two of us. The others have been variously lost: storms and sea monsters; one destroyed by pirates; and one lost in a regrettable card game for which I blame Windeyer entirely.

There is still the house, the white stucco and iron-fenced mansion perched on the gentle hill above the port. But it is mostly emptied of furniture, all but our bed and cooking utensils for those brief times when we are at home and not scouring the sea for some kind of commerce. We stop short of piracy as much as possible, transporting as many small cargos and paying passengers as we can to keep body and soul together. I have had to let the crew go, one by one, to ships where they are guaranteed pay.

I could, as Windeyer taunts, marry: there are several suitors, all rich and corpulent and well connected. They would keep me in a sugar-spun web of boredom, leave me to learn to embroider and raise round, haughty children, the boys replicas of their father, and the girls tiny versions of a caged mother slowly going mad.

‘Sirens’ bones,’ he said to me and might well have been a siren himself (he carries their blood, though diluted by years and generations). ‘Remember mine? Think of what pure Sirens’ bones will fetch.’

When my father ordered Windeyer clipped, he had the great black wings nailed to the main mast of the *North Star*. They stayed there until at last the feathers and flesh fell away and left glorious bright bones that clattered to the deck and proceeded to sing. Father had them bundled up and sold as soon as we made port. With the proceeds he bought another ship.

‘Why would the Sirens give up their bones to us, Windeyer?’ I asked.

‘We only need one set – we don’t even need a *full* set. We don’t need to ask. The bones will be lying about.’

‘How do you know?

‘They build wooden towers for their dead. They leave the bodies to rot. The towers fall and the bones litter the island. I read it in Murcianus.’

‘No one is allowed on the island.’

‘Pilgrims are. Navigators are. *My* kind are welcome.’ His eyes darkened and I couldn’t quite divine if he was bitter or pleased.

And I agreed, at last, even though I knew he had told me truth with a lie rolled up tightly inside.

* * *

The Sirens are not simply eaters of flesh. They guard the gates to flight and to death. They are the deal makers of the gods. They grant wishes and collect the price of them, for both men and Navigators.

Sirens' bones. Iridescent. They are sold powdered to improve longevity. Musicians seek them as beguiling flutes. A house built with Sirens' bones in the foundations will remain firm and strong long after other buildings have crumbled, and the family living therein will have unbridled prosperity. A woman wearing jewellery made of this substance will have any man she desires and will keep his attentions so long as she keeps the trinket. Shaped into weapons, they are the surest, most deadly means of dispatching an enemy. A ship with a compass of Siren bone will surely return safely to its harbour.

There was nothing and no one more magnificent than Windeyer, with his long black hair and his great black wings, striding through the streets when we docked. He was treated as my father's son. Other captains warned Balthazar that he was inviting disaster by refusing to clip the boy, but he scoffed.

Then there came a woman, Gwenllian. No more than a port-whore, no better than Windeyer's mother had been; but lovely and with a silken tongue and heated kisses. A woman so lovely that she caught the eye of a great lord and he took her away. She stoked a fire in Windeyer and brought all his wildness to the surface. He was not trying to flee. He was merely trying to find her.

I told.

I didn't know what my father would do. I didn't know what a man would do to someone he loved. I didn't know how his rage would kindle, how in his fear of betrayal he would do something unthinkable. That he would take from Windeyer the most precious thing he had.

I was a child still, though cusping thirteen. I did not want Windeyer to leave, and so I told my father where he might find him. Even though I did not know what would happen, I told. I wanted him to stay and I told.

And some days he has said, 'You did not know.'

But the simple fact is that I *told*.

And in telling, I took the very thing that made his life wonderful. Guilt and love are my constant companions. So even when I knew he lied, I pretended I did not know.

In the darkness of the small cabin, I lie half in sleep, half awake. I feel his hand against the small of my back, sad and familiar. His tongue licking at the sweat on my skin, his lips salty and firm on mine; I rise to meet him, take him inside me.

I believed him because I wanted to; because there was longing and love and remorse and that most destructive thing of all: hope. Hope of forgiveness, hope of redemption, hope that we might be saved.

'I loved you,' he says. I'm surprised to find I still have tears left. He laps them from my face as if they are something worth stealing.

* * *

Above the island fly bright creatures too large to be birds. Their wings flash in the sun. Windeyer stands beside me, taut as a bowline. In the distance, I can spy the towers, built along the cliff tops, near the very edge.

'See that path? We go that way.'

The towers are made of something that shimmers. Not wood. Bone, I realise. Sirens' bones.

'Come on,' he says and makes his way to unhitch the rowboat.

* * *

They are all tall, long limbed. All women. They are only black or white, there are no other variations in their colouring of hair, eyes, skin. They are naked and they shine; their only feathers are on their wings, which are, without exception, so beautiful I could cry.

We have reached the tops of the cliffs and wandered through crowds of these things. We tread on sacred ground. These towers do not fall. The winds sing through them, howl around the bone frames and make a song that is terrible and sad and lonely. There are no bones gathered at the base. There is nothing to harvest and these creatures will not let us take anything from here. And Windeyer knew this. And I knew it too.

We stand like pilgrims, like beggars. They recognise him – like calls to like. The Sirens can scent their own blood in his. Not so mine. One, the tallest of them, stands near the very edge of the cliff and we approach her. I can hear the crash of the sea below.

'Your wish?' she asks, flashing Windeyer the whitest of teeth from her ebony face.

'I want my wings back,' he says and his longing stabs at me. She grins, nods.

‘Your sacrifice?’ she replies. Her lips and tongue tangle around the word. She points a long slim finger at me, tipped with a diamond talon. ‘What is this one to you?’

He struggles, I’ll give him that. He struggles to say *nothing*; to say *something.*

I smile and save him the trouble. I can give him back the one thing that was taken from him. When he has that once more I will no longer have *him*; but I have held him for too long.

No last words between us.

I take a pace forward, then another, and another until the ground beneath me is uncertain, nothing but scree between me and air. I turn around, hold out my arms and take the final step. The wind rushes past; the smell of the sea is stronger and stronger as I fall.

Above me comes the dark cruciform of Windeyer, launching himself into the sky and blotting out the sun. At first there is simply the shape of a man, his arms spread wide, then there is the sound of tearing, of stretching, of great wings unfurling and beating against the air.

Soon, the water will be hard beneath me.

THE ANGEL WOOD

We wake only when a sudden stop almost jerks us from the seat. Now, with the plague-ridden city just a memory, the air is so fresh it creeps up our nostrils and makes us sneeze at its strangeness.

Jeremy-Charles lies quiet in my arms while Milly and Tildy snuggle, one either side of me. Outside, Mother's voice is tense as she says she carries only victims. A man answers that she lies – who would bother to transport the dying so far from Breakwater? I bid my siblings be silent, and peek through the gap between the doorframe and the curtains that cover the windows.

Two men sit astride fairly fine horses – surely stolen – their faces wrapped in scarves, and pistols casually aimed at my mother. I don't think they've realized that she is a woman, tall as she is, dressed in Father's clothes, her voice deep. Her red mane is caught up under a hat.

One of them ambles his mount toward the carriage. I slide one of the guns from under my cloak and hold it in both hands, trying to steady it. When the door opens, the highwayman's eyes widen in the moment before I fire and his face turns to red. A second shot, then a third, rings out and I fall from the conveyance. Behind me, the children scream.

The other man lies on the ground, victim to the weapon Mother carries. The third shot seems to have gone astray.

My siblings continue to howl until Mother yells at them to be quiet. As she has never raised her voice to any of us before, the shock has the desired effect.

'Tie their horses to the back of the carriage, Henrietta. Hurry up about it.'

I do as bid with shaking hands. As I move to climb back in, my stomach heaves. The grass is soft when I fall and vomit as if my innards are trying to leave my body. Mother's palms are cool on my forehead as she holds my hair back and strokes my face.

'Is Henri sick, Mama?' Tildy's voice trembles. Mother shakes her head, blue eyes warm and pitying.

'No, Henri is not ill. She's just upset. Stay in the carriage, Tildy.' She helps me up, lowering her voice. 'First things are always hardest, Henri. It will be easier next time.'

She bundles me in and shuts the door, hard. We rock under her weight as she climbs back into place. The horses start forward and I return to sleep, curled around Jeremy-Charles, my sisters watching me cautiously from the opposite seat. My dreams are disturbed, patterned with shades of crimson.

* * *

The house in the Angel Wood seems to stretch forever back into the trees.

It had been an abandoned castle when my mother's family first came here, but succeeding generations added to it without much thought for aesthetics. It is now a hybrid thing, with a tower of black stone, a white and brown E-shaped house sitting around it, and a variety of outbuildings that really belonged nowhere else. The outer walls are now tumbledown. The ancient green forest, Mother said, simply kept encroaching – whenever it was cleared away, it grew back as if nothing had happened, as if human will and action counted for naught.

Like puppies shut away for too long, we children tumble out into the late afternoon. My feet touch the earth and the ground seems to hum in welcome, a tremor passing through me. My blood dances in response, washing away the red of my dreams and any lingering distress. I belong here – I don't know how I know this, but it comes to me with an undeniable certainty. This is my home and I will be welcome.

Jeremy-Charles takes faltering steps when I set him on his feet and the twins run almost to the entrance of the house. Mother swings down wearily from the driver's seat, pulling hat from head, hair hanging stiff with a paste of sweat and road dust.

The door opens and what appears to be the oldest woman in the world strides out. She does not seem a witch, does not look malicious, merely more aged than anyone I have ever seen. Her skin is tanned and her hair such a white that it shines like mother-of-pearl. She is quite tall, not at all stooped, and she gives Mother a weary look.

'Are you home, then? With all these?' She jerks her chin toward us, her eyes catching the sun and flashing amber. I wonder who she is to speak to my mother so; none of our servants would ever have even considered a word out of place. 'Where's their father?'

I notice that she does not say *your husband.* Mother stoops to collect Jeremy-Charles, gasping as she straightens; I fear she is very tired. She faces the old woman, somewhat subdued.

'Dead of the plague.'

'And you thought to bring the contagion here?' But she does not seem in the least bit fearful. I think *she* is afraid of nothing.

'We are none of us sick, Agnes. I would not have come otherwise, but I needed to get the children away. Where are my uncles?' She looks beyond her adversary, as if expecting further welcomers.

'Fenelon, George, and James are all dead. Old age, you see, and we've no young blood to continue on. We are much reduced, Susannah.' She looks at us for a long moment, sighs and steps aside. 'Come along. There's plenty of room for you all.'

I am surprised by the amount of light inside; there are many windows, an expensive luxury at odds with the apparent shabbiness. Through the glass I can see the Wood; things flit from trunk to trunk in the shadows. Birds? Squirrels? I wonder if the house in the Angel Wood was like this when my mother left or if it suffered for her leaving.

'Do your offspring have names, Susannah?'

'This is Henrietta – Henri. These are Millicent and Mathilda. The boy is Jeremy-Charles.'

'How old are you, Henri?' She addresses me directly.

'Sixteen, madam.' She is probably not a servant – or if she is, she is one of that strange breed who have no care for place or manners, and are forgiven by some grace.

'I'll see to the horses,' Susannah says – so much more *Susannah* than *Mother* now.

'I will see to the children,' Agnes answers, as if we, too, are animals to be fed and watered.

I take my brother from Susannah and she slips from the room. Jeremy-Charles insists on going to the old woman's arms and I let him rather than risk screams. We tramp along to a large kitchen where a hot stew waits, and soft cheese and slabs of bread are put out for us. We eat in silence until my curiosity gets the better of me.

'Who are you?'

'Agnes Woodville. I'm your grandmother.' She pours milk for the girls and they happily slurp it as if they've been ill-bred. 'Your mother hasn't told you about me?'

I shake my head. 'I did not know she had any family until Father died and she said we would come here. She has never mentioned you before.'

'No, I don't suppose she would.' Jeremy-Charles snuggles close to her as she feeds him bits of cheese. 'She ran away from us. Married your father instead of staying here to do her duty. She—'

'Enough, Mother. Enough poison in my daughter's ear.' *My* mother stands in the doorway, pale and shaking.

'When is truth poison, Susannah?' Agnes asks. 'If you stay they will know soon enough.'

'For now, leave them be.' Mother strokes my hair, red like hers. 'Eat up, then we'll find some bedrooms.'

Susannah sways, weary, and strangely bloodless. When she falls, her cloak opens to show a bright red stain on her white shirt.

* * *

I help carry Susannah upstairs. She lies, pale as her pillows, while Agnes washes the wound. When my grandmother remembers I am still there, she sends me out. I am to choose rooms for us, any that do not seem too full of dust, and put the children to bed. We will speak later.

There is an old nursery, with a huge bed and a cradle intricately carved and dark with age. Tildy and Milly think their new bed is a boat for sailing on the seas of sleep. I do not contradict them and bundle Jeremy-Charles into the crib where, presumably, generations of my mother's family dreamt their earliest dreams.

Across the hall I choose a bedchamber with a four-poster hung about with green drapes and curtains. I am irrationally pleased to have this to myself. In the city, I shared with the twins and, much though I love my sisters, I am thoroughly sick of them stealing my ribbons, playing with my dresses, and leaving my books in a mess. The sturdy lock on the door brings a smile to my face as I turn the key, even though at this point I have no treasures to hide.

* * *

'We were not always like this, Henri.' Agnes leans back in her chair and sips at the mulled wine. Although it is spring, the air still has enough of a chill to warrant a fire in the evening. We sit in one of the parlours. Another day has passed with Susannah sleeping, her breath shallow and her brow fevered. The children once more are abed after a day of exploring the house like persistent mice, finding all the crannies of their new home.

I am tired and a little drunk from the heated beverage I have been allowed – Agnes does not watch as a parent might. There is a strange familiarity between us, two women who have never met but are joined by blood. I do not find myself disbelieving her, or distrusting her as I would a stranger.

'How did you get so poor?' I ask, rudely but without spite – there is none of the wealth of my own first sixteen years evident here. There are no servants. The only horses in the stable are those we brought with us. The chickens in the yard are so thin they look like feather dusters; the cows bags of bones wrapped in leather, empty dugs hanging sadly from their bellies. The poverty seems to go beyond a mere lack of money; it's a lack of vital force. It is hard to believe my mother came from this place.

'We – this family – have been here over five hundred years. This land, this forest have been here even longer. We became part of it, Henri, because we learned how to best serve the Wood. In return we prospered; we were one of the richest families around almost beyond memory. But we had to fulfil our part of the bargain.' She pauses to take another drink, sighs.

'And we did not? For some reason, we did not.'

'It was your mother's duty, your mother's burden, one that has been carried by the oldest daughter for these many, many years. An obligation that has ensured the health and wealth of the Woodvilles for time on time.' Her voice chips on sadness, fractures, then strengthens. 'Your mother chose otherwise. She left with your father and there was no one to take her place. No new blood to replace the old.'

I stare into the fire, watching the yellow and orange flames battle, writhing one over the other. I want to sleep, to be away from this conversation and the blame it lays at Susannah's door. But I also want to *know*.

'Why did she run?' I ask.

Agnes shrugs. 'She was my only daughter. I spoilt her, assuming she would go willingly.' She raises an arthritic hand to her thick white hair and I am surprised by this sign of human weakness. 'In giving way to her all her life, I did not teach her to be dutiful.'

'And what burden, Grandmother? What burden did she refuse?' My voice falters even as I ask and she is free to pretend she has not heard. Agnes rises and touches my hair, as if comparing it to hers.

'It's late, Henri. Time for bed.'

'What burden, Grandmother?' I repeat so she *cannot* pretend not to hear.

‘Perhaps tomorrow, perhaps the day after, I’ll tell you. We shall see what time reveals.’ She leaves the room and I sit for a while longer, watching the fire die, wondering that Susannah could have let this house fall.

* * *

I venture out to see if the chickens have, by some miracle, laid. There are no eggs, which means that Agnes will have to traipse to the nearest neighbour and buy some at ridiculous cost. I could go but she does not yet trust me to haggle the price down.

I turn and see a horse, watching me from the edge of the forest. At first I think it is one of the animals we acquired on our journey here, but neither of those mounts is white. At its hooves lies a green basket, woven of vine and leaf. The beast snorts and stamps, dips its head to beckon me closer.

The hamper contains a dozen or so eggs, large and brown, bigger than chickens’. I wonder at this gift, run my hand down the horse’s nose and notice that its eyes are blue. I step back in surprise and it neighs, then trots away into the Wood, glancing at me once or twice before it disappears.

When I put the receptacle in front of Agnes she stares, disbelieving. I repeat my tale twice, then refuse to do so again and storm out of the kitchen. Not too much later she finds me, flicking idly through books in the library. She sits beside me.

‘You wanted to know, Henri, why this house is so diminished?’

‘What did my mother do wrong?’ I ask, all plans for subtle enquiry flown.

‘She refused to be the bride of the Angel Wood.’ Her voice dips low. ‘On her sixteenth birthday she should have entered the forest, and come out a bride. She should have born a child to the Wood, but she chose *not*.’

‘Why?’

‘Perhaps fear. Perhaps she simply didn’t want to.’ She shrugs, an old woman’s movement, replete with weariness; she is dissembling and there are things she will not tell.

‘How can someone be the bride of the Wood?’

‘The prosperity of this family depends upon the provision of a daughter, to own this house and protect the forest and its people. After that, the bride can marry whomever she chooses – as I did. The eldest Woodville girls have been brides for centuries. Your mother chose otherwise.’ She leans close. ‘Will you be different, Henri?’

I stare at her, at this offer of inheritance, then walk away from her again, unable to breathe in the close air of the library.

* * *

The boughs of the forest creak although there is no breeze. Dark green shapes dart between the trunks of trees, and the occasional flash of an inhuman eye gleams at me.

'They will grant you a boon, you know.'

I leap high in fright though it is only Agnes. I swallow air, feeling sick.

'What?'

'They will give you a boon. Those who dwell in the green, the forest folk.' She moves nearer, her hand touching my elbow gently. 'They will grant you a wish as your bride price.'

'What would I ask of them?' I demand.

'Your mother's life.' Her answer hits me like cold water. 'Susannah's fever is high and I fear death will draw her down.'

I stare, wondering if she has determined to deceive me.

'I would not force you, Henri, though our salvation depends on it. If you do not choose willingly then there is no power in forcing you.' She smiles. 'You have the look of the brides, Henri. If you do this, we will all be indebted to you, but you must choose quickly.'

Upstairs, Susannah is the colour of milk on the turn, the hue of death feathering her skin. I lean across the bed and whisper to her that she must hold on, that all will be well, that I will do my duty.

Agnes and the white horse wait in the stable yard. My grandmother hands me a coronet of golden leaves and emerald stones, and a silver knife, its handle cunningly wrought like twining vines. I settle the coronet on my brow, and a sweat breaks out over my body, a dizziness spins in my head and a darkness seeps across my eyes.

* * *

I blink, moments later, my eyelids fluttering like the wings of startled birds. The courtyard is gone and I'm somewhere deep in the woods, although I have no memory of movement.

He sits in the clearing, naked and unmoving. He is tinged green and brown (more brown than green, as if he is dying), and his hair is leafy. I touch his skin and find it rough, like new bark. Thc wings on his back are branches, and where feathers would sprout on a real angel, leaves and vines grow in a tight thatch.

Still, he does not move.

He has the look of a neglected thing, of an unloved husband, and that, I suppose, is what he is. A beard, straggling, the colour of dead grass, covers the lower part of his face and I can barely see his mouth. His eyes are closed, heavy-lidded, and the rise and fall of his chest as he breathes is almost imperceptible.

I don't know what to do.

I kneel before him and take one of his large hands in my own. It moves stiffly and only with great effort on my part. There is a loud creak as I shift it. I touch my lips to his palm.

'My lord, I am here. Your bride has come.'

For a moment there is nothing, no acknowledgement, and I feel the bitter sting of failure pricking. I squeeze my lids tight, but salt water creeps out.

A hand touches my face and I open my eyes to see a tear, carefully lifted from my cheek, trembling on the tip of his index finger before it disappears, soaked into his skin. His lips brush mine.

I fear he will absorb me as he did my tear, suck my youth away until I am a husk, but I feel nothing except pleasure in his touch. He tastes sweet, and smells as sharply fresh as newly cut grass. When we part, his handsome face is beardless, his flesh decidedly greener, the dead brown fading away. He reaches for me again but I rest one hand on the broad plane of his chest.

'My bride price, lord.'

He nods, but does not speak.

'My mother's life. Heal her.'

His face splits into a smile, as if this is the smallest thing he has ever been asked. Relief surges through me and I fumble with the fastenings of my gown, eager to fulfil my part of the bargain, and perhaps not only for the sake of my family. His hands are gentle as he helps slip the fabric from my shoulders and his lips, on my pale breasts, are hungry.

* * *

When I open my eyes again, Agnes is kneeling before me, the pavings of the courtyard hard beneath her knees. She smiles at me with pride, relief, no fear. She lifts her head, offering her neck. I grasp her long white hair and pull it back firmly so the skin is tight under the dagger as it slips across her throat. Slowly, my grand-mother folds forward, a crimson necklace dripping down, the warmth of her lifeblood spurting on the hem of my dress.

Susannah, pale and silent, watches me from the open door. This is the price my mother would not pay. She would not replace the old blood with new. The tears on her face are matched by my own, but I will not be ashamed of doing what was needful. I lift my chin in defiance.

* * *

The house is mine now. I don't think Susannah expected that (although she should have), and I think she may resent it. She is my mother, but I am the bride of the Angel Wood. In choosing not to do her duty, she lost the right of inheritance.

The child grows quickly inside me and I am thankful that I am young and strong. She kicks often and with great force and I wonder if she will look like her father. My mother sometimes runs her hand across my distended belly in wonder, but does not mention what I have done. I want to remind her, sometimes, that first things are hardest.

We buried Agnes under one of the oak trees. I like the idea of her enriching the soil. She knew this would come, what I would have to do and she chose her own end. One day, I too, will choose such an end.

Those who live in the Wood bring us gifts, offerings for the bride. Sometimes it is ancient gold and gems found who-knows-where, other times it's fresh silver fish or a brace of rabbits. The hens have begun laying madly, giving more eggs than we can ever use, and every cow is brimming with life, heavily pregnant.

This is not the life my parents would have chosen for me. My memories of *before* fade quickly, and their loss troubles me not at all.

I often walk in the Wood – the child is most active then, sensing this is her place as nowhere else can ever be. Leaf and bough, sap and stream will flow in her veins.

Sometimes I sense him, my husband, but I can never quite see him. Agnes told me that brides do not meet him again. Once we have done our duty we are free but I live in hope that I will touch him once more. I do not like to think that there will only be that one moment, in the gentle green hollow on a bed of soft moss, when I felt connected to every living thing in the forest.

I live in hope in the Angel Wood.

ASH

The water flowing beside this small, remote castle runs as cold as a serpent's blood. The mist curls up from the surface of the river, reaching into my lungs, and drawing out deep, damp coughs. I shiver, a tremor that goes through every part of me. The autumn night gives a hint of what winter will bring. I pull the shabby fabric of my old cloak close around me.

The first time I came here I had nothing to fear, no crimes to regret, no sins to repent. I was an invited guest, honoured and, most of all, needed. But even a short span has wrought changes I could not foresee.

Eyes no longer linger on me; they slide away. Scars mar my skin, pulling tight like unevenly placed stiches. They itch and ache, remind me constantly of their presence.

Three years ago, I was still young. Three years ago, I had a countenance that made men pause. The last time I floated in under this stone arch, the boat rocking as we moored, the man-at-arms with brown hair and worried eyes stared a long time at the pale moon of my face, troubled by what his mistress might want with my kind. Then he wrapped me tightly against prying eyes and tugged the hood of the fine grey cloak I then wore far down over my features so no one would see me and later know me.

That day led to this one. I go before the same woman, by the same secret ways, under the same witch's moon. I do not think I will walk out alive. My bones will sleep under dirt and stones somewhere within these stout walls. No one will look for me; no one will care. Some bargains, once made, should not be revisited. Indeed, some bargains should not be made at all.

Stairs are hard for me. My bones were never properly set. I ache. I might forget, sometimes, that my hair has faded, and my face is other than it was – that no man will share my bed willingly – but the pain reminds me. It is merciless. I tell myself I do not care about the loss; that it makes no mind to me, what is there and what is not.

When I am alone, I can oft-times believe it. No one has been there to gainsay my lies. Until now.

The room has not changed, really – a tad richer, more luxurious. Her lover is generous, perchance to make up for his long absences. He does not often leave Lodellan and she is left to while away her time far from him. I wonder how her days pass; a loom waits silently in a corner and the walls are hung with tapestries. Perhaps my question is answered thus. How many days, how many wall hangings to measure a life? How much time in front of the tall silver mirror, watching her face change, her beauty slowly lessen? How does a woman so lovely that men fought for her favours bear this?

Gwenllian occupies a comfortable chair near a wide window, and the moonlight angles in upon her. She, too, has aged, though less dramatically than I. She is older than me but looks younger. Her existence has been cushioned by wealth. There are lines on her face but her make-up cunningly disguises them. There are no flecks of silver in her dark hair. The sleeves of her dress are slashed (not for fashion, but I know why she wears them thus) and I can see the skin there. Her face, neck and forearms are peaches-and-cream, youthful, expensively bought. My best work.

She surveys the cross-hatching of *my* face, the uneven set of my shoulders. Does she wonder why I have not healed myself? Does she think I could not? That I have lost my gift?

'It has been a long time, Blodwen.' The voice lilts, a flower on the breeze, her low origins almost disguised by practice. I merely nod. This is less courteous than she is used to and it makes her frown. Here in her castle, with her servants, she is queen and law. Perhaps her isolation has made her think herself God as well. 'You have been ill?'

'My lady is observant.' My tones, once dulcet, are no longer so. There was a time when I could bewitch with my speech alone. Now I sound like a crow in human form.

'Your tongue is still sharp.'

'It's all I have left.'

We stare at each other for a moment, the Lady Gwenllian and I. There are no attendants – just like before. No witnesses to our bargain. Her eyes drop to stare at her arms, then she raises her hands to touch her cheeks and the smooth curve of her throat. When last I came here, they were still weeping from the burns she'd suffered, the flesh red and raw like a side of half-burnt beef, and the stench septic.

Her lover was here three years ago, just before Gwenllian's accident. He has sent word that a tour of the surrounding countryside will bring him this way. He wishes to see their daughter, who should be six. This much I have from my surly escorts, the men who sought me out in the cesspit of a village where I have lived these last few years. This much and no more.

'Your face…' she begins.

'I was dragged behind a wagon. My legs were broken, too. Not everyone is kind to my sort.' I sit, without invitation, on a chair opposite her. She says nothing; she knows that this small comfort is the very least she owes me. There is the low sound of my joints cracking as I bend.

'You did not…' she gestures, once again not finishing her question. 'You could not?'

I am silent, thinking of the pain of those days and months. Of the strange weight of loss – how is it that in having something taken away from us, we suddenly feel heavier? Now there is merely the lightness of ceasing to care.

'What I do carries a price – I would not pay it,' I say. 'I am not you. My blood is still warmed by conscience.'

Guilt shimmers across her face then dissolves in a cloud of rage. She starts violently from her seat, looms over me, but I am a tired woman. Anything she does to me will be a lifting, a relief. I think she sees in my face that I will welcome any end.

With an effort she speaks quietly. 'What you did for me.' She lifts her arms (as if I do not know her skin as well as my own). 'What you did for me was a miracle and I judged the price fair.'

'But?'

'But I need what I gave you. I need her.'

I laugh so loudly it hurts my ears; the stretching of my mouth makes my jaw ache. My stomach convulses with bitter mirth. It takes me a long time to calm myself and by then her fury is palpable, uncontained. This is why she had me found, hunted like a fox and brought here. I have not strictly hidden, but I have not lived in plain sight.

'I want the child back. I *need* the child back,' she hisses.

The daughter she gave me in return for her healing. Three years ago she was eager to sacrifice the little girl if only she herself could be smooth and whole again.

'I no longer have her,' I say. 'She is not mine to return.'

'Her father comes and he will wish to see her.'

'Tell him what you did.'

'I cannot!'

'Show him another,' I say.

'No other has her birthmark.' She spits the words out. I remember the small red crown on the child's shoulder. Her father saw her when she was born; he will know if his mistress tries to substitute another.

'Tell him she died – he will forgive that.'

'He will *not*! She was my price.' She gestures around us, to the room, to the comfort of her surroundings. 'He warned me to keep her *safe*.'

'You should have thought of that when you were giving her to me.'

Her fingers are at my throat, strong and warm and tight.

'Where is she? Tell me and I will send my men to collect her. I will keep you in my household for the rest of your life. You will be safe and warm.' Her soft words belie her cruel hands. If I had a child I would not give it to this woman.

'I will not tell you.'

She presses hard against my windpipe. The edge of my vision blackens. She lets go, quickly. That would be too easy a release, and she still has hope she can pry information from me.

'You would not have given her away. It was the child you asked for. Life is too important to you – or you would not have been able to do this.' She throws back at me every lie I once told her as she points at her face, her neck as triumphant proof. She does not know me as well as she would like to think.

'I will not tell.'

She snarls, and her teeth are sharp and white.

'If you do not give me the child, you will burn. You're a witch, it's only fitting. You have until daylight.'

She sweeps from the room and the door is bolted behind her. I lean back against the soft padding of the chair and try to swallow the ache in my throat. I think of the little girl laughing, those chubby arms and the smell of warm child. And gone so quickly.

In truth, I do not tell the mother what happened to her daughter, for I do not wish her to know how alike we are, Gwenllian and I. How my contempt for Gwenllian is so firmly rooted in contempt for myself.

The child I demanded for my services I paid to another in turn. I made a deal with an old man who taught me every scrap of magic I knew. I lived in his house for two years learning everything I could, but I did not warm his bed. When first I asked him to teach me, he refused my offer of the usual favours; told me he would have his recompense but that he would name it later. Was I prepared not to know what it was?

Blinded by the desire for knowledge, I said *Yes.*

When at last he said it was time for me to clear my account and sent me to Gwenllian's lonely bower, I did not argue. He told me what to ask for in return. I came back to the cathedral-city, in love with my own power, floating on the cloud that healing Gwenllian brought, feeling as if nothing was beyond me. The child was on my hip and my heart felt full. I wondered why he did not take the girl himself, but who was I to question his long game? *Who was I to gainsay such a powerful man?*

She'd be a princess, I told myself. She'd have the best. I handed her over with barely a qualm. And I woke the next day to find myself sleeping in the street and the house not merely empty, not merely stripped of all the familiar things I'd come to expect, but simply gone. The place I'd called home all gone in the night.

It was a big city, but I could have found them. I could have sought him out and asked *Why*? He'd gone to such trouble, though, to hide – it would be stupid to make him angry by following him. I did not think myself stupid. The child was not mine. She would have a good life, little Jessamyn. The best I could do was to leave her there. I was not her mother, after all.

But I know, too, that when I gave the child away, all my luck turned bad.

Now I would not ruin the happy existence I'd imagined for her by telling her dam where she might be found.

* * *

The first ray of light brings Gwenllian back to my prison. She sees my expression and does not ask again. My answer is plain, even among the scars.

Out in the courtyard a pyre is waiting. They tie me to the stake and throw pitch over me and the wood, so we will burn faster. I think of the girl, how Jessamyn cannot be worse off. How even death would be preferable to life with this woman who gave birth to her with no more thought than an apple tree puts forth fruit.

A small crowd of servants has gathered. There is a young girl with the whitest of hair and dreaming blue eyes. She holds a doll that's almost as big as she is. We smile at each other, but a woman, who might be her mother, hurries her away. 'Bitsy, don't look, her kind will curse you.'

The Lady Gwenllian does not come down, but I know she watches from the tower. As the smoke reaches my lungs, I cough, this time a dry hack that gasps for air. I feel the flames nip at my toes, catch my dress, and I tell myself that I am being warmed by an inn fire. I can almost believe it until the pain licks through me. My last comfort comes with Gwenllian's screams.

My magic lives only as long as I do. In that high room, her arms and neck and lovely face are prickling and peeling and burning, a smell of pork filling the air. When I am gone she will not forget me, nor her broken bargain.

THE STORY OF INK

The girl is thin, flat-chested and badly dressed, but her hair is dark and glossy and her cheekbones high. Her skin is clear and glowing. The torn sleeve of her dress shows the tiny red flash on her shoulder I've been told to look for – Get closer, he said, and it will be a tiny red crown. She's easy to recognise, all things considered. The old man's charge, a runaway.

He's paying. I've got instructions; he says she's his ward, *so* she's his ward.

I watch a while longer, the better to know my quarry. She laughs and jokes with the stall-holders in the market and the other whores – these girls work the streets, they've not got the protection of one of the pleasure inns. This isn't the fancy market at Busynothings Alley either. It's just as busy but nowhere near as clean, nor as reputable. This is Half-moon Lane, out in the slums, where people live packed on top of one another, where the truly desperate find a home in the sewers and some even live in the hollows at the base of the city walls.

Strictly speaking, it's far too wide for a lane, more like an avenue or a boulevard but, well, there you go. Here you can buy the usual bits of food and spice, pots and pans, but there are also potions and poisons to be had. If it's an assassin you're after then try any of the taverns that line the pavement, and if it's love you're in need of and don't want to pay the overheads of an inn-bred whore, then we can fulfil those requirements, too. Girls just as pretty but cheaper, and with a shared room at the top of one of the perilous staircases that cling to the sides of the buildings. Just watch out for the pimps, that's all.

How this pampered princess came to be here is a mystery. You can see she's had a soft start in life, it shines through whatever's happened to her on the streets. But almost everything else is as the old man said it would be. *Almost.* What I didn't expect, what he didn't tell me, probably didn't *know*, is what she's carrying: a baby. Wrapped in ragged but clean blue cloth, a boy if tradition's anything to go by, maybe a year old.

I rap my cane on the roof of the carriage and the driver knows to gee-up the horses and pull us over to the other side of the thoroughfare, stopping just near the girl. Pennyworth gets down and opens the door, unravelling the fine metal steps so I can descend.

Around me the noise stops and I'm pleased with the effect I have. My outfit is cut like a riding habit, although I've never been on a horse in my life. Blue velvet the same shade as my eyes, the short jacket is fitted and detailed with silver braid; the skirt is full and falls like water. Around my wrist is a pearl bracelet and on my right index finger, a white-gold ring, filigreed, with a moonstone setting. I love the tricorn hat that perches on my dark red curls. The silver-topped cane I clutch in my right hand is another fine gift from my employer. (He said I should be protected and showed me how to slide the blade out from the bottom section.) The fact that I'm only eleven completes the strength of the impression I make.

I take small precise paces toward the girl, holding my skirts so they won't drag in the mess and muss. She watches me, the corner of her mouth lifting in amusement. There's nothing unkind in it, but it annoys me, that she doesn't take me seriously. My outfit, my poise, my position were all hard won and here's this street-whore laughing at me.

I taste the acid of resentment, but I paste a smile on my face. No point in showing her what I feel. *You catch more flies with honey than vinegar*, my old mum used to say, when she was sober enough to say anything.

'What's your name, lovely?' I ask her and she laughs. She really is beautiful.

'Jessamyn, but for a quarter-gold it can be whatever you like.' She grins to let me know she's joking. She jiggles the baby on her hip and looks at me amiably. 'You're a little young for my services, darling.'

'I make you a proposition on behalf of my master,' I tell her, lifting my hands in a magnanimous gesture, the cane twirling in the fingers of one hand, then hopping across to the other. I'm still thinking, trying to figure out what to offer her, what will tip the odds in my favour.

'Indeed? And what does he propose, this man who sends a child into the streets?' Her face displays distaste now and I can't help myself.

'What I do, I do *willingly*. Don't be fooled by my size, missy. I choose to be here and I am no man's whore,' I hiss, displaying more of myself than I would like. She recoils and looks ashamed, to have shown herself judging of me when she's the one walking the streets, some stray get on her hip.

'I'm sorry,' she says and I can tell she is. 'Let's start again, shall we? I'm Jessamyn.'

I take a deep, calming breath and smile brightly. 'And I'm Livilla. My master asks that you come to visit. Perhaps that you will stay, if you find his house and company agreeable.'

'And how does your master know me?' The baby's strong little hands curl around her fingers and she gives him a distracted smile. How hard is her life with this one to keep? But she has not let him go like so many of them do. She did not get rid of him by drinking some witch's brew. She keeps him close; that should tell me something about her.

'He has driven by in his carriage.' I gesture over my shoulder at the fine black conveyance with its silver trappings, but conspicuously lacking a coats-of-arms or any device that might mark it out. 'He's an important man, is my master, and it wouldn't do for him to be seen approaching a woman on the street…'

'Indeed not,' she says and gives a laugh. The baby giggles too, hearing her. He grabs a handful of her lush black hair and gently plays with it. I wonder what my master will do with this little man. Farm him out? Send him to one of the orphanages? Keep him at home and raise him right? I cannot tell.

'Just come and see. One visit. A good hot meal for the boy-bee. Nice bath for you. I'll look after the boy-bee. Nothing too strenuous, for my master is venerable.'

'Isn't venerable just a big word for *old*?' she asks, all mirth.

I ignore her and go on, 'Just one visit and if you like it then think about staying. Better to be in one of the fancy houses. Better to raise the boy in a safe place, to let him be educated by tutors, rather than thieves. What do you want him to grow up to be? Honest man with a good trade, or a pickpocket?'

Her eyes darken. The child rubs his face against her neck like a puppy seeking a pat. She runs a hand over him as if to check that he's not too thin, not too deprived. He's a fat happy baby, but I don't tell her that, don't offer reassurance.

'Alright,' she says.

I try to simply look pleased and not triumphant, as if this is a happy result for both of us. As if this won't bring me a longed-for reward. A place of my own, one of the tiny townhouses that border the richer cantons, newly built for the newly respectable, in the row that burnt down last year in a conveniently tidy fashion (a most controlled conflagration, it has been noted). A little house over four floors and no one to share it with, new-fangled plumbing and a handkerchief garden out the front. All my own.

Pennyworth's waited by the coach, now he bows politely as I usher the ragamuffin in and follow her quickly. I flutter my lashes at him and he knows to turn the lock after he rolls up the steps. The door on the other side of the coach has been long ago fused shut.

Inside we rest on velvet red seats, comfortably firm, but soft to touch. We both sit so as to face forward when the carriage moves. In the middle of the seatback is a panel and I slide it smoothly out: a small contraption with a crystal decanter and two glasses sitting in their own elegant case. Some freshly-made sweetmeats wait in a fine dish suspended in a kind of silver cage. I know they're laced with an opiate, so even though they make my mouth water I cannot partake. Although, perhaps, for later, when I need to sleep, I will pocket one.

I pour her a drink and she accepts it graciously, nodding to me over the rim of the glass. The baby tries to grab at it and she gently shushes him. He whimpers but settles. I break off a corner of a sweetmeat and push it into his mouth; it will calm him if nothing else. I offer her a fresh piece but she shakes her head.

'I prefer apples. Lost my taste for sweetmeats after I gorged myself sick on them once,' she says and I curse inwardly. The tokay isn't drugged – the old man insisted she would take the sweetmeats, so he didn't drug the alcohol, so I could have some too and not raise suspicions by insisting she drink alone.

She lifts one of the shades and looks out the window. She goes pale; she must recognise the way we're going.

'No,' she says. 'No!'

'C'mon, love, I'm taking you home,' I try to sound sympathetic, but it doesn't seem to help. Her eyes go wide and she's panicking, but she still doesn't hit me. That's the advantage, I guess, of being a kid. She tries the door on her side and finds the handle useless, then pushes past me to get to my door, but all for nought.

'You don't understand. You don't know what he's like.'

'Come now, calm down. He's your guardian and he just wants you to come home. Be a family, like.' I twist the top of my ring and the minuscule sharp spike pops up. I grab her arm and scratch the skin, carving a thin furrow that fills with red. She yelps but it doesn't take long for the poison to work. I have to grab the baby from her so she doesn't drop him as she falls into a deep, deep sleep.

* * *

'And then,' I say, feeding the boy another spoonful of stewed apples, 'the girl unravelled her hair and let it down the side of the tower so the prince could climb up.'

'Don't know why you're filling his head with nonsense,' grumbles the cook. She doesn't like kids, which was why I was such a cause of concern when I came along just over a year ago. She ranted that she'd only taken the job because there were no children – didn't complain to the gentleman who pays our wages, mind. Eventually she had to admit I wasn't really a child, only in my form. My brain is as sharp as an adult's with a man's ambition and a woman's perseverance. My master would often comment on what a force I would be if only I were grown. He says he saw it in me even when I was an urchin – that's why he plucked me off the street. But I can wait. I will grow.

'He's just a baby.'

'Brat it is, street-get,' she sneers. 'Boss never could resist a stray.'

She eyes me caustically. She speaks as if he acts out of altruism. That's a laugh.

Jessamyn is upstairs, sleeping. The driver carried her to her old room. Master saw the baby and I didn't like the look that crossed his face. He's been searching for the girl for over a year and I think – I *know* – he wanted her to still be pure. The child is an irrefutable sign of how impure she's become. *No matter, no matter*, he muttered.

* * *

I wander up the stairs, the baby in my arms. He's sleepy and I think to put him on my bed. Perhaps to take him to see his mother, first. The room is locked but I carry a key on my chatelaine's belt. Now the daughter of the house is back, my place will not be the same – no matter, for I will soon have my own abode and my own servants.

I smile as I push the door open.

She is not there. The coverlet is disturbed as if by the tossing of a body in anxious sleep. She should not, could not, would not have woken by herself so she has been taken. I put the slumbering baby down, surround him with pillows so he doesn't roll off the high mattress and break and wail. There is a drool stain on the shoulder of my fine blue velvet.

I take the staircase that winds up to the attic room.

It is unlocked, which means His Lordship is being unusually inattentive, distracted no doubt by this new acquisition. There have been other girls over the years, but I've never known any of them to cause my master to lose his customary caution. I don't usually come here; I know he doesn't like it, but I feel compelled to go on.

I open the door. It is well-oiled and makes no sound. I slip inside and stand in the shadows.

The ceiling is high and hung with censers and lanterns, but the light doesn't make it to the very corners, as if darkness insists upon residing here and will not be defied. The scent of dead roses and incense is strong. A long window, running almost the length of the room, looks out over the city. There are benches and cupboards and chests, and bookshelves line the walls, although their contents have spilled onto the floor in some places. There is a disorder I do not associate with this man.

Jessamyn lies on a high table, naked on top of a clean white sheet and face down. Her head is turned to the side so she can breathe; a trickle of spittle shines at the corner of her mouth. Her eyes are open but glazed. She looks frail and pale, there's nothing round or soft or curvy to suggest she's a young mother.

Archbishop Bigod has set aside his red and purple robes and wears a plain black cassock. He is tall and thin like the girl, and appears to be in his middling years. Pennyworth whispered to me that our master is older than he looks. Iron grey hair is brushed back, a widow's peak making his visage seem even longer than it is. His cheekbones are high, sharp and angular. His eyes are dark, dark blue. Something in the cast of his face and hers tells me that their blood is closer than he would have me think. He runs his hands down her back, checking for imperfections. Satisfied, he leans away and breathes deeply, eyes closed.

Bigod takes a bottle from the bench next to him and cracks the seal of wax around its sturdy neck. He pulls the stopper out and throws the bottle into the space over Jessamyn. I can hear him intoning an incantation.

Ink spills out, staining the air, but only the vial falls to the floor, empty. The liquid hovers above the girl's back. Then the old man claps his hands and it sounds very loud in the silence of the attic. Black tendrils float down and settle onto the snowy skin. It moves around like snakes and beetles, writhing until it has formed a pattern.

'Livilla,' he says and I jump. I should have known he would sense my presence.

'Yes, sir?'

'Come closer, so you can see better.' He doesn't even glance over his shoulder at me. I step into the lit part of the room and stand on the opposite side of the table to him. He gestures to the canvas of his ward. 'This map will cost me dearly, but it will lead me to the place I need to go.'

'She is really your daughter?' He is not often talkative, so I will take this chance.

He nods. 'Lost and now found, soon to be lost again. A long game, this one; having her in secret, then stealing her away.'

I don't understand. 'Why hide it? All of it?'

He gives me a withering look. 'An archbishop with a child? A child fathered for this single purpose? I must be patient with my flock's sins, Livilla, but their tolerance of *my* sins is not so great.'

'Is it worth it? This map?'

'Not just a map, but a conduit. It will give me dominion over the dead,' he says as if that is an answer. 'There is a price to pay, of course. All things of value must be purchased, little one.'

He bends down and whispers something to his daughter. The girl rolls over, her smile lazy. A dagger lies on the bench and he takes it up, puts the point of it against her chest, not right in the middle where he'll get stuck on the breast bone, but to the left a bit. At first there's just the shadow, then a dent in the flesh, next a pinprick of blood bursting through the skin and finally is a great jet of red and Jessamyn sighs. I can almost see her spirit go, fleeing her mouth.

'She's both a map and a conduit and I must set her or she'll be gone in a few minutes.'

'Gone where?'

But any answer he may have given is lost in the sound of the front door being broken open; the shouting of Cook and Pennyworth rapidly stilled; the thunder of many booted feet coming up the stairs, up towards this room. Bigod's mouth hangs open, he who has always been so assured is now unsure what to do in the face of such blatant disobedience. Who breaks into the Archbishop's house?

I step away from him and into the shadows. I work at the stiff lock on the arched window that shows me the night sky of the city, the Cathedral spire a sharp silhouette against velvety blue-black and cold diamond stars. My fingers feel thick and stupid on the reluctant metal; I tear a fingertip on a sharp edge and the blood makes things slippery, but it also seems to lubricate the mechanism and the lock moves slowly with a scrape.

I look at the room behind me and the door bursts open. Men pile in, dirty and unkempt, hung about with weapons. No soldiers these – brigands, thieves. At their head is a tall handsome man with a wolfish smile. The Archbishop still has the dagger in his hand and he lashes out, nicking the man's chin. A thin red line opens up and the man's smile widens as he runs my master through.

Bigod makes an *o* of disbelief. I push open the window and it does me the courtesy of sliding silently. I scamper onto the sill and then step out. The night air is fresh – it's only a matter of moments before it sneaks into the rooms and snuffs the candles and the outlaws notice me. Still, I risk one last glance.

The Robber reaches for Jessamyn's body. He doesn't even look at her face (wouldn't know her if he saw her again), just flips her over to view the map. He grins when he sees the tattoo-work on her back and pulls a knife from his belt. The man is about to strip the skin from her but she begins to fade. His hand and the knife pass through her as she becomes ghostly. I'm pretty sure I see her eyes fly open, dead girl though she be, and they're alive with surprise and fear. Then she's gone. A map and a conduit.

I gingerly make my way along the ledges. I think the bandits will have been far too disturbed by what happened inside for them to notice anything else. I scamper across the roofs like a stray cat, hampered by my pretty skirts and my fine footwear. I kick off the shoes and tie up my skirts like I've seen the washerwomen do, like my old mum used to do when she still had the wit to hold down a job. I think about the jewellery and the coin I had set aside for my future. About the little house that would have been all my own. I think about the baby boy lying on a bed his mother will never find.

I wonder how long I will take to forget.

LOST THINGS

I'm just a boy, I keep telling them. A common footpad.

No one believes me. Which shows that (a) they're a suspicious bunch, and (b) not as stupid as they look. But still, it would be nice if someone believed me just once. It's partially true anyway: I've been working as the cook's boy (although *working* is a very strong word) for this group of robbers and thieves, but I'm actually a girl. And I'm a map. *The* map.

Well, maybe not *the* map in the greater, more universal sense, but the map for which this lot are looking. They just don't know they've got it. Or, they didn't until yesterday afternoon when I tried to dodge under the Boss's arm (strictly speaking, he's a Robber Bridegroom but that's a bit of a mouthful every time you address him) as he tried to swipe me for some infringement and grabbed my shirt. The damned thing's so old it's got no strength left in the weave. The moment pressure greater than a summer breeze got hold of it, it tore and left me in all my small-breasted glory as an object of unhealthy interest for the merry men.

I've been able to get away with being a boy because I am seriously flat as a board, no bosomy wench me. In fact, the worst that could have happened as a girl would have been a bit of rough shagging, but the Robber Bridegroom saw the map, didn't he? So I was stuffed, wasn't I? I mean, my virtue's safe 'cause he's got me under lock and key (as far as a withy cage in the back of the outlaws' cave counts as lock and key), with orders that anyone who touches me will be strung up from the nearest oak tree and left to hang until the flesh drops off his bones.

I'd like to tell them that I'm a princess in disguise running away from an arranged marriage, but I've got no hope with that porky. My accent screams "nasty part of town" with bells on, and when I lived in the city I spent more than enough of my time dodging the Peelers, I can tell you.

I'm no one important, not really, but someone who *was* important got their hands on me for a time. He inscribed this bloody map on my back, about ten inches by ten inches, the map to the places where lost things go. The Boss has been looking for it for a while apparently.

The door to the cage creaks opens, and I jump. The breakfast delivery may be a chance for escape. I tense in case I can get past whatever idiot they've sent. I must appear for all the world like a rabbit set to bolt – which is to say pretty silly, really.

Faideau, a tall wiry boy not much older than me, stands in the breach, in one hand a lump of bread, in the other a wooden cup of what is probably curdled goats' milk. I'd have called him *friend* until yesterday.

He gives me a look of exasperation. 'Honestly, you're just determined to piss him off, aren't you? Where are you going to run to?'

'Oh, shut up. Give me that, I'm hungry.'

He hands over the bread and the cup. I hate goats' milk but it's the only thing will soften the bread. He pulls something green from his pocket and waves it at me, teasing.

'An apple! You stole that from the Boss's private stash,' I breathe in admiration. He grins and sits down beside me on the bed of dried bracken. With surprising strength, he twists the fruit in half and hands me my share. As I grab at it, Faideau eyes the tattoos that cover my right index finger, but politely doesn't mention them.

I bite into the juicy sharpness. I don't even mind that it's not a whole piece – it's the first bit of fresh produce I've had in three months for the Boss is a dog-in-the-manger when it comes to this sort of thing. Whenever we manage to hijack a shipment of vegetables and fruit, there is no sharing. Although I don't know why I thought the lair of a band of footpads would be a haven of tasty treats.

To be honest, I wasn't thinking at all. I had a *minor* misunderstanding with the Authorities in Lodellan and well, I hid in a cart that was rolling its way along Busynothings Alley and out under the main gate. Didn't realise it was going to be stolen, did I? I fell asleep and didn't wake up while the whole stand-and-deliver business took place.

At least, that was the story I told them when they found me. I said I wanted to stay, that my name was Tobias and I was a young-thief-on-the-make. The Robber Bridegroom advised me quite kindly that I'd be seeing some illegal things and I'd better work out which side my bread was buttered on. I saluted him smartly and set about making myself useful. I attached myself to the cook because it seemed like a good idea at the time. I thought there might be extra portions, spoons to be licked – and we know how well that went.

Plans are strange things, never moving in the direction you'd like them to go. This is something I've known all my life but still I get that fizz of surprise when something goes wrong. I guess I'm what you'd call an optimist.

'No cutlery?' I ask politely, thinking a knife might have been useful. He snorts.

'Who do you think you are, Lady Muck?'

'Well, it's not so much for me as for your own sake, my sloppy friend. The Boss does like his cutlery and if you're going to be doing my job, you'll need to sharpen up your act, boyo.' I warm to my theme. 'I mean, I may have been slack, but I never forgot the cutlery.'

'*Slack* is the least of your worries, Jezzy. You should think about the other words the Boss's been using, like liar, cheat, sneak, thief...'

'That's a bit rich. We've fallen in with *thieves*, Faideau. Maybe he didn't mean me specifically,' I say.

'He started the sentence with your name, put in a few profanities, then inserted the foregoing adjectives.'

'Strictly speaking, I think they may be nouns.'

This is what my life has come to – arguing points of grammar with a skinny brigand. I should never have run away from home – or perhaps I should have run further.

'Whatever.' He shrugs. 'And by the way, what did you think you were going to do if you got out? How far do you think you'd get?'

'Well, I wasn't really thinking,' I huff at him airily. 'The Boss, did he use the phrase *skin alive*?'

'No, but only because he probably hasn't thought of it yet. He'll be sending someone else soon, I reckon, when he calms down and starts to think of this as fortuitous.'

'Where did you learn these big words, Faideau?' I tilt my head, examining him closely.

'My mum brought me up proper,' he says ungrammatically, as if he can fool me; but I know better. I know he's lying. His mother taught him nothing because she wasn't about. I run my tongue around the cave of my mouth, checking hopefully for any stray bits of sour-sweet fruit. No such luck, so I start on the stale bread, dunking it into the bitter milk.

'Thanks, Faideau.' I really am grateful.

'Welcome,' he says gruffly. I want to ruffle his dark curls but that might be taken the wrong way. He finishes his half of the apple and stands. 'Better tell the Boss what he wants to hear, Jez. It will go easier for you.'

I roll onto my side, feeling less grateful, and don't bother to watch him leave. The door clacks shut behind him and I'm left looking at the damp rock wall, watching the trickle of moisture wind its way through dark green moss.

* * *

'You knew I was looking for it.'

'Well, strictly speaking, sir, I didn't,' I hedge. Faideau rolls his eyes in despair and the Boss turns his glare upon me. His eyes are a fetching blue, I must say – and he's got a good face. There's just that thin scar on his chin, gives him character – makes him look, well, rakish. Is it any wonder he's got brides lining up to throw themselves and their wealth at him? He's charming and I suspect some of them would still succumb even if they knew how badly things were going to end. A true Robber Bridegroom, he believes in death doing couples part. He seems to be getting a bit tense. I sigh.

I'm half-naked with the second-in-command, Jones (a nasty fat little man), holding me still, with the third-in-command, Hopney (a nasty skinny little man), running his hand down my spine. I hope he's washed his hands. We're in the Boss's personal cave, and the only other audience member is Faideau, of whom our host seems fond in a roughly paternal type of way.

The Boss waggles a finger at me.

'You *knew* I was looking for it and you deliberately concealed it from me.' He emphasises my sin with a poke to the breast bone. It's quite forceful and takes my breath away. I don't like being poked. Faideau is watching my face, then his eyes drop and he squints at my chest, at the raised scar over my heart.

'I'll thank you not to stare, young man.'

'Focus, Tobias – oh, I'm sorry, what is it now?'

'Jessamyn. Jez.'

'That's better. Now where was I?'

'About to let me go?'

'I don't think so. Oh, yes. You knew that map was of an abiding interest to me and you wilfully concealed it from me.'

'Honestly, what did you expect me to say? I know we've only just met, Mr Robber, but would you like to see the map on my back? Your record with the ladies isn't so good. I don't know you from a bar of soap, but oh well, why don't I just trust you with my life?'

'And you were the worst cook's boy I've ever seen.'

'I'm not actually a boy, am I?' May as well be hung for a sheep as a lamb, I figure.

'I should have known from the mouth on you,' he notes, wise in hindsight. His voice softens. 'It must have hurt – who put it there?'

'A man. An old man, who found me on the streets.'

'This old man…' he prompts.

'That's all, an old man with money, strange tastes and powerful friends. He took me in, said I had lovely skin, that I was a wonderful canvas – I thought he was going to make something of me, a lady.'

'Silk purse out of a sow's ear?'

'Something like that,' I agree, taking no offence. 'But all he wanted me for was the map. Tied me to a bed when I was finally fed and healthy and a bit fleshed out. Inked me up.'

'Why did he let you go?'

'Who said he did?' I raise an eyebrow. 'I scarpered across the roofs as fast as I could and disappeared for a time. Don't know what happened to him.'

My lies and the fragments of truth I remember mingle so well that I can hardly recognise which is which. I cobble them together like a beggar's cape. I don't tell him that I've jumbled the order of events, that I knew the old man. I don't tell him about what I left behind.

'Where did you hide?'

'No point telling anyone is there, if I have to do it again?'

He nods in an offhand manner. The Boss gives me a measured look that says he recognises part of this as a giant lie, but he doesn't push it. He knows more than he's letting on; wish I was brave enough to ask him a few questions.

'Then I ended up here,' I say truncating my tale as much as I dare. 'I joined your band and have been masquerading as the world's worst cook's boy ever since.'

'You were pretty dreadful – but you never forgot the cutlery.'

I give Faideau a triumphant look. He jerks a couple of fingers in the air to tell me what he thinks of that.

'So, what am I going to do with you, Jessamyn?' asks the Boss. I know it's a rhetorical question, but I can't help but hope.

'Dishonourably discharge me from your service and send me on my merry way?'

'Not going to happen, I'm afraid. I need what's on your back.'

'Well, as long as you don't plan to separate me from my skin, I guess I'll stick around,' I advise resignedly. 'Perhaps I could have my old job back?' In truth, I have no intention of staying. Unfortunately, he seems to realise this.

'Nice try. You're my map to where the lost things are, Jez, you're not going anywhere.' He sits in the old armchair covered with green velvet; there's only one for no one sits in this room but him. 'What about the finger? Is that part of it?'

'No, got that later, just for decoration.' I take a deep breath. 'Boss, it isn't a good idea.'

'Shut up and stand still.'

'I'm cold.'

'And will get colder still if you don't shut it.'

'Look, I'm just going to say this, then I'm done,' I announce and continue before he can bellow at me. 'There's a reason things get lost, and by lost I mean dead.'

'She's not dead, she's lost,' the Robber Bridegroom grumbles. I shake my head.

'Lost is a euphemism for dead, Boss. "Dead Things" just doesn't have the same alluring ring to it. What I'm saying is that you won't be finding your missing socks there. Some lost things are meant to stay that way and it's best not to go looking. Sometimes the lost things – they look back.'

'Are you quite finished?' he asks politely.

'Quite.' And he takes a bandana from his pocket and stuffs it in my mouth, tying it tightly at the back of my head. I try to say 'That's totally unnecessary' but it doesn't come out anything like that. The Robber Bridegroom runs his hand across me, as if he's reading the map with the tips of his fingers, as if my skin will commune with him. He begins to croon.

'So close. Much closer than I thought. We'll be there soon, together again soon.'

* * *

'You could let me go, you know.' Hopney and Jones are bullying some of the underlings into preparing packs for us: rations, ropes, axes, the usual going-to-visit-the-land-of-the-dead travel kit. Faideau is escorting me back to the withy cage.

'Yeah, right. Perhaps you'd like my testicles to wear as earrings while we're about it?' He gives me a firm push.

'Sarcasm is so unattractive.' I'm disappointed in him. 'You could come with me. This isn't a life for you – you're not like them.'

'They looked after me. A man's got to have some loyalty.' He should be a bit fussier about where he gives it. 'Your finger?' he asks, jerking his head towards my tattooed digit. 'Did that happen at the same time as your back?' I shrug. He pushes me into my cage and starts to close the door.

'Oi!'

'What?'

'What's he want with lost things?'

'He was very fond of his mother,' says Faideau and leaves me to ponder that.

'Oh, no.'

* * *

I sleep deeply – there's no telling when I'll have that luxury again. Daylight comes early as does my escort. It's just me, the Boss, Faideau, Jones, Hopney, and some stolen horses. We ride for a day (which seems nowhere near long enough to me, and yet far too long to the Boss, who takes his foul temper out on everyone), then set up camp. Or rather they set up camp and I watch – the advantage of being mistrusted is that I get to be tied to a tree and rest while they do all the heavy lifting.

'More wood,' I say to Hopney when he drops a few branches in the centre of the clearing, right where the campfire will go.

'Shut yer cakehole.'

'Fine,' I reply, 'But this is the forest, in case you haven't noticed. The *woods,* and we are uninvited guests.'

'So?' he asks, but he's less belligerent. I nod behind him at a spot between the trees and he turns to look. In the lowering dusk there are shapes, some wolfish, some humanish; none of them are sharp-edged even though they should be. All are, well, smudgy.

'The ones who live here,' I say pointedly, 'don't like fire. Now *me*, I like a good fire.'

He yells to Faideau and they both start collecting more wood with a speed that borders on the impressive. I feel the weight of a gaze and notice the Robber Bridegroom is watching, eyes narrowed as I boss his men around. I give him a bright smile and whistle a tune, off-key.

After an imposingly bad meal of beans and stale bread (I never thought I'd find it in my heart to miss our cook), we all lay close to the fire, wrapped in blankets. Out beyond the limits of the firelight, things move in the darkness, never coming near enough to be seen. Sometimes beneath the crack and pop of the burning wood, I can hear a breath, a sigh, the click of teeth.

Faideau and I are closest together; the tether on my ankle is attached to his wrist.

'How did you get among this lot, Faideau?' I whisper when I think the others asleep.

'Why do you want to know?'

'Because I'm bored and I'm tied up and I don't think you belong with them. You don't *seem* like a cut-throat.' I take a deep breath. 'No family?'

'No. I – no. The Boss brought me up – if you can call it that. There were some other people, but I had to leave them.' He's silent for a bit, then, 'Do you think you can be forgiven, no matter what you did?'

'Oh, I hope so,' I reply with a bit more fervour than I intended.

'Why? What did you do?'

'I left someone behind. I didn't mean to and it wasn't really my fault. And I've been trying to make it up for a very long time.'

'I – what I did, I meant to do. I'm sorry for it, but I meant it.'

'How old were you?'

'Nine.'

'I'm pretty sure kids' stuff is forgiven, Faideau,' I tell him, I hope kindly.

'Sometimes kids do the worst stuff,' he begins.

'If you don't shut up, Jez, I will cut your tongue out. I don't need *it*.' The Robber Bridegroom says it so pleasantly and so calmly that I might almost be tempted to not take him seriously. But I'm not an idiot, so that puts an end to the conversation.

* * *

A few hours after dawn, we come to a lake, wide and flat, with an island not quite in its middle. A surprisingly steep mountain rises from it. We find a jetty and a rowboat moored there. I see no houses around and assume the boat is the only dry way across. We all five of us pile in – at one point I think about throwing myself overboard, but to what end? We're going in the same direction.

Faideau looks less than happy about the whole situation but I note he's still not questioning the Boss. I feel a despair so deep, one that I've felt only once before, in the utter depths of my life, at the end my life, in fact.

'Please, Boss. I'm begging you. Don't do this. Leave it be.'

'No. Grab her, gents, and keep her close.'

Before they can get me, I tear open my shirt to show the scar, puckered and a bit purplish after all these years. I point to where my heart used to be, where the flesh was parted and the all-important organ torn out. A red birthmark glows on my shoulder. 'This is how I died.'

They stare.

'This is how I became a lost thing. I died eighteen years ago.' I'm so desperate, I trip over words. 'I found myself here, where all go when they shuffle off. When he tattooed me, the old man thought only to make me into a map. He just wanted my skin. He didn't want me, I wasn't *special*. But he tattooed me and he took my heart. He would have flayed me too had he not been interrupted. But it wasn't my time. I died too soon so I made a *deal*: they gave me flesh once more. I found a way out, a way home. I went back to find my son. Time passes differently in there. When I got back, he was a young man, gone from the city and wandering the forest in the company of thieves.

'There are rules to these places. I'm outside of them for the moment. One day I'll go back but only when my deal is done. You, on the other hand, don't belong here at all. The dead you *look for* will feed off you, pull you down, keep you here. You can't take them back with you. You're *food* to them.'

'She's my mother, Jez,' he says gently, as if speaking to a moron. 'She'd never hurt me.'

'The dead have no loyalty.'

The boat grinds aground and we step out onto the small beach. Jones and Hopney take an arm each and frog march me into the undergrowth and onwards to where the mountain begins. The Robber Bridegroom has the light step of the mad. Faideau brings up the rear; I glance over my shoulder at him, try to will him to *do* something.

The door in the mountain is huge, carved from stone. Conversely, the keyhole is very small, room enough for a slightly bony finger to fit through. The Boss tells me to open it, to let him into the kingdom of the lost things. I refuse and start to scream. I struggle so hard they can't get me near the door. I break away, manage a few yards before Hopney brings me down and Jones sits on me. The Robber Bridegroom, by now frustrated beyond all measure, places his foot firmly on my hand, then takes his long knife and slices off the finger in question.

He takes the severed thing, holds the bloody end gingerly, and stuffs it in the lock. Things churn and creak inside the mechanism until it opens with a *thunk*. His henchmen step away from me and my gouting hand. Faideau kneels beside me though, and wraps a none-too-clean hanky around the wound. If I wasn't so busy swearing, I would thank him.

The Boss stands at the open door, searching inside the darkness for something, someone he recognises and loved perhaps too much. Particles coalesce in the dim light of the cavern, forming and re-forming until a woman stands before him.

She is beautiful, truly beautiful, long golden hair, generous breasts and hips and a tiny waist, a crushed-berry smile, with laughing eyes. If I didn't know better, I'd think her enchanting and entirely harmless. I grab Faideau's arm with my uninjured hand, to make him tear his eyes away from the vision that is the Robber Bridegroom's mother.

'Don't think of anyone you've lost. Don't do it or you're gone,' I hiss, pinching him so he'll take me seriously. His eyes slide towards the Boss's mother and I pinch him again, this time so hard his flesh splits, just a smidgeon. He swears at me, but I've got his attention. 'The Robber Bridegroom has to go. There's no helping *them*. I'd prefer *you* didn't end up with them. Help me stand.'

He does, although he looks at me suspiciously now, as if I'm something dangerous, no longer vaguely amusing. I limp over to the doorway. Just inside, the Robber Bridegroom and his mother are entwined in a "nice to see you again" embrace that is a bit too friendly for words. Jones and Hopney have wandered past them and are well into the throat of the cave. I see them pause, crane their heads forward to peer into the blackness, then give strangled cries as things, dead things, swarm out of the shadows and engulf them. Many of the lost things are recognisable as women: the Boss's former brides. There are so many.

His mother looks less delectable now, her face is that of a dried-up crone, skin cracked like old parchment, nose eroded by the rot of death. She opens one eye and gives me a slow, wicked wink. Her son moans. I don't know if he could see her as she really is even if he opened his eyes. Behind them, the darkness has swallowed Jones and Hopney and now it surges forward, towards the light, towards escape.

I put my shoulder to the stone and push, weeping and sobbing and dripping blood on the dirt at my feet. The door closes with a scrape, and I scrabble about at the keyhole, pulling at the tiny bit of flesh to get a hold on it, finally jerking it from the lock. The cogs and wheels turn and creak, sealing the lost things in their home once more. I drop to the ground and cry until snot drips from my nose and I hiccup until I vomit. All in all, an attractive picture. From inside the mountain comes a thin scream.

In the end, Faideau picks me up, wipes me off as best he can and we stagger back down to the beach. He climbs into the rowboat and holds out his hand. I shake my head. 'I can't go with you. My deal is done.'

'There are things you need to tell me,' he says.

'I wish I could tell you more. I was a stupid girl, sold myself for food on the streets. I had you.' I nod.

'Will you tell me?'

'No.'

'Let's go home.'

'I can't go with you,' I repeat and I throw my finger out into the lake, food for fish.

'Mother...'

'Don't call me that – it just sounds somewhat unhealthy at the moment.' I smile and it feels all wobbly on my face. 'You have to go, though; this isn't a good place to be.'

'I can't leave you,'

'Faideau, this was my deal – to save you and I did so. If I leave, they'll come after me and we don't want that.'

'You can't get back in. You've thrown away the key.'

'There are always other keys, other doors. Don't come back. Promise me.'

'Jez...'

'Promise me. Row away and don't come back. Make a life. Love someone. Give me grandchildren. Promise me.'

'I promise.'

I hug him for the shortest long time I can, him in the boat, me on the shore. My child. It's been a lifetime since I held him, since he was a small warm, wet lump of baby-smell and soft flesh. We pull away at almost the same time and he sits down heavily, wiping his eyes and sniffling. I push the boat off the sand and wave.

He drifts for a while then begins at last to row, digging the oars deep into the water. I sit on the beach and watch him go back the way we came.

And then I remember I didn't ask him what he did, what was *his* sin. I didn't remember to ask and so give him some kind of absolution. I watch my boy float away, and think that he looks as broken as my heart feels.

A GOOD HUSBAND

The water here is sweet.

This pool is wide enough and deep enough to give me the space I crave. At the northern end a stream flows in from a larger river many miles distant; at the southern end a tributary retreats far, far away to the ocean. There the taste changes and becomes salty, the colour murky. Fine enough for my cousins with their scaled tails and sharp nails, frilled gills and tiny teeth. Well and good for the Sirens, ever more distant relatives, creatures who cannot decide between elements or even themselves, whether they are fish or fowl. Such a bitter home is not my choice though, oh no.

I love this place. It's somewhere between a small lake and an overly large pond, a strange in-between thing, to be sure. The important point is this: it's mine and mine alone. In some spots there are reeds, in others rocks for sitting while I comb my hair, grassy banks, and a thick screen of trees providing cover from the casual onlooker. I get visitors, oh yes, but only the women of Briarton (the town beyond the trees and over one hill, nestling in a gentle valley) come here with any kind of regularity.

It's mostly the unmarried girls. The Lake of the Mari-Morgan is a place they have claimed for themselves. They come to dance and sing and play. Before a special occasion like a wedding, they will conduct their toilettes here, washing their hair to make it shine and their skin so it glows (the water here is said to have beautifying properties – it's true, my little kindness to them). With gifts, large and small, they beg my favour, pray, cry, gives thanks, rail at fate or me (whichever pops into their heads first), yearn and sometimes get what they want. If I can satisfy a request, I generally do. Sometimes I chose not to, simply so they do not take it for granted; on those occasions they seem to assume their wish was not worthy, or their offering even less so.

I do quite like them, humans, with their funny hearts and minds, their queerer souls. If I am honest, I find them amusing. If I am even more honest, the company they offer is worth the expenditure of magic to give them their heart's desire. I am a solitary creature but sometimes isolation makes me ache.

Seldom do I show myself nowadays. Not that I am less beautiful or less vain, but I am infinitely more tired. If they see the weariness in my face, then what prospect for them? If an ageless being looks to have lost her spark, then…? I speak only when I choose and it seems to work best as a disembodied voice – perhaps it's the god-like quality. When I do appear it's to make a point, a scene, a statement. Sometimes a clever girl will express, in front of her companions, disbelief that I exist. She might stand on my favourite rocky seat, the one a long step from the shore, and declaim her cynicism. What better way to prove her wrong than to be seen, gliding over the lake, all a-glimmer?

Their mothers stop coming after they wed. I have often wondered if their hope dies then, or marriage was simply what they wanted. Having achieved it, they are content to chew on that same meat. But they pass the faith on to their daughters.

This one, this tall thin woman who comes all hesitating through the trees, is different though. This one I am fascinated by, oh yes.

She leans down close to the liquid mirror of the lake. She has visited here since she was a little girl, always bringing a tiny offering of some kind: flowers, sweetmeats, salted fish, embroidered pieces of rag made beautiful with her cunning stitches. She has never asked for anything in return, not ever, not even before her own wedding. The name the other girls call to her is "Kitty"; she sews for them. They have attired themselves in marriage and ball gowns of her making after bathing here. I have seen those very dresses wrapped in sheets and draped carefully over bushes and branches until the moment they are required. I've watched Kitty sewing them by the water's edge, smiling gently as her companions laugh and dance around her while she toils on their behalf.

This day, this hour, the scars on her face are still fresh, the reddish-brown of dried, scabbed blood. Two parallel lines run across the bridge of her nose before dropping down her left cheek. She will never be pretty again – and she *was* pretty, I will tell you that. Large blue eyes, a doll's pouting mouth and hair that was most glorious – is most glorious still, yet looks like a joke now perched on the mess of her countenance.

When first it happened, she came here to weep. Blood flowed and mixed with her tears to drip into the water. That got my attention: grief and blood. Sacrifices very few ever make, although she did not know it for a sacrifice and there was no one to tell her.

Her friends urged her to wash the injuries in the lake and it did some good, made the healing faster, but in truth the scars will never be gone. There was too much force behind them and too much spite – that's what makes them so deep, the spite. It bites not merely the flesh, but also the soul.

Kitty stares at her reflection, her features set in a determined way. She peers intently as if she might be able to see me through sheer force of will – she cannot although I lie right beneath her, studying her through the pane of water. The wounded woman opens her mouth and says, 'Help me.'

Her tears start again and I can taste their salt as they drop down, forming ripples in my home.

'Help me,' she repeats. 'Mari-Morgan, please help me.'

I kick away but make no disturbance in the glassy stillness. Blood and tears she gave me already, all unknowing. For this reason alone I must make answer to her summons. She will ask something great of me, something I may not be able to deliver. I can only throw out an obstacle for her and hope she will give up.

Rising, I become visible, walking across the surface as if it is solid. I know how I must look to her when she's so *ruined*. I can see my reflection in her large eyes: silver-green hair, silver-peach skin, eyes like a deep lake that cannot decide between blue or green or black, and a not-quite-stable outline. I ripple, I shimmer, my element is also my essence – in a bright light you might even see through me. I defy the eye to focus properly.

'What would you have of me?' I ask in a voice that sounds like a rushing flood. She shakes her head at this hoped-for appearance and I can see that she did not quite believe it would happen. All these years she has brought offerings to a creature she was not sure existed. I am both touched and vaguely annoyed.

'Make him kind. Make him love me. Make him a good husband. Make my life better.' Her long hands move to her scarred visage even though she seems not to notice. She doesn't quite touch the wounds and they must ache still, stretching tight and itching as they dry and knit. Kitty knows how much she asks.

'What will you give me?' I demand, as if the dripping blood and flowing grief were not enough. 'Nothing can be granted without something in return, oh no.'

'What will you have? Ask anything,' she says unwisely.

A long time ago when I loved to be seen, when I was younger, less tired, more arrogant, then, for a time, I asked for dresses. I wanted, silly conceited thing, to wear the pretty clothes the human girls did, to adorn myself like the colourful birds that nest in the trees along the banks. And the maidens brought them to me, exquisite things, almost works of art and oftentimes more than the girls could afford – I'm fairly sure some of them dropped their own wedding dresses in. I marvelled over them as they were held above the surface, watched as the sun glinted on buttons and silken bows, crystals and beads and velvet ribbons. They looked so lovely out there in the light when they were *dry*. Their owners would throw these glorious gowns into my lake and they would grow heavy and sink. I would scoop them up and struggle into the saturated frippery and find the garment, bereft of air and sun, had somehow *died*. Swimming in wet clothing is difficult to say the least. Shimmering and shimmying, floating and darting through water and lake weeds is neither easy nor pleasant when attired in a sodden drape of fabric. So I stopped asking for this particular kind of gift. I gave up and embraced my watery nakedness, my uncertain outline and the translucent nature of my body.

But now here is a clever, clever girl with brilliant, cunning fingers who sews the way my sea cousins create storms, with the same aplomb and passion.

I make my request and see her heart sink. My unkindness will save her further distress, I tell myself. If she cannot fulfil my price, then both our lives will be easier. One should not ask for what one thinks one wants, it is never the same as it seems when you are not in possession of it; like those dresses, so lovely in the sunshine, so disappointing in my hands.

* * *

I do not expect to see her again, certainly not a week later when blood covers the moon and casts a curious light upon everything. Moonlight is ordinarily strange enough, but this moon, this night, this light… there is both a weird clarity and a distinct gloom, shapes at once sharp and blurred. It is through this odd illumination that I see Kitty slip, nervous as a cat. A leather satchel hangs at her side, the thick strap angling across her chest, dark against her pale dress.

When she reaches the edge of the lake, she kneels down, heedless of grass and dirt stains on her skirts. She removes the satchel and opens it, the metal clasp giving a *snick* that sounds shockingly loud in the stillness. She takes out a book, its ancient leather cover corrugated like a toad's skin. I can see gold lettering on the spine, a large elaborate script. *Murcianus* it reads. *Murcianus' Little-known Lore.*

I feel unaccountably excited.

Next she pulls forth a pair of large shears such as you might use to cut a thick or stubborn material. Then a small patchworked hedgehog of a ball stuck full with pins and needles. Finally, a spool of fine thread – it gleams and I know it cannot be mere silk. Oh, there is silk in the mix certainly, but there's also flax and spider's web among other things, fused and bound together by sheer dint of sorcery. Someone else has created it – this girl is not *that* kind. I will be surprised if she manages her task for I don't sense any great magic in her.

Kitty takes the great scissors and leans out over the water. Tonight it shines like quicksilver. She has propped the Murcianus open on a flat rock and checks over the spell before proceeding to cut as if something lies *just* above the surface.

I *think* I can see it, the fabric of night and fluid at which she snips. I can see it ruche and crumple and fray, but I'm not sure how much *she* can see. Still and all, as her confidence grows and her fingers become steadier, as she begins to *believe*, the panels take on a dark form, shimmering like rogue satin.

She lays the pieces on the grass beside her as she finishes each one. Next she reaches into the lake and pulls up handfuls of water plant, long ribbons of it, green and slippery with algae. Carefully she washes it off and lines it up next to the water-fabric. At last she begins to sew. It takes her hours but the strange luminescence of the sky remains strong. She refers occasionally to the pages of the book and I wonder idly where she got it.

She hardly seems the type to own such a tome, but they've been floating around for years, various volumes and guides to the arcane. I have a vague memory of the author himself, or someone claiming to be him, visiting here and begging me to make myself appear so he could sketch me. Now that I think about it, my quite-passable-likeness graces the frontispiece of *Murcianus' Mythical Creatures.* Mythical! How a man who sat there drawing me when I'd very nicely solidified for him could call me *mythical* is beyond me.

But I digress. I've watched her all this time and become so fascinated that I've risen out of the water and gradually, very gradually forgotten to concentrate on not being seen. She notices me, but we don't speak. By the time the dawn is almost here I'm perched on a rock near the bank, avidly willing her to finish, oh yes. She places the last stitch, bites the eldritch thread and holds the dress up for me to inspect.

It has long, long skirts, a scooped neckline, a tight bodice and fitted sleeves to the elbow. It is embroidered with a design of silvery fish and flowers, and bows made of lake-weed decorate the sleeves and waist. It's the loveliest thing I've ever seen. It is the colour of my eyes, green and black and blue and all shades in between.

I move to the bank and stand still while she slips it over my head, laces the stays tight. The touch of it is cold and damp and it feels like a second skin. It moves ever so slightly, with the same gentle current as the water in my lake.

I'm so happy I could shout. Kitty stands back to survey her handiwork. Her eyes are red and there are dark smudges beneath them. The red-brown lines are vivid against her pallor but she smiles, seeing what she has done. For a time, I do believe she has forgotten her misery.

The sun comes up and strikes us both. She becomes a silhouette against the burning dawn and I a shining patch of liquid and light that must surely hurt my seamstress's eyes.

The moment passes, the sun lifts and I am as I am. I smile at Kitty.

'Thank you,' I say, marvelling that she has succeeded where so many would have failed. Joyful, even though I know that fulfilling my part of the bargain will not be easy on either of us, but that I am *obliged* to fulfil it.

'Make him love me. Make him be kind. Make him a better man.'

I am silent for a moment and she seems to stop breathing in that space of time. 'Bring him here this evening and I will make your life better.'

I turn and dive then wink out of sight just before I hit the glassy face of the lake.

My new dress does not hamper me; it flows and floats, part of the water and yet still separate from it. Not impeding my progress, it's nothing like those gowns of old. There is no drag, no gentle sluggish sensation of being wrapped in a wet winding sheet and of thinking, 'So this is how they feel when they drown'.

I dart off into the depths, down to the cave where I keep things that have caught my eye.

I do not sleep here – I prefer any number of rocky shelves,

sometimes on the very bottom, cocooned in weeds. But I rest here, with these few things, these trophies.

There is a mirror, demanded long ago for I do-not-remember-what favour. The gilt frame is chipped and peeling, the silver beneath the glass is pitted with black circles as if diseased. A few stacks of bones that belonged once to lovely-looking men. They drowned and I kept them for as long as I could while they still retained a hint of their beauty. I should throw the skeletal refuse out but I like its bright white.

I curl up on a pile of discarded, wetly crumbling dresses. The smell of mould and dank drifts up from them. I nestle there content in my fine and perfect attire – I feel, however irrationally, that I have conquered this stinking heap of disappointments. I run my hands over the flow of my new skirts and think of how to reward its maker.

* * *

He's not a handsome man, but he's big and strong. Too big to be hitting a woman; too big to be harming a wife who loves him; too big to be treating someone so kind so badly.

How she coaxed him here I've no idea. He looks displeased to have been drawn from his home into the deep blue of the evening. How desperate is she that she risks this? Knowing what he has done to her once, and what he has the potential and will to do to her again, still she obeyed me.

'Go to the edge,' she urges like a mother trying to get a difficult child to eat. He does so with ill grace, grunting. I can see his fingers are thick with muscle and he's clenching his fists as if desirous of hitting something. Before he turns on Kitty, I make myself visible, standing on the water, just a few yards from the bank.

He looks amazed to find me *real*. So many men simply think me a women's story, a myth, a jape. In his face: fear, desire, shock, but mostly greed. A tale is told, I believe, of the Mari-Morgan's treasure and perhaps that's the hook Kitty used to lure him. How can she, knowing something so venal would bring him, still love him? Still want him? I might shake my head were I so inclined.

I smile, gesture for him to come to me. He does this willingly, heedless of the liquid he splashes through even though it soaks his boots and trousers. He reaches out to take hold of me – as if he will hang on until I tell him where riches lie, as if I should be afraid of him, as if he might do me harm. His hands pass through my body because I do not wish to be touched. *My* hands, though, are solid enough, strong enough to take a good grip on his shirt.

I pull him down. Kitty's screams grow softer and softer as we go further into the muddy-green, dulled by the depths.

He struggles for a while, but is no match for my age-old force. He may as well fight against a statue. The bubbles escaping from his mouth at first obscure his face, then he stops trying to breathe, to live, and simply gives up. Stops moving. The tiny spheres dissipate, heading urgently away as if they might carry his screams and release them into the dry-world. The water turns his face a sickly shade. I let him go, watch as he disappears into the deep dark, rolling and rolling, the white of his shirt like a fish's belly, until I grow bored.

I float upwards.

Kitty is weeping with all her might. She does not see me for I keep myself hidden. If I leave her here, she will cry her heart out, pouring salty tears into my home. She will put on widowhood and wear it until her dying day, as if the man I drowned deserved her devotion, as if he was such a wondrous husband she could not bear to take another. She will waste the time left to her. I have made her life better, but whether she can recognise it I am doubtful. If I leave her to her own devices, she will curse this place and me and perhaps no one will come anymore. I waver, reach out.

I put my hand on her head, feel her soft thick hair; she starts. Before she can rise and run, I sink into her. She will feel it as a splashing on her skin, cold and momentary. Then I am swimming through the entirety of her: blood, heart, lungs, mind, soul. The soul, oh yes! How fascinating a thing. I do not have one, so I think it most peculiar.

This soul, this heart, this mind all work in concert to create a human and this one is ineffably *sweet*. She truly believed her husband could be changed, that he *could* and *would* be changed. She still loved him no matter what he did to her face. I could have told her he was not sorry for it. That he marred her only so no one else would want her. So she would believe herself worthless and never think to leave him. I cringe away from this cloying need I sense. I push down my contempt – I owe her this much. I can and will give a life of freedom; what she does with it will be her own concern.

Oh my, and the feelings surging through this lovely girl! How they taste! So strong, viscous and bitter as the ooze at the bottom of my lake. The ache of love and longing and of not being loved. The sharp fear and nagging guilt. At last, here at the very base of it is the tiniest, sharpest of all: relief. Hidden deep down, but it is there. And a thrill at the idea of liberty, if only she will allow herself to recognise it and not be so ashamed that she refuses to let it fly.

I walk her to the edge of the lake and jump in.

* * *

We swim.

We swim for almost a week. I do not let her rest often, but only when I have no choice, when it seems she will drown, that her body will simply give up and sink like a stone through sheer exhaustion. Remaining inside her is tiring for me – being confined by blood instead of my natural element makes me sluggish, but I do not leave her for I know she will run if released of my hold. So I stay cooped up inside the cage of her.

The stream becomes wider, then turns into a tributary, then it spills into a great river. We pass castles and towns, villages and farms, mills and ruins. Sometimes people see us – see her – and they watch until we are out of sight. Kitty looks a strange soaked creature for there's nothing of the water-sprite about her. She simply appears to be a depleted girl, wet as wet can be, slowly making her way against the current.

At last we come to the cathedral-city and I can take her no further. Neither of us will last: I feel poisoned by my imprisonment and she can barely lift her head. I do believe, though, that she will be far enough away that she won't think to return to Briarton. And I have spent these days washing through her mind, watering down her memories and her hurt and her painful pointless love, trying to give her a clean slate and a heart that isn't so spotted with blood. When I leave her, I hope she will be free, that she will not feel the memory of love as a tug in her stomach, as something that will draw her to the past.

She climbs out of the water and I let her go. I pool at her feet and then run back into the river. I do not take up my shape in front of her, for fear she will see me and remember. Back in water, I resume my form with relief. I feel the liquid cleansing me of the reek of humanity. I let the current take me as it wishes. Eventually, it will lead me back home. Until then I am content to drift.

A PORCELAIN SOUL

'Now. Slice it thin.'

Mater Lucina's voice is soft, barely heard in the cool of Tertiary and her tone belies what she's asking me to do. The gossamer substance floats in a small glass box that's been carefully placed on the beaten bronze bench top. It is the closest thing in consistency to that of a soul. Pious mothers bring newborns here and donate their babies' breath, so we students of Tintern Doll Makers' Academy will have something on which to practise. It doesn't hurt the babes at all: just a few aspirations into a vial and it's done, no one even misses it. Harmless enough 'prentice work materials for us, before we start using our own souls.

'Slice it!' A sharpness, because I hesitate when I shouldn't, weighted down by the worry of failure.

So I go at it in a panic, conjure a blade and see it form inside the box. Another part of my mind holds the floss steady and I slide the knife through it, so a thin, thin piece peels off. Thinner than the soup in an orphanage, thinner than the horizon. A sliver so waif-like that for a few moments it doesn't even know it's been cut. It wobbles, finds itself unanchored from the clotted mass, shivers and falls with the elegance of a fainting dancer.

Shuddering with relief, I wipe the sweat from my forehead. It was better than I deserved to produce, so much better. Lucina knows it, too, and she tells me as much. Her tiny mouth bunches and puckers in irritation. I cringe, knowing that making her angry won't help my cause.

'For that,' she finishes, 'for the hesitation and a result you did not warrant, you will clean out Primary tonight.'

I stifle a groan. Primary Workshop means clay, slops, slurry, shards of fired and discarded porcelain, the broken pieces of dolls that did not make it, and all the dust and coughing that goes with it. Then there's the dryness you cannot get out of your hands for days. But I need to be obedient, I need to be the best.

She smiles at me, not unkindly, but with a certain disappointment that hurts. 'You have to learn, Bitsy, to be decisive and to earn what you get. You can't simply rely on your talent to give a good enough outcome. One day your luck may run out. One day very soon you'll be doing this to *your* own soul and believe me, you don't want to make mistakes then.'

I nod, but don't say anything. My throat feels constricted with the efforts of the afternoon. I start to clear away the tools but Mater Lucina shakes her head. 'Selke will clean up in here; her punishment for that mess last Sunday.'

I hide a smile. Selke slipped five homunculi in amongst the church choir. A harmless enough trick and, if anyone had paid attention, they'd have noticed the blankness on the ill-painted faces and known them for the soulless abominations they were. She set them to explode when the hymns were sung. Not all together, mind – they were timed to go off at different pitches, so through the service there were these little explosions of glitter, fabric and false flesh. And the squeaking, the God-awful squeaking they made just before they popped.

The tutors don't like us playing with homunculi – too inhuman, they say – but Selke and obedience don't seem to mix well. She *is* quite brilliant. Her toys are bizarre and dangerous and spectacular. She really shouldn't be here; she should have gone to one of the Armourers' Academies where she could set her mind to things that are meant for war. Truly that's where she'd rather be, but an accident of birth got in her way. So, she's here instead and it presents a problem for both of us.

* * *

It's late when I finish Primary, and I miss dinner. Luckily the kitchen mistress likes me and I find a small basket of food waiting on the steps of the workshop when I step out. I lift the red and green cloth: a hunk of cheese, black bread, two chicken legs, a fat slice of gooseberry pie and a small skin of milk.

I pass by Secondary, its lights already extinguished (no one else required punishment this eve) and then see there is a glow from inside Tertiary.

Selke is still there. She isn't, however, tidying.

A wolf, just a small one, barely beyond a pup, lies where the box of breath was earlier. There's no rise or fall of its chest. It looks beautiful and sad. Beside the body is a lead coffer, about a foot square, which Selke is opening.

'What are you—'

'Sssssssh. Stay out of my way or help,' she hisses. Her red curls are piled up in a haphazard mess on her head, damp with sweat, and her green eyes look through me like a cat's.

I put the basket down and lock the door behind me. 'But Selke, what are you…' I wave my hands in despair.

'Stand there and watch.'

I look around for something, anything to use in case this goes wrong. She drops back the lid and it gives an angry clang. Up floats a cloud of something that whirls and spins in a tight ball, like chaos barely contained. Animal souls are erratic and volatile; they have none of the calm inertia of a human one. Selke's mind-knife appears and she takes a slice.

'Too thick,' I tell her. 'Far too thick; too much *anima*.'

'Shut up, Bitsy!' She frowns and sweats as she manoeuvres the piece of roiling grey to lie just above the dead beast's chest. Then she lets it sink into the fur to dig deep into the meat of the animal. The wolf shudders, his entire body shaking as part of it becomes transparent, part of it remains solid, in a kind of incomplete decay that surely must hurt and confuse it. The creature is now half spectre, half rotting corpse, mad and in pain.

There's no time, really, between this and when it rolls to its feet and begins snarling. Selke is frozen, transfixed by the thing she's created. It gathers its legs beneath it to spring, every stable muscle straining, but the ephemeral sections shiver and shake as if a strong wind might blow them away.

I bring the hammer down on its head, which has, luckily for us, remained real and stout. It releases a tiny whimper and gives up the ghost one more time. The grey of the soul seeps out and slowly dissipates, freed of the spell that held it.

'Shit,' she says, then glares at me. 'Now I have to start again.'

'Not tonight you don't and not without a tutor here! You're not good enough to keep it contained. You still can't get the balance between light and dark right. Selke, you're amazing, but this just isn't your skill!'

She looks set to argue, so I say, 'Another word and I will tell your aunt – then you'll be cleaning Primary for the rest of your life.'

Selke subsides. The last thing she wants is for Lucina to hear about this – it may tip the balance the wrong way for her.

'Peace offering?' I say, holding the wicker basket high. We are not bad friends, but at the heart of matters we are rivals and this causes tension. Oh, others here have their special talents – Kina can make pretend birds that sing you an aria, Lalla can paint a doll's face so it seems to have a different expression depending on the direction from which you view it, and Talia's soft fake foxes will curl about your feet and purr like cats – but Selke and I have, as Mater frequently tells us, the most developed abilities. Some days I think Lucina says this to make us opponents so we will strive harder. It's worse, still, that Selke is being offered what I so desperately want when she has no desire for it at all.

'Nice to be the good girl,' she sneers without heat, and takes the chicken leg I offer.

'Oh, c'mon. I'm not the one with the exploding simulacra. What did you think that would get you? Top of the class?'

She shrugs and says, 'Still and all, it was pretty spectacular, wasn't it?'

I have to agree. We eat in silence for a while, then she asks 'So, has she set your final task?'

A successful graduation piece gets you admitted into the Doll Makers' Guild and then you can find gainful employment in one of the town or city fraternities. Some might have the luck to be taken in by one of the houses rich enough and large enough to employ a dedicated doll maker. Some may take to the roads, as itinerant wanderers and makers of toys, living hand to mouth. Or some can teach – if you're really fortunate you might be asked to join the staff of an academy, like Tintern, which may be small, with no more than forty students, but our work is respected. And we have a powerful patron, which counts for a lot.

'A special commission. You?'

'Well, *if* she lets me graduate—'

'Avoid the exploding things and you should be fine,' I interrupt, halving the piece of pie and sharing it. Selke will graduate whether she wants to or not.

'Shut up. The wolf – Rennak of Lodellan wants guard dogs for his cathedral.'

'You mean…' I bite down on a gooseberry and its juice is sour. 'You're reanimating for the Archbishop?'

She grins in a way that strikes me as obscene. 'As soon as I can get the balance right, the slices thin enough.'

'How does that count as *toy making*, Selke? If it were clock-working I'd understand.'

'Oh, c'mon. You think your *puppets* are any better? I'm using existing materials to create something different. Same as you. And don't get onto your reanimation soapbox – when you're fully fledged you'll put a sliver of your own soul into each doll.' She makes a face as she, too, gets a bitter berry. 'Anyway, you know I'm not interested in the stupid dolls.'

She never has been. If she manages the wolf then martial households will fight for her services. In fact, if she pleases the Archbishop, she'll find a place in his grand home. That is if, and only if, Mater Lucina lets her go. 'Besides, clockworking is unreliable. Eventually the damned things run down, they need maintenance. The wolves are another matter entirely. Anyway, the point may be moot.'

'Selke, she's let you learn the art – no one else has been allowed to deviate from standard instruction – she's letting you do the wolf. She'll let you go.' We both hope I'm right. If she is allowed to go, then perhaps I will be allowed to stay. Resources are finely balanced in a small academy – there is only room for equilibrium.

She shrugs, morosely. 'What's this special commission anyway?'

'A doll for Lord Holgar's daughter.'

'Will you use one of these?'

I look at the rows and rows of porcelain shells lining two of the four walls of the room; all empty and waiting to be filled with a tiny piece of humanity. I shake my head.

'No, I'll start from scratch. She needs to be right. I don't want it to be… easy.' I smile.

'You won't have any trouble with making her beautiful.'

'No, it will be the slivering. It will be keeping steady when I do the soul.' I've made dolls before, lovely ones, perfectly gorgeous toys that we've sold at great profit, but the little piece of spirit inside has never come from me; one of the tutors has always done that. I know all the theory; I have done all the practice with breath; but this will be the first time I've worked on my own soul. Everything rests upon this. But even if I succeed, there's no guarantee I will be given what I want.

We finish the cheese and bread then turn down the gas lights and go to the Dormitory. Before I sleep I remember that tomorrow my cousin will arrive with Lord Holgar. I have not seen Benedict for some time. I wonder if he will look different.

* * *

Tintern Academy sits inside a rectangular, walled compound about half a mile from the city proper. We have three workshops, a kiln-house and a cooling room, stables, guesthouse, kitchen and refectory, a student dormitory and a main house with classrooms on the lower floor, and tutors' accommodation on the second. The entire third level is Mater Lucina's domain.

In her library-cum-office, the smells of ink, paper and beeswax polish are strong. The flat plane of Mater's wide desk shines and I know from experience that if you put a cup down on the surface with too much enthusiasm it will speed across like a skater on a frozen pond. The bay window behind opens onto a small balcony that looks over the yard of the Academy's enclosure. Strong morning sun pours in and highlights the dust motes that float and whirl, in spite of or because of the enthusiastic cleaning I gave the room this morning when it was still dark.

Mater wears her guild attire, a purple robe with dagged sleeves over a long blue tunic with all the embroidered badges of her station running from the top of each shoulder down almost to her knees. The floppy black cap has three feathers, one blue, one red, one green, which all stand to attention. Lucina's greying-brown hair is tucked up and hidden. Her fingers, thin and scarred, are weighted with gold rings. I notice that she has applied the most subtle of make-up to brighten her sallow complexion.

She stands in front of her great bureau, and I, in my only passable tunic, wheat-coloured and washed out, beside her. In my hand I still have the key to the room, and my palm is sweating. I slip the big black lump of metal into my pocket. The door opens and Duke Holgar, lord of Tintern and its surrounds, strides in as if he owns the place. I keep my eyes downcast as Mater Lucina taught me – the man expects humility, he demands people know their station. His entourage follows him.

I know he has left a company of ten troops down in the yard and our grounds master is directing them to the stables and the small guest quarters in the eastern corner of the compound. Those deemed fortunate enough to accompany the Duke number five: two huge blonde men, obviously soldiers; another man who looks like a warrior-scholar; a dark, angry youth; and last of all, my cousin Benedict in his grey robe with white rope belt. The soldiers take up position by the door, brooding presences filling up more space than seems physically possible or indeed reasonable.

I risk a peek at the Duke. He is tall and richly dressed in blues and greys. His hair hangs in two thick long plaits and his beard and moustache are pale gold – I suspect he is very vain of them.

When the welcome is done, Mater launches into business. She seems unafraid.

'This is Bitsy, my lord,' says Lucina. 'A final-year apprentice, one of my best.'

I blush warmly to hear her say that, although it would be better had she called me 'the best'.

He catches my glance and nods before he addresses me. 'This doll is not merely a gift for my daughter. It is a lesson.'

Holgar looks behind him at the young man slouched between Benedict and the warrior-scholar. He's olive-skinned, with shorn black hair, and a raised and recent scar running the length of the left side of his face. His expression contains enough hatred to make me nervous. I take an involuntary step back and bump against the desk.

His companions look askance at me. The warrior-scholar is in his thirties, muscular and broad, but his shoulder is hunched as if once broken and never properly healed. My cousin is older again, in his forties with greying hair and a weary face. I wonder how life in the Duke's household is agreeing with him. Holgar's attention returns to me.

'A lesson,' he repeats, 'to those who would disrespect their betters. Alexander.'

The hunch-shouldered man comes forward. 'My lord,' he says and hands over a black silk pouch, which Holgar in turn gives to me. I upend it. A ruby oozes out onto my palm like a large, slow drop of blood. I lift my eyes to the Duke's proud, cruel face.

Behind him, the boy vibrates with rage.

'You can use this?' Holgar asks. I nod and he continues, 'Then let it be done.'

I see the boy's face again and know that this is designed to cut him to the quick: a great gem like this to be set in a child's doll.

I speak without thinking, quickly, wanting the Duke to know how much I will put into this piece, how important it is for me; what good work I will do for *him*. I think of the hours I shall spend working the clay, 'I'll mix in gold and pearl dust so the skin looks real. A woman from Tintern, her daughter died last year, she donated the girl's hair – that will be perfect. The eyes, the eyes should be green. The ruby I'll use as the heart – I can create a panel in the chest and your daughter will be able to open it and watch the gem pulse—'

'The work will begin tomorrow, my lord, and may take up to a week,' Mater interrupts swiftly and I stop, bewildered. Holgar, I realise, is completely uninterested in what I have said, bored with my maundering. The dark boy glares at me and his hatred feels like a dagger. Benedict is shaking his head, not angrily, but pityingly. Pity that I thought this was somehow about my skill, my future and my success. It's not; it's about Holgar's revenge and whatever hurt he can inflict upon this young man.

Mater is still speaking. 'I invite you to take your ease with us this evening, my lord. The guest quarters have been prepared; tomorrow perhaps you would like to watch Bitsy work? Or perhaps not. Will you dine with me or take supper in your own room?'

I look at the floor, to the thickly patterned whorls of the rug and wish my cousin was not there to witness the raw ache of my embarrassment.

* * *

Outside, between the walls of the compound and the sluggish summer river, lie the gardens, filled with vegetables for our meals and the herbs required for our work. The juniors (some as young as five, none older than ten), are bent over flower beds picking what they need for their practice. They will make simple corn-dollies, stuffed with a combination of leaf and petal that will give the things a brief life while the ingredients are still fresh in the hollow space of their husk bodies.

I remember my first: it got me Mater Lucina's attention and shifted from me being kitchen scrub to student. Sent out to harvest produce for a meal, I watched instead the pupils playing, not following instructions, or doing so and simply failing. I forgot my task and made my own tiny creature. It danced like a mad thing for two days. I got in trouble with the kitchen mistress, but it didn't matter: Mater Lucina had seen something in me and the next day I was in class with the others. I promised myself I would be exceptional; I promised that I would not let Lucina down.

More and more Mater is letting me teach. I hope it means something good, I hope it means she will reward me with the position left vacant since Venantis' death last winter. Today, I'm overseeing the juniors in the loosest of ways – normally I'm not so lax, but I do not see my cousin often. We sit on a fallen tree trunk, smoothed into the shape of a seat by weather and backsides.

It's almost a year since Benedict last visited and he looks hollow, as though his duties as spiritual adviser to Holgar's house are eating him away.

We are cousins at some remove or another; when I was orphaned

Benedict brought me to the Academy for he could not bring up a small girl. He begged Mater to find a position for me. He did not think for anything too great – my mother was a castle kitchen maid, why should I hope for better? He is kind and good. He spent most of his years in the monastery, but when the Duke came to the Abbot seeking a house-priest, Benedict, concerned he was not in the world enough, volunteered. I used to see him more often before he left for Holgar's and I believe he regrets his decision. We hold hands, a small familial comfort. Our news has been sparse. I do not share my hopes and fears as I do not wish to hear a sermon on the evils of ambition, of desiring to rise above one's allotted place. It is easy for me to distract him with questions about his own situation, and about other people, for Benedict's single vice is gossip. I ask him about the boy and, in his roundabout way, he tells me.

'One of Holgar's vassals, Robert Velatt, held back part of the crop tithe he was bound to give, so his own village would have enough food to get through the coming winter. The Duke marched on the rebellious holding. To teach him a lesson, Holgar took *The Luck*.'

'What's that?'

'The ruby you held in your hand not many hours since; it's been in the Velatt family for hundreds of years. Having it put into a doll and given to his daughter is Holgar's idea of how to best display his contempt for the family.' Benedict shakes his head. He cannot find service with his lord very fulfilling.

'And the boy?'

'Velatt's only son – taken as hostage for good measure – to ensure he is brought up to be an obedient vassal. Velatt has three daughters – not one of them survived the Duke's visitation with virtue intact.' He holds his breath and then lets it all out in a rush of words, 'I do not like my lord, Bitsy, he is not a good man.'

I open my mouth to try and offer him some reassurance, but am cut off by the sound of mirth, girlish and sly.

Selke comes out the small side gate. She is wearing a purple gown and her usually unruly hair has been brushed and held in place with mother-of-pearl combs. With her is the dark boy. Hanging behind them is Alexander, close enough to be a bodyguard, far distant enough to give them privacy. His expression is one of concerned helplessness, as if he thinks he should intervene but is not sure why.

They are laughing, however I see in both their faces a kind of cunning assessment, a measuring. I wonder if each recognises it in the other? I think it strange Selke is making friends with anyone, let alone this boy who bears the ire of her aunt's patron. She sees me and hesitates, gives a half-smile and re-directs the boy, first with a gentle hand on his elbow, then more boldly, with a firm press to the small of his back. They move away, further into the gardens, nearer to the river, heads close together as they speak.

'What's his name, Benedict?'

'Dante.'

'Will he be allowed to go home?'

Benedict hangs his head, dispirited. 'Holgar has taken three hostages in the last ten years. None of them has lived to be returned to their families.'

'No wonder he's angry.'

'Angry doesn't even begin to touch the sides, Bitsy.' My cousin lowers his voice. 'And he hates me. I have tried only to comfort him, but he swears if he ever has the chance he will cut out my tongue and stop the endless stream of my advice.' He clears his throat. 'But this doll you shall make? Will you tell me about it?'

He is being kind, humouring me when he knows I must still sting from the Duke's snub, from the cut inflicted by my own ignorance. I smile and squeeze his hand and begin to tell him.

* * *

The week passes slowly, strangely. I spend my mornings in the workshops and in the afternoon, I go to Tintern and do good deeds. A doll maker's soul requires regular replenishing. In preparation for slicing the piece I will put into this doll, I help at the hospital and the poor-house, I serve meals in the orphanage and sew simple clothes at the charitable society run by Dorcas Tanner on Samhain Street. I do so many good works that I think I must surely begin to shine with virtue or sprout a halo.

In Primary, the first morning, I stand in direct sunshine and check my hands for any nicks or tiny cuts, anywhere an intrusion might occur. Finding none, I wash them in the consecrated font, and wait while a thin layer of water forms over the top of my own skin. In effect a fine pair of fluid gloves, so I am both protected and still able to work with the materials.

I open the clay-safe, an iron-clad box the height of a middling-sized man; a hefty padlock hangs stubbornly, keeping it closed. Inside, the clay is finely grained, almost white. There are eight drawers, vertically stacked, and I slide one out. Although it's packed tight, the substance still shifts and strains within the confines, sluggish from the warmth of the safe. Dug from cemeteries, replete with the juices of the once-living, redolent with the scent of rot, it costs Mater a small fortune. It must be worked rapidly for it is *not* like ordinary *mud*; its quickening and shaping and setting happen so much faster. It fires more quickly and at a higher temperature; strangely, it cools more swiftly. Living clay is almost a second chance for the flesh of the dead.

I empty the contents onto the marble bench top and cut away a large hunk, then dump the remains back in the container, which I replace in the clay-safe. I begin to mould the pliable stuff, feeling it push up ever so slightly against my palms, objecting, for a time, to being *shoved* about so. I croon as I fashion it and it grows calm. I tell it who it will become and how beautiful she will be. I wash it down with water to keep it moist, but not too moist. When it is at last as malleable as I need it to be and willing to absorb other things, I sprinkle gold and pearl dust over the glistening surface and begin to knead it in, until it's evenly distributed. It gives a lovely sheen. I take the small vial into which I bled and spat earlier this morning and now I fold that in too; tiny pieces of life.

Then I begin to model it in earnest, sculpting from her delicate feet with their tiny toes, to the chubby ankles and calves to the dimpled knees, then the thighs, the rounded hips and pert bottom, the waist, flat chest, the neck with a line or two to suggest the last of the puppy fat. The face, the pouting lips, cherubic cheeks, the nose with its tip ever so slightly tilted, and the eyes-but-not-eyes, the carefully carved out pits that watch me blankly as I work.

Taking a length of wire caught between two wooden handles (a tool as fit for an assassin as for a worker of clay), I cut her carefully in half, down the median line. I hollow her out, thin her skin until she is sturdy but fine. I slice a panel from her chest, halve it and set the pieces carefully aside, making sure to maintain their gentle curve, so they will fit once fired and hinged. When this is achieved, I mix an adhesive slurry and gently push the two halves of her back together.

I wait while it dries and sets.

Across the skull, I place tightly curled spirals of red hair. When I have planted a good two dozen, I whisper softly and smear further layers of extra moist clay over them until they are covered, the head is smooth and no one would suspect the seedlings I have put there.

The air of the kiln-house is thick and dry. The oven I'm using has been heated to just the right temperature – it is the one I always prefer, the one I am so used to that I could feed it and fire something in it in my sleep. I slip the doll and the pieces of her chest onto a tray, which I slide onto the shelf, being careful not to burn myself.

If I could, I would wait inside, anxiously watching as the porcelain child is baked, but the heat is too fierce. I sit outside on the steps, paying attention to no one, answering no questions, merely hoping and praying she will survive this phoenix-birth.

* * *

Secondary Workshop is the house of colours. Subjected to intense heat, fed on blood and sputum like a plant on manure, the brilliant red hair is beautiful. Under my hand the locks are soft and thick; they will not grow much longer, but already they hang beyond her shoulders and halfway down the curve of her back.

The blank sockets have been filled with a rapidly setting adhesive and I slip the glass eyes in and rotate them gently until they sit just right. The merchants of the port city of Breakwater travel far and wide, saving their best wares for Tintern; they know Mater does not stint on materials. The orbs are as green as a pond and seem to have the same depths so cunningly are they made. I think if I did not love doll making so, I would like to work with glass. To finish, I stick on thick black fringed lashes, made from feathers.

When these are set, I take the tints and permanent powders Mater has loaned me. Her very own set, the best quality I am ever likely to see or use.

The brows I paint are black and arched. I tint her cheeks like the first blush on a rose. I add some shading to the dips and hollows of her face, so her expressions seem more real, her face more mobile. I tip the nails of her fingers and toes a pearly white. I splash crimson over her lips, darker and redder than they should be – for she, in my mind, is fearless and bold and her mouth should say so, even though everything else about her may whisper "doll".

I set her aside and wait for her colouring to dry.

* * *

On the second to last day, I walk her to Tertiary. Her clothing has been handmade and even though this is not one of my strengths, you would not know it from the garments laying on the table beside her. The dress is cloth of gold, embroidered with tiny green flowers.

The bodice has an insert of gold lace that can be removed easily to view the contents of the chest. The skirt has panels of deep green velvet and the sleeves are tight to the elbow, where gold ribbons circle, then they flare out like wings. There are underclothes, too: delicate drawers made of fine cambric, with lace on the hems of the legs. A cobbler in Tintern with far greater skill than I has made her boots and gloves in soft green leather. A velvet cloak with a fur-lined hood also waits for her.

She is a proper lady and I catch my breath at the thought of how she will look when she can move just slightly and blink her eyes. When you can watch the ruby pulse and beat.

The hinged doors of her chest fit perfectly and are open, sticking up like abandoned ribs on an empty spine. I hold a small network of copper wire, which I twist to the left to compress. It concertinas down so I can slip it into the cavity. Once released, it springs back to the correct size and lodges its claws against the insides of the doll, safe and sturdy. There is a compact niche where an ordinary crystal would have sat as home to the fragment of soul. Now it's where that grand ruby will reside.

I think about it again – I have looked at the gem, touched it every one of the past four days, felt the smooth oiliness of its skin, measured it carefully, over and over to make sure I made the cage the right dimensions, so I might calculate the size of the sliver needed to animate the creature. I have stared at the reflection of my own face in its dark red surface and wondered what else I might see there if I simply watched long enough. I still have the key to Mater's office, so I might come and go as I need to examine the jewel.

I wrap the doll in a length of thick black velvet and put her into a box, about two feet long. I slide the lid closed so she may sleep. The clothes I hang carefully on tiny hooks so they will be ready for her.

Tomorrow I shall embed the jewel. I will cut into my own soul and make a thing that almost lives, almost breathes. A tiny abyss for a child to pour affection into. A beautiful emptiness.

And if I do it well, perhaps I will win my heart's desire. And if I do it well, perhaps I will not. Perhaps it will not matter.

* * *

I have hardly seen Selke in the last few days. I've been falling exhausted into bed as early as I can and she has been entertaining her new friend. When we have crossed paths, we've exchanged very few words, as if we've had an argument and are now uncomfortable with each other. In truth, there's been no such event. It's distraction and self-obsession that keep us apart, secrets and wishes and hopes that we fear to share lest they be found stillborn if spoken too soon.

This night, though, I cannot sleep. I toss and turn in my worry-creased sheets, feeling the coverlet as either too heavy or too light. I am troubled by everything, the weight of my hair, the way it bunches beneath the skull, how my nightgown rides up or twists about my legs and waist, how my toes are oppressed by the tight-tucked sheets at the end of the bed.

'Did you see it?' Selke whispers, even though our beds are crowded into an alcove at the far end of the dormitory. We can talk into the night should we so wish with the least disturbance to the other girls.

'What?'

'You know what. *The Luck*.'

'Oh, that. Yes. Saw it, held it, measured it, weighed it.'

'They've kept it in Mater's office, haven't they? Do you still have the key?'

'Yes,' I say without thought.

'Bitsy, will you show me?'

'With your sticky fingers?' I joke. 'Oh, no.'

'What kind of friend are you, not to trust me? Tomorrow you'll finish and it'll be gone. This is my last chance – I'll never see its like again. Be kind, Bitsy.'

'No, Selke. I only have the key because Mater trusts me. I won't betray that.'

She's silent and then venomous. 'She's not going to give you the position, you know. We discussed it tonight. She's making me take it.'

I feel sick. My head throbs and I want to vomit, but fear if I start I will not stop.

'So, you see, it doesn't matter how good a girl you are, Bitsy, how lovely your work for Holgar is – Mater is still forcing the position on me. You'll get your guild badge and that's all. There'll be no room for you here.' Her voice slithers. 'Poor Bitsy, all that devotion, all that loyalty so ill-rewarded.'

Every one of my nightmares seem laid out and realised before me: where I'm out on the streets of Tintern, trying to make a living, offering to create toys for food. I dream myself starving in the depths of winter, not good enough to find a place in the lowliest of fraternities; left with no option but to sell myself.

'But Bitsy, what if I'm not here? She won't be able to give it to me – she won't. If I'm not here...' In her voice is a catch that tells me how much of this she's planned. Clever Selke, always thinking. I know she's manipulating me, but still I listen, I let her pour misery into my ears.

'There's no need for you to run away, Selke,' I say weakly. 'Talk to Mater, she'll let you go. She'll know it's best to have an ally in Lodellan – if you're ensconced in the Archbishop's household, making unholy terrors for him, it can only benefit the Academy.' I feel her fear; I know Selke sees nothing but the boredom of the classroom for her, days and days stretching end on end without ceasing.

'She won't let me go. She won't, you know. I loathe teaching, I loathe being here but she'll make me stay. And you'll have to find somewhere else to go, all because my aunt insists we keep it in the family.'

I let a whimper escape me and leave my bed, bare feet silent on the rug-covered floor, and look out the window. It's not yet frosted with winter's breath, but the milky moonlight feels cold. Below, there is movement in the thick darkness. I squint and see Dante gliding past the kiln-house and the cooling rooms, across the packed dirt of the main yard. He slips along the wall of the wash-house and the kitchen and refectory wings. To the side gate, not the main one, but the one that leads out to the gardens.

'Selke,' I hiss. 'Selke! Look – that's Velatt's son.'

She is beside me in a heartbeat.

'No,' she says in a strangled voice. 'He said—'

'Selke, what have you done?' I feel heavy with dread.

'He just wanted to go home. I gave him a key to the room they've got him in, so he could escape. And he promised me...'

Dante opens the gate and instead of slipping out, he pulls it back and solid shadows pour in – they are not Holgar's troops, not the large blonde Northerners. These are shorter with cropped black hair, and they carry swords rather than the double-headed axes the Duke's men favour.

'What have you done, Selke?' I repeat and grab her by the arms and shake her.

'He promised me a place in his house. He promised his father would 'prentice me to their Armourer. If I helped and brought him *The Luck*, he'd take me with him.'

'Oh, Selke. You idiot. He hates Holgar, he doesn't care who he hurts. Our friends and family are in danger all because of you.'

'I have to warn my aunt.'

'We need to lock the doors here – soldiers and little girls don't mix. Then we need to go to Holgar.' I remember the fate of Dante's sisters and don't like to think anymore upon it.

'Holgar?' asks Selke.

'He will be with your aunt,' I say and she looks at me strangely. How can I know so much about Mater and she seemingly nothing? Does she not see the sideways looks that pass between the two? Or is she so caught up in her own doings, her own plans that nothing else penetrates? How can *Mater* not know this?

We wake the others in the dormitory and urge them under their beds to hide. There's no way we can escort forty weeping things along the corridors – the sounds of fighting are now clear, travelling quickly through the night. The girls are afraid but they listen to us. We bid Kina, the oldest, to lock the door after us.

The hallways never seemed so long or dark. There's nothing but moonlight to guide our feet and we pelt along towards Mater's rooms.

Selke is well ahead of me (she has always been more fleet of foot) and she takes a corner wide, abruptly stopping short. She flicks a frightened glance at me and I duck behind an oversized urn, my knees shaking. Into my field of vision steps Dante Velatt. I can hear other men crowding the corridor behind him, but none of them dare to move ahead of their young leader, so I cannot see them and do not know how many there are.

The thought strikes me that perhaps Selke will betray me. I have the key on me. Perhaps she will betray us all; perhaps her finger will at any moment point towards my hiding place.

'You lied,' she says to the dark boy. I cannot tell from her tone if she is more upset at her loss or at being deceived.

'A little. You didn't expect me to pass up the chance to put Holgar and his whore to the sword, did you? But you can still come with me. I'll give you your dearest wish.' He raises a hand to her face and traces a line from her temple to the tip of her chin. I see a movement in her throat, a convulsion and she spits in his face. Her disgust is as much for herself as for him, I think. I turn, hearing the sound of a slap as he tells her precisely how much dissent he will tolerate.

I take quiet steps on tiptoe and go the opposite direction. I slip out a window and stand in the shadows of the main yard, trying to catch my panicking breath.

On the night air I can hear blade against blade, the clunk of swords countered by shields, the whoosh of the double-headed axes;

all these noises crowd in my ears and render me deaf and afraid. I imagine the sound of heavy boots behind me, but there are none, at least not yet. I swallow the taste of fear and make my way to Primary.

Gaining the workshop's door, I slip inside; I do not turn the lock for there will be no hope if what I create cannot get out.

I look at all the porcelain shells on the walls; perhaps fifty in all. They range in size from large babies to small children. Most have eyes, but their faces have not been painted to distinguish them from one another. I do not need them to be distinguishable.

To take one piece without Mater's overseeing, without having done the proper preparation, would simply be indelicate, slightly dangerous, but I would survive. I would be disoriented when the soul is slivered, for a skerrick of the mind goes with it; the two are inextricably linked. I know the theory of it, all the magic. But what I must do, the thing I must make happen, the only way I can think of to save the people I care for, will ruin me forever.

Holgar's men are too few and taken by surprise. Only an army will save us.

I take one of the heavy bronze knives from the shadow-board that hangs on one wall. It is sharp and has a good weight. Time to be decisive; I fill my lungs, pause for the briefest of moments then slash the blade across my palm, my wrist and in the soft curve of my elbow where the flesh is tenderest. Blood comes. I begin to chant, low and steady, my voice timing in with the beat of my heart and the cadences of my breath. The cuts hurt, but I ignore the pain and concentrate, breathing deeply.

This is the last time I will be me. This is the last time I will be clever. This is the last time I will tell any story.

There is a heated agony in my chest and a lightness in my head as my soul and mind begin to slip their bonds, tiny pieces of each fusing together and marching out of my mouth in between the words and notes of my enchantment. They lodge in the bodies of the dolls. I see each of those strange manikins begin to move, to kick their feet and flail about with their arms; they climb down from the shelves clumsily. Some fall and smash, but others learn quickly how to use their limbs. They come to rest in front of me, a fragile battalion awaiting instructions. I fold an order, a command, into the animation spell.

I feel sick and dizzy and begin to sway, but I keep up the chant, even though I grow weaker and my voice begins to fade and eventually, I am so empty I forget who I am and was, and I faint.

* * *

'Shall I tell you a story? The tale of what you did?'

Selke stirs honey and cream into the bowl of porridge, just the way Bitsy likes it. Tears have fallen in, too, but she doesn't think Bitsy will mind. Bitsy doesn't mind anything much now. On a chair beside the blank-faced girl sits the doll, with vivid red hair and green, green eyes. She will not be without it in the days since the Academy was saved; she carries it around like a talisman, like a child, like a sibling.

'You should have seen them, Bitsy, when your little army came. Dante and his men weren't expecting them to be dangerous, so they laughed when they saw those toddling monsters. Some of the soldiers picked them up to cradle like babies. Then the dolls latched on and sucked their breath out. When that was gone, they began on the blood.' Selke sits down and spoons the porridge into her friend's waiting mouth. Bitsy seems to find this funny, this daily feeding, but until her arm heals she cannot feed herself, she's too weak and the pain from the cuts is such that she cries. Like a child, she doesn't understand why she hurts and this makes her weep all the more.

'They killed Dante, too, you know, no less than he deserved. All his men are gone and no one knows what I did. Not even you anymore. I'm sorry about your cousin, though, truly I am. Dante had no call to cut out his tongue.' She spoons in another mouthful, then wipes the escaping dribbles from lips and chin.

'You gave up everything you were to save us. That's what you did. I know it's no good to tell you, but I need to. Mater says you'll never come back, but I need to hope that you can and if you do, you should know what you did.' Selke looks into her one-time rival's pale blue eyes that have forever lost their focus and fierce intelligence. Instead there is just a wide fey stare and a gentle, idiot's smile. 'I would never have done it. Could never have done it.'

She puts down the now-empty bowl and unwraps a cloth bundle. The enormous Velatt ruby lies on the rough linen wrapping. 'Holgar left this. He was so scared of you! But he wanted nothing more to do with this thing and he needed to show he was grateful. I'll give this to Fra and it will help him look after you properly. Perhaps he can get a good price for it in Lodellan.'

Bitsy's fingers trace the lineaments of the jewel. Selke lets her hold it and it sits heavy as a life in the palm of Bitsy's hand. The girl stares into the depths of the stone, as if her eyes might find secrets beneath the facets. Inside the gem something moves and it makes her laugh, a sound that startles Selke. The laughter is pure and lovely and rings like a crystal bell.

Selke's head droops like a flower too large for its stem, weighed down by sadness. She hopes and prays that one day the urge to cry will leave her. She hopes and prays that she never wishes or wants for anything ever again.

THE BONES REMEMBER EVERYTHING

I walked for three days.

I had not left a note for Rilka, left her no clue; I had not thought of my lover when I entered the woods. The wolves were shadows and did not bother me. Need for neither food nor drink slowed my progress. There was only the voice, which no longer simply inhabited my dreams, but hummed through the waking hours like a daylight lullaby. I kept going until I reached the place where I was told I needed to be. *Ingrid, welcome home.*

The path ended abruptly at a prickly barrier; a hide of thorns so thickly grown and woven that I couldn't make out what lay beyond. The bushes stretched as far as I could see. Left and right, the briars had melded with the usual flora, and there was no way past to be found. I reached up in frustration, to touch one of the branches, but I misjudged and snagged a finger on a long barb.

I put the digit in my mouth and sucked away the welling fluid, tasting its metallic tang. In front of me, though, the drop of blood remaining on the tip of the spike gleamed then began to eat away the brambles just as acid attacks metal. Soon, there was a wound in the wall, big enough for me to walk through. I gave one final look back to see the obstacle continuing to be erased as if it had never been.

Ravens hopped across an untamed lawn and a grey stone tower rose up in the middle of the clearing. Lining the crenellations were statues – not gargoyles but cats. A single door at the base stood ajar. I did not hesitate; the voice urged me on.

Inside, at the bottom was a disused kitchen; then halfway up, a library with shelf-lined walls; finally at the very top of a spiral of age-smoothed stairs a circular room waited. Four arched windows, set across from each other, to the four compass points, let in light. In one area was a spinning wheel covered in cobwebs; a stool was placed in front of it. A four-poster bed crumbled quietly, its hangings all decayed, and bookshelves had been picked bare by birds and mice looking to cushion nests. Only a tiny cat and raven, cleverly carved in stone, lay overturned on the splintered wood. Against another part of the wall hung a frame made of bones; stretched across it was a covering of skin. At its foot stood a rough-hewn table and on that table were thread, a needle, a quill and a very large jar – almost a glass pail, really. At first, I thought it filled with ink, but closer inspection showed it to be a sluggish dark red, uncongealed. The lid came away with surprising ease. The scent of iron made me dizzy.

The very air seemed to be waiting

The quill was sharp, and when I picked it up, I felt a tingle in my hand that thrummed up my arm and made my shoulder ache. I dipped the nib into the ichor-ink and stood in front of the strange canvas. I swiftly sketched a woman, the one whose voice sang from my dreams. Without knowledge I understood that she shared my blood. The liquid soaked straight into the surface, did not run or smear; it knew where it was to stay.

When the drawing was done, I waited for the outline of the face and body to dry. I picked about the chamber, trying to find a trail, a story in the leftovers of a life. There was little enough and I realised that the only truth was that of the bones.

I closed my eyes and saw a girl sitting by a window, the north-facing window of that very tower, spinning. The thread her efforts produced was long and fine, flax entwined with strands of her own dark hair – she had been at the work for some time. Every so often she pricked her finger and the crimson welled, then was absorbed into the filaments as she caressed them with something like love, something like hate. The pain didn't bother her, for she was spinning her own life, making herself into a tale, her own tale of blood and flesh and bone, and she would endure for the bones remember everything. And they will call.

I shook myself and opened my eyes. The fine silver needle was surprisingly easy to thread. As I sewed and embroidered, the fibres took on the required colour: ebony for hair, white as new snow for skin, red as a ripe apple for lips. I stitched and stitched, and wondered what would happen when I finished.

Still I did not sleep; day and night no longer mattered. I did not mind, though, for the voice called me by my name and told me its story.

* * *

Once upon a time, there was a Queen. She was beautiful as they all must be but she was sad as they aren't supposed to be. Her husband loved her and he wanted children. She did not. In the course of time, though, she fell pregnant and two daughters were born.

The pain of the first, the pale twin, she tolerated but the second caused her such agony, such a rush of hate that she cursed the child. The dark twin did not cry, she was and always would be, a well of silences and depths no one could plumb. The other was shiny and shallow, a sprite of light and laughter. Two babes of the same womb, of the same birthing, should have been loved equally, but they were not. We were not. I was not.

Ultimately, love hangs on acts, however unimportant they may seem at the time. It attaches to what people do or say and our memory of those things. Gestures that travel to the heart and lodge there for a while at least. They build a foundation for kindness and love from which a child can learn.

I have no memory of such acts. I remember the chill of indifference. I remember living in the shadows of my mother's unhappiness. I remember being famished my whole life, yearning for a crumb of affection, just one that might somehow quell the hunger inside me.

But I starved. My sister ate her fill and her heart grew expansive and happy. She did not know want, she did not know how sharp your soul grows when it's deprived, how its ribs stick out like dead trees on a bare landscape. She did not know what it was to never be sated. She could no more escape her fate than I could but even knowing this, I hated her. Hate her still, I think; perhaps more than I hate our mother. I don't know why; I just know that I do.

From my earliest years, a cat would find me, no matter where I was in the castle. The day my mother found the nursery filled with the creatures, Marietta and I in our gold beribboned cribs and my delicate sister sneezing wildly, was the day Mother banned felines from the court. They stole the breath of babes, she declared.

My nurse, Ella, told me otherwise. She kept her own cat, thin as grief and black as sorrow, hidden in her room. 'Your mother is fearful,' she explained. 'Cats don't steal breath – they simply help souls cross the lonely spaces between life and night.'

She was dark, Ella, and beautiful; her olive skin burned by the sun when she spent her hours outdoors picking herbs and bulbs. She was different from the other women of the royal retinue; quieter but far more self-assured. They were bright parrots, gaudy and loud; she was a hawk, watching, always assessing. Sometimes she would look at me as if she could not quite decide what action to take. I think, in the end, she surmised I would do more damage left to my own devices.

It was Ella who fed me, brushed my ebony locks each night before bed, rubbed creams into my skin to keep it luminously white. She taught me magic ran in my veins, and how I might tap into it when needed. Hers were the hands that sewed my wedding dress, and hers were the hands that washed the blood from it after everything fell apart. Hers was the kindest touch I knew, but we did not share blood so it did not really count.

She was not my mother.

Life was not unbearable, though, until the wedding day. I was not loved but I had no reason to punish anyone. I existed in shadow, spent my time reading, learning from Ella, building a store of knowledge that I thought I would never use. I merely existed.

My father, having demanded children, gave us only passing attention. When at last he began to feel the weight of his years, his thoughts turned to the matter of succession. We were mere daughters, but princesses can produce heirs. My mother had failed to provide him with a son, so he had to find sons-in-law who would do him proud. As the oldest, Marietta had been married off a year earlier.

Raised properly, we did not question the men chosen for us. I was simply happy that Father had selected a handsome boy, tall and dark, not some old man whose breath stank as he rotted away from the inside. My betrothed was not too bright, but his kisses were intoxicating. I thought perhaps I might love him, with time. But he was merely a possession, something that I acquired through no virtue of my own.

My sister's husband did her the disservice of falling from a horse three days before my wedding. She did mourn him, I believe this, and quite sincere was her grief. But it did not last long.

My wedding dress was ivory, a miracle born of Ella's fingers, yards and yards of silk and tiny pearls torn from the sea far away from our little kingdom, and bought from the man who once had wings. Ella braided my hair into glossy ropes, intertwined with strings of gems. When she was done, I dripped with diamonds and emeralds (never wear emeralds they said, they will bring heartache – but I loved the stone more than I feared the risk).

In the mirror was a beautiful girl, seventeen, but behind her lurked another image. A second woman waited, older, but still me, ephemeral, standing like a fetch, dressed in black, hair wild as if a mighty storm inhabited it. I leaned closer, peering hard because it seemed that I was becoming fainter, while she grew more solid. I did not fear – what had I to fear from myself? But I did wonder why she was there; then the door opened and my parents stepped into the room.

My sister was to have my husband. She was the eldest, her need was greater than mine, the kingdom required a prince to replace my father or at least to get an heir. I would, eventually, be found a new husband. But not today. Not this wedding day. My sister would have this one.

I looked back at the mirror and watched the girl in the wedding dress fade. The woman in black froze into focus.

I nodded to my parents. Would my sister like my dress? My jewels? They went with the husband, did they not? They did not hear the sarcasm, I was a shadow child, after all. Send my sister to me and she will get her prize.

Golden Marietta with her fat, happy heart waited in the corridor. She entered and I told our parents to leave us so we could swap clothes. Only Ella remained, watching us with a wary eye as we undressed. I think she waited only to see what harm I might do, what havoc I might wreak, how I might reward her training.

I laid the ivory silk gently on the bed like a dead child. Marietta let her black mourning gown pool on the floor as if casting off a mood. When we stood naked, the light twin and the dark, reversed images, I moved close and placed my hand on her smooth belly, settled it over her womb and thought of heat.

'Nothing will grow here, I swear it. You will get no joy of these stolen things, Marietta. He can plough you nightly but nothing will take root; a hundred men may labour over you but nothing will come of it, sister.'

I slapped her and blood spurted from her nose, staining the pale cloth of our wedding dress. She reeled back and stared down at the mark on her belly; the shape of my palm and fingers stood out like a brand. She watched as I dressed in her widow's weeds, pulled the gems from my hair and let it loose as a storm cloud.

'Help my sister dress, dear nurse. Then pack my things for I will leave this place.'

I found my erstwhile fiancé in his chamber, surrounded by valets and groomsmen readying him for his bride. He preened before the mirror and as I stood behind him, he started; perhaps he saw my double image. I sent his men from the room, opening the front of my gown before they had even pulled the door to.

'Any bride will do, it seems. Give me this one thing, my love, my heart. I ask but this and I will leave you free to marry my sister and have this kingdom.'

He made no argument, but lay back as I rode him like a witch, like a whore. He cried out and I felt his seed take hold inside me. I left him spent.

In the few days it took for Ella to arrange our departure, I passed through the corridors of our tiny castle like a whirlwind; none stood in my path. My mother I saw several times in whispered conversation with my nurse, telling what things might go and what things must not be taken. My father merely watched with a kind of horror when I entered a room. Courtiers stepped aside as if too close contact might contaminate them. I did not see my sister in those final days.

We rode out early one morning, a fine carriage for myself and my nurse, and a cart piled high with possessions. Four men accompanied us as guards.

We came to this tower; it seemed we wandered aimlessly, but I wondered later if Ella directed our path all the while. The men hefted the furniture and belongings up the winding steps and then disappeared into the forest in short order, taking both carriage and cart with them.

There were people living nearby, forest folk, hunters and the like. Cottages, huts and hovels housing women and children who waited for husbands and fathers to return from elsewhere. Others still lived alone, women and men both, happy with only the silence for company. For a while we saw them every few days; Ella would trade for provisions, bartering her healing skills. I paid them no mind, stuck to my round room and brooded as my belly grew; read the books Ella had brought with her and those in the library beneath; consumed the knowledge therein. Eventually, they disappeared, those forest dwellers, moving away to places where, presumably, they did not feel quite so uncomfortable with my brooding presence in the tower. Soon enough, the animals as well deserted our part of the woods. There was no longer even the familiarity of birdsong.

There was a child, though. Of course there was. When she was born, I called her Dowsabel so she would be sweet and gentle, and gave her to Ella to take to my sister. To let Marietta raise the baby I'd stolen from her womb. It may have seemed kind, it may have seemed like forgiveness.

Ella did not return. I don't think I expected her to do so.

In this tower I delved deeper and darker into magic; living as long as I could, until I sensed illness sinking its claws into me. Young still, yet I sickened and could not cure myself. I wondered if the evil I had done poisoned me. The more I studied, the more I realised the only way to cheat death was to wait.

I began this work. I put in place spells that needed simply the final word to set things in motion. I delayed though, drinking in whatever life was left to me until the day I felt the tightness in my chest was not going to release, that the harshness of my breathing would not ease. The cyclone of magic that tore me apart peeled the skin from my flesh, filleted me, built the frame and made the canvas, then liquefied my organs and poured them and my blood into this jar. I sundered myself piece by piece, using every bit of craft I had learned.

And I waited. I waited for you.

* * *

My hands move lethargically now, putting the last stitches in place. My golden hair is gone. It has been woven into the design; patches of skin are missing from my arms, and the torn bodice of my dress shows that I have used a knife to take squares of my own hide from there, too, small swatches to quilt the thing on the wall before me. So many needle marks mar my fingertips that the flesh is a mass of tiny wounds; a pallid pink jelly seeps from them. Where the canvas is marked with this pigment, a tiny pageant has made itself – my lover, her journey, plays itself out.

I watch as I work, my attention divided between finishing the tapestry and taking in the tiny Rilka as she searches for me in a sparsely sketched series of scenes.

I see her miniature simulation leave the Battle Abbey and ride to the love-nest in which she'd installed me not many months since, when I'd come from the cathedral-city. I had thought to find some peace, somewhere to flee the years haunted by memories of my dark-hearted mother and my strange half-sister. And the soul-blackening guilt that I had failed each of them in turn – being neither obedient daughter nor protective sister, and in the process losing them both.

In truth I had wandered without plan – I simply *fled*. Had I thought about it, surely I would have realised that the convent was one of the Church Militant's outposts and would not likely be a haven of serenity. Rilka was the Abbey's Marshall and she tried to be discreet, but the reality was that the Church did not need her order to behave as did other nuns. These women conducted their holy worship by sword and fire.

'You don't belong here,' Rilka had said and the honey of her voice took the edge off the words. I was in the laundry, folding newly boiled sheets, and applying the heavy iron heated on the wood-fire stove to shirts and breeches of rough cloth. I remember the warmth of her breath on my neck, the firmness of her grip, the muscles in her broad back.

Rilka convinced me that my path did not lie in the cool of the cloisters, nor on the training fields, nor indeed with any of the offices. What she offered seemed as good as any other road open to me.

In the tiny cottage, comfortable and bright, somewhat like the one of my youth, the idyll was agreeable. But the haunting began that very first night.

'There's a voice in my dreams,' I told Rilka.

'Dreams? That means you've not enough to occupy yourself; you need exhausting.' She grinned and pinned me to the bed. She had no concerns about leaving me alone. I thought of those moments as I watched the tiny figure inscribed in red ride into the clearing to find the cottage empty. She rested only long enough to stuff a sack with provisions.

I wondered if Rilka questioned why she hunted for me. By her own admission, there had been many women before. Perhaps it was love, perhaps it was lust. Or perhaps she did not like being *left*.

The wolves follow Rilka. She does not dismount from her tall horse during the day unless she must, and she keeps her sword unsheathed. At night, she builds a huge fire and sits close by it. She does not sleep. When she comes at last to the tower, she approaches the door, and finds it locked. Her head cocks to the side as she listens to the conversation floating out the windows and gliding down to her. Rilka stands back and kicks at the door, again and again until the lock collapses under the onslaught of her soldier's boots. She mounts the stairs.

When she enters the room at the top, I give her a weak smile. She doesn't seem to notice, or at least she doesn't return the greeting, but rather looks past me at the huge tapestry I have made my work. It moves – it is *not* moved, but *moves*. The woman inside it dances about. She smiles and laughs, filling all three dimensions. It is only a matter of time before she steps *out*.

‘There was not enough,’ says the woman on the wall.

Rilka looks at her, uncomprehending. She holds her sword, but seems to have forgotten she has it. Rilka’s eyes flick to me but she cannot bring herself to approach.

‘There was not enough,’ repeats the woman as if to a simpleton. ‘I needed more to live, to be *well.*’ She smiles. ‘And this great-granddaughter of mine has given me almost all she had.’

There is still more that I might give. For once, I can commit to giving what is needed, and when I do, the pain will stop, the ache will cease. The quill lies on the floor beside my feet and my fingers are slippery when I pick it up. I put the sharp end to my throat and jam it in deeply, then pull it out. Blood spurts over the hanging, which soaks it up like a sponge. The tableau shudders, giving birth and the woman walks forth as I slide slowly off the stool.

‘The bones remember everything,’ the woman says softly. ‘And in their memory they call out to the ones we need.’

She barely glances at me. My vision blurs and it feels like looking through water as I watch her move close to Rilka and raise her hand to the dark lovely face. She strokes my lover’s skin as if it’s another material she might use. ‘Her blood tells me what you meant to her.’

She leans in and presses her lips to Rilka’s. She stops only when the nun’s blade slides between her newly animated ribs, and my grand-dam deflates like a punctured wineskin, loosing a sigh that wants to be a scream but cannot quite make it. Such a waste; such a waste, yet soon I will be free of this flesh and its memories.

Rilka kneels beside me. I wonder if she will carry me down the stairs; I am very light. I do not think she will return to the Abbey. I think she will go in the direction of a place where she might lose herself and ignore the calling of bones that are not her own.

SOURDOUGH

My father did not know that my mother knew about his other wives, but she did.

It didn't seem to bother her, perhaps because, of them all, Tildy had the greater independence and a measure of prosperity that was all her own. Perhaps that's why he loved her best. Mother baked very fine bread, black and brown for the poor and shining white for the affluent. We were by no means rich, but we had more than those around us, and there was enough money spare for occasional gifts: a book for George, a toy train for Artor, and a thin silver ring for me, engraved with flowers and vines.

The sight of other children in other courtyards, with Father's uniquely gleaming red hair, did not bother Mother at all. After he died, I think she found it comforting, to be reminded of him by all those bright little heads.

Our home was in one of the squares at the edge of the merchants' quarter – the town was divided into 'quarters' that weren't really quarters at all. Seen from above, Lodellan was a large square, made up of groups of much smaller squares (tall houses built around a common yard). In the centre was the Cathedral, high up on a hill, then spreading around it in an orderly fashion were rows and rows of city blocks, the richest ones nearest the Cathedral, then the further out you got, the poorer the structures, streets, inhabitants. We sat just before the poorest houses, not quite good enough to be in the middle of the merchants' rows, but still not in among the places where rats shared cradles with babies. We had several large rooms mid-way up one of the slender houses, and Mother leased out the big ground-floor kitchen for her business.

From the time I could walk I would follow Tildy around, learning her art. For a while she was simply annoyed by my constant presence, as I got under foot, but when I learnt to sit on the bench next to the huge wooden table on which she kneaded the bread, and be quiet, she decided to share her knowledge. I was her firstborn, after all, and her only daughter.

When I could see over the top of the table, I started to help. Baking tiny child's loaves at first for practice, much to Mother's amusement, then making the dark, "poor" bread for those who could not afford refined flour. Finally, I was allowed to create white bread to grace the tables of the rich: those born to wealth and knowing nothing else, the extra-successful merchants, the Archbishop and his sort. I began to create complicated twists of dough to look like artworks. At first Mother laughed, but the orders kept coming for them, so she watched and imitated me.

One morning, after we'd finished baking for the day, I began to play with the glutinous leftovers on the board in front of me. Soon a child formed, a baby perfectly copied to the life, with tiny hands and feet, an angel's smile and a sculpted lick of hair on its forehead.

Mother came up behind me and stared. She reached past me and squashed her fists down on the dough-child, pushing and kneading until it was once again a featureless lump.

'Never do that. Never make an image of a person or a child. They bring bad luck, Emmeline, or things you don't want. We don't need any of that.'

I should have remembered the dough-child, but memory is a traitor to good sense.

* * *

There was to be a wedding, arranged, a fine society "do" and we were to provide the bread.

The parents of the groom – or rather, his mother – insisted on being involved in every decision pertaining to the nuptials, so there was a power struggle in train between her and the bride's mother (two titans in boned bodices). Things were getting tense, apparently – this information we had from Madame Fifine (less exotic than her name might suggest), the confectioner who was to supply the bonbons for the wedding feast. We were to appear at the groom's parents' house, goods in tow, to show our wares.

Mother and I tidied ourselves as well as we could, pulling flour-free dresses from chests and piling our hair high. Artor and George were press-ganged into carrying the wooden trays of our finest white breads to the big house near the Cathedral. We were shown into a parlour almost as big as our ground-floor kitchen.

As soon as the boys gingerly laid the trays on the big table,

Mother shooed them out. I knew they'd be in the stableyard, bumming cigarillos from the stable and kitchen lads, eyeing the horses longingly, waiting for the day when Mother could afford a horse and carriage (that day was a long way off, but they hoped the proceeds from this venture would speed up the process).

The sitting room was awash with boredom. The parents sat stiffly across from each other on heavily embroidered chairs whose legs were so finely carved it seemed that they should not be able to support the weight of anyone, let alone these four who almost dripped with the fat of their prosperity. The bride, conversely, was thin as a twig, nervous and sallow, but pretty, with darting dark eyes and tightly pulled hair sitting in a thick, dark red bun at the base of her neck. The groom did not face the room: he had removed himself to the large French window and was staring at the courtyard below (probably watching my brothers watching his horses). He had chocolate brown hair, curly, that kissed the collar of his jacket, and he was tall but that was all I could tell. Madame Fifine had said he was called Peregrine.

Mother nodded to me and I took the first loaf from one of the trays, showed it to the clients so they could observe its clever shape (a church bell with bows), then placed it on a platter and cut it into six for them to taste. The two mothers, the two fathers, the bride all took their slices and there was silence but for their well-bred chewing. I crossed to the groom and offered him the last piece. He didn't turn, merely raised his hand, no, and shook his head. I noticed his palm bore the stain of a port-wine birthmark.

'It would be a shame, sir, to waste something so fine.'

Perhaps struck by the fact that I spoke to him, he looked at me and broke into a smile.

'Yes. You're right. It would be a shame.' He took the bread, green eyes bright. 'What hair you have, miss.'

I blushed.

'Emmeline.' Mother called and I began my task over again: now the loaf shaped like a flower, now the one like an angel, now all the animal shapes (rabbits, doves, kittens, a horse), the one like a church. Each time I saved his slice until last and we spoke in low voices, he asked me about my life and laughed at my pert answers. When the tasting was finished, the mothers began to argue: the design to choose was the cause of combat. Finally, they turned to the girl, Sylvia, and made her decide. She had the look of a trapped animal and I felt sorry for her.

'Perhaps...' I began and all eyes lit upon me, the mothers' brimming with affront, the fathers' with boredom, the groom's with amusement, my own mother's with something like dread, and the bride's with hope of rescue. 'Perhaps Miss Sylvia has a favourite animal or flower. We could make the bread to her choice if she does not like what we have brought today.'

'A fox!' she cried, clapping her hands to her mouth as if she had said something awrong or too bold. I smiled and she said more firmly. 'Yes, a fox. That would please me.'

'As you wish, Miss Sylvia.' Mother's voice was a relieved breeze. 'My Emmeline can make anything with her hands; she has great skill.'

So it was settled. The bride had spoken, and defied both her mother and future mother-in-law. Tildy and I hefted the wooden trays scattered with the remains of butchered loaves and made for the door. Peregrine was there before the footman and ushered us through. He smiled and I felt as warm as bread fresh from the oven.

* * *

In the months before the wedding he came to me many times.

The first, I was alone in the kitchen – Mother was ill, spending half her day sleeping, the other half shouting delirious orders (which I ignored) from her bed. Artor and George took turns delivering the bread and sitting by her side, while I kept the kitchen running.

I dropped the tray when I saw him at the door. I was covered in flour, my hair caught up by a scarf, and barefoot because I loved the feel of the kitchen flags cool and dusted with flour. He laughed and held out the largest bunch of flowers I had ever seen. I examined it as he picked up the fallen tray and placed it on one of the benches. This was no posy picked from the fields outside the city, these were exotic blooms, blossoms grown in hothouses and afforded only by the rich.

'Hello, Miss Emmeline. Are you baking for me yet?'

'That's months off, young sir, as you well know. How would it look to serve stale bread at your wedding feast?'

'It would be appropriate, more appropriate than you know. My fox bride might even tell you that herself, if she were truthful.' He touched one of the florid roses in the bouquet and smiled. 'Do you like these?

'They are very fine, sir. Fit for your bride.'

'But I think you will like them best.'

'Yes.'

We did nothing more, that occasion, than talk. Subsequent times were very different, but that visit, I think, made us friends and stood us in good stead. He brought gifts, even though I told him not to; something for me always, sometimes things for Mother and the boys. Artor and George, hostile and suspicious initially, were won over when he brought the horses. Two of the finest creatures I've ever seen, with a red-gold fleck to their coats and white stars on their foreheads. Peregrine told me later that their colouring reminded him of our bright hair. The most beautiful thing he gave me was a ring, rose-gold with a square-cut emerald.

'A dangerous stone,' I told him.

'What do you mean?'

'An emerald will crack, if given by a lover whose heart is unfaithful,' I replied. He laughed and dragged me down.

'Yours will be safe.'

I had no expectation of marriage – I was friend and mistress. He would marry his fox bride, as he called Sylvia, and I knew it. I only expected constancy and for many months I had it.

When my belly began to swell, he laughed with delight, his fingers lightly dancing over my taut skin, stroking the curls at the apex of my thighs, and gently showing me how pleased he was at what we had made together. I thought then, briefly, of the dough-child, but put it from my mind.

One day, a fortnight before his wedding, he ceased to visit. Instead, the fox bride came as I kneaded dough in the kitchen.

She was different to the nervous girl I had met months ago. She eyed the kitchen – and me – with disdain, as if she might find some uncleanness clinging to her silken skirts from the mere proximity of such a place and personage. I put my hands to my stomach. She snorted, a brief, sharp laugh that cut.

'You will not have him anymore,' she said. 'He will be my husband.'

'You do not love him,' I replied. It had not occurred to me that the fox bride would not *share*.

'But I want this marriage. I want to be away from my parents. I want to be mistress of my own house. But if he keeps running to you, keeps loving you more and more then he may decide not to marry me.' She glared. 'I will not allow that to happen.'

'Stay away from here. Stay away from me. I will tell him.'

'He does not remember you.' She laughed, came close, and

showed her sharp white teeth in a smile. 'Why do you think he isn't here? With his love, watching what he's planted grow? You're not the only one who can make things; potions are more powerful than bread, little Emmeline.'

Her hand shot out and she laid her palm against my belly. I moved back, almost falling over an uneven flag. 'Watch nothing goes into your food, Emmeline. You wouldn't want to lose this last piece of *him*.'

I heard her laughter even as she walked down the street. I thought only to run to Peregrine, but my nose began to bleed and my belly contracted so hard that I did fall this time, and mercifully found the dark balm of sleep.

* * *

Their wedding day dawned grey and overcast as summer slipped into autumn. The weather kept all but the most enthusiastic of wedding goers at home – the old women who wait outside the church, knitting and yammering, commenting on all aspects of the event: how the bride looked, how well her dress suited (or not), if she was glowing and if so, why (*honeymoon baby, my sainted aunt!*), and how long the marriage would last.

It was with these ancient birds that I waited on the first day I had managed to leave my bed.

The child had come too soon, a boy, looking not unlike the dough-child, and leaving me bereft. Mother had barely left my side, worrying that I would not speak, would not touch the still body before she took it away. Artor and George brought me posies but they only made me cry. I missed the brief funeral that was held for my son, confined to bed by a bleeding the sad, gentle doctor could not stop. Mother brought an old woman one night who gave me something foul to drink and applied a sweet-smelling poultice of moss between my legs. My body started to repair itself then.

Mother told me that the boys had tried to speak to Peregrine; he had gazed at them in bewilderment, saying he did not know who they were. They had hidden the horses he had given them in a stable at the outer edges of Lodellan, in case someone accused them of theft. Mother had presented herself at the big house, ostensibly to discuss the wedding bread, and Peregrine looked through her. She felt that she must be a ghost, so empty was his face. The old woman who had tended to me told her there were things that could bewitch a man's mind and make him forget his dearest desire.

The fox bride was more than she seemed.

I watched her as she left the Cathedral on her husband's arm. I would have let her have this; it had never been my intent to take it from her, but she had stolen my lover and my child was dead. She stepped into a puddle of mud as she headed toward the carriage, and shrieked her distaste as her silk shoes and white lace hem turned the colour of chocolate. I smiled in spite of myself and slid the hood from my head, my bright hair shining out in the dimness of the day. Peregrine looked up from his wife's distress and saw me. His face twisted, distracted and uncertain, but he did not know me. His attention turned back to his bride and I slipped away before she could see me and triumph.

In my kitchen, I found the remnants of the wedding bread dough and began to sculpt another dough-child. I fashioned it as cunningly as the first but this time with intent and not a little malice. Such magic requires only intent and ill-will but no great skill.

I drew from my finger the ring Peregrine had given me. The emerald gleamed at me, intact, unbroken; his heart was never unfaithful, only his memory. The ring was pushed into the thing's stomach. I made a bellybutton to cover its ingress.

When it came from the oven, it had a fine golden crust and looked like a cherub. I delivered it to the cook at the house the newlyweds were to share; she was a friend of Mother's and took the loaf gladly.

'Tell them it's for fertility, to bless them with a child.'

She nodded. 'They shall have it for supper this very eve, Emmeline.'

* * *

He told me later how the dough-child had been served to them on a silver tray, with butter and a selection of jams. Sylvia had *ooh-ed* and *aah-ed* over the silly thing and happily cut herself a thick slice, slathering it with sugary conserve. Peregrine ate the bread dry and unadorned. When the sourdough touched his tongue his memory returned.

The fox bride continued to eat as he railed at her. She greedily chewed and swallowed great bites, laughing at his rage and talking around her food, telling him she would do it again, too. Then she began to choke. Her face went red, then blue around the lips as she struggled to draw in air. She pointed at her throat, threw things at him as he stood, staring in horror. When she was finally still, he called for aid.

The doctor, the one who had attended me so unsuccessfully, found the emerald ring lodged in her throat. He, I'm sure, recognised it and placed it in Peregrine's hand, closing the young widower's fingers around the piece of jewellery. 'Someone will be looking for that, young man.'

I no longer wear it very often, knowing what I did with it, although I do bring it out now and then to remind myself of his constant heart. We live in another house, as far away from his parents as he could get, but still in one of the nicer squares. My mother runs her business out of a real shop not far from us, and has two young girls 'prenticed to her.

'They don't have your touch, Emmeline,' she sometimes says but she knows why I will no longer bake, why my hands will never again knead dough. She is happy, for she knows her grandchild comes. I am content to visit the small grave where my first child lies. I speak with him often and tell him about his father and sister, who comes to us soon. I tell him I am sorry I could not protect him and that I will never forget him. My memory is true.

SISTER, SISTER

The final hymn is being sung off-key and I suspect the choir-master will not be pleased. I smile, imagining his scowl as he tries to locate the culprit amongst those angel-faces. Imagination is all I have at this distance, there's very little to see from the arse-end of Lodellan Cathedral. Pillars, posts, baptismal fonts, and other members of the faithful all ruin the landscape. My kind are tolerated in church, but only just. This is not the view I used to have; once, I sat in the pews up front, those with gates on the side to let everyone know how special we were. Once, I was *on show*.

I still am, I suppose, but now it's looks of pity, occasionally of contempt. Always curiosity. I'd have thought that after six months it would have died down, but apparently not. I hold my head high, meeting cold stares with one even frostier until *they* turn away. But I tolerate this, continue coming back once a week for my daughter's sake. Just because I've lost faith doesn't mean Magdalene should be denied the possibilities of its comfort; besides she loves the theatre of it as only a child can. When she is older she can decide for herself whether there is something genuine to be had.

The Archbishop lifts the chalice, makes his final flamboyant gestures, bows his head and bids those within range of his voice to go in peace. This much I know from memory. Those in the front rows rise and I think I see the flash of Stellan's golden hair and a hook twists in my gut; but I could be mistaken. No sign of the other one though. The rest of the flock rises with the rhythm of a wave. One advantage of our lowly seating is its proximity to the door. We, the inhabitants of the Golden Lily, are out in the sunlight before the exalted few have managed to move two yards.

Magdalene's hand creeps up to twine fingers with mine, her grip tight and clammy. In the shade of the portico at the top of the steps sit the Archbishop's six hounds. Grey and silver in the shadows, insubstantial until someone with ill intent crosses the threshold, then they become suddenly solid, voracious and vicious. No one wants a resurrected wolf hunting them down. I have explained, over and over, to my little girl that they will do *her* no harm, but there is a core of fear in her that not even her mother can touch.

From across the square comes the sound of a carriage and four. It is the white ceremonial one I rode in on my wedding day. The sheer curtains are drawn but I think I see pale blonde hair as the occupant peeks out. Polly, who has yet to attend a church service in all her time in this city. My sister makes no pretence of religious zeal.

Behind us the wolf-hounds growl and Magdalene wails, climbing up my skirts like a terrified monkey. She holds me so tightly I can barely breathe. Grammy Sykes pats her back and talks in a low voice to the creatures. They react to her tone, settle back to sit in the shadows, the exiting crowd giving them a wide berth. I wonder who among the press of bodies set the beasts off. Grammy pokes me to move along and we head for home.

As we pass by, I look through the lychgate that leads into the churchyard. The red-haired woman kneels beside a grave, brushing it clean with her hand. Beside her plays a small girl, not much older than Magdalene. The woman is there every Sunday. I admire that she has the will to avoid Mass; that she is freed from faith.

* * *

The inn is old, so old that if you cut into the walls you might find age rings like those in the great trees of the forest beyond the city walls. The wood panels have been darkened by years, hearth smoke, sweat, tears and alcohol vapour. If you licked them (as the children sometimes do), you'd taste hops as well as varnish.

The bar itself, where Fra Benedict serves the drinks, is pitted with the marks of drinking vessels slammed down too hard, the irresistible will of dripping liquid, and the musings and graffiti carved by the bored, the drunk and the lonely when the barman is distracted. The glassware gleams, though, as do the metal fixtures and the bottles behind the bar are kept clean (although it's not as if they stay undisturbed long enough for dust to settle). There are booths with seats covered in balding velvet, and the hiss-hum of the gas lamps (lit low for daytime) is a constant comfort.

Things are quiet in the Golden Lily at the moment, Sunday afternoon, most of our clients still pretending their piety after Mass this morning. There's only Faideau in a corner booth, his breeches slung low and his shirt stained with wine. He's a poet, he says; drinks like one at any rate. He snores loudly. Fra Benedict will go through his pockets soon for the money he owes, then roust him to move on, to spend at least a few hours out in the sunshine.

In one corner is the crèche, where we whores and wenches leave our children (those of us who have them) under the tender, watchful eyes of Grammy Sykes and her half-wolf, half-something-or-other, Fenric. The small space is scattered with books and toys, which miraculously stay within a reasonable radius. Two boys, and three girls, one of them Magdalene, three years old and still clad in her red Sunday robe. My little girl, the only reminder that I was once loved.

In the kitchen I can hear Bitsy dropping pans. A few seconds later Rilka chases her out, swearing mildly, which is about as angry as anyone can get with Bitsy, who now stands in the middle of the room, unsure what to do next. Fra Benedict makes his particular peculiar noise to catch her attention, jerks his head for her to come and sit at the bar. He is mute; legend has it that his tongue was torn out many years ago in some monastery brawl. Bitsy hoists herself onto one of the high stools and sips at the weak ale and blackberry shandy he pours for her.

Bitsy is older than me though her face bears the blankness of youth and her long straight hair is a white blonde. She used to be a doll-maker. Not all of them go the same way; she made a special kind of doll, putting tiny pieces of her soul into them. Beautiful dolls, they were (I saw some in a museum, once), but each one, so the story goes, left her emptier. Now she's touched, little more than a doll herself, with just enough wit to sometimes take drinks to tables, wash dishes, and lie still when a client with no need for a real response climbs aboard and lets her giggle beneath him. Fra Benedict is kind to her; I think they are distant cousins.

Rilka's dark head pops out of the kitchen. 'Finished with them peas yet, Theodora?'

I shake my head. 'Soon, Rilka.'

She disappears with a profanity. Rilka was a nun, in her better days. Now she's just like us. Some men pay extra for her to lose her spectacular temper and hurt them. Her *special gentlemen callers*, she says with a laugh. Tall and muscular, cedar-skinned Rilka doubles as cook. Kitty thinks Rilka killed someone, tells how she talks in her sleep.

Kitty mends our dresses, sitting in the corner, working on one of those I brought with me, taken apart and made over to fit others. I had no further need of finery. Kitty pulls hard on her final stitch, makes a knot then cuts the thread with her teeth, etching more deeply the tailor's notch in her left front tooth. Her hair is brassy-bright, a touch of red, a touch of gold; it's beautiful and distracts clients from the scars on her face: two running parallel across the bridge of her nose before dropping down her left cheek like deep gutters, relics of an unkind husband. Her eyes are blue and sad.

She holds the frock up for me to see: the red and gold brocade is now short enough to show off Livilla's fine legs, and tight enough around the waist to push her breasts up so they will spill from the top of the bodice. I nod approval just as we hear one of Livilla's loud sighs floating down from an upstairs room. A few seconds later there is a satisfied, bellowing grunt from her client. She has earned her fee for the day.

Fra Benedict and Grammy Sykes, his common-law wife, don't make us take all comers. Most of the men are regulars who know Fra and Grammy keep a fair house with clean, cared-for girls. Sometimes there are women, too, anxious for something soft and gentle as a welcome relief from their husbands' violent prongings. We need only bed one client each day, any after that are up to our discretion. The fee here is high enough and the need for us to work as bar wenches outweighs the pull of the money to be made in excessive bed-sports. One of the advantages of Fra and Grammy's lax policy is that men are anxious to have what might be refused them, so we always have customers, banging on the doors, hoping to pay for our favours.

Grammy Sykes was a whore once herself; she remembers what it was like, the constant line of hard, demanding cocks. I think she prides herself on being kinder to us than anyone ever was to her. Livilla whispers that Grammy was a great beauty in her day, although there is scant evidence of it now.

Grammy and Fra will both tell you how many of their girls have gone on to better places, indeed, so many of their old employees are now the wives of rich and influential men that upper-class dinner parties sometimes resemble a whores' reunion; can't throw a silken shoe without hitting some woman who used to earn her living horizontally. The comfort of a prosperous future is for the other girls. They don't tell me this story.

I finish shelling the peas then turn to polishing the silverware Grammy keeps for the private parlour. I hear the front door open behind me, see the sunlight flare in momentarily before the door closes and the cool dimness is restored. I don't turn around until Fra nods to indicate that the customer is waiting for me.

Prycke was, still is, the Prime Minister. He wanders the capital with minimal guards as if he is as unimportant now as he was when he was born in the lower slum areas, out near the abattoirs in the furthest, poorest quarters of the city. He's not overly tall, has a stern sallow face, but his eyes are kind. Clad in dark colours, you might not realise how fine the fabrics of his breeches and frock coat are unless you look carefully. The buckles on his shoes catch the light of the gas-lamps and it seems he has stars on his feet.

'Have you a moment, mistress?'

I nod, feeling the precarious pile of dark curls on my head sway; one long tendril breaks free and snakes down my neck. He watches it fall. 'My time costs nowadays, sirrah.'

He is taken aback, reaches into a pocket and draws forth two gold coins. I raise one finely plucked brow but say nothing. I remain silent until he has extracted seven gold coins, then tell him to pay Fra Benedict.

Prycke follows me upstairs. I choose the room with blue velvet curtains hanging around the four-poster bed and a view of the city, an expanse of roofs and, if you look straight down, the Lilyhead fountain and children playing in its greenish waters. I tug at the loose stays of my dress with one hand and at the single clip in my hair with the other; the russet velvet falls to the floor and torrents of hair tumble down to my waist, obscuring the jut of my breasts. I sweep the tresses back so he gets his money's worth.

He gulps, removes his shoes first (so sensible! So practical! So strategic!), then his coat, and unbuttons his breeches, letting them drop. His legs are pale, hairy, strong. The tip of his cock peeps from under the hem of his shirt, shy, not quite ready. He didn't expect this encounter, I'm sure, at least not this *kind* of encounter.

I lie on the bed, splayed like an open flower, and wait for him.

When we are finished, he avoids my eyes. He slips, calls me *Majesty.* I laugh long and hard at that.

'Would you come back, Ma – madam? If you could?'

'Even if I wanted to, I would not, could not. Another sits in my place.' I fix him with a stare, blue and cold.

'Your step-sister, madam, she never sets foot in…'

'My *sister*, Prycke, neither step nor half. Only full-blood can hate so well.'

'Your husband sent me.'

'My *husband* heard me called "whore" and believed it. My *husband* heard his daughter called "bastard" and believed that, too.'

I hiss the words at him, spittle gathering at the corners of my mouth, and curse that I still *feel* anything. 'Five years together and I gave him no cause to doubt me, but the moment my sister *swears* to him that I had taken lovers he believed her.'

'Madam, I was not in the city when it happened. I would have counselled him otherwise,' he stammers. He feels badly for *me*. But he did nothing *for* me.

'For all the good it would have done. My husband brands me *whore* and takes my sister to his bed. So, I embrace my new title, Prycke. I am whore to whoever pays for me.' I sit up, step into my gown, lacing it tightly; I have earned my keep for today and tomorrow.

He dresses quickly, a handy skill. 'Madam, your sister has a strangeness about her. She is peculiar… she does not attend…'

I raise my hand. 'No more, Prycke. No more.' He reaches for the doorhandle. 'Prycke?'

He turns back, face hopeful.

'Tell Archbishop Willem I will see him on Tuesday, at our usual time.'

* * *

'Illustrious company we're keeping,' snipes red-haired Livilla, but it's a half-hearted dig. She's feeling generous after her early earnings.

Fra Benedict gives me a grin and flips me a gold coin. I more than double-charged Prycke and the spare is mine.

'My thanks, Fra.' I smile at Livilla, then take pity on her and snap the disc down the middle, along the shallow groove meant for such making of smaller change. Livilla, for all her ill liver, has stood me well in the last six months; this is a small price, to share with her.

'Pippet, moppet, dolly-doll-doll!' Bitsy sings from the crèche, where Magdalene has crawled onto her lap.

'Watch yer childer,' slurs Faideau. 'Watch 'em after dark.'

'Shut up, you sot,' Livilla throws in his direction.

'Childer going missing, mark me.' Faideau subsides back to his stupor.

'Man at his finest,' sneers Rilka. 'What a wonderful husband he'll make.'

Livilla shrieks with laughter.

'When I remarry,' says Kitty dreamily, 'I want that fancy bread they make. Queer shapes and all.'

'The girl, Emmeline's her name, don't do that no more and she's the one you want. She moved in with some rich fella, the one whose wife choked on *their* wedding bread.' Rilka sniggers. 'Sure that's what you want?'

I had Emmeline's breads at my wedding, but I don't tell them that.

Kitty tosses her curls. 'I want what rich folk have. Her mother still makes the fancy bread; not so good, but still it's the best can be had.'

Grammy finishes the argument. 'Stop yer yammers. Time to get ready, my girls, clients be here soon, almost five of the after.'

We troop upstairs to tidy ourselves. Those who've already earned their horizontal fee take less care than those who have not. Livilla and I will wench this eve; one of Rilka's beaters is expected, Kitty and Bitsy have no appointments and so will take whoever they like.

* * *

Restless, I leave my bed and sit at the attic window.

Through the frost-dimmed glass I can see square after square after square, all the way up to the giant square that is the epicentre of this city. All the way up to the Cathedral with its vaunting spire and gothic towers, flying buttresses – as if all possible styles were thrown together with no thought for taste. Right next to it lies the Palace, my once and former home.

A small palace but respectable nonetheless, perfectly appropriate for the size and wealth of our city, with sufficient halls and ballrooms and bedchambers and kitchens and wine cellars to ensure we were not embarrassed by the standard of our royalty. Gilt and glass and crystal in all the right places, the chandeliers kept shiny and bright, the wood panelling polished to a warm, rich finish, the brocades and tapestries thick and elaborate. Just the right number of winding staircases, deserted towers and hidden passageways.

Above it all flies the full-faced moon, soft and cold.

I look at Magdalene, curled into our bed like a kitten. This is the child I did not want. She was the change in my life that was utterly undesired. Stellan, though, he wanted her, wanted an heir, proof of his potency. I spent my pregnancy in a stew of discontent, resentful of being subject to the rhythms of another organism, of a heart beating not quite in time with mine. It was Stellan who would rub my swollen belly, caress the hot distended skin and whisper to what grew within. He made plans for her, told her about the city that was her inheritance. He created a future for her then forgot it just as quickly.

In truth, for me it did not happen with speed, the change of heart. I resented her as much in the first few weeks of her life as ever; I shudder to think on the bitter milk she drank from me. I do not believe there was a single moment when it altered: I simply found myself going willingly to her one day, craving the serenity of the times when she fed and I merely sat, we two in our tranquil little bubble. And Stellan stood outside where he was prey to others, although I did not know it at the time.

Bitsy and Livilla and Livilla's sons sleep in the room on one side of us, Rilka and Kitty and their respective daughters in the room on the other; they will hear Magdalene if she wakes. I drop a kiss on her sleep-damp forehead then slip a long black woollen dress over the top of my nightgown and pull on a heavy coat, belting it tightly around my waist. Under Bitsy's door I can see a splash of light – we have candlelight up here, only gas on the floors below. I tap lightly and go in. Bitsy is in bed, wrapped around a large doll with red hair. Livilla sits in a rocking chair, half-moon glasses balanced on her nose while she reads a scandal-sheet.

'Listen out for Magdalene? I'm going for a walk.'

'Bring her in here?'

'Only if she wakes.'

'Cost you half a gold coin.' She grins wickedly.

'I'd say I'm in credit.'

I hear her low laughter as I close the door. My boots I carry downstairs lest I disturb the others. Grammy Sykes is sitting by the fire, asleep, Fenric at her feet. Fra has gone to bed, leaving her to doze. He used to wake her up but sometimes she has fearful nightmares and one evening she almost took his right eye out, thinking he was one of the things that hunted her in dreams.

'Cold to be going outside, Theodora,' she rasps, surprising me and Fenric, who growls grumpily, rolls over, farts, and goes back to sleep.

'Got the wanders, Grammy, itchy feet, bed doesn't feel right.' I sit next to her, basking in the warmth of the fire, trying to store up its heat as I put on my shoes. 'Livilla is listening for Magdalene.'

'Watch yourself on the streets. Not just children that go missing.'

'I'll be careful. We're not in the worst parts, Grammy, I can handle myself.' I lift the knife from the pocket of my coat, its curved length gleaming.

She nods. 'Beware all the same. There's a little girl needs you to come back.'

I kiss the salt and pepper hair peeking out from under her white cap. 'I promise.'

The cold steals the breath from my lungs, the winter nights far worse than the days, when we get sunshine to take off the chill. I walk up the middle of the street, trusting that I will see or hear anyone moving in the shadows. I make my way quickly along the cobbles, accompanied by the sound of my own footsteps, the occasional feline yowl, the barking of a stray dog, the rumbling anger of households in turmoil. I feel the houses reaching up, towering over me. I can see under entryways through to the courtyards at the heart of each block, all with a well or a fountain, some with dark gardens and sculptures, some as bare as a newborn.

Soon the Cathedral is in front of me, crouching like one of the gargoyles that embroider its roof. The doors are open, and lights burn inside although it is well after midnight. The Archbishop likes his house of worship to be open at all hours; and he trusts that the wolf-hounds will discourage any vandalism. I hold my hand out to the closest one. A shiver passes through me as it pushes its strangely wet, ghostly nose against my palm, and whimpers for a pat I cannot give. I call it sweet and handsome and it settles back to its post. I walk through the great double doors.

Up the aisle, then to the left of the enormous altar, into the small Chapel of the Thirteenth Apostle hidden by a rich tapestry depicting the growth of St Radagund's very fine beard. Behind the elaborately carved *prie-dieu* my fingers find the catches carved into its underside and pull. Stone scrapes across stone and a hole appears in the floor at my feet, flagstones whirling aside like a child's puzzle. I take a torch from the wall. The steps are familiar under my boots; the skeletons sleeping in the wall niches feel like old friends.

This passage leads into the Palace, into the rooms I once called my own, before my sister took my place. Specifically, into the fountain room, *my* fountain room. A misleading name, really, as it's actually a bathroom, a marvel of white and blue marble, gold and silver tiles, and crystal and nacre inlays. The roof is made of a continuous sheet of rock crystal, so it seems open to the sky; it's especially beautiful at night. The soles of my shoes make a lonely noise as the steps begin to rise, and so I go on tiptoe. I open the hidden door and step out from behind a screen of gold, engraved with a fairytale pattern: Hansie and Greta and their adventure in the cottage made of sugar.

My footsteps sound hollow in this place where once I used to tread so confidently. There are fountains to decorate each corner, cushioned couches and benches, a small wooden hut for steaming oneself, hot and cold plunge baths, and a big swimming pool right in the centre of the room; I stop at its shallow end. The water is dark in spite of the moonlight, almost dirty, thick as blood or treacle. I can see ripples, though, sluggishly coming toward me. I suck in a sharp breath and retreat, back to the shelter of the screen, peering out through the tiny pinpricks in the metal.

It heaves from the depths and shambles up the pool steps to stand in the milky-white moonlight. I can see it clearly: tall but hunched and twisted, straggly black hair, hooked nose, wrinkled skin, long fingers and teeth razor-sharp, empty dugs half-way down its chest and a great shaggy pubic thatch at the junction of its thighs.

A troll-wife come out of the forest and into the city.

It sniffs the air, treads toward my hiding place with deliberate paces. I don't want to take my eyes from it, but feel my bladder threaten to fail me. At last I look away and slam myself through the doorway; the panel clicks shut behind me with barely a whisper.

I rest my forehead against the cool stone, try to steady my trembling legs. On the other side I can hear cold, hungry breathing, sense uncertainty. Sometimes they have trouble knowing how fresh a scent is but they have been known to follow an old one for days, to finally track a meal down, some unwary traveller who thought himself safely home.

There's a low growl that becomes a laugh: knowing and ugly. I turn tail and run.

* * *

'Mama, you're hurting me!' I've clung to my daughter so tightly that I've woken her. Morning light trickles in, grey and grim.

'Sorry, my love.' I roll onto my back and stare at the ceiling, at the intricacies of the thatch-work that keeps us dry and safe from the weather but nothing more sinister. Magdalene falls back into a doze.

Downstairs, Faideau still snores in his corner; Fra must have given up trying to wake him and send him home. I pour out a measure of mulberry brandy and wave it in front of his nose, an incentive and a bribe. The smell wakes him as surely as frizzling bacon wakes Fenric and makes him dance on his hind legs.

'Breakfast?' I offer.

Red-eyed, he takes the pewter mug and tosses back its contents without a pause. I wince on his behalf but he seems to neither need, nor notice, my sympathy. He lets loose an eye-watering belch and I try to wave the fumes away, but the stench is stubborn.

'I swear your breath comes straight from Satan's arse, Faideau.'

'Language, your Majesty.' He waggles a finger.

'You'll hear worse soon if you don't drop that.' I tap the back of his hand to get his attention. A map is tattooed there. 'Faideau, you said yesterday that children were going missing.'

He nods, sombre, if not sober, as a judge. 'Six months or a peck more. From all the squares – but mostly from the poorer ones – families as don't have much food and too many small mouths lining up for it. Sometimes they mind and report to Prycke's Peelers, sometimes they don't.'

'Any children from around here?'

'Not yet. Careful of the inn's childer, Theodora.'

I tip another generous slug of brandy into his mug and am rewarded with a smile. 'Keep an ear to the ground, Faideau?'

He nods, asks: 'Do you know anything, Theodora? Only you look afraid this morn and you never looked afraid the whole time I knowed you.'

'I… I think there… no, Faideau.' I shake my head. 'I don't *know* anything.' I turn toward the kitchen to begin the day's breakfast, glance back to him. 'Faideau? Are you really a poet?'

His index finger rises and taps at the side of his nose. 'Poets are folk what can't write full sentences,' he says.

* * *

'After this, madam, just one more payment,' says the stocky man, handing me a scrappy receipt. 'The house is in good repair, and the estate around it. You can hire labour from the village.'

'No need for that,' I tell him, tucking the scrap into the deep pocket of my skirt. In return I give him a pouch heavy with gold coins, the third such in the past few months.

'Thank you, madam.' He hesitates. 'I must say I had no idea your particular line of work was so lucrative.'

'It's amazing how much men will pay.' True, but also true is the fact that I have gradually sold off the gems and jewels I had sewed into the stomach of Magdalene's favourite toy fox when I sensed trouble brewing in the Palace. And of course I have other means of funding our escape.

'One more payment, madam,' he repeats. 'May I ask when…?'

'Soonest, Mr Spittleshanks, soonest.' I stand, take a look around his study as I always do. 'Your business is doing well, sir. I see another volume of Murcianus's treatise on folk tales.'

He beams that I've noticed. Even a fallen princess is a princess. 'Perhaps madam would like to borrow something to pass the time?'

I laugh. 'What a kind offer, but I have plenty to occupy myself, Mr Spittleshanks.' He reddens and I add, not unkindly: 'Perhaps soon, sir, when my life… changes.'

We part on good terms. I go to his house for our transactions, entering by the back garden – I prefer no one to know my affairs, there might be questions – and we deal only about the house I am buying. None of my usual "commerce" gets done with him. If I thought it would decrease the cost of the house I would have no compunction, but Mr Spittleshanks is a canny businessman, with a plump, comfortable wife. I suspect he fears anything more – energetic – with me might stop his heart and he would certainly not think bed-sports worth a discount on a property.

I pass through the market at Busynothings Alley and buy the fruit and vegetables Grammy asked for, and a loaf of fancy bread shaped like a fine shoe to amuse Kitty and the girls. Some brittle sugar candy for the children takes care of the last of the pennies in my pockets, but there is always more can be earned so it bothers me not. The sunlight makes me feel happy, safe; I can almost forget last night.

I don't go through the front door into the main bar, but pass under the archway into the courtyard where Fra's two superannuated black horses stand with their heads over the half-doors of their stalls, hoping for a pat. I pull two carrots from the string bag and offer them up to eager teeth and tongues. I note that there are already fresh carrot and apple fragments on the cobbles. 'Greedy.'

In through the back door to the kitchen, where Rilka is waiting impatiently.

'About time, Theodora.'

I poke out my tongue, dump the groceries on the large scarred table. I put the candy there, too, and point. '*That's* for the children.'

She makes a rude noise. I pick up the bucket and go back to the courtyard to draw water from the well in the centre. The pail drops down faster than it should and there is a scrape and a splash. I draw it up, and check the contents to make sure it's clean enough. Distracted, I examine my reflection. Still beautiful, strangely unmarked by my recent trials, only the eyes are cold now, pain frozen and held there.

Another face appears beside mine in the fluid mirror. I push away from the well, the bucket falls and the liquid splashes all over my visitor's fine footwear.

My sister does not look pleased.

Did she ever move so silently when we were small?

'You've ruined my shoes, Theodora.'

'They were probably mine in the first place, Polly,' I say.

'I've long since finished with your cast-offs.' She reconsiders. 'Well, except your husband. I'll keep him a while longer.'

'You're welcome to him, sister.' I circle away from her, uncertain why I am so unsettled, our recent history notwithstanding. Beyond the archway I can see the coach that brought her here, and two liveried footmen as well as the driver. I never used a coach in the city, I walked or rode my own horse. I smile in spite of myself; of course Polly would choose all the trappings, she thinks they make her legitimate.

Around her neck is the diamond necklace Stellan gave me on our wedding night. Strictly speaking, it's part of the crown jewels (although relatively new, only made a couple of decades ago) so it was never *really* mine, but it still sickens me to see it on her. Its entire length is set with diamonds and the central stone is a ruby the size of a bantam's egg. I tear my eyes from it. I have not truly seen her since the day she ruined my life. Prosperity agrees with her. Her face is plump, fleshy; she looks well fed.

She takes a step to follow me.

'No. You will not enter here,' I tell her. 'This space is mine.'

She shrugs as if it is no matter. 'I came to ask a favour of you, Theodora, and you are being so rude to me.'

'Ask and be gone and consider yourself lucky when you leave.'

She pouts. 'The Archbishop.'

I say nothing.

'Willem is an especial friend of yours.'

I shrug.

She stamps her foot, small and damp, and water squelches. 'He will not grant your husband a divorce.'

I laugh and laugh. I laugh until tears run from my eyes and my jaw aches. Her face, pale as her white silk dress, turns an angry red.

'And so you can't marry him!' I say. 'Ah, sister, you are just as much a whore as I.'

'If you ask the Archbishop he will consent,' she almost shouts, remembers to be ladylike and lowers her voice. I'm sure my husband has yet to see one of her rages. 'If you ask it of him, then I will be able to marry.'

'Oh, you idiot. You still think you can get your way as you did when we were children. Throw a tantrum and wait for everyone to give in.' I breathe deeply. 'Polly, there's no one here to make me give in to you now. No mother or father begging for a quiet existence. Let what you've already taken from me be enough.'

'I want to marry! I must marry! If I marry, I—' she stops herself, reeling the secret back into her mouth.

'What, Polly?' I scoff, unable to fathom this need of hers. 'You'll live happily ever after?'

Her blue eyes, paler than mine, narrow. 'Do you like your daughter? Do you love… Magdalene, is it?'

As if summoned, my daughter appears at the open kitchen door. She stops when she sees the snowy vision that is my sister, her face uncertain.

I stand so close to Polly that she can feel the heat of my breath on her cheeks and the spittle that flies from my mouth. 'If you so much as say my daughter's name again, I will kill you, *sister*, have no doubt of that.'

'You've made your choice then,' she says flatly.

* * *

The clients have gone but the inn's residents are awake late this night, children included, so we sit by the hearth downstairs, drinking warm goats' milk made sharper by Fra's home-made whisky. The children have straight milk and some crumbly butter biscuits. We are a strange family, but a family nonetheless.

Kitty is singing: a soft, sad song about a disappeared lover and his forever-faithful woman when the fire wavers and almost dies. The room goes cold and a frost creeps across the mirror behind the bar. We are silent, listening hard.

There's a snuffling at the front door. The handle rattles but it has already been locked. Fra throws the sturdy bar down across it. The wooden shutters on the windows have been long-since pulled-to to keep the heat in. Whatever is outside grunts angrily, shakes the door again. Fenric growls but does not move; he is afraid, his fur in such sharp peaks that he looks like a large hedgehog.

'The back door!' hisses Kitty and Rilka bolts through to the kitchen. We hear a thump as the bar slides into place there. The upper windows are out of reach.

We all cower by the fireplace, clutching our children and each other. It's quiet. I creep to the front door and put my eye to the small hole Fra drilled there so we can see who comes a-calling. A yellow orb stares back at me. I scream, scaring the thing as much as it scares me. It stumbles back and I can see all of it, and know it's the troll-wife come to sniff me out. It turns and shambles back up the street, away from the inn. It was hoping for surprise, to find me alone in my bed, asleep and vulnerable, not safely locked up with friends. It won't risk confrontation with a crowd.

'It's gone,' I say, voice shaking. Magdalene climbs into my arms and I sit by the fire; it takes me a long time to get warm.

Grammy asks: 'What is it?'

'Troll-wife,' I answer. 'I saw it last night. It's got my scent.'

Grammy is quiet for a while. 'Are you sure that's all?'

'What do you mean? What more can there be?'

Fra hands me another warm cup, but I can't taste the milk for all the whisky he's put in. Grammy begins to rock in her chair. Fenric sits close, careful his tail does not get caught under the rockers, but close enough that Grammy can bury her hand deep in his thick, syrupy-gold fur and soothe him.

'I mean, Theodora, that everyone knows *your* story. A woodcutter father who took a runaway princess to wife. The girl who freed a lost prince from a wolf-trap and captured his heart so he brought her here on his gleaming white charger.'

'It was black, actually,' I say.

'A happy princess, wife and mother you were until your sister arrived. We know your story, Theodora, but,' she pauses, rocks hard, 'what's your sister's story?'

'That thing isn't my sister,' I protest. 'She's mean and spoilt, but...'

'Yes?'

'She stayed behind in the forest with our father when I left, to take care of him. I said they should come with me, but they both refused. My mother has been dead for...' Something comes to me, drifting up from the depths of memory. 'When we were small – I was three, she just a few months old – our mother was washing clothes by the stream. I was playing with a doll and Polly was sleeping. Mama turned away for just a moment and Polly was gone, basket and all. She stayed gone for the better part of a day, all the while Mama held on to me and screamed and shouted.

'We found her, though, further downstream, somewhere we'd already looked. One minute she was gone, then back, no different.'

Grammy speaks slowly, pulling old knowledge out of a deep well. 'Trolls will take human babies and leave their own offspring in place, re-shaping their children's flesh and putting a binding spell on to hold it for sixteen, seventeen years, or until the troll-child is about to come to adult. When they're small, not fully formed, they're protected from their kinds' ailments, and sometimes so well disguised that even their own kind don't recognise them.

'Some troll-parents will come looking for the child. Sometimes not, and the thing has to find its own malicious way.'

'What happens to the human babies?' asks Kitty, holding her little girl close.

Grammy purses her lips. 'Some are kept as slaves under the earth. Most times they're eaten. When it's grown the troll-child learns to change back to its true flesh. Some choose to stay like that, retreat to the forests and mountains and caves and live out their long, miserable lives. Others choose to stay with humans, but some things they just can't hide – even in human form, stepping on hallowed ground makes an adult troll sick as sick can be. And they don't lose… their appetites.'

'All the missing childer,' moans Faideau from his corner. We jump, having forgotten he was there.

I shake my head. 'No, Grammy, no. She's mean but not… not my sister,' I finish lamely.

* * *

The Treasury is situated, contrarily, in one of the worst parts of the city. I like the irony, though, of the Treasurer and his attendant parasites, bankers and moneylenders, daily making their way through a sea of honest thieves and pickpockets.

It is a newer building but that doesn't mean it's without hidden ways. I take the secret tunnel from deep in Bingle the wine merchant's cellar. When I was princess, the Treasurer Pinchpen entrusted me with the city's finances – at least in word if not in deed. It was more for the sake of form, to honour the history of the thing, the princess's purview has always been holding the civic purse strings. Pinchpen didn't show me the passages, I found them for myself, pushed by boredom into exploring on the days when all I had to do was wait for the clerks to count taxes, balance books, and the like, so I could stamp the seal into the hot wax gobbet on the records.

The passage comes out somewhat inconveniently behind a bookshelf in an antechamber, not directly inside the vault. In the dark, when I generally undertake these trips, it's not a problem.

Today, in the light of the afternoon, it *is* a problem because my husband stands at the high window that looks out onto the grubby street. I catch my breath and he turns.

'Theodora,' he says. The sunlight hits his blonde hair and his tanned face gleams as if coated with gold dust. But he looks unwell. There's something grey under his skin, dark shadows beneath the green eyes.

'Hello, Stellan.' Nothing for it but for but to brazen it out.

'You're here. I haven't seen you in so long.'

I give him a look that says quite plainly he's an idiot and he has the good grace to seem ashamed. I don't want to prolong this but still I ask, 'What are you doing here?'

'End of the month book balancing. I have to do it now you're…'

I am thankful, for once, for his self-centredness, which means he doesn't think to demand what *I'm* doing there. 'I must go,' I say and turn on my heel, away from my goal, cursing silently. It will have to wait, until darkness falls and I must risk the streets.

'I sent Prycke to speak with you,' he said. I'm willing to bet Prycke didn't tell him the details of our negotiations. 'Was I wrong, Theodora? Was I wrong to listen to her?'

I stop. 'If you need to ask, Stellan, then you know the answer.'

He grabs my arm, forces me to face him. Between his pearly white teeth he hisses: 'Theodora, there's *something* in the Palace.'

I cannot shake him off. 'I *know*. I know.'

He drops my arm. 'Why didn't you tell me?'

I laugh. 'And how would I have done that? Since you banned me from my former home? Should I beg my loving sister to take a message to you? For her to whisper it in your ear at night as you lie together? Is she sweet and gentle?' I lower my voice. 'Don't you wonder that there are nights when she does not come to you? Does she go to the Cathedral with you, Stellan, every Sunday?'

His mouth moves but nothing comes out. His eyes are filmy with tears. How could I have loved him? How could I have thought him brave, charming, strong? I should have left him in the wolf-trap.

'How is Magdalene?' he whispers.

I step away. '*Don't* you speak her name. You have no daughter and you have no wife. You have a city that's losing its children, a palace that's haunted and a foul creature in your bed.' I don't hate him anymore, there's just a kind of sad, hollow pity. 'I wish you joy of them, Stellan.'

* * *

'Hold her tight, watch her close.' My words circle around in my mind like confused birds, the words I spoke to Bitsy when I entrusted Magdalene to her earlier.

In the stables, Bitsy lies, torn from groin to sternum, innards spilling out onto the fresh straw. The black horses stand as far away as they can, both trembling. The air in the dim, enclosed space is rich, foetid, choking.

There is no sign of Magdalene.

I told Bitsy to look after my daughter, and I condemned her to this, because Bitsy would never have let Magdalene go without a fight.

Kitty is frozen next to me, staring at our dead friend.

'Who came?' I ask, unable to breathe.

She doesn't seem to understand. I grab her shoulders, shake her violently, unfairly. 'Who came?'

'Your sister!' Two voices, Kitty and Rilka together, Rilka at the entrance to the stables, her shadow long, making Bitsy's corpse almost invisible. 'Your sister came.'

'I saw the carriage,' says Rilka, 'but she didn't come in.'

'Must have gone around the back,' gulps Kitty, tears starting. She falls away from my hands, sinks to her knees beside Bitsy.

'Where's Magdalene?' I ask, and they both turn pale, even Rilka under her cedar skin. I moan, hold my head, feel sick, but I don't indulge for long. I can't.

I run, pushing through waves of people who seem to have materialised just to slow me down. My breath sounds loud to my ears and I'm sure everyone can hear the thud of my heart, matching time with the clacking of my boots on the cobbles. The knife in the pocket of my skirt thuds rhythmically against my thigh. The spire of the Cathedral comes into view, looming over other rooftops. I round the corner and cross the square, lungs aching, take the steps to the portico two at a time, ignore the shimmering shapes of the bored wolf-hounds pacing there.

Up the aisle, past silent, wide-eyed parishioners. Into the chapel, anxiously waiting for the stones to shift aside, not fast enough, not fast enough. Along the tunnel through cold, damp air, the flame of the hastily grabbed torch flickering, guttering with my speed, but staying stubbornly lit.

I don't know, I don't know where they are, but this is the place I will start, the place where I first saw the troll-wife, the only place I can think of.

The panel to the fountain room slips aside. Heedlessly, I throw down the torch and without caution step from behind the screen.

Magdalene sits on one of the benches, nervously swinging her feet, face pinched and pale, bright curls damp and darkened with sweat. One of her shoes is missing and there is a tear where one of the sleeves meets the rest of her dress. She sees me, face lighting up. 'Mama!'

'Oh, my heart.' The distance to her seems so long. I kneel down, hold her tight, blink away the burning tears. I pick her up, and discover why she did not come to me when first she saw me. A rope runs from her left ankle to the leg of the bench, which is embedded in the floor.

'Oh, how adorable! What motherly love! How delightful a reunion.' Polly's tone is poison. She steps out from behind the little steam hut and stalks towards us. Her dress is pale pink, silky, her tooled leather shoes a matching hue. Around her neck is the diamond necklace, the master stone lying snugly just below the hollow of her throat.

'Polly,' is all I can manage.

'No, no, don't thank me.' She gleams at me. 'Really.'

'That was hardly the thing on my mind.' I push Magdalene behind me. She clutches at my skirts, tiny terrified hands pinching at me.

'I have tried so hard, Theodora. That is what you don't understand.' She sighs. 'What I am – what I was born – I have tried to escape, to change. If I try hard, ever so hard – if I live as a human, then perhaps I can *become* a human. Live a normal life, keep my human skin tight around me. Marry a human. Then maybe, just *maybe* it will rub off on me.'

Here is the heart of my sister's desire: humanity. I push Magdalene further behind me. 'I'm taking my child, Polly, we're leaving the city.'

'Oh no, not good enough. I've been thinking, sister dear, divorce really isn't good enough at all. You'll still be in his thoughts; he'll always wonder if he was right about you or not. He'll think about his daughter and how she's growing up without him.' She smiles and it brings a cold rush of air into the fountain room. 'Missing is better. Dead is best.'

She begins to change, to elongate, to increase in bulk; her skin loses its sheen and firmness, darkening and corrugating; her shining hair dims, becomes thin and black, writhes like snakes; her eyes grow wider, turn sulphur and bloodshot; her teeth, no longer uniform pearls, grow sharp and brown; hands lengthen and nails turn into talons. When her slender dress begins to split, I am released from my horrified fascination and pull the knife from my pocket to slice through Magdalene's bond.

'Run,' I tell her, pointing to the gold screen and give her a push. I turn back to Polly, who is now half a human taller than me and looking at her new hands, flexing them, listening to the sound of her over-sized knuckles crack. She laughs and lunges.

I sidestep and jam the knife into her stomach. She roars and stumbles. The silver handle protrudes from her belly, black blood wells where the hilt meets her flesh. I am backing away. She looks at me, and quite deliberately pulls the weapon out, slowly. The blade is gone, eaten away by the substance of her troll blood. I lose my nerve then and flee, gathering up Magdalene at the mouth of the tunnel, hitting at the lever to shut the door and running blindly down the steps into the darkness. I hear a grunt behind me and risk a glance. Polly has jammed her hand into the gap between the panel and the doorframe and thrust the panel back. I keep running as my sister's shape fills the doorway and blocks out the light.

I am thankful, in some tiny, screaming part of my brain, that my feet know this passage, have the memory of it embedded in their soles. I do not stumble.

Magdalene clutches tightly to my chest like a limpet.

I move through the tunnel, imagining hot breath and long, reaching fingers at my back. Soon, I see gentle light slowly seeping down to illuminate my path. I swear I fly out through the opening, I swear I grow wings in that moment, until I trip, my foot catching at the top step just as something tugs at the hem of my dress from the darkness below.

I keep hold of my daughter, twisting in mid-air as I fall so as not to crush her beneath me. I slide along the smooth flagstones and watch as the troll-wife leaps from the hole, the remnants of Polly's gown hanging in tatters on the grotesque form, the diamond necklace tight around the creature's much bigger neck, almost embedded in the flesh. She is all hunger, no caution, seeing only me.

She takes three thundering steps towards us before she falters, stumbles, senses something is wrong. Her eyes goggle around and she howls when she realises we are in the Cathedral. She tries to throw herself forward to get at me. She should have gone back down to the tunnel while she still could. Her fearsome noise is drowned out by the growls of the Archbishop's hounds.

They've become solid, substantial, heavy in the presence of the troll-wife. And they are *hungry.* All six wolf-hounds leap and knock her to the ground.

I hide Magdalene's eyes.

It takes them a long time to eat Polly. She is alive right up until the end as they shred her flesh, gnaw on her bones, tunnel through her ribcage to get at her large, meaty heart, and slurp on her steaming, stinking innards.

In the end there is only lank black hair, and sad pink strips of silk on the floor of the Cathedral. The wolf-hounds lick up the blood and, sated, begin to assume their usual ephemeral outlines. One coughs, seeming to choke, but as his form softens, becomes smoky, the object drops through his insubstantial throat and jingles on the flags at my feet.

The diamond necklace. I pocket it as a ruckus begins at the front of the Cathedral.

The Archbishop will be pleased to see how well his hounds earn their keep. I do not think my husband will recognise his mistress.

* * *

Night has fallen and Stellan is waiting outside Spittleshanks' house as we exit. Magdalene hides behind my skirts. She remembers her father, she simply does not like him. I refuse to leave her alone ever again. I hope we will soon be able to sleep the night through. Untroubled slumber is the balm I long for; for nights when Magdalene does not wake and whimper, and when I do not clutch at her in my sleep, terrified of finding her flesh changing in my hands. And I pray for nights when I do not dream of my sister, my *real* sister, dead or worse, toiling under-earth, never seeing the light of day.

'Will you come back to the Palace now?' My husband is crying. 'Come home, be with me. We will be a family once more.'

In the carriage under the street lamp my other little family waits: Grammy and Fra and Rilka and Kitty and Livilla and all their children (and Bitsy's doll, so we never forget) are wrapped up in warm coats and scarves. The windows of the inn are now dark. Faideau will not come: he says he is afraid of trees; I have left him a stack of gold coins to keep him in food and drink.

Within my grasp is my past, my former life. It slips and slides under my fingertips like treacherous silk. And here once again is my husband, who is beautiful still for all his flaws. Memories of *before* conjure rich flavours: Stellan *before*, our love and lust *before*;

luxury and leisure, never knowing want or hardship. If I just stretch out my hand it can yet be mine. But there is a sour aftertaste; there is what happened, and what was done. There was loss and betrayal and it can never be erased.

I shake my head. 'No. Better we take our chances among the whores and thieves. They're more honest, more loyal.' The deed parchment and the remaining half of the diamond necklace and its ruby sit heavy and solid in my coat pocket.

I take my daughter's hand and turn away, setting our feet on the wet cobblestones, shining like a path to a better place, to the dark coach that awaits to take us far, far away.

LAVENDER AND LYCHGATES

My mother's hair catches the last rays of the afternoon sun and burns. My own is darker, like my father's, but in some lights you can see echoes of Emmeline's bright fire buried deep.

She leans over the grave, brushing leaves, dirt and other wind-blown detritus away from the grey granite slab. A rosebush has been trained over the stone cross, and its white blooms are still tightly curled, with just the edges of the petals beginning to unfurl. Thomas Austen has rested here for fifteen years. Today would have been my brother's birthday.

To our right is one wall of the Cathedral, its length interrupted by impressive stained-glass windows that filter light and drop colours onto the worshippers within. My father, Grandma Tildy and my twin brothers, Henry and Jacoby, are among them, listening to the intoning of the mass. I can hear the service and the hymns as a kind of murmur through the thick stones. Emmeline has refused to set foot in there since Thomas's untimely demise. I used to attend, too, but only until I was three or so, when I made plain my preference for my mother's company over one of the hard-cushioned pews. Peregrine gave up arguing about it long ago, so here I sit, a thirteen-year-old heathen.

I've been perched on the edge of Micah Bartleby's tomb, weaving a wreath. I braid in lengths of lavender to add colour. I put the finished item beside my mother and tap her on the shoulder to draw her attention.

'Thank you, sweetheart,' she says, voice musical. Her face is smooth and her skin pale; only the flame-shaped streak of white at her widow's peak shows that she's older than you might think. Her figure remains trim and she still catches my father's eye. 'Don't go too far, Rosie.'

She says this every time even though she knows the graveyard is my playground. When I was smaller, Emmeline would not let me wander on my own. She knew – knows – that things waited in the shadows, bright-eyed and hungry-souled. Now I am older she worries less for I'm aware of the dangers. Besides, the dark residents here want only to steal *little* children – they are easier to carry away, sweeter to the taste. She believes I am safe. I drop a kiss on the top of her head, feel how warm the sun has made her hair. She smells of strawberries.

I take my usual route, starting at Hepsibah Ballantyne, ages dead and her weeping angel tilted so far that it looks drunk and about to fall over. Under my carefully laced boots crunch the pieces of quartz making up the paths, so white it looks like a twisted spine. Beneath are miles and miles of catacombs, spreading out far beyond the aboveground boundaries of the graveyard. This city is built upon bones.

The cemetery devours three sides of Lodellan Cathedral; only the front entrance is free, its portico facing as it does the major city square. High stone walls run around the perimeter of the churchyard, various randomly located gates offering ingress and egress. The main entrance is a wooden lychgate, which acts as the threshold to the home of those-who-went-before.

No rolling acres of peaceful grass for our dead, but instead a labyrinth, a riotous mix of flora and stone, life and death. There are trees, mainly yew, some oak, lots of thick bushes and shrubs making this place a hide-and-seek haven. It's quite hard, in parts, to see more than a few feet in front of you. You never know if the path will run out or lead over a patch of ground that looks deceptively firm, but is in fact as soft and friable as a snowdrift. You may find yourself knee-deep in crumbling dirt, your ankles caught in an ancient ribcage or, worse, twenty feet down with no one to haul you back into the air and light.

I am safe from these dangers at least, for I recognise the signs, the way the unreliable earth seems to breathe, just barely.

You might think perhaps that becoming dust would level all citizens, make social competitions null and void, but no. Even here folk vie for status. Inside the Cathedral, in the walls and under the floor, is where our royalty rests – the finest location to wait out the living until the last trumpet sounds. Where my mother sits is the territory of the merchant classes, those able to afford a better kind of headstone and a fully weighted slab to cover the spots where the dearly departed repose.

Further on, the poorer folk have simple graves with tiny white wooden crosses that wind and rain and time will decimate.

Occasionally there is nothing more than a large rock to mark that someone lies beneath. In some places sets of small copper bells are hung from overhanging branches – their tinkling plaint seems to sing "remember me, remember me".

Over by the northern wall, in the eastern corner, there are the pits into which the destitute and lost are piled and no one can recognise one body from another. These three excavations are used like fields: two lie fallow while one is planted for a period of two years. Lodellan does not want her dead restless, so over the unused depressions lavender is grown, a sea of purple amongst the varying greens, browns and greys. These plants are meant to cleanse spirits and keep the evil eye at bay, but rumour suggests they are woefully inadequate to the task.

In the western corner are the tombs proper, made from marble rather than granite, these great mausoleums rise over the important (but not royal) dead. Prime ministers and other essential political figures; beloved mistresses sorely missed by rich men; those self-same rich men in neighbouring sepulchres, mouldering beside their ill-contented wives, bones mingling in a way they never had whilst they breathed; *parvenus* whose wealth opened doors that would otherwise have remained firmly shut; and families of fine and old name, whose resting places reflected their status in life.

My father's family has one of the largest and most elaborate of these, but he is banned from resting there – as are we. Even after all the scandal with his first wife and the kerfuffle when he set up sinful house with my mother, Peregrine had his own money. His parents saw no point, therefore, in depriving him of an inheritance and left him their considerable fortunes when they died. What they *did* refuse him was the right to be buried with them. They seemed to think this would upset him most, which caused Peregrine to comment on more than one occasion that it was proof they really had no idea at all.

Once upon a time I liked to play with my dolls in the covered porch that fronts the Austen mausoleum, imagining these grand-parents I'd never met. But now I'm older, I don't trouble with dolls anymore, nor do I concern myself with grands who didn't care enough to see me when they lived. I feel myself poised for I know not what; that I stand on a brink. Grandma Tildy tells me this is natural for my age. So I simply wait, impatiently. I walk up the mould-streaked white marble steps and sit, staring into the tangled green of the cemetery.

Across the way a veil of jasmine hangs from a low yew branch, and something else besides. Something shining and shivering in the breeze: a necklace. I leave my spot and move closer to examine it without touching. There's little finesse in its making, the blue stones with which it is set are roughly cut and older than old. The whole thing looks pretty, but raw. I know not to take it. Corpse-wights set traps for the unwary. There are things here the wise do not touch. Should you find something, a toy, a stray gift that seems lost, do not pick it up thinking to return to it for chances are its owner is *already* contemplating you from the shadows. There are fetishes, too, made of twigs and flowers, which catch the eye, but nettles folded within will bite. Even the lovely copper bells may be a trick, for many's the time no one will admit to hanging them.

There's a rustle in the boughs above me and I see a face, wrinkled and sallow, with yellowed buck teeth, the brightest green eyes and hair that is, in the very few parts that are not white, as fiery as Emmeline's. The creature seems a "not-quite" – part human, part something else. Troll? My heart stops for a few beats as I stare up at the funny little visage; its gnarled hands hold the leaves back so it may peer at me clearly. Then it tries a smile, a shy strangely lovely expression, which I cannot help but return. I do not think this being is associated with the shiny temptation on the branch below it.

'Rosie! Rosamund!' My mother's shout reaches me. I back away and race through the bone orchard, my feet sure.

Emmeline is standing, stretching her arms up to the sky. In her hand is her sun bonnet, which she wears less than she should, its ribbons fluttering. She smiles to see me. 'Afternoon service will be finished soon.'

I'm almost there when my foot catches on a tree root I could swear was not in existence a moment before and I fall towards my brother's grave. My hands hit the rough-polished granite and while one stays put, merely jarring the wrist, the right one skids across the surface, catching on the letters of his name. I feel the skin peel from my palm and let out a squeal of shock and pain. A slew of hide and a scarlet stain mar the stone. The ring my mother gave me, silver vines and flowers all entwined, is embedded into the flesh of my finger and I think I feel it grind against bone. I knock my knees against the sharp edge of the slab, too, ensuring impressive bruises in spite of the padding of my petticoats and skirt.

I may be almost an adult, but for all that I wail like a child while Emmeline fusses about with her lacy handkerchief.

'Oh, oh, oh, my girl! Come along home, we'll get those seen to. Your grandma will have something we can put on that.' She helps me up and dabs at the seeping blood while I howl. My abused flesh stings and burns as we pass out under the lychgate. Shadows crowd above us in the angles of its ornate roof.

As we hobble away, I remember that I forgot to whisper good wishes to my brother.

* * *

My father has streaks of grey at his temples and furrows on his forehead. He says it's because he is given to thinking deeply. Peregrine looks tired and gives me a weary smile as I kiss his cheek and go to my place at the table. The breakfast room is painted a warm lemon and the curtains are pulled back so as to catch all the natural light.

There is a sideboard loaded with food, but no sign of servants. Cook and her girl set out our meals, but neither Emmeline nor Tildy could get used to being waited upon. 'No point pretending we're better than we are,' they said. I think Peregrine, only child of aged and proper parents, loves the chaos of this household. When he was growing up, he told me once, *everything* had a place, including him. Heaven forbid he should stick a toe out of line. 'Your mother,' he said, 'rescued me from the tyranny of order.'

'Bad sleep?' I ask, refilling his cup and pouring tea for myself.

'Emmeline was restless, so neither of us slept well. Or rather, she slept but didn't rest.' He stifles a yawn. 'She kept kneading the covers and the mattress as if she would change their shape. I suppose I should be grateful it wasn't me.'

I, too, feel tired. Last night Tildy painstakingly cleaned the wounds and smeared them with a salve that reeked of lavender, before applying bandages. The three drops of valerian she put in my milk ensured I slept without pain, but my slumber was fraught with dreams of mud and dirt closing over me, sucking the moisture from my skin and turning me into a cold dry husk. 'She's still abed?'

'Preparing the boys,' he says, grinning. My parents take turns-about rousting Henry and Jacoby. It's not that they are hard to wake, it's that getting two nine-year-olds washed and dressed in the morning is a challenge. No one parent should have to deal with that every day. My younger brothers are wild but not bad, and Grandma Tildy (a twin herself) says they will calm down in a year or two. It should be noted, however, that she no longer takes the morning shift.

‘And you didn’t think to take her turn after she’s had such an awful night?’ I ask primly. My father throws up his hands in defence.

‘It just so happens that I *did* offer, and it just so happens that your mother refused, Miss Bossy Boots,’ he grins and butters a piece of toast, then continues, ‘And shouldn’t *you* be getting ready?’

It’s a Monday and that means the pain of four hours at Miss Peach’s Academy for Accomplished Young Ladies. When I got too old for governesses, Peregrine insisted I be equipped with an education suitable for a young woman of Lodellan’s *Quality*. He said there was no need for me to become the wife of a rich man and even if I chose not to join *society*, I should at least know how to behave. Forewarned and forearmed, if you will.

Grandma agreed with the sentiment in principle, but she said I should have a trade, just in case life took me in a different direction. After all, today’s heiress is just as easily tomorrow’s guttersnipe – Emmeline’s path upwards might very well be a slippery slope downward for me. Peregrine replied there was enough time for me to learn a trade after a few years of becoming *accomplished*.

Tildy got that look she sometimes gets and took me to the bakery anyway. It’s run now by Kezia and Sissy, the ’prentices she took on when Emmeline stopped baking. My uncles, George and Artor, married them, so when Grandma finally admitted her hands no longer had the strength for the work, the business stayed in the family. Tildy concedes with gloomy pride that everything seems to be running smoothly without her.

She tried to teach me how to make the fancy bread for which she and her daughter had been famous. Alas, even though I was most willing, I showed very quickly that I had no talent at all. I think Tildy was more disappointed than she let on, but she shrugged it off.

When Emmeline, who’d been apathetic at best about Peregrine’s plan, heard about my first attempt at a trade, she was not happy with her mother. My fate at Miss Peach’s was sealed.

The door to the breakfast room is flung open and the twins fly in, clean and dressed, but no less frenetic for it. They aim themselves at the platter of bacon, from which I have already taken more rashers than is considered proper for a delicate young lady. Emmeline follows them, dark circles under her eyes, a tired smile on her lips. She stands in front of the sideboard, contemplating the breakfast options with something like confusion. Peregrine, rising, steers her to sit down while I put a mix of munchables onto a plate for her. She gives us a look that says *I'm quite capable of doing this for myself, you know*, but eats what she's been given and asks, 'How is your hand, Rosie?'

I display the offending limb: apart from a few pale scars there is no trace of yesterday's injury. Tildy, at a loose end when her baking days ended, started brewing things instead – not beer, although she's a dab hand at wheat ale. She took lessons from an old friend who used to do her best business after the *real* doctors had paid their expensive visits to patients. My grandma takes a particular pride in the things she can now do with herbs and mixtures, ointments and potions.

Emmeline nods. 'You grandmother will be pleased with herself.'

* * *

With the twins safely delivered to the hands of their schoolmaster (private tutors do not last too long with them), I continue towards Miss Peach's. A few streets away, I can hear the noise from the market at Busynothings Alley, siren-song subtle but strong. Any absence from school will be reported (as I know from bitter experience), so it's hardly worth the trouble. Lateness, however, although frowned upon, isn't generally met with anything more than a tut-tut from the principal's pursed lips.

I hesitate at the corner of Gisborne Street and Whortleberry Lane and contemplate my options.

Today is needlework. Tuesday is charity day, when we all troop down to the kitchen and make meals for the *less fortunate* (but I have a theory that all those dinners end up on Miss Peach's very own table). Wednesday is painting. Thursday is healthy outdoor activities: walking to a park and sitting under trees to protect our complexions. Friday is deportment. The older girls have extra classes to learn beauty and styling techniques, how to manage households and how to best have and raise children. Apparently, accomplished young ladies don't need to know anything else. Trifles such as literature, science, history, maths and geography are taught to me by Peregrine, or I pick them up by my own reading in our impressive library at home.

I think of needlework and how many times I am likely to prick my fingers, how much blood I am likely to spill on the fine sampler fabric. I *am* early, and I also know that while forty-five minutes is counted as "absent", thirty minutes is merely "late". My decision is thus almost made for me.

Whortleberry Lane is where books are born.

There are three tiny printeries, which never seem to lack for business. Two specialist paper-makers inhabit long, thin shops and will create a paper for whatever purpose you require: invitations, thank-you cards, sympathy cards, sketch sheets, even the special black-edged paper for the desks of those in mourning. Three bookbinders have premises in the lane and they will cover your books, fix old and ill ones or make you your very own journals and diaries for writing, stamping your initials on the cover in gold or silver flake. An ink-maker has strange, ill-ventilated little rooms in which it can be hard to breathe. And then there are the bookstores proper where you might find all manner of ordinary and extraordinary tomes.

My favourite of these is run by the pretty Misses Arbuthnot, two sisters who will find you any book you care to ask for, or may suggest something you just might like – should you be in the mood for a suggestion. The place, although very neat, has crooked staircases and leaning bookshelves and the smell of old knowledge embedded in the walls. Some days Tildy asks me to request the Misses Arbuthnot to find her a particular book. Invariably I will bring it home wrapped in brown paper with string tied tightly about to keep the busybodies out. She's a good library in her rooms, does Grandma.

Today, the younger Miss Arbuthnot (the one with the blonde curls) is minding the store. She gives a smile when she sees me slip in, but otherwise goes on with her inventory. The newly arrived books are in small wooden crates, some with the lids already jemmied off, presumably with the small ladylike crowbar lying on the counter. As I go past, I can see some of them have their spines marked with a fine golden "M". The younger Miss A subtly moves her body to obscure my view and the message is clear: *too young for these ones*.

I take the first flight of stairs, then the second, then the third and am puffing, just a little, by the time I reach what should by rights be an attic. There were customers on the lower floors, but this one is empty, the aisles between the shelves all deserted as far as I can see as I scamper up one, down the next to check. This level exists in a kind of clever deshabille, seemingly disorganised unless you know the system. These are the books *about* books. They are arranged in what might be called Birth, Life, Death – the making of, caring for and disposal of books too injured to go on.

This is my favourite place.

Carabhille's *Birth of the Book* waits just where I left it. I hide it away on a lower shelf, out of its ostensible order so no one else might buy it before me. Moneyed family or no, I still have to earn my pocket money and nothing by Carabhille is cheap. It will be another good month before I can make an offer. This one has a tooled leather cover in blood-red, the lettering on its spine and front is silvered. Open it and you find a hand-illuminated manuscript in brilliant colours with gold leaf highlights; no woodcuts, no moveable type. The frontispiece depicts a great tree from which hangs strange fruit: more books, each one tiny and beautifully detailed. The edges of the pages are rough – hand-cut by their first owner, whoever that may have been. The book smells old. It's weighty and I feel as if I'm *holding* knowledge.

'How's your hand?' A voice asks. It's a pleasant enough voice, not quite broken, but I still shout in fright. I turn around and see a tall, handsome-looking lad, dark-haired, pale-skinned, green-eyed.

'What?' Strictly speaking, I know it should be 'Pardon?' but he's taken me by surprise.

'Your hand. I saw you leave the churchyard yesterday with your hand all bloody. I wondered if you were all right?'

I'd not seen him, nor anyone else, but then I suppose I was not at my most attentive.

'Oh,' I say. 'Fine.' I show him. He looks impressed and gives a low whistle.

'Someone's clever.'

'My grandma.'

'Not your mother?'

'No, not yet. Maybe one day she'll ask Tildy to teach her.'

'What's she do now, your mama?'

'Paints.'

'Houses?'

'Portraits. Pictures of rich people and their unattractive children,' I say and poke out my tongue like a brat. My manners, thus far, have not been up to scratch, so why change tack now?

'Naughty,' he says. Before I can reply there's a scuttling at his feet. A fox comes out of the shadows of the shelving and weaves about his boots. He seems to think there's nothing unusual about this. It spits out a bark and gives me a long measuring look. I crouch down and offer my hand, hoping it will let me stroke its pretty red fur. It moves toward me as if it will, but then tries to nip my outstretched fingers and runs away, back into the shadows.

'Not very friendly.'

'Picky things, foxes.'

I look up and find the boy is gone. I wander between the shelves, searching for him but he's nowhere in evidence. I put the Carabhille back in its hiding place and make my way down the stairs, a little shaken. I check each of the floors to see if he made it down before me, but there's no sign. He must still be hiding upstairs, in some spot I don't know – although I cannot imagine where that might be.

Outside the sun is very bright and blinds me for a moment so I don't see who grabs me by the arm and gives me a bit of a shake. When my eyes adjust I find my father, his handsome face dark with an anger he so seldom experiences he doesn't seem to know how to wear it. Luckily I bit back those swear words I'm not supposed to know.

'What do you have to say for yourself?'

'I was just… I was only… I was late, not absent.' In truth, I'm too perplexed to be afraid of Peregrine's temper, and I also know he never can maintain a rage for very long. Sure enough, I'm rewarded by the clearing of his expression the same way a strong wind blows away storm clouds. 'And anyway, what are you doing here?'

'Collecting a book for your grandmother about the uses and tasteful arrangement of lilacs.' He pulls a face. 'How much do you hate that school?'

'It bores me rigid, Papa, you know that.' I lean my head against his shoulder. He smells like aftershave and wool. 'The instruction is mindless and I fear my brain will atrophy if I'm left there much longer.'

He snorts. Peregrine is especially bad at being authoritarian. 'Then, my Rose, what *do* you want to do?'

'Well,' I say slowly as if I haven't been thinking about it. 'I do believe Grandma was right when she said I should learn a trade.'

'It won't be baking, my heart.'

'Yes, I think we all know that even if it weren't for Mother's objections, I have absolutely no talent in that direction anyway.' I sigh unconvincingly. 'But what I would like to try, Father dear, is bookbinding.'

'Bookbinding?' He looks startled as if this would never have occurred to him in a hundred years – and truly it would not. It's only been in my head for a couple of months.

'I'm sure someone will take me on – if not as a proper 'prentice, then at least someone will teach me, surely?'

'There's a Mistress Kidston who is a bookbinder of great repute – she's in the one at the end of the lane,' he says, considering. 'She's repaired books for me before, made my diaries and ledgers. I think she would be appropriate.'

I love that my father knows this. He wouldn't have me 'prenticed to some smelly old man. I also love that my father doesn't insist on me becoming a lady too fine to tie my own laces or pour my own milk. I love that he's given up on my current education as a bad joke.

'This, of course, is on the condition that you promise to attend better to your 'prentice studies than you have thus far to your young ladies' studies. And you will confess to your mother what you've done. And what agreement you've forced me into.' He rolls his eyes upward like a saint being martyred.

'Cowardly cat,' I scorn, but hug him hard. 'We have an accord, sir.'

'I suppose there's no point in sending you off to – what is it today?'

'Needlework.'

'Oh, messy. Now, come on home. May as well get into trouble sooner rather than later.'

* * *

In a week, I will start my 'prenticeship. Emmeline met my announcement with an amicable and rather relieved 'Thank Heaven'. Grandma grumbled but accepted it. Henry and Jacoby looked at me with a new respect, for a while at least. Now it's time to gather all the accoutrements for my new trade. Peregrine has ordered the tools from a man Mistress Kidston recommended. Had it been up to my father, each and every instrument would have been handmade and carved with my initials, but I think he sensed the pain of embarrassment this would cause me. I must admit my excitement as the craftsman listed all the things I would need: the nippers, the frottoir, the paring and lifting and skife knives, the polishing irons and the ever-so-elegant spokeshave, but to turn up on my first day like a princess with her own engraved tools was a little too much.

Tildy has taken it upon herself to organise the uniform part of my requirements. Miss Lucy's tiny *modiste's* is set below street level, but bright in spite of it. The full-fronted glass of the shop draws in light, and the artfully made gas lamps are all alight and cast a golden glow over the white and green rooms.

'I'd prefer overalls, you know,' I grumble, flapping at the outfit being pinned on me. It's calico, a practical fabric and hardwearing and perfectly suited to a 'prentice. What's not practical are the skirts, which are almost as voluminous as those of a party dress; the pockets are good, though, and deep. Lucy Pye, tiny silver spikes held precariously in her mouth and stuck in the silken cushion on her wrist, puffs up at me, mumbling about *little misses*.

'I know,' sighs Grandma. 'But it's enough you're being allowed to be a 'prentice instead of going to that fancy school, isn't it?'

I grudgingly admit it is.

'Can't expect to dress like a boy too, my Rose. Now go and change. We'll pick these up in two days, Miss Pye.'

I go behind the curtains into the cramped dressing room and strip off the frock, careful to avoid the pins. I can hear the whine of the seamstress as she talks at Tildy.

'No point, if you ask me, in your young miss to be 'prenticing. What's she need that for? Got money and a fancy home; no doubt her father'll find her a husband to look after her. Why does she need a trade?'

'That's enough out of you, Lucy Pye, keep your fingers to stitching and your lips from flapping and making a breeze,' says Tildy mildly. 'My granddaughter won't depend on chance in her life – she's smart enough to know the only person she can rely on to look after her is herself. That makes her smarter than most people I know. I never relied on anyone, nor did *you* so don't go looking down on my Rosamund for not being a lazy brainless girl with nothing in her head but sequins and beads.'

'Might have been nice,' snipes Lucy, 'to have the choice, though. Do you really think I'd have spent all these years sewing if there'd been some useful man around to take care of me?'

'Take care of yourself. Can't ever be sure when a man's going to die or change.' I hear the clink of coins on the glass top of the counter. 'Be thankful you've only yourself to rely on.'

I struggle back into my own frock and do up the buttons on the front of the bodice, cursing every one of them. I tidy my hair and step out. Grandma Tildy stands and nods to a chastened seamstress. 'We'll see you Friday, Miss Pye.'

We walk out the white door that looks like a wedding cake, then take the steps leading to the street. You can tell it's a good neighbourhood because crevices like this don't smell like cats' pee.

'Honestly, Lucy Pye and her opinions everyone's got to hear!' Tildy clicks her tongue in annoyance. 'Now, a few years back there was a seamstress who sewed like an angel, you've never seen such dresses for all that she worked in the Golden Lily. Gentle as a doe and never said a mean word about anyone. She's one I miss.'

'What happened to her?'

'Moved away,' says Tildy shortly, and I recognise the tone she gets when she realises she's begun telling a story she doesn't want to give you the end of. I'm about to start pricking at her to ease out more information when a tall shape appears a few paces ahead of us in the gathering afternoon. I see him only briefly; he gives a sharp-toothed smile and then slides into an alleyway. I think I see a flash of dark red at his heels.

I turn to Tildy, whose hand convulses on my arm. Her face is stricken-white.

'Who is that, Rosie? That boy?'

'I don't know, Grandma. I met him a few days ago at the bookshop.'

I can feel her shaking and worry that she will fall. 'Come away, Rosamund, we must get home.'

'Tildy, are you alright? Do you need to sit down?' There's a tea shop not far down the street.

She shakes her head. 'No, love. We just need to get home.'

Tildy insists we cross the road even though it takes us out of our way – but it also keeps us away from the mouth of the alley, which is black, toothless. 'Rosie, promise me you'll stay away from him if you see him again.'

'Why? I barely know him, Grandma.' I protest, not about the ban on him, but the idea she seems to have about my connection with the nameless boy.

'Let's just get home, Rosie.'

I heard from some of the girls at Miss Peach's how their grand-parents went soft in the head, but with my fierce grandmother it seems unlikely. Still she's frail and afraid and I've never seen her like that before. It frightens me.

She spends much of our walk looking back over her shoulder as if we might be followed.

* * *

Emmeline has gone to bed early, troubled by a headache.

After dinner, I leave Tildy and Peregrine to talk and take the boys upstairs.

When they are washed, sleepy and in their pyjamas (the ones with the feet in them), I agree to read them a story. They always choose the one about the Robber Bridegroom because, they say, the clever girl wins. So I give them the tale and only when they are drifting off do they let slip a disturbing fact.

‘Met your boyfriend today, Rosie-rose,’ singsongs Henry as I pull the covers up to his chin.

‘Boyfriend!’ chimes Jacoby, who holds tight around my neck before I tuck him in too.

‘I’ve not got a boyfriend, as you both know.’ I kiss two warm, shiny foreheads.

‘He said he knew you,’ mumbles Henry. ‘He was waiting outside the gates of our school and talked to us.’

‘What’d he look like?’ I ask the drowsing children. Jacoby mutters that he is tall and dark-haired, which tells me very little, but makes me cold. There’s no further news to be had from the twins, both are asleep and even if I had the heart to wake them I doubt I’d get much more information.

I look in on my mother. Her nightgown has ridden up as she’s tossed and turned in distressed sleep, her hair is damp and sweat beads her brow. Beneath her lids, her eyes dart here and there, searching for something. Her hands clutch and clench. I wipe her forehead and cover her with the sheet lest she take a chill.

Peregrine and Tildy are talking still, and I can hear their voices raised. This is unusual in and of itself.

I creep down the stairs, careful to avoid the ones I know will protest my weight.

‘I know what I saw, Peregrine. I saw him look at Rosamund and I *saw* him true.’ Tildy’s voice is hard with urgency. ‘He’s a cold lad.’

‘Oh, Tildy. Don’t be ridiculous. I don’t believe in any of that nonsense.’ But Peregrine’s tone is more bravado than truth and Grandma hits back at him with undiluted scorn.

‘You don’t believe! How can you say that? You of all people, when you know what Emmeline did! You know what’s *possible*.’

What Emmeline did. Why my mother no longer bakes. Her power and its consequences, her revenge and how awful it was. What Emmeline did.

I don’t pay attention to his reply for there is a shifting of the air behind me and my mother walks past. Her eyes are still closed and she moves toward the other stairs that lead down to the kitchen.

I stick my head in the door of the dining room and beckon my arguing relatives.

They follow and by the time we get to the stone-vaulted basement kitchen Emmeline is a whirl of white nightgown and red and white hair. Her eyes are closed, but she moves with graceful assurance around the room and finds everything she needs. Emmeline begins to make the bread mixture she's not dipped her hands into since before I was born. On my mother's face is an expression which plainly says that she does this against her will. She mouths 'no, no, no' but her hands keep mixing, mixing, then she dumps the dough out onto the tabletop and begins to knead it angrily. I am frozen, unsure of what to do; Peregrine and Tildy watch with a kind of fascinated horror that pins them to the spot.

Emmeline makes no recognisable shape. I think her mind resists even in sleep, and whatever has pulled her from her bed has failed. When at last she stands, unmoving, her head low and her tears dripping into the leftover flour on the bench, then I put my arms around her. She doesn't start or cry out. I talk to her in a low voice and Peregrine and Tildy do the same. We walk her out of the kitchen, up the stairs and back into her own bed. We do not wash Emmeline's hands for fear the touch of water might wake her, so we gently try to pick off the remains of any dough, and hope she will not remember this night's venture.

* * *

The day is miserable, grey and dull. It has been raining constantly, monstrous great drops of moisture hit the windows with a savage sound and pour down the panes like small violent rivers.

Emmeline retreated to her bed again soon after breakfast. We none of us have spoken about her nightly excursion and she senses something is wrong and it makes her short with us, as if she knows we are not telling her something important. That we are treating her as if she's a child. She pleads weariness and a headache and no one doubts it. Tildy gives her a tincture of valerian. In return, I do not tell my father what the boys said last night about the slender young man. I do not wish to worry him, although I'm certain Tildy would be happy to crow a victory over that piece of information.

The twins have been bickering since early this morning and by the afternoon it has worn thin. Peregrine has, uncharacteristically, lost his temper and sent them to their room. This caused no end of uncomprehending distress and many tears. My father maintained his rage long enough for the boys to disappear up the stairs, pathetic sobs wafting down behind them as they slowly closed their door as if waiting for the reprieve that did not come.

I give my father a severe look and he has difficulty meeting my eyes. The trouble with being so easy-going is that people start acting as though you've no right to a bad mood. It is unfair but unavoidable.

'Oh, all right!' he huffs and makes his way up the curved staircase, his boots thudding with displeasure on every step. The boys will think themselves in line for a hiding now. I smother a grin, and Tildy stomps out of the front parlour. Her humour is no better than anyone else's in the house at the moment.

'Shouldn't you be doing something?' she demands. Idle hands and all that. I sigh.

I try to look saintly and put-upon. 'Saturday, Grandma, and even the worst of the wicked get a day off.'

'You little…' she trails off so I never hear what she thinks of me. Her eyes dart past my shoulder and out one of the front windows. I turn and follow her gaze.

Through the decoratively etched glass panes on either side of the front door I can see the youth, impervious to rain or so it seems. I fling open the door and make to go out, but Tildy grabs my arm and pulls me back. She charges past me and I can feel her fear like an icy breath coming off her skin. She's terrified but she will protect me no matter what.

'Who are you?' she yells. 'What do you want?'

I see his mouth curl up at one corner, part contempt, part fondness, as if he knows her better than she might ever think; as if he won't do her harm because he's terribly, irrationally, mysteriously fond of her.

But then she slips on the soaked stone steps and falls like a sack of potatoes down our long front stairs. The expression on the boy's face is one of distress in the moment when he's still there. I look to my grandmother, flick my eyes back up and he's gone yet again.

The rain is *cold* and hard against my skin as I kneel down beside my grandmother.

'Tildy! Tildy, are you all right?' I'm too scared to move her. Did she hit her head? Did I hear bones crack? Is there blood anywhere? Will she be all right?

At first there is a silence, a lack of response that makes my heart contract to the size of a pin. And then the sound of salvation, the most beautiful noise in the world: Tildy cursing up a blue storm.

Peregrine has heard the commotion. He looks impressed at the range of his mother-in-law's profanity. Indeed, there are things I'd like to write down – one never knows when one will need a decent curse.

'Can you get up, Tildy?' My father speaks to her as if she is better beloved than his own mother – which she is.

'Everything aches and it will be worse tomorrow.' She moans, lying still. I try to feel for any broken bones. She tolerates it for a moment, then brushes my hands away. 'Enough, child.'

'I'll send for the doctor,' says my father, and puts his hands under one of Tildy's arms, and gestures for me to do the same.

'Never mind that. I'll go and see my friend – she'll have something that will dull the pain better than any of those sawbones will come up with.'

'She's on the other side of town.'

'A walk will do me good.' She's being stubborn. She doesn't want to go out alone, doesn't want to encounter the cold lad again.

'Take her in the carriage, Papa. It won't take you more than an hour. I'll keep an eye on things.'

There is no more debate when Tildy gives in and admits that although nothing's broken, she is not in a state to walk the streets and she will need some kind of treatment to ease her aches.

They climb into the carriage, Peregrine's driver at the reins, just as the afternoon bruises into night.

* * *

I ask Cook to throw together a light supper. I go upstairs to check on the twins and find them both asleep, curled beneath their beds as if they hid there after Peregrine's tirade. Dark, damp curls are infested with dust-bunnies.

I open the door to my own room and immediately something feels wrong. The carpet underfoot squelches, saturated as if someone dripping wet paused there. On the cream coverlet of my bed I can see paw prints, large but fine, in a mud that may be almost as red as their owner's fur. The prints trek across the wide expanse of the mattress, then show a leap onto the small stool with its covering of cream and gold brocade, then a slight skid across the glossy painted surface of the duchess.

I go through my trinkets, the shiny things in the small cut-crystal bowls, all the bits of jewellery I've been given over the years by my parents and Tildy. The only piece missing is the ring twisted out of true by my fall and still stained by my blood. Given mother to daughter and then again, as I expected to do to my own daughter in turn.

There's the sound of a door opening somewhere in the house. At first I think it my father and grandmother, but realise it's too soon and the tenor was surreptitious, sneaky. I go out to the corridor and peer over the railings into the entry hall.

The front door is wide open.

I thought it too soon for Peregrine and Tildy to return; now I know it is too late.

I take the curved staircase at a dangerous pace, careful not to fall. In the drying shallow puddle on the stoop I can see the outline of two smallish feet as if imprinted there by the moonlight. At the end of our street, seemingly so far away, I see a flash of white and know it for my mother. I slam the door behind me and run into the road, my shoes slapping against the cold wet cobbles. Sometimes I almost slip, slide along, then regain my balance.

Always just in front of me, always just at the end of the next street is the flickering flag, leading me on. I cannot believe she moves so fast.

At last I gain our destination – I should have known it all along. The graveyard is lit in part by the lambent light from the portico of the Cathedral. The Archbishop's wolf-hounds strain as if against leashes; they cannot leave the bounds of their building. Then there are the corpse candles dancing around the graves; I follow the grim path to where more of them helpfully serve to illuminate my mother's grisly task.

Emmeline kneels in the muddy mess of the bone pit. She is scooping up great hunks of mud with her cupped hands, gathering it to her as if it is an injured child she can put back together. When she has enough, when it clumps together like clay – do I see it *move* in the moonlight? Shuddering with breath? – then she begins to mould it as she once fashioned loaves of bread. When she finds a bone, she sets it aside – will she find a use for it later?

The boy watches her, sitting cross-legged on a grave so old that the elements have removed any trace of the name of its occupant. His expression is fond and unhealthy all at the same time. I step as quietly as I can but the quartz is no friend to me this eve. I know these ways, these paths, but then, I suppose, so does he. This is as much his playground as it ever was mine – more.

'Hello, Rosie.' He doesn't even bother to look at me as I creep along. I give up all pretence and stand next to him, watching as the captive sleeper sculpts the graveyard mud. I take steps towards her, but he holds up his thin hand – I notice for the first time its port-wine birth mark, a match for the one my father bears. On his finger, loose and worn wispy by age, is my silver ring. 'Uh-uh. It's not safe for anyone to wake her but me now. Besides, my mummy's got work to do.'

'What's she doing?'

'Building a body. Of course it will be just a shell to start with, but once it's tempered with your blood, sister-dear, it will be a vessel fit for me.' He smiles. 'And when I settle my soul inside, I will walk out under the lychgate, Rosamund, and I will have everything you stole.'

'I didn't steal anything from you.' I want to turn and run, but I will not leave Emmeline behind.

'Oh, yes you did, my life and my place here. You stole my mother.'

'She's *our* mother, Thomas.'

'*Mine*!' When he yells his face elongates, the rims of his eyes seem to dry out and crack, his mouth opens to ridiculous size and his tongue, red and sharp, is split like a serpent's. The moment passes and he's a handsome youth once more, rather like my father in looks. *Our* father.

He calms and continues. 'I should have been first, but you sat in my place. You took her.' He sighs lovingly, his eyes moist upon my mother. 'But she remembers me. That's what kept me here, you know. Her memory is true. She really just wanted me, never you. Just me.'

I am silent and he continues, 'I must thank you, though, that taste of blood and flesh you gave me for my birthday was just the thing I needed. Of course it's the very least you can offer, little thief.'

'Have you spent all these years thinking that?'

'*She* told me.'

'Emmeline?' I ask, my heart breaking. Surely not my mother. Surely not my Emmeline.

'No, *her*.' He jerks his chin towards a tree and next to it sits the fox, now unnaturally large as if it may change its size at will. As the moon shifts and clouds obscure part of the silver disc, there seems to be a woman in the animal's place, with neat dark hair and sharp features, watching spitefully as my beautiful mother drudges in filth. The moon's face clears and once more there is merely a fox. 'She has been my friend all these years.'

'What's her name, Thomas?'

'Sylvia.'

'Do you know who she was? What lies has she told you?'

'The dead don't tell each other lies,' he sniffs, but it's unconvincing and I feel I can go on.

'She was Father's wife. She's the one who killed you.'

There's a sharp bark from the fox. I can't tell if it's a protest or a laugh.

'You're lying. You'll say anything to stop me living.'

'Thomas, if you wake Emmeline and ask her, she'll tell you. You trust her, don't you? You trust *your* mother.'

'If I wake her she won't finish.'

'Yes, she will, if I'm lying! She'll want to show you – she'll want you back, you're her firstborn.' *Oh please, oh please, oh please let it be a lie!* I need to know as much as he does, how true our mother's heart is.

He's reluctant. I wonder that the fox-bride doesn't take on her human body, yell at me, stop my dissident tongue, but perhaps she can't. Perhaps this is her punishment, that she can only flicker between one form and another, never able to hold onto a woman's shape try though she might; never able to speak with more than the bark of a fox and in a tongue only the dead can understand.

'Wake Emmeline, Thomas. Wake her. If I lie, then what's to lose? If I lie then why should your friend object to me being found out?' Above the fox I can see something stirring the leaves of the tree, ever-so-subtly, ever-so-quietly that not even Sylvia notices.

Thomas doesn't see either. He shifts his attention to our mother and calls out softly. 'Mother? Oh, Mother-mine, wake up.'

Emmeline blinks and shakes her head. She takes in her hands and the black marks on her nightgown and the dark stains of clay and mud streaking up her forearms. Thomas stands over her and helps her up. None of the muck on her rubs off on him, as if his substance will not allow anything to stick.

Emmeline looks at me, her eyes confused, her expression pleading. *Oh, please explain, my Rosamund.* How to do so? How to say it without angering this frightful spirit?

'Emmeline.' I'm wary of calling her *Mother* in front of so jealous a brother. 'Emmeline, this is Thomas, your firstborn. He has a question for you. He has been waiting for so long to come back to us – to *you*.'

Her eyes flash and I hope I see understanding there. Emmeline and her talented hands, Emmeline and her strong will; Emmeline who did what she did all those years ago. My mother is clever and quick.

'Mother, how did I die? How was I lost to you?'

She flicks a look at me and I give a barely perceptible nod. I have known this story as long as I can remember, heard it at Tildy's knee before Emmeline could stop her. Heard it so I might know who my mother was and how special she was, what she could and would do to protect her family.

'Your father's first wife cursed me.'

Thomas howls as if stuck with a knife and the fox barks sharp enough to hurt my ears. She makes to disappear into the shadows but a dark lumpen shape drops from the boughs above and scoops her up, holding tight as tight can be so she can neither nip nor struggle. The hands are gnarled but very strong and they wrap around the animal's throat with an astonishing speed and begin to squeeze. One moment it is a fox, the next a young woman with a thin neck, the next a fox again; one barks, the other cries out; in the end both are silent. A limp red carcass dangles in my strange friend's grip.

Now there is Thomas to deal with.

He looks so stricken and already he seems… thinner. I think I can see through him to the faint outlines of gravestones. He has been held here by belief and memory, and now his foundation has been shaken to its core, shown to be false.

I feel sorry for my brother.

He shakes where he stands. The mud at his feet seems to suck up at him. 'Mother,' he weeps. 'Don't you want me back?'

'I never really had you, lovely boy. I miss you, Thomas, I truly do.'

'Wouldn't you rather me, though? Me, not her? I was the one you were supposed to have.'

'But I do not love Rosamund less. She did not take anything from you, she did not replace you. You must understand, Thomas, that I would not have you instead of her. You were taken from me so long ago. I grieve every day, but I know I cannot have you back.'

'You don't mean that,' he screams. The mud is now most certainly sucking at his lower limbs but he does not seem to notice. Emmeline smiles and nods.

'Yes, I do, my darling boy. I love you but I will not exchange my *rosa mundi* for you. And I will not forgive you if you harm your sister.' She reaches out to put a gentle hand on his chest. Her palm meets something not quite solid, sinking further into his flesh than it should.

'Mother,' he whimpers and he weeps. 'Don't you love me?'

'Ah, so much, so much. Yes. And I will miss you forever.'

He sinks to his knees, suddenly weak. Emmeline kneels beside him and cradles him against her. I *can* see through him, now, to the ground beneath. She strokes his face but her fingers begin to dip beneath the skin as he loses solidity, loses his form.

Thomas wanted nothing more than to be loved, to have his chance with our family. He had only a child's selfish desire for something with no idea that there are some things we cannot have. This night, I understand my brother. One day I may weep for him and one day I may forgive him. Until then I give him what I can. I sit next to him and hold his rapidly fading hand. He looks at me with moon-washed eyes; I'm not sure he can see me anymore.

Robbed of his power, of Emmeline's yearning memory, he becomes shadow and recollection, nothing more. In a few more beats of the night, he is gone and there are only Emmeline and I and our strange ally.

We rise and move towards the creature, who is hunched and wizened. It's dressed in rags that were once proper clothes. The fox's corpse is rotting now, quite rapidly and the not-quite-human-not-quite-troll throws the body as far away as it can.

I notice that Emmeline's green eyes more or less match those of the weird human-ish thing. It – she, it is obviously a she – gives a shy smile and a curiously graceful curtsey. My silver ring, which fell into the mud when my brother's hand dissolved, is cold in my palm. I hold it out to her. She looks pleased and slips it onto one enlarged knuckle and pushes with determination until it pops over and dangles around the thin digit. With a nod of thanks, she turns to the yew tree once again and climbs swiftly, her large feet and hands finding holds not obvious to the eye.

'Who is she?' I ask.

Emmeline shakes her head. 'My father had varied tastes, Rosie. I think the hair and eyes tell a story.'

She holds me close and there is no place nicer or kinder than in my mother's arms. I think of Thomas, deprived of this, a cold lad his whole life. I hope the last memory of our mother holding him sustains him in his final sleep. I hope he will not be forever alone in the dark.

UNDER THE MOUNTAIN

The sight of the inn picks at the stitches of my memory. The splintered shingle, emblazoned with a faded golden lily, swings in the breeze. I stare at it for a while, trying to catch at the recollection, mentally trying to scratch an itch I can't *quite* locate. I push the aged door and it swings to easily. The place seems deserted, but in a corner, wedged in the angle of a padded bench beneath a hissing gaslight, is a man, pieces of parchment gathered in front of him. His hair was black and he was handsome, once. Now the hair is shot with iron-grey and he's crumpled, body, face, and (I suspect) soul. His bearing speaks of loss.

'Faideau?' I ask. He blinks, and I realise I am nothing more than a silhouette against the light. I close the door so he may see me clearly: tall and strong, long blonde locks, high cheekbones, ice-blue eyes. No sign of the unwellness, of the ache in my bones that comes from hard riding. I find the shadowy space a relief.

'Who wants to know?' He is not drunk, but he is aggressive. His eyes are dark.

I did not need to come here. I had no requirement to speak to anyone but those who would have sold me fresh provisions and stabled my horse for the night. I know where I'm going, having studied Theodora's books and the notes she left behind. I did not *need* to visit this place. I don't really know why I came.

I do not remember him, but this is the man Theodora mentioned with a sad amusement, a pang for what might have been. This was the one who did *not* take advantage of her favours after her fall from grace. When she changed from princess to whore and embraced her new calling as much to embarrass my father as to soothe her own pain, *this* was the one man she did not hold in utter contempt. Thus, she told me later, she did not sleep with him.

'I'm Magdalene.' I see him all uncomprehending. 'Theodora's daughter.'

'Theodora.' In his voice is such love and ache for my mother that I am embarrassed for him, to see his heart so naked. 'How is she?'

How to say, to tell anyone *how* she was? How her night terrors had been getting worse. How thirteen years of them had made her gaunt and thin, drawn shadows under her eyes and washed their pale blue to the grey of a sickly sky. How long streaks of silver-white had threaded through her hair. How Theodora, whose beauty once made kings and clergy weak, had begun to fade.

'Gone. She's gone,' I say and he misunderstands and I think the heart will flop out of his chest. 'No, no! She is alive, but she is gone. She – left me.'

'You? Left you?' And I know he is thinking back to that night when Theodora ran through the streets of Lodellan and saved me from the thing posing as her sister. And he asks himself what I have asked myself: *how* could Theodora leave *me*?

'She slipped away in the night, left me a letter. Went to search for Polly, her *true* sister. She said even if all she finds are the bones, it will help.'

He slumps even further down as if the mention of Polly adds weight to him. When he raises his eyes to meet mine I see secrets there, pushing their way to the surface. But I don't want them.

'Do you remember? Any of it? The time when childer went missing?' he asks, peering at me. I take a seat opposite as he continues, 'You don't look like her, you know. Not at all.'

I shake my head. 'I do not remember.'

But sometimes I dream of a pretty blonde woman. She grows and changes. Her voice remains honeyed even as she turns into something that will eat me; something that is *all* appetite. I fear my mother had similar dreams, for she would wake clutching at me, feeling to make sure my flesh was my own. That it did not shift and change into something *other*. He wipes a hand across his face and I see the map tattooed there. Curiosity shimmers.

'What's that?'

'A reminder,' he sighs and looks at the marks on the back of his hand as if they are foreign to him. 'How are the others? Grammy, Kitty?'

'Kitty and Livilla and their children left a few years ago.' I do not tell him why. I do not tell him how they feared for their offspring in the face of my tempers; how their last words to Theodora were bitter. 'Fra died last spring. Grammy and Fenric are there, old but well enough. Rilka we see sometimes – she comes and goes according to her own counsel.'

He looks sad to know these things. 'Have you gone to see your father?'

'No, why would I?'

'Why would you come *here*?'

I hesitate. 'I don't know. I had to stop somewhere.' I cannot tell him about our fights, Theodora's and mine; about the rage, about my guilt, about my last words to her, but I think he may guess. 'I just stopped here for one night, for supplies. I remembered the inn, or at least I seemed to.'

'You should stay then. Plenty of beds.' He grins without humour. 'Take your pick.'

* * *

The blue room has a view out over the Lilyhead fountain, but I don't look down. Instead I stare straight ahead and concentrate on the sculptured lineaments of the Palace. I have no memory of living there; I recall my father following us when we left that funny little man's house on the night we fled Lodellan. I remember his blonde hair, and his lovely green eyes shining with tears in the lamplight. I remember how disgusted Theodora's expression was when she gazed upon him. The sun is setting, all red-gold and raw, burning the sky as it plummets. Below I can hear the clank of pots in the kitchen like a call to arms.

Faideau has a disreputable apron tied around him, the lacy frills hanging torn and frayed. I see no sign of the drunkard of whom Theodora spoke so sadly and fondly. His hands are steady on the knife and his movements, though slow, are assured. He sees me in the doorway and smiles. I wonder what Theodora would have said had she seen him like this.

'Did you find everything you need?'

I nod. 'Thank you.' Wondering how much small talk there can be between we two.

'Why did your mother leave you?' he asks without preamble.

I lie. I lie because I don't want to think about it. 'I don't know.'

He doesn't believe me, begins to tell me his story, perhaps in the hope that one confidence will draw out another. 'When I was a boy—'

'I do not have time for this!'

'You have plenty, missy, you're not going anywhere in the night.' He will reel out this tale at his own pace and I have no choice but to listen.

I'm old enough to know that secrets don't spill quickly, they bleed, they seep.

'When I was a boy, I was adopted by a very bad man. I was brought up by brigands but left to my own devices an awful lot. Often I'd sneak away to another part of the woods and watch a family who made their home there. Mother, father and a daughter, they were happy and loving. I'd watch all three, unseen. I was very careful never to let my foster-father or any of his men know. That family was my secret – I kept it to keep them safe.

'I made friends with the little girl. I was treated so very well in their home. The first tenderness I ever experienced came from them. I wanted nothing in life but to be loved, to belong to *that* family. I would lie on my bed of bracken at night and dream of four walls and a hearth, of the sounds of people who loved me sleeping nearby.'

'Faideau.' I itch to shake him, to stop him, but he ignores me. I have enough shadows of my own; I do not wish to carry those of another.

'Your mother, even then, was as beautiful as a new day. Then the baby arrived and I was displaced. The mother was preoccupied and Theodora wanted only to play with the new human doll. I interested her not at all. Perhaps if I'd been older I would have known that things would return to normal if only I'd the patience to wait. That their love hadn't gone, merely been distracted.' He frowns as if he could tell his younger self these things and thus avoid all that had come about.

'In the woods, Magdalene, there are wolves, trolls, men who turn into beasts at the first sign of the moon, women who do worse. All in all, witches are the least of your worries. Things in the forest speak, things that shouldn't, and they know what's in your heart. A troll-wife found me hiding, watching Theodora and her mother and new sister at the stream.'

My heart clenches. His confession will hurt us both. 'It – she – told me I could win their love if only I did her a favour. It was a joke she said, no one would get hurt – that sometimes we needed to use tricks to get what we really, really wanted.'

And he told me how he stole away the true Polly lying fresh in her basket, and took her to the doors of the kingdom under the mountain. How the troll-wife gave him another child in return, a misshapen lump of flesh, a wailing thing that she touched and moulded until it took on the appearance of the infant he had brought. How he returned it to where Theodora's mother might find it and his head was filled with thoughts of how much this family would love him. But the guilt ate at him, night and day, so any joy he might have had was bitter. He was uncomfortable and afraid that somehow he might be discovered. That the mewling changeling might somehow betray him. His fear transmitted itself to the family and so they became ill at ease in his presence. After a while he stopped going to visit.

I could have told him, even *I*, that such an act will return a greater pain to the perpetrator than the victim, how selfishness is *never* rewarded. How, when I had screamed at my mother and wished her gone, the very next day she was. And how on the morning I found her missing I could not imagine a worse ache than that of the loss of her.

'How could she not know you, Faideau? To meet you again?'

He shrugs. 'When she came to Lodellan as the prince's bride, all royal and shiny, there were so many years between us and I wore another name, once, when I was small. And I was so much *less* than I had been. The boy had faded from her memory; the man was a drunk. And so this,' he gestures as if a shared history is spread before us rather than the components of a meal, 'is all my fault.'

'But you were only a child,' I say.

He smiles coldly.

'Someone else said that to me once, or something very like.' He shakes his head.

How do I judge this man? How *dare* I judge him? Had he been stronger, had he been better, Theodora may not have married my father and we would not have been as we were. My aunt would never have been stolen away; we would not have fled the city; we would not have had this vein of agony running through our lives. I would have had a different father; or I would not have existed at all. I do not find that last thought painful.

'So, I ask again, Magdalene, why did your mother leave you?'

But I do not say anything, do not give him even a scrap and he hands me a plate. 'I think you should leave very early. I don't want to see you again.'

I almost open my mouth then, but he continues, reluctantly, as if he now gives me information against his will. 'Your mother is known, Magdalene, in the forest. She travelled its ways long before she came to Lodellan. She knows its dangers. Be careful. Don't stray from the path.'

* * *

'Starving,' Grammy had said. 'I left her because we were starving.'

When I'd found Theodora gone, it was Grammy who listened to me curse and cry, Grammy who dried my tears, who fed me a hearty breakfast, who quietly watched as I stuffed a satchel full and just as quietly took everything out and repacked it with things that might actually be of some use. I followed her as she stumped about the house, adding a compass and a dagger from Kitty's room (still kept as she left it, just dusty); a loaf of bread, the last of the dried meat that Fra Benedict used to take into the woods with him, a small wheel of cheese, a bladder of water from the pantry; and the sword with which Rilke had trained me.

It was Grammy who explained how a woman might leave a child behind.

'We'd grown so thin, Fenric and I, that you could almost see the sunlight through us. I gave up whatever I could for the baby, to keep her healthy, but it was winter and harsh. I could find milk only so often. Sometimes I fed her on blood from the animals Fenric was able to hunt up. I was barely more than a child myself. We were cold and hungry and I'd promised I would see the child safe and protected, but I was doing a worse job of it than even I thought possible.' She lowered herself heavily at the bottom of the steps, wiggling the satchel about so its contents sat just right.

'In the forest, there was less snow – the trees were so thick most of it didn't make it through and while it wasn't warm, for a time it was better than it had been. I wanted so badly to lie down and give up and sleep forever. But I kept going; Fenric would nip at me and growl if I stopped, if I napped. And Olwen, Olwen would wail. In my memory it was constant, but perhaps not. I remember her being heavy, too, but I know that's not right – she was so light, so underfed. We kept going.' Fenric, at her feet, watched her devotedly as he always did. She ruffled his fur and smiled.

'Just before nightfall, we found a man and a woman weeping over a small mound, a child's grave. I no longer recall their faces, but I thought they looked kind. I thought they looked in need. Their cottage was small and neat, with bright flowers that lit up the garden as surely as fire does night. The door was ajar and I went inside while they were distracted. At first I thought only to steal some food. Then I saw the cradle, empty, but fitted with a fine layette made with such care. Olwen was asleep. I placed her in the cradle. She looked as though she belonged there, tiny scrap that she was. She sighed in her sleep and I thought 'This is better. This is best.'

'I slipped away like a shadow. I thought I might die out in the winter, but she at least would live. I knew I would not return for her. She was no longer my burden.'

'Why tell me this?' I demanded.

'Because you need to realise that sometimes mothers have to leave children behind. Even if they don't want to, sometimes they must,' she said gently.

'She did not *need* to leave me! She did not need to choose her sister over me,' I howled. 'Did I make her so miserable?'

But I knew the answer.

Could I have alleviated some of Faideau's agony if I had said to him *We had been fighting, Theodora and I, constantly it seemed and equally constantly it seemed about nothing. A glance, a sigh, a word, a breath out of place could birth a conflagration as surely as a spark onto a pile of tinder. Whenever my words were particularly hurtful I would catch something in her expression as we glared at each other, something that said* I pulled you from the jaws of a troll-wife and look how you turned out*!*

If I had admitted to him that my own mother seemed to fear and distrust me, would that have helped either one of us? But I did not share any of this and the time has passed for a confession to have any gentling effect. I have neglected that chance. So I leave, as instructed, without saying goodbye.

The sky has barely warmed, still streaked with the cold grey of dawn. I've wrapped my cloak tightly about me and am thankful for the gloves Grammy gave me, leather lined with fur. I rest my hand on the hilt of the sword. There are few folk out at this hour, mainly merchants preparing for market trade. I feel eyes on me, pricking holes in the back of my neck, but no one speaks to me. No one yells *Tell her father she has returned*. No one knows me, no one cares. I do not belong here; I am passing through.

I ride out under the city gates and follow the road until it is eaten by the forest.

The trees are thick and it's dark underneath their canopy. I rely on my mount's sturdy hooves to keep us on the path. There is a peculiar silence all around, no birds sing, nothing scampers or pads, flits or slithers. Above me the air is thick with spider webs, silver and disturbingly sturdy-looking, but empty of all but the remains of morning dew. When we come to a clearing the light is shocking.

I take the chance to consult my map, hastily scribbled on a parchment as I prepared to go after Theodora. All I can think of is how much I want to rage at her, scream and cry and give vent to a disappointment I never thought I could name. To tell her she has made me ashamed by running away, by denying me. For the first time in weeks I give in to tears, to the weakness that her departure left me, to the wailing child I've kept bottled up inside.

'Please, miss, will you help?'

One is whey-faced with blonde hair not unlike my own; the other has very dark straight hair. The one who speaks is of medium height, wiry; a bit older than me. His smile is nervous. His hands, clasped pitifully in front of his chest, are shaking. The dark one is younger, smaller and keeps his eyes lowered, as if too afraid to look at me.

'Help with what?' I ask gruffly, embarrassed to be caught with tears on my cheeks and making such a childish racket.

'There's a woman over there.' He points vaguely into the depths of the undergrowth. 'We found her – my brother and me – I think she's hurt.'

I wonder if it's Theodora and because I wish for this to be at an end, and because some part of me *does* want my mother lying injured somewhere, I dismount.

Immediately the younger one raises his eyes and they are filled with rat cunning. He gives a grin punctuated by black gaps of missing teeth. He grabs for the bridle and my horse rears. I stumble out of the way. Only now do I notice how well the dirty shades of their jerkins and breeches help them to blend in. Brigands.

I draw my sword and the boy who's trying to steal my mount charges at me. I run him through and the sword parts his flesh like butter. I've never killed anyone or anything before. Never felt how the steel moves through *meat*. Never understood what Rilka was trying to teach me when she trained me all those long hours.

He makes a terrible noise. I did not expect that either and surprise loosens my grip. He staggers away from me and pulls the weapon from my hand. I watch him drop and die.

The older one comes at me then, his arm sweeps up in an arc and he slaps me with such force that I am knocked off my feet. He is hard upon me, tearing at my belt, pulling at my doe-skin britches, laughing out loud at my stupidity. He digs his fingers into the softness of me and I know that if I think myself helpless then so I will be. I fumble for the dagger and find it gone.

He keeps talking, puffing hard as he tries to manoeuvre. 'Got some other mates who are gonna love you, dimwit. But I want first taste and now I don't hafta share with *him*.'

I reach up and grab his neck. They feel powerful, these white, girl's hands. I *squeeze*. His eyes pop as much from shock at the power he senses constricting his breath as at the loss of air. He ceases trying to poke me with his white worm of a cock, starts trying to break my hold, clawing at my face, but his strength fades rapidly. He bats at me like a kitten with a ball of wool until at last he is still.

I roll his limp form off me, lie there for a moment, feeling the fallen leaves and pine needles littering the ground, the rocks, the twigs, all the detritus of the woods beneath me like a carpet. Above me is green, some patches of blue and white. In my ears ring the words 'Don't stray from the path' and I curse the tears that heat my eyes.

Lying here, I feel a recurrence of the illness that's troubled me for months. The ache in the joints, the crunch of bones, the pressure behind my eyes, feeling as if I'm not in the right shape – feeling as if I've got growing pains after all these years. I stay there for a while until I feel stronger.

* * *

The horse is gone and I could not find it, damned thing. The long walk has given me blisters and I can feel them swell and pop inside my boots, the fluid oozing out with each step. I regret this journey with every pace, every mile, every breath.

I come at last to where the doors should be, the spot where *Murcianus' Magical Places* told Theodora she might find the kingdom of the trolls. Where her stolen sister might still draw breath.

I can see nothing, no crack in the cliff-face, no place where one might apply pressure or insert a key. There is, however, a well with a faded red roof. A bucket is suspended on the crossbeam, waiting to be lowered and fulfil its function. When I look more closely, I notice there is a curve of steps cut into the interior of the well so that one may take the dark path downwards. At the bottom I can see water with the reflection of flames dancing in it. I move over the lip of the well and carefully take the steps. They are slippery with moss and I find holds for my fingers in the walls to keep myself steady.

At the bottom, I tread in three inches of water, thick as treacle. It soaks through my boots and it tickles my feet, soothing the burn of the blisters. I feel an itch at the bottom of my spine, the ache at the base of my neck, each follicle on my scalp stings. My skin seems to be trying to crawl off my flesh. I ignore the discomfort.

The passage is mercifully short, lit by torches and it terminates in a low-ceilinged room. A table and chairs wait at the far end. The water deepens to my knees. At the table sits a thing in the shape of a child, made of dried earth; its feet are held well above the flood. It blinks and dust floats from its eyelashes. It smells of baking earth and death. On the table in front of it is a goblet of blue and gold glass; muddy fingerprints mar its sides. The hands have been partially eaten away, the fingers mostly gone, their stumps are wet as if the fluid has melted them.

'Girl,' it says, all cracked and crumbled. Particles puff out of its mouth. 'Help, girl.'

'How? Will you drink?'

'Water is death to me.'

'Then what?'

It smiles, eyes on my wrists attentive as a lover.

'Key,' it says. For a moment I don't understand, then it dawns on me. All things have a price.

The dagger Grammy gave me, rescued from the forest floor, is sharp. I cross to where the thing sits, careful to not splash lest it lose any further form. I draw the blade across the fleshy part of my hand, and the blood wells willingly. I put the bleeding breech to the dry mouth and the thing slurps happy as a babe at the teat.

I let it suckle until I feel faint. I say *Enough* and it relinquishes me.

I sit on one of the other chairs and examine the creature. It is now brown and moist-looking, skin with an almost oily sheen.

Her smile is bright.

'It's thirsty work waiting for guests. Not too many come down here.'

'How do I get inside the mountain?'

'Hasty, hasty.' She shakes her head, a gesture older than she seems.

'I need to find my mother.'

'Mayhap you will. Mayhap you won't.'

'Where's the key?' I ask, irritated enough to grab her arm – my fingers sink into the stuff of it, finding it sticky and warm. I pull away; some of the substance adheres to my palm and digits. I wash it off in the water as the thing watches me with a vague distaste. I wonder if it was given it this shape to make people sorry for it? Gods know, I would feel a twinge of sympathy for any child left behind.

'Never fear, the door will open for you.'

'That's it?' I feel robbed, betrayed. Surely there should be more, something concrete. I'll not relish going down this well again should this thing be lying to me.

'What more do you want?' It asks with a strange kind of exasperation. 'Magic?'

I want to reply *Yes, that's exactly what I want*, but I don't. I trudge back along the passage, through the thick water. The darkness swirls around me, touches me, wraps itself like a cloak over my heart and I cannot shift it.

Back in the light, I feel dizzy. My temperature seems to rise with every step; my head aches, as do my teeth. My eyes are dry in their sockets and my ears ring with a noise like that of hammers beneath the earth.

The doors are visible to the eye now, their price paid in blood. They are stone and wood and old as time; huge. Meant to be moved by giants. I put my hands out, my tiny hands, and give a despairing push. There is a creak and a groan. Blackness spills upwards and out, staining the day around me. It disperses like smoke or steam and I look down into a sloping tunnel. There are weakly flaming torches clinging to the walls.

Behind me is sunshine; it feels too bright and makes my eyes water.

I step into the darkness. My skin burns.

* * *

Under the mountain, deep inside its heart, beneath layers of earth and rock and other old things, I find my mother.

What did I expect? Theodora wrapped tightly around a skeleton, her hands buried in the emptiness of the ribcage? Theodora broken open, the marrow sucked out of her bones? Yet here she is, serving at the great fossilised tables of the trolls, her hair turned almost all white since last I saw her. Her face is painted with contempt and scorn for these things that live in the dimness, that steal away children, that feast on tender morsels and leave their own offspring as cuckoos in the homes of humans.

How can these creatures see what is written so plainly and let her live? How is my mother so completely without fear? Another woman shuffles along behind her, carrying an enormous platter with difficulty. Her hair is all white and she looks decades older than Theodora, but I can see in the slant of the eyes, the tilt of her chin, an echo of my mother's face. Polly. Her leg drags; an old injury? She is emaciated.

My skin feels… it feels lighter, thinner. The pain is disappearing. Perhaps like a fever it comes and goes. I draw my sword, but as I pass through this hall packed tight with benches inhabited by so many, many trolls I realise I am regarded with merely a lazy curiosity. Not a one of them thinks me worthy of fear. Not a one of them pauses more than a few seconds in their chewing and slurping to attend to me.

The attention from the high table eventually fixes on me as I get closer. There is a hum and the air vibrates with the noise from a multitude of throats. The troll-queen, shaped like a malformed lump of clay, sits on her rough-hewn obsidian throne. Her tiny black eyes blink at me and she grins, jagged-toothed, and utters one word: 'Child.'

That stops me. That recognition. That ache, that thrum, that sense of truth from this mouth so foul.

'No,' I say. I look at Theodora. She doesn't seem to recognise me. How can she not run to me, call me 'child'?

Again I say, 'No. There is my mother. I have come for her and my aunt.'

And the troll-queen answers, pointing a gnarled finger at her own solid chest, 'No. *Here* is your mother, she who moulded your flesh, who sent you into the world.'

Theodora weeps then, her reserves all gone, and this is what convinces me. That at her very core she knows, that she believes, that her heart tells her this is so by its breaking. And my own heart continues to pulse in a calm slow reptilian rhythm; that there is no shock or shame for me in this truth. That after all these years as a cuckoo in Theodora's nest I at last recognise myself.

Who is she to me now? What do all her years of care and love weigh? How much do I love my once-mother? My not-mother? How much do I love this unknown aunt? This not-aunt? Is my affection real or simply learned as a result of rote instruction? Are they merely *meat* to me? Do I offer them up here as not-so-fatted calves?

How much do I care? Enough to stay? Enough to let go of this flesh, this humanity? Do I dare dig beneath my skin and see what really lies there? Do I dare find where I belong?

'Let them go and I will stay,' I say to my true-mother; this horror of a mother whose blood recognises mine.

She snorts. 'You lie. You will flee. You will cling to your life of light and soft flesh, just like the other one. You will not choose our kingdom of underneath. You are too much *her* creature.' She gestures to Theodora as if my once-mother somehow ruined me on purpose.

'No. I say I will stay. This bag of bones is no blood to me, but let her go for the years she gave me succour. And let her sister go or this one *will* return. I tell you that I will *stay*.' My body, released from its magical bonds, knowing at last its own larger limits, stretches and reaches and grows into my *true* shape. I do not need a mirror to tell me how different I appear.

I look at Theodora, drink in her pain, her distaste and her hatred. See how my transformation has washed away every trace of affection. All the love she poured into me, all the care she took, the protection she gave, all were for nought. The knowledge that she was too late to save her own child so long ago, that she already sheltered a *thing*, will weigh on her forever, I think. She will not return for me this time. I am no longer hers. I never was.

'My *own* child?' she asks the other mother, her voice raw.

The creature makes a sound that might be a laugh, might be contempt. 'Was delicious.'

I wonder if this will break Theodora, but no; she is stronger than that. She straightens and takes Polly by the arm. Will she return to the manor, take her sister there and try to make up for the life she missed? Perhaps she will return to Lodellan, find Faideau once more. Perhaps he will tell her the truth of it all and she will forgive him. She is still young enough to have another child, if she is brave. Part of me wants to ask what she will do. Part of me is too cold to care.

To see the light one last time, I follow the two women as they shuffle up the ramp towards freedom. They slowly move between the great doors into the fresh air and I reach out my hand, let it bathe in the sun. It turns white, delicate. I look at it, at what I was. I retract my arm and embrace my new skin. The doors close slowly on the sight of my not-mother's back.

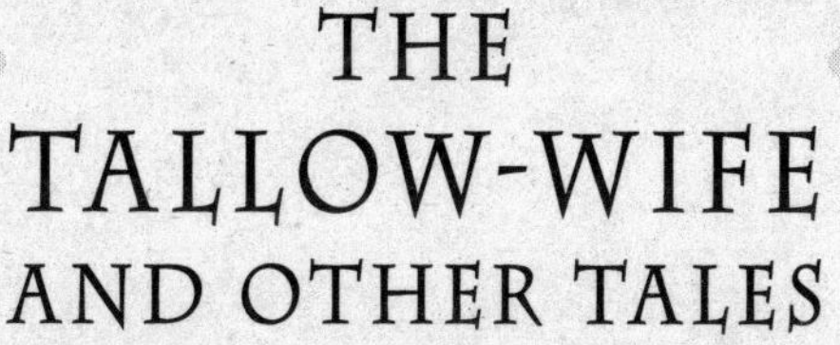

In olden times when wishing still helped...

THE PROMISE OF SAINTS

In the Church of Guinmarie's Mercy, which sits upon a hill in the tiny town of Jago's Rise overlooking the sea, there lies a bejewelled saint. She's attended by nuns of various vintages; not a man will go near her for the last who did – none can say *when*, only that it *did* happen – dropped dead whilst scoffing at her. Whether this was by design or happy accident is unknown and unknowable but it did its job and now only visiting priests set foot in here, gingerly stepping around the place where she lies. Girls and women come to her to pray or beg (some would say there's little difference) for one thing or another. Sometimes it seems she hears, other times not. Or perhaps life simply takes its path without her attention or otherwise.

Back when she died and was laid here – so very long ago – her attendants, the sisters-that-were, dressed her in the richest of robes, a cloak with an ermine collar as if to keep the chill from her bones. There's no flesh on her nowadays, merely a fragile canvas of thin-thin skin, so she's also been wrapped in fine netting to keep all her component parts together and in roughly the right order and shape. Her organs were purportedly removed by her first curators and kept in jars, but no one's found them in many a year, so possibly they were carried off by someone with strange tastes, or simply thrown out by a careless custodian.

Her teeth are fitted with braces made of rubies set in a gold framework; sapphires that might or might not echo the missing eyes wait in the sockets; and her skull is covered in a bonnet that looks like a constellation of diamond daisies. Epaulettes made up of a rainbow of gems sit on the shoulders of her cloak, and beneath is a cloth-of-gold vest over a dress that helps keep her ribcage intact. The bony hands protruding from the bottom of the sleeves are encased in items that are a combination of rings and bracelets. Her legs are covered and if anyone's ever lifted her red woollen skirt (the hem worked with silver embroidery) to see if there's any adornment there, no one is admitting to it; indeed, no nun has any memory of her being moved for several lifetimes. The skeletal feet have been hung with silver chains dangled with tiny engraved foxes and bells.

She's been here a long time, the Sainted Maiden, lying on a bier in the tiny alcove to the left of the altar. Tales are told, as they often are when the truth is lost, and they say she moves around at night. They say she dances across the green and purple marble squares of the nave as if at a wedding. Some say her dance is one of exultation, some say of defiance. But the fact is that no one knows anything about her, what her name was, who her people were (for no one in the town claims kinship), or even how she came to be venerated so.

Unprotected by barriers of any kind, the dust settles freely upon her, but no one's game to touch her – everyone's aware that disturbing the holy dead with anything more than entreaties is never a good idea – not even the Sisters who tend to her as the years of their lives march away. Certainly none of the supplicants, and there are many, can bring themselves to offer her the slightest contact. All they bring are demands, generally marital in nature.

Jago's Rise is small and the jewelled corpse in the little church is the town's main claim to fame, one of the few reasons any traveller or pilgrim comes here on purpose. That and the remains of the great battlefield, once so littered with dead that none would even contemplate the task of burying them all, so the earth was watered with blood and gore and fundamentally changed forever.

The Hallowed Girl, it's said, was once a bride herself – although no one knows if the marriage was completed and consummated, or aborted, so her titles are varied and perhaps contradictory – and that's why these others come to beg what she may or may not have had.

* * *

Adalene first brought Elspeth to see the Saint when she was five. The child had shown no interest, no gratitude nor enthusiasm for her mother's hopes, but kept her eyes downcast, stepping deliberately on the cracks in the floor for all she was worth, little bitch. Adalene's grip on her daughter's hand was desperate and hard even to her as she pulled Elspeth along. Finally, they halted and Elspeth still didn't look up.

Not until Adalene said, 'That'll be you, one day.'

The girl raised her eyes then, took in the skeleton caught in its cocoon of tulle and wool and fur and gold. The gems encrusting it sucked in the light of the torches but threw out less than they ate, it seemed. Elspeth looked at the skull with its jaw slightly askew, slightly ajar, no eyes except those gleaming sapphires hard as hearts, and she screamed.

Elspeth thought her mother meant she'd be dead. That someone would stick her with shiny pins and make her into an exhibit, as pretty and useless as a butterfly under glass. She took it for a threat, and it was a long while before she calmed. A long time before her mother could get her to listen that they were there to ask for a blessing: that Elspeth was to beg the Sainted Maiden for a good husband.

Elspeth had no such desire and couldn't imagine ever wanting a husband, good, bad or indifferent. At that very moment all she truly wished and wanted was to never lay eyes on the hallowed, hollowed girl ever again.

It was then that one of the nuns – the youngest of them but already nearing fifty – drawn by Elspeth's screech, came over from whatever task she'd been attending to in the shadows to place a broad palm against the girl's cheek. The woman was terribly tall, her face gentle and her smile absent-minded, but there was something about her touch that leeched away much of Elspeth's fear, or at least enough that she could ask a question.

'What's her name?'

'She has none, only titles.'

'Everyone should have a name,' said Elspeth.

The nun looked at the girl properly this time, actually focused on her and the smile was different, not simply something she aimed at everyone. 'And yet she has none.'

It made Elspeth terribly sad and she wished aloud for the Bride to be named and loved; she wished with the same strength as her mother had wished for her to be well married. Such very different things, one propelled by a kind of greed, the other by a sort of kindness. And that latter desire removed whatever vestiges of fear might have remained, so that Elspeth did something no one had done in untold years: she touched the Hallowed Girl.

Small fingers to skeletal digits, the most glancing of contacts – soft flesh against dusty bones, a small shudder of shock – but it was a touch nonetheless. The first in so very, very long. Whether it was that or the sort of magic stirred up by wishes will never be known. Whatever the cause, something was woken.

* * *

That night, the Maiden visited Elspeth for the first time.

It would not be the last.

Perhaps it was in her sleeping or perhaps her late waking – it was so difficult to tell, but Elspeth could have sworn she felt the tender touch of bony hands, felt the shifting of her bedclothes and mattress beneath a weightless weight, felt the breath that was not breath flowing across her face as the Maiden whispered to her. The Hallowed Girl, the Sainted Maiden, the Immaculate Bride told Elspeth that she would be her one and only. That Elspeth was her truest love and would tend to the Saint as lovingly as any wife. Elspeth would require no husband for, in return, all of her needs would be met in the Church of Guinmarie's Mercy. And that the Saint would, on their wedding day, offer her the highest of bride prices.

In the moonlight that flooded the room the Hallowed Girl touched a finger to Elspeth's, the one that leads straight to the heart, and in her dream or waking she saw a silver ring – tiny foxes chasing each other, nose to tail – form on that finger and glint. It soon sank into her flesh, but the following morning she could still feel it there beneath the skin. A promise and a chain.

* * *

Adalene took her daughter to the Saint all those years ago and hasn't she had reason to regret it ever since?

What she'd hoped would result in a profitable match had seemed to simply have developed into a religious mania. From that time forward Elspeth had spent part of her days (and some of her nights, however Adalene did not know *that*) in the Church, tending the shrine of the Hallowed Girl.

Frankly, Adalene had despaired. It's tremendously hard to match-make if one of the parties has a tendency to not appear when they are meant to. Numberless days was Adalene left clutching a damp scone and rapidly cooling cup of tea in the sitting room of some other mother-on-the-make, while Elspeth failed to arrive for a meeting with a potential suitor and his dam. Nothing Adalene said or did made a whit of difference.

But then, ridiculously, one of those potential suitors found her daughter's lack of interest appealing. Fascinating, apparently. He pursued her in spite of his own mother's warnings – oh, Adalene knew there'd been warnings, she'd seen the woman's expression as her son's questioning about Elspeth became positively fervid.

'Can she weave?'

'Yes.' *Barely.*

'Can she manage a household?'

'Of course.' *An outright lie that would only be discovered too late.*

He'd nodded. 'She carries herself well, I have seen her around town and her posture is notable. She will wear finery beautifully, that is an important thing for a rich man's wife.'

'Yes.' *A truth at last.*

Elspeth's husband-to-be is prosperous, precisely the sort Adalene would have wished for herself if she'd got another chance, but her combination of ill temper and a face rendered plain by discontent has closed that avenue. Had she been sweeter of one or the other, she might well have had suitors lining up at her cottage door. As a widow, she was regarded with pity by the young women of the town; the older ones, knowing better, called her blessed. She views them all with contempt though she smiles politely at them in the market square and when she takes in their mending, or whenever she'd offered her daughter to wife.

But this oncoming son-in-law pleases her for the moment – he will no doubt disappoint in time, but for now he is sufficiently unknown a quantity to provide a sort of contentment for Adalene. He'll furnish some financial stability too and that will smooth over a multitude of sins.

Adalene only knows she'll be as close to happy as she's likely to get when Elspeth is wed, and that day cannot come too soon, before the girl ruins even that.

* * *

The Saint had promised so many things.

In the silent space between the shadows of the Church, and in the dim twilight of her visits to Elspeth's bedroom, words had come as covenants on a breath that smelled like nothing from the living. *Freedom. Love. Eternity.*

Some days, when sunlight brings clarity and burns away faith, Elspeth wonders if she is mad. If that moment all those years ago when fear seared through her like wildfire hadn't consumed her sanity. Her mother certainly thinks so, what with her refusals to marry, her defiance. Though Adalene can be unpleasant, Elspeth loves her. She believes her mother loves her too despite the terrible things she says. The girl knows her parent wants to provide for both their futures, but Elspeth's was mapped out sixteen years ago, wasn't it? And through Adalene's own actions did she but know it.

Her mother's despair was what caused Elspeth's seeming acquiescence when the suitor appeared at the door, avid and ardent and determined. That and the promises her Saint had made, that there'd be no wedding, no matter what Adalene coaxed or cajoled or threatened. That and the knowledge that skeletal saints are notoriously bad at providing a dowry or portion for a widowed mother's old age. That and the suspicion that perhaps she was addled, holding onto the promise of a stale fever dream. So she'd remained silent when the proposal was made and accepted; she behaved like a girl about to be wed to the man who sought her.

But she clung, too, to a thin thread of hope. To the fact that the Saint on one of those nights of shadows and breaths and caresses, also promised the one thing that no one else has ever had, or at least not in the longest time, so long ago it wasn't recorded or remembered.

Ultimately Elspeth knew that the vow she'd held most dear was the promise of the Saint's very own name.

* * *

Jasque is a wool merchant, or rather the son of a recently deceased one. His mother still holds the reins of enterprise, but Jasque is free to act as though he makes important decisions. He's quite happy to live with a heavy purse and light responsibilities.

He could have chosen a better bred, but less beautiful bride – indeed his mother, Ernestine, had urged him in the direction of a girl whose left eye turned just a little, and whose family owned many flocks of sheep. Yet he decided the lovely Elspeth was for him precisely because it seemed he could not have her.

Ernestine knows how troublesome beautiful girls can be (she was one herself), what with wills of their own and everyone falling over themselves to please in hope of their favours, or even just a glance, kind or indifferent it matters not. But her son's a fool for a pretty face and all she can do is love him anyway and shrug. Oh and tie up whatever parts of the business she can in legal machinations, and hide profits so it's hard for her boy to fritter them away on expensive offerings, and harder still for a girl to extract gold from the spinning of wool like some voracious fairytale princess.

However this girl, this Elspeth, doesn't seem to want anything; she makes neither demand nor request; she's nothing like that grasping parent of hers. She's polite when given a gift, and there's seemingly no greed in her; and she's pious, too, spends part of every day at the Church, helping the last aging nun to tend the shrine. This makes

Ernestine, quite naturally, suspicious. She's never known a girl to look at her very fine son with his very fine robes and very fine face (which, admittedly, will go to fat soon enough just like his father so she'd best get him married off quickly), and the heavy coin purse at his belt and not want *something*. Therefore there must be, she reasons, something that rides beneath the surface, some need or desire that cannot be seen by daylight.

She doesn't say this to her son, for her mother's heart is soft, no matter that her mind is practical and wary. Besides, fewer things drive a man into another woman's arms than a mother's displeasure and, though her son's already made his decision, there's a tiny hope in her breast that something will happen to make the machinery of this match fall apart. On the morrow her boy will marry and that will be the end of it, and Ernestine will have plenty of time to discover her daughter-in-law's faults and flaws.

Jasque, however, has his own concerns though he'd never voice them to his mother.

Tomorrow his bride is to walk barefoot along the path from her home to the Church of Guinmarie's Mercy. She'll be dressed in a gown heavy with seed pearls and silver thread (paid for from Jasque's pocket). Then they'll stand in front of the altar and say their vows before the god-hound (the sort who travels the countryside for precisely this kind of event, living his life away from the eyes of those further up the godly ladder). Jasque knows that the source of his disquiet will be lying not so many feet away, just out of sight, yet there all the same, like some mote in his eye that cannot be removed.

Another thing he's never mentioned to Ernestine: Elspeth's acceptance of his proposal was made by *her* mother. He'd had to propose in front of Adalene for the woman protected her daughter's virtue like a dragon on a mound of gold, and Jasque has no good reason to claim she was wrong to do so. But when he'd offered his suit, it was the older woman who'd said *yes*. The girl had looked over his shoulder as if there was someone standing behind him, someone else to whom she might answer.

She'd smiled, batted her lashes, and seemed to acquiesce.

But she has ever refused to meet him at night, no matter how he's pressed her, and she's also refused to stop her devotions at the Church. She did so gently and politely as she does everything, yet her refusal was no less adamant. The last of the Sisters would soon be gone, Elspeth said. For all the many girls who came to beg favours of the Bejewelled Bride, none seemed inclined to swell that thin rank of those who cared for her; someone must be there to take the old nun's place.

He had been displeased, but was smart enough not to press. Yet, spoiled only child of too-indulgent parents as he was, Jasque was not one to take "no" for an answer.

And Jasque was certain that she could not serve what no longer existed.

* * *

Elspeth wears her wedding dress to church the next day, although the Hallowed Girl has promised there is to be no wedding, at least not to Jasque. The gown is beautiful and it seems perfect for the occasion. When will she get a chance to wear it again? Besides, it seems only right to come to the Bride in such finery.

As she walks, barefoot, she notices that there's no one by the side of the road and a weight lifts from her shoulders. This is good: she takes it to mean the Saint's promise is true – otherwise there would be crowds, waiting and watching, throwing flower petals and wishes for happiness, fertility and long life. Her steps become much lighter, swifter. Yet when Elspeth turns into the last windy street, the one that runs up to the hill upon which Guinmarie's Mercy sits, it is *there* that she sees a crowd, and the breath in her stops for long seconds.

She continues on, however; she cannot turn tail and run, not now. And as she approaches the congregation she realises there's no sense of revelry and no one looks happy; this gives her courage. Townsfolk cluster in the churchyard, gossiping in groups.

Elspeth keeps walking. At the great double doors with their bands of silver engraved with a series of skeletal figures dressed in funereal finery are Adalene and Ernestine, both wailing in the arms of the remaining nun – the one whose touch first brought Elspeth's heart to the Bride. Ernestine's howls are renewed as she sees the daughter-in-law-to-be, but the energy is mostly spent, the emotion behind them is broken. Adalene echoes her much as a cat does another, trying to outdo a rival. Elspeth wonders how long they have been here.

The elderly nun, expression serene, makes no effort to stop Elspeth as she enters the church. Whatever lies inside is meant for her gaze. Around her finger, she feels the ghostly ring shifting, moving up to the surface of her flesh, strangely painless.

Light comes in through the coloured glass of the windows, painting the aisle and pews in a rainbow, yet the Maiden's bier remains in shadow, so it takes some moments for Elspeth to make out the details of the scene.

On the floor are gems that have fallen off the corpse, and a thick wooden cudgel too, as if dropped by a careless hand. The Hallowed Girl still reclines in her place, skeletal head on a red velvet pillow, jewels catching the light and eating it.

But Elspeth's Bride does not lie alone.

Jasque is in her arms, held tight as a lover, *his* head tilted to rest on *her* shoulder as if he sleeps, though his eyes stare. There is blood, quite a lot of it, dripping down and pooling and seeping through the cracks between the purple and green tiles; some of the spatters look like flowers blooming. As Elspeth draws nearer she can see that the Bride's ribs have broken through her fine netting and entwined with Jasque's just as lovers' fingers might.

Elspeth's first duty as a wife will be to unlock them.

The promise of saints is expensively bought.

But soon she will know her beloved's true name.

THE TALLOW-WIFE

Cordelia does not think about the things she has lost.

She does not think on the children, or her husband, or the fine house in Lodellan. She does not think on the jewellery, or the dresses, or the shoes. She does not think on her former status, on the Sunday afternoon teas, the Saturday morning bruncheons, or the Friday night balls. She does not think of her sister, or her friends, or the shades of her dead parents who surely grow even paler with shame. Nor of all the handkerchiefs with knots tied in them to ensure good luck, every one of which failed dismally to do its allotted task.

No, Cordelia thinks only of the lengths she must cut with the dull knife. Of the quantities she must measure so carefully to ensure neither wastage, nor excess. The turnkeys who appear daily at the barred window only ever hand out the precise amounts needed to create three dozen candles at a time.

Any less and there will be trouble. Any more will be an equal calamity, for it means she's skimped on the quality and girth, that the women who want these things will know they are lesser... women like she once was... and they will not buy them. Or, worse still, they will buy them, find them wanting, and return them, demanding their good gold back. Either way Cordelia will be punished.

She wishes the candles were of a much different sort.

But at night, after she extinguishes the tiny ceramic stove where she melts the wax, when she closes her eyes, when sleep will no longer be denied, when the groans of other inmates and creaks of the old prison ship recede, when the rock and pitch of the hulk is gentle as a cradle, then she dreams. When she fingers the raised edges of the scar on her shoulder, traces the rough petals, the scabby stem. When she curls herself into a cold ball, settles her hands on the concave stomach that should by now have been convex, then she dreams of all she has lost. She dreams and it feels so real that she prays not to wake up. She prays that sleep will take her and hold her and keep her. She prays death will come while she slumbers so the memories she carries with her into darkness are those of life before.

* * *

The front parlour is cold when Cordelia enters, and she glances immediately at the hearth, which is stacked full with logs, none alight. She rolls her eyes; the tweeny cannot take instruction, or refuses to do so. Not enough lightwood, again. Not enough care or attention paid when Cordelia has gone to the trouble of so oft crouching beside her and showing her how to do it *properly.* The girl is sullen, or has been noticeably so for a sennight. Cordelia refrains from thinking *stupid*, for it seems unfair – she's seen Merry embroider some exquisite kerchiefs and shawls, make cutwork and bobbin lace finer than anything they've ever imported, sew the most sublime dresses and frockcoats. Not stupid, no, but perhaps merely resentful of things that do not revolve around her talents.

Cordelia sighs and kneels, removes the excess wood, replaces it with extra kindling: twigs, shreds of old broadsheet, and the tiniest length of char cloth. She breathes the prayer Mrs Bell taught her when she was little, an invocation to the hearth-sprites. She finds the flint and steel where Merry has discarded them, and strikes, once, twice, then the tinder takes. Soon delicate golden flames are licking at the larger pieces, seducing them, convincing them to burn. Cordelia smiles. This is her favourite task, though it's beneath her nowadays. She loves the simple ritual with all its power and import. So elementary, yet so essential.

She gives the blaze a last nod, a grateful thanks whispered, then stands, her palms rubbing against each other to remove any dirt or dust, finally smoothing out the cream and blue skirts of her dress, making sure no soot has impressed itself on the fine fabric. She won't speak to Merry, no, but she will tell the housekeeper, Mrs Bell – the tweeny's aunt – to tend to this chore herself. They have an understanding: Mrs B had worked for Cordelia's parents, cared for the girl from her cradle, then accompanied her when she'd come to Lodellan to marry. Sometimes Mrs B still calls her "dearling" when no one else can hear. Cordelia does not wish Merry removed or harshly berated – gods know she wishes the girl some happiness! – but she would like on winter days to come down in the mornings to warmth and a fire crackling sweetly.

Out in the hallway, there is a breeze, colder even than the unlit parlour was, and Cordelia frowns. She soon finds the source. One panel of the front double doors with its frosted and etched crystal panes is wide open, chill pouring in and bringing with it the smell of newly baked bread wafting up from Bakers' Lane. She makes an exasperated noise – not a curse for that would be ill-bred – and bustles forward. Merry is too careless; with the recent robberies in their neighbourhood *this* is utterly reprehensible! Despite Cordelia's weakness for lame ducks and a belief that better human nature can always spring forth, given the right encouragement, she does have her limits. But when she steps onto the black marble stoop (which gleams – for all her faults, Merry ensures it's brilliant, as well as rubbing coarse salt into it once a month to keep away ill-luck), she loses impetus.

The clamour of carriages and horses masks Cordelia's footfalls, and Merry, whose attention is focused on the lad at the bottom of the stairs, does not hear her. The youth is tall, flame-haired, sapphire-eyed, milk-skinned. Cordelia recognises him only because she's seen him at Belladonna Considine's home. A footman Bella had apprenticed to the aging valet whose service was coming to an end. The boy would learn from and care for the old man at the same time, ensuring that the House of Considine was always tended by loyal staff. Cordelia had hoped for something similar with Mrs B and Merry, which is why Annie, the parlour maid, has been freed of several of her duties: so Merry might learn by doing. Cordelia believes strongly that managing can only be done when you understand a task fully through experience, and if Merry is to replace Mrs B in the fullness of time, she must be properly prepared.

This young man is certainly pretty to look at, definitely prettier than their own footman whose plainness of face is quite astonishing. But this one, oh this one! The breadth of his shoulders, the slenderness of his waist and hips, the length of his legs in the fitted trews, demand attention. Pretty, yes, but oh! Now Cordelia notices that Merry is shivering in her mint-green brocade frock with white lace at the collar and wrists. No, worse, more than shivering, this is a tectonic tremor, the girl is shaking from head to toe as if in the throes of a fever. Cordelia raises a hand, opens her mouth—

—the boy spies her and the shift in his gaze makes Merry turn. Cordelia feels all her annoyance drain away. The girl's face is deathly pale, her eyes red-rimmed, and tears have drifted down her rounded cheeks. Her dishwater-blonde hair is untidy as if she's run troubled fingers through it, and her bottom lip trembles. Cordelia is face-to-face with another's agony and it makes her throat seize up. And Merry, poor Merry does not wish to be seen like this. Her gaze at first burns with hatred and resentment to be found thus, then it softens as pain comes to the fore, overwhelms her pride.

At last Cordelia swallows.

'Don't forget to lock the door when you come in, it's cold,' she says quietly and Merry nods, as if grateful to have an excuse to cut short whatever is passing between her and the pretty boy at the bottom of the stairs.

Inside, Cordelia rests her head against the wood of the doorframe, listening carefully as if she might hear something from the mummers left on the stoop, but there is nothing, merely the noises of the street, strangely louder.

'What are you doing, Dellie?'

Cordelia jumps, pushes away, and moves down the hallway to where her sister waits at the entrance to the library. She doesn't want Bethany to see Merry's pain; she's been aware for some time now that the two do not get along. Nor do they need to, she supposes; Bethany isn't a servant and Merry is, but sometimes Bethany goes out of her way to be mean. Perhaps it is because they are closer in age, because Merry grew up in Cordelia's house and Bethany came to it somewhat later.

Bethany's golden hair is several shades darker than Cordelia's, and her eyes a paler shade of green, but there is no denying they are sisters. Bethany is taller, despite being the younger; where Cordelia is buxom, Bethany is a willow; where Cordelia will pour oil on troubled waters, Bethany will often put a match to the oil purely for the sport of watching things burn. But not all the time; only when she's taken by a spirit of mischief. There's no true harm in her sister, thinks Cordelia.

'What are you doing, Dellie?' repeats Bethany, a novel in one hand, her burgundy skirts bunched in the other as if they are an impediment to movement, though the young woman is quite still. 'Is it Merry mooning over that boy again?'

Cordelia does her best not to show surprise, but of late her sister has been different. She wonders if it's Bethany's age. She herself was married and a mother by the time she was eighteen. Once they'd shared everything, now it seems Bethany keeps secrets and lets them out only when it will embarrass others. Cordelia has often thought this behaviour stems from her sister feeling untethered in the household and their best efforts, hers and Edvard's, to make it otherwise, appear to have failed. Or sometimes at least.

It's not as if Bethany's some penniless maid who must marry where she can for security. Cordelia and Edvard have always made it clear they plan to settle a considerable sum on her as well as a house – not one in the Cathedral Quarter, no, but certainly a more than respectable merchant's abode, something only Bethany will own – either upon her wedding or her eighteenth birthday, the latter event being but a few weeks away. The former is a different matter entirely: the marriage proposals, which once flew thick and fast, have become rarities. The bucks of the city initially thought Bethany a challenge, yet the sheer constancy, the unwavering tenor, of her refusals had beaten them down. Cordelia has heard her sister described as an unweddable, unbeddable Atalanta, and worse, when the men who come to drink her husband's brandy and smoke his cigars think she cannot hear. She wonders if Bethany has heard them, too.

'I thought I would take the children to the fair after lunch, Bethany. Will you come with us?'

'I'm otherwise occupied, Dellie, I'm sorry.' She smiles impishly, a child again. 'But will you bring me a bag of sweeties? The hard sort, the rock that crunches between your teeth and makes your tongue fizz so! You know I love such confectionary.'

Cordelia laughs; her concerns melt.

'Of course! I—'

A clamour comes from the floor above, from Victoria's bedroom by the sound of it. Cordelia's only daughter is shrieking, a sound so high she can barely discern any words at all – the girl's pitch, tone, and projection demonstrate the singing lessons have not been wasted. In response Torben shouts he didn't take her precious brooch, and Victoria parries that *he did, he did, he did.* Whatever thoughts Cordelia might have expressed to her sister are lost, and she gently touches Bethany's shoulder in apology, then picks up her pace, mounts the gold and black wrought iron staircase, girding herself for the battle.

* * *

The travelling show comes to Lodellan once a year, and Cordelia is sure she recognises faces amongst the older members of the troupe. The children look forward to the event, although Henry's expression is torn between excitement and embarrassment, as if he feels himself too told to enjoy such pastimes. But he did not refuse to accompany his siblings, and he has his arm linked with hers as they walk beneath the makeshift archway the travellers erect every year to claim their space outside the walls of the city. Merry, her expression serene and sweet as if nothing untoward occurred this morning, is a little ahead with Victoria and Torben, one on each side, their hands in hers. Cordelia drops several coppers and one quarter-gold into the palm of the wizened woman at the entrance and her generosity is rewarded with a smile, no less genuine for its lack of dentition.

Around them is all manner of noise: laughter, shrieks of shock and delight, howls of terror from children who pretend to mislike strangeness, gasps from women, and guffaws from men. The carnival is small, but takes up more space than it seems it should. Everything is rich and colourful, if a little worn in places; a maelstrom of movement and light, hue and shadow. The Parsifals pass stalls packed with impossible amounts of things: bottles of perfume and potions, tonics and tisanes; scarves and dresses, cheaply and sloppily made, but bright and pretty, items poor girls would be perfectly happy with if given as gifts by otherwise inattentive suitors. Cordelia wonders if Merry's ever received such things from the boy on the front stoop.

There are stands with sweet-smelling soaps, and flowers carved so finely the wood might be paper. Some merchants offer knives designed to deliver injury and cutlery for meals, plates of metal highly polished. There are pots and pans, tobacco and cigars, pipes of ivory and horn and stone. One hawker shows antique jewellery she claims has magical properties, made by the hands of the finest jewel-smiths trained, she so swears, by those who once lived in the city of Cwen's Reach before the Great Fall of the Citadel – such women could have coaxed the sun and moon into something more lovely if they'd but taken the notion. Another stall has only boxes, but all manner of them, made of materials imaginable and otherwise: ceramic, glass, bones, quartz, skin (*not* animal), hair, silk, stiffened and held in shape by strange means. *This'un*, promises the salesman, *is constructed of naught but breath and wishes*. Cordelia examines it as closely as she is allowed, but remains certain it's simply extremely thin-blown glass.

They pass from the merchants to the showfolk, and this is where the wonders are.

On a slapdash stage is a boy, a youth really, of middling height with blond curls, whose face is not his own. He remakes it at will into imagined creations or does a fair imitation of someone in the crowd – male or female – which is never quite right and guarantees a laugh. His cerulean velvet frock coat is worn but very fine, embroidery creeping across the lapels: leaves in green, cherries or apples in red, creatures that begin as birds but flow into beasts, all picked out in silver that catches the winter sun whenever it peeks from behind the clouds.

Elsewhere is a man who juggles stone spheres in a three-ball cascade. At the end of each circuit in the air, one of the rocks becomes a bird which flies into the sky, wings flashing with quartz, then returns to settle in a basket at the man's feet so he may reach in for new material. On another platform a woman swallows glowing coals, then spews forth great gouts of fire as if it is nothing out of the ordinary; beside her an old man drinks water from a bucket then farts out cubes of ice that clatter from his trouser legs and onto the stage. Yet another has two young women, scandalously under-clad in the cold, their breath steaming around their heads like dragons' exhalations; they throw frayed-looking ropes upwards, which become still and stiff and remain where they are put. The young women smirk at the crowd and shinny their way up the strands, the sequins and fringes of their tiny frocks waving at the crowd as the girls reach a particular height and then evaporate, becoming pale mists of pink and purple.

'Oh! Fairy floss! Mama?' Torben is the one who shrieks, but Victoria's expression is equally avid. There is a truce, for the moment at least, in the War of the Brooch.

'Don't spoil your dinner,' Cordelia says automatically, but reaches into her reticule and pulls forth bits of coin. 'Henry, you're in charge. Not too much.'

Her eldest child gives a sweet smile and leads his siblings off to where two middle-aged women, their white aprons stained with the bright food colours they add to the candy cobwebs they make apparently from air. Cordelia senses Merry standing beside her, fidgeting as if unsure whether to follow the children or not; Henry is at that in-between age where he is being given more responsibility, but the bounds of it are as yet uncertain.

'Merry?' says Cordelia

'Yes, Mrs Parsifal?'

'Merry, are you happy here? With us, I mean, in Lodellan.' The scene she witnessed this morning coupled with her own concerns about the girl's behaviour in past months, have sat heavy on Cordelia's mind. The girl gives her a blank sort of look. 'I only ask because you've seemed out of sorts lately. If I can help in any way, tell me.'

The girl's lips open and close but no sound comes.

Cordelia begins to feel foolish, which makes her annoyed at herself; her tone is clipped as she asks, 'Do you need new things? New tools for your work? New things for you personally? Would you like to take a trip somewhere, perhaps to learn from the Master Seamstresses of Mistinguett's Lace, or somewhere else? We would be happy to send you, to pay your expenses… or do you… do you perhaps wish to leave us? Find a position elsewhere?'

'Whyever would I want to leave? Whyever would I want to leave you and my aunt and the kiddies?' Merry's pale hazel eyes fill with tears, as if she's astonished that Cordelia has asked. As if she's not considered the idea herself, not even once. And then, with dread, 'Do you want rid of me, Mrs Parsifal?'

'Oh no!' Cordelia's distress is sharp, high-pitched. 'I hope you never leave us! Even if you marry, I hope you'll stay with us, Merry.' She grasps the other's hands, feels the calluses and places where needles and pins have left their mark over the years. 'I only want you to be happy, Merry, and I feel as if you've not been. Never think I'm trying to get shot of you. Let us say no more of it, but you must promise to tell me if you think of anything that will make you happier?'

Merry nods, sniffs back her tears. Cordelia gives her a little push towards where Victoria and Henry are bickering over who gets which hue of floss. 'Kindly deal with them, Merry.'

The girl moves away. Cordelia takes a deep breath and rolls her shoulders to loosen the tension gathered there; she lacked the courage to ask about the boy on the stoop. She closes her eyes for a moment, and another and another, only opening them when a voice grabs her attention.

'Difficult when there are so many paths in front of you.'

Cordelia looks around, finds a woman to her left, tending a cart. The flat surfaces are stacked with candles every colour of the rainbow. The woman sits in front of it, on a low stool by a small fire, over which is suspended a pot. The woman holds a long white strand of what looks like string and every few seconds she dips it into the contents of the pot. With each immersion, the string comes out thicker, the blue of it intensifying.

Wax and wick, Cordelia realises. The woman is a tallow-wife, a candle-maker.

'Pardon?' Cordelia steps closer to watch the work.

'So many choices for you and yours at this moment. Who can

know which is the right one?' says the woman pleasantly. She's got a cloud of ashen hair with small silver charms and favours woven through it; there are bells which give a tiny but clear peal when she sits up, stretching her back and allowing the candle a few moments for the latest layer to dry.

'My, what patience you must have.' Cordelia looks at the range of the woman's wares, thinks they would be lovely in the sitting room and on the dining table for formal dinners with the Agnews and the Considines. 'I'd never be able to wait for so long.'

'Ah, we never know what we can do until need forces it upon us. What will you have, mistress?'

'The jade and the lavender, please,' she says reaching into her purse, but the woman is shaking her head, her mouth pulled in a sad smile.

'Ah, they're not for the likes of you. The green is for fertility and I doubt you need that, and the purple's to make a woman cautious, but you're too far gone for *that*, my dear. There's blue to lift a heart, yellow to bring light into a life, and the reds make passion blaze. But you… best to take the black, they'll do what needs doing, they'll show the darkness at the heart of your path.'

Cordelia's hands begin to shake. What does this woman know of her? She doesn't appear to offer a threat, but her words imply she wishes Cordelia ill… or believes it will befall her. She is about to ask what is meant by the unpleasant things the old woman had uttered, when Victoria's voice carries clear to her: 'Mama! Mama!' Primed for fear, prepared for the worst, Cordelia looks up, desperately searching for her children, but sees them precisely where they were, eating the coloured floss, Merry watching over them like a hawk, while a man stands beside Henry, speaking earnestly with him.

It takes a moment for Cordelia to recognise Mr Farringdale. Edvard's factotum, a man of many talents who acts (as his own father did, rather less successfully, for Edvard's father) as a mix of legal adviser, accountant, and personal secretary. Not, as Cordelia's momentary panic would have her believe, someone new, a stranger, a peril; the candle-maker has her at sixes and sevens.

Isambard Farringdale has been in the Parsifals' lives for so long they can barely remember a time when the short, dapper man was not there. As she watches, he hands Henry a leather-bound journal, Torben a model ship, then turns to Victoria and offers a doll; not one of the rag moppets suspended from various stall roofs and marquee support poles, or sat in the forks of trees. No, this is a porcelain treat with red curls and creamy kaolin clay skin, a dress of crimson and purple in satin and lace. Cordelia sees tiny black leather shoes with silver buckles peek out from beneath the hem as her daughter takes the doll with a delighted squeal. Cordelia says under her breath, 'How kind.'

'Come now, mistress, take 'em as a gift.' The older woman's voice intrudes. 'I don't often give my wares away. Only when there's need.' In the woman's tone there is bitter amusement and sadness and Cordelia cannot think why. She only knows she wishes to be elsewhere.

'Thank you, but no,' mutters Cordelia, recalling now the whispers she's heard about such women, that their candles aren't simply for the production of light.

'Mark my words, there's fire and water and air coming for you, mistress! And a long while to battle 'em afore you sleep in the earth.' But the woman sounds resigned now, as if she's done her best and a refusal is not her fault.

Cordelia moves away from the tallow-wife and stumbles towards her children. Unnerved by the candle-maker's words, her steps are less assured than she would like. She wonders if the woman makes more money from scaring people than by selling her candles, fleecing the gullible. Does she double as a fortune-teller or is her portrayal of a distraught prophet of doom merely part of her sales technique? What can that woman know of Cordelia and her life, her family, her future? Cordelia fixes a smile and holds her hand out so that Mr Farringdale might bend gallantly over it and press his thin lips to the cool kid of her gloves.

* * *

Although Edvard is some twenty years her senior, Cordelia has never truly felt the age difference, never thought of him as an old man, until tonight. In their shared bed with all its hangings and posts, high firm mattress and fine snowy linens, he is propped against pillows, a book in his nightgown-covered lap, eyes closed as if asleep. She regards him in the dressing table mirror as she brushes her hair, applies night-cream, and she can see from the rise and fall of his chest that he is still awake. That his breath has not yet settled into a rhythm of which he himself is unaware, yet she knows well from the hours she's watched him sleep and dream.

His features have not relaxed despite the shuttered lids; they remain taut, the muscles standing at attention. His brow is lined, the fine skin beneath his eyes dark and thin and dry; his lips, rough when he kissed her cheek earlier, are peeling as if from sunburn. Patches of grey have infiltrated the ruddy brown locks she loves so. He is a man under a burden, she decides, and though she does not know what it is, equally she *does* know he will not tell her.

Her husband's firm beliefs are as affected by change as the path of the sun around the Earth, which is to say not at all. Edvard holds that a marriage has two participants, two spheres of influence, and the captain of one shall never set a hand to the tiller of the other. In all their time together he has never confided anything to do with Business (and it is always *Business*, not merely *business*) to his wife. The responsibility for making money, ensuring they are financially secure, is his, and an entirely unsuitable thing for her to learn about; in his endeavour he is helped by Mr Farringdale. Her task is to tend their home and raise their children, ably assisted by Mrs B. In this way and this way alone does their partnership function.

When Cordelia was younger and braver, wilder, she tried on a few occasions to *adjust* his attitude. She'd reminded him, when they were first married, how her parents had given her charge of dealing with the buyers who came to the Singing Vine Vineyard as soon as she'd turned thirteen. How her presence and charm had ensured greater sales every year. She bid him remember that was how they met when she was just seventeen, that his order for the SV Rouge Felix was the largest there'd ever been. She reminded him that he'd proposed marriage very soon after that. Edvard, far from convinced, had spent days voicing his disapproval of her father for allowing a child – and a girl-child at that! – to be exposed to commerce in such a fashion.

Cordelia let the matter drop, let his umbrage subside, learned to quietly do what she was allowed. Then, just after the birth of Henry, thinking that surely her husband would soften since she'd provided his heir, she tried to cajole Edvard into teaching her about import and export, the ships and their ventures, all the ins and outs of their shares in the Antiphon Trading Company in far-flung Breakwater. He'd refused, gently at first, citing her fragility. She, annoyed, pointed out that as she'd had the fortitude to push his gigantic son through a very tiny fundamental hole, she was certain she could weather the rigours of buying and selling. He'd been so offended by the coarseness that he'd refused to speak with her for a week and, only after she'd apologised in floods of tears, had he relented.

Her parents, when discussing dowry terms with Edvard, had

frequently praised her biddable nature: *Cordelia has the habit of good behaviour*, they would say, though they did not mention she'd learned it through hours locked in a cupboard, with belt-stripes across her backside. She found in obedience a form of camouflage, and she'd taken refuge in it as soon as she'd discovered her husband to be no more flexible than her parents. Apart from the occasional moments of rebellion, which never lasted too long, she'd done her best to behave as a dutiful wife. Her mask was so effective that she managed to convince even herself, forgetting for long periods who she was, what she'd wanted.

In some ways the habit has stood her in good stead as far as a contented marriage was concerned, although it has blinded her to other matters, and given her a firm conviction that her abilities are limited, her capacity for suffering and pain minimal, and her resilience non-existent. She tells herself she does not resent Edvard for *she* made the choice to let the less docile aspects of herself go, to bury the knowledge of her own strength and resource. To let them wither, if not die. She could have fought, certainly, until their life together was a scorched earth; she could have won if she wished, but she made the decision to be submissive and that at least was her choice alone. Cordelia is nothing if not fair-minded.

'Are you all right, my love?' she asks quietly. He startles, as if he'd forgotten she was there, jerks his knees so the book in his lap falls, and stifles a curse. In the looking glass she sees the pages in brief flashes, numbers and columns, until the ledger hits the thick carpet with almost a sigh. There is a flare of annoyance on her husband's face, then he laughs and his eyes light up. He swings his legs off the bed, fine ankles on display, and bends to retrieve the tome, which he tucks into the top drawer of his bedside table.

'Of course, my dearest. Just mulling over some figures.' He crosses the room to stand behind her, his hand caressing her waves of hair, smiling at the reflection of her green, green eyes. She smiles back, thinks how handsome he still is, and he slides his other hand over her shoulder, down to cup her breast, leans in to whisper, 'Come to bed, my good wife.'

Afterwards, when she knows he is sleeping, when she recognises the tiny catch that presages the loud snoring she has learned to block out, she rises, sweat cooling rapidly on her naked form even with the fire blazing in the hearth. She quietly extracts the ledger from the drawer. It's curiosity more than anything, a tiny rebellion; but she doesn't understand what she sees. So many digits, neat and tidy, most in black but some in precise red, which come more and more frequently the closer she gets to the last pages. All those ciphers so conscientiously written in Mr Farringdale's tight little script. She shakes her head, thinking with a small grief that she has left it too long to learn these things, has let her mind atrophy, let too much of her intellect run out with the breast milk she's given generously to their three children. Too much energy put into selecting weekly menus and daily dresses, planning parties, running a household.

Cordelia returns the book, careful to make sure it's in the exact position she found it. Her mind may feel stagnant, but she is no fool.

* * *

In Cordelia's dreams, Bethany is small, so small, nothing but a little girl, her parents' late bliss. The child she'd bade farewell to when she left Singing Vine to marry. The child she hardly knew, for such wee folk are barely formed before they are five; the fifteen-year age gap made her sister a beloved stranger, someone for who she had affection as a result of obligation rather than any great knowledge of who Bethany truly was.

Cordelia conjures a time she knows only from her sister's occasional tales, stories sobbed after waking from nightmares. Of the time when the Blight came, traipsed in on the boot of some traveller, or dropped from the beak or shit of some bird flying from one land to the next. How it came mattered not at all; that it happened is all that mattered. She dreams of parents who, she tells herself, are not the ones she knew, not the people who shared their good fortune with those who wandered, footsore and starved, from one place to another; whose prosperity enriched the town huddled at the foot of the hills upon which Singing Vine was set. She dreams of a man and woman who'd become thin and malnourished, their mouths sunken where teeth had fallen out, bellies swollen with hunger, hair shedding in clumps as despair made its home in their hearts.

She dreams of the night when the Lawrences drank down some of the vineyard's best reds, all liberally laced with a gentle poison that made them think themselves young once more. She imagines her sister, almost ten, accepting but not drinking the draught offered by loving hands. She imagines Bethany watching their parents die. She thinks of the little girl found by neighbours unable to feed another mouth, who sent her off to an orphanage in Seaton St Mary. A little girl who, when finally located almost twelve months later by Mr

Farringdale's exhaustive investigations, stared at her elder sister with a gaze so empty and old that she was barely recognisable as the golden-haired cherub who lived in Cordelia's memory.

Cordelia thought that child would never forgive her, but then Bethany had fallen ill with fever and spent nigh on a month in bed. Sitting beside her, night and day, almost ignoring her own offspring, Cordelia waited to see which side of the divide between life and death the girl would choose. When Bethany at last awoke, her eyes were clear and new, and she smiled at her sister as if she was the loveliest thing ever seen. For the longest time, though, Cordelia was roused by terrified screams as the nightmares rode Bethany hard, and there ever remained some questions about life at the orphanage which her sister refused to answer.

* * *

In the small dining room, not the formal one, Victoria sits beside Cordelia and glares at her younger brother; the truce is dissolved. The brooch has not been found, nor has Torben admitted his crime. Unable to find any evidence of his culpability, Cordelia will not mete out punishment; she spoke quietly with him earlier, emphasising her disappointment if he *had* taken the trinket. Henry, at fourteen, has grown out of tormenting his sister, yet Torben, at seven, still finds joy in the act. However, he swore his innocence, brown eyes awash, and she chose to believe him.

Edvard, at the head of the table, has been discussing with Henry the next stage of his schooling.

'Whitebarrow, Father. Or St Isidore's Mount, at a pinch.'

Edvard, as yet not convinced the boy truly wishes to become a medical man rather than a merchant, lifts a brow and suggests Pennworth. Henry, tall and handsome, already a copy of his father, manages to keep his expression neutral and nods consideringly. Cordelia frowns for the both of them: Edvard had agreed to abide by the boy's wishes. Pennworth is not noted for its medical curriculum, but commercial… that and the fact that it is known to be… *economical*, the sort of place people lower on the social scale than the Parsifals send their sons in the hope they'll learn to make money. Such an alma mater may well cost a young man certain positions, certain advancements. Henry's tutors have given glowing reports of his abilities, supported by the results of the entrance exams he'd sat some weeks ago, which showed he was more than capable of undertaking the studies at Whitebarrow.

Cordelia smiles at her son, encouraging, hoping he will remain strong, and not be swayed by another's wishes. Stronger than she has chosen to be. *The problem with appeasing others*, she thinks, *is that it becomes a hard habit to break*. Should she tell her boy this sooner rather than later, or point out to Edvard that he has three heirs, not simply one, if he would but open his eyes? Torben will settle, when he's older. Victoria… she gives her daughter a surreptitious glance and worries that she's made the girl too readily into what she herself has striven, by denial of self, to become. Is Victoria helpless, will she drift until she finds a husband to tell her who to be, what to do? Cordelia swallows the disquiet and resolves to speak with Edvard after dinner, to remind him of his promises; remind him if she must that, according to his own rules, the children are *her* purview and she will see them follow their hearts.

Bethany's place is empty but Cordelia gives Merry a nod to serve the rare roast she's been carving at the sideboard. Cordelia rubs her stomach surreptitiously; a new life is growing there. She wasn't certain until this morning, when her bloods failed to appear – she has been regular as the moon ever since her twelfth year – and now she knows. Cordelia is uncomfortably aware of the tallow-wife's words at the fair. She is unsure how she feels: three children have done enough to drain the life from her. It's not that she doesn't love them, but she'd thought Torben the last. She has been looking forward to a time when she might convince Edvard to let her travel with him, to leave landlocked Lodellan and go thence to the sea. Perhaps even to make the journey *home*, up into the mountains to where the old vineyard lay, to see what might be salvaged, perhaps to try her hand at a new venture and see if her parents' sacrifices might still be worth something. She hoped, when the children were independent, but this… this would delay any such freedoms at least another fourteen years.

She squeezes her eyes shut, keeps them that way until she senses someone at her elbow. Merry stares at her, a little moodily, a little concerned, the fresh pot of coffee in a pin-and-needle-pricked hand. Cordelia smiles and nods for her to pour the steaming bitter brew. Edvard has always disdained her habit of drinking it with dinner, but he has ceased to comment. She adds cream, but no sugar, and sips; feels the thing in her stomach, however small – two months, no more – squirm and protest. All her children were thus, all objecting *in utero* to the beverage; to this day Victoria screws up her nose at the smell. And every day Cordelia bids her not to do so for the wind may change and leave her face all a'turn. Well, the girl would not need worry soon enough, for this new pup will curtail her mother's customs if she wishes to keep any food down at all.

She wonders if she might refuse to go through with it. She is almost thirty-three: hasn't she done enough? Hasn't her body done enough? How many more dark purple veins will pattern her hips and thighs? How many more crêpe-ripples will emboss her breasts, her belly? How much higher will her hairline reach, how much thinner will her hair get, how much will fall out this time? And will it recover as well? Will it regain its thickness, its sheen, its weight? *Who would I go to? Who might know of such things*? Nowadays the city is filled only by male physicians; the cunning women have been hunted, driven to ground, and are few and far between. Magic and old medicine have become elusive, rare, endangered in the years since the Prince's daughter was led astray by a witch. Even Mrs B's tiny habits and rituals, her acts of household enchantment – hanging a toadstone pendant around the children's necks when they were ill; putting little purses of graveyard dirt beneath pillows when a member of the household could not sleep; all the tisanes she brewed for any number of ailments – all are carefully hidden lest someone see and talk; lest someone burn in consequence. And the lords of the church in Lodellan always find a witch or three for an annual incineration.

Her reverie is broken by Bethany's bright greeting, and she removes the hand from her stomach so no one might notice. Her sister offers an envelope to her, and an inky broadsheet to Henry. Cordelia recognises the lilac stationery and gold wax seal, and breaks into a relieved smile, which Edvard echoes. She barely notices her sister's excited glow as she sits beside Henry, hand lighting on the lad's shoulder so briefly. The boy buries himself in the news, while Bethany's attention is concentrated on Cordelia.

This missive is coveted in Lodellan: a summons, really, to the Winter Solstice Ball thrown by the Princess Royal. This is the second occasion in a row that the Parsifals have garnered such favour. To be invited one year and forgotten the next, replaced by newer, richer, more amusing callers, is to be dreaded! A repeated request means one automatically passes onto the standing guest list for years to come. It is precisely the sort of invitation Edward spent ages seeking – subtly, of course, without appearing to do so. He's rebuilt the family fortune his grandfather frittered on dancehall girls who were more expensive than one might have expected, racehorses that were slower than they should have been, and a variety of alchemical experiments meant to create diamonds and gems and gold by the molehill, by the mountain.

'What will you wear, Dellie?' asks Bethany, tone sly. 'Though why I ask when you've spent so much of your time on this important decision…'

Cordelia chooses to ignore the dig, and toys with the envelope flap, reluctant to break the resplendent seal; then she carefully slips the length of her pink nail beneath and gently encourages the wax up, all in one piece. The small triumph makes her smile. 'The purple, I think.'

The dress has often felt like a daring, audacious thing, made in *hope*. Merry has been working on it for months and Cordelia watched the last stitches being placed in the hems not two days ago. She has worried, sometimes, that it has been too cheeky, a challenge to fate; others she simply revels in how lovely it is and that it is hers.

'A decision worthy of the intellect devoted to it,' says her sister, as if it's a joke, as if there's no edge to her words, and nods at Merry. The girl brings the wine decanter, pours for Edvard and Bethany; a half-glass for Henry, which is then topped up with water as he's never liked the taste. Cordelia shakes her head when the girl lifts the vessel in offer.

'Then this is the perfect time, my love,' says Edvard. Cordelia concentrates on him, on his eyes, mouth, then glances at her sister's fervid expression as she, too, watches Edvard. It makes Cordelia uncomfortable; it brings to mind this afternoon when she came upon her husband and sister, standing close and whispering, huddled like conspirators, Bethany's posture reminiscent of the women on Half-moon Lane, those not fortunate enough to have a place on Courtesans' Row. She pushes aside the fears that have crawled up her spine, have curled in the pit of her belly. She brightens her gaze, widens her smile.

In Edvard's hand is a burgundy velvet box.

'For you, darling, to ensure you are the belle of the ball.'

Her fingers slip and shake as she accepts, and seeks the latch. By clever design, the lid flips open when the catch is released and inside, lying on a bed of dark red, is a necklace. Her sister smiles and claps with delight, but no surprise. *This*, Cordelia thinks with relief, is why her husband and Bethany have been speaking secretly. Her relief is too great, yet she chooses not to examine what that might mean, and contemplates the gift.

An enormous amethyst is the heart of the piece; it is glorious, cut many times over to give the perfect shape, to glean every bit of light from the candles, the fire in the hearth. It seems to have impossible depths, a darkness and a lightness dancing within and without its hallucinatory purple hue. It is surrounded by a band of alternating emeralds and diamonds, set in an opening lily of white-gold, each petal perfectly recreated. All hangs from a chain of tiny elegant interlocking silver spirals.

Cordelia drapes it around her neck, ensures it's secure. It feels warm against her flesh as she rises to stare at her reflection in the gilt mirror above the small fireplace. A few dark spots on her creamy skin distract her – a sure sign of a babe on the way; lemon juice solution will help. She attends to the necklace again, primps and preens, smiles at her second self in the mercury, the one who is free from all the burdens she bears, all the burdens she has consented to. Her smile dims when she recalls that the Winter Solstice Ball will be the last time she can fit into that glorious dress for a long while. She touches the amethyst absently.

Edvard calls, 'To the table, my love, and your dinner. You must eat, you need your strength.'

And Cordelia realises, then, that he *knows*. His smile is too smug, his words too weighted. He won't mention it yet, will consider it something for her to announce, but his knowledge gives her no options, other than deceit. The thing around her neck turns cold as she recognises it as a bribe, a sop, a pretty thing to wear while she grows fat yet again. While all her chances for change disappear. Still, Cordelia is skilled at hiding her true self, and she smooths her expression until it is pleasantly bland, then takes her place beside her husband.

Merry brings out the first dessert and places it on the sideboard. The boys eat quickly and will be through their main course well before the rest of the family.

'Henry,' Cordelia says, noticing the broadsheet beside his plate leaves smears on the snowy cloth. 'Put that away, you're making a mess.'

'The Agnews,' he says sombrely, folding the pages and handing them off to Merry without even looking at her, as if she's not there. Cordelia is caught between reprimanding him for that small impoliteness, and preoccupation at his words. Preoccupation wins.

'What of them?'

'They've been murdered – Master and Mistress, Mrs Agnew's parents, the four children, and the three servants.'

Cordelia's hand goes to her throat, finds the gem, grasps it. The amethyst curls into her palm as if it belongs there. She seems to feel the echo of her heartbeat deep in the stone.

'Do they know…?' begins Edvard, unable to finish a question with so much potential, so many gaps, and mysteries, and lacunae, so many possible answers. The Agnews were one of the city's most prominent families, certainly one of the richest; not bad folk, generous to those beneath them, kind to their servants and those in their employ, charitable, philanthropic. The spate of robberies has been bad enough, but now, *this*.

Murder.

And not a slaying in the road, not a battle of lowlifes, not a fight between tarts that's gotten out of hand, not an over-enthusiastic debt-collector, nor a constable taking his duties too seriously. But a killing in a fine house barely three streets away. A killing of a fine family who should have been touched by no more than time and the rigours of old age, not by violence. Not by something so…

Henry clears his throat, he is pale; he'd been friends with the oldest Agnew boy. 'A robbery gone wrong. There was another body. They think someone interrupted the thief, who tried to eliminate all witnesses. Perhaps Mr Agnew managed to kill him even as he himself was dying.'

'Who?' asks Victoria through her tears. She would no longer play with Ozanne and Oriel Agnew, her closest companions.

'An employee of the Considines', their valet-in-training… Japheth something or other.'

Cordelia's twists in her seat, gaze going immediately to Merry, who has dropped the second dessert tray. Meringue and cream and fruit compote spread far and wide across the expensive silk carpet. The girl holds both hands to her mouth, face drained of all colour, and Cordelia thinks, foolishly, that she is quite lovely when not scowling. Merry's eyes are huge, the pupils so large there is almost no white left around the irises that at this moment look more green than hazel. Before Cordelia can go to her, the tweeny flees, sobs trailing behind her like black mourning ribbons.

* * *

The last notes of the requiem mass still hang in the air when the Parsifals leave by the great arched doorway of Lodellan's Cathedral, passing by the six ghostly wolf-hounds – age evident in their fading outlines – that guard the holy house. The family is in the front half of the dolorous procession following the Archbishop; the line of mourners snakes across the portico, down the stone steps, then along the footpath to where the lychgate breaches the walls surrounding the graveyard. Cordelia looks up at the elaborate roof and see shadows shifting in the steep angles there; then the moment is gone, and she is through the strange bottleneck and pursuing the safest paths. The ground is treacherous in places, the unwary who wander are likely to find themselves breaking through the crust of the earth and turning an ankle in an unsuspected grave, or worse. The trees, mainly yew and oak, are ancient, branches and roots entwine from one to the other, and thick bushes fill any space in between; beneath the canopy the atmosphere is cold, and Cordelia hears the chattering of teeth behind her. *One of the children*, she thinks, *Victoria*.

Ahead, she sees the flickering torch the Archbishop carries to light his way into the Agnew vault.

The cortege sweeps past the graves of the poor, marked by simple white crosses or piles of stones. Next come the merchants' plots, which are tidier and larger, the slabs and headstones made of better material, more marble and granite, the statuary showing signs of artistry. There is Micah Bartleby's tomb, black quartz glistening in the skerrick of sunlight that's fought its way through, and here an angel leans drunkenly, its features all but erased by the elements and the only trace of a name left is *Hepsi... tyne*.

At last they come to the mausoleums, where Lodellan's richest and best lie, and the great snake of mourners splits around the pink marmoreal structure where the Agnews will take their final rest, and forms a line either side. No distant cousin or such can be located – the family has been utterly annihilated – so Belladonna Considine, wrapped in shimmering black bombazine, undertakes funereal honours. She wears a veil of netting so thick one can barely make out her features.

How must she feel? wonders Cordelia. *Knowing her own servant visited such catastrophe on her dearest friends?* Belladonna takes the fat golden key from the Archbishop's hand and inserts it in the lock, then gives the heavy door a good push. There is neither creak nor groan of hinges, for the edifice is kept in good repair. Belladonna steps into her husband's politely waiting arms, and the clusters of pallbearers trail the Archbishop and his blazing brand down into the darkness of the crypt.

Cordelia is grateful she does not have to go beneath, to feel the blackness pressing in from all sides. She puts an arm around Victoria, who stands close, shivering. The cold on the girl's shoulders is so intense it bites through the leather of Cordelia's glove. She looks at her daughter and sees, to her left, in the space between Victoria and Torben, a pale white formless mist. Cordelia blinks, but is careful not to draw attention. She glances at the crowd then realises no one else can see the icy cloud; she manages a motion that is part-rub, part-wave, and her fingers pass through the thin fog, leaving traces and trails in the air. Soon it dissipates and Victoria's tremors ease.

Cordelia takes a relieved breath and finds Bethany, who holds Henry close, looking at her. Cordelia smiles and focuses once more on the mouth of the sepulchre, where the first group of attendants returns to the light, quickly moving aside so the next can deposit their own burden. She'll not tell her sister about the strange vapour or how it felt; Bethany needs no encouragement to laugh at her. She does not wish to be regarded as mad as well as weak, but Cordelia knows as surely as night follows day that around them, in the trees and foliage which weave their way through the graveyard, there are things, *other* things, which move and watch, breathe and sleep, dream and desire. Things that the clever rich folk of Lodellan don't believe in for it is not *fashionable*. But those with less money and more sense still leave offerings on the graves; the sexton still plants lavender over the common burial pits where the indigent and unloved lie, in hope of ensuring they rest in peace. Mothers in the slum quarters still warn their children not to listen to the sound of the jingling copper bells hanging from some of the yews and oaks in the bone orchard. Though she's told no one Cordelia has seen them on occasion, the things that shift and threaten, when she's come to visit the grave of one friend or another. She holds her daughter closer.

Later, at the wake at the Considine house, Cordelia finds herself alone with Belladonna. A small bubble of quiet, of suspended time, forms around them; outside it there is well-mannered noise, conversation, people attired in haute-couture black weeds moving in a strange kind of dance. Cordelia touches her friend's hand gently and says how sorry she is. Belladonna pauses, tugs at her veil and shows her face. The transformation is terrible: the once-silver eyes are dead grey ice; the elegantly high cheeks are hollowed and the skin drawn tight, with a yellow tint; the pouting mouth is slack, the lips strangely thin, and poised as if a howl might force its way between them at any moment. There is such guilt and such burden.

'How can I go on? Knowing we – *I* – harboured a viper in our bosom?' Belladonna's voice is so low that Cordelia can barely hear. She squeezes the other woman's arm tightly, hoping for sympathy and strength to flow into her. She thinks, although she tries not to, how Bethany told of the boy Japheth's body: thrown onto the midden heap outside Lodellan's walls. While she can understand the urge, she still considers such an act vindictive and short-sighted: no carefully constructed coffin to either help him rest easy or keep him from haunting the city until the last trumpet sounds.

'My dear Bella, you have no need of guilt. You did not employ him in an ill house, did not subject him to evil influences. However his heart and mind were turned, the cause was not here. Not you.' Cordelia lightly strokes the other's sleeve. 'Mourn our friends by all means, but you had no role in their deaths, please set aside that woe.'

Tears flood the other woman's eyes, as if the kindness is unbearable. She pulls from Cordelia and flees, to the upper levels of the house, covering her face as she goes. Cordelia is empty, bereft. She shakes her head; her mind is adrift, her emotions high with the tragedy striking so close to home. She just needs time, as does Bella, to recover, to feel as if the ground is solid beneath them once again. Blinking, Cordelia turns to the ballroom – the only room big enough to hold the crowd – now hung with black crepe and wreaths of lily and rowan, acanthus and asphodel.

Henry, Victoria, and Torben will be in one of the auxiliary parlours, playing in desultory fashion with what pass for friends amongst the children of the rich. Across the room Cordelia spies Edvard, part of a group of sombre-looking men. Their expressions are carefully maintained, but she suspects she knows what they hide: a combination of judgement and fear. Judgement of Leon Agnew, that he did not protect his family, and fear that he *could not* do so. Fear that there but for the grace of God went each and every one of them. Edvard has spent the past few days ensuring weapons are hidden throughout their house, that Henry knows where they are and so do the coachman and footman. Not Cordelia, though, nor Victoria nor Bethany, nor Mrs B, nor Merry, for if their menfolk failed to defend them, what could the women possibly do?

One of his companions says something and Cordelia watches as Edvard's face pinches, sours. His reply makes the other man wither and shrink, and she wonders what has lit her husband's serene temper so quickly. She senses someone beside her: Bethany, pale and lovely, hair beneath an ebon lace mourning bonnet, her dress of charcoal satin with tight pintucks that Merry's clever fingers took hours and hours to achieve. At her breast is an oval brooch, glass-fronted, showing the coil of blonde hair that belonged to their mother. By rights it should have been Cordelia's but it was the sole possession Bethany managed to keep during her stay at the orphanage and Cordelia never had the heart to insist when her sister had already lost so much.

'What do you think he said?' she asks idly, wistfully. 'What are they discussing?'

'Surely, sister, you've enough gumption to find out?' Bethany's tone is sharp and it cuts. 'Why don't you ask him yourself? Keep at him until he answers?'

Cordelia knows her shock and hurt are writ large on her face; Bethany shows no sign of caring, and continues, 'Why do you insist on being wilfully ignorant? I swear, Cordelia, you were never such a fool when we were small.'

Cordelia thinks that unfair; Bethany was so young when her older sister left Singing Vine. What recollections could she possibly have? She has the uncomfortable feeling, though, that Bethany is right; as a child and young woman Cordelia was outspoken and inquisitive, insistent, and always, always, gained the knowledge she wanted, needed. She did not dwell in ignorance, and no one ever told her certain things were not her concern. How did she become as she is now? Did she give up all at once? Or bit by bit, unaware of how she was changing? *Lessening* just to make life easier? She turns her mind from the idea of growing dim, of diminishing. It seems too hurtful, too fearful. She blinks, feels Bethany's hand on her arm.

'I'm sorry, sister, I should not have spoken so. It is… the grief.' Bethany bats away tears or so it seems. 'They speak of men's matters, of commerce and the like. They will discuss Agnew's failure as man and husband, protector and guardian of his family. They'll opine how terrible a monster that boy must have been to do this thing, to overcome one such as Leon. Then they will grow quiet and discomforted until someone mentions a mistress to break the tension, the residence he keeps her in on Courtesans' Row, the clever things she does, and how happy it makes him to know she is his refuge from a demanding wife and puling offspring.'

Cordelia wonders if Edvard is one of those men, if he visits another woman in a tall house that she can imagine all too vividly: red velvet drapes, luxurious sofas, beds hung with silks and fine netting, walls decorated with erotic frescos from which inspiration might be taken. Cordelia shakes her head; Mrs Bell sewed a swan's feather into Edvard's pillow the day of their marriage, a sure way to safeguard fidelity she'd said. Cordelia feels quite unstable already without the weight of her husband's possible secrets tumbling onto her. She absently pats Bethany's cheek and moves off before her sister can say something even more disturbing; she feels, yet again, that she no longer knows the girl she raised as her own. *It is her age*, she thinks, *she is finding herself.* Bethany will settle, eventually, and they shall rub along nicely once more.

* * *

Cordelia tries to change the direction of her dreams, encourage them back towards happier terrain; she knows, though, that they will not obey her entirely, or indeed for long. But still it seems she succeeds as the days before the Winter Solstice Ball run together. In her sleep, she could swear the fire is real, that the scent of burning wood and roasting chestnuts tickle her nostrils. She picks pleasant scenes as she once did the sweetest cherries from a bowl. She is sure she can hear the crackle and snap of twigs, the small avalanches of cinders and glowing coals through the grate, that she can hear the laughter in the house. She turns in her slumber, enjoying the warmth, the memory... yet all too soon that changes once again.

* * *

The air in the house is thick with mourning. Cordelia finds it hard to breathe, harder still to see the expressions of shock on her children's faces. They've never experienced loss or grief in their short lives; she feels she has failed to prepare them. Edvard's parents were long-dead by the time he married, and her own parents' deaths occurred when Henry was very small; he did not know them, besides. Their world has been intact, hermetically sealed from heartache, and she searches desperately for a way to make them smile again. Cordelia leaves Merry at home, does not even mention that they are going out. The girl has been heavy-eyed, inattentive, hard of hearing since news of the Agnews and their murderer; she has refused to discuss the matter though Cordelia has tried to offer comfort. Even Mrs B has failed to draw anything from her, or so she has told Cordelia. Cordelia wonders if the girl has been outside the city walls, walking the paths that have been worn through Lodellan's great midden heap by scavengers who go on two legs as well as four, looking for the body of the boy she loved.

Yet taking the children to the carnival the morning of the Ball is a mistake, which she understands only as they step beneath the archway entrance, and she once more trickles coin into the toothless old woman's hand. This is the final day, the crowd is thin, and the troupe are already packing up: there are fewer toys and gewgaws on the stalls, most of the makeshift stages have been pulled down and only the girls who climb the enchanted ropes are performing. Their air is one of boredom, barely concealed impatience; they're the last act, thinks Cordelia, the one most likely to attract attention. Does this happen every time the show moves on or is there a ballot and the girls drew the short straw on this occasion?

Her offspring remain listless, indeed their languor seems to increase as if infected by the apathy of the dying carnival. Cordelia sighs heavily and Bethany, strangely compassionate, takes her arm as they wander aimlessly through the partially deconstructed landscape. Torben, Victoria, and even Henry amble in front of them like lambs. Bethany does not even rouse herself to make disparaging remarks and Cordelia is grateful her sister has at last developed some kind of restraint.

The sight of her babies so passive, so downhearted, is depressing. Normally she would have to shepherd them, drag them back into easy reach, or have Merry do it. The longer she watches, the heavier the oppression becomes, but she fights it until she sees the cart with the coloured candles – much fewer than last time, whether due to sales or packing she cannot know – and the woman who makes them, the tallow-wife, who stares at her with an unfathomable gaze. That is when she feels her chest compressing, compacting, growing tighter; finds the air harder to pull into her lungs no matter how deeply she breathes.

'Take care of them for me, Bethany,' she gasps, pulling away from her sister. 'I must walk.'

And Bethany nods and lets her go, as if recognising what Cordelia needs most right now is solitude, not worry nor sympathy.

Cordelia pushes and shoves her way through the dwindling mob as if she's a fishwife on the docks of some town that actually has an ocean, has something more than the river that's become sluggish and brown over the years. It's all she can do to keep from breaking into a run. She's out now, beyond the enigmatic gaze of the tallow-wife, gone from the press of bodies; the noise and chatter diminish behind her as she walks faster and faster and her ladylike shoes beat a desperate rhythm of escape along the main road.

Farther away from Lodellan, she feels she can breathe again, and she slows, stops. Between the trees is a building, a low dilapidated affair of wood bruised by time and weather. Cordelia moves toward it; the roof has fallen in at some point, a tree grows through the western wall, the door hangs by one tenacious hinge alone, and the windows have long been shattered. She searches her memory and finds something at last, snags it, draws it up. Tales of a woman many years ago, the city's finest coffin-maker though none recall her name. Her demise was murky and led to whispers and rumours, dark tales about her true goings on, yet Cordelia cannot recall precise details try though she might.

She looks at the tumbledown structure, at the wreckage of what someone had built. She thinks of her parents, of the Singing Vine and what its loss meant to them. She thinks of the Agnews, how their lives were taken but their possessions remain, to do no good to anyone. She thinks that the destruction of *things* should not mean the ruination of a life.

Cordelia glances over her shoulder, looks at the road that leads away, is struck by the scandalous idea that she could simply keep going.

Then she remembers the child that grows inside her, remembers the children she has already birthed, recalls Mrs B and Merry, Edvard and Bethany. She thinks on the pillars of her existence and is ashamed she could contemplate such cowardly flight. Cordelia turns on her heel and returns to the carnival, breath frosting on the cold air.

The old woman on the gate lets her through, waving away the coins she offers. More, she points the direction in which she might find her family. Cordelia gives the candle-maker a wide berth.

She espies the children at a tiny petting zoo. Victoria and Torben seem more animated as they fuss over the baby animals: there's a bear cub, a pony, a lamb, a calf, and a wolf pup; kits of snow fox and badger. Henry kneels, with no thought for his expensive kerseymere breeches, beside an exotic kitten with fur of black and orange stripes, which eyes the other animals as if they might provide its luncheon.

For a few moments she cannot see Bethany and anger begins to boil at the perceived lack of responsibility. Then she is there, her tall slender sister with her golden curls held in place by fine black netting, wearing yet another exquisite gown, this one pale gold, made by Merry's clever, miserable fingers.

Bethany is gesturing at someone Cordelia cannot see until her sister moves aside and there is Mr Farringdale again, this time gripping a magnificent bouquet of flowers: red roses, asters, carnations, daffodils, daisies, forget-me-nots, and hyacinths… in fact so many blooms that are out of season Cordelia wonders how he got them and how much this tribute cost. This token, however, goes unnoticed, uncollected, unaccepted by the object of his affection though he still holds it out in offering. Cordelia is pierced by the expression of loss on the little man's face.

Oh, poor Mr Farringdale, to carry a torch for such as Bethany. Bethany, who's refused the richest, handsomest, finest bucks of Lodellan. What chance could he possibly think he might have?

And her sister turns then, as if she senses Cordelia's presence, her thoughts. And in that moment Bethany's face is naked: Cordelia doesn't recognise this girl whose expression is so fierce and feral, shows too many wishes and wants, too much greed, lust, abandon, arrogance, and pride. And in that moment Cordelia feels as though there is more, much more than an age gap between them…

… then Bethany sees her and grins; she is herself again, sweet though mischievous, sometimes cruel but never too much so, a little bold, but not too bold, eyes warming and dancing. She is Cordelia's little sister once more, not a woman standing on the precipice between light and shadow. Cordelia tries to smile, finds her lips stiff and unwilling, for the memory of her sister's changed face is too fresh, too raw; it leaves a residue of fear that Cordelia cannot comprehend. She forces the corners of her mouth upwards; dismisses the moment for it is too unreal.

As she approaches, Mr Farringdale scurries away, bouquet in hand, no doubt to nurse his heart with the aid of the mulled cherry wine and blackberry port of which he is so fond. Cordelia will speak to Bethany, yes, but not today, not tonight. Tomorrow, after the Ball. There has been enough unpleasantness, and Cordelia is determined to rebuild her family's happiness. They will stay here as long as the children wish, as long as she can see their joy returning if only in some small measure, for it is a start.

And Mr Farringdale, poor Mr Farringdale… she will make enquiries and investigations. There will be women in Lodellan who would welcome his suit, who would see him as a good, solid investment, someone who would appreciate their kindness and wifely efforts on his behalf. Someone who would mend what Bethany in her youth and hubris has injured.

Tonight is the winter solstice: the longest night. Tomorrow will be a time of new beginnings, the day to start over. Yes. Everything can be fixed.

* * *

The dress is exquisite, a raw silk that contains within its warp and weft all possible variations of purple: lavender, lilac, fuchsia, violet, amaranthine, magenta, periwinkle, mulberry… every tone and shade and hue. It skims Cordelia's trim-for-now figure perfectly, though Merry has had to let it out twice in the fortnight before the ball. She has done so with lips pursed, gaze judging, as if Cordelia has been overeating, doing it on purpose. Alas, all the adjustments – and Merry's grieving inattention – have left one of the appliquéd roses, which encircle the waist and trail down the skirt like a cascade, somewhat loose. A few quick stitches are required before Master and Mistress Parsifal depart.

Cordelia's hair is swept up onto the crown of her head, pale sunlight curls tumbling artfully, although it took more than two hours to get them to look so casual. The gown shifts and changes its colour and mood with every movement, and the necklace, oh the necklace! It is pure magnificence. There will be nothing like it at the Ball.

Merry's room is at the top of the stairs, a large attic space fitted with rugs and hangings to keep out the winter chill, a comfortable bed with a richly embroidered quilt full and fat with goose down. Part of the area is set aside for the girl's sewing: there are three tailor's dummies, a workbench for cutting patterns and material, a series of shelves with skeins of silk, and drawers wherein lie needles and pins and scissors of various size and shape and sharpness, each intended for a different purpose. But of Merry herself there is no evidence, which makes Cordelia puff an exasperated breath. Yet she'll not entrust this small task to Annie the parlour maid's ham-fisted efforts.

No matter. A tack or two is all that's needed, a service she did for her own mother many years ago. As long as she is careful not to prick herself and bleed on the fabric, it will be a simple task. She eyes the range of threads and finds the correct tint, then opens the drawers one after another seeking the right gauge of needle. In the last compartment something catches her eye, a flash of silver and gold and green and nacre, a small brooch in the shape of a spray of lilies. The one she gave Victoria for her twelfth birthday, on the eve of her Presentation Ball, the item the girl wore on the pearl organdie gown with argentella lace. The very brooch Torben has been accused of stealing.

And it is *here*.

In this drawer.

In this room.

In the possession of this girl…

Cordelia's throat tightens as she thinks of having this girl, this dangerous girl, this sullen, angry, moody girl in her house, near her family. This girl… this girl whom she'd welcomed when Mrs B had taken in the orphaned niece as a baby, who'd been raised beside the Parsifal children, to whom she'd given a position, a wage, and much patience. The thought that this girl should so requite her kindness in a petty dishonest manner, that this girl had been associating with a killer…

Her fear makes her angrier than she might otherwise be; it washes reason and kindness away. Deliberately, Cordelia reaches into the drawer and finds a tiny silver pin. Her hands shake as she fastens the wayward rose in place, and it's only by sheer force of will that she completes her task without drawing blood; it will do. Then she picks up the brooch, all her anger, her fear, her umbrage, pooling, roiling and boiling as she makes her way downstairs to the basement kitchen.

Once again there's no sign of Merry, but Mrs Bell has not yet retired to her small suite of rooms behind the pantry. She is tidying after supper, grey-gold tendrils peeking from under her mob cap. She smiles as Cordelia enters, eyes lighting up, expression fond as fond can be, but finds no answering grin. Cordelia holds out her fist, fingers opening like petals to show the spray of gilded lilies there. Mrs B is perplexed.

'Where did you find it, madam? Did Torben—'

'It was in Merry's room,' says Cordelia tightly.

Mrs Bell stares, then shakes her head. 'She's a good girl, Mrs Parsifal. I know she's had a hard time of it and she's been a challenge for you, but she's a good girl for all that.'

'She has to go.' Cordelia's tone is arctic, and it chills the housekeeper who's never heard such a sound from her mistress's lips.

'Perhaps Miss Victoria misplaced the brooch when she was in for a fitting…' The excuse is weak even to her ears: Victoria hasn't had a new dress in months. 'You've known Merry all her life, Mrs Parsifal. She's not bad, no more than Miss Bethany's ever been. I'm sure…'

The older woman's pain begins to crack Cordelia's icy determination, but she steels herself: she will not be defied. Not in this. The house is the one sphere over which she has control. Her husband keeps secrets from her; her sister is becoming a stranger; this is the sole change she can enforce.

'Make sure she's gone by the time we get back tonight, Mrs Bell,' orders Cordelia, blinking hard to keep the tears confined. They cannot be allowed to run or they will take the black lash powder and eye-paint with them, cut swathes through the glimmering pearl foundation powder, drop onto and ruin her dress. 'I'm sorry, but I really must insist.'

'There's no bad in my niece, Mrs Parsifal.' Mrs Bell wrings her apron with dry, red hands. 'I beg you to reconsider, my dearling.'

'Not much good either it seems,' snaps Cordelia, fighting the effect of her childhood nickname, then watches as Mrs B's aspect freezes. All her affection drains from it.

'If Merry goes, then so must I, mistress,' says Mrs Bell quietly, her own tears utterly unfettered, pattering on the white of her apron front. Cordelia is stunned, hurt, possibly as stunned and hurt as Mrs B, but this doesn't occur to her, nor will it for weeks to come. Her face burns while her heart closes – that her old nurse would choose such a girl over her! – and she draws herself stiff and straight.

'Do what you must,' says Cordelia, breaking a lifetime's bond too easily, and spins about, hurries up the stairs into the hall where Edvard waits impatiently. Annie, beside him, has her mistress's fur-lined cloak waiting. She drapes it around Cordelia's shoulders as she gently draws on the lavender silk gloves that are meant for show, not warmth; then Annie disappears, subtle as a ghost. Cordelia keeps her head down so Edvard cannot see her expression, will not ask what is wrong and delay their departure. Had she but taken the time to steal a glance at *him* she would have observed his distraction, his pallor, and the fact that his eyes do not quite light upon her at all, as if she is simply an amorphous thing on which he cannot focus. But, caught up in her own web of upset, she does not notice that her husband is distressed to the point of inattentiveness as they step outside to where their coachman awaits with a carriage and four.

* * *

In her sleep, Cordelia imagines the baby is still inside her. She feels it turning and twisting, making her stomach bubble as if in the grip of terrible indigestion. As if a small sea creature does somersaults in the very pit of her. She could swear it's real, could swear it's solid and true – though it's months since her belly carried anything but hunger. She imagines that when she wakes it will be to the sweet, demanding cry of a newborn seeking milk, of a child wanting the comfort of its mother's arms, the warmth of her familiar flesh.

She dreams that the unwished for child is still hers to have and hold.

* * *

The coach takes them the short distance to the palace, pulls up outside the grand wing which Armandine, the Princess Royal, has made her own since her brother's marriage. Though the Prince of Lodellan will not be in attendance tonight – he seldom partakes in his sister's soirées – his wife will be, for this is the woman with whom Armandine herself was, and still is, in love.

Some whisper the Prince's bride has no aristocratic lineage at all, that she was selected for her peasant heartiness, the width of her hips, the generosity of her breasts – for her perceived fecundity. Thin blue blood, fussy breeding habits, and limited marriage pools have failed the ruling family, and the days of large broods are done with. It is said that Princess Armandine has given up her lover Ilse in the daylight hours only when propriety still holds some sway, that she and Ilse yet meet on all but those nights when the royal physicians deem her most likely to conceive. As a result, Ilse is round, set to provide the longed-for, much-needed heir, an heir with its mother's robustness, to be born of a woman whose bloodline has not been weakened by its *purity.* There's a fortune-teller kept in Armandine's household (who's thus far managed to avoid accusations of witchcraft) and she swears it's a boy.

But Cordelia doesn't think of the rumours. She doesn't think on the importance of this invitation, of the culmination of Edvard's ambitions, of the beauty of her gown and the splendour of the necklace lying cold around her throat. She thinks only of Merry and her betrayal, of Mrs Bell and her ill-placed loyalty. She thinks of a home without Mrs B's warmth, of the absence of a woman she only now admits she loves better than she ever did her own icily beautiful mother; the woman who protected her from the worst of her maternal parent's rages and punishments. She shakes herself as the footman rolls out the metal steps, and Edvard helps her from the carriage. She makes a concerted effort to forget all that's happened, to concentrate on the Ball, on being Edvard's fine wife, on doing him justice.

They sweep in through the first set of doors, wood and fittings faded by the elements, up stone steps covered in a crimson carpet for this eve only, along a phalanx of men-at-arms in shining livery, and join the receiving line waiting outside a second set of doors, great arched things of highly polished ebony banded with gold. Cloaks are taken by maids and whisked away. When their turn comes, Edvard offers the pale purple leaf to the chief doorman, whose expert eyes scan the contents. Satisfied it's no forgery, he gives a nod to the lesser doormen, who push open the panels and let them through. Their card returned, they step inside, onto a landing high above the ballroom floor. A herald, now, takes the invitation and reads out their names at the top of her lungs, so all heads swivel to look, to see, to judge.

Proceeding down the red marble staircase they are engulfed, briefly, by friends before joining the next section of the receiving line. Cordelia notes, amongst the already-arrived, already-welcomed guests, Belladonna Considine in an exquisite sable gown covered with shimmering jet beads. Her very public mourning is tasteful, understood, yet no one would expect her to forego the Winter Solstice Ball. Cordelia fixes a smile for her, part greeting, part sympathy, and flutters her fingers to catch the other woman's eye. Belladonna's lips begin to lift in answer, then stop, her glance hooked and caught by… something. Cordelia wonders if she's been found somehow unfit, her dress has been compromised by errant snowflakes, stained or marked in the kitchen during her confrontation, but a downward glance reassures her.

Belladonna moves off, swiftly. *Is she embarrassed by her outburst at the wake*? Before Cordelia can comment to Edvard they are swept onwards to a raised dais where the scarlet-clad Princess Royal, platinum-blonde locks carefully braided into a crown studded with gem-encrusted pins, awaits on a high-backed chair. Beside her, on a chaise longue set slightly lower, lounges a woman with fiery red hair and bored yellow eyes that glitter suddenly at the sight of Cordelia's ornaments. Her cheekbones are broad, her head quite round but for the sharp little chin, and a heavy belly presses against the fine chiffon underskirts displayed through the slit of her amber high-waisted outer gown. It's all Cordelia can do to resist the urge to touch her own stomach in sympathy.

Edvard bows and Cordelia curtsies. The Princess Royal's appreciative glance takes in the dress and necklace. She offers her hand, long and pale fingers weighted down by many rings. First Edvard, then Cordelia, bow over them, kissing the cool stones and even cooler flesh. One of the diamonds catches Cordelia's bottom lip, just a little and she feels a tiny cut, and a minuscule spring of ruby red. She licks it away and raises her head to meet Armandine's gaze.

'What a delightful ensemble, Mrs Parsifal. You must tell me the name of your seamstress.'

'A girl of our household, Your Highness,' she replies, the lie heavy in her mouth.

'You must let me borrow her,' says the Princess.

Cordelia nods. 'Of course, Your Highness.' She does not know how she will make this happen.

'And come visit with us, take tea.' She waves at the thin woman in green standing behind her chair, book and pencil in hand. 'Rada, make arrangements for next week.'

The clerk nods, takes a note, and the Parsifals are moved on. No one bothers to introduce them to the woman with auburn hair and yellow eyes. The woman who is ostensibly the reigning Princess of Lodellan, the mother of the city's next ruler. A woman who'd have no true place here if the Prince's daughter from an earlier marriage had not run away; if his first wife had not inconsiderately died of shame and grief before she could provide a new heir.

Now they are free to mingle in the to-and-fro of the crowd's waves, to shift and dance across the mosaic floor of gold and gem tiles that shows scenes from the city's history, good and bad: the miracle of the twice-born prince; the queen who let a dark woman lead the violet-eyed royal children astray and ended her days walled into her chamber; the troll-wife who almost stole the crown and her defeat at the hands of the unloved princess; the Archbishop who raised the new cathedral yet disappeared before its completion; the lost children turned to wolves by the bite of a grieving widow; the bakeress whose creations caused more trouble than they should… all this and more collected in the stones beneath them, now ignored by heedless feet whose owners no longer find miracles and magic fashionable, but actively suspect.

The Parsifals gravitate towards a group of friends – two groups, really, the men and women forming separate circles close enough that they might each hear the others' conversation, but not take part. While she chats with the wives, Cordelia begins to relax, almost forgets the drama leading up to this point. She basks in compliments about her dress and necklace, although part of her is dedicated to listening to her husband's discussions, determined to learn any way she can the things he keeps hidden. Determined to prove Bethany wrong.

'The profit we made on that latest Antiphon expedition has equipped three more ships!' bleats one youngster, hair black and thick as a fleece, but with no discernible moustache or saving sign of a beard. A son of one of the merchants, too foolish and wrapped up in himself to keep his boasting more private.

Edvard frowns. 'You turned a profit?'

The gentlemen around him nod. He seems confused. 'But we *lost* money on the deal.'

The others, older and wiser, look elsewhere so he might not see their pity. Their lack of comprehension. Edvard shakes his head, and the young cumberground laughs loud and spiteful. 'Forgotten how to count, old chap? I'd find a new accountant if I were you.'

And Cordelia watches as the blood leaves her husband's face and he shakes as if suffering a sudden palsy, as if a terribly misplaced trust has been revealed. She tries to go to his side, but a hand grabs her arm, nails scratching the skin. She turns and meets the eyes of Belladonna Considine, filled with hatred and grief so palpable that Cordelia feels the gaze almost as a physical force. Then she notices the men-at-arms on either side of the woman, stern-faced, implacable.

Belladonna points at Cordelia, at her throat. 'That's it. The necklace Leon had made especially for his wife for this ball. Odela showed it to me not two days before the murders.'

Cordelia says gently, though her voice trembles, 'No, Bella, you are mistaken. My Edvard gave it to me.'

Belladonna shouts, 'Do you think I wouldn't know it? Do you think I'd not recognise it? How dare you? How dare you do this and come here wearing the spoils of your evil labours?'

'There must be some mistake. Edvard, tell them…' Cordelia looks to her husband for support, but sees he is in the custody of two guards, taller even than himself, as though specially chosen for his apprehension. 'Edvard, tell them!'

But though he struggles, though he tries to throw off his captors, though he shouts their innocence, their outrage, no one listens. The crowd around them simply grows, as if the Parsifals form the vortex of a whirlpool from which there is no escape; in which the couple will be dragged a'down.

Finally, one of the guardsmen, tired of Edvard's dissent, draws back a meaty fist and hits him square in the mouth. There is blood, a tooth flies across the gathering to be lost in a sea of shoes, and her husband crumples so he must be carried from the ballroom. Cordelia, dragged along behind and protesting all the way, finds herself drained of sympathy. She wants to shout at him, to rail, pull a response from him, but he has left her to face this shame on her own.

As they pass through the crush, people step away as if a stench has attached itself to the Parsifals. Cordelia hears the whispers, the snippets that cut like cold winds, like sharp knives: *financial problems, lost his edge, murders, living beyond their means, thieves, shame, driven to it by her demands.* Rumours growing wings and flying so fast!

And then out the doors they'd so recently entered in triumph, taken across the courtyard with its frozen air, marched over the uneven flagstones to the entrance of the palace gaol. Snow and sleet come down hard, chilling them, marking them. The dread iron gate is opened, then closed behind them with a terrible clang, and in a dingy chamber rough men strip them of all belongings but their clothing. The cool absence of the necklace makes her flesh burn.

Next it is down, down, a'down into the dungeons that stretch beneath the city. It is barely warmer here than in the winter wind outside. They are delivered to separate cells so far from each other that even if he would answer her cries, Edvard could not hear them.

* * *

It is almost a week before Cordelia sees anyone other the gaoler and his hateful wife. That woman brings her stale bread, stew that smells richly of ferment – of which Cordelia eats no more than she must – and water that is sometimes fresh, most often not, but cannot be ignored. Though she isn't supposed to talk to the prisoner, Mistress Lamb does for the first few days, taking time to spout spite as she shoves the food through the bars, happy to see someone like Cordelia fallen so far, so fast.

'The pieces have been put together,' she says with glee. *'The broadsheets have traced the coincidence of the Parsifals' waning finances with the spate of robberies. No one, of course, believes* her *guilty of being but an accessory – anyone who knows Cordelia Parsifal swears she's too dim to think up anything so devilish clever. But then equally,'* the woman continues, *'no one believes she did not know what he did. No one believes a husband wouldn't confide his deepest failures, his darkest solutions, to the woman he loved,*

and their devotion to each other is well known,' sneers the gaoler's helpmeet.

'But why?' asks Cordelia when she can get a word in edgeways. 'Why would we do all this and then flaunt the spoils in such a stupid manner?'

'Oh,' Mistress Lamb says, 'the penny-papers know that's where they ran aground! The necklace was new, assumed unseen by anyone but the dead. Edvard rashly, arrogantly, presented it to her. How fortuitous that Mrs Considine – wonderful woman, devoted friend – had been shown the thing by poor Mrs Agnew before her untimely death!'

'Where are my children?' asks Cordelia, over and over, never getting an answer, but it does not stop her asking again.

By the third day, though, the goodwife has worn out her bile, and even in her malicious stupidity she realises that Cordelia's hurt bewilderment is not an act; no mummer, this sad and terrified captive. She has stopped spitting in the water and simply hands over the meals, although their quality remains unimproved. And still Cordelia has seen no one, no lawyer, no representative of the courts, no friend or acquaintance, no priest to offer succour or damn her soul; not even Mr Farringdale – who could surely clear up any financial questions! – has been. No one has formally presented the charges to her, though she cannot help but know of what she accused. She's wondered if all matters have simply been addressed to Edvard, if she's been wrong in her anger towards him; if her husband is negotiating – nay, fighting for – their futures. Their lives.

On the sixth day, when the gaoler's wife brings the morning repast, she also leads in Bethany and Cordelia dares to hope.

'Bethany! Are the children all right? Are they safe?'

'They are safe, sister, never fear. I have the care of them.'

The tears she's held in, even two days ago when she began to bleed and cramp, and knew the child – suddenly, strangely precious – was gone, spring at last. Cordelia's heart, so battered and bruised, leaps, certain somehow that she is saved.

But Bethany's mournful expression tells her soon enough that *this is not over*. They hold hands through the bars, and sink to sit, Cordelia on filthy straw, Bethany on cold stone flags. The goodwife watches for a few long moments, then shuffles away. From her beaded velvet purse, Bethany pulls a wrapped napkin and passes it over. Knowing that the children are in no danger makes Cordelia ravenous, and she wolfs the smuggled pastries so quickly that she feels sick; the queasiness doesn't make her stop eating.

'Have you seen Edvard?' she asks, watching greedily as Bethany hands her another napkin, more pastries. 'Has he spoken to the lawyers? To Mr Farringdale? How much longer will this misunderstanding go on? I simply don't understand, Bethany, how it happened, why Bella would say such a thing.'

'Dellie, you must prepare yourself. Life is going to be very different.'

'It will take a long time for us to live down the humiliation, certainly. But once we're released, once people realise this has all been a terrible mistake…' she takes a sharp breath. 'A trial…'

'There will be no trial, Cordelia,' Bethany says. 'There will be no public shaming – or at least nothing worse than there has already been.'

'We may be grateful for that small mercy then.'

'But they say there must be seen to be a reckoning.'

'But we are innocent! Bethany, you know we are!'

'Yes, sister, I know you are. But…'

'What of Edvard and Mr Farringdale? Are they not mounting a defence? Edvard was with me on the night the Agnews were killed.'

'Ah, but you would say that, wouldn't you?' Bethany's eyes are weirdly bright, then she looks away. 'Or that is what *they* will say – and the newsmen have already judged you – what dutiful wife wouldn't lie for her husband? And they consider you a dutiful wife, Cordelia, if a stupid one. They think you merely obeyed your master's wishes.'

'But what about Edvard? What has he told them?'

Bethany pauses, as if choosing her words carefully to spare feelings, then realises that there is no gentle way forward. 'Dellie, my dear, your Edvard is dead.'

Seeing incomprehension, she goes on, kindly, 'He took his own life, hanged himself.' She points to the wall behind Cordelia where there are metal shackles set high, but not so high that a man of Edvard's height couldn't reach to loop his own belt, then wrap it around his neck and lean forward slowly, oh so slowly, until all his breath was gone in a terrible, slow asphyxiation. 'It's as good a confession as anything, Cordelia. He gave up his right to defend himself – and you.'

Edvard is gone. He's left her alone, alone in this hole, in this morass. Her husband, her *protector*, the man who could not bear to allow her a speck of independence, is no longer here – by his own choice.

'He was weak, sister, like they all are: with fortune frittered away, he was a failure as businessman, husband, and father.' There is a flash of contempt, quickly covered, as if she realises now is not the time. 'And all the humiliation of the past days, having everyone who counts think he's a thief and a murderer…'

'But you do not, do you?' asks Cordelia quietly.

'Of course not. But with his money gone through bad investment, wasted on foolish ventures it certainly makes him look guilty. For God's sake, Dellie, he was the only man not to make a profit from the Antiphon venture!' Bethany says in disgust and the comment hooks into Cordelia's memory; she begins to think, trying to swim through the numbness. She is not really listening.

'I have some money put aside, I can take care of the children. Henry can still go to university. I will teach Victoria to be self-sufficient. And Torben will learn to grow up soon enough.'

'How did you know about Antiphon?' asks Cordelia.

Bethany pauses, thinks, answers, 'Edvard told me.'

'No, he didn't,' Cordelia says. Had her sister said she'd read this information in one of the penny-papers, Cordelia would have believed her without question. 'He didn't. He didn't tell me, he certainly wouldn't have told you. I heard them talking at the Ball: everyone else made money, but he seemed to think we had not.'

Bethany remains silent.

'The woman here tells me we'd been having financial problems, problems Edvard never mentioned.'

Her sister's face freezes, as if she's deciding what to do, then she finally smiles: the deception is no longer worth her effort. The mask peels away, leaving the true Bethany utterly unveiled before her, the Bethany Cordelia has only glimpsed as if in a bad dream.

'Oh, sister,' she pleads, 'what have you done?'

'What I wanted to.'

'Why, Bethany? We never refused you anything!'

'I lived as a beggar in your house! Everything I had I had to ask for – you gave me nothing of my own! Always let me live on your charity.'

Cordelia's mouth moves, but no sound comes.

'So I started taking what I needed at first, then what I wanted. Others have been willing to help… and those who were not were easily enough disposed of.'

'That boy…'

'A pretty distraction, useful until he got squeamish, until your

Merry maid gave him a conscience. He didn't want to…' says Bethany, almost reluctantly. She looks at Cordelia, shakes her head, and repeats, 'He didn't want to hurt them. Wasn't averse to stealing, but he lacked the backbone to kill, even though leaving them alive would mean our discovery. Men are weak like that.'

'You gave Edvard the necklace. You stole it from the Agnews, murdered them…'

'He told me to find something *special* for you. Fool. Didn't ask where I'd found it, didn't question the amount I demanded.'

'He set aside his pride, asked for your aid. He opened his home to you and you…' Cordelia seems to feel the sticky warmth of Odela Agnew's blood on her neck where her jewellery had once sat. 'How did you… how did you take *our* money? He'd not have asked your advice about investments…'

'Mr Farringdale can be most accommodating when given the right incentive.'

'Mr Farringdale…'

'I have found, sister, that once you discover someone's secrets you hold their heart in your hand.'

Cordelia thinks of Mr Farringdale and his spurned suit, his hopes and heartache; how long has Bethany strung him along? What promises has she made that he would betray his employer? 'My children—'

'—will be safe so long as you are compliant. I have enough money to save the house, indeed, to buy up all those buildings Edvard owned and rented out to butchers and bakers and candlestick makers! – they will be sold cheaply to get rid of them, to wipe out the shame. Mr Farringdale will kindly see to that for me.'

'Why would he—'

'Have you ever been to an orphanage? Have you visited the one in this fair city?' Bethany rocks back a little as if easing the stiffness of sitting on the floor. 'Oh, I know Edvard gives – gave – regular donations, but I don't think either of you ever actually went to see the conditions. Of course, it is considerably better than the place you left me for over a year.'

'We came and got you! As soon as we knew what had happened we came! As soon as we could.'

'But you didn't, did you? *You* didn't come. You sent Mr Farringdale, didn't you? Thin, yearning Mr Farringdale, with his darkest of desires, desires that could only be sated on a child… but you sent *him*.' She gives a bitter laugh. 'Oh sweet sister, how innocent you are. Now consider Victoria: she's older than I was when he came for me… perhaps she'll be safer.' There is a moment when every particle of Bethany's hurt, her agony, shows in her eyes, and Cordelia thinks the girl might cry; she reaches a hand, all scratches and grimy nails, to her sister. Bethany pulls away, straightens.

'Bethany, I'm so—'

'Don't say you're sorry, sister, it's far too little, too late,' she quietly says, then hisses, 'Bad enough you left me with Mother in the first place! Bad enough you took Mrs Bell with you when you left, took away the only person who might have protected me!' Bethany swallows. 'I was her best girl, but with you gone, who do you think she turned on?'

Tears pour down Cordelia's cheeks, streaming through the filth. She thinks on her own hours locked in the cupboard by their mother, learning hard lessons that made her only too glad to leave when Edvard offered that avenue… not considering who she left behind, not caring that whatever she escaped would be visited on her sibling. She takes in the change in Bethany's face, the expression that says her sister is a husk hollowed out by her past, eternally washed through by need and greed; a shell that can never be filled. There is a fire in her eyes that says her steps across the precipice have been taken, that she's chosen the dark over the light.

'And when – oh when, sister! – I at last arrived here what did I find but that you'd all but adopted Mrs Bell's bastard daughter! Don't look like that, Dellie. What an idiot you are: can you not see it in their faces? Their eyes? That little nose with its tilt? Oh, you're so blind you deserve everything that happens to you!' Bethany sits back from the bars, shaking, and Cordelia isn't certain whether it is from laughter, sadness or hatred, or perhaps some strange mix of all three. 'You'd taken in that little accident, that stray, that base-born by-blow, and left me to the tender mercies of Mother, then Mr Farringdale!'

'Oh, Bethany, I'll tell. I'm going to tell.' But Cordelia is trembling, rocked by her sister's revelations and betrayal, by her own crushing guilt.

Bethany shakes her head a little wistfully. 'No, you won't, Cordelia. You really won't.'

'I will shout until someone listens. Edvard still has friends, influential friends—'

'Edvard is dead, sister. He is a disgrace; all those friends have distanced themselves from you both.' She smiles, as if reasonable.

'Mrs Bell—'

'Is gone, sister, as is Merry. Clever tarts, scarpering like that.' She laughs, mirthless. 'Your beloved Mrs B took her *true* daughter and left you to rot.'

'The brooch…' says Cordelia, wishing she could apologise to Merry for every ill thought she'd ever had about her. Feeling the loss of her and Mrs B almost as keenly as that of her children.

Bethany's eyes are lit with malevolence as she answers obliquely, 'Little sweet thing with her principles. The moment Japheth set eyes on her, spoke with her, he turned soft. He was as bad as you, setting me aside for Merry.'

'It wasn't enough to take him from her?'

'It's never enough, sister!' shouts Bethany, spittle shooting from between her lips to splash hot on Cordelia's hand. Then she calms down, takes a deep breath. 'You are utterly without allies. Everything you once had is mine. Now, think on this: what will you do to keep your children from harm?'

Cordelia says nothing, feels ice forming in her throat.

'Your husband took the easy way out. Perhaps you might do the same? A strip from the hem of your so lovely gown would be a tidy noose. No? Then as I said, justice must be seen to be done. If you confess to being Edvard's accomplice, I will take care of your children. Keep your mouth shut, sister, and your babies will be safe.'

Cordelia stares at Bethany, trying in vain to see the little girl who'd come to live with her so long ago. She thinks of Merry rubbing salt into the doorstep to keep wickedness at bay, all for naught when they didn't know the wickedness was already inside the house.

Bethany leans forward again, her voice soft. 'One word out of place and I will drown the little darlings, I promise you. It won't matter if anyone believes you because by then your beloved hearts will be dead, I swear.' She fixes Cordelia with a hateful glare and speaks in a clipped fashion. 'The Prince has agreed: one year in the Rosebery hulks if you confess. Not such a long time. One year and your *dearlings* returned to you and I'll let you all go far away – but if you ever say a word of this, sister, I will find you. What do you think, Cordelia? Willing to risk it?'

* * *

Before dawn, Cordelia is woken and her dress, now a ruined purple rag, is taken and in its place she is given a bleached calico shift, rough and itchy, and a coarse woollen cape too short to offer any real warmth. Other women are led up from the depths beneath Cordelia's cell, and she is chained to them. Their ankles are fitted with shackles already speckled with rust and dried blood, which immediately bite into tender flesh, drawing new vital fluid to add to the old. Cordelia, eyes grainy with an excess of tears and a lack of sleep, not to mention the dust that rises constantly from the flaking stone walls and the straw on the floor of her cell, can feel only the sting of the rose tattoo they applied to her shoulder as soon as she gave her confession. Though the process took barely five minutes, rubbed by the coarse fabric of her attire the scarring burns constantly, as if the acid is daubed over and over.

The women, all twelve, are hustled out through the cobbled courtyard. As they wait to be loaded into an enclosed dray, Cordelia looks around, sees the portcullis, and in the voids between the metal latticework finds two faces, familiar and haggard: Mrs B and Merry. She'd know them anywhere though they've covered their bright hair with scarves and have thick travelling cloaks drawn around them. How could she not have seen? When a newly stout Mrs Bell left to collect her niece all those years ago, the gift of a dead sister never before mentioned, how had Cordelia not realised? Both reach a hand through the bars as if to touch her, as if to pull her to safety. Cordelia clasps her own hands and presses them to her heart; fights the urge to run to them, screaming questions, begging.

Instead she nods, then the gaoler prods her in the back hard enough to leave a bruise, and she mounts the rickety stairs up into the body of the wagon with thin wooden benches on either side, and only one window, set in the door, too high for any of the seated passengers to see much but the blue of the winter sky. Six a side, those at the farthest reach must stretch their legs to accommodate the short span of the shackles. Cordelia, at the end of the human chain and nearest the door, is spared that at least. The woman beside her has no front teeth and her breathing is harsh, the exhalations rotten. Two inmates across from her begin to talk, low voices, low words. They gossip because it makes them feel better, to know someone is worse off than they are.

'The rich ones got no backbone, not strong enough to live through loss,' one says, and laughs to show she too has fewer than the usual complement of teeth.

'Position's all they care about. When they lose their place on the ladder…' the other shrugs, looks at Cordelia as if she knows who she is, leans in to speak directly to her. 'Well, they're brave enough to do their terrible deeds, but too weak to take responsibility for 'em.'

Cordelia merely stares. She stares so long that they become uncomfortable, they shift and shuffle, avoid her gaze, stop talking.

And though she wants to, she still does not fight. She does not scream or shout or leap to her feet. She feels instead a stiffening in her back, realises it's the spine Bethany always said she'd lost. She knows pleas will fall on deaf ears, that no one will believe the tale she might tell. She does not fight because of her children, because in her silence lies their salvation.

So she says nothing, ignores the gibes and the acid-burn of the tattoo. She sways with the motion of the carriage, all the rattling, rolling, clattering way to Rosebery Bay. Three days with the other women and the smell they make, not allowed out for piss breaks except in the morning and the evening, fermenting in the back, the rank stench of body odour and shit and vomit.

All on the road to Rosebery Bay.

* * *

Cordelia dreams of the fire, of the warmth and the heat, of the sound of the logs as they crackle and burn and weaken, shifting as they become less solid. She dreams of the time that Henry once tucked chestnuts in the coals. In reality, they popped and exploded, giving all and sundry a fright. In her fancies one flies from the hearth, is propelled towards her skirt. The fine lace, highly flammable, takes the spark like a lover and the trail of flame speeds up her dress, up the bodice, then up the left sleeve. She uses her right hand to try to pat out the flickering red-gold, and succeeds only in burning her fingers. The dream-flames bite into her upper arm, her shoulder.

She does not like this fantasy – it is not the refuge she has come to expect, to desire, to need. She shakes herself awake and finds, much to her distress, that the flames have jumped the slender gap between sleeping and waking; she can see them through the barred window, an orange glow brightens her tiny cell despite the white-grey billowing in the passageway, trickling under her door. She has woken to shouts and cries and screams and coughs, but no sound of the turnkeys coming to release any of the women on this ship.

Cordelia curses, despairs that the smoke did not take her as soon as it could, that it did not kill her while nestled in the memories where she wished to lie. She backs into a corner, and the space she has just vacated is gradually filled again: at first there is ash, then cinders, then embers, and finally blackened and half-eaten planks as the ceiling caves in. She stares through the dust that shifts on the breeze, giving her glimpses of the open maw of the night sky, with its twinkling teeth of stars.

Freedom, above.

So far away.

Briefly she thinks of stepping into the smoke, breathing deeply. Or onto the flaming timbers that begin to crackle once again, slowly burning their way through the floor on which they've landed. Asphyxia or incineration are her only choices.

But no. Somewhere in the back of her mind she knows that if she's survived everything thus far, she will not give up lightly. She pulls the thin straw-filled sack of a mattress from the cot she's slept in all these months – not a proper bunk as she's in one of the last cells to be added to this ship, which does not sail anywhere, so no care has been given to ensuring beds are nailed down and secure – and exposes the slats she feels against her bony back each night. Cordelia throws the mattress-sack away; it lands on the pile of planks and the fire grows large with new fodder. She heaves the rickety frame onto its short end and prays it will be strong enough and long enough.

As she steps to the first rung, her skirt kicks back with the movement and brushes against the inferno of the mattress. The line of flame she'd only imagined becomes a reality, leaping up her poor calico gown, strangely focused as it moves to her left forearm, upper arm, shoulder, nibbles at her hair. She hears the creaking and complaining of the ship as its body is consumed and in the coldest part of her brain she knows that if she stops to swat the flares, she will surely die; she will lose her chance, her momentum, her precious few seconds to get out.

A burning brand of a woman, she scampers up her makeshift ladder, and scrambles onto the deck, which is beginning to tilt. The flames on her shoulder are eating, eating, eating at the rose tattoo that was put there to show her as a thief, a sneak, a convict, a murderer for all they said "accessory". It scorches like the acid used to etch the design there in the first place. She bats at the tiny, deadly flashes as her eyes take in the swaying masts, the last of the dirty canvas sails, that are orange then black, then crumble in the wind. She wheels and turns like a dancing doll, out of control, turning in a decaying spiral that finally sees her at the rails. She hits the strakes, loses her balance, and pitches headfirst over the side.

For moments she is free, she flies, the fire seems to pull away from her and her skin does not know that it's been hurt, then the waters of Rosebery Bay meet her, hard black glass. At first she is against it, then she is through it, and finally she is lost, travelling a'down, a'down, a'down, farther and farther from the dark sky and its starry teeth. Farther and farther, to where dreams no longer live.

A'down, a'down, a'down and Cordelia Parsifal, wife, mother, sister, tallow-wife, lets go of all that she is, of all that she has been. She is free, suddenly light, spinning away as if a great pressure had been released... yet in a moment there is a change, vital and irresistible. She hears the voice of the woman in the prison coach, her sly dig that the rich ones got no backbone, not strong enough to live through loss. Something finds her, pulls at her, drags her back to her body, insists her spirit remain.

She does not have the energy to fight life anymore than she did death. The impulse will not let her go, it takes possession of her limbs, her aching arms and legs, and makes them move, kick and stroke, kick and stroke, kick and stroke.

Up and up and up. Above her the surface of the water is silver and midnight blue, where the moon sits and waits for her return. Waits for her to make herself anew.

WHAT SHINES BRIGHTEST BURNS MOST FIERCELY

Mr Isambard Farringdale knew he was being followed by someone well versed in the art of not being seen.

He'd had the sense of it for some days now; it began as a kind of low-level itch at the back of his neck and grown as time passed, creeping across his scalp like a spider, slithering down his thin spine until it coiled at the base like a loving snake he couldn't shake. Yet every time he looked over his shoulder as he travelled the streets of Lodellan, either crowded or empty, there was nothing and no one in sight. He thought to become cleverer, more cunning, slipping swiftly around corners then peeking out to catch any pursuer unawares, but it never worked. All he managed was to frighten several servant girls on their way to the Busynothings Markets, to startle a costermonger who was understanding, and an ironmonger who was not.

Then he'd thought perhaps the explanation was less simple than he'd at first believed: that the occurrence was not mortal, but *other*. Rumours and reports have trickled through the city in recent days, tales of strange things walking by day as easily by night, of eldritch influences taking flight, of spectres and spirits making their displeasures or whims known. So many fearful whispers running through Lodellan at all levels that the Prince has demanded explanations of the church prelates. Isambard's heard that god-hounds have been sent forth to investigate; with the city's pre-eminence as a place where no witchcraft will be tolerated, how can they do anything but?

This evening, though, the gentleman in question has shrugged off his disquiet – for some urges are too strong for even amorphous fear to defeat – and attended at his favourite private club for entertainment few folk would enjoy, admit to, or even countenance. Mr Farringdale knows full well that his pastimes would draw, at the very least, opprobrium from upstanding citizens and he is careful to ensure the truest nature of his pleasures is kept under wraps. The kind of people who share his predilections are equally circumspect; and the objects of their intense interest… well, they are given no opportunity to complain.

Puffed with indulgence and warmed by copious cups of mulled cherry wine and blackberry port, Mr Farringdale steps from the unprepossessing doorway which hides Madame Arkady's House of Curiosities (a name unknown to all but its clientele) and into the cobbled back street that runs off Half-moon Lane. He draws himself up to his full height, all five feet two, does his best to stride in a dignified manner in the direction of his home. But the alcohol gets the better of him and the best he manages is a sort of strange listing canter, the heels of his buckled boots making a *tap-tap-clack* on the stones beneath his feet. He giggles. He giggles quite loudly and for quite some time, until the sense of being watched starts to haunt him again, and the spider-snake twitches awake. Isambard sobers a little, quickens his step, tripping more than he would like, until at last he is at his own door, fumbling the keys, forgetting to lift the latch so he panics, thinking himself shut out… then calms and does what needs doing.

Inside, he turns the lock with shaking fingers, shivers. He allows no servants to live in, so the hearths have been set but not lit in anticipation of his return. Mr Farringdale presses his forehead to the polished oak of the entrance and waits for his heartbeat to slow, for his pulse to stop thrusting against his skin; he swears he can see the thud and thump of it at his wrists where the veins are terribly blue.

The house – new, purchased with his ill-gotten Parsifal gains – is silent, so quiet. There is no noise at all. Nothing, no sound of drawn breath as a warning, nothing except the words, 'Good evening, Isambard.'

Mr Farringdale takes one great dancing, twisting leap to face his visitor. His eyes seek the shadows in vain until there is the scratch and spit of a vesta and a tiny flame throws a halo on a round face. Soon illumination spreads through the rich front parlour where no one spends much time at all – Mr Farringdale has neither need nor wish for clients nowadays – the caller lighting lamps and candelabra as he finds them, then finally touches the spark to the kindling in the hearth. Mr Farringdale's dark eyes follow his movements.

The guest is neither tall nor short, but somewhere in between. His hair is a mop of golden curls. His face is a series of soft circles, the rosy cheeks, the eyes, the mouth, even the tip of the nose, but not in a clownish way. All are well formed, perfectly proportioned and pleasing, as if the features are constructed to not excite the least fear or concern: a visage with no angles, no edges, is far less threatening. Or Mr Farringdale suspects he is intended to find it so, although he doesn't know where that thought comes from.

'Good evening, Isambard,' repeats the young boy – youth? man? – and gives his unwilling host a smile meant to allay fears.

Mr Farringdale's fears remain firmly unallayed.

The boy's outfit says "affluence": the trews are a dark velvet (midnight blue? hard to tell in this light), his cream shirt sporting a frilled collar trimmed with golden thread, and his frock coat cerulean, velvet again, embroidery creeping across the lapels: leaves in green, cherries or apples in red, things that begin as birds but flow into beasts, all picked out in silver. His footwear, however, tells a different story. Although well made, the boots are dusty and worn, the toes scuffed; they whisper of a life hard-lived, of steps taken on rough paths, many under trying circumstances. These boots give lie to the dandy's indolent air.

Then the youth's smile widens and he bends into a flourishing bow, his left arm sweeping back like a wing, the hand at the end of his right executing a detailed sort of dance. For a moment, he is a grandee of some great and mysterious court. Then he straightens and once more he's a misplaced jester or ringmaster, Isambard can't quite choose.

'My name is Jacopo,' says the boy, 'and I am come to offer you an exchange that will benefit us both.'

Mr Farringdale raises a brow, feeling the sweat break from his sloping forehead, the telltale itch begin at the tip of his beaky nose, the surest sign that his fear has peaked and now he is planning for his own advantage. He relaxes slightly, his curiosity piqued at the thought of a bargain, though he has no need of money. Feeling less endangered, his bartering instinct rouses, however. He does not wish to be won over too quickly, appear too easily placated; no one blamed him outright, but the people with fortunes wondered how it was he allowed so much of Edvard Parsifal's to slip away, and he's no longer welcome in polite society. Many question how he afforded this house when his master finished his life at the end of a tightly knotted belt. Fortunately, he has reserves, many of them, skimmed off the top of the Antiphon profits, but it won't hurt, he thinks, to have *more*. If the Parsifals' tale of woe illustrated anything it's that life can be most unexpected. And he has a belief – often shared by those who began with very little – that greater funds might help his position. Might make him acceptable once more.

'Were you following me? Was it you?' His voice is higher than he would like, but the question is out, too late to change his mind.

The youth's face falls, his expression a pretty mix of shame and regret. His body moves, a tremor that transmits itself down through his torso, thence to arms and legs, hands and feet. As if a current has passed through him. Isambard is fascinated, although part of him wonders if it's an act designed to distract, to charm and disarm him. If Isambard's interest ran to boys, it might work.

'It was indeed, and I offer my humblest apologies if my observations caused you some distress. But as a man of intellect, not given to rash actions, you will understand my desire to make sure you were whom I sought. My employer bid me be circumspect. It would not be wise to approach the wrong individual with what I am offering – and I do feel now that you are precisely *the* man with whom I wish to deal.'

In spite of himself, Mr Farringdale is flattered. 'Your employer?'

The lad continues. 'I'm aware that what I ask for is valuable – as is your time, which is also rare and irreplaceable – so I am prepared to give something equally valuable, rare and irreplaceable. A one-of-a-kind *objet* in return.'

The youth produces from his pocket a strange item: a chrysalis of a thing, translucent, transparent. It starts out the size of a pellet, then grows before Isambard's astonished gaze. An egg – chicken, goose, turkey, eagle – until it is an ovoid a foot high, about eight inches in circumference and takes up all the space between Jacopo's palms and threatens to overflow. Mr Farringdale shuffles closer and the boy turns so he might better regard what is being offered. The shell is glowing, pellucid: through it can be seen what lies inside.

It is a girl, like a smallish doll. Isambard makes out the dark golden hair, the high cheekbones, the rosebud mouth, the chin jutting forward, a little pugnacious and, when she opens her lids suddenly, the bright green of her eyes. He realises why she is so very familiar: it is Bethany Lawrence as she once was, so delicate and defenceless. Not his first, not by a long shot, but certainly his most desired, most earnestly yearned for, his most dangerous, and longest loved though she's grown well beyond his preferred *vintage*. She'd lodged inside him, however, and refused to leave; he wonders if it was some revenge magic of her own, or if he has, somewhere deep down, a conscience, guilt for all the pain he caused her. In part, it's why he could never refuse her anything, especially the demands she at first couched as requests. To a certain extent, it is because he feared – fears – being exposed for what he was and what he'd done… and continues to do to others. He shakes at the idea this boy knows.

'She'll grow, but only so much. She'll never be any older than when she was *yours*, when you took her.' The boy's voice trembles and Mr Farringdale looks at him, suspicious, but there is nothing in Jacopo's face to say he disapproves, that he judges. There is only a strange brightness that Isambard realises provides more of the light in the room than the lamps. But the girl in the chrysalis takes his attention again, her gaze meeting and holding his. Mr Farringdale's fingers stretch forth, almost touching the oval until, at the last moment, Jacopo pulls it away.

'She'll be yours again, on one condition.'

Isambard is unsurprised but resentful to hear that this will not be free. Yet he knows himself well enough: he will have this thing. He will do whatever it takes to have her again as she lives still in his mind. His one love, did she but know it. No, he thinks, she knows full well and uses it to her advantage; it's that she doesn't *care*. He doesn't dwell on the irony of the girl he so injured and possessed so very young, now having a grip on his soul.

'How do you know?' asks Mr Farringdale, dread limning his very being. 'How can you know?'

'Ah, Isambard, my ways and means are my secrets, and that's how it shall stay. It's sufficient that I – and my employer – *know*, don't you think?' He waits until Isambard nods unwillingly. 'So. You'll have your heart's desire on one simple condition. In exchange, Mr Farringdale, I ask for something that weighs nothing! Light as a feather, you'll barely feel it go: information.'

Isambard shivers. He knows that substance is *not* light. It does not float. It is a thing to weigh one down. The right kind will drag a man to the bottom of the sea and keep him there until flesh rots from his bones. Information, when it is known, comprehended, when its value becomes obvious to the holder, then it is *knowledge*, and that is the most dangerous burdensome thing of all. He says none of this however.

'I need to know two things. Firstly, what happened to the necklace, the Agnew Necklace? Secondly, I need an address for Mistress Bethany Lawrence and the Parsifal children. I know she no longer resides in this fair city.'

Isambard blinks; his mind darts like a caged thing. He will tell one thing quite willingly, the other… he plays for time.

'The Princess Royal has the necklace.' He hurries on, seeing Jacopo's disbelieving expression. 'There was no one left, of the Agnews, you understand. The estate wound up in the royal coffers, as will happen when there are no heirs, and Armandine claimed the jewellery for her own. She had greatly admired the piece at the Ball, so imagine her delight to find it… orphaned.'

He does not mention the rumours of the effect this had on the royal household, of the discontent it sowed between the Princess Royal and her lover, each of whose desire for said necklace apparently outstripped their desire for each other. He does not think it will matter to the boy. After a long moment, Jacopo nods, accepts what he's been told. Isambard can tell, though, that the lad is calculating some sort of odds.

'And the other matter, Isambard?'

'I cannot… You must understand: she put her trust in me.'

'You can and you will.' Jacopo holds the chrysalis in front of him so Mr Farringdale can better see the girl inside. She bats her lashes and smiles, pulls at his dark core. The youth's tone changes, becomes less friendly. 'Miss Lawrence left you, Isambard, she left you here all alone. After everything you'd done for her. For *your* Bethany.'

The warning voice in Mr Farringdale's head becomes smaller, quieter as the other voice, the one that tells him he is the injured party, that he deserved better, becomes louder, more strident. Angry not at him, no, but at her, she who caused his misery, who complicated his life, who demanded and took so much, then deserted him. Here. Alone.

'Breakwater,' he says, his pitch rising even as his heart thrills at the betrayal and the thought of the girl in the egg.

Jacopo nods as if it is something he suspected. 'I will need proof, of course.'

For a moment, Isambard's mind is blank, then he remembers the letter, the one and only communication. He rifles through a drawer in the corner bureau, until he finds it, pressed between the pages of an old diary, finger marks visible as are port stains; he imagines there are tears, too, their ghosts blotting the onion-thin paper. The tears are his. It is all business, this epistle, but it contains the address to which he was to send the last of the household goods, and details of her new bank accounts for a final transfer of funds. She kept no property in Lodellan after all; perhaps she found its streets unexpectedly haunted. He holds the sheet with a traitor's shaking hands, but the voice in his head assures him that when he has the girl in the chrysalis, what need will he have of this cold folio?

His faltering steps bring him to within a few feet of the youth and he holds out the letter, which flutters only a little with his emotion. Jacopo takes it, barely glances at it and thrusts it into his pocket, crinkling it so that Mr Farringdale must bite down on a gasp of imagined pain. Then the boy says, as if an afterthought, 'And the children? She took them with her? *All* of them?'

Isambard shivers, swallows. The girl in the egg nods at him encouragingly. 'She took the boys.'

'And Victoria?'

'Sent away some months before. To a cousin, Miss Lawrence said.' But he knew now just as he had known then, there were no cousins. 'I don't have an address, but I believe it was to Seaton St Mary.'

Mr Farringdale thinks the boy blanches, his glow dimming briefly, then Jacopo nods again.

'Thank you, Isambard. I do believe you've played fair with me. But I am no fool. I must ascertain what you've told me about the necklace – what good would I be to my employer if I were easily duped?' He smiles. 'I'll leave this here with you as a gesture of good faith, but be aware that she will not be freed – will not be yours – until I return and open this clever cage. If I do not locate what I am looking for in the palace, I shall simply take her away. Do we understand each other?'

Mr Farringdale nods. He has told his truth, his only fear is that the boy will fail to find the jewellery, will think him a liar and refuse his prize.

Jacopo snatches a knee rug from the back of an armchair no one ever uses, to make a nest before the fireplace, then carefully balances the egg on it. He stands, dusting off the knees of his trousers as if Mr Farringdale's day-maid's labours leave much to be desired, then he points at the chrysalis.

'Tend the fire, Isambard, it will benefit the egg. But don't touch it – the egg, I mean – it is not yours until I return and gift it to you, after I've tested the quality of your information.' He gives a smile, as if between friends sharing a great joke, but Mr Farringdale notices how Jacopo's teeth show and how sharp they are.

* * *

There were other ways he could have taken what he needed from Mr Farringdale, but he didn't fancy swimming around in the man's memories. Didn't want to carry that with him. Besides, *she* was very specific about how he was to deal with Isambard; she was quite intent that things be done in this manner.

Jacopo pushes all other thoughts from his mind and concentrates on finding his way to the square, the great square. He is not familiar with this city, having only been here once with the troupe, and despite the past few days of following his prey, mapping his habits. Jacopo likes to know his mark as well as he possibly can. He's been in the house on more than one occasion, sometimes when its occupant was at home, sometimes not. He has flicked through the contents of wardrobes and dressers, walked around the special room with its rose-pink curtains and coverlets where the small visitors stay, however briefly, before they are inevitably found to be not quite right. Part of Jacopo understands Mr Farringdale's wanting and dissatisfaction, but no part of him understands the man's desires.

He steps out into the well-lit public space that flows around the Cathedral like a moat. The building is huge, a vaunting spire, gothic towers and flying buttresses, yet all in a strange harmony. There are no guards, at least no human ones; on the portico of the Cathedral he can see the smoky flashes of the wolf-hounds, the resurrected beasts who serve as ecclesiastical guardians of the structure. They are rare, these things, and old, the knowledge of their making lost when the church crushed the Doll-makers' Guild, claiming the toys (and beasts) they made offended against God. There was an old tale, flimsy with age, of the fox-haired woman who'd created the guardian wolves, seduced the archbishop of the time, then fled. No god-hound had ever found her – she was a witch, of course – and Jacopo's grandmother Theodora had observed that with no small amount of satisfaction.

The wolves harm only those with ill-intent, Grandmamma had said when he was a little lad dandled on her knee. I've no ill-intent *here*, thinks Jacopo, and hopes his logic works; inside the palace things will change. He straightens his spine, stands tall and sturdy, and crosses the square, thinking determinedly of anything but what he plans to do.

Jacopo recalls Grandmamma's stories: of how she learnt the secret byways of the palace and Cathedral through boredom and accident. Fated to wait once a week while Pinchpen the Treasurer tallied all the taxes that might be counted as Theodora's in her role as Princess of Lodellan (she was required to affix her seal to his ledgers), she'd wandered and explored while the money-rat concerned himself with his counting. As he lost himself in the various coffers and caskets of gold and silver, crates and sacks of goods in kind, she meandered, and in doing so she found secret passages and false walls, hidden doors and staircases that went deep, deep, deep, joining the palace with the great Cathedral and a variety of other buildings of varying degrees of salubriousness, mansions and public houses, dens of iniquity and shops frequented by the rich and richer. She'd wondered every time she saw the piles of coin – small avalanches that threatened to cover the feet and ankles of Pinchpen's minions – how many children went hungry, how many families slept cold, how many farms and businesses failed all so Lodellan's Prince and Treasurer and Archbishop might hoard all this like bipedal dragons. So that the few might be assured of yet one more ermine cloak, one more purple silk robe, one more golden tasselled cushion for the comfort of tender buttocks. Jacopo remembers how she told him she'd ensured the leftovers from the royal table always went to the orphanages, and to inns whose charitable staff gave the foodstuffs to the beggars who gathered in alleyways at night.

Six silver-grey shadows wait for him at the top of the steps. They are faded and he wonders how long it will be before they disappear entirely, remaining only as a disembodied bark, a sly nip, a cold shiver. Boldly, he moves forward, stops, opens his palms so they can sniff at him to their hearts' content. They are puzzled; he wonders if they catch a whiff of his grandmother, long dead, embedded in his being. More likely they think him a strangeling, something like themselves, although not reanimated; just *different*. With confused whimpers, they fall back, let him through, watching him pass over the threshold, their fine large heads tilted to the side, pale eyes questioning, teeth very white. If they notice how Jacopo shudders when he steps inside they give no sign.

There are things buried beneath, he can feel it; unhappy, exhausted things, used long beyond their intended years. The bones are cursed, and more: they are caught in place by their function, to act as a surety for the foundations, not even a pale shade can shuffle through the stones; but they seem somehow newly active, newly angered. They should not be… moving about, however. He senses them, although they were never mentioned by Grandmamma

Theodora in her tales, tales she told him so many times they've become like his own memories. This place, he supposes, has stood for a long time, longer than Theodora lived near it. She could have learned only so many secrets, for not all are spoken, not all leave a trace.

His footsteps echo on the flagstones as he approaches the monumental altar; it's covered in gold and he's sure its value could feed the entire city for a year or more. To his left is the tapestry hiding the entrance to the Chapel of the Thirteenth Apostle; he passes through, notes the arras is becoming threadbare, that St Radagund's very fine beard has thinned and he can see back the way he came. There is the *prie-dieu*; looking closely he can see it's carved with a mix of sea monsters, wolves, and trees. Running his fingers along its underside – and gathering splinters as he does so – Jacopo locates the catch and pulls.

There are aching moments when nothing happens. When he wonders how best to proceed… but then comes a reluctant scrape and scratch of stone on stone and the flags before him whirl aside like a child's puzzle. At his feet there is a square of black, a mouth without teeth but no less daunting for that. *How long since anyone walked this path?*

Jacopo's glow, which he'd dimmed to walk the streets lest anyone see, increases as he enters the darkness to show his way into the catacombs. He tries to ignore the feeling that the earth is closing over him, that the things beneath are stirred by his presence just as the dust is by his well-worn boots. The sense of the unhappily departed grows stronger; Jacopo feels a juddering as a rhythm up and down his spine, a throbbing where the back of his skull meets the nape of his neck. He shakes his head, lets the motion become a shudder, and his radiance wavers.

For all the things Theodora had imparted, drilled into him for whatever reason, all those years ago, she'd not mentioned the buzzing. The angry vibration that began moments after he kindled his own luminescence, as if this sign of his difference caused offence in some unearthly quarter. At first it is simply a noise like a cluster of midges are pursuing him. He picks up the pace, conscious that his footfalls signal nervousness. He cannot help but feel that behind him something shifts and shuffles, its form summoned into being by sheer malicious will, yet it is only when he feels a stab between his shoulder blades – not deep, but painful – that he can force himself to turn and face his demon.

Not far from him, drawing ever closer as the boy's light diminishes from fear, is a man – or the remains of one at least. An old man in the rags of a white cassock trimmed with purple and gold; the brownish stains might once have been bright blood. A ragged cloak retains some evidence of a cobalt hue. As he drifts, his head is sometimes entirely skeletal, others with a thin tight covering of discoloured skin over the frame of the skull, bare of all but a few clumps of yellowed hair. At the end of knife-thin fingers are nails long and sharp, almost waving at the boy.

For a dreadful moment, Jacopo's terror is so great that his flesh loses its gift and he's plunged into darkness as surely as a drowning man plunges through the ice in an unseasonal thaw. He stumbles over his own feet, goes down on hands and knees, feels the scrape of his palms on rough earth. There is no sound, though, nothing but his heartbeat's staccato: where is it? The spectre?

Theodora never mentioned such a thing! At the thought of his grandmother, the light in him stutters, flickers back into being. In its weak flare, the old man – dreadfully closer – flinches, hisses, scuttles away. Jacopo concentrates on memories of Theodora, reading him books, telling him stories, holding him tight, tucking him into bed, and the glimmer around him becomes stronger. His pulse calms when he sees the phantasm cringing. Jacopo climbs to his feet, confidence bolstered. He's incandescent, illuminating the tunnel far ahead of him, and he notes that the ground begins to slope upwards; the coffin niches are filled with nothing more than skeletons and dust and cobwebs. He doesn't turn his back on the haunt, though, is careful as he walks with a lolloping sideways gait, that takes him forward but allows him to keep an eye on the strange wispy thing behind.

At the top of the stone steps, Jacopo locates the hidden door, which proves more stubborn than the entrance to the catacombs, and requires a shoulder to make it budge even after the lever is pulled. The panel pops out unwillingly and Jacopo steps into the magnificent fountain room, dimly lit by sconces, that always featured in Theodora's stories of the troll-wife. He almost slams the panel behind him, but the creature did not follow him up the stairs, had given up any serious pursuit when it realised he could no longer be intimidated; that he had good memories to serve him well. Yet his heart still hammers inside his chest, there is a cold sweat slicking his skin, and he clenches his hands into fists to stop them shaking. He'll not go back this way if he can help it.

Jacopo lets his brilliance go low, until he is blinking to readjust to the dim chamber. The gilded privacy screen Theodora always mentioned, of Hansie and Greta and the sugar cottage, is missing and he's disappointed; he'd waited so long to see it. The tiles are still of gold and silver with crystal and nacre inlays, and the tubs, basins, fountains, and benches carved from white and blue marble remain. Jacopo sees the moon through the ceiling, a sheet of rock crystal. There is the tiny steam hut, the smaller pools – and the larger one, the waters of which move.

A woman rises from the night-dark liquid. Her hair, though damp, flashes fire. She is short, stocky, her hips broad, her breasts heavy, legs muscular. Jacopo is surprised; Grandmamma always said the Lodellan royal family were tall without exception, and slender with extraordinary platinum blonde tresses. But this woman is… not regal. She walks with a determined, plain gait, there is no elegance in her stride. Her face is pretty enough but her expression's dissatisfied. Discontented. Sour. He wonders who she is, but in the end decides it doesn't matter. The palace will have changed since Theodora's day, there are new rooms, new wings. This woman is what he needs at this moment.

He hitches his most charming smile to his lips, takes quiet steps – not silent ones for he does not wish to frighten her – and collects the deep red bath sheet that is lying on the bench closest to the pool. He holds it to cover his attire, so she'll not realise immediately that he is not a servant. He need not worry, she sees him but pays no attention, takes his presence for granted, assumes he is here to tell her something, bring her something, do something for her. She walks into the towel, and this close he can see her eyes are topaz-hued, large. He wraps the thick fabric around her, holds tight for she is not much smaller than he and he suspects she has a peasant's strength. When it becomes clear to her that she's been swaddled, she looks askance at him.

'I'm sorry,' he whispers. 'It's just for a little while.'

And before she can struggle, he fixes his lips to hers and draws the very breath from her and with it all the knowledge she carries. Jacopo feels the transformation coming quickly, and he lays the woman on the bench before he falls.

Memories and emotions rush into him, pressing down on who he is, compacting everything that makes Jacopo, Jacopo. Sedimentary layers of feelings, years of yearning, hurt, thoughts of Amandine that *ache*, ecstasy and exaltation run like mercury through his mind – and his body is changing too. His cock shrivels and pulls up inside him, his hips broaden, his legs shorten, his chest is heavy with tits so big he doesn't know how the woman – Ilse, her name is Ilse, he picks that from the rising swarm of new information – manages to balance. A single drop of milk leaks from a nipple and Jacopo is dizzy with the thought that she is nursing, knows it's the second child, not the first, that she's a breeder for the weak-blooded royalty of this great city. Thinking how quickly she'd become pregnant once more, that the first was barely out of her before the next took hold.

When all the changes are in place, when his own mind reasserts its dominance over the stray recollections, the new knowledge, then he stands. He finds her clothing, a dress of lilac and gold, crumpled on the floor not far away, next to a pair of bejewelled jiffies in soft leather. He puffs out a breath and undresses, folding his own garb neatly. He looks down at Ilse, surveys the fountain room, lights upon the steam hut; she must be hidden in case someone comes in looking, and he cannot have her form for too long, not beyond two hours or, disconnected from her own essence, she will perish.

The air in the hut is cool. The fire has not been lit, the rocks are cold; Ilse will be safe here, she will not be scalded or scorched, nor suffocated by steam. There is a mirror running along one wall and Jacopo pauses. He carefully examines his face, which is hers without a doubt. No one will suspect a thing. He takes a moment, picks through her scrambled memories, finds a thread and pulls it. Follows it. It will lead him to the place where Ilse's malcontent begins and resides.

* * *

Isambard sits cross-legged on the rug, an unaccustomed position he's not adopted since childhood. There's a grinding in his hips that he tries to relieve by rocking from side to side, a protesting tightness in his knee joints, and where his thin ankles touch the floor, pain radiates. He stretches both legs straight out, the heels of his shoes hit the stone of the hearth and make a noise too loud in his empty home, one that startles him even though he knows its source.

Mr Farringdale looks around, embarrassed as if he might be watched, then giggles at his own absurdity. Perhaps there is still too much alcohol in him? He'd have thought it all frightened out in that initial rush of terror when the youth appeared, when he spoke of things he should not have known.

Isambard considers rising, searching through the drawers of his desk or bedside table to find one of the weapons he keeps for just such an eventuality: dealing with a thief. It's not really a threat he's faced much in Lodellan, not since the fall of the Parsifals, which ironically enough was when malfeasance went on the rise. Anyone inclined to criminal activity became quickly acquainted with Bethany Lawrence, and equally quickly came to realise she was not to be trifled with. Mr Farringdale, as her representative since she'd relocated to Breakwater, is virtually untouchable – or thought himself so.

Now he wonders if he dare flee, take the egg with him, run back to Madame Arkady's House of Curiosities, beg her protection. But then… what might happen to the precious thing he's been promised? Its opening depends upon the boy's touch – or did he lie? Is there some magic in his skin? Or might any touch do? Dare Isambard risk it?

* * *

The suite of rooms, hung in shades of green, is decorated like a bower. Seats and tables are in the shapes of flowers, couches and chaises like velvet hillocks, scattered with cushions made to mimic floral fields. The carpets are thick and deep as spring grass, the curtains are ephemeral things, veils of petals falling in a shimmery cataract of cleverly sewn fabric. There is a fountain, delicate and tall, like a calla lily in shining mother-of-pearl.

In very last chamber he finds the bed. It is round, wide, and above it is suspended a canopy in the form of a bluebell, but in a diaphanous olive. Its coverlet is the same colour, an overlapping series of tulip-shaped pieces, so they look almost like dragon scales. Bedside tables of rosewood sit to the left and right, their mirrored backs carved like foxgloves. There is a slatted door leading into a dressing closet. One wall of the bedroom is taken up by a cabinet, a conglomeration of drawers and glass doors. Through the vitreous front, Jacopo sees the glitter of all manner of jewellery.

Chokers and pendants drape around busts of ebony. Bracelets and bangles wait on sculpted hands of the same material. Rings drip from the branches of tiny trees made especially for this purpose. If this is what's on show, the youth wonders at what might be hidden in the drawers. A striking miniature catches his eye, of a girl with palest blonde hair, violet eyes, who stares haughtily from the porcelain; it's so lovely he almost reaches for it, but Jacopo is no thief, or not a common one at least. Everything gleams by lamplight in the quarters of the Princess Royal.

And the thing he has come for has pride of place in the centre of the magnificent repository; there would be no joy in hiding it away. That is the amethyst *she* described, there can be no other like it. Multifaceted, it drinks in all possible illumination, holding the rays in its depths so it seems to pulse and dance with both darkness and a lightness. The band of alternating emeralds and diamonds around it are perfect in the white-gold setting shaped like an opening lily, and the elegant interlocking spirals of the chain are starkly beautiful. Jacopo trembles at its nearness; it is so exquisite yet it feels… there's something icy about it, even from here, as if he can sense grief embedded in the thing.

It is his for the taking. There is neither lock nor latch on its door and in a trice Jacopo has his fingers on the strikingly cold necklace, feels the hardness of the gems, the nip of the precious metal. He retreats from the cabinet, the treasure hung over two fingers, throwing watery colours around the bedroom. But, in his reluctance to crumple it like paper or fabric, he waits too long to hide it. And he knows it in the moment just before a voice spears from behind him.

'Whore,' someone hisses.

Jacopo turns and is struck by the sight of the woman: tall and slender, those eyes, that silvery hair. The Princess Royal herself. He notes the resemblance to the girl in the miniature; he does this as he forgets, momentarily, who he is: not simply Jacopo with his charm and cunning, but now Ilse-Jacopo, with all the baggage of Ilse's loves and hates and hurts. He tilts his head forward, lets his shoulders slump in an attitude of distress; considers his options. They are few; all are brazen. He settles his new features differently, consciously refusing the pull of the malcontent expression on Ilse's face when first he saw her, the one that has become her habit. He smooths out the disappointment, the dissatisfaction, the disaffection. He washes away the reproach – not guilt, no, but the blame she daily apportions to her husband and his sister, for the choices they gave her. As if she had no say in yea or nay, as if she had not grasped at what they offered – a choice of beds, property, glittering rewards when she produced the long-for heir, the unassailable position of mother of the next prince of Lodellan, and more rewards with each and every child she bore – with both greedy hands. All the things she had had, and still had.

Instead Jacopo drops a veil of grief over his visage, softens his eyes, shows the affliction and longing that are buried deep within her, all that she has hidden in her stiff-necked pride. He lets tears collect and bank precariously. His lips part, just a little, and his chin quivers with the force of his – her – pain. Her heart shows in his face; she is naked before her lover for the first time in long, long months.

And Jacopo sees the effect it has on the Princess Royal. Armandine is so struck, so pierced, it is as if she is staggering under a blow. Her own porcelain veneer of disdain cracks as surely as a teacup dropped on a marble floor. She reaches out to Ilse-Jacopo and follows through with a step, uncertain, then another and another, until the tall ethereal princess has her sturdy inamorata in her arms, in an embrace that is unbreakable. Jacopo has no choice, he gives himself up to this, to these sensations, to this love, this reunion. If he makes excuses, tries to flee, he will be caught. He does all the clever things to her that the gypsy girls taught him, all the clever things he'd hoped to do to Tove before she'd disappeared. He takes part, terribly conscious of the minutes ticking by, relieved, at last when Armandine falls away, exhausted, and begins to snore.

Swiftly Jacopo dresses once more, pocketing the necklace that had been discarded on the combined skirts of their fallen robes. He traverses corridors dripping with treasures and art, giving regal nods to any men-at-arms he sees guarding doorways, chatting to pass the hours, and unerringly finds his way to the fountain room. His spine tingles unpleasantly at the thought of the risk he's taking, fighting with the knowledge that he could leave in this form, depart through the grand palace entrance and not be anywhere near the underground passages where the haunt lurks; but then he would leave the woman to die, and Jacopo will cause no more deaths than he must.

He steps inside the overblown bathroom, and releases all his pent-up breath. The steam hut remains closed; at its door, he drops the gown, puts on his own clothes, ill-fitting for the moment, then opens the hut where Ilse sleeps deathly still.

His puts his lips – still tasting of Armandine – to hers and carefully breathes her back into herself. There are moments when he is sure he is too late, then she sighs, hiccups, and starts, eyelids flickering like butterflies. She stares at him and he gives his most reassuring smile… until she screams.

It is a piercing shriek, and he knows it will have been heard by the guards. He slams the door of the steam hut and runs, his carefully thought-out plans in ruin, and darts as quickly as he can through the panel, shoving it closed, bolting into the darkness with only his skin to light his path. He has no choice: he must go back the way he came or risk being found by a mortal threat.

* * *

Mr Farringdale nurses his injured digit: the right forefinger was badly burned where he touched the egg and he'd cried out.

The pain made him weep, made him angry and vengeful. He would run, the prize be damned. He would have Madame Arkady send two of her largest hoodlums, the ones who'd hired themselves out of the assassins market in Breakwater, back here to wait for the youth. To hurt him as much as humanly possible, to get whatever he knew from him, before finally putting him down. And whoever had sent him would know that Isambard Farringdale, right hand of Miss Bethany Lawrence, was not to be taken lightly.

But then he caught sight of the egg, of the lass inside pressed up against the translucent shell, her expression one of concern. And was that… a tear glistening on her pale cheek? Isambard held his hand closer, lost himself in the gaze of the girl in the oval, lost himself in how like the *old* Bethany she was. That expression, just like the first time he'd found her, the first time he'd loved her, and every time he was able to do so again before he had to hand her over to her sister, the uppity Cordelia.

That expression… not unlike the one on Mrs Parsifal's face several times in the weeks leading up to the family's grand disgrace. Did she suspect the pillars of her existence were being chipped away? By her nearest and dearest? Isambard feels, though he will not admit it, that the sting of his finger is minuscule compared to Bethany's and Cordelia's agonies. He feels a fleeting guilt at his part in causing it, but reminds himself that both acts were done from his love.

The tiny girl in the chrysalis holds his gaze, her compassion and kindness are drugs to him; he thinks she appears poised to dance, like the ballerina in a jewellery box. All thoughts of flight subside as he watches, breathless with anticipation.

* * *

The haunt is waiting when Jacopo reaches the bottom of the stairs, drifting back and forth like a stalking wolf. There's a gleeful expression on its malicious face. Despite everything, Jacopo's heart becomes cold with fear and his light flickers drastically.

This is what the spectre has been waiting for and it swoops at him. The boy falls backwards, cowers, cannot force even one greater glimmer from his skin. He watches the creatures come closer, closer, closer…

Then it stops.

It tries again, throwing itself forward and stopping just short of the prone youth. Jacopo is bewildered, yet grateful. Surely it's not the trace of Ilse on his skin? Or the Princess Royal? Then he recalls the one new item in his possession: the necklace. Does the cold grieving thing repel this malign thing? His employer did not tell him its history, but perhaps it is steeped in sins or glory greater than this spiteful wisp ever committed? The apparition hisses in frustration, and over the top of that angry exhalation Jacopo hears the sound of many hands beating on the secret panel not so far above him. He rolls to his feet, radiance flaring, making the spectre cover its eyes with those horrible hands, and the boy runs for his very life.

Behind him are a splintering of wood as a door is broken down, many boots on stone steps, and then… and then…

And then screams.

Screams as the phantasm of the catacombs finds victims who have none of Jacopo's protections. Can it go beyond the level of the dead, will it float up and go through the palace at its leisure? He thinks not, senses once again that it cannot. Then he shakes the thought away and concentrates on finding his way back up into the Cathedral.

* * *

Breathless, Jacopo enters Mr Farringdale's house. The owner had locked the door after his guest left, but locks are no barrier to Jacopo.

The first thing he gazes at is not the egg, but his host's hands, which hang loosely now, almost touching the floor as he sits cross-legged in front of the fire, as if he never moved. The chrysalis remains in its tidy nest, resting between Isambard and the hearth. Jacopo scans the man's digits and lo! What he seeks is there: a sear mark on the soft pad of the right index finger, its existence given away by a slight glimmer, the same sort of luminescence that Jacopo emits. The youth is pleased to know he'd assessed the man so correctly. Mr Farringdale couldn't resist *touching.* Jacopo wonders how long it took between his departure and the moment Isambard's curiosity got the better of him. He wonders if the wound still throbs and aches. He wonders if the man realised that the thing is made of wax.

'Couldn't help yourself, Isambard?'

The man's expression is studiedly neutral, but his eyes are filled with fear that this prize will be snatched from his grasp. Jacopo smiles to show he understands. That it's all right. That nothing has changed. That Mr Farringdale has not ruined his chances. The man's features relax, and for a moment he glows as if a little of Jacopo's shine has rubbed off on him.

'Did you…?' Mr Farringdale's voice is raw.

Jacopo nods, draws his hand from his deep pocket. The necklace drips from his fingers, trailing light and colour.

Isambard catches his breath. He only ever saw it that once, when Bethany showed it to him (it still dripped with Agnew blood), before she gave it to Edvard Parisfal. She'd boasted then how new it was, that everyone who knew about it was dead – except its maker and she was too far away to make a difference – so it was perfect to fill her brother-in-law's request, to pull him further into her debt. She'd gotten cocky, he thinks, and things had fallen apart so quickly, though he'd admired how smoothly she'd managed to shift all the consequences to others, to her foolishly blind sister. If she hadn't, he was aware, he'd not be living a life that gave him such pleasure; yet he was also aware that she might have used him a scapegoat, just as easily, had she not needed him for a little longer.

The boy shoves the gleaming thing back into his jacket and breaks Isambard's meditation.

'And so, Mr Farringdale, you have upheld your part of the bargain.' Jacopo kneels on the other side of the chrysalis and the flames from the hearth turn half of him red-gold, throwing the other half into darkness. He reaches out, his long fingers with their carefully tended nails touch the very top of the oval, ever so gently, and a word leaves his lips though Isambard cannot hear it for it is only a whisper. The girl looks directly at him and the egg begins to grow.

His breath is trapped in his throat for so long that Isambard fears he may pass out. Just before the thing gets too large, just as he is about to doubt the lad's promise, about to believe she will get too big, too old, too mature, everything stops.

A crack forms at the apex of the shining ovoid and zigzags its way to the floor. The girl raises a small fist and gives a single, sharp punch. The waxen shell shatters into pearly shards and the girl, his girl, *his* Bethany, steps out and away from the wreckage. Her dress is white, lace and satin, a child's frock. Her shoes, equally white, have silver daisies embroidered on the straps. Her hair hangs in two thick plaits of darkest gold and her eyes are glittering green, her mouth a rosebud of red-tinted pink.

A great sigh escapes Jacopo as he rises out of his crouch. Mr Farringdale had forgotten, for the slimmest of moments, that he was there. 'Good luck, Isambard. You have certainly earned your reward.'

He nods at his erstwhile host, pretends not to see the hand the man offers in farewell, and strides into the darkness. There is no sound of the door opening or closing, but Mr Farringdale does not notice. He turns back to the girl and reaches out.

He brushes one of her plaits and finds it adheres to his fingers. He cannot pull away. His other hand goes to the rescue of the first, and it too is caught in the spider web of her locks, and against the skin of her neck, which proves equally gummy. The girl makes a noise, something like a snicker, something like a snarl, and she winds her arms around him, pulls him closer and closer until they are body to body, and stuck thus.

No matter how he struggles, Isambard is held fast. The girl is adhesive, a wax baby, a tallow trap. From her very pores, from her mouth and nostrils, eyes and ears, pours forth a sticky substance. It bubbles up, over her owner's shoulders and down his back, his front, stomach, crotch, legs, until it meets up and covers him and her utterly, sealing both of them in. Or rather, Mr Farringdale alone, for the girl is gone, become a sea of waxy foam that has surrounded him, is in his mouth, his throat, his ears and nostrils, pushing against his eyeballs. Slowly but surely the new chrysalis begins to cool and tighten, to shrink, compressing Isambard, crushing him down and down and down, until there is only a shining pebble on the rug before the hearth.

Jacopo, now taller, steps from his place in the shadows and pockets the strange stone with barely a glance. His own features have changed, no longer so round and inviting, that gilt sheen of his has dimmed, the face elongated, the jaw is harder and squarer, the cheeks angular, and the nose crooked, showing it was broken at least once. These features have been lived in, not borrowed; they are his and worn with pride, no longer secret. He is older, a young man, no longer a boy barely out of puberty.

Before he leaves he goes through the drawers and cupboards one last time, liberating any and all valuables he can find in the house – with Isambard gone, with no live-in staff, there's no one to recognise and report a theft. There's a considerable stash of gold and silver, full coins and bits for change; Mr Farringdale had feathered his nest very nicely indeed. Jacopo's *employer* will welcome new funds for her endeavours. He's unsure of her plans for the necklace.

There are other things he finds, however, things that obviously once belonged to some child or another. He sets the pieces aside until he is almost ready to leave, then Jacopo gathers them up – dolls, stuffed bears, tiny shoes, hair ribbons – and takes them to the hearth. Each one is sent on their way there, blessed by fire and air so they might find their path home, back to the hands that loved them. He thinks the Burned Woman, the Cinder's Sister, will be pleased and the idea brings a smile to his lips.

EMBERS AND ASH

The witch saved the ship the best – the only – way she knew how.

The great waves had lifted the caravel and propelled it towards the sheer rock face below the wreckage of the Citadel at Cwen's Reach. The woman summoned every sorcery she could and threw it at the variegated sheets of granite and, for a moment, the very earth softened, grew not simply porous but quite ephemeral. And in those precious seconds the ship – timbers, nails, cargo – all passed into the substance of the cliffs… then the magic ran out and solidity reasserted itself, embedding the *Silver Branch* in a constricting rocky grip. Any passengers unfortunate enough to be in the for'ard section were petrified or crushed – no one really knew, the only certainty was *trapped*.

The witch hoped it was the former, just as she hoped that one day she might find the power to reverse what she'd done. But she'd been drained in that last act, her very bones stripped of any and all enchantments, so nothing remained but that painfully weighty yearning for what was lost. It perched upon her day after day as she and three saved sailors waited for aid.

Eventually, folk from the nearby village – built in the foothills and named Cwen's Ruin to distinguish it from the destroyed city above – managed to make their way to the stranded ship. Where no paths existed, they were made either by means of sturdy planks and walkways or by cutting steps into the stone. And when they finally clambered aboard, they discovered the survivors quite healthy if not happy – with only four of them the stores of food and drink (those not fossilised) lasted a good while – but where the sailors were most anxious to leave, the witch was much less so.

Lis had grown comfortable, ignored day in and out by the mariners who'd seen her stupendous and terrible deed and found her an object of terror. They would not eat with her, would not speak to her, and slept out on the deck no matter what the weather rather than share a confined space with her. She was a woman: who knew what she might do? She was a witch: they knew what she *had* done. They'd not even risk trying to throw her overboard for fear she'd not fall but fly.

The rescuers, however, had seen and heard of things far stranger; generation upon generation had grown up with tales of how the Citadel atop the cliffs had been destroyed in a single night by one man's malice. Yet victory was snatched away by the will of the Little Sisters of St Florian, who had dispersed on the wind like birds, with precious books grasped in their claws. Not all the books, however. Though the village was small, a poor place compared to the original city, it was proud of its heritage. Each home held ancient tomes given in trust by the Little Sisters with strict instructions for their keeping (and for the fostering of young girls who sometimes accompanied them). Other volumes had been found after the soldiers marched away and the last inhabitants of Cwen's Reach crept up to the destroyed bastion. It's whispered how they found nothing but ashes, broken books and the bodies of two nuns.

The tales of those times are repeated and passed on. The fostered girls grew, some married in and some left forever. The volumes held in anticipation of the Little Sisters' return. Yet of them and their highest order, the *Murcianii* scribes, there has been no sign for hundreds of years. Still, the villagers kept faith. They've carried the knowledge of the loss for centuries and are neither fearful nor ignorant: a woman like Lis who'd done such deeds was nothing new to them.

So when she offered those who'd come to save her ale and bread and dried meat and wheels of cheese from the *Silver Branch*'s copious supplies, they'd accepted. They found her company jolly, she carried a sweet tune, spun a perfectly timed joke, and listened to maudlin recountings with a kind ear. She took all in good humour but wasn't slow to slap a face or box an ear when required. One of the guests joked that the caravel would make a fine tavern and she a fine innkeeper. His fellows offered hearty agreement and Lis, head tilted to one side, decided it was a fine idea; a fine place to wait. A fine place to hope.

That's how the *Silver Branch Inn* came to be.

Or so the story goes.

* * *

The woman is very tall, and something tells Lis that, in her youth, she was awkward, self-conscious. Now there's a glide in her step, a confidence that comes of long command and of being loved well for who and what she is. Her hair is covered by the hood of a travel-stained dun cloak, but fox-red wisps have curled their way out to frame a face which appears both strangely young and strangely ancient, though it bears no wrinkles, no traces that might tell the truth of her age. It is as if time quite deliberately has not left its marks on her, but rather erased them. Bright yellow-green eyes glimmer beneath emphatic brows, and their expression is kind but distant, a little weary. The lips are full, the mouth a touch too wide, yet she *is* lovely. Not even the teardrop birthmark beneath her right eye – a thing that makes her hard to miss – detracts.

However, something troubled runs under her skin, some turmoil makes her features seem not entirely solid. A distress, a constant worry that she fights to control. Lis thinks it's been weighing on her for some time.

When the newcomer had stepped in from the night, she'd paused, her gaze sweeping the assembled patrons (some few travellers, most inhabitants of Cwen's Ruin who preferred the *Silver Branch's* the village's more conventional inns). Lis notices that none of them have taken the woman's interest for disappointment settles on her face – an old disappointment, not a surprise – then she commits to the room with firm steps. The stranger's glance finds the tavern keeper and her lips lift. Lis smiles in return, but feels a roiling deep in her stomach, a ridiculous anxiety for the woman's story, for the relief of someone new.

'What will you have?' she asks as the guest takes a seat at the bar.

The woman's smile widens, sweetens, and Lis senses… senses… a *pull*, a *need* to please. She's still witch enough to recognise it and raises an eyebrow, leans forward and says quietly, 'Don't do that. Don't try to charm what's not freely given.'

'Ah!' the visitor says and grins ruefully. 'I should have known, I seemed to sense something but you're… different. Drained.'

Lis shrugs, uninterested in sharing. Such a rude beginning! The woman would have to make up for it before Lis offered much of herself. Instead she asks again, 'What will you have?'

'Food and drink and such information as you'll part with only by your own will,' the woman says.

Lis nods, acknowledges the unspoken promise that no more tricks will be played. She's not entirely mollified, but does not judge the other too harshly, for she spent enough of her own early years using the same skills to get her way as and when she needed. After plating up a half a loaf of brown bread with fat slices of cheese, thin slices of beef and pickled plums on the side, she carefully pours an ale to make sure the head isn't too large, that there is more draught than foam. Lis names a price and the woman pays with a coin that's not scored for breaking into bits. The gold is bright, brighter than what is passed about nowadays, and on one side is a crowned head, the outline of which appears uncertain as if made of smoke shifted by a breeze. If she didn't know better – if her eyes did not feel so unfocused – she'd swear the crown was made of whistle-wood branches, each finial topped with rich black alder-buckthorn berries.

So.

This woman is far more than she appears. Lis blinks, bites the piece suspiciously, finds it gives in just the right way, there is no cheaper metal concealed inside; she pockets the thing. When she hesitates on how to make change, the other shakes her head.

'Information as well, remember?'

'Of course. What will you have? Location of treasure? Prediction for your future? A spell to guarantee love or to cheat death?' She can offer none of these.

A cloud passes over the visitor's face and Lis recognises it as pain, regrets her flippancy. All these things, she realises, the woman could arrange for herself, if she's a powerful as Lis suspects she is.

'I'm seeking a girl. No, a woman by now. My… daughter.' She clears her throat, then amends, 'My husband's daughter.'

'You'll need to be more specific, my lady.' Lis has assumed the woman's veins run more blue than is usual, but the twitching grin makes her consider if she's wrong.

'She is called Ella, or used to be. Where she treads, children disappear.'

Lis turns away, reaches for a goblet to buy time. When she looks back the woman's expression is keen, so Lis says lightly, 'There's a name I've not heard in many a year: Dark Ella, the Plague Maiden. She's a fairy story, is she not? A hobgoblin to scare the naughty ones.'

'She's real enough.' The woman's eyes are bright. 'And I think you know that.'

Lis shrugs. 'Everywhere's got a tale of her or someone *like* her. That she roams hither and yon, taking childer as she wishes; a plague maiden's a convenient excuse for a missing child. It means you don't have to go looking, or at least not for too long. No one blames a parent who gives up after a day or two if their offspring's been snatched by a bugaboo.' Lis snorts. 'It's said she cleared Iserthal of its babies over three hundred years ago, that she stole away the royal offspring of Lodellan a hundred years ago. But in recent times, mentions are few and far between… perhaps she's gone?'

'She's not gone. I've tracked her, across the length and breadth of so many lands I might lose count if I weren't careful.' The woman lifts her tankard but puts it back down without taking a sip. She's not eaten anything either. 'I've found whispers of her, she leaves trails, a stolen child here, a lost lover there, sometimes she's behind justices small and large, sometimes fomenting mischief… Ella still wanders for she's nowhere else to go. But she's hidden herself and I must find her.'

'Why?'

The woman's gaze seems to look elsewhere as she weighs her words. 'Her father is dying and only she can save him. If she does not come home there is nothing I can do. If she does not come home… well, his death will have consequences, in this world and others, above and below.'

'Such as?'

'Hollowed out as you are, you can still sense some things, yes? Do you hear voices and sighs? Feel cold fingers as the passing dead reach out?'

Lis has heard noises, yes. More recently her nights have been disturbed by sounds that have no source, sudden icy spots on the ship. She's even thought there have been moans coming from the part of the vessel embedded in the rock.

She nods, but they both are silent, the one failing to eat or drink, the other polishing a goblet that was clean some while since. They do not look at each other, but the gathered clientele watch as if their glances are drawn against their will. As if they sense a stirring, a brewing, a knitting, a *making* of a moment after which everything will be irretrievably changed.

'There will be more of such occurrences if his death comes to pass,' the woman says.

'I might ask around,' offers Lis at last. 'I might find something.'

'You might,' agrees the other patiently.

'What would you be willing to give in exchange?' asks Lis, casually as she can.

'You've already had gold of me, innkeeper. What more can you possibly want?' The woman's tone is steely; she'll not be trifled with.

'I want whatever power you have.'

The woman clicks her tongue as if disappointed at the demand. 'Whatever power I have was gifted by my husband. It cannot be passed on, cannot be given away. And if he dies, it will die with him and I will be… I do not know what I will be without him.'

'You misunderstand me. I've no wish to bear such potency again –' *How much trouble did it get me into last time!* – 'I would merely have it briefly employed in my service.' She sees the other's expression and laughs, not unkindly. 'Not for ill, no. I wish you to undo something.'

The woman hesitates, sizes Lis up with a gaze more knowing than the innkeeper is comfortable seeing. She can barely stop herself from fidgeting. At last, the woman nods. Lis decides an assessment's been made of her character that is more flattering than it deserves. The answer is, however, less than a ringing promise: 'Perhaps.'

'Can you… can you melt rock?'

The woman tilts her head, considers. 'Why?'

'There are those trapped whom I would have free.' Lis gestures over her shoulder, as if the other might see through the wall, into what was once the captain's cabin (he went overboard well before Lis did what she did), to the place where wood and stone had melded. Quickly she explains what happened during the storm (not all of it, though, not what came *before*), what she did to try and save the ship.

The guest shakes her head slowly. 'Melting isn't what you want, that will simply burn and drown those trapped within. And if you interrupt the balance between ship and rock, the angle… it's a miracle it's lasted like this for so long.'

'I think whatever magic left me lodged here.' Lis taps the bar, meaning everything: the caravel, the cliffs. 'But if not melting, then what?'

'You want air. You need precision.' The tone is judgmental, just a little, implying that Lis' solutions would likely cause more trouble than her original troublemaking.

The innkeeper gives an annoyed wave as if to say if she'd been much of a witch at the beginning of all this she'd have done things differently. She'd have managed to save everyone. She wouldn't have started matters in the first place. 'How ever. Can you do it?'

'I can try. I promise I will do my best.' The woman holds up a warning finger. Lis notices it's a pale blue, as if the woman works too much with ink, or has done in the past. 'But this is *only* if you lead me to Ella and *only* if she agrees to come with me.'

Lis pushes out a breath, considers protesting, then thinks that might reveal too much. 'Agreed. I'll see what information I can glean.' She places the over-polished goblet on the servery. 'Come back tomorrow morning. There's a house in the village below that will offer you a bed. I'll give you a note for the landlady.'

The woman shakes her head, says, 'I shall be *above*.'

'There's nothing there,' Lis protests.

The woman shrugs. 'There are memories. That will be enough.'

Lis watches the woman rise, then as an afterthought asks, 'Do you have a name?'

Lis suspects she will not answer.

'I am Mercia and once I trod the corridors of the Citadel.'

And she is gone before Lis can say, *But it fell three centuries ago.*

* * *

Mercia moves slowly, as if her true age is finally showing itself in her bones. It feels like she's been searching forever. She takes the path that once led to a thriving town, not quite a city but certainly more than a village; a place prosperous, clean, its citizens educated and cared for by the Little Sisters of St Florian. A place proud of its commerce, its fine craftsfolk (jewel-smiths and weavers whose works were sought far and wide), and of the Citadel sitting atop the promontory. Of the women dedicated to collecting and keeping and sharing all the great knowledge of the world, ensuring it remained, in books big and small, scrolls and bibles, grimoires and journals, scraps and notes of vellum, all cradling tales of the famous and the infamous and the very ordinary, valuing tiny lives as much as those lived large.

As she walks through the broken streets lined with roofless houses, shattered walls, she understands why no one could bear to rebuild. How to live on tear-salted earth, reminded every day that the Sisters were gone?

Word of the Fall had reached Mercia only a century after it had happened, when she was *beneath*, when it was too late to do anything but grieve. Too late to help or take revenge. Too late to do anything but ponder and weep, and then to forget. Forget until Gwern began to sicken. She'd spent so long forgetting that it was a surprise to discover her hunt for Ella led this way. Then again, perhaps it was not a coincidence: if she'd learned anything at all it was that unfinished business had a tendency to seek out its own completion. She had no choice, so the desire to flee that beat like a frightened bird in her chest had to be ignored. Her solution and Gwern's salvation, bitter though it might be, was here.

As she roams the desolate byways she cannot help but think of the paths of her life.

Fathered by a ghost, a wicked weaving of spite and moonlight, she'd found a proper home at the Citadel, a place of safety, surrounded by books. Mater Friðuswith, who'd taken Mercia under her wing, taught her such a fine hand, taught her the secrets of making the mind blank in order to remember what tales were told and write them down later. Had taught her all these things so she might earn her entry into the ranks of the *Murcianii*, the Blessed Wanderers.

The Misses Meyrick of St Dymphna's School had the only extant copy of the *Compendium of Contaminants*, the greatest of poisoners' bibles, one of the lost tomes of Murciana, the first of the Citadel's roaming scribes. They had refused access to it time and again, so Mater Friðuswith had sent Mercia in the guise of a student. She'd come to the Misses on the pretence of learning the art of assassination, she'd taken their friendship and care, and betrayed them. She tells herself, in her darkest moments, that they died because of her, but in truth Gwern would have killed them anyway for what they'd done to him. Saving Mercia from their rage was merely a bonus.

She thinks of her first sight of Gwern on the day she'd arrived: a tall crooked-shouldered man, dressed rough, held prisoner by the Misses, his blood stolen to provide a most potent poison for purchasers of such things. How he was when she last saw him above the earth: man-shaped but almost twice as tall, features shifting as if made from soot vapour and dust and ash, on his brow a crown of stripped whistle-wood branches, each finial topped with rich black alder-buckthorn berries. How he was when she at last found him again, at last made her way to the under-earth. How he was when she left him this time in his kingdom *beneath*: lethargic, sickly, shrunken, devastated as a tree shattered by a lightning strike.

Mercia had spent years searching for her lover, years when she'd thought him lost forever. Had she but followed him down that last day! Had she been *able*. But her final sight of him in the grove of Alder's Well had sustained her, although some days she doubted the details of her memory. Some days she resented the years lost; others she reminded herself that the Erl-King was eternal and they had forever. Or so it had seemed.

In the days after leaving, she'd returned to the Citadel for a time, handing over the Poisoners' Bible, earning her place, but she did not wander again. No. Mercia spent her days in the Library, reading and researching everything she could find about the kingdom beneath, about its ruler (her lover), about how she might make her way to him. Days, weeks, months, years in which despair often threatened and she doubted her memories. But at last, in one book she found the tale written by a Sister Rikke (long dust) of the coming to Iserthal of the Plague Maiden, Ella, of her father the Erl-King. In another she found the secret of passing through the alders, to underearth: mandrake in the veins.

She'd left the Citadel. She left under cover of darkness, taking only her quills and inks and parchments – she still records even now, even beneath the earth, even on the road as she searches. She asked no permission. Mercia felt that she had given enough to the Little Sisters, enough for a lifetime. She left without a word of farewell to anyone, not even her blood sisters who still lived in the town of Cwen's Reach.

Mercia recalls locating an alder grove near Iserthal, drinking the deadly mix and, with equal measures of hope and dread, reaching out to the trunk of the largest tree, which shone like angel wings. She thinks of holding her breath until the bole at last split, to show a dark trail *beneath*. She does not think of the route she trod down, nor the parts of herself she gave up on that journey, she does not think of the wounds she bore by the time she came before Gwern's throne, or the sickness in her belly that grew as she drew closer. What if he had forgotten her? What if there had been nothing between them? What if it had all been lies in the service of his escape? What if she had left everything behind for… naught?

She stumbles as she comes to an empty space in a street she recognises. Not even rubble remains of the pretty house that once stood, a home that for a while held her family: mother Wulfwyn, sisters Delling and Halle. Here were mother's last terrible days played out: haunted by the ghost of her own brother, Mercia's father. Here her sisters had settled into quiet lives as jewel-smiths. She wonders if anyone went looking for her, sisters or Sisters. But she will never know: all were long-dead by the time the Citadel fell.

Finally, Mercia reaches the spot where enormous wooden gates once hung. There are only gigantic rusted hinges left, barely clinging to the weathered stone. In her imagination she recreates it as it once was: the main tower wherein dwelt the library, the dormitories, the dawn and dusk chapels, the kitchens, gardens and refectory, the stables and the dormitories, the infirmary and lavatorium. The buildings of butter-coloured stone, the windows of stained glass, the stream that ran around a fountain in the shape of a labyrinth. With a breath that feels inhumanly cold even to her, she steps into the courtyard of the Citadel.

But the illusion will not hold, the reality is too stark, too hard. Undeniable.

The tower had collapsed, its length crashed into the kitchens. The stables still show signs of fire that not even centuries of wind and rain and snow can wash away. There are, incredibly, books – or rather their corpses – scattered across the flagstones, abandoned, unloved. Dead. The stream has dried up. The roofs of the dormitories have fallen in, the gardens are home to weeds and wild roses sprung up over two ancient graves. She can barely make out the names on the headstones… Goda? Dyla? Dylis? Sisters she never knew, but who *might* once have heard tell of her in the same way she had heard of Sisters who'd left for good: a tale, a legend, a ghost story.

There's a fragment of yellow, peeking out from beneath a tumble of masonry and she can't quite believe it. It can't be. She bends, gently retrieves it, finds the book mostly intact. A little thing, so small, barely more than a pamphlet. In faded letters on the cover *A Brief History of the Alder Well*. How many years since *he* handed it to her that night? How many years since she brought it to the Citadel to sit on shelves beside all the other volumes of lives great and small? Oh, that *this* greets her now! Mercia clutches it like a lifeline.

Mercia takes in the destruction and remembers the secret she shared with her sisters before she left for St Dymphna's, even though she'd been warned it was one not meant for the ears of anyone not a Sister: that she would join the *Murcianii*, the Blessed Wanderers, the travelling scribes. Mercia wonders now as she has since the day she heard of the Fall if that was *why* the Citadel was lost. Logically, she knows that the years between her words and this grand ruination were many, that those she knew and loved would have been dead well before. Yet still, she wonders if the weight of those lost souls, destroyed books, those fallen stones, are on her shoulders for the secret she told.

Then, crushed by the loss, Mercia sinks to her knees and begins to weep.

* * *

The ship, when it met with the cliff, did not pass through entirely solid rock for in places the stone was already permeated by tunnels and chambers, some naturally formed, others hollowed out by workman at the behest of the Little Sisters. The caravel, fortuitously and firmly stuck, was on such an angle that the unembedded part did not sheer off from its own weight and plummet into the sea. Lis wished she could call it intentional but it was, as with most of her life's efforts, pure luck.

She'd had a door made in the hull, for the captain's cabin had come to rest in a cavern where once there'd been a kind of pool, its circumference broken and breached. In the early years she'd wandered through the tunnels that led off that chamber, always careful to mark her way with chalk. Those going up led, eventually, to the ruins of the Citadel, while those going down went to the beach and sea caves, but they were treacherous, slippery and often lost to cave-ins. Although Lis did not tell Mercia, she'd stopped going into the caverns in recent months because that's where the whispers grow louder, the cold touches stronger. Whatever is dead or *other*, is more active there. It hasn't seemed to bother Ella, however.

The cabin is comfortable, outfitted with a large bed, fine hangings, luxurious furnishings, more lanterns, thick carpets on the floor that told stories in their very weave of mermaids and pirates and monsters. The *Silver Branch* does an excellent trade, and as no one has ever arrived to lay claim to it as salvage, the once-witch makes a good profit. There is a large roll-top desk where Lis does the monthly accounts with clockwork regularity, and a round table meant for dining but more often than not is where her lover passes out. This evening, after Lis sends the stragglers home she wipes down the bar, washes the goblets and platters, sweeps the floors and makes sure everything is in readiness for the next day's trade, then prepares for what will come.

At the entrance to the private quarters she pauses, steels herself, steps through.

Ella's moods shift like the sea, though Lis knows she's not of that element: she's too earthy, some days she gives off the scent of roses gone to rot. Mostly, she stays in this room and makes her way through Lis' alcoholic stores, but some nights she'll sit in the bar, not speaking just watching, and no one speaks to her for no one's a fool. Lis explains her away, whenever she must, as a distant relative. But the locals have simply grown used to her and are adept at pretending she's not there; if they call her anything it's *Maid*, although never to her face. It was pure luck, really, that Ella wasn't in the tavern tonight when Mercia came looking, pure luck that Lis hopes to turn to her own advantage.

Ella's been known to disappear into the warren of tunnels, leaving Lis to worry and curse for days on end. When she finally returns – for she always does – she brings souvenirs, mostly old books, no longer readable, sometimes rocks she likes the look of with shiny quartz veins, others shaped like ribs or fossilised shells, once an old skull. All these things are lined up like offerings on a shelf. Lis hopes that Ella has not decided to begin one of her jaunts tonight.

She's in luck: her lover is cast in rainbow shades of ruby and emerald, amethyst and topaz, rays thrown out by multicoloured lanterns imported from far-off places. Ella is also slumped at the table, staring into the depths of a wine glass. Her long dark hair is tangled and she is still in her nightgown, which is spotted with a very expensive claret. Lis wonders how many bottles are left.

'How long are you going to stand there?' Ella asks without looking. Clearly this will not be a tender night.

Lis gathers her herself and says, 'Someone came looking for you.'

Ella's struck with a stillness Lis has never witnessed, then asks: 'Who?'

'Said she's your mother. Or your father's wife, at least.'

'I've no mother, nor memory of one,' says Ella and her voice, which so recently held the promise of bitterness and strife, is suddenly stripped and hollow. Almost childlike.

'She says your father is dying.' Lis clears her throat. 'Didn't know you had a father.'

'Did you think I sprang from an egg? A titan's skull? A witch's brew?'

Truly, Lis has cobbled together just enough snippets over the years to realise that she shares a bed with a plague maiden, a stealer of children, or at least a former one, but she has no idea where such creatures come from. She keeps her pitch steady: 'Will you speak with her?'

Ella is silent.

'I think you should.' A tremor; Lis slips a hand in the pocket of her ash-grey skirt, makes a fist, feels her nails bite at the palm.

'What's it to you?' Ella turns her agate gaze upon Lis, who

shrugs. It wouldn't do for Ella to realise that there's something in it for her lover; even on her good days, she's not kind. Wouldn't do for her to know there are plans afoot, plans that would thoroughly unseat Ella. Lis calms herself against every screaming instinct and pretends she does not care one way or the other.

'It can't hurt to hear what she has to say. Perhaps there's an inheritance in it for you,' Lis says, though she cannot truly imagine what that might be.

But the comment makes Ella laugh and the bitterness returns, swelling richly in the air, seeming to make the colours from the lanterns vibrate and tremble.

Lis shrugs again and turns away. She will draw a bath, she decides. Will pour herself some of that claret if Ella's left any. Will rest, resolute, in the knowledge that she's done all she can, though it is little enough. She'll not push for fear of showing her hand.

'She waits above, in the ruins. Her name is Mercia,' she says, uncertain why she let that slip. Lis sets about preparing to bathe, and ignores the looks she feels Ella throwing at her.

Given her time again, there are many things Lis would not have done. Lis would never have welcomed Ella into her bed, no matter how lonely she'd become or how beautiful the other woman was. She'd never have invited her to stay at the *Silver Branch*. And she'd definitely not have summoned that storm in the first place, all in the interests of impressing a princess.

* * *

Ella waits until she hears Lis slip into the tub behind the carved screen, then she rises. No matter how much she drinks, she's never drunk, not truly, and her steps are steady as she pads to the far end of the room where the large bed waits. She doesn't climb in, however, but presses her ear to the odd surface that's not quite stone, not quite wood. Somewhere beyond it are those passengers who hid in the bow, neither drowned nor saved, but petrified or dead, eternally strung between the two.

'Are you alive?' she whispers to the wall. She only cares about one who might hear her.

Ella thinks of the times Lis has drunkenly told her Ballad of the Heedless Witch and the Runaway Princess. She'd wondered what the girl in the rock looked like, until Lis had let slip that her lover was from the royal family of Lodellan. Ella knows them of old. Once, standing so close, she would have been able to hear if their hearts still beat. Once, before her father took her powers as punishment for fleeing under-earth, she could have rescued them with no more than a touch of a hand, a whisper to soften the granite and make it give up its prisoners. Once, she was not so cruel.

Some days Ella finds Lis leaning against this wall, her whole body pressed firm, risking splinters from wood and rock. She sighs and sings to the stone girl. Even though there is no love between them – lust, convenience, loneliness, yes – Ella is jealous. Even if she was still able to free the trapped, would she? To give Lis back that for which she grieves?

Ella has lost so much, why shouldn't someone else suffer?

The thought turns her mind to the woman waiting above…

Ella can neither sense nor feel her power. She'd always known, however, when eldritch creatures were close by, which suggests the interloper is something else, both more and less, something beyond Ella's experience. The woman claims the Erl-King as husband? The last Ella knew of her father he was held captive by Orla and Fidelma Meyrick in that trap she'd helped them set for him all those years ago.

How had he escaped?

How had he come to have a wife?

How had the Erl-King come to be dying?

Why had this *wife* come to her now?

She'd never wished death upon her father, or not consistently, for without him there would be no hope of going home. Yet when she'd heard he'd begun searching for her after so many years of exile, she took the chance for a petty revenge, condemning him to life above the earth just as he'd done to her.

Home. It's such a very long time since she's touched a mirror to see if she might travel between, even longer since she's seen a shadow tree and begged it to open for her. Many years even since she sent a child through a gaping, shining trunk, trying to pay her passage back with the Erl-King's preferred coin.

Ella wrestles now with that idea: *home*.

She struggles with its meaning, its weight, its value after the centuries of banishment.

She wonders how much – if – she still wants it.

* * *

It is almost morning by the time Ella ascends the honeycomb passages inside the cliff. She picks a path through what is left of the ruined kitchen and refectory. The corridors are dark and littered with dusty debris, but her eyes see everything, the last remaining gift of an upbringing in the kingdom of under-earth.

At the doorway leading to the great courtyard, she pauses, sweeps her gaze across the ancient devastation; the destruction might have happened only yesterday. Ella almost misses the woman, so still she is, kneeling in the middle of the rubble. She's gathered around her piles of ruined books, their spines twisted out of true, and there's a small yellow one in her hands as if it's the most precious. The woman's shoulders heave – Ella wonders how long she's wept – but that's not the movement which first catches Ella's attention: it's the foxes who congregate at the woman's dark skirts. All shapes and sizes, colours and breeds.

Ella does not recognise the woman, but the foxes are the Erl-King's dogs, ever have been. If they come to this Mercia's side in such numbers then she is more than mortal. Her father has elevated this… thing.

A toy, a whim.

No.

More than that, Ella thinks, contempt swiftly changing to resentment. He has given her power. This close Ella can tell: the woman has *command.* If she has come from beneath then the shadow trees open for her. If she has tracked Ella then she is determined and clever.

At last the woman senses herself watched and scans the landscape; by the narrowing of her eyes, Ella knows she's been spotted in the pre-dawn gloom.

Mercia rises, reluctantly letting the ruined books fall from her lap, all but the yellow one. The foxes, with a reproachful glance, slowly fade into the devastated landscape. She appears unembarrassed to have been found so vulnerable and Ella marvels at that, for her own weaknesses have been carefully shielded and hidden. Or at least until she'd stumbled into Lis' tavern and her bed. She tries not to think about why she let her guard down around the former witch, why she trusted her with some of her truths; perhaps because she sensed a kinship with another stripped of her gifts – or perhaps she simply felt Lis was no danger to her.

Arrogance. Ella does not like to think on that. She wonders now if she's trusted Lis too much, underestimated her entirely.

'Hello, *Mother,*' she says, pushing herself away from the doorframe, and approaches.

Mercia looks a little discomforted. 'Ella. I am Mercia.'

'My father's…?' Ella does not say *plaything* or *whore* but her tone implies such insult and Mercia knows it. In a flare of light, she is suddenly even taller, her cloak replaced by an ebony gown that shimmers. Around her head lies not a hood, but a crown of stripped whistle-wood branches, each finial topped with rich black alder-buckthorn berries that catch the first light like gems. Then the moment is gone and she's ordinary again.

'Gwern is my husband, my king,' says Mercia, and her voice is heavy with a history Ella suddenly aches to comprehend. *How does this woman know him by* that *name?* The secret name she herself had only ever given to the Meyricks. What were the details of their meeting and mating, the depth of their connection to one another – what made *this* woman special enough to be chosen, for there is no doubt in Ella's mind that Mercia is an equal to the Erl-King. What made *this* woman a queen?

But she does not ask the questions she ardently yearns to for she'll not show weakness. She says carelessly, 'Lis tells me a tale of his withering. What is this, some new ploy to entrap me, to punish and torment me?'

'You know,' begins Mercia, then pauses and licks her lips, changes her tone. 'You know how the Misses Meyrick bound him.'

Ella can tells she restrains herself from saying *The secret given away by his own child.*

'I removed the mistletoe but it left a taint in his blood, so small even the alders could not detect it, and he was able to travel home.' Mercia shakes her head. 'But over the years the poison has grown. His dying has been slow, as of a wound gone unhurriedly septic. Dying for so long that at first we did not notice. But the mirrors closed to us first. Then… then the shadow trees sickened too, it became harder to travel *between*, and the creatures beneath… they are all connected to him, and they too began to fail. I did what I could to arrest the decay but as he fades so do they.' She licks her lips as if parched. 'All our children…'

'Children?' asks Ella sharply; the idea of anyone replacing her tastes keen and bitter.

'Those you have sent to him. They have become *mine*.' And Mercia smiles in spite of everything. She opens the little yellow tome and reads: '"The Erl-King who rules beneath has been sighted in Alder's Well for many a year. Inhabitants of the town claim to have seen him roaming the woods on moonlit nights, as if seeking someone. Parents are careful to hide their children, and the Erl-King is often used to frighten naughty offspring into doing what they're bid. My own grand-dam used to threaten us with the words 'Eat your greens or the Erl-King will find you. And if not him then his daughter who wanders the earth looking for children to pay her fare back home.' Legend has it he travels by shadow tree."'

'Huh.' It's meant to be a noise of contempt, but somehow it leaves Ella as if it's been punched out of her. She has spent centuries stealing kiddies as a payment, an ever-unacknowledged bribe to her father and now this woman claims them? That smile, however, that smile: it is so very kind, so very happy, and it dampens Ella's rage. She wonders that the years beneath have merely lightened Mercia's skin, not darkened her soul. If this woman set Gwern free then she is bold and brave and daring. She is made of a fine mettle, one from which the dimness of under-earth cannot leach the strength.

'I read about you,' says Mercia and the declaration is sufficient to stop Ella in her tracks.

'Me?'

'Before I knew of Gwern. When first I came here.' Mercia gestures to the broken walls, the ruined stones. 'As a novice, I read all the tales the Blessed Wanderers gathered and yours was amongst them; one of your tales at least. How you were found in the ice by a girl called Rikke.'

A name Ella had not thought upon in so very long. She thinks of the young girl's kindness when the worst of things had happened. She thinks how she sent all the children of Iserthal, except Rikke and her newborn brother, down to under-earth.

'Rikke came here, did you know? Became one of us, a chronicler.' Mercia sighs. 'But she was gone by my time, into the Dark Lands.'

'Is that what happened to you? You did not stay? My father took you away?'

'I met him. I chose him. He chose me.'

Ella crosses her arms. 'What do you think I can do? What do you think I *want* to do?'

'Come home. Come home and begin anew,' says Mercia, yellow-green eyes bright. 'Let all your burdens and your past go. In order to start again, you must first *stop*.'

Ella tilts her head.

Mercia rushes on, 'We need your blood, Ella. With that he can heal.'

Ella shudders, realising what the woman means. In all her years above, of wandering, of aching, Ella has never thought to end her own life. 'And what of me? What of all I am and have been? What of the sum of my parts? Am I to forget all of that?'

Ella hears herself as a wounded child, begging to know where her treat is. *Haven't I been good enough?*

'Is your life worth so much now? How many kindnesses have you committed? How many parents are left to weep while you send their babies below to pay your way back?' Mercia's tone is suddenly shrill. 'And when Gwern came looking for you, when you could have gone home, what choice did you make then?'

Mercia's despair and fear press against the bounds of her self-control, and Ella has a sudden image of this woman gathering like lost lambs all the strays Ella sent to the Erl-King. She suspects she sent the worst of children to the best of mothers and does not know whether to laugh or cry or rage.

'I want to go home,' wails Ella. 'I want to go home as I am!'

Mercia shakes her head. 'You cannot.' She sighs. 'Ella, Ella. When you reject a world, it rejects you in turn. I know this of old. I left the upper-earth to join your father and everything changed: when I am above, the way the air curls around me, the way the light touches me, all cause discomfort now. I may only remain in the daylight hours for short periods else the world leaves marks of its disdain upon me.' Mercia rubs her hands together as if to stop them from begging. 'Please, Ella. I promise I will aid you. I promise you I will bring you home, but you must let everything go. You must start anew. You will be changed. But you will be home. You will be mine. Your father will live.'

Ella remains silent.

Mercia tries again. 'It is not merely the world below, but this one. With Gwern's dying comes a loosening of ties and laws and boundaries. Otherly creatures, ghosts, wolves and worse, those that are neither properly one thing nor another… are becoming untethered. Bold. Will you help?'

Ella stills as the dawn light breaks over the jagged walls of the Citadel. She freezes for the longest of moments, watches Mercia flinch as the rays hit her, then Ella shakes her head. 'No.'

Mercia presses her lips together, a thin line. She nods. Turns on her heel, and returns to the downward path. Ella smiles, certain in the knowledge the woman has given up. That whatever Lis had hoped for is no longer on offer.

* * *

Lis waits anxiously.

She'd pretended to sleep when Ella slipped out in the wee hours, and before that they'd lain on the mattress, not touching, cold as effigies. Lis wanted to scream, to cry, to demand that Ella help Mercia, so that Lis might regain her heart's desire. Because when Lis had what she wanted, then Ella and her demands, her tantrums and tempers, could be damned and gone.

But she didn't. She kept a tight rein on all she wanted to say. Not simply because the wrong word would see her hopes dashed, but because she had finally admitted she'd come to fear her lover. She knew enough of Ella's history to know she was not human, not properly. That, while she suffered and wept, laughed and bled like everyone else, there was a core of ice inside her, and it made her able and liable to do terrible things. Ella's heart was a cold thing.

Now Lis waits to see who will return first. When the door opens at last, it is Mercia who enters, her expression is so hard that Lis' heart drops to the soles of her feet.

Ella has refused. Lis has failed. This woman will not expend her power. Life will go on in its never-ending cycle of anger, demands, chill sex, no love, hours pressed against a wall of rock and wood.

But then Mercia marches over and offers her hand.

'Take me to the place where you believe they are.'

'Ella has agreed?' asks Lis in disbelief.

'No. But you tried to help me and I value kindness.'

Lis does not question, does not say it was for her own benefit, merely takes the proffered fingers and leads Mercia to the cabin, to the spot where hope and fear have resided for so long.

'How many?' asks Mercia.

'Four,' she says, then admits, 'perhaps five. I did not pay much attention to the others.'

The woman says nothing though her eyebrows quirk. She tells Lis to move away, and places both palms against the strange surface. Lis stands by the table where Ella's empty bottle from last night lies. She steadies herself on a sturdy chair and waits, thinking she can hear Mercia whispering, but the pitch is so low that no words can be made out.

Lis watches, not breathing, and for long moments nothing happens.

Was she's wrong? What if this magic is beyond Mercia? What if the woman isn't special, merely convincing in her madness?

Then the wood and rock begin to change, to shift, to become

something neither solid nor liquid, but smoky, a mix of air with soft molecules. The grey swirls and one, two, three, four figures stumble through, fall to the floor, gasping, cursing, praying. Four forms, four men. Lis feels a wail begin deep in her throat, creep up, up, up, then expire as a tall slender woman with white-gold hair falls from the mist. She reels across the floor and into Lis' arms as the once-witch's cry turns to joy.

Mercia steps back and the wall solidifies again.

From the door comes an equally loud cry, of grief and rage. Lis cannot be bothered to look at Ella, not when the face before her is the one she's longed to see for a decade.

* * *

'You did this on purpose. You knew.' Ella's voice is empty.

Mercia's hands are shaking, either because the effort has cost her or because the last of her anger has washed through her. She says, 'Nothing holds you here any longer.'

They watch Lis and her stone girl in each other's arms. The princess traces the lines on her lover's face with trembling fingertips, marvelling. She says she has no memory of the time that has passed; it was merely a tender slumber.

Mercia wonders how long this will last, this thing that Lis has held in her heart. How much is guilt and how much is love and how much sheer dreams spun of hope. Will the embers catch again or simply snuff out?

Ella's eyes glitter as much with unshed tears as with outrage. 'You did this to spite me.'

Mercia doesn't deny the spark of vicious pleasure the other woman's hurt gives her. 'Did you value her? Lis? Did you love her and warm her, cosset her and keep her? Did you tell her she was of abiding importance, that she had a place in your heart? What did you sacrifice for her, Ella?' Mercia shrugs. 'Or was she simply the place to hide, the port in the storm? Is that what you're truly lamenting? A convenient rut you'd fallen into and she'd consented to tolerate? Well, you are both free of that.'

Ella does not answer. When Mercia touches her arm she pulls away.

'Will you come home now?'

'No,' Ella says maliciously. 'Not for anything in this world or the one below. Let him die. Let him cease. Let all things that owe their existence to him wither.'

Mercia's hand falls. She pulls her hood over her head, and its shadows throw her features into a strange relief. 'If you should change your mind—'

'I will not.'

'If you change your mind and are swift about it, then come to where all your sorrows began. I will wait each night of the full moon for you, so as long as I am able until the doors are closed to me.'

'Do not hold your breath, *Mother*.'

Mercia says nothing more, merely turns and leaves.

The tears Ella has held in burn their way out and sear down her sallow cheeks. Mercia's truths will not be denied, they've hooked their claws into her mind, burrowed so they cannot be ignored: her safe harbour is destroyed. She must wander again, or find it in herself to help her father. To give up all she is and all she has been.

The stone girl's presence pushes at her, steals the oxygen, taking all of the attention Lis had once lavished on her. *Taking it back*, she corrects herself. The girl is merely reclaiming what was hers; what Ella usurped for some short years.

Ella will go forth. She will keep moving. She will make herself harder to find.

She will not go home.

She will remain herself.

BEARSKIN

Torben knows he has only one shot. The crossbow shakes in his grip. There is a single bolt and even if there were more he has not the strength to reload for the weapon belongs to Uther, the woodsman, who has left the boy to wait in the small, smelly blind set between the trunks of three ailing alders. The walls are of woven rushes and withy. The flimsy roof fell in who knows when and Torben feels the drip-drip-drip of snow-melt from above – not that the weather's warming up, but it seems the unhealthy branches won't allow the ice to remain on their limbs much past daybreak.

The boy is cold in his pale wolf furs, despite their thickness. He never had a taste for hunting though Edvard, his father, tried to teach him. Henry, his brother, took to it like a duck to water, but Torben refused to attend what Edvard patiently told him. He'd not learned the knack of willing himself warm either, of wiggling his fingers and toes to keep the blood moving. Beneath the fur cap, cold sweat darkens his muddy blond curls. Uther does not bother to instruct, or even try, he simply slaps the boy about the ears each and every time he fails at one rough task or another. Torben suspects the man rather enjoys it and encourages missteps whenever he can. Edvard was always kind and tolerant, going over the same lesson time upon time, never punishing his youngest child's inattention. Perhaps that's why the lad suffers so now.

Thoughts of his father bring, as usual, hot tears which the boy wipes away – he does not want them to freeze on his face. He has learned that much. He bites his lip and steadies his aching heart. He dare not think of his mother.

Torben presses an eye against the matting, but there is nothing beyond except a vastness of white broken only by thin naked trees. There is no canopy above of evergreens to offer any cover. He squints, trying to see if Uther is returning, slinky through the forest, quiet despite his hulking size. No, there is not even the icy comfort of Torben's gaoler on offer.

Gaoler. Not the word Aunt Bethany had used. *Guardian. Teacher*. Master to Torben's apprentice. He'd asked over and again *Why*? Why did he need an apprenticeship when Henry would be allowed to go to university? There was plenty of money – it seemed all the problems his parents caused had been solved by his aunt's cleverness – why was he not to be given the same chance? Wasn't that why they'd moved to Breakwater? To be closer to the university town of Whitebarrow? So Henry could study medicine as he'd desired, coming home regularly during semester breaks to be embraced by Aunt Bethany with that enthusiasm she reserved only for him? It was a few more years, certainly, before Torben would be old enough, but his tutor said he was terribly bright for his age, that he had great prospects, great possibilities. It hadn't occurred to Torben then, though it had many times since, that his repeated interrogations of Aunt Bethany were the reason he now found himself huddled in Edmea's Wood in the depths of winter, yearning for the company of a man he couldn't stand. A man whose face wore the scars of a bear attack. A man who'd grown so tired of Torben's stumbling and tripping, his barely swallowed whimpers, that he'd left the boy alone in the decaying blind with instructions to *Fecking wait* while he went and checked the traps on his own.

Torben sits back, tries to get comfortable; he can barely feel his feet and his backside has gone to sleep. Everything will hurt when he stands, when the blood flows back into his flesh and muscles – oh yes, he has muscles now, not big ones, but they've replaced the baby fat he'd had in copious store *before*. The physical labour, the sparse diet, have stripped the excess from his bones. He is constantly hungry, a gnawing in his belly day and night, but he doesn't dare steal. Uther is keenly aware of the quantity of provisions in the larder, and Torben is certain that the quiet, scrawny girl who keeps house would be unwilling to risk the woodsman's wrath all for the sake of the plump little rich boy who came to them weeping some months ago.

He listens carefully in case Uther is sneaking up behind to scare him so he pees his pants again. Torben would have thought that trick one to grow old quickly, but apparently not. All he can distinguish is the wind rattling branches, the creak of frozen wood, the whoosh of his own breath as it makes dragon's mist in front of his face. Put him in a library and he can identify the title of a book by the sound of its fall, but here… here he is lost. He clears his throat; it seems terribly loud in the sighing of the snow. A bird calls overhead, a melodic thing, and he thinks of Victoria, his sister, gone before him. That should have been a warning, he thinks, a sign that Aunt Bethany would brook no dissent no matter how much she professed to love them. And hadn't Henry given him cautionary looks? Hushed him so very many times? Yet Torben had not understood, had not taken notice, for his questioning had never before had such a consequence; he'd not been able to conceive that his sister's fate might somehow also become his. Henry will be safe, Torben thinks, Henry has the habit of obedience and Aunt cares for him best of all.

There is a noise outside, closer than it should be. Something has stalked him, gotten into proximity, and he all oblivious. To one side it shuffles and snuffles… his finger tightens on the trigger of the crossbow… whoever or whatever is there moves nearer… Torben's finger twitches and the bolt is released, punching through the withy screen. A thud, then a brief sigh-sob, then the sound of a small body falling to the snowy ground.

Heart in mouth, Torben scrambles up, fighting his way out of the blind; unable to find where the door latches, he tears it in panic. He falls through the rip and discovers that he has murdered a bear cub.

The cub is not especially large and his dark brown pelt is thick and matted. He should not have been out, thinks Torben in distress, he should have been sleeping the deep winter's slumber, not wandering about – Torben assumes it's a "he". He kneels and feels for a pulse, however, there is nothing. The barb is embedded right where the creature's heart should be. Blood has dripped, making crimson blossoms on the white carpet. The fur and flesh beneath Torben's hand are warm, so warm, but he knows the heat will flee soon enough. Copper eyes glazed over, bewildered, snout damp, teeth sharp beneath the sweet upper lip. The boy begins to weep and does not try to stop; tears drop like liquid stars onto the dark coat and stay there, held on the tips of the bristles.

He cries until he hears a new noise, a crashing and a thrashing somewhere amongst the trees of Edmea's Wood. Not Uther; the woodsman would never make such a racket. That is when Torben flees; he doesn't see anything but his imagination has always been worse than what might be real. He struggles through drifts, uncertain if he is heading in the right direction, driven only by the desire to escape whatever is behind. He doesn't care what punishment Uther will inflict on him for not staying put. He only knows he must run.

It is almost an hour later when he stumbles, more by luck than design, into the white-swept courtyard of the small stone house in the woods.

* * *

Tove took pity on him when he threw open the door and staggered over to the roaring fire in the large front room. She handed him a mug of heated winter-plum brandy. It was liberally sweetened with molasses and made smooth by a knob of butter, and took away what little breath he had left. But it warmed him and quickly, pressing life back into his extremities, even those he was sure had been frozen forever.

'Thank you,' he croaks to the girl. She doesn't speak and he wonders, not for the first time, if she cannot or simply won't. He's never heard her answer Uther, nor have a conversation, not that the man is much of a one for such pleasantries. She watches everything though, he's noticed that. Her dark blue eyes seem everywhere at once, as if taking in all possible threats, all available exits and places to hide. Torben feels for the first time, as she refills his mug, that he may stare openly at her, at the fine dark blonde hair, and the small stubs of antlers that poke through it on each side of her head. They are not fully formed and have not changed in the time he has been here. Tawny velvet covers them and he wants to run his fingers over it.

'I killed a bear cub,' he says as she stirs the stew pot on the fire. She pauses, shoulders tensing, goes back to it, then speaks the first words he's ever heard from her.

'What sort of bear?'

'Brown. A brown bear.'

'No, idiot. Was it a true bear or a one that's a bear only some of the time?'

'Is there a difference?' he asks, then wilts beneath her gaze, is burned by the contempt he sees there. His world is cracked open, his firmly held idea of who and how she is shatters. He wonders if this is why Uther does not touch the girl, does not abuse her. She's not his daughter, Torben knows that much for so the woodsman told him when he'd asked, *No, she goes with the house*. But Torben thinks she doesn't go with the house at all, that she belongs somewhere else entirely and is just *here* for a while. He says, 'I'm sorry.'

She stills again, then relaxes, seeming to shrug away the tension. Her lips are no longer set in a sharp line and her gaze seems gentler. 'You're not to know, I suppose. City folk are ignorant.'

That stings from this strange girl with her barely born antlers, her silence. He blurts, 'At least I'm not some superstitious country clod. Bears are just bears, all the time. My parents—'

'Your parents?' she sneers. 'What about them?'

He stops, wonders what she knows. Wonders what she's been told and by whom. Wonders if she knows how Edvard ended his life in gaol, and that his mother… oh, his mother. They stare at each other for long moments while the drink in his hand goes cold, and the stew on the hob, unstirred, becomes agitated, bubbles up and spatters on the flags. It breaks the spell, and he says softly, 'What are you?'

But their brief connection is lost. She turns away and does not answer.

* * *

When Uther finally comes home a few hours later, a brace of fat bone-coloured coneys slung over his shoulder, he doesn't yell as Torben expected. Isn't angry at all, just curious. Strangely proud. He hands the catch to Tove, then eyes the boy.

'You kill tha' cub?' His voice is deep and raw, rough as elm bark looks.

Torben cannot find a reply so he merely nods from where he sits by the hearth, the aching cold almost out of his bones.

'Should ha' lugged it home,' the man says, seating himself across from the boy. The fire plays shadow and light over his face, making the scars seem to dance. 'Not much you can do with th' hide, but meat's sweet so young.'

'I…' Torben croaks. 'I heard something else after it, coming for me. I thought it might be the mother.'

Uther nods. 'Might ha' been. Mayhap she woke early too, found him missing.' He leans forward to unlace his boots. 'I'd ha' run too. You did th' smart thing.'

Torben is surprised and disturbed. Surprised that the man has addressed unnecessary words to him, words of comfort and approval; disturbed that the worst thing he has ever done, though it was an accident, is the one thing this man approves of, is the one thing that might make his life here easier if only for a while. He cannot find it within himself to be glad, not even a little. He swallows hard, nods so Uther will think they are in harmony however briefly, and will not suspect that the boy is so sickened by himself he's thrown up three times in the privy out back. That every time he closes his lids he sees those copper eyes staring at nothing at all.

'Ne'er fear. I brought it back. Skinned it afore I came in, meat's in th' smoking hut. He'll no go to waste.' Uther rises, leaves his boots to dry by the flames, lands a heavy hand on the top of Torben's head, not in violence, but a kind of rough pat as he stomps to the washroom where Tove has heated water in the tub. *Good lad*, it says and Torben wants to weep again. His stomach rebels at the idea of eating such flesh, or indeed anything. The winter-plum brandy is long gone. His skin crawls to think of the hide made into shoes or a hood. He refuses the bowl of stew Tove wordlessly offers and makes his way upstairs to his small room under the eaves.

* * *

The stone house is uncontaminated by reading matter of any kind and it is beyond Torben as to how anyone can occupy their hours without tales of some sort. The lack still claws at him. He was forbidden by Aunt Bethany to bring any books, yet he managed to smuggle a copy of Murcianus' *Mythical Creatures* – a gift from Cordelia – and it lies beneath the mattress. He limits himself to a single page each night to stave off the time when he feels driven to either beg Uther for a new volume or bargain with the woodsman for something in exchange; he does not know what currency might work with the man.

Torben does not read this eve, for he is exhausted. Sleep comes quickly, with dreams chasing its tail like nipping pups. His mother, Cordelia, sits at his bedside. Cordelia as he last saw her, not as Aunt Bethany said she'd become – blackened, charcoal, *crisp*. His mother loving and laughing, telling him he was her sweetest, her best darling, her last child, and her only light. That he was special.

It's so long since Torben felt special.

He wakes himself before the dreams turns to nightmares, almost throwing himself from his mattress.

He stares out the tiny window into the darkness where nothing can be discerned until the full moon rises over the reaching fingers of skeletal treetops. Everything is bathed in silvered indigo. Torben looks down at the lean-to; he can just see the edge of the cub's skin stretched over the tanning rack. In the moonlight it's paler than he recalled, and it appears as if there are stars at the end of each bristle.

The stone house sits in a small clearing. To the left is a frozen rill, where Torben and Tove must hack at the ice to melt it for drinking and cooking and bathing. To the right is the lean-to and the outdoor privy. Behind is a barn-cum-stable where the jersey cow and two Clydesdale horses share straw with chickens, ducks and geese. The front garden is dotted with rose-beds, the plants oddly blooming all year round. The coloured blossoms look like jewels against the moonlight-blue snow.

Torben's attention is caught by a hesitant movement at the edge of the woods. A shape materialises, taking slow steps. At first he thinks it a bear, but the size is too small, the gait too elegant, and the owner walks on two feet, not four. The smudge resolves itself into a woman, her skin dark olive, her hair a blackish-brown running down her back, past her waist, to her ankles where it drags in the deep powder. She is tall in a dark dress, heavy-boned, large around breasts and hips. Her face is gentle, her eyes flash amber. She raises her head and Torben sees how she sniffs at the air.

She drifts towards the lean-to, her hands reaching out to the cub's hide. Just before she touches it, she looks up as if sensing Torben's gaze. His tears have started again and course down his cheeks. He wonders if the woman can see them glinting. Her expression does not change, she merely stares at him for long moments, then helps herself to the fur, carefully unhitching it from the frame. She cradles it in her arms and returns to the forest.

For a long time Torben watches the space where she no longer is. When he's half-frozen again, he crawls back into the bed with its goose-down quilt and pillows, the only luxuries Aunt Bethany sent with him. He trembles with fear that the nightmares might overwhelm him, but his dreams when sleep will no longer be denied are empty, and he is safe.

* * *

In the morning Uther finds bear tracks outside, where Torben had watched the woman walk.

'Did you see ought?' he asks, scars twitching, and the boy swears he did not.

Uther grunts and strides towards the barn.

Torben knows the woodsman keeps his great crossbow there, one Torben has no hope of lifting left alone arming, and the bear traps, cruel things with steel teeth. He shivers in the cold as he looks down. The prints are huge, almost three times as long as his own foot. He cannot reconcile the woman he saw with the traces she left behind.

No, perhaps not her. Perhaps a bear came after he slept. Perhaps a bear followed the scent, hers or the cub's, and obliterated the woman's footprints. His heart constricts, then: what if the bear stalked the woman? What if it found her with her gentle face and wondering eyes? Neither woman nor bear deserve Uther's attentions, he decides.

He looks to the house and finds Tove regarding him from the back door. She stares hard. The girl's barely paid him any attention since he arrived, yet here is the second day in a row that she's met his gaze. That she's let him know again she disapproves.

Tove sleeps on a pallet in the kitchen; he's often wondered why, for there is a tiny spare room beside his. Is she leery of slumbering too close to the menfolk? Or is there another reason? Are charms buried beneath the fireplace like those Mrs B used to tell him about in their old home? How, when she and Cordelia had first moved to Lodellan, she'd ordered the footmen pull up the ingle stones so she could hallow the hearth? Does Tove feel safer there, near whatever might have been used to sanctify the heart of the house?

He wonders whether Tove slept last night or was she awake as he was? What did she see through the window? Would she tell him even if he asked? Torben opens his mouth but the only thing that comes is heated mist before Uther shouts from the barn: 'Hurry up, boy. We're hunting bigger game today.'

He envies Tove that she gets to hide even as he is afraid of what she might say if he spoke to her again.

* * *

It is late in the day when Torben catches the trail. The light is beginning to fade and they are deep in Edmea's Wood, where the trees though leafless grow oh-so tightly together, and the shadows are lengthening. Torben has thrice been lost, but managed to right himself again before Uther realised and had to come and find him, swearing as he went.

The prints are strange, sometimes they disappear for large spans, with nothing to show how the creature got from one spot to another. Torben hoped every moment that the woodsman would not pick up the spoor again, but the man is tenacious, bloody-minded. The scars on his face, the memory of the claws that put them there, drive him. But this time… oh, this time, it's Torben who has found the tracks. He looks at the direction they lead, peers amongst the close trunks but sees no hint of the creature that left them. He spins on his heel as well as he can in the sluggish white and tramps back towards where he last saw the woodsman.

Breaking from a stand of singing winter grass that croons as he passes, he spies Uther on the other side of a clearing, heading straight towards him. The boy increases his pace, almost jogs, trying to ensure the man stays as far from the evidence as possible.

He is breathing hard when they meet, but it covers his nervousness about lying.

'Anything?' rumbles Uther, dark eyes scanning the direction from which Torben came.

The boy shakes his head. 'Nothing.' He pauses. 'It's… it's not a normal bear, is it?'

For a moment the man hesitates, then he nods, a sharp jerk, says, 'No.'

'Was it…' Torben, almost stricken by unwonted audacity, points to his own face as if he is scarred, '… the one who did that?'

'No. Tha' one's th' rug on my bed.' Uther looks around, stares up at the greying sky that seems to deepen every second. 'Home now. Light's going. Try again tomorrow.'

On the return journey to the stone house, Torben's heart is light, his feet lighter still, and he does not feel weary though they have traipsed the length and breadth of Edmea's Wood for hours. There will be hot stew tonight and a warm bed, and perhaps he will allow himself two pages of the Murcianus, though he is already part way through *P* and the *Plague Maiden* awaits his attention (he looked for *Bears* and found nothing). Relief leads his mind elsewhere, as if he's carefree once more. Perhaps Tove will forgive him, talk again; her voice was sweet.

* * *

Tove remains silent when they enter the kitchen and all the way through the meal, although this is not unusual. It is only after Uther has clattered up to his bed in the master chamber that Torben is able to approach the girl. But when he tries to engage her she glares and calls him *lackwit*.

'Why?' he asks, bewildered.

'Because of the bear,' she hisses.

'But, but… but I led him astray. Though I found the tracks, I did not tell Uther.' He feels a tremor starting in his legs. Torben had expected something nicer, if not a kind word then at least not this sort of spitting rage. 'Won't it?'

'You think that will be enough? He'll be out there tomorrow and the day after that, then the next. He won't stop until he's found her.'

'Her?' His tone wavers though he knows she speaks truly, gives voice to what he suspected but did not wish to believe.

'And it's all your fault because you're a frightened little baby.' She looks at him as though she hates him. He thinks if she had full antlers she'd do her best to impale him, and not regret it at all.

'I didn't ask to come here,' he stammers, wanting to cry, but he will not let this hard girl see his tears.

'I would you hadn't,' she hisses. 'Why did you? Why did you come and bring this misfortune?'

He has no answer for her or none he wishes to give. How to say *My parents are dead*? *My Aunt has no love for me*? *Father killed himself in despair and Mother... oh, my poor mother. Mother burned to a crisp on a prison hulk right in the middle of Rosebery Bay*? *In all that water, Cordelia seared and smoked, scorched and singed, blistered until her skin split.* How to say *My Aunt told me all of this with a smile and a laugh*?

He swallows and settles on, 'I ran away… I tried to find where my sister had been sent… but I didn't get far… was dragged home… I'm not very good at anything, really. I couldn't even run away properly.'

He turns his back so she will not see the unshed tears. They are not friends. They will not be friends. The realisation is sharp. He crouches by the fire and does not move, not even when he hears her boots come close, then move away; even when he hears her return to the kitchen and settle on her thin bed there.

Torben thinks of Victoria, of their childish arguments; he thinks he'd give anything for an hour with her once more, either in peace or bickering he doesn't care. He thinks of Henry, his brother, who said nothing when Torben was given his marching orders, merely shook his head as if the boy should in no way be surprised. If asked, he could not tell what thought is uppermost for everything seems a maelstrom of emotions and images, of things long lost and desired to reappear. The flames die down as the hours pass and Torben becomes an invisible lump in the limpid leftover glow. He only comes back to himself when he hears two things at once: a creak on the stairs, and the sound of something falling outside. Frozen by uncertainty he remains immobile. He's so still and small, so saturated by shadows, that Uther does not see him when he creeps past. The woodsman has the great crossbow held at the ready; the sight takes Torben's breath away.

Uther undoes the latch and slips out. Torben stands, limbs throbbing painfully as his circulation speeds up. He follows the woodsman.

The lean-to is empty though the tanning rack has tipped over, and there are footprints, man and bear, leading towards the barn, where the door hangs open. Torben takes only a few steps before he hears a rumbling roar, and a shout. One of the building's walls splinters under the weight of an ursine charge, and a brown she-bear tears into the silvery night.

She streaks towards Torben. He can see fear in her amber eyes, and steps aside for he instinctively knows she will not slow down. Her one thought is of escape. She rushes by and he can smell musk and fear. Uther stumbles from the barn, dark stains on his winter furs where the bear's claws made their mark. He curses, then plants his feet apart, and lifts the crossbow into position.

The seconds seem long between the release of the bolt and when Torben steps into its path. He knows the she-bear will run in a straight line making her an easy target. He knows she has come here because of him, because he killed her cub. Because he fled and left it for Uther to skin. He led her *here*. He cannot stand to be responsible for her death too. He knows his life is the very least he owes her. Or perhaps he simply knows that if he remains, he will carry her grief as well as his own and it is a burden he does not want.

The angry thud of the missile into his chest pushes all air from his lungs, and he falls. He stares at the winter stars. The pain comes, and Torben finds it hard to breathe. The snow beneath him is soft yet brittle, melting slowly. He sweats, the droplets freeze, and soon he has a layer of ice over his skin. He prays that death will come quickly. Perhaps he will meet his mother again. He wonders if Cordelia's ghost wanders, looking for her children.

Then the sky is eclipsed as something huge soars over him. There is a scream which cannot possibly come from Uther, but must: high and terrified, and abruptly cut off as the sounds of flesh tearing and bones breaking become so terribly loud. Then heavy footfalls come towards Torben and, once again, the sky goes dark. Though he cannot make out the features above him, something wet and warm rains down on his face; from the odour, a mix of blood and spittle. He manages to roll onto his side, though it hurts; he does not wish to see the yellowed teeth descending. He wonders if Tove is watching from the kitchen window, her breath making distressed shapes on the glass; if she nods, thinking *This is right*? The she-bear bends forward and takes the scruff of his fur collar in her mouth; a tooth sinks into him, pierces the fleshy part of the shoulder where it meets the neck. He cries out, but it is the least of his agonies.

Torben is dragged like a sack of meat from the yard, into the woods. He is soon so cold he barely feels it when he hits a rock or a log, when something sharp tears his clothing. He is part-pushed, part-pulled into a dim pungent burrow. He lands on something soft; as he grows warmer his wounds bleed afresh.

His lids flutter open and he sees the woman again. She has large hands, and brown furry feet; toes tipped with long claws peek out from under the hem of her dun-coloured gown. She ambles about the burrow gathering things he cannot see, hunched over to ensure her head does not scrape the roof where luminescent roots poke through, throwing a glow across walls, floor, everything. There is the sound of mortar against pestle, and he ponders if perhaps he's been dreaming all along, if he dreams still.

But there can be no dreaming when she kneels over him, puts one large hand on his left shoulder to hold him down, then pulls the bolt from his chest in a single powerful motion. He feels the blades in the tip tear new lacerations in him and it seems his breath tries to escape with it. Then, there is a new pressure on his chest: his strange physician is stuffing the wound – with moss? It hurts, but he is in no position to resist.

When she's done, the bear-woman holds his head and makes him swallow the powder she has ground. It's bitter, bitter, then sweet. He opens his lips to beg for water, and she spits into his mouth. Startled, he swallows that too, finds it is not foul, but quenches his thirst, eases his aches. Darkness begins to pull at him and he thinks it is death. He tries to say *I'm sorry* to the bear, to the woman, because he thinks it is important that she hear it. But his tongue is going numb and seems to grow; his teeth feel more numerous.

She pats his head and whispers *Hush*, or at least he thinks that's what she says. Perhaps it is simply a bear noise that he interprets as he wants – needs – to. His failing gaze paints Cordelia's image on the bear-woman's face. His mother smiles fondly and says *Hush, all will be well*, and Torben thinks he smiles in return. A hand brushes his hair, then he feels the soft thing beneath him being adjusted, wrapped tightly around him. The hands fall away but the fur rug does not. It grips him snugly and grows, along his limbs, up over his head, down his forehead, nose, cheeks, jaw, neck, over his chest… and Torben thinks he imagines it as he surrenders to what must surely be his final slumber. His last thought, with some regret, some relief, is of Tove. He will never know what she is, who she was; she's a mystery he will never solve.

* * *

Torben is surprised when he wakes. He knows he has slept long.

He rolls over, finds himself changed, but is not overly concerned; his fur is lighter than it was when it belonged to the cub before him, now closer to the dirty blond of his once-hair. On his back, he twists this way and that, trying to scratch the itch along his furry spine, enjoying the sensation more than anything he can recall in life. A tree, he thinks, outside there will be a tree with rough bark and he will rub the length of himself against it and it will be most satisfying. He rolls again, receives a gentle swat for his troubles, a warning not to wake his mother sooner than he must. She has had a busy winter, with her sleep interrupted.

He raises his large head, looks to where the snowfall had once formed a door to their den. It is gone now and in its place are puddles of melt, and beyond it the sight of Edmea's Wood, the trees bristling with new leaves, branches, and bright colours. Birdsong rings through, the sky is a warm blue. At first he thinks to bound forth, to try out his new shape, the four paws with their powerful claws, then another swat, a little less gentle, and he settles, curls back to back with the she-bear. There will be plenty of time to learn the world anew, he thinks sleepily; he knows what happens to cubs who stray from their mothers too soon.

THE NIGHTINGALE AND THE ROSE

The girl's voice is divine; it rises higher and higher, as if to reach the heavens, which might be appropriate in a less profane setting. One by one the specially blown glasses vibrate and shatter much to the delight of patrons. The shards do not spread too far nor too wide; the things have been carefully calibrated – and equally carefully enchanted – to ensure no one is cut by the disintegration. It is the house speciality, the melodic cherry on the theatrical bordello cake that is the Chaucer Theatre in Seaton St Mary. Lovers of music and lovers of destruction flock in equal measure to hear The Nightingale sing.

Oh, the girl can and has lifted her voice higher: most particularly on the day when Madame Arkady (proprietress of the House of Curiosities in Lodellan, and silent partner in this more respectable – a relative term, of course – more well-known venue) delivered her here with rough and capable hands, and bid her demonstrate her gift before Adonijah Hart's sceptical eye and ear. *Go on*, the fat woman had demanded, *Sing*. The maiden, weary-eyed from the four-day carriage ride, obliged and every single piece of glass, from tumbler to windowpane, from mirror to vase, had exploded. Fortuitously, it hadn't been in the evening when customers filled every inch of the music hall, from velvet-covered wall to velvet-covered wall. Master Hart, whose eyebrows met in the middle, dusted shining fragments from his shoulders, hair and beard, and shook his head to dispel the ringing, then suggested, with a glint in his yellow eyes, that it would be cheaper to simply get rid of her.

'And you'll explain to her aunt where she's gone, then?' asked Madame Arkady archly. She knew full well that Adonijah for all his front was as afraid of Bethany Lawrence as she was, and with good reason; he had the missing finger on his left hand to remind him how tolerant she was of dissent. 'The girl must not be harmed, must not be *hunted*, must be left intact in all fashions. Her true name should not be spoken for there will be those who remember what happened to her family –' Madame would have employed the girl in her own House in a heartbeat had she not feared the consequences of someone recognising her or of her aunt finding out – 'She's to be kept safe and she'll turn a profit soon enough, I'll guarantee.'

Reluctantly – as if he had a choice! – Adonijah Hart agreed, but as the Madame's ample bustled backside settled itself into one of the plush armchairs so they might discuss her share of that profit Victoria Parsifal was to make, he grumbled, 'She'll bring nothing but trouble, you mark me.'

So, the girl was installed in one of the empty attic rooms, and no one but Venetia Volkova was told her true name, though each and every theatre employee (lesser singers, better dancers, all flesh for hire) was warned that they were responsible for her remaining safe and sound, locked away except when she performed. They resented the watchfulness her presence forced upon them. Deals were struck with the city's Glassmiths' Guild for the production of the right kind of items to ensure the Chaucer's new acquisition was a showpiece, not a liability, including windows resistant to the vibrations of the girl's voice. Yet even Arkady's predictions were short of the mark: the songbird had pulled in such a large clientele that she'd paid for herself and the glassware almost fifty times over by the end of a month. Her earnings outstripped even those of the gambling den in the basement, and the discreet whores on the second and third floors.

The girl has never tried to run in the six months she's been held here. She stays not merely because of the close watch kept on her, nor because she's never allowed to set an unaccompanied foot outside. She stays not merely because of the threats which she's got no doubt both Hart and Arkady would make good on to hunt her down. She stays because defiance got her into this predicament. She stays because she has nowhere else to go.

* * *

Victoria seldom looks at the audience. Or rather, she looks but does not see them as anything but a mass, a moving swaying, toe-tapping, amorphous crowd. She does not examine individual faces – she'd done that on her debut and it had terrified her. The sheer greed, the fervent desire, running rampant across visages male and female, whether from love of music or love of the grand wreckage she caused, it did not matter. She'd felt like nothing so much as a treat to be devoured. That memory was, if she was honest, another reason she did not run; a prison the Chaucer might have been, but one that as effectively kept the monsters out as it kept her in.

This night, however, oh this night, something draws her attention to the tables, the long chaises, the stools that line the well-stocked bar, up to the balcony booths where the more affluent sit so they may look down on all, or indulge in their vices behind embellished wooden partitions painted gold and red. Something pushes and pulls Victoria's gaze hither and yon, and when her green eyes finally latch onto a point in the middle of the great room, onto the only table occupied by a single figure, when that happens, she is disappointed: she cannot see more than a silhouette. The stage lights do not help, and the main floor is lit just enough for waitresses to ferry drinks through the maze of furniture and patrons – and dark enough that said patrons cannot divine if their beverages appear somewhat weak, somewhat watered.

The girl narrows her eyes without actually squinting, mindful of Mrs B's long ago warning about wrinkles. The thought of Mrs Bell brings a surging ache, and other faces rise in her memory. *No, no, no!* Not yet. She pushes them down for if she thinks of those beloved features she will weep, and if she weeps she will ruin the act, and then she will be punished. Victoria Parsifal steels herself in unconscious imitation of her mother. There is only this last aria, only the final pieces of glass set around the room to shatter in a few moments. She focuses her attention, stares at the silhouette sitting so far from her; a woman, she thinks, straight-backed, thin shoulders, a long neck and tilted head, a hat that appears as a dark construction of veil and lace, ribbon and bow. But no fine detail. No. Nothing further to see. A veil at night? Victoria wonders, then thinks it not so strange if the woman wishes to enjoy this particular diversion incognito as many do; some in Seaton St Mary have enough reputation to protect.

Aware of the build in the music from the small orchestra pit, Victoria takes a deep breath. She closes her eyes, lets the memories come now, lets them break her heart as they do every eve. The pain is how she knows she is still alive. She holds the note until she hears the telltale bursting of vitreous items, then lets it go on a little longer as if that might squeeze the last pang from her, finally allowing it to drop away as the applause soars to meet her, overwhelm her, touch her.

When she opens her eyes again, the table where the woman sat is empty, and Venetia is beckoning from the wings so the next act might take to the boards.

* * *

'Did you hear?' The voice has a lilt to it and a lightness, which one might think would translate to a fine alto. Alas, by some strange alchemy the spectre never manages more than a squawk whenever she tries to accompany Victoria's private serenades. It might have something to do with the large gash still evident in her ghostly throat.

Victoria has not been able to ascertain why it was Ozanne Agnew who attached herself when Oriel and Victoria had always been closer friends. Yet Victoria's never seen hide nor hair of the other twin, and Ozanne chooses not to answer whenever questioned about this matter. Truth be told, it's quite a while since Victoria asked for she's become something of a pragmatist, taking comfort where she can. Ozanne is there. Ozanne connects her to the past. Ozanne helps her to remember. Ozanne is the only one who calls her by her name and not simply "girl" or "Nightingale". The past weeks – almost two months – she has not felt alone.

And Ozanne, who passes through walls and floors and ceilings, who is seen by no one else, collects snippets of gossip and information from around the Chaucer, though she says she cannot go *outside*. At the end of each day, she tells who is fighting with whom, which of the harlots has found special favour with which client and which other strumpet's nose has been thus put out of joint. Ozanne knows who is pregnant, who thinks they are safe in short-changing Mr Hart and how wrong they are; she knows precisely what Mr Hart is beneath his skin.

'Did you hear?' she repeats urgently.

'Hear what?' Victoria asks, using a damp cloth to wipe off the thick stage make-up Venetia applied. The fabric comes away smeared with red lip wax, black eyeliner, blush-pink rouge and malachite-green shadow. She scrubs the last of the maquillage until she can see her own pale skin in the mirror, then begins on her hair. It's the same ruddy brown as her father's was, backcombed and styled, forced upwards and held in place by myriad pieces of folded copper and the spray Venetia mists onto it each night. Even when all the pins are gone, the style does not shift; it is only with the aid of a tortoiseshell brush that Victoria can deconstruct it. Venetia is only ever there for the building phase; Victoria thinks she does not like to see her illusions pulled apart.

'The hind-girls have been seen in the woods on the outskirts of the town,' whispers Ozanne and Victoria is unsure whether it's an intentional lowering or if the breeze passing through her severed larynx is insufficient to create anything louder.

'Have they? They're coming close, then,' says Victoria, pausing in her coif-related ministrations to watch as Ozanne nods and begins to move around their attic kingdom; a tarnished gilded cage where everything is second- or third-hand. It's not lost on Victoria that Merry used to occupy a room quite similar in the Lodellan house.

"The hind-girls dance along the narrow forest courses, throwing their heads with such abandon that sometimes the antlers of one get caught in those of another. But their feet are sure on these paths of beaten earth for they known those ways of old," Ozanne rasps the tale her mother had read from an ancient book, the one passed down from Odela's own mother and grandmother and great-grandmother. And the spectral girl dances, too, mimicking the steps of the two-legged hinds, the girls who have chosen to be *so*, to be free of all civilised constraints. Ozanne's grace is increased by the fact that she floats above the carpets installed by Master Hart to ensure his songbird does not catch a chill. Ozanne moves like a cloud, like a mist across the surface of a winter's lake.

Victoria sighs. Hair finally down, if not entirely tidy, she rises and makes her way to the bed, which is almost new and not previously used by the girls of the Chaucer. She snuggles beneath the quilt, which has only three darned patches. Ozanne is still prancing, not in the least bothered by items of furniture or the sharply sloped roof, for she passes through both – it is the closest Ozanne comes to leaving the safety of the Chaucer, for she tells Victoria that she is held *here* – though she does not explain how or why, just as she is somewhat fuzzy as to how and why she came to find Victoria. Sometimes she says *Summoned*. Sometimes Victoria could swear the ghost girl brings flakes of snow in with her when she draws her head back inside after it's been through the ceiling. But she cannot be sure; the things, if they exist in the first place, disappear too quickly.

'Tell me the story again, Ozanne,' she begs and the other girl pretends not to hear, as she does every night. But Victoria is patient and lies still. She closes her eyes; past experience has shown that when her companion senses herself no longer watched, she'll stop her gambolling and drift towards the bed. Soon enough Victoria feels – or thinks she does – a slight pressure on the quilt as if her friend can bring any weight to bear. Victoria senses – or thinks she does – cold thin fingers on her forehead, and the whispery voice begins anew.

"Once upon a time on the far side of yesterday, in a land that never was, in a time that could never be, there lived girls who chose their own fate…"

Victoria drifts to sleep, wrapped in the familiar words and a promise of freedom for which she dare not hope. She sleeps through the click and thud of the door locking, as she does every evening when Venetia comes to ensure she is secured, and she continues to slumber, not so much later, when there is scratching and scraping at the skylight, which is sealed by pitch. This too is a frequent occurrence, and the thing persists in a hope every bit as evergreen as a forest glade.

Ozanne is not aware of this visitation for she has gone, passed through walls to plant seeds in other dreams.

* * *

'We could leave.'

Venetia's tone is sultry. She's lying, half-dressed, on the magnificent bed that takes up a large chunk of real estate in the manager's rooms. She wonders if Hart would try to remove her, should he tire of her; decides he'd think it not worth the trouble she'd cause. Besides it's a long time since she shared space with the other women of the Chaucer, and that period was so brief that she can barely remember it. But he won't tire, she's sure, not with their shared skins, their hidden selves known only to each other. Their sort are rare enough nowadays, and that bond is worth more than any entertainment he might find with someone younger, more biddable.

'And go where?' asks Adonijah as he removes his jacket. Here, away from prying gazes, from faces eager for a sign of weakness, he allows himself to look tired. Venetia knows there are shadows beneath his eyes for she'd applied the concealer herself to help him keep his mask intact. But his sleep has been interrupted for weeks on end, he mutters things under his breath that she's not been able to coax from him in the morning when he claims he cannot remember anything.

'Anywhere. You have money put aside. I have money put aside. Let us go. We board a ship and sail towards the horizon, find what lies beyond it.' She sits up, one strap of her corset slips from a creamy shoulder, but Hart merely raises an eyebrow and gives a weary grin; mostly these blandishments work but not tonight, not regarding this. 'We've been here long enough,' she says as if they've a history *before* they met at the Chaucer.

'And *where* would we go?' he insists

'Anywhere,' she replies with equal vigour. 'We travel. We are not tied to one place.'

'Do you think we'll be so easily allowed to *retire* from what we do?' Hart holds up his hand where there is a vacancy in place of the pointer finger. 'I've no desire to lose more than this.' He sinks onto an ottoman and begins to unlace boots that seem to never lose their shine.

'Then we run. We can disappear. We go north.' She juts her chin towards him as if he's the direction in question. 'We go to the cold and the snow; go back to my places.'

'You fled them for a reason, my lovely girl.' He gives her a smile that no one in the Chaucer would recognise: an expression of trust, humour, patience and love.

'The Dark Lands, then,' she says, and wonders how she became so desperate so quickly. 'To Caulder and then beyond.'

He pales at the thought. 'Even our kind, my love, I do not think would do so well there, not with the leech lords.' Hart rises, goes to the bed and fits himself against the curve of her back, weaves his fingers into her almost-white hair, kisses her shoulder. 'What is this fear, Venetia? Why now?'

She shakes her head, swallows hard; the distress coincides, she thinks, with his terrible slumbers. 'I say to you what I'd say to none other: I am afraid. Every day misgiving creeps like a tide through my veins. I am not used to such a feeling and I do not like it.' She hisses, 'I do not know what is happening, but *somethin*g is happening.'

'Such mortal terrors!' he says and laughs though he knows it will anger her. 'What do we have to fear from such things?'

'And yet I am afraid.' She sighs hard as if it might become a sob if not carefully controlled. 'Can't you sense it? Swear to me you cannot. All is not as it should be, on the streets, in houses, in the woods; the world is *turned*, Adonijah! I see things in the corner of my eye that are not there when I look directly at them. There are cold patches in the corridors of the theatre where once were none. I find it harder to hold my shape! Tell me your dreams are not disturbed and distressed! And the hind-girls, Adonijah, are growing bolder. I hear tales; so few things know us, so few things stand against us.'

'My dreams will pass, my love. You are tired because I keep you awake with my restless slumber. All will be well, and we will stay the course, Venetia.' They both know he lies. 'Besides, we cannot leave the girl. I lost money and Bethany Lawrence took my finger: if we neglect our charge, my lovely Venetia, what do you think she'll do?'

'Feed us to the wolves,' she says morosely, then they both laugh, knowing *that* won't be their fate.

'We have the girl, that is something. Bethany Lawrence doesn't want the child gone, or at least not quite yet. We hold the little one as long as we must.'

'Not so little any longer. She needs new clothes, Adonijah. There's no more room for her to fill out what she brought with her.'

'Can't you… mend something?' asks Hart.

Venetia laughs. 'I'm a whore, not a tailor.'

'Not a whore anymore,' protests Hart and Venetia is pierced by his sincerity.

'Nonetheless, the girl must have new things. Her tits will pop out on stage and what will you do then, when customers think she's for sale?'

'Have a seamstress call here,' he grumbles. 'You're too soft on that girl.'

'She's an investment,' says Venetia quickly. 'No, I must take her out. The only seamstress worth having is new in town and does *not* do house-calls.'

'If you've already made enquiries, my dear, you've already made up your mind,' he says pointedly, 'so why are telling me this?'

'To give you the satisfaction of thinking you're in charge!' Venetia's tone is light with laughter. She'll get new clothing of the expedition as well.

'Do not overly abuse my pocket,' he warns, and she kisses him to stop his mouth, then continues to kiss him to stop the hollow pulse of fear in her veins if only for a little while.

Ozanne watches them from a corner of the room, perching with no visible support. She watches as they take their pleasure in each other, as they sample experiences that have been stolen from her by her death. She waits until they are done, waits until their breathing is slow and steady in sleep. Then she floats to the bed, leans over Adonijah Hart and begins to whisper into his dreams.

* * *

The air is cold and there's been a light fall of snow overnight, so all the market stalls have a fine, crisp layer on their canvas roofs. Now, flurries of white puff through the square and Victoria thinks she sees shapes form in them, ghostly as Ozanne's, but then they are gone almost as soon as she spots them. Venetia, wrapped in a full-length fiery fox-fur that makes Victoria want to weep and stroke it at the same time, has a firm grip on the girl's wrist, and Victoria is sure she can feel a pulse of distraction passing between them. Her own cloak is velvet over thick layers of wool, goose down, and woven ribbons; the hood is raised over a knitted cap, and around her throat is a scarf that feels too tight, but upon which Venetia insisted. Gods forbid anything should happen to that voice!

Victoria would have liked to enjoy one of her rare trips outside in a more leisurely fashion, but the woman is impatient, even more so than usual, as if she's anxious to be out of the cold, in where four walls might keep things at bay. *Venetia is not so bad*, the girl thinks, when compared to Aunt Bethany. Venetia wasn't supposed to care for Victoria, had no connection of blood to her, yet she wasn't needlessly cruel. Perhaps, reflects Victoria, she might have had an easier road with her aunt if she'd not been so defiant, if she'd not refused to forget her mother despite Bethany's reassurances that it was for the best that all memory of Cordelia be left behind.

Yet Victoria had found in that subject – Cordelia – a cause, a light, something to hold onto: she refused to stop telling Torben tales of their mother and her care for them, so he wouldn't forget; refused to listen to Henry who counselled her a quieter path; refused to stop asking when they might make their way to Rosebery Bay and visit with Mama. Refused to stop grieving when Bethany had told them of Cordelia's fate on the burning hulk. She'd refused to love her aunt as she demanded to be loved. Refused and refused and refused again until Mr Farringdale – with his staring eyes and fingers that landed on, then left, exposed flesh too quickly to be commented upon – was sent for, and Victoria and all her things were taken to Madame Arkady for *disposal*.

Victoria wonders what might have happened if she'd known then what Ozanne had told her some weeks after she'd first appeared in Seaton St Mary: that the ghost girl remembered most clearly the night she and her family died. Victoria wonders if, with that knowledge, she'd have repeated to her aunt Ozanne's tale of the frightful wakening as a knife danced its cold path across her throat, of the sudden gushing warmth as her life flooded out. How the ghost girl recognised the face looming over her, coming suddenly into the beam of moonlight from the window, the dark blonde hair, the eyes so green, the face enough like Victoria's that Ozanne, even dead, sometimes shudders to see her friend.

Victoria's experiences since her exile have taught her to be more circumspect in how she deals with those around her, how blatant she is in stating her beliefs and dislikes; she has learned the art of dissimulation. What if, in a passion, she'd thrown that terrible knowledge at Aunt Bethany? Might she too have felt the cold kiss of steel on her flesh? Thus she is respectful even when her contempt burns most brightly and makes her stomach clench. She is amicable when all she wishes to do is scream and shout. Unfortunately, this obedience, so harshly learned, has made of her a fearful creature; her courage, pushed down so long, hides itself too well. She trusts no one except Ozanne, for the spectre can neither carry tales nor betray troth.

'Hurry up, child,' hisses Venetia, somewhat dampening Victoria's fondness for her. Her voice is husky and she tugs at the girl.

'Your throat is sore?' Victoria asks and her companion throws a withering glance. But Victoria nods towards one of the stalls where an old woman, her hair tucked under a scarf in peacock shades, stirs a large steaming pot. The cloud is thick but the scent is not unpleasant. 'Perhaps a ginger tea, Venetia? My mother used to give it to us when we were ailing, with honey in it.'

Venetia slows, finally stops, then drops Victoria's hand. She reaches into her purple silk purse for slivers of coin and exchanges them with the old woman for a wooden cup, polished smooth and shiny by many hands. Venetia sniffs, then chugs the contents down, all at once. There is a moment when both vendor and Victoria hold their breath… then Venetia gives a resounding burp, her eyes bulge, and she laughs.

'Better,' she says to Victoria, as if they are friends rather than prisoner and escort. She snaps off another sliver of coin for a drink for Victoria.

By the time they arrive at the *modiste's* place of business, Venetia's mood has improved and she is humming, with her hand pressed to the girl's shoulder to gently guide rather than either drag or push. They pause at the door with its diamond-shaped glass panes; when Venetia presses it open, a bell above sings their presence. They wait for a response and Victoria uses the time to examine the shop, which is exquisitely decorated: white and grey marble parquet floors, the walls painted grey-blue and the brightest white on the skirting boards, cornices and covings. The windows are large to let in light, and hung with thick muslin curtains, swan-coloured. Gaslights (expensive and rare in Seaton St Mary) augment the product of the weak winter sun. But what she notices first of all is the scent: at various spots around the shop candles of pink and cream burn, a mingle of rose and jasmine, not overwhelming but subtle. Victoria feels the tension melt from her shoulders and chest, and thinks she sees Venetia undergo the same *melting*.

The room is spacious: one wall taken up with mirrors; a corner is curtained off for changing in private; a row of chairs with curved legs, winged backs and well-padded seats, in a deeper blue-grey than the walls; intricate silver hooks are provided for the hanging of cloaks and overcoats. From the roof is suspended a single item: a dressmaker's mannequin, hewn from polished mahogany and embellished with gold pegs and bolts, screws and handles, the turning of which will make the form expand or contract as required. Victoria wonders if there are others elsewhere, less fancy, more for practical use, less for show.

'So much for too busy.' Venetia snorts, eyeing the empty space, then calls out, tone sharp as cut glass: 'Hello?'

After a few moments, there is a shuffling, a noise like a mouse, and a door, cleverly concealed behind one of the mirrors, swings open. The seamstress is not much older than Victoria, and she is neither plain nor pretty, but somewhere in between with her face unadorned by any kind of colour or tint, and her hair almost entirely concealed by a delicate cap, beautifully embroidered with columbines and phlox; a few curls, red as flame but looking more dyed than natural, peek out from beneath the brim. A pair of silver-framed spectacles are perched on her nose, topped by very dark brows. Victoria thinks her familiar but she cannot quite place the combination of features. The *modiste's* dress, an olive serge, shows off oyster-hued underskirts, and the leg'o'mutton sleeves are decorated with tiny bells, so as she moves a frivolous *tinkle* sounds; for all its sombre colours the craft and skill in the making of the gown are obvious. Her expression is serene, confident: she knows what she does and how well she does it. On the right upper bodice is pinned a small brooch in the shape of a spray of lilies. Victoria blinks; she had one just like it once.

Victoria thinks Venetia unlikely to take to the young woman but when the seamstress smiles and offers her hand, Venetia accepts it without hesitation.

'Mistress Volkova?'

'Mistress Asher. Thank you for seeing us.' Venetia's politeness surprises Victoria, but then, she reasons, surely even Venetia must know that some situations call for manners. Or perhaps it is the civilising effects of the candles' perfume.

'And thank you for making the trip, I know your time is valuable. I am new to Seaton St Mary, and must devote as much of my time as I can to my craft. At the moment, no house-calls are possible.' The other woman also knows the required form, knows the steps of the dance. It occurs to Victoria that she has lost the art of socialising: it's so long since she had playmates, and the circle of people she interacts with is so very small, and most of them are hostile – many of the Chaucer's girls simply ignore her and have done so ever since she first arrived. Loneliness hits her like an unexpected storm.

Mistress Asher takes their cloaks and hangs them on the beautifully wrought silver hooks, then leads her clients to the chairs. She produces a decanter of cherry brandy and pours three measures into finely blown glasses etched with a mother-of-pearl hue. When they've had a sip, she asks, 'And what do we need today, little miss?'

Victoria is struck shy, and she looks away, peeking through the mirror-door to the workroom where she can see rows and rows of dresses, some finished, some half-made, pinned to headless mannequins. There are bolts upon bolts of cloth, seemingly in all colours, a striking range of patterns, most with a sheen that suggests they will be become dresses for ladies and whores.

'Something that fits!' says Venetia, who gulps at her brandy; Victoria wonders how strong the beverage is and sets hers aside. 'She's fair bursting out of that child's frock. She will need stage clothes for her performances, too – Mistress Asher, you must come and visit, listen to our little Nightingale sing! – and some everyday robes, simple long-wearing things.'

'And nightgowns and some undergarments,' adds Victoria, feeling bold, and Venetia nods, waves her glass in agreement.

The seamstress's eyes travel to Victoria's boots, noting how scuffed they are. 'Perhaps new shoes too, I think. I have some.'

Victoria flashes a grateful smile.

'You're a cobbler, too?' Venetia laughs, helping herself to another measure of the cherry brandy.

'No, but I know that ladies like to have properly coordinated outfits, so I keep some stock. I do believe there will be something to fit the little miss. But, dresses first.'

Venetia and Mistress Asher discuss colours and cuts; the first of the stage gowns will be delivered to the Chaucer two days hence. They must be dramatic, drawing attention to the girl, yet modest: *Here are the goods, you may not have them.* The day frocks are an easy matter, as there are already several ready-to-wear that can be fitted quickly for when a client is in a great hurry. From the back room the seamstress brings a primrose bombazine with small white embroidered flowers, an unadorned dove grey serge with snowy cuffs, and a lavender brushed cotton, with silver animals embroidered along the hem, a chain of dancing badgers and foxes and owls, which makes Victoria exclaim with delight.

In the dressing room, Mistress Asher hangs the dresses, then stands back to usher Victoria in. Pulling the thick curtain closed behind them, she quickly unbuttons the girl's too-small dark green woollen dress, then leans over her shoulder to whisper – much to Victoria's confusion – 'Be ready, Victoria.' When the girl turns her head to look at the seamstress, the young woman lays a needle-scarred finger to her own lips, then steps out to leave Victoria alone. It's the first time she's heard her own name spoken by any lips other than Ozanne's in so very long.

Perplexed, Victoria lets her frock pool at her feet, then kicks it aside as if she hates it. The primrose bombazine is easy to pull on, less easy to button the tiny pearl nubs. Outside, the seamstress engages Venetia in conversation about the sort of outfit *she* would like. The girl hears the whisper of silk and satin, and knows wares are being show, the temptations of finery deployed. There are rapturous *oohs* and *aahs*, and the *clink* and *glug* of more drinks being poured.

Just as Victoria's fingers reach their limit, just before she calls for assistance, she notices a crack appearing in front of her – no, not a crack, but a slit, a sliver, a widening abyss betwixt wall and mirror. A panel, not quite a tall as she is pushed open, and a passageway is revealed, dimly lit by torches. There is just a silhouette at first until a woman steps forward to the edge of the opening, but not into the dressing room. Her dress black as coal, black as night, and a veil, very thick, covers her face; Victoria thinks the woman's mourning must be very deep indeed, her grief a bottomless well. The woman holds up a gloved hand, the right one, and beckons.

Victoria does not move, and the woman speaks softly.

'Victoria, come now, please, we must away.'

She knows the voice, so soft, the tones so tender. The girl leans forward.

But something is wrong. There is a slowness to the speech, an impediment as if the speaker is making sounds underwater. Her mother's voice, but as if she drowns in the air. Her mother who was reported dead and gone; why is she in the wall? The girl reaches out and pulls the heavy veil away, tears the hat from the head and finds, in place of Cordelia's sweetly remembered features, a monster, or half of one at least.

The left of the creature's face is melted, there's no other word for it; a mess of scars and raised angry red flesh, the lid drooped and partially fused over a white, sightless eyeball. One side of the scalp is hairless, although Victoria can see places where the filaments once gold, now cindered, have burned themselves into the skin. The left corner of the mouth is joined, almost to the halfway point. There is nothing in the world for Victoria but that ruined wreckage of a face.

The grotesque grabs at her wrist, holds so tightly, so tightly, hands clawing up her forearm, and the girl is convinced the thing will burn her too. That although its inferno seems dormant, this thing holds within it the very essence of fire, and at any moment the flames will burst forth, lick at her, taste her skin, her flesh and lap it away until she too is nothing more than a mound of burned *meat.*

Victoria has no fear of ghosts, but this is a monster, something from Ozanne's storybook tales, a ghoul, a corpse-wight, come with her mother's voice to lure her then steal her soul.

She screams.

She panics.

She pulls away.

She tries to run.

Tripping over the skirts of her new dress and the old, she falls, taking the curtain with her. There is a terrible tearing, and Victoria is covered, blinded by the thick fabric. She is certain the beast will yet take her as she falls into the shop.

She is still shrieking when Venetia drags her free of the drapes, and slaps her to silence. Victoria points at the dressing room, now bared before all eyes, but there is nothing. The mirrored panel is closed, hidden. Venetia strides into the alcove, looking for a bogeyman. In those seconds, the seamstress kneels beside Victoria, meets her eyes and shakes her head. And in those seconds, Victoria recalls that at no point was the seamstress told her name, and she recognises at last Merry's sorrowful gaze.

And in those seconds, Victoria realises what she has done.

She has the wit at least not to say anything more.

* * *

'What a show this one put on,' sneers Venetia as the door to the Chaucer closes behind them.

Hart is leaning against the bar. He directs a yellow gaze at Victoria, who's wearing the newly fitted primrose dress and doing her best to keep the tears in.

'Indeed?' he says, and gestures to the barman, who pours a mulberry gin.

'Screaming and crying as if a wish-hound was after her.'

'I got a… fright,' offers Victoria lamely. 'I imagined it, I know. Just a fright.'

'Well, we have larger problems than that.'

'What?'

Hart nods towards one of the padded booths, up close to the stage, where Madame Arkady sits, a barrel swathed in red and purple satin. Her fat little hands are raised to her hair to remove a hat with two stuffed bluebirds in a nest of tulle perch on the brim, then ensure not a one of her glossy dyed black curls is out of place.

'What does *she* want?'

'No doubt she will tell us.'

'May I go to bed?' Victoria asks meekly. 'My throat is sore and I would rest it before tomorrow's performance.'

'Not yet, girl, for the Madame has asked especially for you. No doubt she wishes to report back to your loving aunt as to the conditions of your care.' Hart's hand with its nails the consistency of glass darts out and grabs her chin. He draws her closer in this way. Her heart skips unhappily. He sniffs at her skin, her hair, her clothing, as if he might extract lies by this means. Then he pushes her away, dissatisfied, distrustful.

'Go,' he commands, and she does not wait to be told twice; she walks in front of Hart and Venetia. Out of her habit of being biddable, she bobs a curtsey to Arkady, then is annoyed at herself.

'Girl,' says the fat woman. Hart puts the glass of gin in front of her, mutters that food will be forthcoming.

'Madame,' answers Victoria meekly. She remembers the day Mr Farringdale took her to the House of Curiosities; she remembers other things from that day, passing by rooms with doors ajar wherein acts were being visited upon small bodies. On her way out, in the custody of the Madame, she saw some of those same small bodies no longer moving, no longer crying, but draped over the broad shoulders of the House's employees like sacks strangely full yet utterly empty. That memory is yet another reason Victoria has stayed at the Chaucer: she's never yet seen anything so awful here.

'Adonijah.' Madame nods, seemingly calm, but Victoria notes

that she does not speak to Venetia, and that fat woman is perspiring. The temperature inside is not so warm as to make anyone break a sweat, so either the woman was unduly hurried in her arrival, or is unduly nervous. The way her eyes flit around the shadowy corners makes Victoria wonder what or who she's looking for.

'And to what do we owe this pleasure?' asks Hart. Neither he nor Venetia sit, but remain standing; they flank Victoria, who is not sure if she feels threatened or protected.

'I come to ask if you have seen or heard from Isambard Farringdale?'

'We've never had direct contact with him,' answers Venetia, a tiny silvering of contempt clear in her tone, and Madame's eyes narrow, her gaze clearly articulating *Why is this whore addressing me?* Venetia moderates a little: 'Such dealings go through you, Madame.'

'What's happened?' asks Hart, who has no time for beating around the bush.

'He has… not been seen in some while.' She swallows. 'He's been gone… I do not know… his day maid only recently noticed his absence – they did not often cross paths – and she reported to me, but no one truly knows when he was last in his home.'

'To be unmissed…' says Venetia with a hint of sadness.

Victoria thinks of the little man who'd been around her family all her life, who'd been so attached to Aunt Bethany, and who'd delivered Victoria to her current fate. He gave her a doll once, but she'd never played with it; it had sat in a corner for a few days before she'd stuffed it as far up the chimney as she could reach. She'll not miss him, and the corner of her mouth rises. Arkady notices and snaps, 'You, girl. What do you know?'

'Nothing. What could I know?' asks Victoria. 'Nothing, but he gave no aid to my parents in their trials. I have no reason to mourn him.'

Madame Arkady leans forward, her ample breasts resting on the table in front of her, and pins the lass with her gaze. 'There are rumours. Rumours of your mother.'

Victoria can't hide her shock, but there's no reason for Arkady to know the true reason for it; she puts the note of a sob into her throat. 'My mother is dead. My mother burned on a prison hulk in Rosebery Bay. My mother never came home.'

'Yet still.' The woman sits back, taps her fingers with their red polish on the varnished surface. 'The Agnew Necklace was stolen from the palace of Lodellan. The Prince's wife has been blamed, exiled. Yet pieces of the necklace have appeared in pawn shops and private collections. They have come to the attention of… colleagues of mine. By all accounts, where they go, ill fortune follows.'

'Anyone might have stolen it,' says Hart reasonably. 'What chance would Cordelia Parsifal have of surviving an inferno that killed fifty other women? The woman was a dunce, a lackwit. Hardly the sort to mastermind such a theft – unlike her sister. If you're seeking a thief, look to Bethany Lawrence before Cordelia Parsifal.'

Victoria wants to object to that characterisation of her mother, but she also knows it's best to remain silent.

'In fact, it sounds very like something Breakwater's Queen of Thieves would do,' sneers Venetia. 'Steal the same necklace twice.'

Arkady shakes her head. 'Only a fool would say that aloud. No. She's been looking for Farringdale high and low since I told her. He knows too many secrets.'

'Why did she leave him alive?'

'He still has value.'

'Perhaps *he* stole the necklace and is funding his flight with the proceeds.'

Again Arkady shakes her head. 'I know him. Isambard is predictable in his peccadilloes, his habits, his tendencies, his devotion to Bethany. He is usually in my House at least once a week, but I was travelling and did not realise the lack of him until I returned.' She finishes her drink, then sets the empty glass to spinning on the tabletop, her eyes following its perfectly balanced reel. 'I could set my watch by that little man; he is not brave enough to flee and of all folk he knows there's no escaping Lawrence. If he is gone it means someone has taken him or he is dead.' She scratches at her forehead, hard enough to leave red marks, and glares at Victoria. 'So, I ask again, girl: have you seen your mother?'

Victoria's heart thuds so hard she is sure it must be heard. 'My mother is dead, Madame Arkady, burnt to a cinder. You must look elsewhere for your culprit.'

The fat woman stares at her for a long while, as if her glare might shake out some truth, but if the girl has learned nothing else at the Chaucer, it is patience.

'If I might enquire, Madame, where did these rumours of my mother's survival come from? Perhaps you might ask instead who might benefit from the spread of such falsehoods.'

And Arkady looks taken aback, as if she had not pondered this question herself. Her mouth moves like a fish gasping for air. At last the woman snorts and waves a dismissal. Victoria is careful not to walk any faster than she should, nor to show any greater desire to leave than might be considered normal. She feels eyes on her back, suspects it's Venetia's measuring gaze. Will she mention once more the girl's episode at the *modiste's*? Will it rouse Arkady's suspicions? Or will she simply shrug it off as Hart did, merely as a sign of Victoria's mental frailty?

In the attic room Ozanne waits, hovering over the bed as if she is sleeping, two feet above the mattress. She gives her friend a smile and floats upright, to almost, but not quite, stand on the rug by the hearth. 'Oh, what a pretty dress!'

Victoria does not answer. She closes the door softly, knows that Venetia will come along later to lock her in; she wonders if it is the time to flee, to take her chances at sneaking past the other inhabitants of the Chaucer, and running to Mistress Asher's – Merry's! – shop. This is the one eve she does not perform: would she be missed? But if she is caught, if she leads them to Merry, to her mother! No. No, she will wait. Mother and Merry will have some new plan; why, in a matter of days she'll be taken back to the shop for a final fitting on the stage dresses. Rescue will come.

Her mother survived! Cordelia survived water and flame and has returned for her daughter! So much effort they'd gone to, such expense by the look of the shop, and Victoria had ruined it all. The girl sits heavily in the rickety armchair by the fire, her knees giving way. Her hands begin to shake and that transmits itself to the rest of her body.

'What's wrong?' rasps Ozanne, drifting to her side.

'My mother. I saw my mother.' Victoria is surprised at how strong her voice is, how steady.

The ghost girl gasps, but with her slit throat it sounds like drowning. She asks, almost fearful, 'She's a ghost? Like… me?'

'No. She's alive. Alive, Ozanne!' Victoria's eyes shine despite the afternoon's failures. Perhaps she does not notice Ozanne's silence because the spectre is oft given to periods of quiet, or perhaps because she is thinking of what new plans might be being made even now. Victoria is determined that, the next time, she will not fail to be brave. Or perhaps she simply forgets the other is there until Ozanne speaks.

'Zilla said the hind-girls killed a man behind the Drowned Maiden Tavern, and carried off two girls into the forest.'

Victoria shrugs. Zilla is Ozanne's favourite girl to eavesdrop on even though – or because – she exaggerates the most. The hind-girls have no need to kidnap women; there are plenty who choose to go to them, to transform, to live as they do. Yet the thought of a man killed by them troubles Victoria not at all. The world, she thinks, would be a better place, scattered with a few more such corpses.

'Tell me something else, Ozanne. I don't care about the hind-girls tonight. They've got their freedom. Tell me a different story, a tale of change and renewal, tell me a tale of hope, of lives pulled back from the edge. Tell me a tale of a fire that does not burn.' And though she speaks firmly, Victoria is not quite sure what she means. She rises, and carefully removes the new dress. She crawls into bed, huddles under the coverlets, and closes her eyes, summoning her earliest memories, of her mother's hands washing and dressing her, for Cordelia would give up care of her children to neither nanny nor governess, wet-nurse nor mother-help. Of Cordelia gently brushing her hair, untangling knots, never hurrying or hurting in haste. Of her mother standing her on the kitchen table, holding her close and dropping a singsong whisper into her tiny ear *Mummy's here, Mummy's here, never fear, never fear.*

Ozanne, nonplussed, wracks her brain for something new, something strange. She's at a loss, having told the same story or a version of it so many times, and now the other tales from her Mama's book seem to have deserted her. But then… there is a spark… a tiny recollection, a whisper from a time when names were forgotten but deeds were remembered.

'Once upon a time, in Badger's Briar, there was a woman who'd lost everything she valued, home, hearth, land, husband, children, family. Injured and bleeding, certain she had nothing left to live for, she threw herself in the graveyard's communal pit where the unloved were tossed to rot. She bore terrible injuries that should have killed her, and in that hollow of decaying mud and vital fluids she stared up at the sky, waiting to meet her maker.

'But she did not die. She slept and when she awoke all her wounds were healed; the cuts and tears, the bruises and breaks, even the wrinkles on her face that she'd earned by her time in the world were all gone. The mud she'd lain in was *argilla viva*, the living clay, and she set her mind to how it might best be used in a new life…'

* * *

Hart's nightmares feel like chains, and no matter how hard he tries he cannot wake. His mouth is dry as a desert and when he attempts to scream his lips are stuck together. In his dreams, they've been sewn in place, stitched by the hand of the girl, Victoria. She's leaning over his bed, a terrifyingly long needle in hand; the length of black thread is still connected to his flesh. The girl gives the smile of a satisfied housewife; as he watches she leans down and snips the thread neatly with her teeth. Then she takes the needle once more, gathers his eyelids, upper and lower, pinches them together and begins to darn them closed.

Outside of the dream, in the bedroom, he does not scream, yet speaks as he tosses and turns but does not stir.

Venetia, however, *is* awake. She gave up trying to rouse him some time ago and has instead been listening to him mutter Victoria's name over and again, in a low feral growl. She cannot distinguish between notes of hatred or lust, having often found them to be intertwined. She only knows she's been kind to the girl and the girl has played her false; why else would Adonijah be moaning those four syllables in such regular, raw rhythm?

She rises and pulls on her dress, then the fox-fur cloak over top, and laces her feet into a pair of stout, low-heeled boots. Though she stomps when she stands – almost in hope – Adonijah does not wake. If she took a moment to examine him further, she might realise his is the stupor of bewitchment, but a red veil of jealous rage has been hung across her eyes, her perceptions, her heart; her course of action has been determined.

Though this was not what she'd planned, Ozanne, floating above the door, laughs gleefully, a wheezing sound that Venetia can *almost* hear as she passes beneath the malign spirit.

* * *

'I should have known, you sly little trollop. Butter wouldn't melt in your mouth, oh so innocent! I should have known it for an act! Got your aunt's blood in your veins, how could I forget?!'

Venetia marches Victoria through the dark and snowy streets. Victoria wears neither cloak nor shoes. Venetia was cunning and careful enough to take her out the back way, through the laundry and the tiny overgrown garden behind the Chaucer so the men on the front entrance would know nothing of this endeavour. Victoria's bare feet are half frozen, and the hem of her nightgown darkens with each step through the melting slush. New layers of white cover their footprints almost as soon as they are made. She trips and slides as she is dragged along. Her skin and lips have a blue tint, and her teeth rattle against each another.

'What will you tell my aunt?' she demands, surprising herself by her boldness. With rescue so close, how can she be fainthearted now?

Venetia laughs and it is more snarl than anything. 'That your mother lives and took you. That she survived Rosebery Bay. Never fear, little songbird, you'll not be found, by either your aunt or your dam. Bethany will be so busy looking for her sister she'll not question *my* story.'

'If you think my aunt so easily distracted then you don't know Bethany Lawrence very well at all,' Victoria says coldly. 'She'll skin you alive.'

Venetia pulls up short, shocked by the sudden fierceness. She gives Victoria a shake, slaps her hard, as if trying to knock fear into her, but the girl doesn't cry. She bares her neat little teeth and that makes Venetia laugh even as she says, 'All my kindnesses to you and this is how you repay me.'

'Your kindnesses were few,' Victoria spits, then asks, 'Tell me what you think I have done, Venetia!!'

'Adonijah,' hisses Venetia, as if this explains everything.

Victoria, still innocent, takes a long while to understand. Then she laughs, and Venetia takes this for an admission of guilt, of triumph of a sort, and slaps the girl again and again until blood drips from her perfect little nose. The woman lets her go and, without any support, Victoria falls to her knees in the mix of mud and melt.

When her ears stop ringing, she looks around. They are outside a tavern, the Drowned Maiden, in the centre of town, but it is so late even the inn's lights have been extinguished. The streets and alleys are empty as far as Victoria can tell, and she knows enough of Seaton St Mary that any shouting on her part would be met with a fastening of shutters and locks; this is not the place in which to expect aid.

'Run,' says Venetia, hands making *shooing* motions, and she laughs again, teeth so white in the moonlight. 'Run, little girl.'

And Victoria does not question, does not query. Though her feet are numb she bolts. She is a bird released, a hind fleeing. She thinks only of finding her way to the forest, to the place where buildings are scarce, and town and woods bleed together, nothing to say definitively *here one ends and here the other begins*. Of losing herself there, and Venetia's pursuit.

Then she recalls Ozanne, who was not in the room when Venetia threw open the door. The ghost girl will not know where she's gone.

Ozanne, waiting and watching, held in place, waiting forever. And then she wonders if, perhaps, without Victoria there, without her fear and need, will Ozanne cease to be?

Victoria risks a look behind and sees Venetia has not moved from her spot, but that she has removed her magnificent cloak and placed it on a water barrel; that she is stripping off her amber silk dress with small deft movements. Victoria's speed bleeds away and she comes to a stop, though her heart warns her not to, yet there is something so compelling about Venetia's disrobing. Victoria thinks of the tales Mrs B told of men whose eyebrows met in the middle, whose palms were hairy… and she thinks that a woman is more likely to pluck her brows to an elegant shape, to use sugar wax on any unwanted hair about her person. She thinks of Venetia's eyes, as yellow as Hart's. Ozanne did not warn her about Venetia.

Venetia, now naked, throws back her shoulders as if she might have their points meet behind her, and Victoria hears not a howl, but a cracking of bones and a tearing of skin.

A voice in her ear, whispery as air from a cut throat, says 'Run!'

Victoria bolts again. There is just the sound of her own breath and the pulse of blood thundering in her ears, and hissed directions – *Left! Right!* – as she tears along streets and lanes, unknowing of where she goes, merely praying that Ozanne is correct in her instruction. Ozanne who should not be outside.

Victoria is not built for speed, she's never trained for such physical activity, is not fit for a prolonged chase, but she's harried on by the knowledge that her survival depends on this and this alone. That and Venetia's ecstatic howls resounding on the sides of houses, along paved pathways, ricocheting off barrels and carts and stairs and windows, all the things that stand between her and Victoria. Ozanne hovers beside Victoria, untroubled by the flight which leaves wisps of her ectoplasmic form trailing in their wake.

There is a moment when town turns to wild wood and Victoria's not sure how it happened; she passes trees, stumps, bushes and shrubs, rocks and small startled nocturnal creatures too slow to flee. She clumsily hurdles things, her nightdress torn by the reaching brambles, threads and shreds festoon branches, signalling her passage for any who might follow. The ground is pitted, churned, as if many have passed this way, not hooves though, nothing cloven, but rather feet that have left half-moon cuts above the toes, where jagged nails make their mark.

Victoria tries to run faster, but a tree root appears as if from nowhere. She trips and stumbles into a clearing, tumbling over and over, feeling her right wrist snap as she falls awkwardly. But she is soon upright again, seeking a sign, a break in the foliage, an avenue of escape.

But there is nothing.

The clearing has only one entrance-exit, the path by which she came. The trees here are so closely grown together they seem almost a single entity. If she were to try to press herself between the trunks she would be caught, easy meat, easy pickings. Victoria turns and turns and turns. Then she stops.

Ozanne, just above the ground, is shaking and shivering like a leaf in a storm. At first Victoria thinks her friend is crying at her failure to provide safe passage.

'It's alright, Ozanne, this isn't your fault.'

'I should hope it is!' whisper-shouts the ghost girl. 'All the time it took to find you, tracking you from Lodellan to thence to this backwater! All that time holding *her* in check until it was just right! So you didn't get off too easily, too soon.'

'What do you mean? Ozanne, how are you outside of the Chaucer?' Snowflakes fall a little harder, catching on Victoria's lashes. She blinks. Somewhere back along the path comes another howl.

'Oh, so little time! Come out, sister, come out and watch! See what entertainment I have made for us.' Ozanne pirouetting and dancing. Beside her something coalesces from the cold air, a hardening of mist and ice particles until her twin is hanging against the night. Her twin, yes, but with injuries far worse: her head barely remains attached to the neck, so vicious was the blow that severed her little throat.

'Oriel!' cries Victoria – her favoured, her friend! – but the ghost doesn't smile, though the lips on the almost-decapitated head draw back in a snarl. Victoria can tell there remains no trace of any fondness that Oriel once bore her. The spectral twin's fingers twitch as if pulling flesh apart.

'Oriel,' says Victoria again, without hope.

'I've had to counsel her to be patient,' says Ozanne confidentially. 'She wanted to deal with you herself, but I reminded her that our ability to affect the material plane is bothersome limited. We're good with dreams, though, tremendously good.'

'Ozanne…'

'She'd have given you nightmares to send you to death. I had to keep her outside most of the time. She'd sit on the roof, watch you sleep through the skylight. I told her that you should suffer, that you should have a life, a little life before we took it from you. It was *your* aunt who did this to us. We deserve this blood.' She giggles. 'I thought it would be the man, but the woman will deliver our vengeance just as well.'

'My aunt won't care that I'm dead. Don't you know that by now? Have I not told you enough tales?'

'You've told me enough tales for me to know that your aunt won't like anyone dealing with her *property* in a high-handed manner.' Ozanne smiles. 'You will have lost everything just when you've begun to yearn for better again. How delicious! Your mother so close! And *we* are beyond the hand of the living.'

Something barrels into Victoria and knocks her arse over tit. She shrieks as her wrist is battered in the fall. She and what was Venetia roll together, now fur, now flesh, now snapping, now screaming, until they fetch up in the centre of the clearing and tumble apart.

Victoria tries to scramble backwards, her fingers dig deep into the mushy ground, her wrist a ball of agony that won't allow her to pull herself too far. The wolf pads over, lays its forepaws on her thighs, and pins her. The lips draw back from long ivory teeth and hot saliva spatters down onto the bare flesh of her legs. Its breath is hot and reeking on her face, though Victoria refuses to close her lids, refuses to be fearful any longer.

The only skerrick of Venetia in the lean face is the eyes, strangely human-shaped, almost at odds with the rest of the features, but there remains nothing mortal in the wolf… except… except…

Venetia's fine head tilts, her gaze narrows and fixes upon the phantasms of the Agnew sisters. Shifted, no longer mundane, she can suddenly see them.

A noise breaks their moment, and each looks around for the source of the low crooning, which rises, from a hum to an angry chorus.

Stepping from between the trees, between those impossibly close boles Victoria could never have fit into, beneath the light of the moon, perhaps fifteen, perhaps twenty, forms materialise. It seems that the trunks shift and shuffle, pull away from each other to let the girls and women, some barely out of their teens, others with white-grey hair streaming from their shoulders – all naked – through. Antlers grow from their temples like strange crowns covered in brown velvet. Their feet bare with mud up to the ankles. They approach, slowly at first, tossing their heads more violently with each step. Their eyes shine red with anger.

Part of her mind is distant, detached, and Victoria wonders whether she has trespassed on sacred ground. She does not have to wonder long, for without warning one of the hind-girls charges, head down. She hooks the wolf with her antlers and tosses her aside, yet she is careful not to trample Victoria as she makes another run at Venetia, who is trying to roll to her feet.

Victoria scrambles away, holding the injured hand to her chest. She reaches the edge of the clearing, sobbing, and leans against a tree, its bark rough through her thin nightdress. As she watches, another hind-girl butts at the wolf, who howls in pain, a red tear along one of her flanks. The hind-girls take turns, either deliberately opening up more wounds, or sometimes merely tormenting her with a shove. Venetia makes terrible noises.

It's murder, Victoria thinks, a slow murder. She considers her time at the Chaucer, of Venetia's rough considerations. Venetia, the only one who'd even been a little kind to her.

'No,' she says too softly. Then shouts, 'No!'

Victoria wades in amongst the herd, finds where Venetia lies, bloodied and kicked back to humanity, no trace of her silver-grey fur except in those places where tufts of it stick to wet patches of skin. In the depths of a rent in one of her shins white bone shines bright beneath the full moon.

The hind-girls back away, still dipping their heads and horns dangerously as if they might change their minds at any moment and charge forth to crush them both. Victoria stands in front of Venetia, arms spread to show the women where they may not trespass. There is a strange silence until a breezy wail of rage splits the evening.

Ozanne and Oriel swoop at Victoria, although only Ozanne is able to give voice to her fury. She passes through her friend, once, twice, but cannot effect anything more than a shiver and a shock. At last she hangs there, screaming into Victoria's face about how unfair everything is, that Victoria has no right to all her luck! That these hind-girls would save her as if she might become one of their own! Victoria is so absorbed that at first she doesn't notice… but then Ozanne produces another noise altogether.

The hind-girls have begun at her feet; the oldest women in the herd, the wisest who know how such phantasms must be dealt with. Oriel, too, is being devoured from the bottom up, but she utters no protest, merely stares at Victoria with a glittering gaze. Ozanne shrieks the whole time as her pale essence is folded up between layers of pink tongues and slurped in like soup.

When their meal is done, one of the younger hind-girls gives Victoria a single nod, a single glance from midnight blue eyes, then moves away. Her sisters follow her down the path with not a glance at the once-wolf.

Victoria helps Venetia to her feet. Though she is battered, she can stand when Victoria steps away from her, fearful that too close a contact will result in renewed captivity. Naked, Venetia shivers, her skin moving with a life of its own, as if it's not entirely connected to her anymore.

'What will you tell them?' asks Victoria, voice shaking.

Venetia hesitates. 'Not what I did. I will say I forgot to lock your door. I will say you spoke of wanting to return to Breakwater. If your aunt thinks you're coming to her, she'll not expend much effort in the finding of you for a while.'

Victoria nods. She steps in, pushes her shoulder beneath Venetia's. 'I'll help you to the edge of town, but no further.'

'That's more than fair, gir—Victoria.'

As they shuffle back along the path, there is little trace of the hind-girls, the mud appears more churned perhaps, but the snow has stopped. Victoria thinks of what she will do once Venetia is propped against some wall, able to hobble her own way back to the Chaucer. She will not let Venetia see the direction she takes, for she's not entirely trusting of the woman. She will find her way to the *modiste's* shop. She will knock on the door quietly-quietly so as not to rouse attention from the neighbours. When Merry answers Victoria will fall inside, will urge the seamstress they must leave immediately. And then… and then she will find her mother waiting for her. Cordelia will hold her upright and stroke her sweat-curled hair. She will croon in her daughter's ear *Mummy's here, Mummy's here, never fear, never fear.*

There will be horses, she thinks, there might even be a carriage to carry them far away. A smile tugs at Victoria's cold lips as she makes her limping way into Seaton St Mary for the last time.

OF GHOSTS AND GLORY

Awake! Awake!

So many days, weeks, months since the birds beneath the mountain – white, blind and malign – had shrieked those words, thrown them echoing down the corridors of stone to bounce around the halls hollowed out of the earth's body. To shake the misshapen forms from their slumber – longer and longer did they sleep, the world above become less and less a place into which they could slip and sidle with ease – and let the creatures know that a thief had crept into their kingdom. That their treasures had been plundered, their sanctuary violated, and the guards meant to keep them safe been slaughtered by a bold and steady hand.

It was worse than a crime, it was an insult.

An insult that could only be wiped away by the liberal spilling of blood.

And so the Queen of Trolls called forth her own child, who had once walked in the sun, to dispense justice.

* * *

'Are you alright?' asks Sabine. She's the mistress of the coffee merchant, having refused to marry him for going on ten years.

Ildikó, weary of answering – she's been asked the very same question three times since she stepped into the market square of Able's Croft – merely nods. Sabine hoods her gaze as if she understands all too well, and hands the jewel-smith a gold-etched glass filled with cold coffee and a stick of sugar, which will melt gradually to sweeten the beverage. Ildikó accepts with thanks, rueful; she thought she'd covered the bruises sufficiently, but perhaps the scratch from Áskell's intaglio ring (carved with the shape of a bear) – somehow vertical, and very near to the hairline – is not as inconspicuous as she'd hoped. She should have known that the townsfolk would watch the mayor's wife far too closely for such a thing to go unnoticed.

'Thank you, Sabine,' she says quietly, then quickly drains the cup, and returns it. The sugar stick is almost still solid.

'Will there be anything else, Ildikó?'

'If you could have your boy deliver two sacks of the blend my husband prefers, today or tomorrow? We have enough to last a few more days, but it would be best not to run out.' She signs her name in the order book; the invoice will be presented at the end of the month. Áskell is scrupulous about the payment of bills, which may well be his sole virtue. 'Thank you.'

'I believe Gerde has something for you,' says Sabine casually.

'Yes,' answers Ildikó. Why else would she have left the house, her face covered with a layer of paint so thick she might be taken for a street girl? But she does not say this, does not let the bitterness loose, for Sabine and the other women of Able's Croft have shown her many kindnesses over the years even though she was not born one of them. Their pity is painful, but this is what she has: it keeps her afloat.

'Good day to you, Sabine.'

Ildikó, one hand holding her basket, the other slid beneath her belly for support, manoeuvres past the sacks and barrels that half block the door. Sabine's shop boy – who is in his sixties – has been slow in shifting stock. Ildikó steps into the sunshine and its steaming air – summer has been long – and sighs. She's too close to fifty, too old to be having this child (any child – though her own mother bore *her* later still), and the pregnancy has been hard. Harder still with Áskell, who is careful not to hit her belly wherein he thinks lies his longed-for son, but who has no qualms about backhanding her face when he considers her in need of such discipline.

At least she's been spared his attentions in bed since they realised she was pregnant. Ildikó's more grateful than she can say to Artemisia, the apothecary's daughter (she knows more than her father ever will for she is not afraid to peer into the darkness of mind, magic and heart), who'd told Áskell in no uncertain terms that he must let his wife alone if he wanted to see his child to term. It is Artemisia, also, who keeps Ildikó in creams that take away the pain and the bruises, that buoy up her body to make this carrying-time not quite so tiresome. Yet there is only so much salves can do.

Ildikó heads towards the butcher's shop. Her feet and ankles are swollen. She will visit Artemisia afterwards, for some dandelion tea and perhaps something new for her face.

* * *

The air tastes different above. Familiar but only just. How long has she been beneath? How many years have passed while she lived in the darkness with strange kin? She travels mostly at night; though she'd lived in the sunlight once upon a time, she finds it uncomfortable now. There are those of her kind who turn to stone in the sun, but she thinks her time before changed her.

Besides she is no longer in such command of her old shape, so each dawn when she finds a place to hide – in a cave or crevice, abandoned cottage or empty barn, even holes she digs in the damp ground with her own long fingers and shovel-like hands – she practises. She changes to the old-her, the once-her before she goes to sleep; when she wakes the form has slid away, she takes up more space and differently. But she feels the transformation becomes easier. Soon, she will be able to appear as she did all those years ago.

Then she will pass by not unnoticed, but noticed in the right way.

* * *

If Bruna was surprised at Ildikó's announcement that she'd go to the market herself that morning, she'd showed no sign. The girl, new to the household (hired for the unexciting features that keep her safe from Áskell's attentions), does not question, even though the groceries were done yesterday. Bruna cannot know (although she might one day realise, if she remains in the mayor's house long enough) that claims the butcher is out of bacon wurst are a recurring event.

Gerde smiles when she sees Ildikó, an expression that dims as the woman draws nearer and the subtle layers of purple-blue beneath the make-up become obvious. Gerde is broad, nuggetty, though there is no fat on her; her hands are square and the skin red as if the blood and meat she deals in have stained them. As she stares, she curls fingers into fists and rests them on her wide hips. Her lips purse but she says nothing except, 'Here it is, my dear,' then passes over three wursts and a letter, the latter of which Ildikó tucks carefully into the deep pocket of her wine-dark dress.

'Thank you, Gerde. I appreciate it.' And Ildikó returns the smile; the expression lights her face.

'You're always welcome. And, Ildikó?'

'Yes?'

'Be careful if you wander. There's word of wights on the roads, of wolves coming close to town, of things that aren't wolves all the time.'

'There's always some tale, Gerde.'

'No mere tales, these. And more frequent the occurrences are. Be wary, my girl, that's all. And the hind-girls have been seen, and it's no fib they whisk away the careless.'

Chance would be a fine thing, Ildikó thinks, but does not say that or point out that the hind-girls only take the willing and the brave.

She'll not risk reading the letter in her cellar workshop even though she can hear the movements of the household above her, would recognise the sound of Áskell's boots if he returned sooner than he should. She does not mind that there is no natural light down there, no windows to provide distractions when she works – though she's done little enough of that in recent times – what does bother her is the lack of escape routes. There is only the door at the top of the stairs and, should Áskell so choose, he can trap her quite easily. She's thought on occasion of hiring local men to dig a tunnel, but she knows it would not remain confidential. Though the women stand guard over her secrets, the men cannot be trusted. They would ask themselves 'What manner of man would keep such knowledge from our fine mayor, so generous, so powerful?' with no thought of the consequences for his wife.

Of course, she also picked up the careful lilt in Gerde's tone. Women born in Able's Croft all practised a kind of singing magic, their cadences designed to soothe souls and temper reactions, an especially handy tool for the management of husbands. Her friends, she has discovered, are not above trying to use the technique on her for her own good, and some days it calms her. Unfortunately for Ildikó, being an outsider, she has never mastered it – though she's wondered often enough if it would matter if she had: Áskell, also born elsewhere and his personality as it is, seems unlikely to be affected.

However, she's determined to have this single freedom. She would rather take her chances with the wights and the wolves and the sometime-wolves and the hind-girls. So Ildikó nods, says, 'I'll be watchful.'

* * *

She's been tracking the thief by his smell. Her kind's been known – in the old days when they roamed further with less consequence – to stalk an unwary traveller for days and weeks, from forest to city in the interests of a good meal, an act of revenge or simple spite. And the thief left his scent behind in full measure, pissing in a corner before he left, spitting on the bodies of the guards he'd murdered.

But...

There had been something else...

Another odour and it had confounded and confused her. Sent her off in directions that had nothing to do with her hunt, her quest. She visited towns and cities and houses and haunts of former days, looking for the ones she'd loved, once. She'd searched and sought and found nothing, not a trace.

Not a trace but that thread of scent like a red line dotting the air.

So, she has wandered longer than she ought, but who will know? Her folk will slumber once again. Her mother... the mother-troll-queen-thing... she might doubt. She always has even though she was the one who ordered what was done to be done. A dislike for the child she'd sent forth to be made and remade, when the fault is hers alone.

Thus some while passes in distraction and diversion, and only now does she return to her appointed task when other streams run dry.

* * *

The forest glade is small, and a little way out of Able's Croft; it's only found by those who know enough to seek the narrow, mostly overgrown path that leads off the main road. By some quirk of nature and weather, blackberries grow here year-round. Ildikó quickly fills the basket with the fruit. Should Áskell be home when she returns, he'll not suspect she's been wasting time and he's got a taste for the blackberry preserves she makes. Although no doubt he'd prefer she spend her days working on trinkets that might bring in more gold, for which he's got a dragon's taste, a troll's appetite. As if he's not stolen a fortune from her already. But Artemisia also told him she and the child would be at risk if she breathed in the dust of her materials, so he's left her in peace.

When she's done and the basket is all but overflowing with the fruit, Ildikó rests beneath a yew tree. She has not seen her son in an age, but he has never ceased to write. His script is untidy, but she has no trouble deciphering the beloved words. His missives are like stories, for Jacopo's life criss-crosses itself like lines on a map, here an encounter, there a misadventure, here an acquaintance made, then lost, and there found once again as a firm friend. But always something new, always something unique, for her son is as changeable as his face.

The tales of his first years in the world were breathless, a constant stream – or so it seemed to his mother – of high adventure. He was a ship's boy on the *Poseidon's Breath*, a merchantman out of Breakwater for a while, amassing a small fortune, in and out of scraps and scrapes with such terrifying consistency that she thought perhaps the captain was not averse to acts of piracy. When he grew bored with the sea, he joined trade caravans, even made an expedition to the Dark Lands. He wrote of the city of Caulder just beyond the border which produced some of the finest silver in the known world, and where a blood-drinker still ruled, though one strangely benign and much beloved, keeping her people safe when others of her kind farmed their mortals like cattle for blood. He'd been granted audience with this Adlisa, found her charming and clever, but so terribly sad. She'd begged him for death – a balm none of her subjects would grant – and which he could not. How she'd been reluctant to release him, until he told the tale of his mother and how much he missed her… that had seemed to touch the ruler and she let him leave.

He'd told of the ruins of the great Citadel of the Little Sisters of St Florian at Cwen's Reach, a place that had once held all the knowledge of the world, yet been reduced to rubble in a single night. One could still see derelict volumes, torn pages weathered by time and elements, fluttering across a courtyard cracked and destroyed by cannon fire long ago. He wrote of the jewel-smiths who'd worked in the town, knowing she'd be interested in those who shared her profession, and of the strange inn, a ship embedded in the honeycombed cliffs below the Citadel and run by a woman rumoured to be an ex-witch.

He'd not so long ago written of the carnival troupe he'd joined once the trade routes began to bore him; how he made a living he didn't need (he'd been clever with his pirating funds) from his skin-shifting, performing on rickety stages to wondering audiences – no one called him a *witch* because he was male. He told, too, of the woman they'd found inside the ring of sanctuary stones just beyond the boundaries of Rosebery Bay. She was barely breathing and badly burned, but Gwyn the hedge-witch and tallow-wife who travelled with them had brought her back to life. Their foundling – she could not or would not give a name, and so they simply called her the Cinder's Sister – had grown stronger, learning magic at Gwyn's knee and assisting her in the making of candles.

In this latest letter, however, Ildikó catches a sense of something that has been missing: excitement. His previous recountings for some time have felt flat, merely a recitation of acts committed or events witnessed, but this epistle… once again her son is breathless.

Dearest Mama,
You'll be most likely delighted to hear that I have left the troupe (for I know how you've disdained my associations with charlatans and jackanapes as you've been wont to call them). You will recall, perhaps, my mention of the Cinder's Sister? Well, I am no longer in ignorance of her true name, though I'll not commit it to paper for letters oft go astray. Suffice to say I am accompanying her – let me call her the Tallow-Wife now for there is none other with whom to confuse her – on a quest which I believe to be noble.

Ildikó makes an annoyed sound, an exasperated sigh. She senses her son will follow this Tallow-Wife to the ends of the earth if he must, yet not for reasons of the heart, or at least not in a romantic fashion. He's made references to girls over the years, however those mentions were nothing so much as butterflies, blooming beautiful and rare for brief moments and then gone. But this is not like that, and Ildikó must suppress the ache that tells her he's attached himself to this woman by way of seeking a mother he might have a chance of saving. She cannot be so stupidly jealous, yet there is still that ache.

Remember the tales Grandmamma Theodora told of the city of Lodellan? Well, my dearest, I have been there in the service of my employer, of course, and what do you think? I entered the grand Palace where Theodora once lived, trod those gilded halls where her dainty feet once touched. The great bathroom of which she spoke? Still there! Intact and just as she said. Not a word of a lie.

What were you doing there, my lovely boy? wonders Ildikó nervously and soon finds out. Although he is unwilling to name his accomplice, he cannot resist mentioning their act.

My employer had been deprived of much, Mama, family, home and wealth. A great injustice, that she has been left destitute and homeless in this world, and unloved. I was able, by means of my unique abilities, to assist. She confided at last that her late husband had gifted her a necklace of immense loveliness (not to mention value), which had been confiscated. I'll keep quiet details of the how and why (though no doubt you can imagine, knowing me as you do, Mama) but needless to say I took particular delight in relieving the Royal Family of that fine city of their prize. I can never forget Grandmamma's tales of her treatment at the hands of Husband the First, her Prince of Lodellan, and the fact that my actions helped another victim of their selfish reign made the victory all the sweeter.

Ildikó swallows hard to think of the danger he put himself in, all for the sake of adventure wrapped in the guise of aiding a stranger. She cannot help but hate the woman who's drawn him into her web, into her troubles. Yet when she reads the description of the necklace, which her boy lingers upon, she thinks she might well faint.

And it is a perfectly beautiful thing, Mama, must have been made by someone touched by the Divine. A magnificent amethyst cut so cunningly that both darkness and light seem to dance within and without its impossible depths! There is a band of alternating emeralds and diamonds, set in an opening lily of white-gold, each petal perfectly recreated. All hanging from a chain of the tiniest, most elegant interlocking silver spirals. Though it makes me feel a traitor to say so, I fear even you, my darling Mama, could not have made such a thing!

And Ildikó feels ill, thinking of the cold weight of that purple stone in her palm as she contemplated how best to cut it; her art had grown in the years since her son's departure and he would not recognise her skill now. She thinks of the kind little man, Leon Agnew, who'd made a special trip to see her and ordered the making of the necklace – and she had been only too happy to use the gems Áskell had dumped on her workbench one day; to get them out of her sight. He'd told her that the amethyst was not to be sold, that it was hers and she was to wear it. She'd not liked any of the jewels from the start and her husband had refused to tell her from whence they'd come. Ildikó did not ask why some had a patina of dried black blood on their surfaces for she'd learned her lesson long ago.

No, she'd not liked any of the stones in that calico sack, but especially not the uncut amethyst, so misshapen, so primal, almost like a hunched creature that might unfurl when the household slept.

She'd misliked it less after she'd finished, when she'd cut away much of its bulk, shaped it to be beautiful, surrounded it with the diamonds and emeralds; when she'd forced her will upon it. Yet it still made her nervous. During the creation she'd been gripped by a fever, seldom sleeping, eating little, obsessed with the thing as if ridden by some demon of fabrication. Ildikó thinks of how delighted Leon Agnew had been once she'd handed over the finished product – and of how relieved and exhausted she'd been to see the back of him and the two burly men he'd brought to keep himself and his treasure safe on the long journey home. She thinks of how Áskell, troll-like though he is, loving gold above all things, had lost his temper when she told him how she'd used the amethyst, that it had been *sold*. And she thinks of Leon Agnew's fate, and that of his family. She thinks of the news brought to her by an amused Áskell who'd heard it from a travelling tinker who sold his wares at too high a price but buffered the gouging with the information. Ildikó knows the Agnews all died by a burglar's hand, so the woman Jacopo has thrown his lot in with – who has turned her son into a thief – cannot be an Agnew, cannot be the kind little man's wife.

She will write; she has always replied to his letters at a poste restante address, at an inn close enough to Breakwater that it's easy for the boy to visit on his travels (for they always seem to take him past there), but far enough from that dreadful city that he might not be too easily traced. She will write and bid him be wary. She will write and forbid him from having anything more to do with the Cinder's Sister who surely drags no good luck in her wake.

Yet Ildikó knows she gave up the right to forbid her son anything when she sent him from home.

After a year of marriage, Áskell realised that the physical hurts he visited on her no longer mattered – her gaze turned inwards, her body went limp, for all intents and purposes she went *away* – so he started on Jacopo. His stepson functioned merely as a means to punish Ildikó; should the boy die then Áskell would find a new way to hurt her soon thereafter. Ildikó, knowing she had brought the monster with a man's face and form into their lives, also knew that the only way she could save her son was to send him into exile.

She made preparations in secret, then one morning, after her husband left for the mayory, she sent the twelve-year-old Jacopo on his way with a satchel stuffed full of food and all the coin she could scrape together. Though it tore at her to do so, she'd no doubt he'd be dead or almost so in the space of a month if he'd stayed. She prayed his face-changing would help keep him safe; he'd done it even as a child. Some mornings she would look at him in his cradle and think *He is not mine!*, but then the next minute he would laugh, he'd be her son, *her* little one, once more. She didn't know where the ability came from, some unsuspected strangeness in her blood or his father's.

Ildikó reads Jacopo's last lines, empty things for the exciting information has already been relayed: hopes for her health, for the child to come, for a reunion between them one day, for his stepfather's timely demise. She closes her eyes, leans against the trunk of the yew tree, rests her hands, still clutching the sheets of onion-fine paper, on her stomach. The baby inside wriggles and kicks against her palms, making the folios crackle and sigh. *There, there. There, there,* she murmurs, just as she had when Jacopo was nothing more than a weight at her waist, and rubs her belly. The motion soothes both mother and child, and soon they fall asleep.

* * *

The smell.

There it is... or part of it. There's someone else... yes. She recognises that too, though it wasn't the one looked for. Female and male: parents. The woman who sleeps against a tree trunk, the pages of the letter tugged from her loosening fingers by the sly breeze, came from two she knew once. The belly's so rounded, so heavy, the woman's got her legs crossed beneath her, sitting like a child. There are lines on her face – oh, they smooth out under the weight of slumber, but they're there and deep for the woman's old to be having a baby. Troll-kind spawn most of their lives, expelling stone eggs and letting them hatch where they fall, then delivering them to human cradles like cuckoos. And she smells another still... that first one...

As the huntress watches, the woman stirs a little, her hands seeking her belly, press at it gently as if it too might be smoothed out. She's never done it herself, this one, never bred, whether through a choice her body's made or some other reason, she's never cared to question.

She steps out from behind the trees, draws herself up, concentrates.

Her bones obey, albeit reluctantly: changing, realigning, compacting to acceptable proportions. The scraggly black hair becomes a flood of gold, the complexion turns creamy, the eyes go from ebony pits to blue pools, the creviced lips pink and plump. The loose skin splits and reforms, folds back on itself, becomes a gown of deepest night.

There. Ready. She strides across the clearing.

* * *

The child kicks, hard enough to wake her mother.

The light in the clearing has changed and Ildikó doesn't understand where she is for a moment. How long has she slept? *Too long.* The shadows have stretched thin; Áskell will be home by now. He'll never believe the truth, that she fell asleep somewhere; he'll think she's been with another man, though she's never shown any such inclination. Indeed, she believes that time spent with her husband would be enough to make any woman swear off the male of the species forever.

She gathers her wits and looks about for the letter. There is only one page still in her hand; the others have blown across the grass. Before she can track them, she notices a movement in the shadows on the other side of the clearing.

A woman, tall and strong-looking, pushes her way between the trees. Long blonde locks stream around her shoulders and down to her waist. Her gown is black as pitch, the sleeves a thin gauze that look like spider's web and the skirts appear liquid, viscous. She smiles, a friendly expression, yet it causes Ildikó's heart to clench. She tries to push herself upwards, but gravity holds her too well.

Ildikó notices that, when the other woman steps into shadow, she changes or seems to. She tells herself it cannot be anything more than a trick of the light. In the shade, the woman transforms, becomes even taller but misshapen, hunched and twisted, her hair now straggly black, nose hooked, skin wrinkled and teeth razor-sharp. Then in the last of the sunlight she is as before, stunningly lovely, so beautiful that Ildikó feels inadequate.

Her own hair is the same dark brown as her mother's, shot through with white rather than silver, as if time chose quite definitely to be unkind. Her skin is creamy, but there are bags beneath her eyes, crow's feet creep outwards from the corners like deltas. Her rosebud lips are past their prime, though no one would notice if she were given to smiling. Her dress is rich and well made, for Áskell will not have his wife attired like a pauper. Yet still Ildikó cannot help but think resentfully that the loss of her husband would take several years from her appearance.

The stranger is beside her now and this close it's clear her eyes are ice-blue. She kneels, slides one arm around Ildikó's back and helps lever her, with no perceptible effort, into a standing position. Ildikó feels faint, sways, and the woman puts a steadying hand to her rounded belly, intimate without permission. The touch is brief, so brief, but Ildikó feels the baby freeze as if to pass unnoticed. The woman smiles, steps away once Ildikó is stable.

'Are you well? You are very pale.' The voice is strong, mellifluous but decisive, with none of the gentle tones Ildikó has come to associate with the women of Able's Croft. Ergo, the woman is not from here.

Ildikó nods, then shakes her head, then nods. She cannot understand her confusion; it is the passing of the hours, she tells herself, the disorientation of sleep. The woman reaches out again, but Ildikó raises her hands, uses them as a shield: *No*. The other's fall away, but the smile doesn't waver.

'I am well,' says Ildikó. 'I am well. Thank you for your help, but I must go.'

She cannot imagine why she wants so badly to flee, but she scoops up the basket awkwardly, stuffing the single folio of the letter under the cloth; she will return later, tomorrow or the day after and find the other pages, but for now she must escape.

'Allow me to assist,' says her uninvited companion, 'for I am going the same way.'

Ildikó does not hesitate, does not pause; she does not offer her own name, for in such things there is power. She repeats only, 'I must go,' and sets off at a stumbling walk-run to leave the bright woman.

But when she is on the main road once again, she throws a glance behind and sees herself followed. She is more concerned with avoiding this stranger, making it to home, than with the terror of her husband's rage when she arrives so late. The thick gold ring he wears on his right hand will no doubt lay the ground for new scars on her shoulders, breasts, back.

When Ildikó at last reaches the fine four-storey house with the brass knocker and diamond-paned windows she owned long before Áskell insinuated himself into her life, the woman is still in pursuit, still smiling gently every time her prey glances around. Ildikó half-falls up the steps to the portico, then against the entrance; she feels faint, wants to give in to the dizziness, but refuses. However, when the door opens with a creak and Bruna looks at her in surprise, Ildikó can no longer help herself: she vomits all over the serving girl, drops the basket of blueberries, and promptly passes out.

* * *

The house... the house is nothing like the ones she'd grown up in. First the palace of Lodellan, then the grand manor her not-mother had purchased for all those who'd left the Golden Lily Inn. After that the open road, a series of inns and barns and cottages. And after that... after that, beneath the earth, in the belly of the mountain with all her stone-hearted kin. She eyes the carven door with its fine silver bands, the shining windows of coloured glass, the small balconies that hang above like icing on a cake.

The woman leans against the door, knock-knock-knocking, and it opens; she falls into the arms of a plain-faced girl, is spectacularly ill. A man, big as a bear, dressed in more colours than a festival day whore, his yellow hair curled and coiffed like his beard, looms there now. His expression is hateful, angry, and it makes her shape shake. Not from fear, no, but because she wants to cause him harm. It's all she can do to remain as small as she can, as lovely looking.

He sees her and his face changes as surely as if he shifts the way she does. But he's human through and through, she can smell that on him. And she can smell on him the scent she'd been sent after. This is the one who'd pissed in the halls of the Queen. He's with the woman, the pregnant woman: that's why she could sniff out this one... all those aromas converge here.

He smiles.

She smiles.

They move towards each other and she stretches forth her hand.

* * *

Ildikó's fallen asleep over the bench when she should be working, fallen asleep in the cellar workshop when there are pieces awaiting her attention: rings, two in silver, one in gold, all lacking their stones; bride-price bangles, five gold and four silver, some of which she must engrave with flowers and rabbits and badgers and owls and swans' feathers; and there is Artemisia's birthday gift, ordered by her father. A chain of intricate interlocking spiral silver links, in her signature design (developed only after Jacopo left her), elegant interlocking spirals. The work requires such concentration, such closeness that her eyes hurt after a while. Artemisia will not turn twenty for another eight months, and this is the most ambitious piece Ildikó's attempted since... there must be a pendant, also, an etched silver locket with a starburst design, tiny sapphires set at the end of each arm.

Too tired to lift her head, she listens carefully for the sound of her husband's boots overhead, stomping across the floor of the dining room. She waits in vain for the scrape of him pushing back his oaken chair carved with the face of a howling green man in the exceedingly high top rail. There is no noise of him striding towards the front hall where he will collect his coat with the rosettes of office decorating the shoulders, the green, blue and yellow knots of fabric that echoed the colours of the town's coat of arms. Is he tidying his reddish beard in the mirror by the hallstand, making sure no crumbs mar his general appearance? Áskell remains vain; he's still tall and broad and only a little run to fat, but his eyes are mean and piggy, and there's more than the trace of a flabby pouch beneath his chin, his jowls softening by the day. How did she not notice that until after the wedding? She holds her breath: is he waiting outside the door of the cellar?

No.

No, she's not sleeping in the workshop.

She's in bed and there are voices, soft and low, which Ildikó recognises.

Artemisia assures Áskell that his wife will be well enough after a few days of repose. The girl is stern, buying some peace for Ildikó by playing on the man's fear of losing his "son". 'Bed rest, absolute and uninterrupted, no stress, no demands, no fuss. Indeed, it would be better for her to have the room all to herself, Meister Áskell, even the slightest disturbance could upset the child's wellbeing.' Inside her mind, Ildikó smiles.

The other voice, however, withers the smile. It makes soothing noises, yet the cadences cling like the wisps of a nightmare. Ildikó forces her heavy lids open, just a sliver. The woman from the clearing stands beside Áskell, her hand with its long, delicate fingers and shell pink nails, touch his arm; they're in front of the brightly coloured tapestries woven by Ildikó's aunt. Áskell is transformed, and she recognises his expression: the one he wore when a pretty new maid was employed – before Ildikó learned to hire the plain girls. The same look he sports when about to depart on a "hunting trip" to the north (which she discovered soon enough meant a tour of brothels he'd invested in). The look that says he has found something he *wants* and is determined to have.

He has never flaunted his mistresses – it wouldn't do to let his constituents know too much – even when he'd showed his truest of colours to his new wife. None of them ever last very long.

Normally, Ildikó would feel relief that his attentions are elsewhere, but this woman… this woman with her beauty and her slow smile that lifts like a hook in the heart… somehow Ildikó senses she is more than clever enough to know how to manipulate Áskell's idiot affections. She'll withhold what he wants, what he begs for, she'll put conditions on his being granted her favours and those conditions will mean Ildikó's setting aside in the most permanent of ways. This woman does not want one such as Áskell – why would she? She can clearly see right through him to the rotten core – therefore she must want something else.

What else can it be but *assets*, feathers for a new nest?

As Ildikó peers through her lashes the guest turns her crystalline gaze on Áskell and says, 'It was my fault. I distressed her, gave her a fright.'

Ildikó's stomach curdles when Áskell coos, 'Nonsense. She has ever been fanciful. As if you could scare anyone!'

He guffaws, thinking himself clever, and the woman's laughter joins his. Ildikó's belly feels as if it is filled with stones; the child does not move there, though whether it is dead or playing possum she is unsure.

'She will recover,' Artemisia says firmly, interrupting their mirth. 'It was such a warm day, she over-heated. She must rest, take fluids. And she must have quiet.'

'Of course,' says the woman and lays a hand on the patient's forehead. Ildikó is overwhelmed by images and memories not her own. As she drops back into the deep well of sleep, she hears Áskell use the woman's name, but whatever he calls her slides from Ildikó's ears like rain on a windowpane.

* * *

It's a long time since she slept in a bed. The first few hours were difficult so after a while she rose and wandered the house. Touched things, smelled them, stared at them a longer while than she could if a member of the household – or indeed any human – had been watching. The tapestries were strange things to see. Made by his wife's aunt, Áskell had said. The not-aunt. The canker, the beginning of the end of her own comfortable life.

She'd only met the woman that once yet the degree of hatred she had for the not-aunt – and she recognises it as a fool's acid, irrational and indiscriminate – was all out of reasonable proportion. All for a sin the woman had never committed. Just her ill-luck to have been plucked from an unguarded cradle a lifetime ago. Her misfortune to have lived instead of otherwise, lived in the darkness and the dank in a manner not intended for mortal morsels. But that hatred was enough to sour the truest love of the huntress's life.

She stared a long time at the things, and when at last she returned to her guest room she slept soundly, almost as soundly as if beneath the weight of the earth.

* * *

Ildikó dreams, although nothing in her head is hers.

She shuffles through dark caverns lit by rude torches, passes table after endless table populated by misshapen creatures feasting with abandon and cackling like a coven. Now, there is a crypt with skeleton-filled niches flying past – her body different, lighter and smaller and she's infinitely more fearful; she's being carried but all she can see is the way along which they've fled, not who bears her. A change of scene once more and there is cold golden sunlight on white hands, and her mother Theodora's features lit by grief and yearning… then the sight of Theodora's back turned upon her as she helps another old woman along a path, up and out of a mountain kingdom. Finally, a great stone door closes behind them, shutting Ildikó-in-dreams in with the monsters for years and years and years. And the resentment, the hatred, such as she's never felt… not towards her mother or aunt, at least.

At some point, the nightmares let her go and she falls into a fever. The days pass in a kind of fugue, some hours she is almost awake, others swimming in sleep thick as treacle. She thinks Áskell is absent, unusually so for he usually makes a point of checking on his "son" daily. Or perhaps she has simply been slumbering when he visits. She thinks she hears noises, one night, grunts and gurgles and the slapping of flesh. Sounds with which she thinks she's all too familiar; she hates the thought anyone might have heard her making them.

But the woman has been there, sharing shifts with Bruna, sitting by her bed, watching, sometimes feeding her hearty beef broths, no doubt on instruction from Artemisia, sometimes helping her from the mattress when she must use the water closet, and sometimes bathing her with a sponge and warm water from a large bowl. The forced intimacy is dreadful, but Ildikó is in no position to complain; she fears that to raise her voice in protest might upset some delicate balance. And she is afraid: she hears Bruna deferring to the pale woman, taking orders about the running of Ildikó's home, and Ildikó feels, when she is conscious enough to feel anything, that she has lost the battle with nary a blow being struck.

* * *

She's not eaten so well in years. Sleeping so long, every ounce of fat has been chewed up by her body and it's all she can do to keep this form from looking gaunt. She's forgotten the taste – so sweet to be reminded of it. So pleasant. And now there remains one last thing to do.

* * *

At last, Ildikó wakes clear-headed, bright-eyed, but still terribly weak. She stares at the canopy above her bed. Then at the rich tapestries hanging around the room. They were made by Aunt Polly who, though rescued from the kingdom under the mountain, never again spoke a word. Never spoke, no, but she wove her story out in the wall coverings: her own taking as a baby by a troll-wife; her childhood in a nursery sometimes filled with the cries of babes both human and otherwise, sometimes silent as the grave; being set to slave the moment she could toddle; scenes from a life of drudgery and constant fear; finally, her finding by her sister. Ildikó takes in the loving stitches that make up Theodora's lovely face, the hair turned silver-white during her own servitude. She thinks of the tales Theodora told her out of Polly's earshot lest the aunt be reduced to tears and moans. Theodora told them to keep Ildikó from straying off the path and being lost forever. Repeated them to Jacopo, too, but with less success: the boy took from them a longing for adventure.

Theodora's fear overshadowed her own life. The fear that Ildikó might suffer the fate of the other child. Become nothing more than troll-shit long before Theodora even knew; replaced with a cuckoo in the nest.

As Ildikó's eyes roam the arras, she takes in the figure that stands behind her mother, there before the Queen of the Trolls, the Queen Beneath the Mountain and again, at last, peering out between the closing doors to the kingdom staring at the bent backs of two old women. And Ildikó recalls at last what Áskell called the woman, finds her name hiding in the curve of her ear where it had fallen like a crumb.

Magdalene.

Magdalene, the disappeared daughter.

Magdalene, the cuckoo child.

Magdalene who cannot be that other Magdalene, yet whose features echo so truly those of the woman from the clearing, the woman who followed her home, the woman who has taken up residence here as if she is Mistress.

The door opens.

Seeing the patient is awake, the woman smiles. As she approaches the bed, she holds up a sheaf of papers. Automatically, Ildikó reaches for them; a quick glance shows it is the lost pages from Jacopo. She smooths the letter as if it is a pet with ruffled feathers. In the woman's other hand is a cloth, speckled white and red, weighty.

'I went back to the clearing.' Maybe-Magdalene grins crookedly, sitting in the chair beside the bed; one hand lies flat in her lap beside the red and white kerchief, the other loosely curled closed as if keeping something hidden. 'I did not think you'd want anyone else to find it.'

'No,' says Ildikó. A moment hangs between them, and a glance. She thinks of how the woman did not tell Áskell where they had met, did not say what his wife had been doing; did not use that information to unseat her at the best possible time. She feels, suddenly, that she may have nothing to fear. 'No. Thank you.'

'The boy?' the woman asks. 'Not your husband's?'

'No.'

'You had to send him away.' It is not a question.

She nods. 'How did you know?'

'Men like Áskell don't tolerate the cubs of others.' The grin has no mirth, is more a baring of the teeth. 'They want their own or none at all.'

'They want sons. Sons they can turn into their image.' Ildikó rubs her belly unhappily.

Maybe-Magdalene says, 'He wouldn't have been happy with *her*.'

'No. No, he won't.' It surprises Ildikó not at all that the other knows what she carries.

They are silent again for a few moments, then the woman asks, 'Why did you choose him? I never would.'

Ildikó snorts a laugh of surprise. 'He was – *seemed* – different. I was lonely. Jacopo's sire was long gone. I thought it would be good for my boy to have a father figure. I thought it would be nice to have a man around my home, to have one to warm my bed, to help.

Well, he helped himself alright, to everything. He charmed the townsfolk – although the women saw through him much faster – and became the mayor.'

'The women here, I've watched them these past days, can sing their husbands – I swear, I've never seen the like! – could they not sing them to see the truth of the man?'

Ildikó shakes her head. 'Whatever power they might have over their menfolk, it's gentle. It does not extend, apparently, to changing their opinion of my husband. Or perhaps Áskell simply had a greater magic at his command, although I've never seen trace of what it might be.'

'Masculinity, my dear. They were admiring of the power he wielded over the household he took.'

Ildikó grunts, recognising the likelihood of that, then coughs. The woman pours her a cup of lemon water from the jug on the bedside table, helps her to drink. 'Your boy – your young man – he speaks of a necklace with a great purple gem at its heart.' Ildikó's blood chills, but the other carries on, her voice silky cold. 'I have been seeking such a stone for some time now.'

'Why?'

'Why do I seek it? Or why this stone?'

'Both.'

'The stone was stolen – it and others – from me and mine. A thief who murdered four of my… family, just to add insult to injury.'

Ildikó licks her lips, decides the truth is the only way forward. 'Áskell travels north every few months. He hunts, he whores, does as he pleases. He… he returned from one such trip with the amethyst and other stones. Called it a *gift*, told me to make something for myself.'

'And did you?'

Ildikó shakes her head. 'I put it away, but then… a client asked for a unique piece for his wife, so I used the stone. Áskell was enraged, but it was worth it. Worth the bruises.' She smiles at the memory of the bitter, short-lived triumph. 'That necklace was the most beautiful thing I've ever done.'

'Ah,' says the woman, but the casual nature of the expression belies the sharpness of her gaze, the way she sits tensed in the chair beside the bed.

Ildikó hesitates, then says what she's never articulated before: 'But it's as if there's been nothing much left in me ever since, no genius, no great art. I manage the small things, gifts to mark milestones in life, rings and bracelets and pendants that are pretty enough, but… but it's as if in the making of that necklace I somehow *unmade* myself, or whatever it was inside me that was… divine.' She sighs with relief to have the fear out, given voice, given form. 'I know I'll never create anything as lovely as that again.'

Maybe-Magdalene gnaws at the corner of a nail, the first sign of nerves Ildikó has ever seen from her. 'You could not have known.'

'I believe it's the necklace of which my son writes and so do you,' Ildikó says.

'Your Áskell was hard to find. He left false trails, and so few know how to do that. A wily thief.' She does not confess to her own wandering that made the finding of him take longer; does not say that had she hurried she might have prevented so much from happening. 'To steal treasure from my people is to bring a curse upon those who hold it – though you might pass it along, the taint never truly leaves; *you* have lost your talent.' She examines her nails, with their strange glassy sheen. 'The effect may have been lessened when you cut the stone, but still there is… contamination. Ill fortune will come home to roost, sooner or later, wherever the thing goes.'

Ildikó can feel her face pulling into a grimace of fear – not for herself but for Jacopo, her beloved thief – but the other holds up a slender hand to still her.

'Such a thing might only be held safely by someone who has suffered and survived the greatest of misfortunes, the worst of injustices. From your boy's letter I suspect this Cinder's Sister is such a one. And your son, his intent was not to benefit himself, I think he will be well enough.' But she shrugs. She doesn't truly know. 'And your ill luck… But your husband…'

'I'd thought… I thought he would go north again soon, that he would leave me for a while. That I might have a chance to flee. But after this… he'll be watching like a hawk to make sure I don't die on him, don't deprive him of his precious *son*.'

Maybe-Magdalene leans forward, the fabric of her sleeves seems to flow like liquid across the sheets, and the woman kisses Ildikó's forehead, a benediction.

'You're her, aren't you?' Ildikó says softly. 'The one who went beneath, the daughter who went under the mountain, into the kingdom of the trolls? You're *that* Magdalene.'

The other does not answer except to say with a terrible longing, 'Where is Theodora?'

Ildikó blinks in surprise.

'You're her daughter,' states Magdalene.

'The child of her old age; unexpected.'

'I can smell her on you – her and the other, Faideau, who loved her.' She smiles.

'My father,' says Ildikó.

'I recognised it the day I saw you in the clearing,' says Magdalene. 'I could smell it in the halls beneath the earth, mingled with your husband's odour. Even after all this time, I know her scent. Where is she?'

'Our mother is dead. So long ago.'

A kind of a slow collapse travels across Magdalene's face, years of hope and disappointment all converge there, like spring flowers dying in an atrocious heat, like a flame long-nurtured snuffed out. A moment fractures and the lines of her blur, and the shape Ildikó had only thought she'd imagined in the glade all those mornings since is truly there clear as day: the troll-wife. She is not afraid, though; if her choice is Áskell's temper when he finds his child is female, or this creature's raging appetite, then she'll make her end in this room.

But then the woman is a woman again. Ildikó can discern the strange bright girl of whom Theodora spoke, the little thing she rescued, the child who went into the kingdom of the trolls and stayed to pay for their mother and aunt's release. Not-mother, not-aunt. The changeling, found and lost.

'You're Theodora's first daughter,' says Ildikó.

Magdalene shakes her head. 'Not-daughter. Un-daughter. The viper she held at her breast all unknowing.'

'I'm sorry,' says Ildikó and she truly is. The other woman shrugs.

'The years pass and I do not notice. There is no sun beneath the mountain.' Tears run down marble-smooth cheeks, and Ildikó is reminded of those days when she would find her mother weeping in the same manner. And, when Theodora espied her, she would scoop Ildikó up and hold tight, and sob into her hair, making her promise over and over not to stray. Magdalene says, 'I wanted to… talk… to ask her things. We parted so quickly, so ill-tempered, there was no time.'

'Your… *other* mother?'

'Lives still. The queen on the misshapen throne. She who did not raise me, and though she chose to place me with Theodora, she never forgave her for making me as I am.'

'And that is?'

'Soft,' whispers Magdalene as if it is a curse pronounced, then grins. 'Too much like a human. I lack certain instincts. I *am* what Theodora made me.'

Ildikó says, 'She spoke of you.'

'No. She spoke of the other one, her true child, the one who was dead before she even knew.'

Ildikó shakes her head. 'No. Only a little of her for she was Theodora's for such a short span – and *our* mother said she never knew quite when the change was made. She had you so much longer. You were the one she knew. It was you she told me tales about, beginning sentences with "Magdalene hated turnips", "Magdalene loved this story", "Magdalene was never so naughty as you!" You were the daughter she knew. Loved.'

Magdalene's shoulders slouch, and Ildikó reaches across to grasp the other's hand, which is now white and soft, now black and gnarled. Ildikó does not let go as the flesh fights for form. She says softly, 'We are sisters, you and I.'

Magdalene wipes her cheeks. Then she holds out her free hand and drops something onto the coverlet over Ildikó's lap.

'A gift, sister to sister,' she says. 'He will not bother you again. When they look for him, tell them he has travelled north once more. His favourite horse is gone, his favourite sword, his favourite pistols. By the time anyone notices he's not returned there will be no trace.'

Magdalene flips open the kerchief in her own lap; it was white, the red is darkening to brown as it dries. Ildikó glimpses chunks of bloody flesh – heart, balls, cock – before her sister hides them again. 'A treat for my other mother.'

Ildikó looks at the object lying on her coverlet: Áskell's thick gold band with the carven bear, a smear of red around the inner edge. And Ildikó recalls her un-sister's earlier statement: *He wouldn't have been happy with her.* Past tense. Áskell is past tense. She sighs out the words, 'Thank you.'

'I think you might find your husband's influence over other men was assisted by that –' she nods at the ring – 'although I do not know from whence it came. I've not seen the like.'

'Take it. I don't want it here.' But her sister shakes her head and the band of gold remains in Ildikó's lap. Their hands are still joined, and when Magdalene tries to pull away Ildikó will not let her. 'Where will you go?'

'Home.'

'You will not pursue the gems?'

Magdalene shakes her head. 'Vengeance was the goal. It has been achieved.'

Ildikó breathes out, all her tension going with the exhalation. 'I will write to Jacopo, warn him, though I do not know when he will get the letter.'

Magdalene rises, squeezes Ildikó's fingers and says nothing further. She closes the door silently; there is no sound of footsteps on the staircase, though Ildikó thinks she hears the other's voice quietly instructing Bruna that the master of the house has taken one of his trips. That the mistress is on the mend and must be cared for tenderly. That she herself must return to her own holdings. Then Ildikó hears the front door opening with its usual creak and closing, and the baby in her belly kicks and turns once again.

A STITCH IN TIME

Cordelia is dying and there is nothing they can do.

Her injuries from the fire, determinedly refusing to heal properly, have gotten worse. The arm and her face are the most troubling, suppurating decay creeping from the dying flesh to the living. The smell in the sick room at Singing Vine is dreadful. The windows are kept open even though outside there is snow. Cordelia, when she speaks, tells Mrs Bell it is good, that the cold numbs her pain.

There is nothing they can do but wait. Wait in the wing they've managed to salvage of the partially ruined house – the roof has fallen in on the other side of the manor. Wait in the hope that the woman Victoria's gone to seek will be willing to come and willing to help. That she exists.

They take turns, Merry, Mrs Bell, and Jacopo, sitting by Cordelia's side. Mrs B bears the heaviest load, the longest shifts. They change her dressings, re-applying the poultice of yellow archangel, and dripping water infused with mandrake, poppy and honey between her dry lips. Merry knows from the moments she spends lingering outside the room that Mrs Bell reads to her charge from a book of fairy and fable, its cover battered and bruised by time, but the name *Murcianus* can still be seen on spine and front. Jacopo makes up his own stories, picking them from his adventures. Merry, having no such resources, simply sews on her watches, knowing that Cordelia ever admired her skill with needle and thread. She'll talk her way through her tasks, instructing this stitch and that, what it's best for and not at all suited to. Sometimes the patient's eyes – one green, the other blind-white – will open. Merry's been making a dress for Cordelia.

'You'll wear it when you're well, Mrs… Cordelia.' Before this final illness, Cordelia had said she no longer wanted to be called by her married name, nor for Merry to address her as if she was the mistress of a great house. That was all in the past. Those who remain with Cordelia are not servants, but the family she's chosen for herself. It's just that sometimes Merry slips into old habits. 'So, you must get well, you see?'

The frock is a simple emerald-coloured damask with plain skirts, but the sleeves are slashed and trimmed with white guipure lace. Merry does not mention the last gown she made for the sick woman, though she suspects it is on both of their minds.

Sometimes Merry rises and goes to the window to see if Victoria has returned. Merry wonders if the others do the same thing, but she doesn't ask. She knows it's silly, knows that returns are seldom seen from afar, that *if* the girl comes back she'll simply appear like a summoned thing. Merry touches the little brooch, the spray of lilies Victoria insisted she keep, and hopes it's soon. She hopes it wasn't a fool's errand.

Jacopo tells stories all the time, not just to the invalid. At dinner one night he shared a tale from his Grandmamma Theodora, of a long-ago Lodellan and its Archbishop Narcissus Marsh who'd wanted his cathedral protected by something more terrifying and immediate than God. He found a woman, toymaker-trained, who'd turned her gifts to dreadful, magnificent things and produced the reanimated wolf-hounds that still flitted around the portico of the great structure. Jacopo had gathered other stories: that the woman had fled the city with the Archbishop's inquisitors on her heels, hunted for sins real or imagined; that she left a trail of salvations and deaths in her wake; that she'd mastered a strange substance, living clay; whispers that she still lived, though she could not possibly. Rumours that she was last seen living in a place that had once been the site of a great battle, such a battle that the earth was watered with blood and gore and the bodies were too many to bury and so they lay there to rot, with no words spoken over them nor lavender planted to keep them safely below.

Jacopo, Merry knew, told the tales in desperation, not thinking beyond entertaining his companions. But Victoria… Victoria had listened in ever-growing hope: she's heard a similar recounting of the living clay – *argilla viva* – from the lips of the ghost girl Ozanne Agnew. It was, she'd said, a sign and she would not be dissuaded. Victoria had lopped her exquisite hair into a boy's bowl cut, taken a pair of Jacopo's old trews, a shirt, vest and coat so as to pass unremarked. Mrs B packed her a satchel of food, with nary a word in dissent and Jacopo was, eventually, coerced into sketching a map of where the woman was last reported.

Merry had sewn seven of the diamonds from the Agnew

necklace – the damnable thing, the source of so much grief it pleased her no end to see it broken apart – into the hem of the vest. The letter from Jacopo's mother had warned of the curse, but also that one who'd suffered misfortune might put the thing to use: Victoria had suffered and was willing to take the risk. As Merry'd helped Victoria into her outfit, she'd almost said *You don't have to do this*, but she knew that wasn't true. Merry understands the younger girl has been trying to prove herself ever since the events in Seaton St Mary. So much preparation and expense, everything ruined by her fear. Victoria would be stubbornly brave from now on.

'Will she be well?' Merry had asked her aunt as they'd watched Victoria Parsifal ride off. Mrs Bell hadn't answered.

That was six weeks ago; Jacopo had estimated it would take her three weeks to travel to Jago's Rise, all going well. There would be the same to return, and any time in between spent trying to convince the woman to help. If the woman existed.

* * *

'It was beautiful,' Mrs Bell had said of the vineyard. She'd been very young when she arrived at Singing Vine to work for the Lawrences, before the children came and brought joy, before the blight came and brought destruction. But Mrs B and Cordelia were gone by the time the latter occurred, and they'd only ever had Bethany's tales of what had come to pass. Her aunt has taken Merry for walks around the estate, pointing out this spot and that where Cordelia did something as a child, and Mrs B smiled fondly. What Merry noticed, however, was that there were no sweet reminiscences of Bethany. She's thought back often enough to the years in Lodellan and cannot pinpoint a time when there wasn't some sort of cool distance between Mrs Bell and Bethany. A politeness, certainly, but no warmth, as if Mrs B did what she did out of obligation not the genuine love that powered everything she did for Cordelia, and for Merry too. Merry might have thought it indifference on both sides but for her aunt's insistence that they flee the townhouse the night the Parsifals were arrested. Somehow she knew that there would be no safety if they remained in that big house with Bethany Lawrence. Her aunt knew enough to *fear*.

They'd found shelter in the dank cellar of the Agnew mansion, abandoned and cold, still smelling of death. They'd stayed almost four weeks as the aching damp crept into their bones – not game to move about too much, never lighting candles to traverse the upper floors lest they be noticed – until that morning they went to see Cordelia as she was harried into the dray for Rosebery Bay. They'd left the city that same afternoon, hair cut back and darkened, dirt applied to their faces as carefully as make-up. They took to the roads for months on end, eventually holing up in a hovel outside the barely surviving village of Bitterwood.

'We'll not stay long,' her aunt had said, 'it's too small. People don't have enough to do with their time, we'll draw attention sooner rather than later.'

'Where can we go? When can we stop running?' Merry had only ever known one home and that had been in Lodellan, with Cordelia and the children. Flight was wearing; Merry found it exhausting. She hadn't lived her life hiding who she was and even though she'd been a servant that was in a grand house with a rich family gaining fame. She'd held her head high when she went forth to the markets or accompanied the children on their outings. She'd been rightly proud of who she was and who she served. The need to hide, she supposed, knocked both the surliness and pride out of her. They'd had to be so careful and Merry had learned to pass beneath notice.

Yet somehow, Jacopo had found them. He'd found them and never said how, but told them that Cordelia yet lived, that she'd begged for them to come. Mrs Bell had been unconvinced of his story until he'd told how Mr Farringdale had been dealt with. *Then* her aunt packed their meagre possessions and allowed the youth to lead them here, to where the carnival troupe had come at Cordelia's plea to bring her home where she could mend.

Through the open window come laughter and shouts, and Merry frowns. Cordelia's sleep is so hard won it shouldn't be interrupted. Merry goes over and leans out the sill to hiss. It's Jacopo and the five troupe children left in their care while the parents are away in Jory's Dell gathering supplies and trading. They race and rush, making snowballs and throwing them at each other. She smiles in spite of herself, and that's the moment when Jacopo looks up and notices her. He grins and her heart flips, just a little; she'd not thought that would ever happen again, not after Japheth. She raises a hand to him, and he to her. They stand like that for a while until one of the children bowls him over and he tumbles, laughing.

'Let them be,' comes a croak from the bed behind her, the voice a fractured thing with just a trace of its former melody. Merry rushes to Cordelia, whose uninjured eye is open. 'Like to hear them play.'

'Do you want anything?' Merry asks.

'Wine.'

They'd found hidden in the cellars some few bottles of the SV Rouge Felix, one of the finest the vineyard ever produced. Sometimes when the poppy tincture isn't enough, Mrs Bell gives alcohol to Cordelia. Singing Vine vintages were always said to bring sweet dreams. Merry pours a measure from the bottle on the bedside table into a pewter mug (they found no glassware intact in the manor).

'Miser,' coughs Cordelia and Merry grins, adds more. She helps her once-mistress to sit then holds the cup to her ruined mouth. A red line trickles out, too much like blood for Merry's liking. She gently lies Cordelia down again, wipes away the stain on her chin, and makes sure she's as comfortable as she can be.

'Mrs Bell?' Cordelia whispers.

Merry shakes her head. 'She went with the troupe.'

Mrs Bell's decision had surprised Merry until she'd looked closely at her aunt, seen the shadows beneath her eyes, the grief that waited in them, the white pushing its way through the blonde hair, the slump of her shoulders. She understood suddenly that the older woman could not continue to watch the child she'd raised die by increments. Merry also understands that her aunt is as broken by Bethany's betrayal as by Cordelia's inevitable end.

Cordelia nods as if she senses Merry's thoughts. The unburned hand lifts with surprising strength from the beneath the coverlet and grasps Merry's fingers. She says, as she has said so many times, 'Forgive me.'

'Always. Now hush.'

Forgiveness.

When Jacopo first told them what Cordelia begged, Merry thought it unlikely. She recalled too deeply how easily Cordelia had dismissed her and Mrs B that terrible night when everything fell apart. That Cordelia had *so easily* believed ill of the girl who'd offered her nothing but loyalty. That, if she owed nothing to Merry, she most certainly owed too much to Mrs Bell to have treated her so shabbily. Even that morning when they'd seen Cordelia loaded into the prison carriage, so thin and dirty and pale… even then Merry couldn't help but feel a bitter satisfaction.

But then…

Forgiveness.

That moment of following Jacopo into the ruined manor house, spying the woman sitting by the hearth in the kitchen, watching her turn so slowly and painfully, and seeing what the fire had done to her. And in *that* moment everything lifted from Merry, every weighty resentment, every petty concern, even the fat oily hatred left by the realisation it was Bethany who'd taken Japheth from her.

It all disappeared with one look at Cordelia's ruined face, the clawed hand, the ravaged mouth; Cordelia, then as healed as she would ever be. The sound of the voice that came from her devastated throat, the sometimes sweet note that broke through the rasping croak, the words that cost her so much pain and suffering, but she said them. Cordelia said them because she owed them, and not even direst agony would stop her from speaking them aloud. She'd begged their forgiveness. She'd begged their help, and Mrs Bell and Merry gave both willingly.

The sweet aimless mistress whose forte had been selecting menus and frocks had become a monstrous general, focusing her efforts on locating the children, on compiling all the information she could about her sister and the new empire in the port-city of Breakwater. It was as if the fire she'd escaped still had hold of her, burning inside to keep her moving forward.

Yet after they'd rescued Victoria, Cordelia had promptly collapsed. Her wounds became infected, and death had begun creeping upon her like an aged husband. Merry began to see how Cordelia's pursuits were wearing her out, using her up. She thinks back to Cordelia describing what went wrong in the *modiste's* shop, how she said that her own daughter had thought her a horror. Merry believes that was the day when her mistress's heart, already covered with tiny fissures, broke and she lost the will to continue. Merry's never told Victoria or anyone else that.

Merry opens her lips to ask a question but notices Cordelia's closed eyes, regular breathing. She slumbers once more. Restless, Merry rises, returns to the window.

Now, Jacopo amuses the children by changing his features. The lean face and crooked nose that are his alone shift, the cheeks become chubbier, the nose a bulbous cherry, his eyes almost disappear in the wreaths of his smile. The hair sticks straight up, black. A clown's face, a made-up thing. Next, the new features belong to a woman, cheekbones high and wide, a feral topaz gaze, bright red tresses. Merry feels a small jealousy stir, suppresses it; wonders yet again what the fantastical Tove looks like. Is this her? Something says *no*.

Then Jacopo relaxes back into himself and the children shriek with laughter as they begin making snowballs again. Merry thinks how easily they let things go, reminds herself she must do the same. It's a habit that's grown less difficult with time, but requires conscious thought. The tiny annoyances, all the bitter seeds, will grow to something larger if nurtured. Tove, of whom Jacopo's spoken perhaps twice, is one of those seeds.

She breathes out, then laughs at the sight below. Jacopo looks up again, and there's a warmth in his smile. *Is it enough*? she wonders, but is distracted by a movement at the edge of the forest.

At first she's hopeful, but realises it can't be Victoria for it's too low to be a rider. Unless the girl lost her horse? But no, the gait isn't right. Merry's heart constricts: a bear out of season? She points and Jacopo turns. She hears him tell the children, 'Go back inside, quickly,' and they obey. Merry swiftly leaves Cordelia's room, rushes downstairs to let them in; colourful lumps tumble past. She directs them to the fire in the large sitting room, then pulls a stout walking stick from the copper rack by the door.

Merry steps out into the white, hefting the cudgel which she's learned to use with effect. Jacopo, she knows, has a long knife at his belt. When she reaches him they stand together, watching the dark shadowy thing come towards them.

'Be ready,' says Jacopo. She gives a nod.

The shape stumbles a little in the high drifts, rights itself with a curse that can be heard at the house. It's a cloaked figure, walking with a slight limp; not a bear to Merry's relief. When it's within five feet of them, it stops and pushes its hood back. The face is old with thin lips and yellowed teeth, a hooked nose. There is silver-grey hair bunched at the shoulders. The hands are gnarled, skin spotted with brown, the nails with black ridges beneath. The voice, when it comes, seems younger than it should, a woman's, though still hoarse.

'I beg the grace of a single night, no more. A warm fire, a bed of straw, perhaps some stew and a mug of ale or mead? One could ever find winter's pity at the Singing Vine…'

'You've been here before?' asks Jacopo.

The wanderer shrugs. 'I've been away a long time, but I remember there was always place for beggars and travellers by this hearth-fire. Have times changed it so much?' Her gaze passes them to take in the fallen roof of one wing, the clear signs of decay. Cordelia had said that in spring they would hire carpenters to repair everything, but Cordelia seems unlikely to make it to the new season.

Jacopo glances at Merry as if it's her decision to make. She hesitates. One old woman. One kindness, she tells herself. It is, she thinks, what Cordelia would do, Cordelia who'd always ensured that vagabonds were fed if they came to the kitchen door in Lodellan. Merry nods. 'One night, and welcome.'

* * *

Dinner has been had and the children sit on the rug in front of Merry's seat while she reads to them from Mrs Bell's book of fairy and fable. Analetta, Florica, Jaelle, Marko and Luca sleep in the house during their parents' absence, rather than in the colourful wagons drawn in a circle in one of the meadows.

The old woman, still wrapped in her cloak, sits apart and very still so that they almost forget she's there. She ate a second helping of stew and bread, but refused anything to drink. Mostly she watches the children intently with that gaze the elderly reserve for the young as if wondering where their own youth went, how they might get it back. Every so often Merry feels eyes upon her, looks up and finds the woman's eyes glittering dimly at her from beneath the hood.

When Merry at last closes the book, having finished the tale of the mari-morgan who wanted a beautiful gown, the children moan and complain, demanding one more story. But she's firm and sends them to brush their teeth and hair, then tumble into the big bed in the room that once was set aside for low-paying guests when the vineyard was a going concern. Jacopo is outside, chopping wood to ensure they've enough to see them through the night.

'I thank you for your generosity.' The woman speaks up as Merry is tidying away the last of the dishes from the table. 'You're young to have so many.'

Merry laughs. 'Not mine, not a one! Their parents are travelling.'

There's the thump of the front door as Jacopo returns, cheeks rosy from exertion, his arms full of split logs. He grins at Merry and nods to the woman, places his burden in the wood box, then heads off to the washroom. His steps are a little hesitant and Merry thinks how he'd drunk more honey-ale with dinner than he was wont to do.

'Ah,' says the old woman, 'That's not your man then?'

Merry feels the words as a nip, a sting, and shakes her head. She moves away, clutching a tower of dishes. A hand snakes out and touches her wrist. The dishes rattle, threaten to fall. Merry is distracted by the whiteness of the skin on the forearm where the sleeve drops away, but then the voice catches her attention again. 'But how you look at him! So naked. And he barely sees you, my poor dove.'

Merry stiffens, feels her face show everything she wants but tries to let go lightly. She pulls back.

The woman continues, though. 'Forgive me, my dear, I don't mean to be cruel. You've shown me kindness and I would repay it.'

Though her lips feel starched and stiff, Merry manages a smile. 'There's no need. Enjoy your rest.'

'I'd offer you something, and it would gladden my heart to do so.' The woman gestures for Merry to come closer, and she obeys instinctively for it's a gesture her aunt uses; obedience remains ingrained. 'I can guarantee you his love.'

Merry almost laughs, manages to shake her head politely. 'No one can deliver that.'

Then, with cunning sleight of hand, the woman's palm is suddenly full. A vial, the length of her middle finger, with a silver cap engraved with nettle leaves and flowers. The liquid inside is an intense purple; it leaps around in the container, flashing iridescent in the firelight. It's so pretty Merry almost reaches for it.

'Slip this into his meal; he'll not notice the taste. As long as he receives the dish from your hands, you'll be the one to claim his heart. No former love, no future devotion, will turn his head from your sweet face, my dove. Only let me do you this one service and give an old woman some happiness.'

Merry thinks about Tove, how much she'd hate the unknown girl if she let her heart have its way. She thinks about Jacopo's expression when he'd spoken that once of her, thinks about what *she* thinks it means. About the yearning, yet she doesn't understand that yearning can have different tenors. Her fingers, though they hesitate a little, close around the cool curve of the glass and feel very light indeed.

* * *

Merry pauses at the top of the staircase, listening.

Silence. No giggling from the children's bedroom, no snoring from Jacopo's.

Their guest, pleading aged bones and stairs did not mix well, refused a chamber. Jacopo had found a pallet for her and set it up by the fire in the dining room. Merry'd piled the thin bed with warm clean quilts.

Before she takes her own rest, Merry checks on Cordelia. She spoons a thin beef broth into her mouth, then when the patient signals *enough*, Merry changes her dressings and nightgown too.

But when she offers the mix of mandrake, poppy and honey water Cordelia shakes her head. 'Don't need it,' she says. Merry tries to argue, and Cordelia says, 'Don't *want* it.' Then she tells Merry to leave her be, and closes her eyes.

The girl hesitates. She might sit up in a chair all night, sleeping in fits and starts, but Cordelia does not want her there, and she live or die whether Merry is here or not. To emphasise her point, Cordelia says, 'Go!' though she cannot manage a shout. With her fingers Merry brushes the few golden locks that have grown back on the devastated skull and says, 'Alright.'

But she closes the window against the cold before she leaves, a tiny defiance against the invalid.

The door to her own room is ajar, and she pauses. Perhaps one of the children has crept in to beg another tale. She steps over the threshold, a scolding ready on her lips.

By the bed is Jacopo, swaying just a little. The collar of his red shirt is open, the silver birds and fish she embroidered there catch the light of the fire.

Merry does not say anything. All her serenity flees as surely as blood does from a wound. Her heart, which she has so often ordered empty, refuses to obey. It fills to bursting. Her feet move of their own volition, fingers fumble with the buttons at the front of her navy serge dress until Jacopo reaches out to help and makes short work of the fastenings. She doesn't object, doesn't say *No, your heart belongs elsewhere*. She doesn't care, just wants, for one night, the warmth of another beside her. The warmth of this one inside her.

* * *

She doesn't know what wakes her, but she heard it beneath the burr of Jacopo's snoring.

Then it comes again, a low laugh, a low voice. Merry tries to rouse Jacopo, his face stripped bare in sleep, but his slumber is too deep. She catches up her violet dressing gown, then pads out bare-footed and silent. At the end of the long corridor she can see the line of light under Cordelia's door; she'd left the candle burning for she knows the woman hates to wake in darkness. Once again, she hopes it might be Victoria returned with the healer, the hedge-witch, yet Merry moves cautiously, placing her feet carefully and quietly. She puts her ear against the thick wood to listen. The voice is familiar, but she must dig deeply for it's been some while since she last heard it.

'You are tenacious, are you not, Dellie? Can you hear me? Are you sleeping or pretending? You were never much of a deceiver, my dear, always so open, so honest. Was Victoria pleased to see you? It took a while but I found out, oh yes I did, tracked down the whore from the Chaucer and made her tell me everything. It could only have been you. I mean, who else would have cared enough to come for the brat? And yours the only body not found in the bay.' There's a sigh. 'Where else would you go but here? Pity you're not awake, I'd have liked the chance to tell you what I've done, how much I've achieved. But, sister, I can't have you following me, getting in the way. It's a mercy, really.'

The voice collides in Merry's mind with a face, and she turns the handle, an inarticulate cry forcing itself through her lips.

Bethany is at the far side of Cordelia's bed, a fat pillow clutched in her pale lovely hands, pressing down on her sister's face. Her hood has been thrown back and the finely made mask lies on the coverlet, a puddle of wrinkled skin. Surely removed so her sister might know her.

She and Merry are frozen for long moments, so many things lie between them. Then Bethany says, 'Ah, gods' shit,' and throws the pillow aside, swiping a knife from somewhere inside her cloak and raising it high.

Merry does not think, does not consider the weapon and the damage it might do, but throws herself forward, up and over Cordelia's bed, her feet missing the sick woman's limbs more by happy accident than intent. Surprised, Bethany retreats but does not turn her back. Merry slaps and scratches at her, leaving livid red marks on the other's face, drawing blood, pulling out hanks of hair. She spits, too, hot wet gobs of hatred that are the only way she can express her rage. A witness, if there were one, might note a similarity in their features, in colouring and set.

But then Merry feels a searing pain in her side. The last eruption of anger rises, more fiercely than any before, and she shoves Bethany as hard as she can. Merry watches with grim satisfaction as the other woman flies backwards into the glass of the window Merry, then through the pane, cartwheels into the moonlit night. Her cloak spreads, eclipses the moon briefly before she's pulled earthward.

Merry leans over the sill, clutching at her flank, and watches Bethany land. At first it seems she's done so safely, but then a gasp of pain and a stream of curses rise into the air. The Queen of Thieves limps away, a dark blot on the blue-white of the snow, and disappears into the trees. Merry turns back to the bed: Cordelia's eyes are open wide, pinned on her saviour.

The girl takes a step but finds her legs don't want to oblige. She sits heavily on the floor, feels the warm red flowing from the wound in her torso. She tries a smile for Cordelia, but her lips are numb and she does not know if they work or not. Merry slumps and closes her eyes.

* * *

In the time in-between, Merry dreams. She dreams she and Cordelia are holding hands and walking across an iridescent purple lake. She dreams she's getting further and further away from her aunt and Jacopo, both of whom stand on the shore, distracted by others. Merry looks over her shoulder and watches: Mrs Bell is talking to Bethany with a kind of sincere urgency that Merry's never witnessed before. Jacopo is beaming at a scrawny girl. Whenever Merry tries to focus on the girl's face, there's nothing there, or at least nothing that sticks in her mind. It's as if she loses the memory as soon as she gets it; she stares at the hair, then shifts her gaze to the eyes and the colour and style of the tresses are gone; she shifts from the eyes to the nose and the former feature disappears. In short, she'd never be able to recognise whoever it is – although surely it must be Tove – even if she saw her again. Cordelia, fingers firmly laced with Merry's, keeps pulling her along, dragging her forward, towards the centre of the lake, which is shrouded in mist. The closer they get to the impenetrable fog, Merry realises there are cries coming from somewhere in there, getting louder and louder. Babies crying, children howling. Then Cordelia's grip is gone, slipped like a harness, and Merry turns to find there's no longer a shore, no sign of Mrs B or Jacopo, and Merry is alone in the white.

* * *

Merry wakes though she did not expect to. She stretches, winces; her ribs are bandaged. She wonders how long she's slept. The window is open and though the air is cool and she can see snow still caught in the top branches of the trees outside, the smell is not the same crisp cold of deep winter.

On the other side of her bed she notices a familiar figure, dressed in a deep red baize gown, the white apron on the front perfectly pressed and pristine. Her aunt is dozing and Merry wonders where Jacopo is; perhaps he's with Cordelia if she's made it through the night. She reaches out, touches Mrs Bell's hand, which is loosely clutched around a barely begun piece of embroidery.

The woman startles, almost tips from the chair, bites back a low curse. She recovers and cocks an eyebrow at her niece. 'Awake at last. You took your time.' Yet she's smiling and it's a radiant thing. Her fingers wrap around Merry's, hold tight.

'How long?'

'A fortnight.'

'Cordelia?' Merry sits up too quickly and gasps at the pain in her side.

'Lie back, lie back. Silly girl. Cordelia is very well.'

'Very well?'

Mrs B's smile widens. 'Victoria found the woman.'

'Oh!'

Mrs Bell leans forward. 'A miracle if anything is, although…'

'What is it, Aunt?'

'The woman's… well, she's strange.' Mrs B shrugs, says, 'You'll see for yourself soon enough,' and won't say more.

Merry gives up, asks instead, 'Where's Cordelia?'

'Gone. To Breakwater and the lad with her.'

'Oh,' Merry says, feeling both robbed and relieved. She's slept so long, yet all her feelings for Jacopo are those of the sweet hours they spent together, memories still fresh and raw. She wonders what he would have said to her, what she would have said to him. 'I'm tired, Aunt.'

'After all that sleep?' Mrs Bell laughs and pushes the damp hair back from Merry's brow. She leans in to kiss the girl's cheek. 'Rest then. I'll bring you up some soup.'

'Thank you.'

At the door Mrs B pauses. 'He stayed by you, you know.'

'Pardon?'

'The lad. The whole while you slept. They only left this morning, but he stayed by you all that time.' She nods and leaves.

Merry rolls onto her side, presses her lips tight and squeezes her eyes shut. The tears, however, will not be denied, and they seep out to scald her cheeks. She indulges them for a while, then at last dashes them away. She reaches beneath the mattress to the small place she found when she first slept in this bed. In the timbers of the frame there is a niche, a hidey hole, originally meant for she knows not what but perfectly fit for the vial she'd slipped in there that night as Jacopo slept.

It's poison, surely. Bethany would have no reason to give her anything else; imagine the mischief if she managed to get Merry to kill Jacopo!

Her fingers fiddle and fetch and finally grab a hold. She brings it up and lays the tiny container on the china-white of the sheets. The shiny purple contents, untouched, look even more intense. Surely it will serve some other purpose. Merry taps her nails against the glass for a long time, a rhythm that eventually sends her back to sleep.

SLEEPING LIKE SNOW

Despite the cold Tove sits in the window seat, the book discarded beside her, staring out on the whiteness blanketing Edmea's Wood; how long has winter lasted? Even the roses that ever bloomed in the garden have died off. Icicles hang from branches like lethal gems, unmelting in the sun; the small rill that runs by the ruin of a barn is frozen hard as a marble floor. The only areas not covered in white are the occasional copses of alders, and those trees are ill, dying, so unwell even the snow will not settle on them, will not stay. They are blots on the landscape and she does not know why this is happening. Tove's been out there, examined them, the ground in which they stand. The dirt shows no sign of being poisoned or unhealthy, it is the alders themselves: thin and withered, sap leaking from what on a person would be lesions. Still, it won't affect her one way or another. Evening is threatening, throwing a cast of purple across the sky, but there's still enough light to see by; some things at any rate.

Tove holds a clay mug between both hands, warming them. The scent of cloves rises from the liquid, mingled with oranges and a heavy red wine. The last time it was this icy was when the soft boy had come to stay, sent by the hard woman. It's perhaps a year, a little more, a little less since he was taken. Since Uther died. Tove's life has not changed overly much since. Or at least, not until ten days ago.

Upstairs are the sounds of the woman who's made the big bedroom her own.

Tove had not buried the huntsman's body. The winter-hard ground would have allowed little more than a shallow depression, and besides she'd not had sufficient fondness for Uther to bother. She left him where he'd fallen, mauled by the she-bear. He was gone in less than a day, food for starveling wolves and foxes, other small creatures of the woods, an unexpected bounty and the greatest good he'd ever done for another being, Tove was quite sure. Within a day the bloodied snow had been lapped up by rough tongues. The meat and bones were dragged off to dens to feed young and old, stored in lairs and larders to help keep alive creatures that Uther had hunted without mercy.

Tove liked that idea very much indeed.

No one had come looking for the boy; she flicks her gaze to the book, which was his.

No one had come looking for Uther, who'd brought the boy, either.

No one had come to the house in Edmea's Wood, which Tove had been *given* after she'd earned her freedom in Seaton St Mary. Although "freedom" was perhaps too strong a word; released but not cut loose entirely. That was the condition of her liberty, that she hold this place open for anyone Madame or the Queen of Thieves sent. Madame Arcady with her houses of ill-repute, of amusements and strange curiosities, depending upon the depths of one's tastes and pockets.

But since the huntsman and the boy there'd been no one else, and Tove dared to hope herself forgotten. She leans back against the down-filled cushion and swirls the contents of her mug before draining the dregs. They taste bitter, as dregs are wont to do, yet she drinks them down; life has taught her not to disdain any morsel for you never know when it will be your last. There's the sound of something being dropped above her head, a curse uttered, but there's no shattering, no breaking, merely the *clunk* of an inconvenience.

No one had come until the strange woman whose skin seemed like porcelain, and moved as if she might break at any moment. She'd carried a large leather satchel, heavy-looking, yet had nothing more than the clothes on her back; she's been wearing Uther's cast-offs these past days. *Selke*, who'd given her name reluctantly when Tove had said it was the price of shelter. The woman has made herself at home.

While Tove watches the woods, something moves through the trees. It usually doesn't concern her unduly – there are bears and wolves, foxes and stoats, badgers and birds of a frosty sort – it might be any of them. Absently, Tove touches the nubs on her forehead, feels the brown velvet of those nascent – no, not nascent, *stunted* – horns. She can forget them most of the time, forget what happened and what they say about her, but when she touches them…

In recent days she's seen footprints, seen the paths beaten to mush by feet made tough with wandering and all kinds of weather.

She's never seen this before. Not here, any road. She thought they'd never look for her. She thought she would never see them again. She thought everything she'd given up was behind her forever, that her single foolish act of kindness had both saved her from one life and condemned her to another.

She thought herself forever lost.

But why would they look for her after all this time? Surely it's just part of the migration, to pass through here at some point? Besides, she's not seen *them*, only traces. She strokes the cover of the book, thinks about the entry in there, the one that calls them "mythical"; a half-smile quirks at the side of her mouth. And perhaps she is wrong anyway. Perhaps those marks are from the bears that sometimes roam, sometimes on four feet, sometimes on two. *But there are no claw-marks*, she whispers to herself. *And it's winter*, she whispers to herself, *the sometimes-bears, they sleep.*

Whatever is moving out there *now*, however, isn't an animal: too tall, walking with too much purpose in the direction of the cottage. Despite the fact that they've found food here before, the animals remain wary of humans. Tove squints. Trousers and boots and a heavy coat and a fur hat; but not the gait of a male. Whoever's wearing that attire and moving through the damson of the rapidly falling evening hasn't learned to walk like a man. She sets aside her mug, touches the knife that hangs at the waist of her plain blue woollen skirt.

Tove rises, watching through the windowpane as the figure approaches until she's certain they're heading towards the cottage, then moves to the door. She pauses at the staircase that leads up and calls, 'Hush a while, someone comes.'

There's no answer but the noises fall away quickly, there's the sound of a body surrendering itself to the bed, the easiest way to not draw attention. Tove waits for the knock. It's firm, polite. She waits a little longer, but there's nothing further. *Patient*, she muses, then makes her decision.

Standing back from the doorstep is a young woman Tove thinks not much older than herself. Pink-cheeked in the frosty air, green eyes, ruddy brown curls escaping from the hat. Her lips are cracked and dried from the cold, there's a bruise above her right eye, and a trickle of old blood stuck in hair that's not been washed in days. The girl opens her mouth, then tips forward.

Tove manages to catch her, but the girl is strangely weighty and they both almost end up on the ground. Tove is stronger than she looks, however, and heaves the girl up against her, props a shoulder under an arm and begins the process of hauling her guest inside. From somewhere out in the trees comes a wail, a howl, a call: hind or wolf or bear, she cannot tell and that is the most frightening thing she's ever encountered.

* * *

Tove hasn't spent much time talking in her past few years – she found she preferred silence – but since Selke's arrival she's been forced to *chat*, a bit. The woman requires little entertainment, mind, and often she speaks to herself with no expectation of an answer. When she wants one, she'll raise one of those fine brows and look directly at Tove.

She's giving Tove the brows now, pointing to the girl lying on the battered loveseat by the fire. 'Who is this?'

'She fainted.' Tove shrugs. She removes the fur cap and lets it drop. Next, she wrings out the cloth she'd immersed in snow-melt. Draping it on the girl's forehead, she watches as the water turns dried blood liquid again to run down into the hairline. 'But something's after her, I think. Did you hear that cry?'

The older woman shakes her head. 'You should put her out. Away from the cottage so it can find her and not us.'

Tove's stomach tightens. 'And if I'd done that with you, Mistress Selke?'

The woman had been starving and fearful; Tove knows the look of a hunted animal (the boy had worn it too). Tove hasn't extracted the full story, but the woman's got the manner of a witch – and doesn't strike Tove as the sort to hide her true self, not even in the interest of self-preservation – and that's enough to make living difficult. But Tove recalled hearing, sometime in her childhood, that women of a kind would help each other survive, offer shelter, so she took Selke in.

'She stays. She stays until she's awake and we know why she's here and what's out there.'

Selke, discontented, moves to one of the windows and stares as if she can see something beyond her own reflection against the night-blackened glass. The green eyes flick back and forth; Tove wonders if she's merely scanning the strange landscape of her own skin so tight and smooth and pale. Not a wrinkle to be seen, and whenever she smiles it's an odd thing to behold: however genuine the mirth, there's nothing more than a lifting of the muscles almost without their permission, a shifting of unwilling flesh. The face looks young yet not, and the hair's that peculiar hue of white that can only have begun its life as bright red.

Tove gives up trying to read the woman and goes to the kitchen, where a pot of stew simmers: vegetables from the root cellar and the meat of a couple of thin rabbits; the chickens, ducks and geese are long gone. It's been an age since any deliveries arrived from Lodellan or Seaton St Mary. When what passes for spring comes she'll need to find a city, buy more food, replenish the larder. Alone, the stocks would have lasted much longer, but with three mouths?

She spoons stew into two bowls, careful to make sure there are as many chunks of meat as generosity can spare; may well as keep up their strength while they can. The snares Uther taught her to set are only big enough for rabbits, and only rabbits are stupid enough to stumble into them. Tove doesn't want to take the huntsman's crossbow from where she hung it over the fire, but there's a chance she will need to before long; to hunt something bigger.

'Selke, dinner.'

But Selke's standing over the girl on the settee, staring with that inscrutable expression.

* * *

Victoria's dreams are wearying.

She's still moving, moving, moving, her legs aching and her feet numb, but she knows she can't stop or they'll catch up. Her companion sometimes carries her, but mostly she can't bear his touch, so she makes him put her down. In her mind, all's a rush of the awful hours in the river, the water was foul and icy and where she thought she would die and fail her mother again; a blur of trees and snow and the broken buildings in which they'd hid. But there was no death, only frozen limbs and a shivering she thinks will never go away.

Victoria knows she's dreaming but she cannot wake. The exhaustion won't let her go.

In her dreams, she's traipsing for days on end, and the cold makes her mended wrist ache. At last, she dares think she might be safe. Safe to sleep in the ruined cottage in the woods. But as she slumbers, she feels hands on her throat, pressing, pressing. She struggles.

And now once again something presses on her face and she struggles, but cannot dislodge the weight.

* * *

Tove sleeps on her narrow bed by the fire in the kitchen. It had never occurred to her to take one of the upstairs bedrooms when she arrived, even though at first she was alone. She sought the light and the warmth because even in spring it is not warm in Edmea's Wood. She wanted, too, a space she could escape from easily (out the back door or through one of the windows that she keeps oiled and every day dutifully chips the ice from), or where she could hide in the concealed cellar, or the hidden cupboard in the back of the tiny pantry.

Tove has a dream she's not had in a long while; she's not had it simply because she's done her best to forget it. She's made herself wake from it so often that it simply seems to stay away, discouraged. But now it returns in its fullest form.

She dreams of the night she saved her mother and lost herself.

She's in the House of Curiosities in Lodellan, stocked with all manner of perverse delights. Tove never knew a father and her mother, Madame Arkady, has told her too many stories about him, most conflicting, for any to be true. Or perhaps there's a grain of truth in each one, but Tove cannot know which is which, cannot know what to listen to and what to discard.

There were days before her mother's prosperity (gained fulfilling the wishes of those with degenerate tastes) that Tove recalls as a series of starvations and near-deaths, wintering in cities where they did not remain too long. Of brief stays in abodes of varying fortune where the master or mistress or both found a use for Madame's talents until they no longer did (until they became ashamed or someone found out about their tendencies). But in this way, Madame Arkady scraped together funds enough to invest in the playhouse in Seaton St Mary when it was doing so very badly. To convince Adonijah Hart to accept her backing and thus soon find himself rich and damned as he agreed to the troupe of pretty women (not actresses) moving in to refurbished floors, for those theatre-goers who wanted something more than dinner and a show. Not long after, Bethany Lawrence came calling, promising rewards in return for Madame's loyalty and comatose conscience. Tove remembers little of Seaton St Mary, just flickers of memory really: the burnt-out shell of an orphanage with a black reputation, tales of wolves who walked on two legs roaming the night streets, and the vaguest recollection of the boy with the shifting face who'd stare at her when she passed through the markets. She can't recall his name.

When Madame Arkady had enough money to move them

to Lodellan, she bought the House of Curiosities, and there she trafficked in all manner of things, the sorts of things she'd allow no one to do to her own daughter. When Tove was ten, however, her mother began to teach her to run the *business*. How to best water down a drink (and how much could be saved a year in doing so). How to decorate a chamber to a theme as cheaply as possible without having it look tawdry. How to roster the courtesans, both male and female, for maximum profit with as little wear and tear as possible. How to note the signs of illness and what to do about it (specific formulas to remedy every sort of venereal disease). How to best stock the rooms for those whose tastes were… alternate.

Tove thinks of her mother's face that night, the expression of sheer terror, the clear belief that she was going to die.

Tove could not recall a time when Madame Arkady didn't fill her with disgust to one degree or another. What made it worse was that she knew her mother loved her. That she was proud of what she'd accomplished, the legacy she was building for Tove to inherit, and Tove couldn't ever quite decide if she'd loved her either. Every time Arkady said that she'd done all these things for Tove's benefit, Tove knew even less. She wore the burden of this knowledge more heavily each day. She began to leave the House of Curiosities and wander the streets, then further afield to the woods despite all the warnings in the world about troll-wives and wolves and things that were only sometimes wolves, sometimes men, and twice as bad all the time, of leech lords even though everyone knew they could not cross from the Dark Lands, of brigands and robber bridegrooms who roamed beneath the boughs. She wandered because she'd come to believe nothing that might happen to her could be worse than what was happening in her home.

And one night she encountered none of those monstrosities, but rather the hind-girls, of whom she'd never heard. The next day she'd asked Cook, tentatively, what they were – lying that she'd eavesdropped on a passing conversation at the markets. Cook, who knew more than she ever let on, had recited the tale: 'The hind-girls dance along the narrow forest courses, throwing their heads with such abandon that sometimes the antlers of one get caught in those of another. But their feet are sure on these paths of beaten earth for they known those ways of old.' She'd said how these were women who'd chosen their own fate; some left marriages or lovers, some left families and rich men. All chose to be something other than they'd been told they could be.

They seemed, to Tove, the most wondrous things in the world, the embodiment of *possibility*. She met them every evening when her mother was otherwise occupied.

It was perhaps a sennight before she felt the nubs on her forehead, then another few days until they began to break through, all bone and brown velvet, painful but not terribly so. They felt *right*. The pain a reasonable price for what might be expected in return: freedom. Freedom from the creeping dread that everything her mother did, did *for* her, contaminated her. Ruined her.

Another seven days, seven nights of sneaking out when she was meant to be abed, of creeping along the sleeping streets of the great city and taking that secret door in the smithy's wall that no one but her mother seemed to know about. It wasn't beyond Arkady to have had it cut for her own purposes, breaching a city's defences for convenience.

And then there was that evening, *the* evening, when Tove knew it was time to go. It was spring, the air filled with promise, her antlers still growing meant that she'd had to adopt a new hairstyle to cover them over. Her mother would be preoccupied as always with welcoming her customers and ensuring their needs were met.

And so Tove left the House of Curiosities in only a fine dress and her thin shoes – the soles of her feet were thickening and she would discard the slippers in the forest but it wouldn't do to be seen wandering barefooted, not before she got to her destination. Yet she encountered no one on her way to the smithy, found the secret door unlocked as always and slipped into the narrow strip of cleared land that formed a break between the city walls and the woods. She followed the path she always had, through the trees and underbrush, feeling the dirt and twigs and rocks and mulch underfoot as she walked. She continued on until she came to the clearing where the hind-girls had danced for her each night on this part of their migration across the land.

They waited, old and young, magnificent sets of antlers growing from their skulls, most speechless for they no longer had need of words, although sometimes they seemed to sing, a communal sweet hum as they moved along the forest trails. Tove kicked off her fine slippers and dug her toes into the grass, ground her heels as if to attach herself more firmly to the earth. And she too began to dance.

A drifting sway, a stamp, a pivot – so swift! – heel-toe, heel-toe, leap! Head, shoulders, arms thrown back, legs balletic in their flight. Tove could feel her antlers growing more in that single moment than in all the previous weeks. But before she could land the soles of her feet firmly in the soil, there came the scream, which shot her from the air as certainly as an arrow would a bird. She dropped, twisted her right ankle, heard a tiny *click* (surely she broke it a little for it aches to this day in this cold, cold place and she limps sometimes more, sometimes less).

Tove looked about and spied her mother at the edge of the clearing, fat pale face shining like the moon itself, hands clutched at her mouth, red lips, red nails like splashes of blood.

And the hind-girls turned towards Arkady (Tove cannot recall if she ever knew her mother's true name) and began to rake their feet through the dirt in preparation to charge. The older ones chomped at the air with their teeth, making clacking noises, the younger snorted like angry bulls. And in that moment Tove knew she had a choice: to join their stampede or to fail this dance.

Her heart let her down.

She ran a limping aching gait towards Madame Arkady and stood in front of her, hands held up and out, pleading, refusing, forbidding.

After a time, the hind-girls went away.

And Tove helped her mother back to the great city, along its streets and into her home. On their way, she told Arkady that she would never follow in her footsteps. That she would flee every and any chance she got. And if that didn't work, then eventually she would be found one morning hanging from the belltower of the Cathedral.

And Madame offered her freedom of a sort: the stone house in Edmea's Wood. That Tove would tend and shelter anyone sent by either her mother or Bethany Lawrence. There was no possibility Arkady could keep knowledge of her daughter's leaving from the Queen of Thieves so she must offer something in return. Bethany numbered bodies in the same fashion the god-hounds counted souls: all to do her bidding.

Tove dreams of the farewell, on the steps of the House of Curiosities, the inheritance she would never have. Of Arkady's face so cold when Tove kissed her cheek, of her eyes so hard as she looked upon her one and only child. Of how the woman offered no goodbye as Tove climbed into the carriage, then turned away, going back indoors before the horses had even begun their first steps.

In the years since, there have been a few rough men passing through for one night on their way to somewhere else. They barely spoke, not even *please* or *thank you* when she fed them, but they left her unmolested and generally brought stores. They give little news but she has picked up happenings such as the growing criminal empire of Breakwater, the burnings of witches, the strange things that wander the land with greater frequency and threat. Her mother has never visited.

* * *

Tove's woken by a sound, muffled, but loud enough. She blinks and squints in the dim light from the embers of the dying fire. Nothing in the kitchen. Then she peers through to the small sitting room. A tall form is hunched over the body on the loveseat, and that body is struggling. She leaps from bed and runs the short distance, a cry working its way up her throat.

'Leave her alone!' The figure moves away with a curse, dropping the cushion it had been using to cover the girl's face. Tove doesn't attack, but rather grabs a poker and stirs the embers in the sitting room hearth.

Selke is lit by its glow. The girl on the loveseat sits up, breathing hard.

Tove barely reaches Selke's shoulder but she's angry enough to slap at the woman. 'Why? What's she done to you?'

Selke doesn't answer, moves a few steps away.

'Selke? Why?'

The girl answers, choking out, 'Because I know what follows her.'

'You know nothing,' spits Selke.

'I know enough that she tried to get me killed once before, left me to the mercies of a mob. Left me to take the blame for her own crime.' The girl points to the contusion on her forehead. '*Her* monstrosity.'

'She's addled,' sneers Selke, then says, 'Tove. Don't you know me better than her? This blow-in?'

'I don't know you at all.' Tove finds a taper, puts it to the coals, and lights the candles above the mantle so the room is not so drear and dim. She looks at the trembling girl and nods.

'My name's Victoria Parsifal. I've been looking for *her* for weeks.'

'Found me, didn't you?' Selke sulks. She clenches her fists as if angry at them for not finishing their task.

'For the second time, and despite your best efforts. I could drag you back to Jago's Rise and have you burnt.' Victoria hugs the large coat more tightly around her.

Selke narrows her eyes. 'But you won't.'

Slowly the girl shakes her head. 'No. They'd burn me right alongside you. Because they're idiots. But you're still a thief and a murderer.'

'Shut up!'

'Do you have any proof?' Tove asks.

Victoria grins, her teeth stained red; the pressure of the pillow over her face has opened the splits in her lips. 'She's got a leather satchel, yes? Go and look. You'll know if I'm telling the truth or not.'

Selke moves to stop Tove, but the girl's gaze – very much like her mother's, did she but know it – makes the woman step back. Tove legs it up the stairs. She finds the bag beneath the bed; there's nowhere else for it, with neither wardrobe nor blanket box, all clothes hanging on wall hooks. She hefts it back down to the sitting room, where Selke remains, now slouched in an armchair across from Victoria. Tove sinks to the floor, the bag between her outstretched legs, and opens it.

Inside there's no gear for travelling or surviving, only one dress. Just that one gown, old and balding velvet, red and tangled. Tove pulls at it. It's heavy, so she digs both hands down under, excavates. Something round is wrapped in it.

She balances the object on one palm, gently peeling away the fabric until the content is exposed. The thing catches the light and at first Tove doesn't understand what she's seeing: it's brilliant, or rather its "cage" is. She holds a skull, covered in a bonnet that looks like a constellation of diamond daisies; the teeth are fitted with braces made of rubies set in a gold framework, and sapphires twinkle in the eye sockets. Tove turns it and turns it with a dreadful fascination. At last she looks askance at Victoria. Selke's gaze is downcast.

Victoria swallows. 'It's the head of the Sainted Bride of Jago's Rise, the Hallowed Girl. *She–*' a glance at Selke – 'stole it. She also murdered its keeper.'

'I didn't… she tried to stop me… Narcissus thought her a threat,' mutters Selke, then bites her lip.

'Narcissus?' asks Tove.

And then comes that terrible cry-roar she heard this afternoon when Victoria arrived. She can hear it clearly, even though it's somewhere outside. She wonders how close it is to the cottage. There are notes of grief and pain in its call.

'My…' Selke searches for words

Victoria interrupts. 'I don't know what he is now… some sort of revenant.'

Selke closes her eyes, smiles strangely. 'He was once an archbishop of Lodellan.'

'Narcissus Marsh?' asks Tove, frowning. 'The cook in my mother's house would tell me tales when I was small. She said…' she concentrates, dredging up memories, '… Narcissus Marsh had truck with a witch and died badly; his tomb beneath the Cathedral was robbed and his bones taken long after his death.'

Victoria tilts her head. 'You know Lodellan?'

'I lived there for a time,' Tove says shortly, then looks at Selke, disbelieving. 'Did you kill him?'

'No sins remain uncovered. But no, not that one, not his death. Not my deed. I don't know how he died. I only knew where he lay.' Selke sighs, then asks longingly, 'Are my wolf-hounds still there?'

Tove asks, 'How old are you?' but Selke ignores her, waits for Victoria to answer.

'Faded, but they remain.'

'I made them for him, for Narcissus, so long ago.' Her pride is evident.

Tove stares. 'Not responsible for his death, but… how does he live again?'

Selke rubs her eyes with the heels of her hands, like a tired child. 'For all the trouble between us, I was… lonely. There were so many years without him. So many years without anyone, really. When everyone around you dies and you… do not.'

'Trouble?' asks Tove.

Selke shrugs as if everything's lost its sting, as though anything might be forgiven with time. 'A dead child, a dead love, his men hunting me from pillar to post. And then he died and they hunted me no more.'

'You were his witch,' guesses Tove.

'Yet you left him behind with that angry horde.' Victoria crosses her arms, licks blood from her lips. Outside, the howl comes again and they all shiver.

'How did you find me? In Jago's Rise?' asks Selke. 'How did you get away from the mob? They seemed quite determined…'

Victoria merely says, 'There are stories about you still. A *determined* person might yet find you.'

'What happened?' Tove demands. 'Why go looking for her?'

'I wanted her help. But I was unsure how she would take being asked. How she would feel if someone knew who – what – she was. So, I watched her all day to learn her patterns, to see where she might be approached most easily.' Victoria nods towards the older woman.

'You'd have done better knocking at my door and being open and honest.' Selke makes a sound of frustration. 'When you've been hunted as long as I, to see someone peeking at you from behind a tree tends to make you nervous.'

Victoria concedes with a lifted eyebrow. 'I followed you to the church, I thought it might be a good place to talk.' She glances at Tove. 'But I entered just as her Narcissus attacked the Sainted Maiden's keeper. The old woman did not go quietly.'

Selke shakes her head. 'Her howls brought the townsfolk. I'm sorry for her death.'

Tove's gaze returns to Victoria, who continues: 'And what should they see but me, a stranger, and the thing she'd made? And what should *she*, their neighbour, do but point at me and shriek that the creature was mine? While they were busy attacking me and her *beloved*, she took the Hallowed Girl's head and fled.'

'You still got away,' observes Selke as if that makes everything alright. 'You're in one piece.'

'Only because it was late and dark, and most of them were half-asleep. And they paid more attention to your Narcissus.'

'I thought they'd destroyed him,' Selke says softly.

'But you didn't stay around to find out.' Victoria says. 'They set him alight. I pushed him into the river – had to leave my poor horse behind. We floated many hours until I thought it safe to leave the water.'

'And was it? Safe?' asks Tove.

'No. The second night, two men came upon me as I slept. Narcissus…' Victoria closes her eyes, swallows, thinks of the sounds of the men's deconstruction at the hands of the revenant. She blinks. 'He followed Selke's scent.' And in truth, she'd have been lost without the creature's unerring sense of his mistress. 'How else do you think I found you?' Selke makes a noise that might be a sob as Victoria goes on in a softer tone. 'And yet he doesn't know that you left him behind. He said you are not bad.'

'Can he still speak?' Selke's head jerks upwards.

'No longer, but for the first few days we travelled together yes. However, the words have gradually been lost. He's… not dying as such, I don't know if he can die like a normal thing. But… perhaps it's like the Cathedral wolf-hounds, and he will fade forever.'

'What did he tell you?' asks Selke and her voice breaks.

'Of your child, and his. Of the loss, how you would not bring the little boy back to life despite his demands. Of how he, Narcissus, was driven mad in grief and you fled. How he sent legions of his god-hounds after you. And how, in the end, he was brought low, drowning after drinking a goblet of imported wine.'

'Drowning… oh, Patience. Patience.' After what seems to be an exhortation to herself, all the breath seems to leave Selke's lungs. She offers no explanation to the younger women, simply pauses before saying, 'And you. *Why* did you come looking, you pestiferous thing?'

'My mother. She's been burned, the flesh will not knit, she's dying.' Victoria blinks away tears. Tove wonders how long she's been strong. 'It's said you've got the power of recreating what's been ruined. I didn't even know if you truly existed or were simply a haunt to scare small children. But here you are. Why did you take *that*?' Victoria points to the skull still in Tove's lap.

'It's a bone lantern, or it will be,' mutters Selke. 'It's something I can use.'

Tove asks, 'What for?'

'That doesn't concern you.'

'It does if someone comes after you and finds me.'

Selke shrugs again. Age, working with death, breathing it, bedding it, have made her unkind. Uncaring and selfish.

'Tove?' Victoria says the name as if testing it. 'You need not remain here alone. You can come with me when I go. There's plenty of room at Singing Vine,' she offers, then returns her attention to Selke. 'Will you help me? I cannot force you.'

'What can you offer?' Selke sneers.

Victoria says boldly, 'What do you need? *Want*?'

Selke laughs. 'My time over again. My friends to be more than dust. My choices to be changeable. The blood of a god. The soul of an unborn child. A cursed gem. The balm of endless sleep.'

Victoria swallows, her fingers fidget with the hem of her vest. 'I can give you but one of them. The gem. Stolen from a troll's hoard.'

Selke's eyes gleam, and there's the merest trace of a change in her frozen expression, something greedy and hopeful. 'What type? Ruby or diamond are no use to me.'

Victoria drops the hem. 'An amethyst, then.'

'Tragedy churns in its wake?'

'My father's death, my mother's burning, my brother lost, and the thief disappeared down the gullet of a troll-wife.'

The older woman draws in a breath that might be a kind of ecstasy. 'Do you have it here?'

'Do I look like a fool? It's where my mother waits.'

Selke nods slowly. 'Then I'll come with you. I'll help. But the gem is mine?'

'I'll give it to you *only* if you save her. You have my word.' Victoria frowns. 'Do you have all you need to do what you must?'

Selke grins. 'In the bag.'

Tove puts the skull gently to one side. She looks at the very bottom of the satchel and finds what she missed before. She pulls out an urn. It's made of brass or copper, the colour is somewhere between the two so she cannot be sure, and it's heavy. Tove twists the lid. From inside comes a foetid breath, and the contents seem to leap up towards the rim. A pale substance, not fluid, but moving like flesh with a life of its own, shifting and twitching.

'Living clay. Harvested from graveyard pits; I spent a year in Jago's Rise, in their great bone orchard where a battle once took place. I had to work at night so no one would know, no one would think me a ghoul or see Narcissus. I had more laid by too, but this was all I could take at short notice. It is the finest quality I've ever worked with and I can help your mother if she's alive when we get to her. I can help her if she's dead as well, but we'll need different ingredients.' Selke rubs her hands together.

'If she's dead she'll stay that way. Do you think I want her in the same state as your Narcissus?' Victoria stares at the urn as Tove reseals it, and carefully puts it back in the satchel. 'Is this your secret? Why you're still alive? Are you as old as stories say?'

Selke, smiles tightly, waving at her own face. 'I've used it too much, I think. At first to replace things I lost: fingers down the gullets of wolves and the like. Then to keep age at bay, smooth out lines, fill cheeks. Now I think it won't let me go, life. Or death won't take me. I'm stuck between them.'

Just when Tove might feel some sympathy for the woman, the terrible scream-roar-growl comes again and reminds her what's been done. She says, 'You must deal with that.'

Selke hedges. 'In the light. I'll not go out in the darkness. We're not going anywhere before dawn.'

Victoria nods. 'In the morning, we'll leave, but you must deal with *that* beforehand.'

* * *

The remainder of the night is mostly sleepless, torn by the cries of the creature outside. Victoria is comfortable with her decision to leave him there. The door would never have been opened to her if she'd had the once-archbishop in tow. Besides, as his speech slipped away, so too did his semblance of rationality; she'd noticed tantrums as they'd walked along, quick losses of temper increasing.

There's little conversation until Selke seems to drift off and Victoria touches fingers to her own forehead, then points at Tove.

'The hind-girls dance along the narrow forest courses,' she says and smiles.

'You know of them?' asks Tove with longing; apart from the Cook, she'd never discussed them with anyone else. Her mother had never asked why her child had grown horns, why she had wanted to do so.

'They saved my life, once. You…' Victoria can't seem to frame the question properly so she simply says, 'What happened?'

Tove is disinclined to relive the details so soon after dreaming them. 'I made a choice.'

'Do you wish you hadn't?'

Tove nods.

'They're in the woods around your cottage, did you know?'

Tove blinks. 'I… have seen tracks, but couldn't be certain. Do you think… there might be another chance?'

'I don't see why not.' Victoria smiles. 'Why else would they be here?'

'Luck. Migratory patterns.'

'You can but try.'

Tove wonders if they might simply mow her down for her betrayal. She looks around the stone cottage, at the silence that hangs in the corners, waiting for her guests to be gone. Waiting for her to be alone once more. She wonders if death might be better.

'The sun will be up soon,' says Tove, and climbs stiffly from the floor. 'Selke. Wake.'

And she does, stretching carefully like an old cat. Selke stands, towers over the two younger girls. From outside comes another cry, weaker this time, mournful. Tove disappears into the kitchen, soon returns with a rucksack, which she hands to Victoria. 'This is all there is that will last you any length of time. And there are two old horses in the barn who'll bear you.'

Victoria rises, and walks slowly towards the window where the blaze of a dawn is beginning to show over the tops of the trees. She looks down at the little padded seat that curves around the semi-circle of glass and wood. There is a book and though she stares at it her mind takes some while to process the sight. Then she realises that she recognises the type of cover, the gold lettering. She reaches down. 'My mother gave my brother just such a volume…'

Little book worm, she thinks bitterly, fondly of Torben.

Victoria runs her fingers over the gold embossing of *Murcianus' Mythical Creatures*, then flips the cover open.

On the frontispiece in Cordelia's handwriting: *To my Torben, my treasure, my light, with all my love. Mamma.*

Then a long row of *xxxxx*. Victoria's heart squeezes with a middle child's jealousy. She quells it. Her hands tremble as she picks the book up and turns to Tove, her voice low. 'Where did you get this?'

Tove swallows as if she's done something wrong. When she hesitates Victoria shouts, 'Where?!'

'A boy. There was a boy sent here.'

'His name? What's his name?'

'Torben.'

Victoria stumbles back, sits hard on the window seat, the book in her lap. 'Where is he? Oh, where?'

'Gone.'

'Gone?'

Tove doesn't quite know how to tell the whole truth, so she simply says, 'He was taken by a bear… the last winter before this one, before the last spring, before this one settled in forever… the sort of bear that sometimes goes on four feet, sometimes on two.'

Victoria's face goes slack and Tove thinks that the heart has perhaps heft her. Perhaps she's simply died there and then, given up.

'Victoria, I'm…' she doesn't know what she is. 'Who was he?'

'My brother. My little brother.' Victoria's eyes focus once more. 'Where is he buried?'

'I… a bear took him. It dragged him away. There was no body.'

Victoria taps her fingers on the cover of the book. 'You didn't see him eaten?'

Tove says, 'No, but…'

'No body,' muses Victoria. Tove cannot know that Victoria has seen the miracle of her mother's return from the dead, of Selke's existence beyond her natural span. Tove cannot understand the improbable hope it has given the girl in this world. A belief in signs and wonders. 'I cannot search, not now, Cordelia, Cordelia…'

Cordelia would want her to stay and find her brother, but Cordelia is dying. 'Do you have a pen and ink?'

Tove, perplexed, nonetheless finds a small pot and a quill. She watches as Victoria opens the book once again and writes a message beneath the dedication. Tove cannot make out the words and they are not meant for her anyway. She thinks perhaps she should have been kinder to the soft boy. Victoria blows on the lettering to dry them, then closes the book. She lays it gently back on the seat and turns away from it as if she can do no more.

'It's time.' Tove says and her own voice sound fearful in her ears.

The three look around. There is just the rucksack of food and Selke's satchel of unspeakable things. It seems strange that they will leave in this fashion, so unarmed, so ill-equipped, but it's the only way forward.

Yet Selke still hesitates. It seems no one will move until Victoria says evenly, 'Selke, you must.'

'What if he…'

'He doesn't know you left him on purpose,' soothes Victoria. Selke shoots a glance at her. 'He thought only of saving you. He thinks you've been waiting for him here.' Victoria smiles.

Selke closes her eyes tightly, yet tears bleed through.

Tove says once more, 'It's time.' She takes one of the old furs from the hooks by the door and hands it to Selke. The woman accepts, and laces up a pair of worn boots; she pulls open the heavy front door and steps out. Tove, conversely, kicks off her fur-lined slippers and does not bother with a coat. She hands the sack to Victoria, then crosses the threshold and shivers.

Victoria gives one glance backwards, to where the book lies on the window seat like a promise. She nods, then leaves, pulling the door behind her.

Moving across the snowy ground between the house and the woods is Narcissus Marsh, swaying as if wounded. Victoria, familiar with him by now, is untroubled by his appearance. Tove's not seen him before and her breath is caught in a horrified snarl in her throat.

He looks like nothing so much as a stain on the world. Naked and beige, he stands out against the snow like a blot. There is no blending, no chance he might hide. As they watch, small fragments of him come away like the sloughing of a skin, an eldritch dissolution. Each shard that breaks off turns black as ash, then falls apart as if eaten by an invisible flame.

He is very tall, covered in desiccated skin – not simply bare bones or naked muscle and flesh – his limbs are long and weirdly thin, the shoulders gallows-wide. The head is round and hairless, the face with an overwhelming expression of bewilderment. One side of his body, from foot to mid-chest, is scorched where he was set alight. Selke's breathing is harsh.

'He's been dying this whole time without you to tend to him, as much as he *can* die. I think he hurts terribly. Can you… give him an end, Selke?'

All Selke can do is nod. She drops the bag in the snow, then moves forward, away from Victoria and Tove, to meet the creature she'd made. Victoria's breathing turns rough: what if she's wrong? What if he kills Selke and all Cordelia's chances are gone? But she stays where she is, not wishing to spook the former archbishop.

Selke reaches her lover and they circle each other a few steps before she touches his face or what's left of it. In profile: Selke's frozen beauty, Narcissus' ruin of a nose, the spot where an ear has fallen off, the wrecked lips that look like scars around a gaping hole. Such a contrast and yet there's a symmetry to them.

'Bride of the dead,' whispers Tove.

The creature's cheek nestles into the palm of Selke's hand. The woman's expression is inscrutable, but her lips are moving. The more she speaks, the faster his substance peels away like ash leaving a fire. The revenant gives one last cry, and his knees slowly buckle. He begins to topple and the disintegration of his flesh is rapid as he hits the snow. Soon there is only a flurry of beige-black particles whirling in the air.

Selke hangs her head.

'What next?' asks Tove. The weight of the question bears down on her. She's never been involved in the matters that have happened in the stone cottage, not truly. She's been a witness, a watcher, sitting at windows, by fires; she breathes and moves but she does not partake, not since she refused to join the hind-girls that night. It feels to her as if she gave up her right to participate in life then, because when she'd saved Madame Arkady – that stupid, stupid act – she made sure her mother would continue to make a living off the skin and bones of children, their suffering and pain lining her fine fur coats and hats, furnishing the houses she collects like toys and decorates with carpets and tapestries and cushions, and things made of polished wood and inlaid with precious gems.

Victoria's hand touches hers, and points to the tree line. Tove sees multiple forms, creeping between trunks. The hind-girls come, all flowing hair with flowers and brambles grown through, all that flesh exposed to the cold with no sign of a shiver, all those antlers growing tall and heavy and velvety.

Tove had never thought to see them again.

'What will you do, Tove?' asks Victoria.

'Will you be safe with her?' Tove juts her chin to where Selke stands, head and shoulders bent. 'I can come with you?'

'As long as I've got the gem she wants, I'm safe. I'll keep an eye on her, never you fear.' And Victoria smiles again. 'And you've got somewhere else to go. Second chances are rare.'

'Thank you.' Tove hugs Victoria; it's an uncertain, unfamiliar motion and she breaks away quickly. She faces the herd, takes a deep breath, then begins to dance.

A drifting sway, a stamp, a pivot – so swift! – heel-toe, heel-toe, leap! Head, shoulders, arms thrown back, legs balletic in their flight. Tove's feet have never gone soft, not even in these years since she first failed.

Selke and Victoria watch as Tove progresses away from them. When she meets the herd, they circle her, sniffing and testing at the air around her; some touch her hair, skin, the tiny stillborn antlers. Finally, the group envelops Tove, and they move off as one, back into the trees, with not a glance at the two women left behind.

'Will she be well, do you think?' Selke asks and Victoria is only a little surprised that the woman has a skerrick of care left in her.

'Never fear,' she says. 'Tove will dance along the narrow forest courses, throwing her head with such abandon that sometimes her antlers get caught in those of another. But her feet will be sure on these paths of beaten earth for her companions know those ways of old.' Victoria grins. 'Come along now.'

CROSSROADS

Bethany holds the fur cloak tightly around her against the long winter's night – how can it *still* be winter? – but the hood hangs loose down her back; she does not care if she is seen. No one will think her a supplicant, not in this part of her city, or any other for that matter. Some will wonder, however, what has gone so terribly, terribly wrong that the Queen of Thieves must venture forth. They'll speculate who is going to lose a pound or more of flesh in recompense, whose head will roll, which crook, bandit, light-finger, fence, or footpad will regret a careless moment.

It's a strain to walk without a limp. The left ankle is still painful even months after the tumble from the window. Henry has told her with more acid than affection that she should consider herself lucky to be walking at all. Her expression is forbidding – she would have given almost anything to remain at home in the house by the Weeping Gate – and passers-by step swiftly out of her way. Bethany Lawrence fumes purely because she has been forced to come *here*.

This particular market, located at the crossroads just outside the main gate into Breakwater is, more or less, an organised riot. There are groups that move and grow and shrink within seconds, stalls displaying wares and weapons, and in some spots there are simply shingles hoisted above a chair or cart where the purveyor of services sits patiently. Folk so disposed may find hirelings of the sort they require, those inclined towards the liberation of others' wealth, or the committing of violent acts which may or may not be of the terminal type. Mostly, though, people come here for the hire of assassins, either alive or dead. The latter are those once hung or buried or burned at these very crossroads, who've not been able to leave the world behind. They stay and make commerce with those who breathe, a death in exchange for some blood or meat, or a piece of a soul. This is the currency of the dead. The living are sometimes more expensive but often less trouble.

Who would have thought there was such a demand for these

services? Well, Bethany did, and she knows those here are not all gathered for missions in Breakwater; those in need of another's death and clean hands come from near and far. There are middlemen and guildmasters, too, with stables of clever killers, establishing a client's requirements then putting them in contact with the most appropriate employee. All of them paying a fee to one of Bethany's lieutenants for each and every contract. Then there's the rental for space in the market. And the taxes on every drop of poison, dagger, cudgel, tool of the trade sold here. All in all, the Queen of Thieves makes good coin from the assassins market.

It doesn't make her feel any happier about having to do this task herself, however. She'd sent Dove with his quit wit, quicker tongue, and deadly persuasive hands to find the one she sought, but he'd returned with the message *She'll only speak to you.* Then stood stoically while she'd slapped him seven ways from Sunday in a rage.

Up ahead she sees the awning of the tent inn she allowed Vasco to set up two years ago; there are rents in the fabric and splits in the sides, tears where knives and bodies have made swift exits. She'll have a word with him; just because he runs a den of thieves is no reason for it to look like a shit-heap. Bethany is particular about her empire's appearance. If the short fat man with all his hair concentrated on his chin in a complicated series of braids couldn't see his way clear to springing for a new pavilion then she'd give the business to someone who could.

The tent flap is tied back with a filthy piece of rope, and an urchin – not much older than Bethany was when she entered the orphanage at Seaton St Mary – stands outside, sing-shouting loudly to draw customers in. Bethany frowns. The urchin thinks it's meant for him and he bows low, almost scraping his forehead on the muddy ground. She ignores this clumsy politeness and sweeps by, steps into the gloom of the Scalded Man. She pauses, catches Vasco's eye and raises a perfectly shaped brow. He nods, points with his chin to the furthest corner. She breathes deeply of the fug of alcohol, smoke and sweat, lets it fill her lungs before she heads towards the place where the darkness seems concentrated.

At a table waits a woman with fiery red hair and feral yellow eyes. She's stocky, sturdy, peasant-bred, dressed in black, a row of silver daggers hangs from a leather strap over one shoulder. She gives Bethany a glance that says *Sit* as if the Queen of Thieves needed to wait for her permission.

'I'm given to understand you've been looking for me,' says the woman smoothly.

Bethany doesn't sit, even though her ankle aches. 'You know very well I want to engage your services. Yet apparently won't deal with any lieutenant I send.'

'Minions make for bad messengers, they mangle words and phrasing, the intent is lost,' the woman says. She gestures to the seat beside her again, and again Bethany does not sit. 'If I speak to the ringmaster rather than her monkeys, I will have the message true. Now, who is it you wish me to kill?'

'You are Tanaquil?' Bethany asks belatedly.

The woman nods.

'And you can do what they claim?'

A ruddy eyebrow goes up. 'Of course. I'd hardly be fronting Bethany Lawrence if I could not. I like my life and limbs intact.'

Bethany thinks of the tales: a bishop murdered in his bed, a prince killed at his coronation as the crown was placed, a duchess slaughtered at a tea party – all by this woman's hand. Bethany gives a sharp nod. 'You will find your target at the Singing Vine Vineyard a day from the town of Jory's Dell.'

Or you would have a few months ago. Now… but Bethany won't admit to her failure. Won't admit to a weakness in front of this assassin. If Cordelia's moved on then let this bloodhound hunt the quarry down. Earn the hefty fee she's demanding.

'What's the name of the one whose death you so ardently desire?' Tanaquil pours herself a shot of brandy from the bottle on the table. Bethany notes the label: it's one of the more exclusive beverages Vasco stocks; not everyone frequenting the Scalded Man is a low-life.

'Her name is Cordelia Parsifal or it was. Perhaps she goes under a different one now. I assume it's within your very expensive abilities to track her.'

Tanaquil nods, mouth quirking with amusement. 'And how does she look?'

'Like me once, but no longer. She's a mass of burns and rotting flesh.' Bethany shrugs, thinks of the sight of her big sister in that bed, of the stare of the one good green eye, of her weak struggles beneath the pillow in Bethany's hands. 'Gods know, she might be dead already. If so, then I'll pay your fee just to bring me the news.'

'That's very generous, Madame Lawrence. So generous, in fact, that it makes me ask why do you hate her so much?'

Bethany hesitates, decides it cannot cost her anything to tell. 'My sister was ever a thorn in my side. When she's gone, there'll be only memories and those can be forgotten easily enough.'

She doesn't believe her own bravado. She still wakes up gasping from dreams of Cordelia burning; Cordelia helpless in the rundown home where Bethany knew only terror after Cordelia left her. A voice inside whispers *No, they cannot. They can be neither burned out of your brain, nor torn from it, nor drowned in any amount of alcohol. They are part of you as surely as your hand or hair or mouth. They are a torment and a blessing and they will never let you go.* But she doesn't admit this to the assassin.

Instead she narrows her eyes, figures out what's bothering her. 'I know you.'

The woman tilts her head. 'Indeed?'

'You were… you were the wife of the Prince of Lodellan!' Bethany shouts with laughter. 'Ah, I wondered what had happened to you after…' She stops laughing when knowledge catches up with her. She remembers that the necklace that had caused so much trouble had been stolen from the royal palace, right under the noses of the guards. She frowns, recalling the reports sent by her spies, of murdered men found in the crypts beneath the Cathedral, of a vicious ghost that took days to quell and exorcise. And the stories of how the wife of the Prince – the lover of the Princess Royal – had been quietly repudiated, her sons kept from her, and she driven out of the city. 'Ilse. You were called Ilse. Did you take it – the necklace?'

Tanaquil leans forward, her elbows resting on the tabletop, hands clasped as if to stop them from doing something else. Her face is a battlefield of emotions and for the first time in a long while Bethany feels she might have bitten off more than she can chew; that she might actually be under a threat she cannot manage. Tanaquil says quietly, 'I saw your sister the night *she* wore that necklace, watched her marched off to prison in the cold. It hung in Armandine's room all those months your sister rotted in a hulk in Rosebery Bay. I wanted it, yes. But I did not take it.'

'Who then?' Bethany'd planned to steal it again herself, once the memory of the Parsifals and their scandal had faded. She thinks of the rumours she's heard from Lodellan, of the little princes becoming ill, of the Prince himself falling into madness. She has not been back to visit since she took the children away. She's not had much decent intelligence from there since Isambard disappeared…

'If I knew, don't you think I would have told them? To stay by my children, to keep the life I had?' Tanaquil shakes her head. 'There was… that night… I have the vaguest memory of a man… he held me, said he was sorry… that's all I recall.' Tanaquil leans back in her seat, crosses her arms over her chest. 'But I believe you owe me something.'

Bethany nods, pulls the leather pouch from a deep pocket inside her cloak. She tosses it onto the table with a chinking thud. 'The rest when you bring my sister's head to me.'

Tanaquil nods but doesn't reach for her payment. She narrows her eyes and asks, 'What did Cordelia Parsifal do to you that you want this so much?'

And there's that brief moment when Bethany cannot remember. It's the brief moment when the truth rears its head and she sees it as a mirror. She knows that all that she's done to Cordelia had been simply a childish resentment carried too far. What their parents did was not Cordelia's fault; what happened in the orphanage was not Cordelia's fault; and what Mr Farringdale did was not her fault either. Then Bethany swallows hard, blinks until the mirror shatters. As she turns away, she throws over her shoulder, 'You have a job to do.'

* * *

'What's a grandmother?' asks Eliza, and Henry curses under his breath.

He's usually a lot more careful when choosing stories to read, but he's tired, distracted. When *Once upon a time when wishing still helped, there was a little girl whose grandmother loved her very much* came from his lips he could have bitten off his own tongue. He knows his daughter well enough: if he tries to change the subject or refuses to answer there will simply be a tantrum at bedtime that might well go on for hours.

'That is your mother's mother, and your father's mother. Everyone has two grandmothers.' He blinks, focuses on the words. *'Her grandmother lived in a small cottage in the woods, far away from people.'*

'Do my grandmothers live in the woods?'

'Yes,' he says gratefully, hoping it might be the end. *'Usually when the little girl visited her grandmother, it was in the company of her mother.'*

'When will I go to see them? Will you take me? Or will Mama?'

Henry sighs and closes the book.

His daughter's bedroom is a treasury of toys and pink frills; Eliza has confided that she does not like pink, however, she is too afraid to tell Mama. Henry's daughter is wise; he's told her that one day she may change it. When she is ten he has promised and, given a firm deadline, she is content. He still has several years to convince Bethany. Oh, he could mention it now but Henry learned some time ago that his aunt's promises seldom eventuate, and early warning just gave her greater opportunity to think up more excuses. She continues to tell him he will be allowed to return to Whitebarrow and finish his studies – he had a brief six months there before she called him home. He dabbles in potions still, sets broken limbs and sutures the wounds any of her men suffer. She'd said she could not bear to be without him a moment longer, yet when he returned he'd found his sister disappeared and his brother about to begin an *apprenticeship*. Bookish, spoilt Torben sent off into the woods. He'd tried to warn the boy to be quiet, but Torben wouldn't listen, his habit of questioning everything undimmed. Henry still wonders if his presence earlier might have kept Victoria from exile; he suspects not.

But then, he thinks, what right has he to expect honesty from anyone let alone the Queen of Thieves?

'Papa?' Eliza is still looking at him. 'When, Papa, when?'

'I'm afraid we can't go to visit them, my sweet pearl, because both have passed away.' Henry hates that phrase, *passed away*, because it doesn't sound permanent, doesn't sound as if it has consequences, doesn't sound true. But Eliza's barely four and clever though she is he doesn't want to frighten her. *Passed away* is what he's said about her pets – rabbits, cats, puppies – and any members of the household of whom she was fond, but who'd displeased Bethany beyond her short tolerance.

Eliza's bottom lip trembles, tears well, and she looks so much like his own mother that his heart feels faint. It's Cordelia's face he sees in her, never Bethany's. He's sitting in the armchair by her bed and she's propped against myriad frilled pillows like a doll, yet she climbs out quick as a hare and launches herself across the space between them and onto his lap. The breath's pushed out of him but he's used to it and she's still small.

'There, there, precious one. How can you weep for something you never knew you'd lost let alone had?' He grins into her blonde curls in spite of the ache. She shouldn't exist, this tiny scrap, her blood thinned by her parents' proximity, but he's glad for her every single day. Even when she reminds him of Cordelia; possibly the most then.

'But now I'll never know what a grandmother is like,' she says and begins to weep into his chest, that little hiccupping whimper that meshes around his heart. She was not expected in his life, not the way she came, but he cannot image being without her. 'And it hurts.'

He holds her tighter, careful not to squeeze too hard, this precious tiny fragile creature. 'I understand, my dove. I miss my Mama terribly.'

'Will you tell me about her?' she pushes back and raises her head so her shining eyes meet his. And he finds he cannot bear to talk about Cordelia, not with this child who looks so like her.

'She was the kindest person I ever knew,' he says eventually, and notes his daughter doesn't say 'Even more than Mama?' for much though Bethany loves their child, she is not kind. 'And I hope you will be very like her.'

Henry thinks of how he found Bethany this week in her study, teaching Eliza about knives, all the sorts that might exist and how they should be used for varied purposes. He'd seen the fear in Eliza's little face and the disappointment in Bethany's. Henry had never pushed an issue with his aunt before, not even about Whitebarrow, but this time… He'd sent their daughter to her room, then yelled at his lover for a full half-hour for daring to teach their child such things. For breaking her word that Eliza would be kept away from all of Bethany's business dealings – that the child's life would not be tainted.

And Bethany had sat silent and cold until he'd exhausted himself, then said *She's my daughter, Henry, she bears my blood. She'll carry on all I've built when you're long dust.*

You're, she'd said, not *we're.*

As if Henry's span might be measured in shorter paces than hers. As if what she'd pass on was an empire to be proud of… and he knew Bethany was immensely proud of what she'd built, of what she'd done. It didn't matter to her that the foundation of everything was blood and bodies. It was *hers.* She would give it to their daughter whether he wished it or no.

She doesn't want to learn this, he'd hissed. *She's afraid.*

She'll learn, Bethany had said evenly.

She's afraid of you. Your own child is afraid of you.

Good. She'll learn faster. She'd turned her back on him and stalked out. She didn't even bother to threaten him for questioning her; he doesn't know if it's because she still loves him especially or because she didn't feel it necessary to remind him of what she might do.

He wonders if Eliza will be allowed to go to school, to university, to learn something other than murder and mayhem. He wonders if all the potential she might have will be betrayed by her very own mother.

Yet as his small daughter clings damp and sorrowful to him, he wonders what right has he to self-righteous umbrage after his own treachery? Not merely turning his back on those who gave him life, setting them aside for a scandalous touch and the promise of more to come. He thinks, not for the first time, how easy it would be to let it all go, to use one of the medicaments that line the walls of his compounding room to bring an eternal sleep and a rest; but then his daughter's face always appears and draws him back. He does not believe in any kind of deity, his early deeds leeched that from him, so he has no fear of any afterlife retribution. What can be worse, after all, than a lover who is his aunt, and his own memory of swearing to the magistrates of Lodellan that he'd seen his father (so soon to take his own life) return home the night of the Agnews' terrible murder, covered in blood and bearing that magnificent necklace?

All because *she'd* asked him to.

* * *

Ella can't quite recall how she got here, or how long she's been in this blackness. Her eyes only adjust so much and no more nowadays, even though she was born in the gloom of under-earth. There are walls of stone (three), and another made of iron bars that spews onto a broad corridor of cracked flags. Across the way are more cells like hers, but none of them are occupied. She's been alone the whole time and this incarceration is her own fault entirely.

Accepting blame is a sign of growth, she's sure, but there's no one to know of it, no one to boast to, no one to hear her say 'Haven't I been good?' Lis would have said *Does it matter at all, then?* And once Ella would have shouted *Of course!* but now? She'd shrug if she had the energy, but he bleeds her every second day and the fight's flowed out of her drop by drop.

When she'd left the *Silver Branch*, left Lis and her violet-eyed lover to their own devices, she'd wandered just as she had many times before. Washing up in Breakwater like driftwood Ella suddenly found herself in need of a means to earn a living; she'd lived quite happily off Lis and the change was something of a shock. But in this strange city of thieves she found few opportunities for any of her talents. She'd lost the art of being pleasing so plying a horizontal trade was out of the question. There were herbalists aplenty and her skills with plants and potions had atrophied – she didn't recall enough to present herself as a master of the profession. But she *did* recall her blood – or rather her father's blood, how it had been drawn from him by the Misses Meyrick at the School for Poison Girls and sold to those with means and malice. She thought her own might be just as vitriolic, and offered it to an apothecary into whose store she'd meandered. They tested the ichor on a rat that had died noisily but swiftly. Ella, however, had become careless in her time with Lis, hadn't truly bothered to hide herself and what she'd been, so she was too frank about where the poison came from. The apothecary, alas, decided that he would prefer to own the source itself rather than buy it at her whim.

A hit on the head while she waited unawares for him to fetch her coin, and she woke later in the cell (beneath his shop, she assumed, in the web of tunnels that ran under the city, some more tidal than others). Twice a day the floor was inundated, the straw floating almost a foot upwards and she with only a narrow pallet bed upon which to perch. There were no windows, just torches lit at either end of the corridor, too far really to give any kind of illumination where she lay. She thought he drugged the food and heavy red wine he brought down once a day; she'd seen no sign of servants, and suspected he was the sort of man to think them not worth the risk. She was too hungry to resist eating, and too weary to care. Eventually, she came to the conclusion that it would end only with her death and, then, that such an event was to be welcomed.

What was against her was her long life, the sole gift her father had left when he'd taken everything else away; and that remained only so she would suffer. But now she found it difficult to be angry at him. There'd been centuries of rage and bitterness that had gained her nothing. He *had* come looking for her to ask forgiveness and offer it… and her answer had been to feed him to the twin assassins Orla and Fidelma Meyrick so they might trap and tap him much as happened to her now.

So long ago.

So very long ago.

She thinks of the woman, Mercia, her father's wife. Thinks of her offer. Of her plea. Thinks of how she, Ella, would not entertain an act of kindness or rapprochement. Thinks of how her death will have no benefit at all. How she'll pass out of the world as little more than a whispered legend to scare children, as crooked words on yellowed pages in books ruined by sun and wind, moon and rain.

Ella closes her eyes and the darkness behind her lids is only marginally deeper than that of the cell. She begins to drift.

* * *

The apothecary's shop is surprisingly well lit so the man behind the counter can clearly see how lovely the woman is when she enters the premises. Tall and buxom, hair a particularly brilliant shade of blonde, eyes the green of an emerald. Her features exquisitely composed and the skin flawless as if it's never suffered a blemish. He cannot tell her age, but she's dressed very well indeed, a gown of ruby silk beneath a full-length coat of silver fox fur. He stands straighter, adjusts his vest and jacket (both in garish purples and yellows, but made of rich fabrics), and brushes a hand over his mostly bald pate to ensure the seven strands are stretched across the empty expanse. He steps out from behind the counter, fingers interlaced, and fixes a smile to his lips. She doesn't look like anyone he's ever seen in Breakwater, but there's a good sized contingent of those who come to avail themselves of the assassins market (he himself supplies its denizens with some of the finest and most expensive poisons to be found).

Behind her he notices at last the young man: red-rough skin, large bulbous nose, dirty blond curls, eyes small in a round face. Taller than the woman and broader, some muscle, some fat. The woman nods at the oaf, who leaves, but not before giving the apothecary a warning glance. So: Felix has learned to judge his clients by those they hire, and this bruiser tells him that the woman is far more dangerous than she might appear. He resets his grin, dims it, nips at the leer, does his best to appear less himself than he is. 'Good day, my lady.'

She says, 'Good morning, kind sir, I trust you are well.'

He is taken aback: his usual clients, no matter their station, never offer such pleasantries. He's charmed despite the recollection of the bruiser at her back. He knows better, however, than to ask her name. 'I am much better for the sight of you, dear lady. How may I assist?'

She offers a smile and it's the brightest thing to ever light this place. 'I seek a particular substance, one that's as concentrated and virulent as a bride's spite. I have it on good authority that you stock just such a poison.'

It is a sign of Breakwater's nature that anyone might walk into such an establishment and ask so openly for such a thing. He nods enthusiastically, then remembers that even though his business is known to many he's never given his truths or wares up so easily. The apothecary tries to claw back ground even though there's no sign of triumph in her face, not a glint of greed in the green of gaze. 'And might I ask from you whom you heard this?'

And regrets it immediately.

'Sir, you know we do not deal in names,' she gently scolds, but immediately purses her lips as if making a decision. She leans forward. 'But I will tell you I am a tallow-wife and my colleagues have spoken highly of you and your commodities.'

The poisoner-chemist tries not to take in too sharp a breath. Tallow-wives come in varied sorts. The simple makers of candles, useful items, no great skill required beyond a steady hand. Then there were those who create the sorts of tapers and dips that might change a mood or a mind, just some small influence. Finally there are those whose work could cause a life to begin or to cease, to amass or destroy fortunes, families and cities. This woman, if he is not very badly mistaken, was one of those last – after all, the other type had no need for what she'd demanded. He could *tell* – and hadn't his instinct led him to trap the dark woman whose blood he'd been bottling and selling to his great profit?

'I need,' the woman says in a low voice though there's no one else to hear, 'your bleakest, blackest poison. I can pay your price, good sir.' So saying, she produces a small purple velvet purse from inside her cloak and tips it onto the glass top of the nearest counter. Three shards of stars bounce, leaving tiny scratches and scrapes. Diamonds. He picks one up and examines it. Goes behind the counter and finds the jeweller's loupe he keeps for just such occasions (he's seldom paid exclusively in coin and he's a clever enough man to know he must be expert in all forms of currency that cross his palm). The stones are exquisite, clear as snow-melt from the highest peaks, cut perfectly. This is more than he would have charged. Even a single one would still be far beyond the value of what he'll sell her.

Licking his lips, he palms just one of the diamonds, then pushes the other two back at her. 'I have a proposition, mistress.'

She raises a brow but says nothing. He leans over the counter and produces one of the small vials of thick green poison he's harvested. The thing she desires. He holds it up to the light so she can appreciate its sheen.

'If you are agreeable, I would avail myself of your gifts. Make me the same sort of candle as I assume you are making for your own use. Ten, that is all I ask.' He touches her on the arm and her eyes flicker, like dangerous shadows passing beneath the surface of water. The apothecary retreats, hands raised to show no harm was meant; he remembers with whom he is dealing. 'I believe I have all the things you need in my own workroom.'

She tilts her head, thins her lips in thought, then she nods. 'Ten candles for ten vials of your poison.'

He almost objects, then remembers the perfect diamond in his palm. He is not being robbed.

He locks the front door and puts a *Closed* sign in the window.

'My servant will return here to collect me, so you must listen for his knock. I would not want him to think me harmed and thus turn his ire on you. He has a dreadful temper and little control.'

The apothecary believes that to be the most delicately put threat he's ever heard. 'I understand.'

'And –' she says, holding up a single slender finger – 'I have one condition.'

'Yes, my lady?' For surely she's a lady.

She touches his arm, down near the wrist where the skin is bare. He shivers, and she says, 'I would know the source of this poison.'

'Ah, my lady. You so recently reminded me that we do not deal in names, yet you would ask me such a thing?' The feeling of her cool fingers against his warm flesh is like a burning brand. He wonders if he'll come away scarred and the idea pleases him.

She bats her lashes, grins, leans to whisper in his ear, 'I am Nerys.'

She's so close and her perfume is suddenly strong though he'd not noticed it before, roses and something else. He should know better than to trust a tallow-wife, but he's not thinking. He muses that, once they are below, once she's seen the source, he'll take her up against the cold damp wall, ruin her fine dress just a little. Then, she'll make him the candles he wants and he'll sell them for a high, high price. And perhaps there will be time later for more, perhaps she will return to him. Perhaps, perhaps.

But he doesn't kiss her now, just in case he's misread the situation. He doesn't want her to flee. Down in the tunnels it will be easier to persuade her. He ceases to think of the oaf in her employ. Women don't tend to report such things for the shame is always theirs. Besides, he's almost sure she likes him even as she steps away, those eyes slanted up at him, the lashes such thick veils behind which she can hide.

'I am Felix.' He says nothing more, merely leads her to the silk curtain at the back of the shop, through it to the sumptuous rooms it in which he lives, and thence to a set of steps, down to the kitchen, where he grabs a lantern from a shelf and lights it with a taper dipped into the flames of the hearth. Next, to a small pantry with a trapdoor in the floor. This he lifts to show a stone staircase.

'The way can be slippery, and will still be wet from the tides. Perhaps leave your coat here?'

She nods and slips it from her shoulders. She hangs it on a hook at the back of the pantry where normally a ring of garlic would wait, but he's run out and yet to go to the markets. When she is ready – when he is done admiring her figure – he goes first, a crabbed sideways walk so he can offer her a steadying hand as she follows.

They reach the corridor of flags without incident. The smell is of salt and rotten straw. As soon as her boots give a wet clack on the floor, she lets go of him and pushes both her hands into the deep pockets of her dress. She doesn't bother to hoist the skirts, doesn't seem worried about the inch of water at her feet, and the mess it will cause; a sure sign of tremendous wealth. Only the very rich can afford to be so very careless of their pretty things; the more he thinks about it, the more he feels this will be a profitable partnership.

'Won't you lead on, my dear Felix?' she says with a smile, and he returns the grins, hoists his lantern. The corridor is straight, and long, stretching away into the darkness. The span between the lit lamps high on the wall is enough that there are pools of darkness in the middle. Finally, they come to a cell in one of those pools. Felix fits the lantern into a niche beside the bars, to better illuminate what lies in the confined space. He and Nerys stand side by side, staring.

Right up against the back wall is a filthy pallet on which lies a long, thin figure in a ragged black dress. The sleeve on the left arm has been torn open and a rough bandage is wrapped around the crook of the elbow. A fall of ebony hair tumbles to the floor, unbrushed and unwashed, its ends dragging in the last of the outgoing tide. The face is pale, the eyes closed.

'I don't know what she is,' says Felix, quiet as a conspirator. 'But she came to me, offered her blood like a fool.'

'And you did this to her.'

Felix feels a punch at his chest and thinks she's slapped him. Part of him rejoices: now he has an excuse for throwing her up against the wall, but then his chest begins to hurt, to sting, to burn. He looks down, sees the handle of a dagger sticking out of him. He has a small second to appreciate the accuracy of the strike, done while she seemed to not look at him at all. Then his knees buckle and he's sitting in the damp, hands flapping uselessly as fish deprived of water.

'It's very fast,' she says, 'and gentler than you deserve.'

And Felix is gone before he keels over and his head hits the stones.

* * *

Cordelia's careful as she pulls the knife from Felix's limp body to wipe the poisoned blade on his coat. She tears a strip from his shirt and wipes the thing before resheathing and putting it back into one of her deep pockets; some nights she's dreamed of doing this very thing to Edvard for being such a coward. Then she begins to search for the dead man's keys. She leaves the damned diamond in the waistcoat pocket where she finds it: she's been careful about where she sends these things to seed, mindful of their curse.

Her face itches; Selke said it would be some time before the sensation stopped – no matter how fast the magic was that remade her face, the entire healing would be long – but it's lessened considerably, acting up only when she's stressed. The rest of her where skin and flesh were regrown has mostly settled. The eye that was white for so long is normal again but sometimes her vision is cloudy and there's a twitch in the eye itself. Again, Selke said that would pass.

At last she finds the ring of heavy keys, attached to his belt, at his back where it's impossible to see, hard to lift. She picks the largest of the bunch and inserts it into the lock. The cell door pushes back with a creak. She has other things to do, important matters to attend to; it's taken weeks to get the information she needed, weeks to locate a shop like this, weeks to make arrangements and plant the falsities required. But she will not leave this woman alone, not locked up and ill; she won't abandon another to circumstances she'd once suffered herself.

Cordelia puts her fingers to the woman's throat because it's so hard to tell if she's still breathing. It would be foolish to let an investment like die this and Felix didn't seem like a fool, not entirely. There! A pulse, thready but definite. She taps the woman's chest, which is cold. 'Wake up. Mistress, wake up.'

It takes a while but she stirs at last. Her eyes flicker open and Cordelia finds herself staring into the darkest pits she's ever seen. She manhandles the woman into a sitting position, leans her back against the rough masonry. From her pocket she fishes a flask, unscrewing it. The woman tries to push it away.

'It's winterplum brandy,' explains Cordelia. 'It will give you some strength. Really, please drink. I must get you out of here. If someone should come looking for him…' She glances over her shoulder and the woman follows her gaze, then begins to laugh. It's a hoarse rasping sound, but a laugh nonetheless. The woman accepts the flask and downs half the contents before Cordelia wrestles it away. 'No point being dead drunk as well as weak.'

'Mother,' murmurs the woman. 'Mercia.'

'No. Cordelia. And you are?'

'You… you didn't come looking for me?'

'I didn't even know you were here… but I'd heard of the poison he was selling and I was… curious. I thought it would come from some strange plant, instead I find *you*.'

'And what will you do with me?'

'Send you home. Wherever that might be, I will make sure you get there.' Cordelia takes in her disbelieving stare. 'Ah. You've probably no reason to trust anyone. You can walk out of here alone if you wish, but I have a last thing to do before I go. So, I'll assist you up the stairs, then you can make your own way, or wait for my friend to return and help you to our carriage.'

'I'll kill you if you lie.'

'Noted. Now, try to stand on your own two feet, you're heavier than you look.'

* * *

'Eliza, don't touch that,' says Henry and hides a grin when his daughter pouts. But she obeys, stops reaching for the discarded doll lying on the muddy cobbles; there are a few shreds of red hair still adhering to its skull. Instead she takes small dancing steps closer to him and slips her fingers into his gloved palm. Experience tells him that the white satin dress with its pink and purple ribbons beneath her blue coat won't long survive this afternoon's outing intact, but its ruination has been delayed at least.

Together they pass beneath the elaborate marble arch that leads into the zoological park. Bethany had suggested its creation to the remaining city fathers – there are some she keeps around for a veneer of legitimacy – somewhere her daughter would enjoy. Exotic creatures were brought to Breakwater and most survived despite trial and error, their diets often enriched and supplemented by the occasional influential citizen whose voice would not be silenced. As her hold on the port-city had tightened, so did dissent lessen as folk either left for safer towns or found themselves turned into food for the collected lions and tigers, bears and devil birds, wyrms and wolves, and other unexpected beasts that inhabited the enclosures.

As they come to the lion house, Henry lifts Eliza up so she can see more fully into the den where the great cats loll about on grassy hummocks and drape themselves in the branches of trees. The little girl taps her fingers against the glass, draws the attention of a black-maned male, who rolls to his feet and stalks over. He sniffs at the barrier, pushes his nose against the surface experimentally, trying to find a way through to the soft meat waiting so tantalisingly *close*. Eliza gives a delighted giggle when the lion bellows a frustrated roar and wanders away, back to where three lionesses watch his optimism with weary stares. This scene has been played before. Thrice a week or more for Eliza never tires of the place. And Henry can suppress a shudder of fear when the lion roars; he's pleased his daughter is untouched by his own fright.

'Papa,' she says, wiggling.

'Yes, my poppet?'

'Wyrms, please,' she says for she loves the great scaled lizards, at least six feet in length though their strangely articulated legs barely clear a foot off the ground. They're covered in thick plated scales. Forked tongues whip the air before they cough out the tiniest amount of smoke and flame, barely enough to light a cigarillo or singe an eyebrow. There are the stumps of things on their backs that might once have been wings.

'Of course, my little love.' He swings her up and onto his shoulders. She laughs and holds tight to his ruddy hair. Her muddy shoes leave marks on his coat but he doesn't care – Bethany buys him fancy clothes by the cartload as if he's a doll for her to dress. He keeps one hand on Eliza's left leg to hold her steady; this leaves the other free to keep a firm grip on the walking stick, a polished walnut thing with a silver wolf's head handle. Inside the shaft is steel blade; a gift from Bethany on the birth of their child. The port-city should not be dangerous for him – no one in Breakwater would be fool enough to do ill to a member of Bethany Lawrence's family – but sometimes criminals new to the city have mistaken him for a rich mark. On those occasions, he's been glad she'd shown him how to use it though he hates the weapon as much as her empire. If she'd not taught him so assiduously and cruelly, given him a dose of her own ruthlessness, he'd not have come out of those encounters unscathed, and if he were gone who would look after Eliza? The child's both a lift to his spirits and a stone in his heart.

They follow the meandering path past the signs that read "Wyrms", though they need no direction. On the path ahead Henry spies another visitor and he's surprised: usually they have the place to themselves. A blonde woman sits on one of the elaborately carved benches shaped liked fallen trees, a dress of ruby silk peeks out from beneath a full-length silver fox fur coat. As he and Eliza prepare to pass by, he raises a hand – he never wears a hat, it reminds him too much of his father – and nods a greeting.

The woman stares at him for a fragment too long before smiling offhandedly. Then her gaze climbs, up, up to Eliza, and suddenly the smile is genuine. The woman's lips tremble, but her voice is steady. 'Good afternoon, young man. What a dear little girl!'

It's only polite to stop, and Henry sweeps his daughter down from his shoulders, sets her on the ground. Eliza, with a child's flare for *show*, grasps the sides of her skirts and executes a curtsey with barely a tremble in her pudgy little legs. Henry watches as she straightens and looks at the woman for approval. The warmth of the woman's gaze is fair solar.

'Graceful and pretty. I wonder, are you clever as well?' The woman asks and Eliza skips over to stand right at her feet. Henry notices that the hem of the woman's dress and petticoats are slightly stained as if she's stood in dirty water.

Eliza says, 'I can count to twenty.'

The woman listens politely as the little girl carries out her threat. When the recitation is done, the woman fishes a lollipop from the pocket of her coat and offers it. 'A reward for being clever and truthful. Truthfulness is a rare and valuable trait in a child.'

The way she moves her hands as she speaks makes Henry pause, the gesture is somehow familiar. Her voice is low, strangely raw as if her throat was injured, yet there's a hint of sweetness, a remaining note of loveliness that has refused to die. Eliza sits beside the woman before she claims her prize.

'Eliza,' Henry says warningly, but both his daughter and the woman give him a look. Again, so familiar, but the face is not one he knows… and yet…

'I am Nerys,' says the woman. 'Allow me to be kind. I miss my own children terribly.'

'Oh. Forgive my rudeness, Mistress Nerys.' He takes a seat on the other side of his daughter. 'Have you travelled far from them?'

'Indeed. Two are lost forever,' she says, and he cannot think of a reply. She continues, 'What of you, Henry. What family do you have?'

He gestures to Eliza, looks away. 'Just my daughter and her mother.'

'No parents? No siblings?' she presses and there is a hard edge to her query that mystifies him.

'None who live.'

'Really? Not a one? How sad.'

Henry's gaze narrows, his hand reaches for the walking stick as he says slowly, 'I… I did not tell you my name…'

'Yet I'd know your skin hanging on a bush, Henry Roderick Lawrence Parsifal.' She leans forward and her voice swoops low as she grasps his wrist tightly. 'Are you sure none of them live? Henry, shall I tell you where they are, your family?' She leans down to the little girl between them who is focused loosening the pretty ribbon holding the protective wax paper in place around the lollipop. The woman takes the sweet, unwraps it, then hands it back. She points to a tree not far away. 'Look, Eliza, dearling, a squirrel!'

The little girl jumps from the bench and tears away towards the red furry thing; her father never allows her to do this but he does not offer protest this time.

'Who are you?' Henry asks, throat dry.

'Your sister is alive and well, does it please you to know that? She'd been sent to a cathouse in Seaton St Mary to sing, but I've no doubt that when her voice gave out she'd have been consigned to earning her keep in the traditional manner of such places. Torben is gone… Your father lies cold in the grave you helped dig for him—'

'I didn't—'

'Mrs Bell told me, Henry, what you said. Victoria too. What you'd sworn before the magistrates. There's the problem, Henry, with secrets and lies: they pass through walls and windows no matter how quietly you whisper, they lodge in heads and hearts, they live beyond their span. They live long enough to bring their malice home to roost.' She looks directly at him and he realises that her eyes are identical to his daughter's, green, tilted.

His nerveless fingers twitch in his lap as he stares. Though the face is different, its shape not quite the same, the skin strangely smooth and not the hue he remembers, it is his mother's face or an echo of it. But he only sees it now, now he knows who she is. It's as if someone else's features have been laid over the top like a palimpsest, but the essence of *her* remains. The expression, so hard and unforgiving, like nothing he'd ever witnessed from Cordelia his whole life. There's been only love, support and forbearance.

All three gone.

There are so many things that should pass between them, so many things that they should say to one another either in recrimination or forgiveness. But no. Not this day nor any other to come for how could he tell his mother the *why* of it? His own mother, about the thrill of it all? The transgression, the danger, of being allowed to drink his fill at the forbidden well his aunt had offered, over and again until he found he could not give it up? It didn't matter that his feelings had begun to fade as his siblings were disappeared, as his daughter grew in Bethany's shadow. That regret had begun to eat him, and the idea of an easy release had grown more and more appealing. That only Eliza kept him rooted in this place.

Instead he asks, 'What happened to you, Mama?'

She flinches at that last word. 'The ship burned. I burned.'

'Your face?'

'I told you: I burned. This –' she describes a circle around her visage, a graceful pivot of the hand on the wrist – 'is someone's work. Someone's remaking of me. I'm no longer as I was.'

'Why are you here?'

'My own sister tried to murder me as I lay in my sickbed. I'd have died anyway, but she could not wait.'

Henry hangs his head. Bethany had not told him where she'd been when she suffered the injury to her ankle. Had not told him why she'd gone, but then she had never answered to him. And that… she would never have told him *that*.

'Why are you here, Mama?' he repeats. 'If she sees you…'

'She will not know me anymore than you did. My own son. My firstborn. How I loved you.'

They are silent for a few moments, then she says, 'Mothers are supposed to forgive their children anything, but I find myself unable to do so. Doubtless I am a bad mother, but I will do worse things before I am done. You would be wise to leave your aunt's house lest you be taken down with her.'

'May I come with you, Mama? Might I come home? Please?'

And though she doesn't say *no*, he knows it's not an option; that the second he spoke the words, the chance was already dead. Had never existed.

'I will take Bethany's world apart.' She points at the little girl, who's crouched in front of a trio of red squirrels now, the creatures bold and curious. 'I shall start there.'

'Mama, you won't—' For a moment he believes she will hurt his daughter right before his eyes. He has been with Bethany too long, he realises. *He* has done the worst of things so he suspects them of everyone else.

Cordelia sees it in his face and the hurt shows on hers. She says quietly, 'She'll not pay for the sins of her parents, Henry, never fear. But she is coming with me whether you like it or not.'

She slips a hand into her pocket and he wonders if she's got a weapon. If she will use it on him. He would welcome the kiss of a blade at this moment. But he also sees, for the first time, the possibility of a relief and a release. Though part of him wails and resists, the cowardly part of him is stronger. *He will let go.*

'Eliza, my petal? Come here.' She does so reluctantly, waving to her furry friends, steps dragging as she returns to him. Henry pulls her up onto his lap. 'Do you remember what we discussed last night?'

'About grandmothers?'

'About grandmothers. When I said your grandmothers were gone? Well, this lady is going to be your grandmama.'

Eliza looks all big-eyed at Cordelia, who smiles. 'A real grandmother?' Cordelia nods. 'Will you knit me a red cape?'

'I myself am not a great one for knitting, but my dear Mrs Bell who looks after my house is, and my friend Merry sews like a dream. She'll make you any sort of dress you like.'

'Trousers?' asks Eliza longingly but with little hope.

'Of course. Trousers and a coat, any colour you wish. A shirt with squirrels embroidered on the collar.'

Eliza takes a great breath of delight, then stops. 'When will we leave, Papa?'

'Ah, now here is the part where I must beg a favour of you. You're my brave girl, yes?' Eliza nods. 'Then I shall trust you to be brave now. I want you to go on ahead with Mistress Nerys… no, Grandmama Cordelia is, I believe her *true* name. I will follow soon.'

'What about Mama?'

'This is a treat that Mama and I have planned for you. You see?

Isn't it a surprise? A journey and a grandmother. You will be well loved, my dove. And we shall see you soon.' Henry lies with such facility that he is almost embarrassed. He'd like to think that he'd not been entirely tainted by his association with the Queen of Thieves, but there is no proof of that.

'Eliza, you will meet my family – your family too. We live in the mountains and I think you will not have been to such a place before.' Cordelia smiles.

'When shall we go?' asks Eliza her father again in a very small voice.

'Today, my pearl, this very moment. And I know you will be a little sad without me, but you are my bravest girl; brave the way your Mama wishes. I will see you so very soon, you'll barely have time to miss me.' *Today please just this one day, do as I say*, he begs. Eliza's lips purse at the mention of Bethany, then she climbs across to Cordelia. She touches the woman's face and hair, stares into her eyes as if she might find truth there. At last the little girl nods and sinks into the other's arms. The speed of it, the acceptance, both relieves and cuts Henry.

'She'll be safe with us,' Cordelia says, Eliza's head nestling into the curve of her neck. 'I wish…'

You would come with me. Things had been different.

'I wish you had been different.'

Henry remains on the bench long after his mother and daughter have disappeared from view. At one point, he thinks he hears the wheels of a carriage from out past the gates, the crack of a whip and the snort of horses. He ponders returning to the house by the Weeping Gate that he's shared with Bethany these past years. She'll be there now, dealing with her lieutenants, planning and plotting for the next foray of the pirate ships that she does not own, but which pay a fee to her for use of the sea and passage of their plunder into legitimate channels via the Antiphon Trading Company, in which Bethany is now a major shareholder. Discussing how more protection money might be squeezed from shop- and innkeepers, merchants and the craft guilds. What grand thefts might be committed if not with impunity then with minimal consequences; what lives might be snuffed out for profit.

But the idea of that house without his daughter…

The idea of life without her…

The idea of telling Bethany what he's done…

No. Best to walk to past that ebony door with its carvings of mermaids and sirens, the colourful stone parquetry façade of the building, the knocker shaped like a coil of rope. Best to walk instead to the end of the wharf that runs furthest out, over the deepest part of the harbour. Best to put rocks in his pockets as he goes.

* * *

In the unmoving carriage, its blinds rolled down but for a slight inch, Cordelia waits, leaning against the rich upholstery, eyes closed but she cannot sleep. The four ebony horses in the traces are snorting with impatience to be gone. How many weeks since she opened her eyes when she'd not expected to do so again? How many weeks since the woman Selke worked her magic and remade Cordelia's rotting flesh? There's not even a trace of the rose tattoo on her shoulder they'd etched with acid at her confession. If she stares long enough, she thinks she can see the faintest imprint but that might well be her imagination – she'd seen it every day of that long year in the prison ship on Rosebery Bay. It's like a veil over her eyesight.

She appears healed but she is bone weary.

Cordelia opens her eyes and glances down at the small girl curled in her lap. She smiles and a warmth floods through her. She does not dwell on Henry. Eliza will weep when it becomes apparent that her father will not be coming; she will ask questions. Cordelia does not know what answers she will give yet. Time enough to work that out. But she will tell the truth though it hurts, she thinks, for lies got them all here. Too many lies and things kept hidden.

She glances across to the seat opposite. The dark woman slumbers there beneath the cover of Cordelia's fur coat. Some colour is already returning to her cheeks. A few days of food and rest and she will be on the mend, physically at least.

Suddenly the carriage door beside Cordelia is violently pulled open. She's careful not to disturb the sleeping child, merely turns to look. A woman, stocky, yellow-eyed, dressed in black with a line of knives across her chest stares at her. From outside, Cordelia can hear shouts and screams; she peers beyond the woman and sees a cloud of smoke rising above the roofs. Felix's shop is in flames. She smiles at the yellow-eyed woman and they share a nod; Jacopo won't change his face again until they are well away from Breakwater, and it's best his brutish disguise – used for the purposes of arson – not be spotted again. Or his own face, for there were years he spent in this city and some might yet remain who recalled his true features.

The door closes and Cordelia settles. In the bag at her feet are two vials of the poisonous blood – she left the rest to burst in the heat of the flames. No need for such a thing to exist in the world after it had served her purpose.

She wonders if she should have dealt with Bethany this time. If she should have simply begged an audience. Her sister wouldn't have known her face and Cordelia might have got close enough to dispatch her like Felix. But no. The core of her still aches for her stolen children, for their brokenness. Cordelia puts her hand on Eliza's golden hair and strokes it as she did with all of her babies. As she would have done to that lost child, bled away forever ago in the Lodellan prison cell.

No. Taking Bethany's child was the first hurt she had to visit upon her sister. Breaking Henry's heart was the second, for her son's love would die from this day. Death so soon was too easy for her sister. But Bethany *would* die for otherwise she'd never stop trying to kill Cordelia – and Merry and Mrs B, Jacopo and Victoria were all at risk.

After the attack at Singing Vine, after Cordelia's healing and the cessation of her slow dying, she and Jacopo had gone to the town of Bellsholm to plot and marshal for the war. Jacopo's network of contacts brought word of Bethany's contract for Cordelia's death; word also of her sister's child and of Henry kept as a pet. The innkeeper Vasco, an old friend of Jacopo's from their pirating days, was especially helpful. Jacopo would forever have the form and feelings of Ilse at his disposal; no more simple thing than to organise for those folk he'd met – who owed him something, who resented the Queen of Thieves – to bring word (rumour, lies, fairy tales) of Tanaquil, the assassin of Bethany's dreams, to her ears. And Cordelia knows her sister of old: the more difficult something is to acquire, the more Bethany will want it. Force her to come to the inn in the assassins market. Have Jacopo play hard to get.

Henry. Henry.

Mrs Bell had told her what Henry had done. Had told her as soon as Jacopo had reunited them. It had been both a spur and a thorn. Though she'd grown well enough to plan and execute Victoria's rescue, she'd fallen into a heap soon after. The weight of one son's betrayal, the other's loss was too much; of her daughter's terror at the sight of her ruined face. Cordelia would have slipped beneath the surface of life if she could, but just as she'd not been able to drown, she'd lived long enough for Victoria – her stout Victoria – to bring the witch Selke.

Cordelia had thought long and hard over the little one, this Eliza.

What to do. In the end, as much as she wanted to deprive Bethany of her child, she wanted to rescue the girl more. To give Eliza a chance to be something other than her mother would try to make her. Eliza gives a kittenish snore and Cordelia's hands automatically pat her. She whispers, 'Mummy's here, Mummy's here, never fear, never fear,' and the child settles with a contented sigh.

Cordelia feels the carriage sway as Jacopo climbs up to the driver's seat, hears him make that clicking sound with his mouth, the gee-up, then there's the lurch forward as the impatient horses take their head. Soon they are out beneath the gates of Breakwater, onto the roads and byways that will lead them home to Singing Vine.

* * *

In the crimson-decorated parlour, Bethany relaxes. There is no sign of either Henry or Eliza, but she is not concerned. Henry won't keep their daughter out in the cool evening air, will not wish to expose her to a chill or an ague. She looks through the window towards the Weeping Gate and the harbour, to the open sea and the ships that ply the waves. Thinks of the profits they'll bring her soon.

She loves this house; it is very fine, though it was a notorious brothel for quite some years and before that home to a prelate who spent more time investigating the depths than the hallowed heights, and before that it had been built by a sea captain with his waxing and waning fortunes. Other occupants have been far less noteworthy until Bethany took it over.

She sips at a mug of buttered whiskey. Her ankle aches still, her entire leg and hip from last night's wanderings. Bethany settles herself into a comfortable wingback chair, stretches her feet out to where the fire can warm them. Tonight she will need some of the poppy mix Henry brews for her. No medical degree but he's kept himself busy learning the art of healing. Perhaps she can bring in a private tutor for him; that might take the edge off some of his rancour, his boredom.

It's time, she thinks, to pay more attention to her beloved. She has been neglecting him, but now that she's certain Cordelia's fate is assured she feels the tension in her spine loosen in a way it has not since before she flew from the window at Singing Vine. Her sister is soon to be gone for good and Bethany feels Henry will be released from whatever vestiges of love for his mother are left; they've remained entwined in his heart, tendrils tight and inexorably drawing him away from Bethany.

Perhaps, she thinks, *perhaps another child might help bind him to her*. He dotes on Eliza. She thinks ruefully of the ravages of the first pregnancy, the lengths she's gone to to avoid a second. But perhaps it would be worth it. She cannot bear the idea of letting Henry go; of letting him drift further away.

She loosens the pins in her dark blonde hair and tousles the locks into waves. She unbuttons the front of her bodice, pulls the fabric away just enough. It's how he likes her best.

Bethany settles back to wait.

AND A YOUNG HUSBAND TO BURY ME

'Are you done yet?' Selke's voice is muffled by the thick wood of the door, but there's no ignoring her presence. Grateful though Cordelia is for everything the woman has done, the witch is fast wearing out her welcome. Selke's fascinated by the tallow magic, by the candle-making. Cordelia needs quiet to work, but the guest is an overly enthusiastic pupil, asking questions from the corridor to which she's been banished, picking at Cordelia's exhausted brain – and Cordelia *is* exhausted. The creation takes not merely time and energy, but something else, something personal and essential, almost as if a part of her soul is shaved off each time she interacts with these materials, this task.

One bottle of luminous green liquid is almost empty; the other she has buried for safekeeping beneath the flagstones of one of the old cellars, this one that's become her workroom. Before the carnival troupe left, the stoutest of the menfolk dug a vertical shaft down for ventilation. Not much use for the fermenting of wines, but essential for an enclosed space where toxins are kept. They'd also done an enormous amount of repair work on the ruined wing of the house, restoring walls and windows and roofs, so the entire place was weathertight and warm. Safe with locks and shutters and bars to keep out the unwanted.

'Are you? Done?'

'Not quite yet.' Cordelia manages to mostly keep her tone civil; she focuses on the shelf at eye height, at the stone that was once Isambard Farringdale, on the glass vial of purple liquid that Bethany gave Merry. 'Will you go and ask Mrs Bell to serve dinner? I'll be along soon and we can talk.'

There's a grumbling, then the fading sound of footsteps.

Selke is waiting for the fruits of Cordelia's labour.

This creation has taken weeks.

Every component – not just Ella's ichor – had to be specially sourced and prepared from wick to tallow, from the dyes to the scents that would cover the odour of poison. The candle is large, too, larger than usual and carved so it looks like a gift, a glorious expensive thing. Three inches in diameter, nine inches tall, the outer wax is crimson (passion and hatred), the inner ebony black (night and death). There is a sheen to it because Cordelia crushed one of the diamonds from the necklace – and wasn't that a task? Thank the gods for Selke and her incantations, all the dark knowledge she's gathered – and worked it into the melted mix. The wick was spun from silk, treated so it would not burn too quickly, and soaked in Cordelia's own blood to bind her to the working and it to her. Then layer after layer, dipping after dipping, one colour, then the other. One colour, then the other until she'd judged it the right size and weight. The right potency.

Next, the carving and sculpting until it looked like a pillar of roses, red-lipped, black-throated. And all that work needed to be done by her hand alone for this wasn't something to sell, not a piece of merchandise. Only she could bring it into being, cut it, bleed into it as she whispered the spells the old tallow-wife had taught her. The hedge-witch Gwyn who hid her true power, her true self – because a witch with any sense did so nowadays – beneath the guise of a maker of pretty, sweet-smelling tapers and dips to decorate households. Items to bring light and a sense of wellbeing.

Cordelia's candle is not such a thing.

Nor is the second one that's hanging by a length of twine from a hook in the ceiling. That one is much simpler, just a long candle in black, wax wrapped around plain braided cotton, but impregnated with those shards of cursed diamond and the luminous green poison of Ella's blood. Selke had asked for one, and even though the witch had earned the blighted amethyst by her healing deeds, Cordelia couldn't find it in herself to say *no*.

The woman had discussed, briefly, her own great working – a bone lantern – but with no fine detail. She had collected the amethyst and the head of the Hallowed Girl already; next came the candle. There were other items, she'd confided, but they remained her concern alone. Cordelia recognised the habit of concealment in Selke – even though the sorceress had grown more relaxed at Singing Vine, she still held her secrets in case she needed them, hoarded them like food for a bad winter. She had stayed at the vineyard and was welcome, but Cordelia suspected Selke would soon be gone after *her* candle was ready.

There's another knock from the corridor.

'Selke, I told you—'

'It's me, my dearling.'

Cordelia immediately rises from her seat at the workbench and goes to let the older woman in. 'Mrs Bell, I'm sorry.'

The housekeeper smiles and opens her arms. Cordelia steps into the lavender-scented hug. 'She's is driving you mad, isn't she?'

'Only a little,' Cordelia admits. 'But I must be patient, she's earned that at the very least.'

Mrs Bell releases her and nods. 'Yes. We owe her forever, my dearling.' Neither of them mentions the witch's initial ill-considered attempts to murder Victoria. She juts her chin towards the red and black candle. 'Is it done?'

'Yes,' says Cordelia and feels a pride that's also a grief.

'And you'll finish her?' Mrs Bell's voice is flat as if she has no feelings one way or another about Bethany.

Cordelia looks closely at the housekeeper, takes in the shadows under the older woman's eyes, the lines around her mouth, across her forehead. How old is she? Cordelia has never wondered; Mrs Bell has been a constant presence, literally from birth. Their only times apart were when Mrs B travelled to bring her newly orphaned niece home to Lodellan, and when Cordelia was incarcerated, lost. Cordelia has never broached the subject of Merry's parentage with the housekeeper, never mentioned Bethany's insinuations that day in prison. Mrs Bell has always looked youthful, but now… the years are beginning to tell. Cordelia will not comment, though, will be kindly silent. She knows herself it's bad enough when a woman *suspects* she's aging, far worse when someone confirms it for her. She cannot help but touch her own face; it's still strange to her in its remaking, but the itching beneath the skin has mostly stopped.

Mrs Bell approaches the bench. She stands in front of it for almost a minute without speaking, examining the candle but not touching it. Cordelia recalls that Mrs B knows enough small magics to make her wary of larger ones.

'And all you must do is light it?'

'That is all.'

'And you will go once more to Breakwater.'

'Yes.' Cordelia links her arm with Mrs Bell's and together they contemplate the candle.

'And have you thought how you will do this? It's no small thing to enter a house in that city, no small thing to break into the home of the Queen of Thieves,' says Mrs B. Cordelia cannot recall hearing Mrs Bell refer to Bethany by her name since everything went so dreadfully wrong. 'It is no small thing to murder your sister.'

Cordelia ignores the last comment, though she thinks how easily Bethany has found it to try to end *Cordelia's* life over and again.

'There are tunnels beneath the streets. I will meet the innkeeper Vasco and he will show me the ways through.'

'Can you trust him? Why would he betray her?'

'He is a friend to Jacopo and he's got no love for Bethany.' Cordelia rubs at her face. 'My sister has no care for anyone's good opinion, my dear Mrs B. She gives and sows offence as easily as a breeze blows. She has been bleeding the merchants of Breakwater dry for years and there's only so long that people will live with that. She takes with one hand and does not give with the other, not even a morsel.'

Mrs Bell's lips purse, one eyebrow raises and she seems unconvinced, but she says nothing more about it. She points to the nearly empty bottle of toxic blood. 'Do you think she does well?'

'I don't know. I hope so. Whatever darkness is in her… I hope she finds peace.'

Ella had stayed with them a scant week. She barely spoke and Cordelia managed only to extract her name. Selke, with her voracious curiosity, had tried to talk to the dark maiden, but even she gave up quickly. Ella would not tell them where she was going, though she took the horse and food they offered, and the bag of coin. She'd said *thank you* as if it were the hardest thing in the world to do. Yet she had done it. Then she'd left, riding off into the unmelting snow – into a winter that it seemed would never end.

'You will go soon?'

'In a few days, when I'm rested and everything is prepared.' Cordelia gestures to the benchtop, which is untidy but for the bare moat around the candle itself. 'This has left me… drained.'

'At least let the boy go with you.'

Cordelia shakes her head. 'Jacopo's done more than enough for me. Besides, I'd rather him be here in case anything happens. And Merry needs him too.'

The little seamstress is growing rounder by the day. Cordelia doesn't know how long she will be gone and she doesn't want Merry to give birth without the child's father around. She wants her to be protected, not suffer the loss she herself did. She wants the girl to be happy.

'I should have…' begins Mrs B, but does not finish. She says instead, 'Strange times, my dearling.'

'For a long while, Mrs Bell.'

'Well, then. Come along, dinner's ready.'

* * *

Over their meal, Cordelia patiently answers Selke's myriad questions.

She watches as Jacopo feeds titbits to Merry, his hand straying to her belly, and his face when he feels the kick of life there glows glorious as quicksilver. Merry's expression is one Cordelia recognises: a guarded happiness, something she won't give herself up to entirely lest it be proven false. Cordelia does not know how to make the girl believe; she does not know whether she should even try. Who can say how long love lasts?

She watches Victoria – her short and terrible haircut growing out so slowly – read at the table. Her daughter's taken to hunting out books on history, geography and folktales. She researches bears and sometimes-bears. Victoria's desperately trying to find a hint of where in Edmea's Wood there might be a den in which her brother sleeps, shifted and reshaped. She tries to find how he might be changed back, to walk on two legs rather than four. She doesn't eat enough and Cordelia suspects her daughter does not sleep much either. When she returns from Breakwater, she has promised they will travel together and find Torben. She'll save one child and the other, again.

Victoria told Cordelia the tale that the horned Tove shared; that she believes Torben yet lives. That nothing the girl in the stone cottage had said convinced Victoria that her brother had died. Cordelia believes her daughter might be correct, but finding her youngest child cannot take precedence, not now, not when Bethany still walks the world with malice. Nothing could convince Cordelia that her sister will stop trying to wipe out her and all those at Singing Vine.

She does not think of Henry, though Eliza brings her joy. The child is snuggled into her side at the dining table, stealing food from her plate and Cordelia does not scold her. During the day, when Cordelia works downstairs, Mrs Bell keeps the girl amused. Victoria tells her stories sometimes; Jacopo changes his face for her; Merry makes her clothes, anything she requests and the child's joy is never-ending, her surprise and delight fresh each day. Cordelia knows Eliza misses her father – sometimes finds her weeping like a kitten – but does not mention her mother.

This night Mrs Bell has brought out some of the last bottles of a heavy Barbaresco from the cellar, to celebrate, she says, Cordelia's achievement. She pours with a heavy hand – even Merry has a glass – and the company is lively. It is late when they finally go to bed, leaving the dishes on the table, all unwashed, an unheard-of event, but no one cares. They feel, though they do not say, that an ending is soon to be upon them. That better days are ahead. That soon they might breathe more easily, when the shadow of Breakwater's queen is no longer looming over them.

But in the morning when Cordelia wakes and washes and dresses, and goes to her workroom to begin the final preparations for departure, she finds that Mrs Bell and the candle both are gone and there is only a letter left in their place.

* * *

Mrs Bell moves hesitantly through the afternoon streets of Breakwater, speaking to no one.

She knew these ways as a child, but the intervening years – and her will – have dimmed the memories. The avenues have not changed their course – thank the gods, for she is exhausted after her journey – but the houses look different. The shops have altered, in places there are charred voids where she remembers was once a bakery or an inn. She keeps the hood of the cloak over her bright hair and hides her features as well as she can, but no one pays attention. She was thirteen when she left here; she's nearing fifty now. She cannot imagine anyone would recognise her face.

As she gets closer to the house by the Weeping Gate, the crowds thin slowly then more swiftly until she is the only person walking this end of the street. Before she goes down the narrow alleyway replete with shadows to the secret entrance, she crosses the road to where the wooden docks stretch out over the waters of the harbour. Mrs Bell stands so still she might be a statue and stares at the façade of the building with its parquetry of coloured gemstones, the windows she once kept so clean and shiny – they are now dimmed with salt grime and cobwebs. She frowns. There are no guards outside the ebony-wood door with its carvings of mermaids and sirens. When she served here, there was always a man on watch to ensure the girls' safety, and she recalls Jacopo's intelligence that Bethany kept two over-muscled oafs at the threshold.

Mrs B waits a little while, five minutes, ten, fifteen – long enough for the day to blink into dusk – just in case this is a ruse or the men have ever so briefly deserted their posts for food or drink or calls of nature. Yet no one comes, and behind the filthy windowpanes she can detect no sign of movement inside the house; no candles nor lamps are lit. It all seems rather odd. She takes a deep breath, touches the heavy satchel beneath her cloak, twists her hands into fists, and walks up to the front stairs.

Instinct alone moves her. She does not knock but pushes at the door. It creaks open.

Back in her day, this entry hall was all burning illumination from the chandelier on the ceiling, but now there is nothing but shadows. On a small hall-table beneath hooks for hats and capes there is a brass lantern; fuel swishes in the reservoir when she picks it up, and the wick is damp. Mrs B finds the flint in her pocket – always kept on her person – and strikes it. The flame flares, tiny but bright. When she's done, she holds the lamp up and looks around.

Once, there was gilded paint on the walls, the floors polished wood that sounded with the heels of pretty, pointless shoes on pretty, purposeful feet. The curtains were a mix of green and gold velvet. There were chaises and sideboards, an elaborate bar took up one entire wall over *there*. Above, she catches a glimpse of the pendants of the chandelier, blinking like crystal eyes. It was decaying, even then, this abode; the house of ill-repute's better days had come and gone. At some point, it has been redecorated into shades of crimson – Mrs Bell detects Bethany's tastes – there are chairs and coffee tables, and the bar has been replaced by tall bookshelves. She wonders idly if Bethany selected the titles; a closer look shows them to be novels, mostly lurid. Yes, Bethany's choices. One wall is mostly a mirror, shattered by some temper, but all the shards still in place as if by a miracle.

Mrs Bell tilts her head and listens.

There's nothing here, no heartbeat.

No one moves through the arteries of the place. There's no bustle along the corridors or in the rooms. She wonders how long it's been since anyone cared for it; the furnishings are rich, not old, yet their air is one of neglect. There is dust on the sills, cobwebs in the corners, motes spinning through the air. This is not a *home*; it's a shell.

Still, there must be a reason for the absence and Mrs Bell has not travelled so far to find nothing. To do nothing. She has come to make an ending of things that began with her. Not by her choice, or at least not at the start, but later. Later, when she made her decisions and matters fell as they did. She chose to go with Cordelia; she left

Bethany behind. She removes her cloak and drapes it over a chair; she puts the heavy satchel beside it and takes out the candle. It's still wrapped in the silk shawl she'd snatched from Merry's pile of mending. She lets the fabric slip away from the thing, to pool around her fingers, her palm, over her wrist.

The diamond shards pick up the lamplight and wink at her.

Mrs Bell. She's been Mrs Bell so very long – though there was never a Mr Bell – she barely remembers her own name; oh of course she remembers her own name! She holds the pillar of carved wax roses in one hand and the lantern in the other. She begins her search of the house by the Weeping Gate, one room at a time.

* * *

My Dearest Cordelia,

When I was young...

When I was old enough to understand...

No. Before I was old enough to understand, but young enough to expect, I was promised a young husband to bury me.

I was in no way special, it was simply what we were told would come in our old age. It was merely the way of my folk, the place where I grew up. That older women would take much younger husbands to care for them as they taught those self-same husbands how to do good by their next wives.

But matters did not go as planned.

Such is the way of life, I have found.

When I was seven, my parents sent me away.

A plague had come to our town, no family was untouched by illness or death, and we began to starve. There was no work to be had, nothing to bring in coin. A man arrived one day, offering to pay for any child offered to domestic service. We would be cared for, educated and fed. That was all my parents wanted to hear and they did not ask too many questions – I had five younger siblings, but I was the only one the man would take.

He did not hurt me and I was grateful, but as I've grown older I simply think it was the very least I deserved: to not be hurt. He took me to the port-city of Breakwater where once had lived the winged navigators – I heard such tales of them but they were long gone! – and delivered me to serve in the house by the Weeping Gate. It had been a brothel many years before – a woman who'd owned it sold all her daughters as merchandise there – then it had fallen to disrepair until this man made it a bordello once again.

I was put to work in the kitchens. And later – much later, for which I was again grateful – in the rooms upstairs.

Oh, not in that way: the man didn't want me for that. I poured drinks, I sang, I made clothes for the girls who did whatever the clients paid for. I think some days it wasn't such a bad life; other days...

Then a merchant took a liking to me. He ran a vineyard far away, he had a delicate wife, Lenore, who was pregnant. He wanted to bring her some help and he said I had a sweet face. But I should have known for the amount of gold he paid for me that he was purchasing more than a maid.

He took me home, home to the Singing Vine.

His wife was a cold and beautiful woman; she lost the baby the first month I was there. When he could not get another child on her, he got one on me. He gave you to his wife. He would whisper in the dark that he loved me, but I never said it back. Of all the lies I've told, that was not one of them. He did not leave my bed after that, and I think your mother did not mind for his demands were not made on her. Although it took a long while, I became pregnant again. And again the child was given to the cold woman. But I brought you up, my Cordelia, though I had to watch her be cruel to you. I kept you as safe as I could. Yet Lenore did not treat Bethany the same way she did you, and somehow Bethany became more her daughter than you ever did. Your sister spent not a moment in that cupboard, was never whipped or slapped, not punished for anything she ever did. She even started to look like her "mother", I think. Whatever ice was in that woman's heart found its echo in your sister's.

I am a bad mother because I was relieved to leave Bethany behind when you married Edvard; she was so small but so unlike you. Unlike me. Even as we packed your trousseau, Merry was growing in me. Had your father known I was pregnant, I do not think he would have let me go with you. He'd have made me stay to give yet another child to his wife.

Three daughters I had to him, though he did not know about the last.

The price of my leaving was Bethany.

I thought it safe for her to stay there.

I was relieved to abandon her.

She'd never sought me out for comfort or treats; she acted as though I were her slave.

Whereas you, my lovely Cordelia, could barely breathe without being taken to task by Lenore Lawrence. You were the sign of her husband's first, greatest infidelity – she suffered for that and so did you.

Do you recall? I know you do.

I know you have tried to forget, my dearling, I know how you tried to make yourself into an obedient girl. You changed and reshaped until you could barely remember how you had once been. You grew out of true. It ached for me to see it, but I thought at the time it was safer for you to hide who you were.

Now I see you… unfolding. It is not an unravelling, but an unfurling. Though life has cut and burned and cauterised you, you are becoming who you were once meant to be.

I have loved you all these years, you and Merry both, yet you first, my dearling.

In all that, I could find no love for Bethany.

And now, Cordelia, I cannot let you murder your sister.

However, Bethany cannot be allowed to remain or she will see you and yours scoured from the face of the earth. I have wanted to believe that there is nothing of me in her, no kindness or love, only will and wish and want. Like her other mother.

Yet there was sufficient ice in my heart to leave her behind. I was relieved to desert my own daughter. The coldness in her did not come from Lenore alone.

She is what I made.

She is mine.

She is mine to take care of.

She is my candle to snuff out.

I should have been kinder to her.

I should have…

I know the house in which Bethany dwells for it is the one in which I served, the one from which your father plucked me when I was still so young. I know how to enter it without being seen; there are hollows in the walls, and there are ways between.

Take care of my Merry, my last child, my final brightness. She is your sister in all her blood, and I bid you be kind to her. You will have only each other, and whatever family you might make for yourselves in time to come. Let her read this letter; I hope she does not judge me too harshly.

I hope you do not judge me too harshly, my Cordelia, my dearling.

Know only that I have loved you with all of my heart every day of your life, and that I will not cease to do so no matter what awaits.

Your mother (finally I shall take this title).

Aurelia

* * *

As Mrs Bell wanders the house it seems that her memories seep up from wherever she'd buried them and plaster themselves over the walls. That room was once awash with silken hangings like a harem; this one was bare of all but a whipping frame; this one was filled only with cushions on the carpet; this one had an enormous four-poster bed fit for five; and this one contained a bathtub big enough for seven.

She cannot call those years "good", but she was in less danger here as a child than she was as a teenager at Singing Vine. She conjures the faces of women and men who worked here, the kind, the cruel, the indifferent; where and how had fate moved them? She cannot recall the man who bought her, however. She frowns. Silver-haired? Or not. Fat or thin? Tall or short? Well-dressed or… or… or…

He will not come, will not be summoned, and she shrugs. It doesn't matter.

She's reached the top floor but one and hears, at last, the sound of another presence in the room at the end of the corridor; the door is ajar and there are sighs and coughs. Mrs Bell settles both lantern and candle on the floor; she takes the flint from the deep pocket in her dress and strikes once, twice, thrice. A spark catches the silken wick and leaps higher than she would have believed possible. Then it settles, diminishes to something that will not draw comment. She leaves the lantern behind and gathers up the candle in both hands – how it seems heavier than before! The smoke from it smells like death and roses; Cordelia had said its effect would not be so quick as one might notice what was happening. That one might escape if one had a mind to; that, after all, had been Cordelia's plan.

Mrs Bell takes a deep breath, another, another. Then she stops, holds the breath in for if she does not she'll stay out there, gulping in air until time freezes and her heart ceases. She pushes back the door and steps over the threshold.

There's no other light in the chamber, so she holds the candle higher, lets the flame flick around much as she did downstairs. Open wardrobes, dresses disgorged; drawers pulled from tallboys and duchesses, jewels strewn across the floor, the tabletops; crystal bottles of powder and paints and perfumes broken, their contents in ruins. And at the end of the chamber, a bed with a canopy, crimson coverlet and curtains, many pillows and Bethany propped up against them, pale as death, hollow-eyed, her hair a bird's nest, the white nightgown she wears stained where she's spilled red wine.

She stares at Mrs Bell and seems not to recognise her until she says, 'I should have told her to kill you too.'

Mrs Bell thinks back to Jacopo's recounting of his meeting with Bethany. She asks carefully, 'Tanaquil?'

'The yellow-eyed bitch disappeared with my money,' the woman beneath the covers says. She looks at the decanter on the bedside table. Mrs Bell wonders how long it's been empty.

'Would it please you to know that she considered it?' The lie is easy. Aurelia Bell has told so many lies in her life. 'Would it please you to know that your sister is dead?'

Bethany blinks as if she's been slapped. She says, 'Yes,' then begins to weep.

Mrs Bell moves towards the bed; she places the candle behind the empty decanter so as not to attract too much attention. She need not worry, Bethany's eyes flit across it and she whispers, 'Pretty,' then cries even more intensely. Mrs Bell drags an armchair over to sit beside her. She watches the wailing child.

Between sobs, Bethany says, 'You never loved me the way you loved her. You never called me *dearling*.'

'No. And it was unkind of me.' That at least is the truth.

'Why?' asks Bethany and the question is the cry of all lost children. Her hands clench at the once-white sheets; there are black half-moons under her ragged nails.

How long has she been like this?

Mrs Bell doesn't know how to answer. What to tell her. *You were forced upon me. That leaving you behind hurt less than the moment when you tore yourself from my hody in blood and afterbirth. You looked at Lenore Lawrence like she was the sun and the moon, and at me like I was the dirt at your feet. You never once tried to please me, not like Cordelia did, nor Merry. Never once.*

And she knows, *knows*, those last two reasons are childish. That she was the adult and it was beholden on her to be kinder and wiser and gentler. And she decides that in order to be those things, the important things, she cannot tell Bethany anything.

She cannot repeat any of the things she wrote in Cordelia's letter. To be kinder and wiser and gentler she can never tell this girl that she is her mother. If she had not left with Cordelia, if she had stayed at Singing Vine, how might Bethany have been? There is no way to know, only that there were myriad possibilities, so many paths untravelled. How many did not lead to this room? To the days of plague that ravaged the vineyard? To the orphanage in Seaton St Mary and the tender mercies of Mr Isambard Farringdale?

'What happened, Bethany?' Mrs Bell gestures to the darkness, the decay. 'I heard you'd made yourself a queen.'

Bethany moans. 'Someone took my daughter. Someone stole her away and none of the useless pieces of shit under my hand could find her.' She rakes at her face. 'Tanaquil. When Tanaquil returns… she can track them… why hasn't she returned? She still has a fee to collect.'

'Delayed, I'm sure. Perhaps there's other work to complete on her way.' Mrs Bell thinks of the tiny blonde girl snuggled asleep in a room at Singing Vine, adored by all, dressed in the pyjamas Merry makes for her. She notes that Bethany does not call the child by name. To distract her, Mrs Bell asks, 'What of Henry? Is he well?'

'Henry…' Bethany's face convulses as if something beneath the skin is trying to break out. Madness and rage competing. 'Henry drowned.'

'Oh.' *Oh*. 'Oh, Bethany.'

'He walked to the end of the pier. He walked past sailors and boats. They watched him. He walked and walked and then he threw himself into the harbour. Sank like a stone.' Bethany's hand rises, then falls as a fist. 'He didn't wash up until a week later.' She stares at Mrs Bell. 'After everything… after all… he left me too.'

And Aurelia realises that there is the greatest offence: that Bethany has once again been abandoned. She opens her lips to speak but coughs; the smoke from the candle is thickening. She feels dizzy, her head fogged. She clears her throat. 'My poor girl. My poor lost child.'

Bethany has slumped back against the pillows, slid down them a little. Her eyes are hooded and her breathing has slowed. 'Will you stay?' she asks. 'Just a little while until I sleep? You never used to – will you this once?'

'I will stay forever, my dearling,' says Aurelia Bell and her voice trembles. She watches as the rise and fall of her daughter's chest becomes less and less, as the lids sink closed. This candle is, she thinks, a mercy that Cordelia has given her sister, Aurelia's broken babe. She begins to sing quietly as she used to for Cordelia when the night frightened her, when Lenore Lawrence had locked the girl in the closet for some infringement or another; Mrs Bell would sit outside the door and croon *Mummy's here, Mummy's here, never fear, never fear.* She is still singing it when her own eyes close, and the darkness becomes real, but she knows it is the song Bethany will take into forever with her.

* * *

There comes, at last, the day when Cordelia feels a burning in her blood. She's reading the letter again. Yet again.

Still? For it feels as if she has not stopped since she found it. Selke commented on the habit the day she left, suggested Cordelia throw it into the hearth-fire. But how does one burn the truth? Flames cannot make the imprint of the words go away.

The searing is not as bad as she'd thought it would be, but it's there because magic always takes a red price from you. She made the candle from her own blood and intent – Ella's was an ingredient only, not part of the wishing – but Mrs Bell has her blood… or she has Mrs Bell's… *Mother…* such a strange word now… yet didn't Mrs B always love her better than her own mother did? Is this such a surprise, in truth? Not-mother. False-mother. Mrs Bell. Aurelia. Hidden-mother. Ever there.

And because Mrs Bell has her blood, or she has Mrs Bell's, she knows that the magic will work. Cordelia knows that Aurelia has lit the candle in Breakwater. The burning lasts a long while, but she sits quietly outside in the garden with a steaming cup of coffee that's rapidly losing its heat, looking over the vines still white with frost. Tears creep down her cheeks and are frozen there. She stays out until Merry (round and puffing and almost set to pop) and Victoria (too thin now, her girl, lean as a hunting hound) find her shivering and weeping. By the time they drag her inside, scolding, the warmth in her veins is cooling, and she knows that Bethany and Mrs Bell are gone.

BY SUCH PATHS

A town will die of shame as surely as a person, thinks Ella as she surveys the ruins of Iserthal.

How long had it taken? For the place to fall? There are no roofs left on any of the cottages, stone walls have tumbled, the white wattle and daub's peeled away and turned to dust. All those little fences to mark out gardens are gone, gone, gone.

How long since she'd been here, trapped beneath the frozen waters of that lake all those months? The lake that's now barely a shrunken swampy pond covered with rime. How long since her father condemned her to walk the earth? How long since Iserthal's folk betrayed her?

How long since she led their children – all but two, the two that kindness kept safe – to the shadow trees. Drew them to the grove, gave them milk with mandrake to drink, and sent them through the glorious split trunks? How long since she tried to follow them, tried to go home but the alders sealed themselves against her?

Too many years.

Ella closes her eyes for a moment, then another and another. Stays like that for so long the horse beneath her grows restless and begins to shuffle sideways in a nervous dance. She lifts her lids, pats the beast's neck gently and soothes it with the clicking of her tongue it seems to like. It's taken her months to get here; she had no sense of direction to follow and Iserthal's not been included on any maps for an age. She spoke to the oldest people she could find in the villages and towns she passed. She's been filled, for some time now, with an admiration for Mercia who'd tracked her with nothing to go on but whispers and rumours.

Eventually, however, she began to recognise landmarks though they were in the process of changing under the combined labours of time and weather. A rock feature here, a stream there, a statue that was a ruin three centuries ago, give or take a decade. And a light layer of snow over everything – was it the beginning or end of the winter? She can't tell. It seems to have been cold forever.

Was it like this at the *Silver Branch*? No. Perhaps the winters had been longer for a while, but it was only after Mercia's visit that she noticed. Gwern's dying, she supposed, had upset the balance in the upper-earth as in the under. On this journey, she'd seen more strange creatures than had ever trod beneath the sky – stranger than *she* had ever been – things that once would have answered to her and her father, but now watched with eyes of yellow and red, giving speculative glances as if to assess what a meal she might make, how easily she might be overcome. Mercia had not lied. And the tales Ella'd heard of whole families disappearing from farmhouses or even tenements in cities, cattle and horses left to die with their blood taken, more children snatched away and not her doing – she'd not sent one to her father in… she could no longer count. She'd found people were more afraid and suspicious the closer she came to Iserthal. As if all rot had started there.

Here. Not Alder's Well, where she'd betrayed her father, given him to be captive to the Misses Meyrick. No. Here, where he'd cast her out.

There was some satisfaction in that, though Ella found less and less grim joy in cruel things. She couldn't say why the change, but perhaps it was something to do with the manner of her capture and rescue. She fell into the one through her own idiocy – too careless, too certain of her own enduring – and the other by pure chance. Only the woman Cordelia's conscience and kindness brought Ella back out to the light. She was reminded of the girl Rikke, the little one who'd found her in the lake. Who'd offered comfort after the Erl-King had exiled his daughter, his only child. Who'd chased away those boys, little rapists, little bastards. Who'd tended her until she began to mend. They looked nothing alike, Cordelia and Rikke, no, but there was something in their gazes, their faces, a gentleness that pierced Ella's armour when she was at her most vulnerable. The way neither of them had taken advantage of her weakness.

Yet she'd seen the same sort of kindness in Mercia, but Mercia had wanted something. Not for herself, no. For Gwern. And back then Ella couldn't bring herself to do anything for the Erl-King. Couldn't bear to let her anger go – how else would she keep herself warm?

But now…

She'd lain on that filthy bed in that filthy cell, the life stolen slowly out of her, and knew that her death would mean nothing. She'd refused to help Mercia, to give up herself, to be nothing… yet she'd been dying for no reason but a man's greed, her own stupidity… she was *already nothing.* Her heart was empty, a hollow place where hurt echoed. She was no better than those children she'd stolen away – always awful children, always the worst of the bunch, as if that made it somehow better – she'd behaved like a brat for more centuries than she cared to count.

The horse shuffles again. Ella gives up and dismounts. Her boots sink into the snow. She hesitates. Should she wander through the village? For old times' sake? She snorts. The alder grove is further on but she's tired of riding, her backside aches. She's sure the horse will be happy to be free of her weight. She'll walk, stretch her legs. There's still enough light, she thinks, to make it to her destination. She wonders if Mercia will be waiting.

How long since the woman sought her out? She cannot remember. She feels a little ashamed. Is she too late?

Has her father died?

Somehow she thinks not. She does not know how the world would have changed with his death. But she thinks it has not changed *enough.* This ever-winter is a sign of his diminishing, she thinks. Does she hope? She doesn't know.

Ella leads the horse, picks her way towards the path that will, if she recalls correctly, take her to where the shadow trees lie.

* * *

The fire was difficult to start and even more difficult to keep going, yet she'd collected a lot of wood with a patience she didn't generally waste on mundane tasks. Ella doesn't usually feel the cold, just as she seldom dreams, but here in this place she shivers. She hasn't bothered to hobble the horse: she's where she needs to be so if the beast wanders off now, it won't matter. She eats the last of the dry bread and cheese in her pack, provisions purchased from a remote farmhouse. The man there had regarded her with suspicion, but the woman was happy enough to help – later, Ella found she'd given double the quantities negotiated and paid for. More kindness. She finds it pierces her nowadays when once she'd armoured herself against its gentle sting.

During the night she dozes a little, sitting upright against the trunk of a declining alder. They'd all looked ill when she at last arrived in the clearing. She realises she's not seen one in the longest time; she'd stopped looking for them some years ago when she ceased sending children down. Or had she stopped sending children because she couldn't find shadow trees?

But they were ailing, the trees, no doubt of it. Would Mercia get through?

Could Mercia get through?

The whispers begin she does not recall when, only that she jerks awake and knows that she's been hearing the sound for a while. At first, she thinks a mist has closed in, a winter fog of snow and ice, but then she realises it's figures, some small, some larger. All children. They stand around her in a wide semi-circle, not coming close, as if afraid of her even now. One steps forward, pushed by the ghostly hands of others, like a reluctant ambassador. It passes through the fire, is burned up like a breath, then reforms a few paces away from her. It leans down, peers into her face.

Ella doesn't hide; she tilts her chin up so the thing – the child, it's a girl – can see her more clearly in the flicking firelight.

Ella looks at them one by one. She does not recognise any faces – how could she? So many, so many. Yet not enough here to number all her tithes sent beneath. Perhaps these are just Iserthal's children. Her first. She doesn't speak to them. Doesn't say she's sorry for she isn't.

She did what she did because she wanted to – to claim anything else would be to lie. To devalue whatever honesty she might give them.

Perhaps she ends like this.

Perhaps this is the price.

Perhaps Mercia does not come.

Perhaps Mercia sent *them* for this sole purpose.

But the ghostly children do not attack. They do not swarm. They make no demands. They simply settle around her, making no marks in the snow – she can see their perches through their wispy flesh – and watch. They do not speak to her though they whisper amongst themselves; she cannot make out the words. Perhaps they merely sing the only way they know how.

Eventually, she drifts off to sleep again.

In the morning, she's alone. The fire is no more than sad embers, the horse has gone, the whispers are silenced. There is no sign of Mercia.

* * *

During the day, Ella roams. She does not believe Mercia will come during the light hours. It has always been easier, she knows, to travel from darkness to darkness. She goes to the ruined town and steps through broken doorways where once she was not tolerated.

She goes into the skeletons of cottages and looks at the fragments that remain. In a corner somewhere she finds a pile of trinkets, cheap jewellery, left behind when the owners fled.

Elsewhere there are shreds of paintings that hung on walls no longer extant. Broken glass in rainbow hues scattered across what was a kitchen floor. In the cottage that belonged, she thinks, to Rikke and her family – Ella cannot remember the parents' names or that of the little boy she helped to deliver – she finds the cabinet where the woman kept her herbs. Inside are still vials containing dust or stains that used to be tinctures and potions. Beside these is a scrap of paper, a painfully neat hand creeping across the page – the script of a child labouring to make each letter just *so*. The same words have been written over and over as if in practice:

It is six years since the children left.

It is six years since the children left.

It is six years since the children left.

It is six years since the children left.

It is six years since the children left.

It is six years since the children left.

And of all the things, it is this one that makes Ella cry.

Didn't Mercia say that Rikke had joined the scribes? The Blessed Wanderers of Cwen's Reach? It had to be Rikke who wrote this, for who else would know? Who else would have cared to record the truth of Ella's undoing? This is where Rikke began, as surely as Ella did. Here was a hand Ella had held in her own. Dust now, dust for so very long. And the words: another kindness.

Not the truth, or not quite. Not *It is six years since the children were stolen*. For Rikke, young as she was, knew Ella's act for what it was: rightful revenge, retribution, a balancing.

She takes the scrap and folds it carefully into the smallest square, then slips it into a trouser pocket.

The child is no more than motes, but Ella would give everything she is to hold that little hand once more.

* * *

By the third day Ella is starving and bordering on delirious. She's had nothing but snowmelt to drink; she's never been a big eater, but even the withered and poisonous alder berries are beginning to tempt her. She doesn't bother to move about, staying by the fire that she keeps burning even during the day purely for the warmth. She cannot be sure, but it seems the cold is getting worse. She sleeps on and off. The children have not returned since that first night and she finds she misses them terribly. None of the other strange things she's seen in her travels have made themselves known. Perhaps they will not come here. Dare not. This is the children's place, after all.

I've waited too long, she thinks.

She should have come when Mercia first asked.

It's too late and this is her only regret. This of all things, to find herself willing to do this too late.

Wrapped in her heavy cloak, she alternates between dozing and weeping. By nightfall, she's deeply asleep when the alder behind her gives a shudder and a shriek. Ella, abruptly awake, scrambles away, narrowly missing the fire. She's never heard the shadow trees make a sound before.

Ella watches as the trunk convulses in the firelight. It pulsates like it's giving birth, and particularly painfully at that. Then there is a tear, a tiny split that grows wider and longer: two hands appear, pushing at the hole until it is at last large enough for Mercia, in a gown of silver-black, to step through. She props a metal rod, forked at each end, into the opening to keep it agape.

Mercia herself is changed. Beneath the crown of alder-buckthorn berries, there's a streak of white through her dark auburn hair, there are lines around her mouth and shadows beneath her eyes that were not there when Ella first saw her. Impossible as it seems, the woman has aged. In one hand is a glimmering obsidian chalice; at her waist hangs a silver knife.

'The children told me you had come. I'd almost lost hope.'

'You took your time,' says Ella, automatically falling into a pout.

'It takes longer to travel *up* than it used to,' answers Mercia mildly, but Ella notices her hands shake. 'And I do not know how long the way will remain open. So, are you ready at last?'

And in spite of everything, Ella wants to say *No* just as she did before. She wants to *stay*. But she knows she cannot; she nods because the words won't come.

'Then lie back.'

'On the ground?' Ella asks in a very small voice.

'Is there somewhere better?' Mercia asks in return.

Ella lies beside the fire, which flares as Mercia comes close. She kneels and places the obsidian chalice by Ella's neck. Ella wonders if it will hurt, then thinks that if the Misses Meyrick trained Mercia it will hurt only if this woman wants it to.

Ella says, 'You promise? You will look after me. You promised.'

Mercia takes Ella's hand, holds it tightly. 'I promised and I stand by that. I will bring you home. Now, close your eyes.'

And Ella does because she cannot bear to watch Mercia take the dagger from her belt. She lets her fingers go reluctantly. Ella feels the cold silver kiss of the blade against her throat, the quick bite of it and she gasps. Her eyes open and she stares into Mercia's face, focuses on the tear-shaped birthmark. The woman's hand seeks hers again.

Ella feels she takes a long time to die. But it's different to in the cell, the slow bleeding away. And it's not such a long while after all, she realises as her eyelids begin to droop and a terrible tiredness creeps over her. She can feel her body beginning to shrink, to flatten, the flesh and muscle diminishing as if all the air has gone out of her. As if her bones have become smaller, smaller, smaller; and they have. She slips out of herself to hover behind Mercia. Watches as the woman stays by her, holds her hand – Ella can still feel the gentle grip! She watches herself deflate until she's nothing but a flat skin on the cold ground. She watches as Mercia proceeds to fold her up, neatly into a packet of skin and hair and bones that rattle only a little. Watches as her stepmother puts the packet into a pocket in her gown and Ella worries, then, that she's badly miscalculated. That she'll be slid away onto a shelf somewhere down below; forgotten.

Mercia hitches the knife to her belt again and rises. She lifts the chalice, which surely must be heavy, as if it is nothing at all. As if the sum of Ella is nothing at all.

Ella recalls that she *has* become nothing at all.

Mercia moves towards the tree where the opening in its trunk trembles, straining at the metal rod that holds it. Then Mercia waits. She glances back to where Ella's shade hesitates; she does not speak, merely nods the spectre towards the hole. At the signal, Ella swiftly floats through the gap. Mercia follows.

It's terribly dark once Mercia removes the bar and the tree shuts with a groan that almost covers the sound of the metal rod dropping. Soon enough, though, Mercia and her dress begin to glow silvery-green, to light the way down. The journey is protracted, Ella wearies even in this incorporeal form, however she has no voice and cannot complain. Along the way, children join them – more than those visitors that first night – who look at Ella curiously, but at Mercia with love. She in turn greets them tenderly by name, and they dance as their mother goes by, never obstructing her path. Ella notices, as they descend, that all the children become more solid; Ella herself does not.

And she begins to recognise places and things as they proceed, routes she once travelled as a child when first she tried to escape under-earth purely because her father had forbidden it – until she found that crack in the world to crawl through. There are statues and gardens, there are buildings made of bone that flares brightly as the group passes. There are forests of luminous black roses. There are ponds and pools and lakes, there are ravens who've never flown against a blue sky, there are wolves and hollow cats who slink between the upper and lower worlds, making brief pacts with this witch then that. There is the trail that shines like the inside of a pearl, there are the great gates carved of some creature no longer seen either above or below, and there's the arena where the Erl-King holds court. There is a raised platform and her father's throne, made of a petrified tree and studded with gems, and another beside it, the same shape and size. Something new and *equal*, thinks Ella, and a tiny spasm of jealousy runs through her not-flesh.

Then her attention returns to her father's seat and she sees what she'd missed.

Gwern sits there, but he appears to be part of the cathedra: as if he's become stone himself. In his under-earth form he's a black shifting mist; when he was bound aboveground, he was a tall man, hunch-backed; now his limbs look like branches, corrugated with roots, hands and fingers spindly, hair burnt grass. He slumps. Mistletoe grows through holes in his chest like an arrow, the only green thing about him.

Too late, she thinks, too late and the fog of her not-body shudders. She wonders if he can see her.

Ella watches as Mercia mounts the dais where Gwern lies and dies; the woman fishes in her pocket with one hand, withdraws Ella's remains, tosses them to the stone at Gwern's feet. Then, using no finesse, Mercia upends the chalice over the Erl-King's withered head.

Ella's green blood splashes and she wants to cry out at the waste, but as she watches it is absorbed into her father's body; a little spatters onto the parcel of skin, hair and bones. So quick!

And Ella feels that she begins to fade. The tiny scrap left of her shrinks much as her body did above. She feels it as a final thing and believes that Mercia has lied. But there's nothing she can do about it. Only some of the children observe her as she watches herself, her attention taken from her father and his consort as she looks down at the fog of her form: it swirls inch by inch backwards, inwards, smaller and smaller and smaller. Feels herself diminish until there's only a burst of darkness before her eyes, until…

She is nothing at all.

* * *

Blink.

Blink.

Blink.

Her lashes feel like butterflies against her face, against the pillows of her cheeks.

She tries to sit up, but she has no strength. She's lying on the ground, on the folds of a cloak, so soft and warm. She's looking up at the faces before her. Her father a black mist once again, his features forming and shifting in the smoke of his substance; Mercia too, her smile so broad and bright as she reaches down for Ella.

Ella looks at her own hands and feet: tiny. New and plump and soft. Baby hands, baby feet, the nails pink as a dawning. Her mind, her own, the memories, but fading so swiftly. She's lifted and held. Cuddled as the old thoughts dissipate and all she knows is that she has her time again.

STORY NOTES

THE BITTERWOOD BIBLE AND OTHER RECOUNTINGS

"The Coffin-Maker's Daughter"

Stephen Jones had emailed asking for a submission 'more horror than fantasy' for a new anthology, *A Book of Horrors*. Florence and the Machine's *Lungs* "My Boy Builds Coffins" provided some inspiration and I started to think about a society that regarded coffin-making not simply as a necessary service, but also as an eldritch art form, required to keep the dead beneath the earth. I knew this had to be a story with layers of secrets. I had an image Hepsibah standing in front of this heavy door, with a short gamine haircut that had started to grow out and curl, wearing a plain brown woollen dress, a bit Jane Eyre-like, and a sort of baker boy's cap. Her father's ghost was with her, and Hector's a nasty piece of work. I could hear his voice and knew how adversarial their relationship was, but that no matter how much Hepsibah hated her father, she shared some characteristics with him and that's why he was still hanging around. The society was a kind of Victorian setting but mixed with some elements similar to the world of *Sourdough and Other Stories*. Hepsibah's one of my favourite characters, a terrible mess of a human, but really fascinating. I wanted to show at the end that she wasn't as well adjusted as she at first appeared. As soon as I'd written this story, I knew I had the start of a new collection because she wasn't the sort of character who would just quietly go away.

"The Maiden in the Ice"

One of my favourite characters in *Sourdough and Other Stories* was Ella, who threaded through the collection as a kind of malign presence. I'd always wanted to write a story to show where she'd come from, how she came to be exiled from her home. I had the title long before the rest of the tale, and the vision of the girl seemingly suspended, but still moving inexorably up towards the surface. "The Pied Piper of Hamlin", Christina Rosetti's "The Goblin Market", and Angela Carter's "The Erl-King" all influenced this one. As Hepsibah Ballantyne floats through *Bitterwood*, so does Ella, though more subtly, with scattered mentions of the Plague Maiden. I wanted the idea of kindness rewarded and bad behaviour punished to be the beginning of her journey through this world. The main character, Rikke, is an analogue of the child who wasn't taken by the Pied Piper because he was lame and couldn't keep up; Rikke was distracted by her books.

"The Badger Bride"

I love badgers, they're beautiful and fascinating, and I've always loved transformation stories, but they generally run along the same lines: one character must be transformed from animal to human in order for there to be a happily-ever-after. That ending assumes that whatever was threatening the star-crossed lovers has been defeated; but, I wondered, what if it's not? What if the threat remains, blundering about, looking for its dearest, darkest desire? What might our heroes do in order to escape? Gytha seeks answers no matter what the cost; there's something rather Gothic about her determination, but she's in no way a fainting, fairly stupid Gothic heroine. I've always loved the ideas of monastic libraries and the preservation of knowledge, due in no small part to Eco's *The Name of the Rose*, and my Uncle Rod, who's also a collector of books and no mean bibliognost himself. And I love the idea that sometimes, just sometimes, though you don't get what you think you want, you get what you *actually* want.

"The Burnt Moon"

I wanted to show a bit of the ex-Abbot Adelbert and Larcwide the Librarian's history, and give readers more information about Gytha's mother than Gytha ever got. In so many books all the mysteries are solved – but real life isn't like that. Much of the time, secrets are held close and taken to graves. If you're lucky, a trace has been left behind; if you're lucky and clever then you *might* be able to track down the puzzle pieces and put them together. Maybe they'll form a full picture, or maybe it'll be a mosaic, with fragments and shards, and voids where things are missing. I liked the idea of having a plague of rats to continue the Pied Piper echoes from "The Maiden in the Ice", and I especially liked the idea of a character telling lies that later turned out to be true, even though he didn't know it.

"By My Voice I Shall Be Known"

I wanted to combine elements of the Lorelei Rock, the rusalkas, and Melusine, all wrapped up with a traditional kind of revenge tale. The title comes, I think, from something I read about one of the Sybils, but I can't quite remember which one and I don't seem to have kept a note about it. That's my story and I'm sticking to it. I love the idea of that bold statement that her voice will be all she needs, even though it's been taken from her. My mother is a very talented quilter and I'm fascinated by what seems a kind of witchcraft. You're creating something that's a protection from cold, insects and monsters (it really is!) – why wouldn't it be magical? Exactly the sort of thing that would go into a glory chest, something to bring good luck, a prosperous and happy future, maybe even something to influence a husband's behaviour? And what if the magic could be made to work in different ways?

"The Undone and the Divine"

Quite a few inspirations feed into this story: it carries on action from "The Burnt Moon" and "The Badger Bride", and introduces Delling, one of the daughters of Wulfwyn. The title comes from a Florence and the Machine song, "Bedroom Hymns", the name Delling (Dellingr) is that of a male god from the Norse Sagas, and the *naglfar* is a boat made from the finger and toe nail clippings of the dead, which will take part in Ragnarok. I don't know why I picked out these very Norse elements, but I just liked the sound of Delling as a girl's name, and the idea of the nail-boat was very rich and resonant for me when I read about it. I also wanted to revisit Southarp and her people, some of whom were complicit in the burning of Hafwen and some of whom were collateral damage of Adelbert's terrible revenge. I liked the idea that they simply carried on in death the way they had in life, and love the idea of Delling come to do a great, selfless work and thus earn release for someone she loves as well as people she never knew. I think the title plays to this: that the town of Southarp and its folk had been undone, and what Delling does is rather divine.

"The Night Stair"

This story had its origins in a visit to Battle Abbey in 2012. One of the signs in the ruins pointed out the night stair that the monks had taken when going to early services. I just loved that name and thought it sounded positively sinister. Where might it *really* lead? I carried the title around for the better part of a year until I started thinking about a vampire tale for *Bitterwood*. I could see Adlisa standing in the selection line, waiting, hoping to be chosen, not for a perceived better life, but so she could *act*, find the truth, and, with any luck at all, get revenge. But, as always, there's a sting in the tale. She's another character I want to revisit later, as Adlisa the Bloodless.

"Now, All Pirates are Gone"

In *Sourdough and Other Stories*, there is a tale called "The Navigator", about ships and sirens and men with wings who act as guides for said ships. There is a nameless narrator who may or may not die at the end, and who may or may not be a pirate… but there are definitely pirates in that world. I had the title, "Now, All Pirates Are Gone" scribbled down for another story that never made it into *Sourdough*. When I was writing *Bitterwood*, I went back to my *Sourdough* notes and found that title and knew that it belonged in the new collection. I wanted a pirate story that was a bit more than seeking lost treasure and run-ins with the authorities; what if the buccaneers were almost wiped out? The tale of the ghost ship Caleuche in Chilean mythology gave me the name of the mysterious island, and connected this tale with the protagonist of "By My Voice I Shall Be Known".

"St Dymphna's School for Poison Girls"

This title came from a friend's throwaway line about St Dymphna's Home for the Wealthy Insane, and I thought "No, St Dymphna's Home for Poison Girls", which conjured visions of a boarding school like the one in Charlotte Brontë's *Villette* except with more murder and fewer French lessons. I thought about the kinds of families that send their daughters to finishing schools, and the strife between grand houses caused by matters of pride and honour, and wondered what might happen if those young women were taught something useful. I wondered about the sorts of young women who might not think beyond what their families were sending them to do, rather than saying to themselves "Sod this for a game of soldiers – I've just been taught these great and terrible skills by independent and terrifying women, why should I go off to die in the service of my family? Why shouldn't I too become an independent and terrifying woman?" The protagonist Mercia is the youngest daughter of Wulfwyn from "The Burnt Moon", and the youngest sister of Delling from, "The Undone and the Divine". She appears again in *The Tallow-Wife and Other Tales*.

"The Bitterwood Bible"

This was always going to be an important story because it tells the history of the actual Bitterwood Bible and Murciana who made it. I'd given a lot of thought to Murciana because in *Sourdough and Other Stories* she is referred to as Murcianus – indeed, there's a whole library of books attributed to the almost-mythical-by-that-stage *male* author Murcianus. The idea was that the usual kind of colonisation had occurred, that something created by a woman had been so grand and widespread that it couldn't be stamped out or eradicated, so it's been appropriated and attributed to a man. Throughout the Sourdough world there are a lot of magic books referred to and all are some version of Murciana's Bitterwood Bible, even the grimoire used by Patience and Wynne Sykes in *Sourdough* ("Gallowberries" – and my novella *Of Sorrow and Such),* known as *Murcianus' Book of Magica.* There are all sorts of copies of this book, partial and full and annotated and extended, all to keep the knowledge in the world and all repurposed by their owners.

"Terrible as an Army With Banners"

This is the story that always make me cry, so I can never read it out loud anywhere. It's a mix of letters and diary entries; and I channelled my relationship with my own sister when I wrote this. I wanted Goda's words to echo the idea that even though we're so different we will always be sisters, our blood will always be shared, and that family flows through you whether you want it to or not. Eco's *The Name of the Rose* describes a character as 'terrible as an army with banners', and I thought it a most beautiful phrase (and eventually realised it was from The Song of Solomon). I still love it and this story also owes some of its DNA to Eco's wonderful book. I adore the idea of libraries, especially of medieval libraries as bastions of learning, as the places where knowledge was kept safe during the "Dark Ages". The nuns at the Citadel of Cwen's Reach are determined to keep knowledge in the world because, good or bad, one day it might be needed. It's also a chronicle of ending, a letter of farewell, but, I hope also a statement of stubborn hope.

"By the Weeping Gate"

This title came from nowhere: I was thinking about pirates and ports, bordellos and brides – as you do – and about a place where you pass from land to sea and those who watch you go or wait for you to come back, weep. I had a vision of a girl who is clever and kind, but terribly plain amongst all her beautiful sisters. The sisters aren't cruel to Nel, but their mother is: Dalita is a terrible woman, the epitome of a mother trying to relive her life through her favourite daughter (*not* Nel). I have a whole history in my head for her, how she fled her own family and marriage, and made her way in the world, how it turned her tenacious nature harsh and hard, and how – even though she's got a strong idea of family – she sees even her own children as a means to an end. Nel finds a way to use her plainness to her advantage, she's able to pass unseen when others would attract attention and so she can collect secrets as well. I love Nel, I love how she learns and changes and *becomes* something else in this story, how she takes her courage in her hands and goes out into the world to make things right, even though she is, at the end, someone who can no longer hide.

"Spells for Coming Forth by Daylight"

The title came from the alternative name for the Egyptian The Book of the Dead: The Book of *Coming Forth* to *Daylight,* and speaks of 'spells for coming forth by daylight'. I loved the phrase and thought it was a good title for the new version of Nel, changed by the magic left on her dead sister's skin, made more than she had been, yet with her oldest protection, her invisibility, removed. Plus I wanted to bring the book full circle to dear screwed-up old Hepsibah Ballantyne, who'd lived well beyond her span by fair means and foul, and also to wrap up the tale of the blond man who, as Sister Goda wrote, "ghosts through our folios like a virulent breeze". They'd had a tenuous collection in their early lives, and they've both moved through the world of *Bitterwood* seeking their own ends and leaving ruin behind. Who better than Nel to witness the final collision of Hepsibah and the Viceroy?

SOURDOUGH AND OTHER STORIES

"The Shadow Tree"

When I started this story I had the phrase "nigra sum sed formosa" in my mind – you can often see what else I've been reading when I've written something, and Eco's *The Name of the Rose* was clearly it (again). I'd been thinking about exiles and home and family, and what family might find unforgiveable. I'd also read Christina Rossetti's "The Goblin Market" and Angela Carter's "The Erl-King", as well as various versions of robber bridegroom tales. I thought about governesses and nursery maids, the sort of people left in charge of other people's children, and how you can never be certain who or what you've brought into your home. And I thought a lot about the idea of leaving the place you'd grown up, then finding you wanted to go back – but could only do so if you paid a huge price. That's where Ella came from, making her first appearance here and she's another character who flits in and out of these three collections.

"Gallowberries"

This was one of the stories I wrote when I was supposed to be concentrating on my MA creative work – there's nothing like an approaching deadline to make a writer do something not related to said deadline. It has the same fairy tale themes but it's not one of the re-written/re-imagined tales that went into *Black-Winged Angels* – I think it's the first story I wrote that was an extension of all that I was studying, both in terms of theory and writing craft; it's a synthesis, something I can look at and say 'That's where it began, that's where I jumped off the cliff to see if I could fly.' It wasn't easy, taking four years to finish, for me to know what I needed to do with it, and realise I'd been writing towards the *Sourdough* collection for quite some time. But that first image I had of the fruits growing beneath a gallows, thinking about what they might be able to do, fertilised by death, that was definitely the start. This is the beginning of Patience Sykes (later to become Patience Gideon), showing her early life, "Sister, Sister" shows her old age, and the novella *Of Sorrow and Such* shows her middle life. She also makes an appearance in *The Briar Book of the Dead*.

"Little Radish"

I've always been annoyed by Rapunzel stories because everything that happens is forced upon her. She's seldom got any agency: she's bartered away by her parents for radishes or bitter greens or whatever-vegetable-takes-your-fancy; she's locked in a tower and turned into a companion who knows nothing of the world; the prince turns up and takes advantage of her; she ends up as a single mother thrown out of the only home she's known and wandering. So, what I wanted for my Rapunzel was choice: let her make decisions instead of being tossed around by everyone else's needs and wants, didn't want her to be an appeaser. She *chose* the tower. She chose a quiet life. The witch has no vested interest in Rapunzel, she's not a lonely old hag, and she becomes a friend. Rapunzel is not sweet and neat. She does a terrible thing on the spur of the moment, all clothed in rage, and she to deal with the consequences of her actions and her life. Her son's called "twice-born", which links him to the king in "The Shadow Tree"…

"Dibblespin"

This story came about at Clarion South in 2009. I had the image of flowers that actually lit up a clearing, a house with a pretty girl in it and a not-so-pretty girl watching her. They were half-sisters I realised, and friends. There was a bitter woman, Olwen, who truly hated the not-so-pretty girl, Dibblespin, because she was proof of the infidelity of her husband (the husband is father to several girls throughout this book). Olwen is the baby Patience Sykes rescues in "Gallowberries"). Dibblespin's part human, part troll, but has no harm in her. She loves her sister, Ingrid, who loves her back but perhaps less, perhaps because of her beauty she's more inclined to expect love than give it. Unlike full-blooded trolls, Dibblespin loves sunlight; she's clever and kind, but judged only on her appearance. Her name's a riff on Rumplestiltskin, the sound of it a little nonsensical, yet kind of melodic, a bit like the girl herself. She appears again later in the story "Lavender and Lychgates", to another of her half-sisters.

"The Navigator"

This is another story that had its beginnings at Clarion South (2009), and began with the image of a man with wings, soaring in the blue sky above a calm sea. I've never named the narrator, who loves the navigator Windeyer, but she's also the daughter of the man who took his wings, so she carries her guilt tightly entwined with her love. The sense I had of her was that her life had shrunk: her parents gone, their shipping empire whittled away gradually, and Windeyer no longer loved her as much as he loved his obsession with getting his wings back. And as things and people were subtracted from her life, nothing came to replace them, so the emptiness grew.

"The Angel Wood"

This story first appeared in the lovely *Shimmer #5* in 2006, and its title came from a late night episode of *Frost*, I think, in which there was indeed a place called the Angel Wood. I liked the idea of mixing something religious with something deeply pagan, as though the wrapping of the name would lull you into a false sense of security, then when you opened it you'd find a Green Man inside, staring back at you. It began with the idea of people fleeing a plague-ridden city and heading towards a place that the mother had once fled. In coming home, she'd have to face the consequences of her actions – but her oldest daughter would have to take responsibility for what came next. Henrietta, called Henri, was an excellent vessel for new experiences. She's a girl who's on the cusp of womanhood and also, suddenly, an entirely new life, but a life that is both old and inherited.

"Ash"

The inspiration for this story came from a couple of sources. Alison Weir's *Isabella: She-Wolf of France* mentions the Dowager Queen being burned and scarred in a fire in one of the royal palaces (the record of this is an old copy of a doctor's bill). I was looking at pictures of the Tower of London's Traitors' Gate, and imagined a woman wrapped tightly in a cloak, sitting in a boat, floating in under such a water gate. Blodwen had once been a powerful witch, who'd done a terrible thing in return for eldritch knowledge. The woman who lives in this castle, Gwenllian, traded her own freedom for a life of luxury – she's the woman loved by Windeyer from "The Navigator". The eagle-eyed reader will note the mention of Bitsy at the end, who appears in two more *Sourdough* tales.

"The Story of Ink"

This follows on from "Ash" in that it traces the fate of the baby Blodwen gave away. Her life isn't the wonderful dream the poor witch imaged for her, but she's got a kind of freedom for a while at least. Its narrator is the very young Livilla (who later appears "Sister, Sister"), and like Blodwen, she's working for a powerful man, a prince of the church, with an interest in matters less ecclesiastical and more arcane.

"Lost Things"

This is one of my personal favourites. It's black comedy, to be sure, but I love Jez and her way of looking at things, I love how she interacts with Faideau and the Robber Bridegroom, even when she's scared she can't keep a civil tone. Most of all I think I love that there's such a vein of sadness running through everything she says and does, though most folk in the story aren't perceptive enough to catch it. This is the last story in the little triptych roughly in the middle of *Sourdough*, with "Ash" and "The Story of Ink" being the first two instalments of her life. I love that she tries to put things to rights, even though nothing that's happened was as a result of her actions, yet, as always in these stories, nothing quite goes according to plan.

"A Good Husband"

This came from my researches into various water creatures – I didn't want quite a mermaid because, well, everyone's got a mermaid, I found mention of the mari-morgan, a Welsh/Breton water spirit. They drown men as well as any mermaid, they're beautiful, they cause floods and disaster. I wanted her to be a solitary creature, worshipped, bored by eternity. a woman's kind of idol, but that should also play into her aloneness. She should have her own yearning, her own thing to envy: lovely dresses. Her bargains never work out, until Kitty comes along, with her yearning for a good husband.

"A Porcelain Soul"

Rainer Maria Rilke's "Some Reflections on Dolls" contains a fascinating idea about dolls as voids, empty spaces into which we constantly throw our affections, affections which are never returned. That became the inspiration for this story, with the question 'What if this soulless, unloving thing *might* be given a little piece of soul? What if it might seem to be animated?' There's a lot of creepy doll potential there, but what if these kinds of dolls were gifts for the daughters of rich men, of princes? The ultimate high-end toy with someone else's very core inside them. And what about the doll-makers themselves? How much might they give up to create these little monstrosities, to create things like children who suck out the very spirit and marrow of the maker, the mother-figure – what might happen if it went unchecked?

"The Bones Remember Everything"

This was a challenging story to write because I'd written the scene of spinning hair and making a tapestry from a body in my head when I was still a very new writer, and knew it was, at that stage, beyond the reach of my talent. So, I had to hang onto it until I could do it justice. The title came from a line of poem I heard read ages ago at a VoiceWorks event, and I thought it an exquisite phrase. I managed to work in both the end story of Dibblespin's sister Ingrid, and the back story of Rilka, a nun and the Marshall of a Battle Abbey of the Church Militant who appears later in "Sister, Sister", and allowed Ella from "The Shadow Tree" to ghost through like a dark presence. It's a tale about blood and families, sisters and loss, about stories within stories, about bones and babies and the prick of a thorn.

"Sourdough"

This was the story that started the *Sourdough and Other Stories* collection, but in a wandering way. I had an image of girl who made bread into works of art. I thought about "Donkeyskin", where the princess puts her jewellery into food baked for the prince and what a silly, dangerous act that was. I'd read Margo Lanagan's tale "Wooden Bride" and the city she described there gave me an oblique inspiration for Lodellan. I chose the name Emmeline for my protagonist because it means labourer and she does indeed labour over the making and baking of her creations, and I chose Peregrine as her lover's name, because it means both a pilgrim and a wanderer, and in this story he does indeed wander for a time.

"Sister, Sister"

"Sister, Sister" has its roots in my childhood: an old book of my mother's was *Norwegian Folk Tales*. In it were all sorts of tales of hulders and trolls, of women whose back side was hollowed out like a tree trunk, and yet others who looked perfectly normal but for their cow tail… but the bit of information that most appealed to me and stuck with me over the years was that trolls were known to steal away human babies and leave their own nasty, mewling offspring in the cradles. Even at a young age I loved the idea of the changeling child – and even more I loved to torment my younger sister (when she was being awful) that she wasn't really my true sibling, but a troll's daughter left in the crib to cause trouble. When I began to think about new stories for *Sourdough* I knew I wanted a troll tale and I wanted to use the changeling child as a motif. The first image was the interior of the Golden Lily Inn and Brothel; I knew who the inhabitants were, many had previously appeared other stories, such as Bitsy, Patience, Rilka, Faideau and Livilla. One of the things that really comes to the fore in this story is how well we do or don't know our friends, how rumour and gossip colours what we know of their history, and indeed how many of these characters have already become the stuff of legend to some small degree.

"Lavender and Lychgates"

I wanted to revisit Emmeline and Peregrine from "Sourdough" in their later life – to know they were happy – and add another dimension to Emmeline's mother: I realised she was one of the twins from "The Angel Wood", all grown up and with a family and personality of her own. The idea of the importance of books and of Lodellan as a place where they were born was important – that, in addition to its degenerate places, it also produced some wonderful things. I had an image of a young girl playing in a graveyard, which managed to entwine itself with a garbled tale of lilacs and lychgates a friend had told me years ago, the precise details of which I cannot remember. I managed to garble it even more, replacing lilacs with lavender. And I couldn't shake the image of shadows swirling in the apex of a lychgate roof above the heads of people passing out underneath, nor the idea of what happens when you hang onto a recollection too tightly.

"Under the Mountain"

This story loops back to the events of "Sister, Sister" and some of the characters, but this time it focuses on Magdalene, Theodora's little daughter. Magdalene was still very young when they left Lodellan, and she's only got brief memories of their time in the city. I figured that mother–daughter relationships are always fraught by the teenage years, and I wondered what might happen if Theodora left, like the mother running away from home. And I thought about Magadalene, growing more angry and unpleasant by the day, unable to really control herself as she wasn't who or what she'd been brought up to believe. She was fighting against a nature she didn't know she was heir to, yet she still loved Theodora fiercely, still had that attachment to her mother that sent her out into the world to follow her and bring her home.

THE TALLOW-WIFE AND OTHER TALES

"The Promise of Saints"

This story was originally written for *A Miscellany of Death & Folly* and I didn't know where it came from. I love the idea of jewelled saints and I've used the image before in "No Good Deed" (in which is the origin story for the Lawrence family). It was only after I finished that I realised it was really a *Sourdough* world tale and belonged at the beginning of this new collection.

"The Tallow-Wife"

This story began with a dream of a woman in a dark room. When I woke up all I knew was that she'd been hard done by and suffered terrible losses… but that she had also survived and was going to take her revenge. Someone suggested the use of candles as a means of doing that, and it grew from there to be a novella-length piece. I interspersed the present action with that of the past to show how Cordelia's life had changed – it's a tale of a fall, and then a very determined rise.

"What Shines Brightest Burns Most Fiercely"

I wanted this tale to connect with the tales in *Sourdough and Other Stories.* I wanted to hark back to characters like Theodora, and show the bloodlines are still running through these books like threads. Jacopo is the son of the daughter she had with Faideau late in life. He finds Cordelia when she escapes from the Rosebery Bay hulk, and they form a bond. I had a vision of this cherub-faced lad who could change his appearance, and also this doll made of wax that held someone's doom.

"Embers and Ash"

I woke one morning with the image of a ship stuck in a cliff – as you do – and I knew I wanted to revisit Ella who stole children away and had featured in both *Sourdough* and *Bitterwood.* I wondered how far she'd wandered in her very long life, and what she'd been doing – even though her powers had been taken, her immortality remained. And I also wanted to see how Mercia from "St Dymphna's School for Poison Girls" had fared – so why not bring them together, these women connected by the Erl-King?

"Bearskin"

This tale follows Cordelia's youngest child, Torben, after his parents are disgraced. He's been cosseted and protected all his life, and now he's under the supervision of a brute called Uther, who tries to teach him to hunt. The only person who might be his friend, Tove, is angry at him most of the time. Tove has her own tale, but of course Torben doesn't ask for it because he's so wrapped up in himself.

“The Nightingale and the Rose”

This is the story of Cordelia’s daughter Victoria after she’s sent away by her Aunt Bethany for asking too many questions. She’s got a strange singing talent, and has been placed in a theatre of ill-repute in a town that’s on the migratory path of the hind-girls. I also wanted to see what had happened to the murdered twins, Ozanne and Oriel. I took their names from my family tree, so it seemed a waste not to explore further.

“Of Ghosts and Glory”

I knew the necklace that Cordelia wears to Lodellan’s Winter Solstice Ball had to come from somewhere and I figured it had to have a dangerous history. So, I made Ildikó my jeweller – she’s Jacopo’s mother and half-sister to Theodora’s first daughter, Magdalene who went beneath the mountain into the kingdom of the trolls at the end of *Sourdough and Other Stories*. And I also knew that Magdalene was going to come *back* out.

“A Stitch in Time”

Poor Merry! In my mind, she was this talented seamstress and more than she seemed, but kept in the background by her aunt, Mrs B (for reasons that become apparent much later). She was only ever seen from Cordelia’s side of things, she’s always the helper, so I wanted a tale from her point of view. After all, she’d suffered too. I guess I just wanted her to have something nice… although let’s face it, my definition of “nice” might be questionable.

“Sleeping Like Snow”

Tove from “Bearskin” hadn’t left my mind, and I wanted to pick apart her history. Where had she come from, this girl with barely born horns on her forehead? And I also knew I wanted to bring her and Victoria together (Victoria who’s trying so hard to be brave after letting her mother down)… and Selke who’s gone a bit strange after all these years (like Ella, she’s had a very long life and her moral compass hasn’t worked in a while).

“Crossroads”

I wanted to hear Cordelia’s voice again in this collection – she’d been mostly silent since that first novella. She’d been remade with Selke’s help, and she was in a position to start putting the last bits of her big plan into action. I loved the idea of her sneaking into Breakwater right under Bethany's nose. I knew that I wanted her to meet Ella, although I wasn't sure how that was going to go. And I also wanted to see Bethany as the Queen of Thieves, and to know that not everything was going according to *her* plan.

"And a Young Husband to Bury Me"

I'd had this title in my mind for I don't know how long. I think I was considering the nature of promises: what we think we'll get in life, what we're told we'll get, and what we do actually get. Generally, that's three very different things. And I wanted my dear Mrs Bell to be one of the voices for this story, because it's her tale after all; indeed, everything in Cordelia's life circles back to Mrs B though she doesn't know it yet. I didn't just want Mrs Bell to be the "devoted servant" – there had to be something more to her actions, her sticking with Cordelia – and her desertion of Bethany.

"By Such Paths"

I have a glorious piece of artwork by Kathleen Jennings (no surprise in that), and it has on it the words "For it is by such paths we reach the world". I thought it was a wonderful phrase and the perfect title for this final tale. We finish with Ella, just as we began with her in *Sourdough*, the first of the books I wrote. Ella's choices have often pushed the *Sourdough* world in different directions, and I liked the idea of the world starting to push back on her. I hope she's happy enough with her ending.

PREVIOUS PUBLICATION DETAILS

THE BITTERWOOD BIBLE AND OTHER RECOUNTINGS – FIRST EDITION, TARTARUS PRESS, 2014

"The Coffin-Maker's Daughter" was first published in *A Book of Horrors* (Stephen Jones ed.), Jo Fletcher Books (Quercus), 2011.

"By the Weeping Gate" was first published in *Fearie Tales: Grimm and Gruesome* (Stephen Jones ed.), Jo Fletcher Books (Quercus), 2013.

"By My Voice I Shall Be Known" was first published in *The Dark*, Issue 1, October 2013.

'St Dymphna's School for Poison Girls' was first published in *The Review of Australian Fiction*, Number 9, Issue 3, February 2014.

"The Badger Bride" was first published in *Strange Tales IV* (Rosalie Parker ed.), Tartarus Press, 2014.

SOURDOUGH AND OTHER STORIES – FIRST EDITION, TARTARUS PRESS, 2010

"The Angel Wood" was first published in *Shimmer* #5, Autumn 2006.

"Sourdough" was first published in *Strange Tales II*, Tartarus Press, 2007.

"Little Radish" was first published at *Crimson Highway* in February 2008.

"Sister, Sister" was first published in *Strange Tales III*, Tartarus Press, 2009.

THE TALLOW-WIFE AND OTHER TALES
– FIRST EDITION, TARTARUS PRESS, 2021

"Bearskin" was first published in *The Dark*, Issue 7, February 2015.

"The Tallow-Wife" was first published in *A Feast of Sorrows: Stories*, Prime Books, 2016.

"What Shines Brightest Burns Most Fiercely" was first published in *A Feast of Sorrows: Stories*, Prime Books, 2016.

"The Promise of Saints" was first published in *A Miscellany of Death and Folly*, Egaeus Press, 2019.

ABOUT THE AUTHOR

A.G. SLATTER has won a Shirley Jackson Award, a World Fantasy Award, a British Fantasy Award, a Ditmar, three Australian Shadows Awards, eight Aurealis Awards and a Premier Ignotus. Most recently, *All the Murmuring Bones* was shortlisted for the 2021 Queensland Premier's Literary Awards Book of the Year and the 2021 Shirley Jackson Award; *The Path of Thorns* won both the Aurealis Award for Best Fantasy Novel and the Australian Shadows Award for Best Novel in 2022; and *The Briar Book of the Dead* was shortlisted for both the Aurealis and Australian Shadows Awards for 2024. She has a PhD in Creative Writing, is a graduate of Clarion South and the Tin House Summer Writers Workshop, and has been a judge for the World Fantasy and Aurealis Awards. Angela's short stories have appeared in many Best Of anthologies, and her work has been translated into many languages. She lives in Brisbane, Australia with a superannuated beagle and a TBR pile which will likely be the death of her. Find her on her website angelaslatter.com and on social media @angelaslatter